# THE INTERIOR CASTLE

# The INTERIOR CASTLE

*Including* BOSTON ADVENTURE, THE MOUNTAIN
LION, *and a new collection of short
stories,* CHILDREN ARE BORED ON SUNDAY

## By JEAN STAFFORD

HARCOURT, BRACE AND COMPANY, NEW YORK, 1953

BOSTON ADVENTURE, copyright, 1944,
by Harcourt, Brace and Company

THE MOUNTAIN LION, copyright, 1947,
by Jean Stafford

CHILDREN ARE BORED ON SUNDAY,
copyright, 1945, 1946, 1948, 1949,
1950, 1953, by Jean Stafford

This omnibus volume distributed
by special arrangement with
Harcourt, Brace and Company.

*Printed in the United States of America
by The Haddon Craftsmen, Inc.,
Scranton, Pa.* 1

# CONTENTS:

# CHILDREN
## ARE BORED
# ON SUNDAY

TO OLIVER

The first four and last two stories first appeared in *The New Yorker*; the others in *Harper's Magazine* and *Partisan Review*. "A Modest Proposal" was called "Pax Vobiscum" in *The New Yorker*, and "The Echo and the Nemesis" had the title "The Nemesis" in the same magazine.

# Contents

The title of this book is borrowed, with many thanks, from the title of the song *"Les enfants s'ennuient le dimanche"* by Mr. Charles Trenet.

CHILDREN ARE BORED ON SUNDAY

# The Echo and the Nemesis

Sue Ledbetter and Ramona Dunn became friends through the commonplace accident of their sitting side by side in a philosophy lecture three afternoons a week. There were many other American students at Heidelberg University that winter—the last before the war— but neither Sue nor Ramona had taken up with them. Ramona had not because she scorned them; in her opinion, they were Philistines, concerned only with drinking beer, singing German songs, and making spectacles of themselves on their bicycles and in their little rented cars. And Sue had not because she was self-conscious and introverted and did not make friends easily. In Ramona's presence, she pretended to deplore her compatriots' escapades, which actually she envied desperately. Sometimes on Saturday nights she lay on her bed unable to read or daydream and in an agony of frustration as she listened to her fellow-lodgers at the Pension Kirchenheim laughing and teasing and sometimes bursting into song as they played bridge and Monopoly in the cozy veranda café downstairs.

Soon after the semester opened in October, the two girls fell into the habit of drinking their afternoon cof-

fee together on the days they met in class. Neither of
them especially enjoyed the other's company, but in
their different ways they were lonely, and as Ramona
once remarked, in her highfalutin way, "From time to
time, I need a rest from the exercitation of my intellect." She was very vain of her intellect, which she had
directed to the study of philology, to the exclusion of
almost everything else in the world. Sue, while she had
always taken her work seriously, longed also for beaux
and parties, and conversation about them, and she was
often bored by Ramona's talk, obscurely gossipy, of the
vagaries of certain Old High Franconian verbs when
they encountered the High German consonant shift, or
of the variant readings of passages in Layamon's
*Brut,* or the linguistic influence Eleanor of Aquitaine
had exerted on the English court. But because she was
well-mannered she listened politely and even appeared
to follow Ramona's exuberant elucidation of Sanskrit
"a"-stem declensions and her ardent plan to write a
monograph on the word "ahoy." They drank their coffee in the Konditorei Luitpold, a very noisy café on a
street bent like an elbow, down behind the cathedral.
The din of its two small rooms was aggravated by the
peripheral racket that came from the kitchen and from
the outer shop, where the cakes were kept. The waiters,
all of whom looked cross, hustled about at a great
rate, slamming down trays and glasses and cups any
which way before the many customers, who gabbled and
rattled newspapers and pounded on the table for more of

something. Over all the to-do was the blare of the radio, with its dial set permanently at a station that played nothing but stormy choruses from *Wilhelm Tell*. Ramona, an invincible expositor, had to shout, but shout she did as she traced words like "rope" and "calf" through dozens of languages back to their Indo-Germanic source. Sometimes Sue, somewhat befuddled by the uproar, wanted by turns to laugh and to cry with disappointment, for this was not at all the way she had imagined that she would live in Europe. Half incredulously and half irritably, she would stare at Ramona as if in some way she were to blame.

Ramona Dunn was fat to the point of parody. Her obesity fitted her badly, like extra clothing put on in the wintertime, for her embedded bones were very small and she was very short, and she had a foolish gait, which, however, was swift, as if she were a mechanical doll whose engine raced. Her face was rather pretty, but its features were so small that it was all but lost in its billowing surroundings, and it was covered by a thin, fair skin that was subject to disfiguring affections, now hives, now eczema, now impetigo, and the whole was framed by fine, pale hair that was abused once a week by a *Friseur* who baked it with an iron into dozens of horrid little snails. She habitually wore a crimson tam-o'-shanter with a sportive spray of artificial edelweiss pinned to the very top of it. For so determined a bluestocking, her eccentric and extensive wardrobe was a surprise; nothing was ever completely clean or completely whole, and nothing ever matched anything else, but it was apparent that all these odd and often ugly clothes had been expensive. She had a long, fur-lined cape, and men's tweed jackets with leather patches on the elbows, and flannel shirts designed for hunters in the State of Maine, and high-necked jerseys, and a waist-coat made of unborn gazelle, dyed Kelly green. She attended particularly to the dressing of her tiny hands and feet, and she had gloves and mittens of every color and every material, and innumerable pairs of extraordinary shoes, made for her by a Roman bootmaker. She always carried a pair of field glasses, in a brassbound leather case that hung over her shoulder by a plaited strap of rawhide; she looked through the wrong end of them, liking, for some reason that she did not disclose, to diminish the world she surveyed. Wherever she went, she took a locked pigskin satchel, in which she carried her grammars and lexicons and the many drafts of the many articles she was writing in the hope that they would be published in learned journals. One day in the café, soon after the girls became acquainted, she opened up the satchel, and Sue was shocked at the helter-skelter arrangement of the papers, all mussed and frayed, and stained with coffee and ink. But, even more, she was dumfounded to see a clear-green all-day sucker stuck like a bookmark between the pages of a glossary to "Beowulf."

Sue knew that Ramona was rich, and that for the last ten years her family had lived in Italy, and that before that they had lived in New York. But this was all she knew about her friend; she did not even know where she lived in Heidelberg. She believed that Ramona, in her boundless erudition, was truly consecrated to her studies and that she truly had no other desire than to impress the subscribers to *Speculum* and the *Publications of the Modern Language Association.* She was the sort of person who seemed, at twenty-one, to have fought all her battles and survived to enjoy the quiet of her unendangered ivory tower. She did not seem to mind at all that she was so absurd to look at, and Sue, who was afire with ambitions and sick with conflict, admired her arrogant self-possession.

The two girls had been going to the Konditorei Luitpold three times a week for a month or more, and all these meetings had been alike; Ramona had talked and Sue had contributed expressions of surprise (who would have dreamed that "bolster" and "poltroon" derived from the same parent?), or murmurs of acquiescence (she agreed there might be something in the discreet rumor that the Gothic language had been made up by nineteenth-century scholars to answer riddles that could not otherwise be solved), or laughter, when it seemed becoming. The meetings were neither rewarding nor entirely uninteresting to Sue, and she came to look upon them as a part of the week's schedule, like the philosophy lectures and the seminar in Schiller.

And then, one afternoon, just as the weary, meanmouthed waiter set their cake down before them, the

radio departed from its custom and over it came the
"Minuet in G," so neat and winning and surprising that
for a moment there was a general lull in the café, and
even the misanthropic waiter paid the girls the honor, in
his short-lived delight, of not slopping their coffee. As
if they all shared the same memories that the little sentimental piece of music awoke in her, Sue glanced around
smiling at her fellows and tried to believe that all of
them—even the old men with Hindenburg mustaches
and palsied wattles, and even the Brown Shirts fiercely
playing chess—had been children like herself and had
stumbled in buckled pumps through the simple steps of
the minuet at the military command of a dancing
teacher, Miss Conklin, who had bared her sinewy legs to
the thigh. In some public presentation of Miss Conklin's
class, Sue had worn a yellow bodice with a lacing of
black velvet ribbon, a bouffant skirt of chintz covered
all over with daffodils, and a cotton-batting wig that
smelled of stale talcum powder. Even though her partner
had been a sissy boy with nastily damp hands and white
eyelashes, and though she had been grave with stage-
fright, she had had moments of most thrilling expectation, as if this were only the dress rehearsal of the
grown-up ball to come.

  If she had expected all the strangers in the café to
be transported by the "Minuet" to a sweet and distant
time, she had not expected Ramona Dunn to be, and she
was astonished and oddly frightened to see the fat girl
gazing with a sad, reflective smile into her water glass.

When the music stopped and the familiar hullabaloo was re-established in the room, Ramona said, "Oh, I don't know of anything that makes me more nostalgic than that tinny little tune! It makes me think of Valentine parties before my sister Martha died."

It took Sue a minute to rearrange her family portrait of the Dunns, which heretofore had included, besides Ramona, only a mother and a father and three brothers. Because this was by far the simplest way, she had seen them in her mind's eye as five stout, scholarly extensions of Ramona, grouped together against the background of Vesuvius. She had imagined that they spent their time examining papyri and writing Latin verses, and she regretted admitting sorrow into their lives, as she had to do when she saw Ramona's eyes grow vague and saw her, quite unlike her naturally greedy self, push her cake aside, untouched. For a moment or two, the fat girl was still and blank, as if she were waiting for a pain to go away, and then she poured the milk into her coffee, replaced her cake, and began to talk about her family, who, it seemed, were not in the least as Sue had pictured them.

Ramona said that she alone of them was fat and ill-favored, and the worst of it was that Martha, the most beautiful girl who ever lived, had been her twin. Sue could not imagine, she declared, how frightfully good-looking all the Dunns were—except herself, of course: tall and dark-eyed and oval-faced, and tanned from the hours they spent on their father's boat, the San Filippo.

And they were terribly gay and venturesome; they were
the despair of the croupiers at the tables on the Riviera,
the envy of the skiers at San Bernardino and of the
yachtsmen on the Mediterranean. Their balls and their
musicales and their dinner parties were famous. All the
brothers had unusual artistic gifts, and there was so
much money in the family that they did not have to do
anything but work for their own pleasure in their studios. They were forever involved in scandals with their
mistresses, who were either married noblewomen or notorious dancing girls, and forever turning over a new
leaf and getting themselves engaged to lovely, convent-
bred princesses, whom, however, they did not marry;
the young ladies were too submissively Catholic, or too
stupid, or their taste in painting was vulgar.

Of all this charming, carefree brood, Martha, five
years dead, had been the most splendid, Ramona said,
a creature so slight and delicate that one wanted to put
her under a glass bell to protect her. Painters were captivated by the elegant shape of her head, around which
she wore her chestnut hair in a coronet, and there were
a dozen portraits of her, and hundreds of drawings hanging in the big bedroom where she had died and which
now had been made into a sort of shrine for her. If the
Dunns were odd in any way, it was in this devotion to
their dead darling; twice a year Mrs. Dunn changed the
nibs in Martha's pens, and in one garden there grew
nothing but anemones, Martha's favorite flower. She had
ailed from birth, pursued malevolently by the disease

that had melted her away to the wick finally when she
was sixteen. The family had come to Italy in the beginning of her mortal languor in the hope that the warmth
and novelty would revive her, and for a while it did,
but the wasting poison continued to devour her slowly,
and for years she lay, a touching invalid, on a balcony
overlooking the Bay of Naples. She lay on a blond satin
chaise longue, in a quaint peignoir made of leaf-green
velvet, and sometimes, as she regarded her prospect of
sloops and valiant skiffs on the turbulent waves, the cy-
press trees, white villas in the midst of olive groves, and
the intransigent smoldering of Vesuvius, she sang old
English airs and Irish songs as she accompanied herself
on a lute. If, in the erratic course of her illness, she got
a little stronger, she asked for extra cushions at her
back and half sat up at a small easel to paint in water
colors, liking the volcano as a subject, trite as it was,
and the comic tourist boats that romped over the bay
from Naples to Capri. If she was very unwell, she simply
lay smiling while her parents and her sister and her
brothers attended her, trying to seduce her back to health
with their futile offerings of plums and tangerines and
gilt-stemmed glasses of Rhine wine and nosegays bought
from the urchins who bargained on the carriage roads.

When Martha died, Ramona's own grief was despair,
because the death of a twin is a foretaste of one's own
death, and for months she had been harried with premo-
nitions and prophetic dreams, and often she awoke to
find that she had strayed from her bed, for what awful

purpose she did not know, and was walking barefoot, like a pilgrim, down the pitch-black road. But the acute phase of her mourning had passed, and now, although sorrow was always with her, like an alter ego, she had got over the worst of it.

She paused in her narrative and unexpectedly laughed. "What a gloom I'm being!" she said, and resumed her monologue at once but in a lighter tone, this time to recount the drubbing her brother Justin had given someone when he was defending the honor of a dishonorable soprano, and to suggest, in tantalizing innuendoes, that her parents were not faithful to each other.

Sue, whose dead father had been an upright, pessimistic clergyman and whose mother had never given voice to an impure thought, was bewitched by every word Ramona said. It occurred to her once to wonder why Ramona so frowned upon the frolics of the other American students when her beloved relatives were so worldly, but then she realized that the manners of the *haut monde* were one thing and those of undergraduates another. How queer, Sue thought, must seem this freakish bookworm in the midst of it all! And yet such was the ease with which Ramona talked, so exquisitely placed were her fillips of French, so intimate and casual her allusions to the rich and celebrated figures of international society, that Ramona changed before Sue's eyes; from the envelope of fat emerged a personality as *spirituelle* and knowing as any practicing sophisticate's.

When, in the course of describing a distiller from Milan who was probably her mother's lover, she broke off and pressingly issued Sue an invitation to go with her a month from then, at the Christmas holiday, to San Bernardino to meet her brothers for a fortnight of skiing, Sue accepted immediately, not stopping to think, in the heady pleasure of the moment, that the proposal was unduly sudden, considering the sketchy nature of their friendship. "My brothers will adore you," she said, giving Sue a look of calm appraisal. "They are eclectic and they'll find your red hair and brown eyes irresistibly naive." As if the plan had long been in her mind, Ramona named the date they would leave Heidelberg; she begged permission, in the most gracious and the subtlest possible way, to let Sue be her guest, even to the extent of supplying her with ski equipment. When the details were settled—a little urgently, she made Sue promise "on her word of honor" that she would not default— she again took up her report on Signor da Gama, the distiller, who was related by blood to the Pope and had other distinctions of breeding as well to recommend him to her mother, who was, she confessed, something of a snob. "Mama," she said, accenting the ultima, "thinks it is unnecessary for anyone to be badly born."

The Konditorei Luitpold was frequented by teachers from the Translators' Institute, and usually Ramona rejoiced in listening to them chattering and expostulating, in half a dozen European languages, for she prided herself on her gift of tongues. But today her heart was in

Sorrento, and she paid no attention to them, not even to two vociferous young Russians at a table nearby. She disposed of the roué from Milan (Sue had read Catullus? Signor da Gama had a cottage at Sirmio not far from his reputed grave) and seemed to be on the point of disclosing her father's delinquencies when she was checked by a new mood, which made her lower her head, flush, and, through a long moment of silence, study the greasy hoops the rancid milk had made on the surface of her coffee.

Sue felt as if she had inadvertently stumbled upon a scene of deepest privacy, which, if she were not careful, she would violate, and, pretending that she had not observed the hiatus at all, she asked, conversationally, the names of Ramona's brothers besides Justin.

The two others were called Daniel and Robert, but it was not of them, or of her parents, or of Martha, that Ramona now wanted to speak but of herself, and haltingly she said that the "Minuet in G" had deranged her poise because it had made her think of the days of her childhood in New York, when she had been no bigger than her twin and they had danced the minuet together, Ramona taking the dandy's part. A friend of the family had predicted that though they were then almost identical, Ramona was going to be the prettier of the two. Now Sue was shocked, for she had thought that Ramona must always have been fat, and she was nearly moved to tears to know that the poor girl had been changed from a swan into an ugly duckling and that it was improbable, from the looks of her, that she would ever be changed back again. But Sue was so young and so badly equipped to console someone so beset that she could not utter a word, and she wished she could go home.

Ramona summoned the waiter and ordered her third piece of cake, saying nervously, after she had done so, "I'm sorry. When I get upset, I have to eat to calm myself. I'm awful! I ought to kill myself for eating so much." She began to devour the cake obsessively, and when she had finished it down to the last crumb and the last fragment of frosting, she said, with shimmering eyes, "Please let me tell you what it is that makes me the unhappiest girl in the world, and maybe you can help me." Did Sue have any idea what it was like to be ruled by food and half driven out of one's mind until one dreamed of it and had at last no other ambition but to eat incessantly with an appetite that grew and grew until one saw oneself, in nightmares, as nothing but an enormous mouth and a tongue, trembling lasciviously? Did she know the terror and the remorse that followed on the heels of it when one slyly sneaked the lion's share of buttered toast at tea? Had she ever desired the whole of a pudding meant for twelve and hated with all her heart the others at the dinner table? Sue could not hide her blushing face or put her fingers in her ears or close her eyes against the tortured countenance of that wretched butterball, who declared that she had often come within an ace of doing away with herself because she was so fat.

Leaning across the table, almost whispering, Ramona went on, "I didn't come to Heidelberg for its philologists —they don't know any more than I do. I have exiled myself. I would not any longer offend that long-suffering family of mine with the sight of me." It had been her aim to fast throughout this year, she continued, and return to them transformed, and she had hoped to be thinner by many pounds when she joined her brothers at Christmastime. But she had at once run into difficulties, because, since she was not altogether well (she did not specify her illness and Sue would not have asked its name for anything), she had to be under the supervision of a doctor. And the doctor in Heidelberg, like the doctor in Naples, would not take her seriously when she said her fatness was ruining her life; they had both gone so far as to say that she was *meant* to be like this and that it would be imprudent of her to diet. Who was bold enough to fly in the face of medical authority? Not she, certainly.

It appeared, did it not, to be a dilemma past solution, Ramona asked. And yet this afternoon she had begun to see a way out, if Sue would pledge herself to help. Sue did not reply at once, sensing an involvement, but then she thought of Ramona's brothers, whom she was going to please, and she said she would do what she could.

"You're not just saying that? You are my friend? You know, of course, that you'll be repaid a hundredfold." Ramona subjected Sue's sincerity to some minutes of investigation and then outlined her plan, which seemed

very tame to Sue after all these preparations, for it consisted only of Ramona's defying Dr. Freudenburg and
of Sue's becoming a sort of unofficial censor and confessor. Sue was to have lunch with her each day, at Ramona's expense, and was to remind her, by a nudge or a
word now and again, not to eat more than was really
necessary to keep alive. If at any time Sue suspected
that she was eating between meals or late at night, she
was to come out flatly with an accusation and so shame
Ramona that it would never happen again. The week-
ends were particularly difficult, since there were no lectures to go to and it was tempting not to stir out of her
room at all but to gorge throughout the day on delicacies
out of tins and boxes that she had sent to herself from
shops in Strasbourg and Berlin. And since, in addition
to fasting, she needed exercise, she hoped that Sue would
agree to go walking with her on Saturdays and Sundays,
a routine that could be varied from time to time by a
weekend trip to some neighboring town of interest.

When Sue protested mildly that Ramona had contra-
dicted her earlier assertion that she would not dare dispute her doctor's word, Ramona grinned roguishly and
said only, "Don't be nosy."

Ramona had found an old ladies' home, called the
Gerstnerheim, which, being always in need of funds,
welcomed paying guests at the midday meal, whom they
fed for an unimaginably low price. Ramona did not pa-
tronize it out of miserliness, however, but because the
food was nearly inedible. And it was here that the girls

daily took their Spartan lunch. It was quite the worst
that Sue had ever eaten anywhere, for it was cooked to
pallor and flaccidity and then was seasoned with un-
heard-of condiments, which sometimes made her sick.
The bread was sour and the soup was full of pasty clots;
the potatoes were waterlogged and the old red cabbage
was boiled until it was blue. The dessert was always a
basin of molded farina with a sauce of gray jelly that
had a gray taste. The aged ladies sat at one enormously
long table, preserving an institutional silence until the
farina was handed around, and, as if this were an alarm,
all the withered lips began to move simultaneously and
from them issued high squawks of protest against the
dreary lot of being old and homeless and underfed. Sue
could not help admiring Ramona, who ate her plate of
eel and celeriac as if she really preferred it to tuna
roasted with black olives and who talked all the while
of things quite other than food—of Walther von der
Vogelweide's eccentric syntax, of a new French novel
that had come in the mail that morning, and of their trip
to Switzerland.

Justin and Daniel and Robert were delighted that Sue
was coming, Ramona said, and arrangements were being made in a voluminous correspondence through the
air over the Alps. Sue had never been on skis in her
life, but she did not allow this to deflate her high hopes.
She thought only of evenings of lieder (needless to say,
the accomplished Dunns sang splendidly) and hot spiced
wine before a dancing fire, of late breakfasts in the white

sun and brilliant conversation. And of what was coming
afterward! The later holidays (Ramona called them
*villeggiatura*), spent in Sorrento! The countesses' garden parties in Amalfi and the cruises on the Aegean Sea,
the visits to Greece, the balls in the princely houses of
Naples! Ramona could not decide which of her brothers
Sue would elect to marry. Probably Robert, she thought,
since he was the youngest and the most affectionate.

It was true that Sue did not quite believe all she was
told, but she knew that the ways of the rich are strange,
and while she did not allow her fantasies to invade the
hours assigned to classes and study, she did not rebuff
them when they came at moments of leisure. From time
to time, she suddenly remembered that she was required
to give something in return for Ramona's largess, and
then she would say how proud she was of her friend's
self-discipline or would ask her, like a frank and compassionate doctor, if she had strayed at all from her
intention (she always had; she always immediately admitted it and Sue always put on a show of disappointment), and once in a while she said that Ramona was
looking much thinner, although this was absolutely untrue. Sometimes they took the electric tram to Neckar-
gemünd, where they split a bottle of sweet Greek wine.
Occasionally they went to Mannheim, to the opera, but
they never stayed for a full performance; Ramona said
that later in the year Signor da Gama would invite them
to his house in Milan and then they could go to the Scala
every night. Once they went for a weekend to Rothen-

burg, where Ramona, in an uncontrollable holiday mood, ate twelve cherry tarts in a single day. She was tearful for a week afterward, and to show Sue how sorry she was, she ground out a cigarette on one of her downy wrists. This dreadful incident took place in the Luitpold and was witnessed by several patrons, who could not conceal their alarm. Sue thought to herself, Maybe she's cuckoo, and while she did not relinquish any of her day-dreams of the festivities in Italy, she began to observe Ramona more closely.

She could feel the turmoil in her when they went past bakeshop windows full of cream puffs and cheesecake and petits fours. Ramona, furtively glancing at the good-ies out of the corner of her eye, would begin a passion-ate and long-winded speech on the present-day use of Latin in Iceland. When, on a special occasion, they dined together at the Ritterhalle, she did not even look at the menu but lionheartedly ordered a single dropped egg and a cup of tea and resolutely kept her eyes away from Sue's boiled beef and fritters. When drinking cocktails in the American bar at the Europäischer Hof, she shook her head as the waiter passed a tray of canapés made of caviar, anchovy, lobster, foie gras, and Camembert, ranged fanwise around a little bowl of ivory almonds. But sometimes she did capitulate, with a piteous ration-alization—that she had not eaten any breakfast or that she had barely touched her soup at the Gerstnerheim and that therefore there would be nothing wrong in her having two or perhaps three or four of these tiny little sandwiches. One time Sue saw her take several more than she had said she would and hide them under the rim of her plate.

As the date set for their departure for Switzerland drew nearer, Ramona grew unaccountable. Several times she failed to appear at lunch, and when Sue, in a friendly way, asked for an explanation, she snapped, "None of your business. What do you think you are? My nurse?" She was full of peevishness, complaining of the smell of senility in the Gerstnerheim, of students who sucked the shells of pistachio nuts in the library, of her landlady's young son, who she was sure rummaged through her bureau drawers when she was not at home. Once she and Sue had a fearful row when Sue, keeping up her end of the bargain, although she really did not care a pin, told her not to buy a bag of chestnuts from a vendor on a street corner. Ramona shouted, for all the world to hear, "You are sadly mistaken, Miss Ledbetter, if you think you know more than Dr. Augustus Freudenburg, of the Otto-Ludwigs Clinic!" And a little after that she acquired the notion that people were staring at her, and she carried an umbrella, rain or shine, to hide herself from them. But, oddest of all, when the skis and boots and poles that she had ordered for Sue arrived, and Sue thanked her for them, she said, "I can't think what use they'll be. Obviously there never is any snow in this ghastly, godforsaken place."

There was an awful afternoon when Ramona was convinced that the waiter at the Luitpold had impugned her German, and Sue found herself in the unhappy role of intermediary in a preposterous altercation so bitter that it stopped just short of a bodily engagement. When the girls left the café—at the insistence of the management —they were silent all the way to the cathedral, which was the place where they usually took leave of each other to go their separate ways home. They paused a moment there in the growing dark, and suddenly Ramona said, "Look at me!" Sue looked at her. "I say!" said Ramona. "In this light you look exactly like my sister. How astonishing! Turn a little to the left, there's a dear." And when Sue had turned as she directed, a whole minute—but it seemed an hour to Sue—passed before Ramona broke from her trance to cry, "How blind I've been! My brothers would be shocked to death if they should see you. It would kill them!"

She put out her hands, on which she wore white leather mittens, and held Sue's face between them and studied it, half closing her eyes and murmuring her amazement, her delight, her perplexity at her failure until now to see this marvelous resemblance. Once, as her brown eyes nimbly catechized the face before her, she took off her right mitten and ran her index finger down Sue's nose, as if she had even learned her sister's bones by heart, while Sue, unable to speak, could only think in panic, What does she mean *if* they should see me?

Ramona carried on as if she were moon-struck, mak-

ing fresh discoveries until not only were Sue's and
Martha's faces identical but so were their voices and
their carriage and the shape of their hands and feet.
She said, "You must come to my room and see a picture of Martha right now. It's desperately weird."

Fascinated, Sue nodded, and they moved on through
the quiet street. Ramona paused to look at her each time
they went under a street light, touched her hair, begged
leave to take her arm, and called her Martha, Sister,
Twin, and sometimes caught her breath in an abortive
sob. They went past the lighted windows of the *Bier-
stuben*, where the shadows of young men loomed and
waved, and then turned at the Kornmarkt and began to
climb the steep, moss-slick steps that led to the castle
garden. As they went through the avenue of trees that
lay between the casino and the castle, Ramona, peering
at Sue through the spooky mist, said, "They would have
been much quicker to see it than I," so Sue knew, miserably and for sure, that something had gone wrong
with their plans to go to San Bernardino. And then Ramona laughed and broke away and took off her tam-o'-
shanter, which she hurled toward the hedge of yew,
where it rested tipsily.

"I could vomit," she said, standing absolutely still.

There was a long pause. Finally, Sue could no longer
bear the suspense, and she asked Ramona if her brothers
knew that she and Ramona were not coming.

"Of course they know. They've known for two weeks,
but you're crazy if you think the reason we're not going

is that you look like Martha. How beastly vain you are!"
She was so angry and she trembled so with her rage that
Sue did not dare say another word. "It was Freudenburg
who said I couldn't go," she howled. "He has found out
that I have lost ten pounds."

Sue had no conscious motive in asking her, idly and
not really caring, where Dr. Freudenburg's office was;
she had meant the guileless question to be no more than
a show of noncommittal and courteous interest, and she
was badly frightened when, in reply, Ramona turned on
her and slapped her hard on either cheek, and then
opened her mouth to emit one hideous, protracted
scream. Sue started instinctively to run away, but Ramona seized and held her arms, and began to talk in a
lunatic, fast monotone, threatening her with lawsuits
and public exposure if she ever mentioned the name
Freudenburg again *or* her brothers *or* her mother and
father *or* Martha, that ghastly, puling, pampered hypochondriac who had totally wrecked her life.

Sue felt that the racket of her heart and her hot,
prancing brain would drown out Ramona's voice, but it
did nothing of the kind, and they stood there, rocking
in their absurd attitude, while the fit continued. Sue was
sure that the police and the townsfolk would come running at any moment and an alarm would be sounded and
they would be arrested for disturbing the peace. But if
anyone heard them, it was only the shades of the princes
in the castle.

It was difficult for Sue to sort out the heroes and the

villains in this diatribe. Sometimes it appeared that Ramona's brothers and her parents hated her, sometimes she thought they had been glad when Martha died; sometimes Dr. Freudenburg seemed to be the cause of everything. She had the impression that he was an alienist, and she wondered if now he would send his patient to an institution; at other times she thought the Doctor did not exist at all. She did not know whom to hate or whom to trust, for the characters in this *Walpurgisnacht* changed shape by the minute and not a one was left out —not Signor da Gama or the ballet girls in Naples or the old ladies at the Gerstnerheim or the prehistoric figures of a sadistic nurse, a base German governess, and a nefarious boy cousin who had invited Ramona to misbehave when she was barely eight years old. Once she said that to escape Dr. Freudenburg she meant to order her father to take her cruising on the San Filippo; a minute later she said that that loathsome fool Justin had wrecked the boat on the coast of Yugoslavia. She would go home to the villa in Sorrento and be comforted by her brothers, who had always preferred her to everyone else in the world—except that they hadn't! They had always despised her. Freudenburg would write to her father and he would come to fetch her back to that vulgar, parvenu house, and there, in spite of all her efforts to outwit them, they would make her eat and eat until she was the laughing stock of the entire world. What *were* they after? Did they want to indenture her to a sideshow?

She stopped, trailed off, turned loose Sue's arm, and stood crestfallen, like a child who realizes that no one is listening to his tantrum. Tears, terribly silent, streamed down her round cheeks.

Then, "It isn't true, you know. They aren't like that, they're good and kind. The only thing that's true is that I eat all the time," and softly, to herself, she repeated, "All the time." In a mixture of self-hatred and abstracted bravado, she said that she had supplemented all her lunches at the Gerstnerheim and had nibbled constantly, alone in her room; that Dr. Freudenburg's recommendation had been just the opposite of what she had been saying all along.

Unconsolable, Ramona moved on along the path, and Sue followed, honoring her tragedy but struck dumb by it. On the way through the courtyard and down the street, Ramona told her, in a restrained and rational voice, that her father was coming the next day to take her back to Italy, since the experiment of her being here alone had not worked. Her parents, at the counsel of Dr. Freudenburg, were prepared to take drastic measures, involving, if need be, a hospital, the very thought of which made her blood run cold. "Forgive me for that scene back there," she said. "You grow wild in loneliness like mine. It would have been lovely if it had all worked out the way I wanted and we had gone to Switzerland."

"Oh, that's all right," said Sue, whose heart was broken. "I don't know how to ski anyway."

"Really? What crust! I'd never have bought you all that gear if I had known." Ramona laughed lightly. They approached the garden gate of a tall yellow house, and she said, "This is where I live. Want to come in and have a glass of kirsch?"

Sue did not want the kirsch and she knew she should be on her way home if she were to get anything hot for supper, but she was curious to see the photograph of Martha, and since Ramona seemed herself again, she followed her down the path. Ramona had two little rooms, as clean and orderly as cells. In the one where she studied, there was no furniture except a long desk with deep drawers and a straight varnished chair and a listing bookcase. She had very few books, really, for one so learned—not more than fifty altogether—and every one of them was dull: grammars, dictionaries, readers, monographs reprinted from scholarly journals, and treatises on semantics, etymology, and phonetics. Her pens and pencils lay straight in a lacquered tray, and a pile of notebooks sat neatly at the right of the blotter, and at the left there was a book open to a homily in Anglo-Saxon which, evidently, she had been translating. As soon as they had taken off their coats, Ramona went into the bedroom and closed the door; from beyond it Sue could hear drawers being opened and quickly closed, metal clashing, and paper rustling, and she imagined that the bureaus were stocked with contraband— with sweets and sausages and cheese. For the last time, she thought of Daniel and Justin and Robert, of whom she was to be forever deprived because their sister could not curb her brutish appetite.

She wandered around the room and presently her eye fell on a photograph in a silver frame standing in a half-empty shelf of the bookcase. It could only be Martha. The dead girl did not look in the least like Sue but was certainly as pretty as she had been described, and as Sue looked at the pensive eyes and the thoughtful lips, she was visited by a fugitive feeling that this was really Ramona's face at which she looked and that it had been refined and made immaculate by an artful photographer who did not scruple to help his clients deceive themselves. For Martha wore a look of lovely wonder and remoteness, as if she were all disconnected spirit, and it was the same as a look that sometimes came to Ramona's eyes and lips just as she lifted her binoculars to contemplate the world through the belittling lenses.

Sue turned the photograph around, and on the back she read the penned inscription "Martha Ramona Dunn at sixteen, Sorrento." She looked at that ethereal face again, and this time had no doubt that it had once belonged to Ramona. No wonder the loss of it had left her heartbroken! She sighed to think of her friend's desperate fabrication. In a sense, she supposed the Martha side of Ramona Dunn *was* dead, dead and buried under layers and layers of fat. Just as she guiltily returned the picture to its place, the door to the bedroom opened and Ramona, grandly gesturing toward her dressing table, cried, "Come in! Come in! Enter the banquet hall!" She had emptied the drawers of all their forbidden fruits, and arrayed on the dressing table, in front of her bottles of cologne and medicine, were cheeses and tinned fish and pickles and pressed meat and cakes, candies, nuts, olives, sausages, buns, apples, raisins, figs, prunes, dates, and jars of pâté and glasses of jelly and little pots of caviar, as black as ink. "Don't stint!" she shouted, and she bounded forward and began to eat as if she had not had a meal in weeks.

"All evidence must be removed by morning! What a close shave! What if my father had come without telling me and had found it all!" Shamelessly, she ranged up and down the table, cropping and lowing like a cow in a pasture. There were droplets of sweat on her forehead and her hands were shaking, but nothing else about her showed that she had gone to pieces earlier or that she was deep, deeper by far than anyone else Sue had ever known.

Sucking a rind of citron, Ramona said, "You must realize that our friendship is over, but not through any fault of yours. When I went off and turned on you that way, it had nothing to do with you at all, for of course you don't look any more like Martha than the man in the moon."

"It's all right, Ramona," said Sue politely. She stayed close to the door, although the food looked very good. "I'll still be your friend."

"Oh, no, no, there would be nothing in it for you," Ramona said, and her eyes narrowed ever so slightly.

"Thank you just the same. I am exceptionally ill." She spoke with pride, as if she were really saying "I am exceptionally talented" or "I am exceptionally attractive."

"I didn't know you were," said Sue. "I'm sorry."

"*I'm* not sorry. It is for yourself that you should be sorry. You have such a trivial little life, poor girl. It's not your fault. Most people do."

"I'd better go," said Sue.

"Go! Go!" cried Ramona, with a gesture of grand benediction. "I weep not."

Sue's hand was on the knob of the outer door, but she hesitated to leave a scene so inconclusive. Ramona watched her as she lingered; her mouth was so full that her cheeks were stretched out as if in mumps, and through the food and through a devilish, mad grin she said, "Of *course* you could never know the divine joy of being twins, provincial one! Do you know what he said the last night when my name was Martha? The night he came into that room where the anemones were? He pretended that he was looking for a sheet of music. Specifically for a sonata for the harpsichord by Wilhelm Friedrich Bach."

But Sue did not wait to hear what he, whoever he was, had said; she ran down the brown-smelling stairs and out into the cold street with the feeling that Ramona was still standing there before the food, as if she were serving herself at an altar, still talking, though there was no one to listen. She wondered if she ought to summon Dr. Freudenburg, and then decided that, in the end, it was none of her business. She caught a trolley that took her near her pension, and was just in time to get some hot soup and a plate of cold meats and salad before the kitchen closed. But when the food came, she found that she had no appetite at all. "What's the matter?" asked Herr Sachs, the fresh young waiter. "Are you afraid to get fat?" And he looked absolutely flabbergasted when, at this, she fled from the café without a word.

*A Country Love Story*

An antique sleigh stood in the yard, snow after snow banked up against its eroded runners. Here and there upon the bleached and splintery seat were wisps of horsehair and scraps of the black leather that had once upholstered it. It bore, with all its jovial curves, an air not so much of desuetude as of slowed-down dash, as if weary horses, unable to go another step, had at last stopped here. The sleigh had come with the house. The former owner, a gifted businesswoman from Castine who bought old houses and sold them again with all their pitfalls still intact, had said when she was showing them the place, "A picturesque detail, I think," and, waving it away, had turned to the well, which, with enthusiasm and at considerable length, she said had never gone dry. Actually, May and Daniel had found the detail more distracting than picturesque, so nearly kin was it to out-door arts and crafts, and when the woman, as they de-parted in her car, gestured toward it again and said, "Paint that up a bit with something cheery and it will really add no end to your yard," simultaneous shudders coursed them. They had planned to remove the sleigh before they did anything else.

But partly because there were more important things
to be done, and partly because they did not know where
to put it (a sleigh could not, in the usual sense of the
words, be thrown away), and partly because it seemed
defiantly a part of the yard, as entitled to be there permanently as the trees, they did nothing about it.
Throughout the summer, they saw birds briefly pause
on its rakish front and saw the fresh rains wash its
runners; in the autumn they watched the golden leaves
fill the seat and nestle dryly down; and now, with the
snow, they watched this new accumulation.

The sleigh was visible from the windows of the big,
bright kitchen where they ate all their meals and, sometimes too bemused with country solitude to talk, they
gazed out at it, forgetting their food in speculating on
its history. It could have been driven cavalierly by the
scion of some sea captain's family, or it could have been
used soberly to haul the household's Unitarians to
church or to take the womenfolk around the countryside
on errands of good will. They did not speak of what
its office might have been, and the fact of their silence
was often nettlesome to May, for she felt they were silent too much of the time; a little morosely, she thought,
If something as absurd and as provocative as this at
which we look together—and which is, even though we
didn't want it, our own property—cannot bring us to
talk, what can? But she did not disturb Daniel in his
private musings; she held her tongue, and out of the
corner of her eye she watched him watch the winter

cloak the sleigh, and, as if she were computing a difficult sum in her head, she tried to puzzle out what it
was that had stilled tongues that earlier, before Daniel's
illness, had found the days too short to communicate all
they were eager to say.

It had been Daniel's doctor's idea, not theirs, that had
brought them to the solemn hinterland to stay after all
the summer gentry had departed in their beach wagons.
The Northern sun, the pristine air, the rural walks and
soundless nights, said Dr. Tellenbach, perhaps pining
for his native Switzerland, would do more for the "Professor's" convalescent lung than all the doctors and clin-
ics in the world. Privately he had added to May that
after so long a season in the sanitarium (Daniel had
been there a year), where everything was tuned to a low
pitch, it would be difficult and it might be shattering for
"the boy" (not now the "Professor," although Daniel,
nearly fifty, was his wife's senior by twenty years and
Dr. Tellenbach's by ten) to go back at once to the excite-
ments and the intrigues of the university, to what, with
finicking humor, the Doctor called "the omnium-gath-
erum of the school master's life." The rigors of a country winter would be as nothing, he insisted, when compared to the strain of feuds and cocktail parties. All
professors wanted to write books, didn't they? Surely
Daniel, a historian with all the material in the world
at his fingertips, must have something up his sleeve that
could be the *raison d'être* for this year away? May said
she supposed he had, she was not sure. She could hear

the reluctance in her voice as she escaped the Doctor's eyes and gazed through his windows at the mountains behind the sanitarium. In the dragging months Daniel had been gone, she had taken solace in imagining the time when they *would* return to just that pandemonium the Doctor so deplored, and because it had been pandemonium on the smallest and most discreet scale, she smiled through her disappointment at the little man's Swiss innocence and explained that they had always lived quietly, seldom dining out or entertaining more than twice a week.

"Twice a week!" He was appalled.

"But I'm afraid," she had protested, "that he would find a second year of inactivity intolerable. He does intend to write a book, but he means to write it in England, and we can't go to England now."

"England!" Dr. Tellenbach threw up his hands. "Good *air* is my recommendation for your husband. Good air and little talk."

She said, "It's talk he needs, I should think, after all this time of communing only with himself except when I came to visit."

He had looked at her with exaggerated patience, and then, courtly but authoritative, he said, "I hope you will not think I importune when I tell you that I am very well acquainted with your husband, and, as his physician, I order this retreat. *He* quite agrees."

Stung to see that there was a greater degree of understanding between Daniel and Dr. Tellenbach than be-

tween Daniel and herself, May had objected further,
citing an occasion when her husband had put his head
in his hands and mourned, "I hear talk of nothing but
sputum cups and X-rays. Aren't people interested in the
state of the world any more?"

But Dr. Tellenbach had been adamant, and at the
end, when she had risen to go, he said, "You are bound
to find him changed a little. A long illness removes a
thoughtful man from his fellow-beings. It is like living
with an exacting mistress who is not content with half a
man's attention but must claim it all." She had thought
his figure of speech absurd and disdained to ask him
what he meant.

Actually, when the time came for them to move into
the new house and she found no alterations in her husband but found, on the other hand, much pleasure in
their country life, she began to forgive Dr. Tellenbach.
In the beginning, it was like a second honeymoon, for
they had moved to a part of the North where they had
never been and they explored it together, sharing its
charming sights and sounds. Moreover, they had never
owned a house before but had always lived in city
apartments, and though the house they bought was old
and derelict, its lines and doors and windowlights were
beautiful, and they were obsessed with it. All through
the summer, they reiterated, "To think that we own all
of this! That it actually belongs to us!" And they wandered from room to room marveling at their windows,
from none of which was it possible to see an ugly sight.

They looked to the south upon a river, to the north upon
a lake; to the west of them were pine woods where the
wind forever sighed, voicing a vain entreaty; and to the
east a rich man's long meadow that ran down a hill to
his old, magisterial house. It was true, even in those bewitched days, that there were times on the lake, when
May was gathering water lilies as Daniel slowly rowed,
that she had seen on his face a look of abstraction and
she had known that he was worlds away, in his memories, perhaps, of his illness and the sanitarium (of
which he would never speak) or in the thought of the
book he was going to write as soon, he said, as the winter set in and there was nothing to do but work. Momentarily the look frightened her and she remembered
the Doctor's words, but then, immediately herself again
in the security of married love, she caught at another
water lily and pulled at its long stem. Companionably,
they gardened, taking special pride in the nicotiana that
sent its nighttime fragrance into their bedroom. Together, and with fascination, they consulted carpenters,
plasterers, and chimney sweeps. In the blue evenings
they read at ease, hearing no sound but that of the night
birds—the loons on the lake and the owls in the tops
of trees. When the days began to cool and shorten, a
cricket came to bless their house, nightly singing behind
the kitchen stove. They got two fat and idle tabby cats,
who lay insensible beside the fireplace and only stirred
themselves to purr perfunctorily.

Because they had not moved in until July and by that

time the workmen of the region were already engaged, most of the major repairs of the house were to be postponed until the spring, and in October, when May and Daniel had done all they could by themselves and Daniel had begun his own work, May suddenly found herself without occupation. Whole days might pass when she did nothing more than cook three meals and walk a little in the autumn mist and pet the cats and wait for Daniel to come down from his upstairs study to talk to her. She began to think with longing of the crowded days in Boston before Daniel was sick, and even in the year past, when he had been away and she had gone to concerts and recitals and had done good deeds for crippled children and had endlessly shopped for presents to lighten the tedium of her husband's unwilling exile. And, longing, she was remorseful, as if by desiring another she betrayed this life, and, remorseful, she hid away in sleep. Sometimes she slept for hours in the daytime, imitating the cats, and when at last she got up, she had to push away the dense sleep as if it were a door.

One day at lunch, she asked Daniel to take a long walk with her that afternoon to a farm where the owner smoked his own sausages.

"You never go outdoors," she said, "and Dr. Tellenbach said you must. Besides, it's a lovely day."

"I can't," he said. "I'd like to, but I can't. I'm busy. You go alone."

Overtaken by a gust of loneliness, she cried, "Oh, Daniel, I have nothing to *do!*"

A moment's silence fell, and then he said, "I'm sorry to put you through this, my dear, but you must surely admit that it's not my fault I got sick."

In her shame, her rapid, overdone apologies, her insistence that nothing mattered in the world except his health and peace of mind, she made everything worse, and at last he said shortly to her, "Stop being a child, May. Let's just leave each other alone."

This outbreak, the very first in their marriage of five years, was the beginning of a series. Hardly a day passed that they did not bicker over something; they might dispute a question of fact, argue a matter of taste, catch each other out in an inaccuracy, and every quarrel ended with Daniel's saying to her, "Why don't you leave me alone?" Once he said, "I've been sick and now I'm busy and I'm no longer young enough to shift the focus of my mind each time it suits your whim." Afterward, there were always apologies, and then Daniel went back to his study and did not open the door of it again until the next meal. Finally, it seemed to her that love, the very center of their being, was choked off, overgrown, invisible. And silent with hostility or voluble with trivial reproach, they tried to dig it out impulsively and could not—could only maul it in its unkempt grave. Daniel, in his withdrawal from her and from the house, was preoccupied with his research, of which he never spoke except to say that it would bore her, and most of the time, so it appeared to May, he did not worry over what was happening to them. She felt the cold, old house somehow enveloping her as if it were their common enemy, maliciously bent on bringing them to disaster. Sunken in faithlessness, they stared, at mealtimes, atrophied within the present hour, at the irrelevant and whimsical sleigh that stood abandoned in the mammoth winter.

May found herself thinking, If we redeemed it and painted it, our house would have something in common with Henry Ford's Wayside Inn. And I might make this very observation to him and he might greet it with disdain and we might once again communicate. Perhaps we could talk of Williamsburg and how we disapproved of it. Her mind went toiling on. Williamsburg was part of our honeymoon trip; somewhere our feet were entangled in suckers as we stood kissing under a willow tree. Soon she found that she did not care for this line of thought, nor did she care what his response to it might be. In her imagined conversations with Daniel, she never spoke of the sleigh. To the thin, ill scholar whose scholarship and illness had usurped her place, she had gradually taken a weighty but unviolent dislike.

The discovery of this came, not surprising her, on Christmas Day. The knowledge sank like a plummet, and at the same time she was thinking about the sleigh, connecting it with the smell of the barn on damp days, and she thought perhaps it had been drawn by the very animals who had been stabled there and had pervaded the timbers with their odor. There must have been much

life within this house once—but long ago. The earth
immediately behind the barn was said by everyone to
be extremely rich because of the horses, although there
had been none there for over fifty years. Thinking of
this soil, which earlier she had eagerly sifted through
her fingers, May now realized that she had no wish for
the spring to come, no wish to plant a garden, and,
branching out at random, she found she had no wish
to see the sea again, or children, or favorite pictures,
or even her own face on a happy day. For a minute or
two, she was almost enraptured in this state of no desire, but then, purged swiftly of her cynicism, she knew
it to be false, knew that actually she did have a desire
—the desire for a desire. And now she felt that she was
stationary in a whirlpool, and at the very moment she
conceived the notion a bit of wind brought to the seat
of the sleigh the final leaf from the elm tree that stood
beside it. It crossed her mind that she might consider
the wood of the sleigh in its juxtaposition to the living
tree and to the horses, who, although they were long
since dead, reminded her of their passionate, sweating,
running life every time she went to the barn for firewood.

They sat this morning in the kitchen full of sun, and,
speaking not to him but to the sleigh, to icicles, to the
dark, motionless pine woods, she said, "I wonder if on
a day like this they used to take the pastor home after
lunch." Daniel gazed abstractedly at the bright-silver
drifts beside the well and said nothing. Presently a

wagon went past hauled by two oxen with bells on their yoke. This was the hour they always passed, taking to an unknown destination an aged man in a fur hat and an aged woman in a shawl. May and Daniel listened.

Suddenly, with impromptu anger, Daniel said, "What did you just say?"

"Nothing," she said. And then, after a pause, "It would be lovely at Jamaica Pond today."

He wheeled on her and pounded the table with his fist. "I did not ask for this!" The color rose feverishly to his thin cheeks and his breath was agitated. "You are trying to make me sick again. It was wonderful, wasn't it, for you while I was gone?"

"Oh, no, no! Oh, no, Daniel, it was hell!"

"Then, by the same token, this must be heaven." He smiled, the professor catching out a student in a fallacy.

"Heaven." She said the word bitterly.

"Then why do you stay here?" he cried.

It was a cheap impasse, desolate, true, unfair. She did not answer him.

After a while he said, "I almost believe there's something you haven't told me."

She began to cry at once, blubbering across the table at him. "You have said that before. What am I to say? What have I done?"

He looked at her, impervious to her tears, without mercy and yet without contempt. "I don't know. But you've done something."

It was as if she were looking through someone else's

scrambled closets and bureau drawers for an object that
had not been named to her, but nowhere could she find
her gross offense.

Domestically she asked him if he would have more
coffee and he peremptorily refused and demanded,
"Will you tell me why it is you must badger me? Is it
a compulsion? Can't you control it? Are you going
mad?"

From that day onward, May felt a certain stirring of life
within her solitude, and now and again, looking up from
a book to see if the damper on the stove was right, to listen to a rat renovating its house-within-a-house, to watch
the belled oxen pass, she nursed her wound, hugged it,
repeated his awful words exactly as he had said them,
reproduced the way his wasted lips had looked and his
bright, farsighted eyes. She could not read for long at
any time, nor could she sew. She cared little now for
planning changes in her house; she had meant to sand
the painted floors to uncover the wood of the wide boards
and she had imagined how the long, paneled windows
of the drawing room would look when yellow velvet curtains hung there in the spring. Now, schooled by silence
and indifference, she was immune to disrepair and to
the damage done by the wind and snow, and she looked,
as Daniel did, without dislike upon the old and nasty
wallpaper and upon the shabby kitchen floor. One day,
she knew that the sleigh would stay where it was so long
as they stayed there. From every thought, she returned

to her deep, bleeding injury. He had asked her if she
were going mad.

She repaid him in the dark afternoons while he was
closeted away in his study, hardly making a sound save
when he added wood to his fire or paced a little, deep
in thought. She sat at the kitchen table looking at the
sleigh, and she gave Daniel insult for his injury by
imagining a lover. She did not imagine his face, but
she imagined his clothing, which would be costly and
in the best of taste, and his manner, which would be
urbane and anticipatory of her least whim, and his
clever speech, and his adept courtship that would begin
the moment he looked at the sleigh and said, "I must
get rid of that for you at once." She might be a widow,
she might be divorced, she might be committing adul-
tery. Certainly there was no need to specify in an affair
so securely legal. There was no need, that is, up to a
point, and then the point came when she took in the fact
that she not only believed in this lover but loved him
and depended wholly on his companionship. She complained to him of Daniel and he consoled her; she told
him stories of her girlhood, when she had gaily gone to
parties, squired by boys her own age; she dazzled him
sometimes with the wise comments she made on the
books she read. It came to be true that if she so much as
looked at the sleigh, she was weakened, failing with
starvation.

Often, about her daily tasks of cooking food and
washing dishes and tending the fires and shopping in

the general store of the village, she thought she should watch her step, that it was this sort of thing that *did* make one go mad; for a while, then, she went back to Daniel's question, sharpening its razor edge. But she could not corral her alien thoughts and she trembled as she bought split peas, fearful that the old men loafing by the stove could see the incubus of her sins beside her. She could not avert such thoughts when they rushed upon her sometimes at tea with one of the old religious ladies of the neighborhood, so that, in the middle of a conversation about a deaconess in Bath, she retired from them, seeking her lover, who came, faceless, with his arms outstretched, even as she sat up straight in a Boston rocker, even as she accepted another cup of tea. She lingered over the cake plates and the simple talk, postponing her return to her own house and to Daniel, whom she continually betrayed.

It was not long after she recognized her love that she began to wake up even before the dawn and to be all day quick to everything, observant of all the signs of age and eccentricity in her husband, and she compared him in every particular—to his humiliation, in her eyes— with the man whom now it seemed to her she had always loved at fever pitch.

Once when Daniel, in a rare mood, kissed her, she drew back involuntarily and he said gently, "I wish I knew what you had done, poor dear." He looked, as if for written words, in her face.

"You said you knew," she said, terrified.

"I do."

"Then why do you wish you knew?" Her baffled voice was high and frantic. "You don't talk sense!"

"I do," he said sedately. "I talk sense always. It is you who are oblique." Her eyes stole like a sneak to the sleigh. "But I wish I knew your motive," he said impartially.

For a minute, she felt that they were two maniacs answering each other questions that had not been asked, never touching the matter at hand because they did not know what the matter was. But in the next moment, when he turned back to her spontaneously and clasped her head between his hands and said, like a tolerant father, "I forgive you, darling, because you don't know how you persecute me. No one knows except the sufferer what this sickness is," she knew again, helplessly, that they were not harmonious even in their aberrations.

These days of winter came and went, and on each of them, after breakfast and as the oxen passed, he accused her of her concealed misdeed. She could no longer truthfully deny that she was guilty, for she was in love, and she heard the subterfuge in her own voice and felt the guilty fever in her veins. Daniel knew it, too, and watched her. When she was alone, she felt her lover's presence protecting her—when she walked past the stiff spiraea, with icy cobwebs hung between its twigs, down to the lake, where the black, unmeasured water was hidden beneath a lid of ice; when she walked, instead, to the salt river to see the tar-paper shacks where the men

caught smelt through the ice; when she walked in the
dead dusk up the hill from the store, catching her breath
the moment she saw the sleigh. But sometimes this splendid being mocked her when, freezing with fear of the
consequences of her sin, she ran up the stairs to Daniel's
room and burrowed her head in his shoulder and cried,
"Come downstairs! I'm lonely, please come down!" But
he would never come, and at last, bitterly, calmed by
his calmly inquisitive regard, she went back alone and
stood at the kitchen window, coyly half hidden behind
the curtains.

For months she lived with her daily dishonor, rattled,
ashamed, stubbornly clinging to her secret. But she grew
more and more afraid when, oftener and oftener, Daniel
said, "Why do you lie to me? What does this mood of
yours mean?" and she could no longer sleep. In the
raw nights, she lay straight beside him as he slept, and
she stared at the ceiling, as bright as the snow it reflected, and tried not to think of the sleigh out there
under the elm tree but could think only of it and of the
man, her lover, who was connected with it somehow. She
said to herself, as she listened to his breathing, "If I
confessed to Daniel, he would understand that I was
lonely and he would comfort me, saying, 'I am here,
May. I shall never let you be lonely again.'" At these
times, she was so separated from the world, so far removed from his touch and his voice, so solitary, that she
would have sued a stranger for companionship. Daniel
slept deeply, having no guilt to make him toss. He slept,

indeed, so well that he never even heard the ditcher on snowy nights rising with a groan over the hill, flinging the snow from the road and warning of its approach by lights that first flashed red, then blue. As it passed their house, the hurled snow swashed like flames. All night she heard the squirrels adding up their nuts in the walls and heard the spirit of the house creaking and softly clicking upon the stairs and in the attics.

In early spring, when the whippoorwills begged in the cattails and the marsh reeds, and the northern lights patinated the lake and the tidal river, and the stars were large, and the huge vine of Dutchman's-pipe had started to leaf out, May went to bed late. Each night she sat on the back steps waiting, hearing the snuffling of a dog as it hightailed it for home, the single cry of a loon. Night after night, she waited for the advent of her rebirth while upstairs Daniel, who had spoken tolerantly of her vigils, slept, keeping his knowledge of her to himself. "A symptom," he had said, scowling in concentration, as he remarked upon her new habit. "Let it run its course. Perhaps when this is over, you will know the reason why you torture me with these obsessions and will stop. You know, you may really have a slight disorder of the mind. It would be nothing to be ashamed of; you could go to a sanitarium."

One night, looking out the window, she clearly saw her lover sitting in the sleigh. His hand was over his eyes and his chin was covered by a red silk scarf. He

wore no hat and his hair was fair. He was tall and his
long legs stretched indolently along the floorboard. He
was younger than she had imagined him to be and he
seemed rather frail, for there was a delicate pallor on
his high, intelligent forehead and there was an invalid's
languor in his whole attitude. He wore a white blazer
and gray flannels and there was a yellow rosebud in his
lapel. Young as he was, he did not, even so, seem to belong to her generation; rather, he seemed to be the re-
incarnation of someone's uncle as he had been fifty
years before. May did not move until he vanished, and
then, even though she knew now that she was truly be-
deviled, the only emotion she had was bashfulness, mingled with doubt; she was not sure, that is, that he loved
her.

That night, she slept a while. She lay near to Daniel,
who was smiling in the moonlight. She could tell that
the sleep she would have tonight would be as heavy as
a coma, and she was aware of the moment she was overtaken.

She was in a canoe in a meadow of water lilies and
her lover was tranquilly taking the shell off a hard-
boiled egg. "How intimate," he said, "to eat an egg
with you." She was nervous lest the canoe tip over, but
at the same time she was charmed by his wit and by the
way he lightly touched her shoulder with the varnished
paddle.

"May? May? I love you, May."

"Oh!" enchanted, she heard her voice replying. "Oh, I love you, too!"

"The winter is over, May. You must forgive the hallucinations of a sick man."

She woke to see Daniel's fair, pale head bending toward her. "He is old! He is ill!" she thought, but through her tears, to deceive him one last time, she cried, "Oh, thank God, Daniel!"

He was feeling cold and wakeful and he asked her to make him a cup of tea; before she left the room, he kissed her hands and arms and said, "If I am ever sick again, don't leave me, May."

Downstairs, in the kitchen, cold with shadows and with the obtrusion of dawn, she was belabored by a chill. "What time is it?" she said aloud, although she did not care. She remembered, not for any reason, a day when she and Daniel had stood in the yard last October wondering whether they should cover the chimneys that would not be used and he decided that they should not, but he had said, "I hope no birds get trapped." She had replied, "I thought they all left at about this time for the South," and he had answered, with an unintelligible reproach in his voice, "The starlings stay." And she remembered, again for no reason, a day when, in pride and excitement, she had burst into the house crying, "I saw an ermine. It was terribly poised and let me watch it quite a while." He had said categorically, "There are no ermines here."

She had not protested; she had sighed as she sighed

now and turned to the window. The sleigh was livid in this light and no one was in it; nor had anyone been in it for many years. But at that moment the blacksmith's cat came guardedly across the dewy field and climbed into it, as if by careful plan, and curled up on the seat. May prodded the clinkers in the stove and started to the barn for kindling. But she thought of the cold and the damp and the smell of the horses, and she did not go but stood there, holding the poker and leaning upon it as if it were an umbrella. There was no place warm to go. "What time is it?" she whimpered, heartbroken, and moved the poker, stroking the lion foot of the fireless stove.

She knew now that no change would come, and that she would never see her lover again. Confounded utterly, like an orphan in solitary confinement, she went outdoors and got into the sleigh. The blacksmith's imperturbable cat stretched and rearranged his position, and May sat beside him with her hands locked tightly in her lap, rapidly wondering over and over again how she would live the rest of her life.

*A Summer Day*

He wore hot blue serge knickerbockers and a striped green shirt, but he had no shoes and he had no hat and the only things in his pants pockets were a handkerchief that was dirty now, and a white pencil from the Matchless Lumber Company, and a card with Mr. Wilkins' name printed on it and his own, Jim Littlefield, written on below the printing, and a little aspirin box. In the aspirin box were two of his teeth and the scab from his vaccination. He had come on the train barefoot all the way from Missouri to Oklahoma, because his grandmother had died and Mr. Wilkins, the preacher, had said it would be nice out here with other Indian boys and girls. Mr. Wilkins had put him on the through train and given the nigger man in the coach half a dollar to keep an eye on him, explaining that he was an orphan and only eight years old. Now he stood on the crinkled cinders beside the tracks and saw the train moving away like a fast little fly, and although Mr. Wilkins had promised on his word of honor, there was no one to meet him.

There was no one anywhere. He looked in the windows of the yellow depot, where there was nothing but a fat stove and a bench and a tarnished spittoon and a small office, where a telegraph machine nervously ticked to itself. A freshly painted handcar stood on a side track near the water tower, looking as if no one were ever going to get into it again. There wasn't a sound, there wasn't even a dog or a bee, and there was nothing to look at except the bare blue sky and, across the tracks, a field of stubble that stretched as far as year after next beyond a rusty barbed-wire fence. Right by the door of the depot, there was an oblong piece of tin, which, shining in the sun, looked cool although, of course, Jim knew it would be hot enough to bite your foot. It looked cool because it made him think of how the rain water used to shine in the washtubs in Grandma's back yard. On washday, when he had drawn buckets of it for her, it would sometimes splash over on his feet with a wonderful sound and a wonderful feeling. After the washing was on the line, she would black the stove and scrub the kitchen floor, and then she would take her ease, drinking a drink of blood-red sassafras as she sat rocking on the porch, shaded with wisteria. At times like that, on a hot summer day, she used to smell as cool as the underside of a leaf.

There was nothing cool here, so far as you could see. The paint on the depot was so bright you could read the newspaper by it in the dark. Jim could not see any trees save one, way yonder in the stubble field, and it looked poor and lean. In Missouri, there were big trees, as shady as a parasol. He remembered how he had sat on the cement steps of the mortuary parlor in the shade of the acacias, crying for his grandmother, whom he had seen in her cat-gray coffin. Mr. Wilkins had lipped some snuff and consoled him, talking through his nose, which looked like an unripe strawberry. "I don't want to be no orphan," Jim had cried, thinking of the asylum out by the fairground, where the kids wore gray cotton uniforms and came to town once a week on the trolley car to go to the library. Many of them wore glasses and some of them were lame. Mr. Wilkins had said, "Landagoshen, Jim boy, didn't I say you were going to be Uncle Sam's boy? Uncle Sam don't fool with orphans, he only takes care of *citizens*." On the train, a fat man had asked him what he was going to be when he grew up and Jim had said, "An aborigine." The man had laughed until he'd had to wipe his round face with a blue bandanna, and the little girl who was with him had said crossly, "What's funny, Daddy? What did the child say?" It had been cool before that, when he and Mr. Wilkins were waiting under the tall maple trees that grew beside the depot in Missouri and Mr. Marvin Dannenbaum's old white horse was drinking water out of the moss-lined trough. And just behind them, on Linden Street, Miss Bessie Ryder had been out in her yard picking a little mess of red raspberries for her breakfast. The dew would have still been on them when she doused them good with cream. Over the front of her little house there was a lattice where English ivy grew and her well was surrounded by periwinkle.

But Jim could not remember any of that coolness

when he went out of the shade of the maples into the
coach. Mrs. Wilkins had put up a lunch for him; when
he ate it later, he found a dead ant on one of the peanut-
butter sandwiches and the Baby Ruth had run all over
the knobby apple. His nose had felt swollen and he'd
got a headache and the green seat was as scratchy as a
brush when he lay down and put his cheek on it. The
train had smelled like the Fourth of July, like punk and
lady crackers, and when it stopped in little towns, its
rest was uneasy, for it throbbed and jerked and hissed
like an old dog too feeble to get out of the sun. Once,
the nigger man had taken him into the baggage car to
look at some kind of big, expensive collie in a cage,
muzzled and glaring fiercely through the screen; there
were trunks and boxes of every shape, including one
large, round one that the nigger man said held nothing
but one enormous cheese from Michigan. When Jim got
back to his seat, the fat man with the little girl had
bought a box lunch that was put on the train at Sedalia,
and Jim had watched them eat fried chicken and mustard greens and beet pickles and pone. The next time
the train stopped, the nigger man had collected the
plates and the silverware and had taken them into the
station.

Jim had made the train wheels say "Uncle Sam,
Uncle Sam," and then he hadn't been able to make them
stop, even when he was half asleep. Mr. Wilkins had
said that Uncle Sam wasn't one of your fair-weather
friends that would let a Cherokee down when all his

kin were dead. It was a blessing to be an Indian, the
preacher had said, and Mrs. Wilkins had said, "It surely
is, Jim boy. I'd give anything to be an Indian, just anything you can name." She had been stringing wax beans
when she'd said that, and the ham hock she would cook
with them had already been simmering on the back of
the stove. Jim had wanted to ask her why she would
like to be an Indian, but she'd seemed to have her mind
on the beans, so he'd said nothing and stroked the turkey
wing she used for brushing the stove.

It was hot enough to make a boy sick here in this cinder place, and Jim did not know what he would do if
someone did not come. He could not walk barefoot all
the way back to Missouri; he would get lost if he did
not follow the tracks, and if he did follow them and a
train came when he was drowsy, he might get scooped
up by the cowcatcher and be hurled to kingdom come.
He sat on his heels and waited, feeling the gray clinkers
pressing into his feet, listening to the noontime sleep.
Heat waves trembled between him and the depot and for
a long time there was no sound save for the anxious telegraph machine, which was saying something important,
although no one would heed. Perhaps it was about him—
Jim! It could be a telegram from Mr. Wilkins saying
for them to send him back. The preacher might have
found a relation that Jim could live with. The boy saw,
suddenly, the tall, white colonnade of a rich man's
house by the Missouri River; he had gone there often
to take the brown bread and the chili sauce Grandma

used to make, and the yellow-haired lady at the back door of the big house had always said, "Don't you want to rest a spell, Jimmy, here where it's cool?" He would sit on a bench at the long table and pet the mother cat who slept on the window sill and the lady would say, "You like my old puss-in-boots, don't you? Maybe you'd best come and live with me and her, seeing that she's already got your tongue." Sometimes this lady wore a lace boudoir cap with a blue silk bow on the front, and once she had given him a button with a pin that said, "LET'S CRACK THE VOLSTEAD ACT." The stubborn stutter of the machine could be a message from her, or maybe it was from Miss Bessie Ryder, who once had told his fortune with cards in a little room with pictures of Napoleon everywhere; the English ivy growing just outside made patterns on Napoleon's face, and in the little silver pitcher in the shape of Napoleon's head, there was a blue anemone. Or it could be the Wilkinses themselves sending for him to come and live in the attic room, where there was the old cradle their baby had died in and a pink quilt on the bed with six-pointed stars.

Jim cried, catching his tears with his gentle tongue. Then, a long way off, a bell began to ring slowly and sweetly, and when it stopped, he heard an automobile coming with its bumptious cutout open. He went on crying, but in a different way, and his stomach thumped with excitement, for he knew it would be the people from the school, and suddenly he could not bear to have them find him. He ran the length of the depot and then ran back again, and then he hopped on one foot to the door and hopped on the piece of tin. He screamed with the awful, surprising pain. He sat down and seized his burned foot with both his hands, and through his sobs he said, "Oh, hell on you, oh, Judas Priest!" He heard the car stop and the doors slam and he heard a lady say, "Wait a minute. Oh, it's all right." Jim shut his eyes as feet munched the cinders, closer and closer to him.

"Don't touch me!" he shrieked, not opening his eyes, and there was a silence like the silence after the district nurse in Missouri had looked down his throat. They did not touch him, so he stopped crying, and the lady said, "Why, the train must have come *long ago!* I will positively give that stationmaster a piece of my mind."

Jim opened his eyes. There was a big man, with very black hair, which fell into his face, wearing a spotted tan suit and a ring with a turquoise the size of a quarter. The woman had gold earrings and gold teeth, which she showed in a mechanical smile, and she wore a blue silk dress with white embroidery on the bertha. They both smelled of medicine. The man touched Jim on the arm where he had been vaccinated; baffled by everything in the world, he cried wildly. The woman bent down and said, "Well, well, well, there, there, there." Jim was half suffocated by the smell of medicine and of her buttery black hair. The man and woman looked at each other, and Jim's skin prickled because he knew they were wondering why he had not brought anything.

Mr. Wilkins had said you didn't need to, not even shoes.

"Well, honey," said the lady, taking his hand, "we've come a long way all by our lonesome, haven't we?"

"A *mighty* long way," said the man, laughing heartily to make a joke of it. He took Jim's other hand and made him stand up, and then they started down the cinder path and around the corner of the depot to a tall, black touring car, which said on the door:

DEPARTMENT OF THE INTERIOR
INDIAN SERVICE

In the back seat there were two huge empty demijohns and a brand-new hoe.

"Hop in front, sonny," said the man. The black leather seat scorched Jim's legs, and he put his hand over his eyes to shut out the dazzle of the windshield.

"No shoes," said the woman, getting in beside him.

"Already noted," said the man. He got in, too, and his fat thigh was dampish at Jim's elbow.

Jim worried about the telegraph machine. Would it go on until someone came to listen to it or would it stop after a while like a telephone? It must be about him, because he was the only one who had got off the train here, and it must be from someone saying to send him back, because there was nothing else it could be about. His heart went as fast as a bobbin being filled and he wanted to throw up and to hide and to cram a million grapes into his mouth and to chase a scared girl with a garter snake, all at once. He thought of screaming bloody murder so that they would let him get out of the car, but they might just whip him for that, whip him with an inner tube or beat him over the head with the new hoe. But he wouldn't stay at the school! If there was no other way, he would ride home on a freight car, like a hobo, and sleep in the belfry of the church under the crazy bell. He would escape tonight, he told himself, and he pressed his hand on his heart to make it quiet down.

From the other side of the depot, you could see the town. A wide street went straight through the level middle of it, and it had the same kind of stores and houses and lampposts that any other town had. The trees looked like leftovers, and the peaked brown dogs slinked behind the trash cans in an ornery way. The man started the car, and as they drove up the main street, Jim could tell that the men sitting on the curb were Indians, for they had long pigtails and closed-up faces. They sat in a crouch, with their big heads hanging forward and their flat-fingered hands motionless between their knees. The women who were not fat were as lean and spry as katydids, and all of them walked up and down the main street with baskets full of roasting ears on one arm and babies on the other. The wooden cupola on the red brick courthouse was painted yellow-green and in the yard men lay with their hats over their eyes or sat limply on the iron benches under the runty trees, whose leaves were gray with dust or lice. A few children with ice-cream cones skulked in the doorways, like abused cats. Everyone looked ailing.

The man from the school gestured with the hand that wore the heavy turquoise, and he said, "Son, this is your ancestors' town. This here is the capital of the Cherokee nation."

"You aren't forgetting the water, are you, Billings?" said the woman in a distracted way, and when the man said he was not, she said to Jim, "Do you know what 'Cherokee' means?"

"No," said Jim.

The woman looked over his head at the man. "Goodness knows, we earn our bread. What can you do with Indians if they don't know they're Indians?"

"I always knew I was an Indian," said the man.

"And so did I," said the woman. "Always."

Jim sat, in this terrible heat and terrible lack of privacy, between their mature bodies and dared not even change the position of his legs, lest he hit the gearshift. He felt that they were both looking at him as if a rash were coming out on his face and he wished they would hurry and get to the school, so that he could start escaping. At the thought of running away after the sun was down and animals and robbers started creeping in the dark, his heart started up again, like an engine with no one in charge.

The car stopped at a drugstore, and the man got out and heaved the demijohns onto the sidewalk. In the window of the store was a vast pink foot with two corn plasters and a bunion plaster. Next door was an empty building and on its window lights were pasted signs for J. M. Barclay's Carnival Show and for Copenhagen snuff and for Clabber Girl baking powder. The carnival sign was torn and faded, the way such signs always are, and the leg of a red-haired bareback rider was tattered shabbily. How hot a carnival would be, with the smell of dung and popcorn! Even a Ferris wheel on a day like this would be no fun. Awful as it was here, where the sun made a sound on the roof of the car, it would be even worse to be stuck in the highest seat of a Ferris wheel when something went wrong below. A boy would die of the heat and the fear and the sickness as he looked down at the distant ground, littered with disintegrated popcorn balls.

The lady beside Jim took a handkerchief out of her white linen purse, and as she wiped the sweat away from her upper lip, he caught a delicate fragrance that made him think of the yellow-haired lady in Missouri and he said, "I want to write a letter as soon as I get there."

"Well, we'll see," the woman said. "Who do you want to write to?" But the man came back, so Jim did not have to answer. The man staggered, with his stomach pushed out, under the weight of the demijohn, and as he put it in the back seat, he said savagely, "I wish one of those fellers in Washington would have to do this a couple, three times. Then maybe the Department would get down to brass tacks about that septic tank."

"The Department!" ejaculated the woman bitterly.

The man brought the other jug of water, and they drove off again, coming presently to a highway that stretched out long and white, and as shining as the piece of tin at the depot. They passed an old farm wagon with a rocking chair in the back, in which a woman smaller and more withered than Jim's grandmother sat, smoking a corncob pipe. Three dark little children were sitting at her feet, lined up along one edge of the wagon with their chins on the sideboard, and they stared hard at the Indian Service car. The one in the middle waved timidly and then hid his head in his shoulder, like a bird, and giggled.

"Creeks!" cried the woman angrily. "Everywhere we see Creeks these days! What will become of the Cherokees?"

"Ask the boy what his blood is," said the man.

"Well, Jim," said the woman, "did you hear what Mr. Standing-Deer said?"

"What?" said Jim and turned convulsively to look at the man with that peculiar name.

"Do you remember your mother and father?" said the woman.

"No, they were dead."

"How did they die?"

"I don't know. Of the ague, maybe."

"He says they may have died of the ague," said the woman to Mr. Standing-Deer, as if he were deaf. "I haven't heard that word 'ague' for years. Probably he

means flu. Do you think perhaps this archaism is an
index to the culture pattern from which he comes?"

Mr. Standing-Deer made a doglike sound in his throat.
"Ask me another," he said. "I don't care about his
speech at this stage of the game—it's the blood I'm talking about."

"Were Mama and Daddy both Indians?" asked the
woman kindly.

"I don't care!" Jim said. He had meant to say "I don't
know," but he could not change it afterward, because he
commenced to cry again so hard that the woman patted
his shoulder and did not ask him any more questions.
She told him that her name was Miss Hornet and that
she had been born in Chickasha and that she was the
little boys' dormitory matron and that Mr. Standing-
Deer was the boys' counselor. She said she was sure Jim
would like it at the school. "Uncle Sam takes care of
us all just as well as he can, so we should be polite to
him and not let him see that we are homesick," she said,
and Jim, thinking of his getaway this night, said softly,
"Yes'm, Mr. Wilkins already told me."

After a time they turned into a drive, at the end of
which was a big, white gate. Beyond it lay terraced
lawns, where trees grew beside a group of buildings. It
was hushed here, too. In spots, the grass was yellow,
and the water in the ditch beyond the gate was slow.
There was a gravelly space for kids to play in, but there
were no kids there. There were a slide and some swings

and a teeter-totter, but they looked as deserted as bones, and over the whole place there hung a tight feeling, as if a twister were coming. Once, when a twister had come at home, all the windows in Mr. Dannenbaum's house had been blown out, and it had taken the dinner off some old folks' table, and when Jim and his grandmother went out to look, there was the gravy bowl sitting on top of a fence post without a drop gone out of it.

Jim meant to be meek and mild until the sun went down, so that they would not suspect, and when Mr. Standing-Deer got out to open the gate, he said quietly to Miss Hornet, "Are the children all asleep now?"

"Yes, we are all asleep now," she said. "Some of us aren't feeling any too well these hot days." Jim stole an anxious glance at her to see if she were sick with something catching, but he could tell nothing from her smooth brown face.

The buildings were big and were made of dark stone, and because the shades were down in most of the windows, they looked cool, and Jim thought comfortably of how he would spend this little time before nightfall and of all the cool things there would be inside—a drink of water and some potted ferns and cold white busts of Abraham Lincoln and George Washington and rubber treads on the stairs, like those in the public school back in Missouri. Mr. Standing-Deer stopped the car by one of the smaller buildings, whose walls were covered with trumpet creeper. There had been trumpet creeper at Grandma's, too, growing over the backhouse, and a silly little girl named Lady had thought the blossoms were really trumpets and said the fairies could hear her playing "The Battle Hymn of the Republic" on them. She was the girl who had said she had found a worm in a chocolate bar and a tack in a cracker. With Lady, Jim used to float nasturtium leaves on the rain water in the tubs, and then they would eat them as they sat in the string hammock under the shade of the sycamores.

It was true that there were ferns in the hall of the small building, and Jim looked at them greedily, though they were pale and juiceless-looking and grew out of a sagging wicker-covered box. To the left of the door was an office, and in it, behind a desk, sat a big Indian woman who was lacing the fingers of one hand with a rubber band. She was wearing a man's white shirt and a necktie with an opal stickpin, and around her fat waist she wore a broad beaded belt. Her hair was braided around her head, and right at the top there was a trumpet flower, looking perfectly natural, as if it grew there.

"Is this the new boy?" she said to Miss Hornet.

"Who else would it be, pray tell?" said Miss Hornet crossly.

"My name is Miss Dreadfulwater," said the woman at the desk in an awful, roaring voice, and then she laughed and grabbed Jim's hand and shouted, "And you'd better watch your step or I'll dreadfulwater *you*."

Jim shivered and turned his eyes away from this crazy woman, and he heard his distant voice say, "Did you get Mr. Wilkins' telegram?"

"Telegram?" boomed Miss Dreadfulwater, and laughed uproariously. "Oh, sure, we got his telegram. Telegram and long-distance telephone call. Didn't you come in a de-luxe Pullman drawing room? And didn't Uncle Sam his own self meet you in the company limousine? Why, yes, sir, Mr. Wilkins, and Uncle Sam and Honest Harold in Washington, and all of us here have just been thinking about hardly anything else but Jim Littlefield."

Mr. Standing-Deer said wearily, "For Christ's sake, Sally, turn on the soft music. The kid's dead beat."

"I'm dead beat, too, Mr. Lying-Moose and Miss Yellow-Jacket, and I say it's too much. It's too much, I say. There are six more down in this dormitory alone, and that leaves, altogether, eight well ones. And the well ones are half dead on their feet at that, the poor little old buzzards."

There was something wrong with Miss Dreadfulwater that Jim could not quite understand. He would have said she was drunk if she hadn't been a woman and a sort of teacher. She took a card out of the desk and asked him how old he was and if he had been vaccinated and what his parents' names were. He wanted a drink of water, or wanted at least to go and smell the ferns, but he dared not ask and stood before the desk feeling that he was already sick with whatever it was the others were sick with. Mr. Standing-Deer took a gun out of his coat pocket and put it on the desk and then he went down

the hall, saying over his shoulder, "I guess they're all
too sick to try and fly the coop for a while."

"How old was your mother when she died?" said
Miss Dreadfulwater.

"Eighteen and a half," said Jim.

"How do you know?" she said.

"Grandma told me. Besides, I knew."

"You *knew?* You remember your mother?"

"Yes," said Jim. "She was a Bolshevik."

Miss Dreadfulwater put down her Eversharp and
looked straight into his eyes. "Are you crazy with the
heat or am I?" she said.

He rather liked her, after all, and so he smiled until
Miss Hornet said, "Hurry along, Sally, I haven't got all
day."

"O.K., O.K., Queenie. I just wanted to straighten out
this about the Bolshevik."

"Oh, do it later," said Miss Hornet. "You know he's
just making up a story. They all do when they first
come."

Miss Dreadfulwater asked some more questions—
whether his tonsils were out, who Mr. Wilkins was,
whether Jim thought he was a full-blood or a half-breed
or what. She finished finally and put the card back in
the drawer, and then Miss Hornet said to Jim, "What
would you like to do now? You're free to do whatever
you like till suppertime. It's perfectly clear that you
have no unpacking to do."

"Did he come just like this?" said Miss Dreadful-water, astonished. "Really?"

Miss Hornet ignored her and said, "What would you like to do?"

"I don't know," Jim said.

"Of course you do," she said sharply. "Do you want to play on the slide? Or the swings? None of the other children are out, but I should think a boy of eight could find plenty of ways to amuse himself."

"I can," he said. "I'll go outside."

"He ought to go to bed," said Miss Dreadfulwater. "You ought to put him to bed right now if you don't want him to come down with it."

"Be still, Sally," said Miss Hornet. "You run along now, Jim."

Although Jim was terribly thirsty, he did not stop to look for a drinking fountain or even to glance at the ferns. The composition floor was cool to his feet, but when he went out the door the heat came at him like a slapping hand. He did not mind it, because he would soon escape. The word "escape" itself refreshed him and he said it twice under his breath as he walked across the lawn.

In back of the building, there was a good-sized tree and a boy was sitting in the shade of it. He wore a green visor, and he was reading a book and chewing gum like sixty.

Jim walked up to him and said, "Do you know where any water is?"

The boy took off the visor, and Jim saw that his eyes were bright red. They were so startling that he could not help staring. The boy said, "The water's poisonous. There's an epidemic here."

Jim connected the poisonous water and the sickness in the dormitory with the boy's red eyes, and he was motionless with fear. The boy put his gum on his lower lip and clamped it there with his upper teeth, which were striped with gray and were finely notched, like a bread knife. "One died," he said, and laughed and rolled over on his stomach.

At the edge of the lawn beyond all the buildings, Jim saw a line of trees, the sort that follow a riverbank, and he thought that when it got dark, that was where he would go. But he was afraid, and even though it was hot and still here and he was thirsty, he did not want the day to end soon, and he said to the ugly, laughing boy, "Isn't there any good water at all?"

"There is," said the boy, sitting up again and putting his visor on, "but not for Indians. I'm going to run away." He popped his gum twice and then he pulled it out of his mouth for a full foot and swung it gently, like a skipping rope.

Jim said, "When?"

"When my plans are laid," said the boy, showing all his strange teeth in a smile that was not the least friendly. "You know whose hangout is over there past the trees?"

"No, whose?"

"Clyde Barrow's," whispered the boy. "Not long ago,

they came and smoked him out with tommy guns. That's where I'm going when I leave here."

For the first time, Jim noticed the boy's clothes. He wore blue denim trousers and a blue shirt to match, and instead of a belt, he wore a bright-red sash, about the color of his eyes. It was certainly not anything Jim had ever seen any other boy wear, and he said, pointing to it, "Is that a flag or something?"

"It's the red sash," replied the boy. "It's a penalty. You aren't supposed to be talking to me when I have it on." He gave Jim a nasty, secret smile and took his gum out of his mouth and rolled it between his thumb and forefinger. "What's your name, anyway?" he asked.

"Jim Littlefield."

"That's not Indian. My name is Rock Forward Mankiller. My father's name is Son-of-the-Man-Who-Looked-Like-a-Bunch-of-Rags-Thrown-Down. It's not that long in Navajo."

"Navajo?" asked Jim.

"Yes. I'm not Cherokee," said the boy.

"What did you do to make them put the red sash on you?" Jim asked, wishing to know, yet not wanting to hear.

"Wouldn't you like to know?" said Rock Forward and started to chew his gum again. Jim sat down in the shade beside him and looked at his burned foot. There was no blister, but it was red and the skin felt drawn. His head ached and his throat was sore, and he wanted to lie down on his stomach and go to sleep, but he dared not, lest he be sleeping when the night came. He felt again the burden of the waiting silence; once a fool blue jay started to raise the roof in Clyde Barrow's woods and a couple of times he heard a cow moo, but the rest of the time there was only this hot stillness in which the red-eyed boy stared at him calmly.

"What do they do if you escape and they catch you?" Jim asked, trembling and giving himself away.

"Standing-Deer comes after you with his six gun, and then you get the red sash," said Rock Forward, eying him closely. "You can't get far unless you lay your plans. I know what you're thinking about, Little-field. All new kids do. I'm wise to it." He giggled and stretched his arms out wide, and once again he showed his sickening teeth.

The desire to sleep was so strong that Jim was not even angry with Rock Forward, and he swayed to and fro, half dozing, longing to lie full length on a bed and dimly to hear the sounds the awake people made through a half-open door. Little, bright-colored memories came to him pleasantly, like the smallest valentines. The reason he knew that his mother had been a Bolshevik was that she'd had a pair of crimson satin slippers, which Grandma had kept in a drawer, along with her best crocheted pot holders and an album of picture postal cards from Gettysburg. The lovely shoes were made of satin and the heels were covered with rhinestones. The shiny cloth, roughened in places, was the color of Rock

Forward's eyes and of his sash. Jim said, "No kidding, why do you have to wear the red sash?"

"I stole Standing-Deer's gun, if you want to know, and I said, 'To hell with Uncle Sam.'"

Jim heard what the boy said but he paid no mind, and he said, not to the boy or to anyone, "I'll wait till tomorrow. I'm too sleepy now."

Nor did Rock Forward pay any heed to Jim. Instead, he said, turning his head away and talking in the direction of the outlaw's hangout, "If I get sick with the epidemic and die, I'll kill them all. Standing-Deer first and Dreadfulwater second and Hornet third. I'll burn the whole place up and I'll spit everywhere."

"Do you have a father?" said Jim, scarcely able to get the words out.

"Of course I have a father," said Rock Forward in a sudden rage. "Didn't I just tell you his name? Didn't you know he was in jail for killing a well-known attorney in Del Rio, Texas? If he knew I was here, he'd kill them all. He'd take this red sash and tear it to smithereens. I'm no orphan and I'm not a Cherokee like the rest of you either, and when I get out of here, Standing-Deer had just better watch out. He'd just better watch his p's and q's when I get a six gun of my own." Passionately, he tore off his visor and bent it double, cracking it smack down the middle of the isinglass, and then, without another word, he went running off in the direction of the line of trees, the ends of the red sash flapping at his side.

Jim was too sleepy to care about anything now—now that he had decided to wait until tomorrow. He did not even care that it was hot. He lay down on the sickly grass, and for a while he watched a lonesome leaf-cutter bee easing a little piece of plantain into its hole. He hoped they would not wake him up and make him walk into the dormitory; he hoped that Mr. Standing-Deer would come and carry him, and he could see himself with his head resting on that massive shoulder in the spotted coat. He saw himself growing smaller and smaller and lying in a bureau drawer, like Kayo in the funny papers. He rustled in his sleep, moving away from the sharp heels of the red shoes, and something as soft and deep and safe as fur held him in a still joy.

*The Maiden*

"I bought the pair of them in Berlin for forty marks," Mrs. Andreas was saying to Dr. Reinmuth, who had admired the twin decanters on her dinner table. "It sickens me, the way they must let their treasures go for nothing. I can take no pride in having got a bargain when I feel like a pirate." Evan Leckie, an American journalist who was the extra man at the party, turned away from the woman on his right to glance at his hostess to see if her face revealed the hypocrisy he had heard, ever so faintly, in her voice, but he could read nothing in her bland eyes, nor could he discover the reaction of her interlocutor, who slightly inclined his head in acknowledgment of her sympathy for his mortified compatriots but said nothing and resumed his affectionate scrutiny of the decanters as Mrs. Andreas went on to enumerate other instances of the victors' gains through the Germans' losses. Evan, just transferred to Heidelberg from the squalor and perdition of Nuremberg, joined in the German's contemplation of these relics of more handsome times. One of the bottles was filled with red wine, which gleamed darkly through the lustrous, sculptured glass, chased with silver, and the other with pale, sunny

Chablis. The candlelight invested the wines with a property beyond taste and fluidity, a subtile grace belonging
to a world almost imaginary in its elegance, and for a
moment Evan warmed toward Mrs. Andreas, who had
tried to resuscitate this charming world for her guests
by putting the decanters in the becoming company of
heavy, florid silverware and Dresden fruit plates and a
bowl of immaculate white roses, and by dressing herself,
a plump and unexceptional person, in an opulent frock
of gold brocade and a little queenly crown of amethysts
for her curly, graying hair.

The double doors to the garden were open to admit
the moonlight and the summer breeze, and now and
again, in the course of the meal, Evan had glanced out
and had seen luminous nicotiana and delphiniums growing profusely beside a high stone wall. Here, in the hilly
section of the city, it was as quiet as in the country;
there was not a sound of jeeps or drunken G.I.s to disturb the light and general conversation of Americans
breaking bread with Germans. Only by implication and
indirection were the war and the Occupation spoken of,
and in this abandonment of the contemporary, the van-
quished, these charming Reinmuths, save by their dress
and their speech, could not be distinguished from the
conquerors. If chivalry, thought Evan, were ever to return to the world, peace would come with it, but evenings
like this were isolated, were all but lost in the vast,
arid wastes of the present hour within the present decade.
And the pity that Mrs. Andreas bestowed upon her Ger-

man guests would not return to them the decanters they had forfeited, nor would her hospitality obliterate from their hearts the knowledge of their immense dilemma. Paradoxically, it was only upon the highest possible level that Germans and Americans these days could communicate; only a past that was now irretrievable could bring them into harmony with one another.

For the past month in Nuremberg, ever since Evan's wife, Virginia, had left him—left him, as she had put it in a shout, "to stew in his own juice"—Evan had spent his evenings in the bar of his hotel, drinking by himself and listening, in a trance of boredom, to the conversations of the Americans about him. The mirrored walls and mirrored ceilings had cast back the manifold reflections of able-bodied Wacs in summer uniforms, who talked of their baseball teams (once he had seen a phalanx of them in the lobby, armed with bats and catchers' mitts, looking no less manly than the Brooklyn Dodgers) and of posts where they had been stationed and of itineraries, past and future. "Where were you in '45?" he had heard one of them cry. "New Caledonia! My God! So was I. Isn't it a riot to think we were both in New Caledonia in '45 and now are here in the Theater?" Things had come to a pretty pass, thought Evan, when *this* was the theater of a young girl's dreams. They did not talk like women and they did not look like women but like a modern mutation, a revision, perhaps more efficient and sturdier, of an old model. Half hypnotized by the signs of the times, he had come almost to

believe that the days of men and women were over and
that the world had moved into a new era dominated by
a neuter body called Personnel, whose only concerns
were to make history and to snub the history that had
already been made. Miss Sally Dean, who sat across
from him tonight, had pleased him at first glance with
her bright-blond hair and her alabaster shoulders and
the fine length of her legs, but over the cocktails his delight departed when, in the accents of West Los Angeles,
she had said she wished General MacArthur were in
Germany, since he was, in her opinion, a "real glamour
puss." The woman on his right, Mrs. Crowell, the wife
of a judge from Ohio in the judiciary of the Occupation,
was obsessively loquacious; for a very long time she
had been delivering to him a self-sustaining monologue
on the effronteries of German servants, announcing
once, with all the authority of an anthropologist, that
"the Baden mind is *consecrated* to dishonesty." He could
not put his finger on it, but, in spite of her familiar
housewife's complaints, she did not sound at all like his
mother and his aunts in Charlottesville, whose lives,
spun out in loving domesticity, would lose their pun-
gency if cooks kept civil tongues in their heads and if
upstairs maids were not light-fingered. Mrs. Crowell
brought to her housekeeping problems a modern and
impersonal intellect. "The Baden mind," "the Franconian mind," "the German character" were phrases
that came forth irrefutably. And the bluestocking wife
of a Captain McNaughton, who sat on Evan's left and

who taught library science to the wives of other Army
officers, had all evening lectured Dr. Reinmuth on the
faults (remediable, in her opinion) of his generation
that had forced the world into war. Dr. Reinmuth was a
lawyer. She was herself a warrior; she argued hotly, although the German did not oppose her, and sometimes
she threatened him with her spoon.

It was the German woman, Frau Reinmuth, who, although her gray dress was modest and although she
wore no jewels and little rouge, captivated Evan with
her ineffable femininity; she, of all the women there,
had been challenged by violence and she had ignored it,
had firmly and with great poise set it aside. To look at
her, no one would know that the slightest alteration had
taken place in the dignified modus vivendi she must
have known all her life. The serenity she emanated
touched him so warmly and so deeply that he almost
loved her, and upon the recognition of his feeling he
was seized with loneliness and with a sort of homesickness that he felt sure she would understand—a longing,
it was, for the places that *she* would remember. Suddenly it occurred to him that the only other time he had
been in Heidelberg, he had been here with his wife, two
years before, and they had gone one afternoon by trolley to Schwetzingen to see the palace gardens. Virginia
had always hated history and that day she had looked
at a cool Palladian summerhouse, designed for witty
persiflage and premeditated kisses, and had said, "It's
so chichi it makes me sick." And she had meant it. How

she had prided herself on despising everything that had been made before 1920, the year of her birth! Staring at the wines aglow in their fine vessels, Evan recaptured exactly the feeling he had had that day in Schwetzingen when, very abruptly, he had realized that he was only technically bound for life to this fretful iconoclast; for a short while, there beside the playing fountains, he had made her vanish and in her place there stood a quiet woman, rich in meditations and in fancies. If he had known Frau Reinmuth then, she might have been the one he thought of.

Evan watched Dr. Reinmuth as he poured the gold and garnet liquids, first one and then the other, into the glasses before his plate. The little lawyer closely attended the surge of color behind the radiant crystal and he murmured, in a soft Bavarian voice, "Lovely, lovely. Look, Liselotte, how beautiful Mrs. Andreas' *Karaffen* are!" Frau Reinmuth, wide-faced, twice his size, turned from her talk of the Salzburg Festival with Mr. Andreas and cherished both her husband and the decanters with her broad gray eyes, in whose depths love lay limitlessly. When she praised the design of the cut glass, and the etching of the silver, and the shape of the stoppers, like enormous diamonds, she managed somehow, through the timbre of her voice or its cadences or through the way she looked at him, to proclaim that she loved her husband and that the beauty of the bottles was rivaled and surpassed by the nature of this little man of hers, who, still fascinated, moved his handsome head

this way and that, the better to see the prismatic green
and violet beams that burst from the shelves and crannies of the glass. His movements were quick and delicately articulated, like a small animal's, and his slender fingers touched and traced the glass as if he were
playing a musical instrument that only his ears could
hear. He must have been in his middle forties, but he
looked like a nervous, gifted boy not twenty yet, he was
so slight, his hair was so black and curly, his brown face
was so lineless, and there was such candor and curiosity
in his dark eyes. He seemed now to want to carry his
visual and tactile encounter with the decanters to a further point, to a completion, to bliss. And Evan, arrested
by the man's absorption (if it was not that of a child,
it was that of an artist bent on abstracting meanings
from all the data presented to his senses), found it hard
to imagine him arguing in a court of law, where the materials, no matter how one elevated and embellished justice, were not poetry. Equally difficult was it to see him
as he had been during the war, in his role of interpreter
for the German Army in Italy. Like every German
one met in a polite American house, Dr. Reinmuth had
been an enemy of the Third Reich; he had escaped concentration camp only because his languages were useful
to the Nazis. While Evan, for the most part, was suspicious of these self-named martyrs who seemed always
to have fetched up in gentlemanly jobs where their lives
were not in the least imperiled, he did believe in Dr.
Reinmuth, and was certain that a belligerent ideology

could not enlist the tender creature so unaffectedly playing with Mrs. Andreas' toys, so obviously well beloved
by his benevolent wife. Everyone, even Mrs. Crowell,
paused a second to look from the man to the woman
and to esteem their concord.

Frau Reinmuth then returned to Mr. Andreas, but it
was plain to see that her mind was only half with him.
She said, "I envy you to hear Flagstad. Our pain is
that there is no music now," and in a lower voice she
added, "I have seen August bite his lip for sorrow
when he goes past the opera house in Mannheim. It's
nothing now, you know, but a ruin, like everything."
Glancing at her, Evan wondered whether she were older
than her husband or if this marriage had been entered
upon late, and he concluded that perhaps the second was
true, for they were childless—the downright Mrs. Mc-
Naughton had determined that before the canapés were
passed—and Frau Reinmuth looked born to mother-
hood. But even more telling was the honeymoon inflec-
tion in her voice, as if she were still marveling now to
say the name "August" as easily as she said "I" and to
be able to bestow these limnings of her dearest possession generously on the members of a dinner party. It
was not that she spoke of him as if he were a child, as
some women do who marry late or marry men younger
than themselves, but as if he were a paragon with whom
she had the remarkable honor to be associated. She, in
her boundless patience, could endure being deprived of
music and it was not for herself that she complained,

but she could not bear to see August's grief over the
hush that lay upon their singing country; she lived not
only for, she lived *in*, him. She wore her yellow hair in
Germanic braids that coiled around her head, sitting
too low to be smart; her hands were soft and large, honestly meriting the wide wedding band on the right one.
She was as completely a woman as Virginia, in spite of a
kind of ravening femaleness and piquant good looks,
had never been one. He shuddered to think how she
must be maligning him in Nevada to the other angry
petitioners, and then he tried to imagine how Frau Reinmuth would behave under similar circumstances. But it
was unthinkable that she should ever be a divorcée; no
matter what sort of man she married, this wifely woman
would somehow, he was sure, quell all disorder. Again
he felt a wave of affection for her; he fancied drinking
tea with her in a little crowded drawing room at the end
of one of these warm days, and he saw himself walking
with both the Reinmuths up through the hills behind the
Philosophenweg, proving to the world by their compassionate amity that there was no longer a state of war between their country and his.

But he was prevented from spinning out his fantasy
of a friendship with the Reinmuths because Mrs. Crowell was demanding his attention. Her present servant,
she told him, was an aristocrat ("as aristocratic as a
German can be," she said sotto voce, "which isn't saying much") and might therefore be expected not to steal
the spoons; now, having brought him up to date on her

belowstairs problems, she changed the subject and drew
him into the orbit of her bright-eyed, pervasive bustling.
She understood that he had just come from Nuremberg,
where she and the Judge had lived for two years. "Isn't
it too profoundly *triste?*" she cried. "Where did they
billet you, poor thing?"

"At the Grand Hotel," said Evan, recollecting the
Wacs with their mustaches and their soldierly patois.

"Oh, no!" protested Mrs. Crowell. "But it's simply
*overrun* with awful Army children! Not children—brats.
Brats, I'm sorry to say, is the only word for them. They
actually roller-skate through the lobby, you know, to
say nothing of the *ghastly* noise they make. I used to go
to the hairdresser there and finally had to give up because of the hullabaloo."

At the mention of Nuremberg, Dr. Reinmuth had
pivoted around toward them and now, speaking across
Mrs. McNaughton, he said dreamily, "Once it was a
lovely town. We lived there, my wife and I, all our lives
until the war. I understand there is now a French or-
chestra in the opera house that plays calypso for your
soldiers." There sounded in his voice the same note of
wonder that he had used when he acclaimed the decanters that he could not own; neither could he again
possess the beauties of his birthplace. And Evan Leckie,
to whom the genesis of war had always been incomprehensible, looked with astonishment at these two pacific
Germans and pondered how the whole hideous mistake
had come about, what Eumenides had driven this pair

to hardship, humiliation, and exile. Whatever else they were, however alien their values might be, these enemies were, *sub specie aeternitatis,* of incalculable worth if for no other reason than that, in an unloving world, they loved.

Mrs. Andreas, tactfully refusing Dr. Reinmuth's gambit, since she knew that the deterioration of the Nuremberg Opera House into a night club must be a painful subject to him, maneuvered her guests until the talk at the table became general. They all continued the exchange that had begun with Frau Reinmuth and Mr. Andreas on the Salzburg Festival; they went on to speak of Edinburgh, of the *Salome* that someone had heard at La Scala, of a coloratura who had delighted the Reinmuths in Weimar. Dr. Reinmuth then told the story of his having once defended a pianist who had been sued for slander by a violinist; the defendant had been accused of saying publicly that the plaintiff played Mozart as if the music had been written for the barrel organ and that the only thing missing was a monkey to take up a collection. This anecdote, coinciding with the arrival of the dessert, diverted the stream of talk, and Judge Crowell, whose interest in music was perfunctory and social, revived and took the floor. He told of a murder case he had tried the week before in Frankfurt and of a rape case on the docket in Stuttgart. Dr. Reinmuth countered with cases he was pleading; they matched their legal wits, made Latin puns, and so enjoyed their game that the others laughed, although they barely understood the meanings of the words.

Dr. Reinmuth, who was again fondling the decanters, said, "I suppose every lawyer is fond of telling the story of his first case. May I tell mine?" He besought his hostess with an endearing smile, and his wife, forever at his side, pleaded for him, "Oh, do!" and she explained, "It's such an extraordinary story of a young lawyer's first case."

He poured himself a little more Chablis and smiled and began. When he was twenty-three, in Nuremberg, just down from Bonn, with no practice at all, he had one day been called upon by the state to defend a man who had confessed to murdering an old woman and robbing her of sixty pfennig. The defense, of course, was purely a convention, and the man was immediately sentenced to death, since there was no question of his guilt or of the enormity of his crime. Some few days after the trial, Dr. Reinmuth had received an elaborate engraved invitation to the execution by guillotine, which was to be carried out in the courtyard of the Justizpalast one morning a day or so later, punctually at seven o'clock. He was instructed, in an accompanying letter, to wear a Prince Albert and a top hat.

Mrs. Andreas was shocked. "Guillotine? Did you *have* to go?"

Dr. Reinmuth smiled and bowed to her. "No, I was not required. It was, you see, my *right* to go, as the advocate of the prisoner."

Judge Crowell laughed deeply. "Your first case, eh, Reinmuth?" And Dr. Reinmuth spread out his hands in a mock gesture of deprecation.

"My fellow-spectators were three judges from the bench," he continued, "who were dressed, like myself, in Prince Alberts and cylinders. We were a little early when we got to the courtyard, so that we saw the last-minute preparations of the stage before the play began. Near the guillotine, with its great knife—that blade, my God in Heaven!—there stood a man in uniform with a drum, ready to drown out the sound if my client should yell."

The dimmest of frowns had gathered on Judge Crowell's forehead. "All this pomp and circumstance for sixty pfennigs?" he said.

"Right you are, sir," replied Dr. Reinmuth. "That is the irony of my story." He paused to eat a strawberry and to take a sip of wine. "Next we watched them test the machine to make sure it was in proper—shall I say decapitating?—condition. When they released it, the cleaver came down with such stupendous force that the earth beneath our feet vibrated and my brains buzzed like a bee.

"As the bells began to ring for seven, Herr Murderer was led out by two executioners, dressed as we were dressed. Their white gloves were spotless! It was a glorious morning in May. The flowers were out, the birds were singing, the sky had not a cloud. To have your head cut off on such a day!"

"For sixty pfennigs!" persisted the judge from Ohio. And Miss Dean, paling, stopped eating her dessert.

"Mein Herr had been confessed and anointed. You could fairly see the holy oil on his forehead as his keepers led him across the paving to the guillotine. The drummer was ready. As the fourth note of the seven struck in the church towers, they persuaded him to take the position necessary to the success of Dr. Guillotin's invention. One, he was horizontal! Two, the blade descended! Three, the head was off the carcass and the blood shot out from the neck like a volcano, a geyser, the flame from an explosion. No sight I saw in the war was worse. The last stroke of seven sounded. There had been no need for the drum."

"Great Scott!" said Mr. Andreas, and flushed.

Captain McNaughton stared at Dr. Reinmuth and said, "You chaps don't do things by halves, do you?"

Mrs. Andreas, frantic at the dangerous note that had sounded, menacing her party, put her hand lightly on the lawyer's and said, "I know that then you must have fainted."

Dr. Reinmuth tilted back his head and smiled at the ceiling. "No. No, I did not faint. You remember that this was a beautiful day in spring? And that I was a young man, all dressed up at seven in the morning?" He lowered his head and gave his smile to the whole company. "Faint! Dear lady, no! I took the tram back to Fürth and I called my sweetheart on the telephone." He gazed at his wife. "Liselotte was surprised, considering the hour. 'What are you thinking of? It's not eight o'clock,' she said. I flustered her then. I said, 'I know it's an unusual time of day to call, but I have something unusual to say. Will you marry me?' "

He clasped his hands together and exchanged with his wife a look as exuberant and shy as if they were in the first rapture of their romance, and, bewitched, she said, "Twenty years ago next May."

A silence settled on the room. Whether Evan Leckie was the more dumfounded by Dr. Reinmuth's story of a majestic penalty to fit a sordid crime or by his ostentatious hinting at his connubial delights, he did not know. Evan sought the stunned faces of his countrymen and could not tell in them, either, what feeling was the uppermost. The party suddenly was no longer a whole; it consisted of two parts, the Americans and the Germans, and while the former outnumbered them, the Germans, in a deeper sense, had triumphed. They had joyfully danced a *Totentanz*, had implied all the details of their sixty-pfennig marriage, and they were still, even now, smiling at each other as if there had never been anything untoward in their lives.

"I could take a wife then, you see," said Dr. Reinmuth, by way of a dénouement, "since I was a full-fledged lawyer. And she could not resist me in that finery, which, as a matter of fact, I had had to hire for the occasion."

Judge Crowell lighted a cigarette, and, snatching at the externals of the tale, he said, "Didn't know you fellows used the guillotine as late as that. I've never seen one except that one they've got in the antiquarian place in Edinburgh. They call it the Maiden."

Dr. Reinmuth poured the very last of the Chablis into his glass, and, turning to Mrs. Andreas, he said, "It was nectar and I've drunk it all. *Sic transit gloria mundi.*"

*The Home Front*

In the back yard of the lodging house, in the top of a dead tree, glib blackbirds swung in the wind on their individual twigs. Now and again, at some signal, they dropped to the ground but presently returned in a flutter of wings. Then the fancy would strike them to clear the tree, every man jack of them and off they would go like a whole company of hysterical busybodies. All the while they were fussing, big silver gulls sailed at their ease, high above them, descending occasionally to sit on the edge of a moored fishing boat that slowly turned round and round at the head of the little harbor. Some of the gulls set out to sea, as straight and sure in their flight as though a great hand carried them out beyond the causeway to the Sound. A savage sunset ignited the windows of defense plants across the water, caused derelict heaps of rubbish to glitter blindingly, smote the khaki wings of helicopters which all day long gyrated over the disheveled land.

Although it was late in April and the day had been warm, the room was chilly and the stout doctor, shivering, drew the heavy Paisley shawl closer about his shoulders, sighed, and settled more firmly into the rocking chair by the window. Steadfastly he stared out. It would be self-indulgent to turn away in displeasure from all the symbols he read in his prospect, unprofitable to admit the intrusion of homesickness or vexation. (He had, of necessity, come to this twilight discipline; in days past he had been so imprudent in his revery that he had often lost all perspective and had thought of the war as a deliberate insult to himself.) And, indeed, it was not so much sad or vexing as it was puzzling that he, a homeless man, native of a distant country, was willy-nilly a part of the "home front," sharing richly in the spoils. As he followed the ascent of a helicopter, he marveled as frequently he did at the wonderful aptness of the phrase, "the home front." Here people lived as headily and impermanently as soldiers on battlefields. There seemed to be no natives unless the babies born here during this long pause could be called such. No indigenous architecture was visible. Probably it existed but it was hidden away behind blocks of temporary structures, by barrack-like apartment houses, sprawling into the yards of churches, huddling in the sulphurous shadows of factories. And although everything was new, made freshly for this especial period in the world's history, it had a second-hand look. Houses, oil drums, buses, people seemed to have been got at a fire sale.

There was a perpetual stirring in the lodging house. All the other tenants were defense workers, and the walls of the corridors were hung with warning pennants: "QUIET! BULLARD WORKER! HELP HIM HELP WIN

THE WAR!" At the most unseemly hours—eleven at night,
four in the morning—-alarm clocks shrieked, taps
gushed, feet crunched over the gravel of the driveway
to the never ending stream of buses. The lodgers ranged
from late adolescence to early senility and they came
from all over the country, from Harrisburg, Pennsyl-
vania; Pueblo, Colorado; Mobile; Galveston; Wilming-
ton, Delaware. They lived three to a room and six to a
bathroom and because there were so many of them and
their existence was so migratory, it was impossible to
tell them apart, to give them more specific designations
than "old" and "young," "male" and "female." Dr.
Pakheiser from time to time received bits of information about them from the Hungarian manageress, Mrs.
Horvath. She tossed them to him, dry and meatless, and
did so without the least good humor. On the first floor
there was (or had been) a Sikorsky worker who owned
a fishing boat and on Sundays went to the Sound for
bass. A lady accountant at Remington Arms had left her
electric grill on for six hours and the pan that had been
on it melted down to nothing, creating a fearful stink.
A foreman at the Bunner Ritter plant had been rejected
by the Army for ulcers of the stomach. A girl at Chance
Vought had, returning from a weekend in Massachusetts,
seen a trainload of prisoners of war passing through the
station in Providence and she had reported that they
grinned shamelessly as if they were on a holiday. But
the doctor did not know whether these adventures belonged to current tenants or to former ones, and if he

had inquired further and had correctly assigned the histories to the right names and faces, it would have served no purpose; by the time he was sure of his ground, they would have packed up their suitcases and moved away and immediately been replaced.

He was sympathetic with their restlessness but sternly held himself detached from it. Had he not done so, he, too, probably would have wandered from one boarding house to the next like a sick person constantly shifting about in his bed trying to find a comfortable position for his aching bones. Refusing to think of himself as a "transient," pretending that there would never be an end to the war or to this exile, he had put up with the chilliness of the house, the unpleasant manner of the manageress, the excessive rent, and had furthermore doggedly transformed the room into *his* room as if he were going to live in it the rest of his life. It was the first time in his three years of residence in America that he had accomplished the transformation, and it had not been easy. In former rooms, though, it had been impossible. This was like one in a hotel which defied any eccentric impress, and in the beginning he had almost despaired, had been convinced that like all the others, it would remain inviolably and complacently itself and that when he finally went away, if his signature were there at all, it would be nothing more characteristic of him than of the tenants before him or the ones to follow: a half-used box of toothpowder and a rusted razor blade in the medicine chest, or on the desk a bottle of ink or a glass ashtray bought for a dime. There was, upon everything, the mark of an absolute and wholly impersonal vulgarity. The furniture was mongrel. The walls were cream-colored plaster that could offend no one; fastened to them here and there were besilvered lamps containing bulbs shaped like fat candleflames that shed a pale and genteel light. The rugs were scrupulously unobtrusive. The sturdy column of the standing lamp was embellished with twists of iron that represented nothing on earth, and the shade, seemingly designed to diminish illumination by exactly half, was silk of a color that could not be named, a color like one acquired by an amateur chemist or by a child experimenting with crayons. The ample bed (too ample for his understanding. It was called a "three-quarter" bed and he wondered whether it was meant for two children or for someone prodigiously obese) was covered with a faded counterpane made of two Indian prints sewn together.

But the room had its virtues. The rocking chair was comfortable, the table was steady, and there were plenty of clothes hangers in the closet. And Mrs. Horvath kept everything clean. Aside from the fireplace which he had been requested not to use, and the only mirror which was hopelessly defective, and the writing desk which had a limping leg, everything was in "good working order."

The exterior of the house was equally noncommittal. It was large, shapeless and built of yellow stone. It stood

behind a high brick wall, its back windows overlooking
an arm of the sea which, at low tide, was a black and
stinking mud-flat. A dump had been made at the end
of the water and here was heaped all the frightful refuse
of the city, the high-heeled shoes and the rotten carrots
and the abused insides of automobiles; when the wind
blew, the odor from the dump was so putrid in so individual a way that it was quite impossible to describe.
But on a clear day, the doctor could look the other way
and see, far off, the live blue Sound and the silhouettes
of white sailboats and gray battleships. And while the
plants, their windows ghastly blue all night, their noises
constant every hour of every day, were almost within
a stone's throw of his window, he had at least the illusion of being in the country. For the lawns in front and
in back were healthy, the trees were abundant, and forsythia was blooming now along the wall. He had pondered often in the year he had lived here why so expensive a house (for clearly it was that; its plate glass
and the intricate furbelows of its façade testified to suddenly acquired money) had been built on so unprepos-
sessing a site, and at last he learned from a taxi-driver
that the original owner had been a rum-runner who had
brought his boats up the narrow neck of water and had
unloaded them at the cottage in the back yard where
now the Horvath family lived. While he was unable to
find more than a humorous token in it, he thought with
certain pleasure of the interview in which the house had

changed hands and become the property of the present landlord, a Roman Catholic priest.

Sometimes, too, he wondered how the bootlegger would regard the changes he had made in his room, a room which perhaps had formerly been the office for the transaction of his illegal business. And how, for that matter, the priest did when he came on his monthly tour of inspection. Very likely both of them would find it prissy and impractical. He had taken down the pictures he found there: a tinted photograph of the Grand Canyon (which he thought must be the most dreadful sight in the world), a subdued study of an English cottage and one of a vase of asters. In their place he had hung a print of "The Siege of Toledo" and one of "The Fall of Icarus" and a photograph of the bridge in Würzburg. On top of the bookcase were three decanters, for kümmel, brandy and Dubonnet, a little white pot of philodendron, and a pewter tray on which stood two heavy wine glasses and a curious pipe. In the shelves were the few books he had brought with him from Ludwigshafen: Dante, Rilke, Plato, some medical books, *Buddenbrooks, Crime and Punishment, The Charterhouse of Parma*, and those he had bought here, in the hope, never realized, of learning to read English easily. Those were *For Whom the Bell Tolls, The Late George Apley, The Golden Treasury* and *The Story of San Michele*. A cuckoo clock hung on the wall over the bed and on the bureau a large wooden nutcracker lay amongst big pecans in a polished lemonwood bowl. On

the bedside table were an ashtray he had bought in
Milan, a brown earthenware carafe, a diary bound in
green leather, and a silver letter opener.

When, at nightfall, he drew the windowblinds against
industrial America, it was not hard to imagine himself
in his student room at Heidelberg. He had never been
rich enough to eat at the town restaurants and he had
disliked the tepid white food at the Mensa of the University, and so he had made little suppers for himself
at his desk. And while now he was quite able to afford
four-course dinners (the dearth of doctors for civilians
had contrived for him a flourishing and gainful practice
amongst Hungarian defense workers and their pregnant
wives) he preferred to remain in his room and eat the
sort of food he had done when he was a young man.
Upon the table he would place the parcels he had
brought from the delicatessen: a little sausage and a
loaf of bread, a bottle of pickled tomatoes, a carton of
Schmierkäse, perhaps a jar of marinated herring. Then,
his meal ready, he would pour himself a glass of Dubonnet, light an Egyptian Prettiest cigarette and sit for
a while in the chair by the window, staring now at the
dark green blind that was punctured here and there,
admitting star-like bits of light.

During the day, Dr. Pakheiser smoked American
cigarettes, but he had found that nothing so completely
and happily restored his student days to him as the smell
of Oriental tobacco, and because he was so busy until
he left his office, he could not afford time for the nostal-

gic meditations it brought. Closing his eyes, he would fancy himself twenty years younger, not yet fat, but even now near-sighted, eating ham and bread and drinking *Rotwein* in the narrow room of Frau Jost's flat. Frau Jost was a pretty, friendly young widow about whom he sometimes had romantic daydreams, and she had a daughter of four, a jolly little girl named Greta. Every morning, as Alfred left the house, Greta came to wish him good-by. She clutched in her arms a black cat who wore a red ribbon about its neck. And as he ran down the stairs, she always said, "Please look up at the window, Herr Pakheiser, and I will wave." Outside, in the steep street, he had to hold his head far back so that he could see the top window, and there she was, on time and faithful every day, to wave her hand and smile at him, still holding her cat.

Although those years at Heidelberg had been rich and full of importance, it was little Greta Jost that the flavor of the cigarette brought back most clearly. While he had had friends with whom he played chess at Burkhardt's *Konditorei* and had drunk with on Saturday nights at the Vater Rhein and while he had even occasionally had a girl, it was his daily encounter with the child that seemed now to fix the days of the past. He had been, even then, a person of strict habit. Once Greta had had chicken-pox and for a week had not appeared at the window, and all that time Alfred had been somewhat inattentive to his lectures and had spent more time at Burkhardt's. But strangely enough, he had not really been fond of Greta—children, in general, made him shy —and he had even found himself wishing that the ritual had never been established since once it had been, it had to be repeated every day without fail for his complete peace of mind. He was even annoyed if the cat did not appear at the window or if it appeared without its ribbon.

But what he would not give for Greta now! With a perversity which he acknowledged frankly, he imagined that he had been devoted to her, that he had called her pet names and had dandled her on his knee. And that his relationship with her mother had been intimate. He could even long for the irascible porter at the medical college, for the torpid *Badmeister* at the public baths who invariably tried to give him a towel which someone else had just finished using. All these people whom he had known slightly or not at all seemed, in his misshapen reflection, to be his friends.

Dr. Pakheiser was not given to self-pity. A scientific man, he looked on facts. He knew that the *Badmeister* had no more been his friend than was Mrs. Horvath and that, in the end, Greta was the only one who had that stature. And just so now, twenty years later, he had again one friend, one companion, a solitary daily relation with a breathing creature. His companion was a gray tom-cat who called on him each evening with the same unswerving regularity that had brought the little girl to the window every morning. The cat came at seven o'clock, announcing himself with a trilling mew outside

the door. He drank the heavy cream his host had poured
into a bowl for him and then he spent the evening, until
about midnight, curled up in the doctor's lap, asleep.
Two or three times in the course of the evening, he
roused himself to make an excursion round the room,
cleverly picking his way through the decanters, patting
the trailing leaves of the philodendron to watch them
sway. He washed a little and returned and slept again.
Half-roused by the turning of a page or the sound of a
match being struck, he would briefly purr as if to say
that his affection had not lessened, that he was merely
preoccupied. At midnight, Dr. Pakheiser took him downstairs, dropped him on the veranda and watched him, revived by the night air, streak across the lawn and disappear over the wall.

The doctor called him Milenka which in Russian, of
which he knew a few words, means "darling." He knew
too little Russian, even, to affix the masculine diminutive. "Milenka," he would say, "I-yi-yi-yi, bad puss!
Bad boy. Ah, Milenka!" Milenka was an ordinary gray
cat with white mittens, a white snout and a shell-pink
nose. He was rather ugly, for he was underdeveloped
and rangy and since he spent a good part of the day in
the coal bin, his paws were always smudged. But he had
a full, healthy purr and a gentle nature. Rarely did he
strop his claws on the carpet, and thanks to the doctor's
weekly application of One Spot powder, he had very few
fleas.

Dr. Pakheiser realized once with half-ashamed amuse-

ment that he had for Milenka a real love, whereas for
Greta he had had only a perfunctory gratitude. It was
chiefly, he supposed, because he was the cat's protector
as well as his friend and had it not been for his suppers
of cream and herring, the poor thing would have had
to shift for himself on the dump. Indeed, he was quite
sure that if he moved away, Mrs. Horvath would have
the cat destroyed, for she had not known, she declared
cantankerously, when she took over the job, that she
would have an animal to care for as well as beds and
bathtubs. No one knew where Milenka had come from.
The landlord disclaimed all knowledge of him; the
former manageress denied that she had ever fed him
or invited him in any way to stay.

The doctor neither liked nor disliked animals. He
had always been indifferent to them, save for police
dogs whom he feared and cocker spaniels whom he
scorned for their somehow homosexual softness. He had
never known an individual dog or cat well. So this
strong feeling about Milenka perplexed him. Was he
turning into an old lady? And would he, together with
his cat-fancying, get notions before he was fifty? But
these speculations did not really worry him; he was sure
that his fundamental motive in helping the cat survive
was that he did not like Mrs. Horvath and by his lavish
purchases of fish and cream, he was deviously repaying
her for her impertinences.

Mrs. Horvath was a dirty, dumpy person in a brown
coverall and a blue work shirt. She was anti-Semitic in

the most extraordinarily forthright way Dr. Pakheiser
had ever seen. On the first day of her regime she had
been introduced to the doctor by the departing manageress, and she had said, "I think you are Jew, Doctor. But
I get rent every Wednesday all same. You don't worry."
Each time he recollected this speech (delivered with a
smile which could not have disarmed a child) he was so
taken aback that he was never able to analyze exactly
what she meant. Evidently it was her intention to announce her antipathy to Jews at the very outset so that
her tenant would not start off under a misapprehension.
It became clear, after a few days, that her rule was firm:
she decidedly was not one of those people who say,
"Some of my best friends are Jews." On the contrary,
she would say, "I hate all Jews." In a way, he preferred
her attitude to that, say, of his office girl, Miss Johnson,
who, with aggressive piety, often congratulated him on
being one of the chosen people. With Mrs. Horvath, he
was dealing with an armed enemy and war, with her,
was war. Miss Johnson, on the other hand, while less
wounding, was more treacherous. She could catch him
offguard when he was fatigued and, sympathizing with
him for being uprooted from his country, could make
him prey to a burning, unobjectified anger on behalf of
his whole race, and to a weepy grief for himself. Then
he would despise America, Connecticut, his cramped
and cluttered office, the strapping great charwoman who
cleaned it, the smell of workmen in the waiting room

and of workmen's cigarettes, but most of all he would despise Miss Johnson.

Milenka was the immediate cause of war between Mrs. Horvath and Dr. Pakheiser. About two weeks after her arrival, she came one evening to collect the rent. Seeing the cat curled up on the pillow of the bed, she wrinkled her low forehead, bunched up her flat Magyar nose and said, "Cat! I *like* dog. I *like* cat. But outside. Not in the house. In Europe, we have dog, we have cat, but all outside. Inside they make their doing on the carpet and all where. Outside, Doctor, I must ask you." Dr. Pakheiser, unnerved, a man who preferred on all occasions to agree, cried, "I see!" and pretended to himself that this was only a humorous crotchet she was airing conversationally. But she remained firm in the doorway even after he had given her the money and then, so suddenly that he scarcely realized what was happening, she bounded forward toward the bed, shrieking, "Out! Out, you!" and Milenka, his eyes widening with terror, leaped from the bed and ran out the door.

The next evening, though, admitted to the house by the man who left for the graveyard shift at Chance Vought, the cat came back, and the doctor, emboldened by his desire for company and his need for continuing custom, again opened his door. Every night thereafter, except on Wednesday when the rent was due, he came and was not turned away. Mrs. Horvath, to be sure, was aware of what was going on. In the morning when the doctor went downstairs, he usually found her indolently

flicking a dust cloth over the newel post or frankly reading the lodgers' postal cards or sitting, sprawled like a
big tom-boy, in one of the chairs of the foyer. She would
give him a look half scornful, half angry and would say,
"I don't know what happen to you when Father come
and see those places on the carpet with sausage marks."
Or she would tell him, jeeringly, that Father was going
to be outraged when he saw the hole in the curtain the
cat had clawed. "I tell *you*, Doctor," she would say, "on
the grass, okay when they lose their hair. Outside, all
right. Inside, on the cushions, hell's bells!" Sometimes
she would simply ask him, in the derisive voice of a bad
schoolboy, "How you find Milenka last night, Doctor?
Plenty good fleas on him, eh?" And once, reaching the
limit of her insolence, she followed him out the door
and paced up the driveway, calling shrilly, "Milenka!
Milenka!"

When he was not in school, the manageress was accompanied by her thirteen-year-old son, a large boy
with a malicious face that forever grinned under a sailor
cap. Occasionally it was he who came for the rent and
Dr. Pakheiser, fumbling in his wallet, felt that the boy
with his obscene leer had expected to find dirty French
pictures on the wall or a light woman in the bed. "Hey,
Doc," he said once, "you like that cat?" And the doctor,
laughing violently, replied, "Ach, yes! Very much."
Freddie continued. Pretty soon now "that cat" had better watch its step for he was going to trap and tame
some birds and if that dope of an old gray dumbbell got

one of them, it would be "good-by, cat." Dr. Pakheiser,
baffled by the assurance of the outsized youth, cried,
"Ach, so!" louder and more amiably than ever.

So far, no birds had been caught, but Freddie, on
Saturday and Sunday, worked all day long making his
traps out of wooden crates, and in time the back yard
was so full of them that it appeared he intended to catch
entire flocks. And the doctor had no doubt either that
Milenka would chase the birds or that Freddie would
cruelly punish him.

## II

On this damp April evening, Dr. Pakheiser was about to
draw his windowblinds and prepare his supper when he
saw Mr. Horvath come out of the cottage bringing a
step-ladder which he set up underneath an apple tree.
At his approach, the blackbirds all flew off, twittering
irritably. Some time before, he had built a bonfire at the
water's edge which now was burning brightly, sending
up bits of charred paper, like smaller blackbirds. The
man called out, "Hey, Freddie, come here a minute."
And Freddie came charging through the door, wearing
a baseball mitt on one hand. There was a colloquy which
the doctor could not hear and then the boy, rushing to
the bonfire, hurling his mitt to the ground, cried, "Oh,
boy!" He lighted a torch and came back to the step-
ladder, sedately so that the flame would not go out,
handed it to his father and then climbed up. At the top,
he wavered a little and let out an exclamation of fright,

but he regained his balance and stooped down to receive
the torch. He was just tall enough to reach the puffy white
tent of caterpillars in a high crotch of the tree. The doctor watched, sickened, saw yellow flames shoot up as the
fat tumor caught fire. Freddie had not thought ahead.
A worm fell upon his upturned face and he screamed
with revulsion and let the torch drop to the ground
where it went on burning and sending up black smoke.
The work, though, was done and while his father beat
the caterpillars to death with the back of a shovel where
they had fallen in the grass, the boy came down the
ladder and went toward the cottage, wiping his face with
both hands as though it never would be clean again. Mr.
Horvath laughed at him and went on killing the pests.
Mrs. Horvath came to the screen door and hooted at her
son, "Ha! Ha!" she laughed. "You keep the mouth open
next time and see what comes in." Restored to his normal spirits, Freddie hooted back, "Yeah, like fun I will!
Yeah, in a pig's valise I will!"

There was a miaow at the doctor's door. He drew
down the windowblind sharply, shuddering at what he
had just seen. There was something primeval in those
people; their communal enjoyment of the annihilation
of the caterpillars was so stupid and so brutish that the
doctor actually retched. Then he let in the refined, soft-
moving cat.

"I-yi-yi-yi!" he said, stooping to pick Milenka up.
"I-yi-yi-yi, my bad puss, my bad boy." Milenka
stretched his head forward and rubbed the top of it

against Dr. Pakheiser's chin, purring loudly. "Milenka," murmured the man. "Ah, my good friend, my dearest one." He poured the cream into the cereal bowl, fetched a quart of Irish ale from the window sill and, sitting down, said to his companion, *"Gut' Mahlzeit."*

When they had both finished and the doctor had put away the food, he settled once more in the rocking chair with the brandy decanter at his elbow. He opened the journal that had come that day and began methodically with the first article, one on the use of sulfa drugs in the treatment of sinusitis. He had read only a few sentences when Milenka leaped to his lap. Dr. Pakheiser ran his fingers under the cat's jaw and around the ears, laid his whole hand on the little gray belly to feel the vibration and read on, at last in repose now that his house was complete. But there was an uneasiness stirring at the back of his mind and although he concentrated and extracted the full meaning from all he read that night, he observed when he rose at twelve to put Milenka out that he had drunk three times as much brandy as was his custom and had made a great inroad into the package of Egyptian Prettiests which he never smoked after supper.

That night he had a strange dream. He dreamed of D-day. He and little Greta Jost had come to wish Mr. Horvath good luck and they had set out to find rooms. The hotels were crowded, for the holiday throngs were tremendous. They sauntered up the boardwalk, admiring the bright tailored shingle where fashionable people were gathered for the start of the regatta. They entered a hotel which was quite deserted save for a man sitting alone on a little mezzanine at one end of the lobby. He sat at a round amethyst-colored glass table, drinking a very pink cocktail, and as they approached, he stood up smiling and cordially extending his hand. They recognized the President and they were gratified when he called them both by name. His address was old-fashioned: he said "Miss Greta" and "Mr. Alfred." Linking arms, the three of them went out. The President said that while he wished the invasion to be as leisurely as possible, it would be folly, would it not, to give the signal too late in the day? Did not his young friends agree that despite our great advances in electricity, there was something essentially *better* about sunlight? Never was there so civilized a man! In the pure, brilliant sky, exquisite airplanes circled and swooped like the loveliest of birds. There was such a profusion of scarlet! In the flags, in the hats of the spectators, on the wings of planes, in colossal bouquets in vases a mile high situated on the beach at intervals of fifteen yards. The yachts were all ready, freshly painted, brightly bannered for the race to Europe.

Alfred and Greta were the first to land. As they walked up the ramp, he noticed the tiny Scotch plaid ribbons that bound her pigtails. Wandering, they could not find the *Konditorei* he had suggested although time and time again they set forth from the Heiliggeist cathedral and took the familiar street. Nor was it possible, as formerly, to see the ruined castle from the bridge, and Greta said, "Herr Pakheiser, I don't believe this is Heidelberg. Now I am afraid and I want my mother. I think we have come to Heilbronn by mistake." But Alfred pointed to the marking that clearly read, "Philosophen Weg," and he soothed her, "Don't be frightened, dearest." They were speeding in a dirty express train through Freiburg, its towers and steeples flattened out like any corpse, its vineyards wasted with drought and disease. The Alps diminished as they neared them. No trees were left. The sun was small and red like an ember. Alfred, receiving a wicker-covered jug of wine from a weeping man who shared their compartment, was too touched and too embarrassed to begin a conversation, but at last he thought of something. "Sir," he said solemnly, "sir, did you ever go fishing in the Sound for bass, using a caddis worm as bait?" The wine in the man's throat gurgled like a death rattle as he looked out at the leveled mountains. "There was a short notice in some review or other," he said, "outlined in black. Even so . . . even so . . ."

In the limbo where he waited a moment before he wakened fully, he thought he was writing the opening paragraph of a children's story in which a little boy lay on his stomach drinking water from a stream. Suddenly his eyes encountered two others, hooded, sparkling with some horrible intelligence. They belonged to a monstrous caddis worm which advanced through the water as he withdrew.

He woke violently. He clasped his hands to his forehead and in the darkness softly moaned. "I must control myself. I must not perish here."

### III

Late in May, Milenka disappeared. Dr. Pakheiser was disturbed but not really anxious until the fourth night passed and he still dined alone. On the fifth morning he diffidently asked Mrs. Horvath if she had seen the cat, and he detected something doubtful, something covert in her reply. She was not arrogant and her eyes seemed unable to focus on his face. She said—uncomfortably, it seemed to him—"No, Doctor. I see him Sunday. My husband see him Sunday. He come back, don't you worry." Then she looked directly at him and smiled, "He know where his sardine is, I tell you." The doctor was smoking and as he went to the table to drop a long ash into the tray there, his hand abruptly shook and the ashes fell to the carpet. He and the woman both briefly looked at them, dispersed fanwise on the green border. And he knew then that she was hiding something, for she did not reproach him for his clumsiness even though she had just finished using the carpet sweeper. He was so angry that he stumbled to the door and his rage so blinded him that he had to lean against the jamb a moment before he could see the steps. It was not, at this moment, that he was mourning the loss of Milenka; it was that he had sensed, despite her near-civility and his own timorousness, as killing a hatred between them as though they were two jungle beasts, determined to destroy one another. "If she has killed my cat," he brooded as he drove through the gate, "then I . . ." but he could not finish the sentence. He could devise no penalty high enough for such wickedness, no penance sufficiently humiliating.

For two weeks nothing passed between the manageress and her lodger. Nothing, that is, but glances boldly indignant on the doctor's part, guilty on the woman's. It seemed to him that the life of the rest of the house had ceased, that all was at an ominous standstill before a final battle to the death. And then, incredibly, the cat came back. When he first heard the mewing outside his door on the dot of seven, Dr. Pakheiser could not believe his ears. Not until the sound had been repeated two or three times did he open the door. His joy at the reunion was less than his shame for falsely accusing Mrs. Horvath and less than his bewilderment at her shifty-eyed embarrassment. Apparently Milenka had just wandered off somewhere as tom-cats do in the spring. He was thin and mangy and his coat was matted with cockleburs and beggar's-lice. His purr had a bronchial rasp and the doctor made a note on his memorandum pad to bring home a worm pill the next night. Nor had he any appetite for the bit of herring which was all that the doctor had to offer him, and after less than half an hour, he asked to be let out. But this strangeness, under good care, would pass. That night the doctor slept well.

"Good morning," he cried heartily as he met Mrs.

Horvath in the hall the following day. "Have you seen my friend, Mrs. Horvath? He came back for his sardine as you promised me."

The woman's eyes opened from their sleepiness, her lips parted in disbelief, and she said, "Back? That cat back?" Dr. Pakheiser assured her that what he said was true and at that moment, to confirm him, Milenka leaped to the window sill from the veranda and sat there in profile, blinking his eyes. Mrs. Horvath stared, "I do not know," she said. "It is like a dream." The doctor surmised, then, that the cat had been put into a bag and taken into the country somewhere and been abandoned. It was scarcely believable that he could be so gross as to laugh triumphantly and almost to sob his words: "Yes, Mrs. Horvath, my dearest friend is restored to me!"

She looked away from the window. "But, Doctor, I do not know. My son, he catch birds all while now. His school finish pretty soon. I think he don't want that cat here."

"It is cruel to catch birds," he said severely, no longer tyrannized over by her now that he had got his cat back. "And *I* want him here even if that boy doesn't." It gave him pleasure to say "that boy" just as she and her son spoke of "that cat."

"But, Doctor, the cat kill birds. My boy don't kill them. He make them into good pet."

"It is the cat's nature to kill birds. But it is not the nature of man to take prisoners."

"No?" she said. The look of cunning returned to her face. "What we fight war for, then, Doctor?"

"I don't know, Mrs. Horvath, I am sure." He was overpowered with disgust that he should be haggling with this obtuse woman over the life of a diseased cat, and that he should be confronted by so irrelevant a question which he could not answer and which, in spite of its fatuous context, made him feel that because he could only say he did not know, like an unprepared schoolboy, his mind was growing dull. And just as he was preparing to bid the manageress good morning and to hurry to his office to plunge himself into work, she threw out a remark more imbecilic than the first but one that utterly confounded him. She said, "My son protect birds from cats just like America protect Jews from Hitler."

For a moment, before he had collected himself, he read an awful symbolic wisdom into this absurdity. Unhampered by learning, in a country where she could not read the language and could barely speak it, where she could be influenced only by the most basic of national prejudices and loyalties, she was truly a natural enemy. Here was the perfect, the pure hatred; the real thing was in Mrs. Horvath's simple heart. He was not so far gone yet as to think that she was bent on getting rid of the cat out of vengeance. Her reasons were more human than that; she did not like cats and she wanted to indulge her son. But at the same time, there was something so sure in her figure of speech that it was as if, from now on, she would implicitly believe it, would even repeat it in later conversations.

In reply, Dr. Pakheiser only smiled. On his way out, he gave Milenka a pat on the head and said loudly, "I-yi-yi-yi, bad puss!" and walked jauntily round the house to his car, whistling. Whistling, as the phrase went, in the dark.

All spring, Dr. Pakheiser trod on eggs. Each evening when he came home and parked his car in the back yard where Freddie was at work on his bird traps, his heart constricted with apprehension. This would be the night, he thought, when Milenka would not come. The boy, grinning even as he pounded in the nails, looked up with a dispassionate greeting. "Hi, Doc. This is for me to get me an oriole in, see? And that there one is for me to get me a purple grackle in. I lure 'em—I know how they whistle and I whistle and they think I'm a bird —and then they get in this little place here, see, and I pull a string and the door comes down and they can't get out. And then I get 'em so tame they'll eat right out of my hand." Once or twice the doctor inquired about his school with the intention of keeping things running smoothly between them. He went to the nuns to whom he referred collectively as "Sister." "Sister flunked me in Latin but she gave me B in Algebra and D plus in English." But it bored him to talk about the contents of his days; he would break off suddenly and pointing to the blackbirds in the dead tree would say, "See them? I don't want 'em but I could have 'em all if I did." And the doctor would look up at the crowded branches, object of his dreamy contemplation every day. "They're dumb birds," Freddie would say as he threw a pebble into the tree and they all disbanded. "They don't know where they're at." Dr. Pakheiser would reply, "I don't think any birds at all know where they're at." They had come to this conventional rite through a mutual understanding: the doctor disliked birds, the boy disliked cats. Neither spoke of his aversion, but under their banter was the serious warning, "Your pet stays where it belongs, or else."

Milenka was soon prospering. His coat came in soft and shining; his purr cleared and his eyes lost the milkiness that had clouded them when he first came home. He was full grown now and, obliged to assume the responsibilities of a male animal, sometimes missed a meal and spent the time with a plump old tabby who howled for him on the stone wall. But good friend that Milenka was, if he failed to come one evening, he sneaked through the door early the next morning when someone went out to the day-shift. The doctor came to enjoy these morning visits even more than the evening ones. He would go back to bed after he had poured out the cream and lie there watching; when the cat had finished, he would jump to the bed, walk carefully up Dr. Pakheiser's legs to the thigh and there establish himself. But there was one drawback to his coming in the daytime. Ironically, a pair of wrens had built a nest under the eave of the corner window and Milenka, hear-

ing them rustle and chirp, would sit up, his whiskers
twitching, his sleek little body poised for a leap. And
whenever this happened, Dr. Pakheiser felt a thrill of
disquiet, afraid the cat would commit a crime during
the day while he was at his office and could not intercede
for him.

Just as Milenka thrived, so did Freddie's successes
multiply and by the first of June, the clumsy home-made
cages in the garage were half full of orioles and robins
and finches and flickers which, at feeding time, gave
out a dissonant and reedy clamor. One Sunday afternoon, when school was over for him and the skies were
full of birds, Freddie stalked a robin in full view of
the doctor's windows. He crept across the lawn on his
hands and knees toward the large unmoving bird. The
advance could either have been for the purpose of murder or for ministration to an injured wing. It was beautiful to watch. There was no sudden nervous jerking, no
change of pace. When he was within two feet of the
bird, his hands left the ground and his lips parted in
his earnestness. His posture and his skill made the doctor think of a praying mantis, one of those miraculously
ugly creatures which he had seen on the road under a
tulip tree and had taken at first for withering seed pods.
Now, a foot away, the hands parted. He was ready for
the capture. Dr. Pakheiser found himself holding his
breath and could not tell whether he wanted the bird to
foil the boy or wished to see it taken. Directly under the
certain hands, the prey was still unaware. Now they

descended and gently took the bird. Freddie stroked its head tenderly with his forefinger and when the captive made a movement to escape, he drew it to his chest smiling rapturously. And the doctor might have warmed toward him, seeing the innocent happiness in his face, had he not bawled out, "Hey, Mom! Got me another one. Boy, oh, boy, am I *good!*"

## IV

Its head high, its tail feathers trailing the ground, the great cock-pheasant moved with dignity out of the shadow of the apple tree into the light where all the glory of its habiliments shone like a sun-struck diamond. Dr. Pakheiser, who had been roused early by an urgent telephone call, paused in his dressing to watch the wonderful bird. He had never seen one before save in pictures which he had not altogether believed. The japanning of its plumage had been masterful: emerald blazed forth beside gold and gold beside scarlet. There was something about it so rich and unusual that he did not think of it as a bird at all but as a costly ornament for the patch of bright grass where now it stopped, surveying the terrain as if this were its own dominion. But the kingly creature was no wiser than its plebeian brothers, and it began to walk rapidly toward one of Freddie's traps. The doctor immediately flung wide his window, unfastened the screen and leaned out, shouting and waving his arms to scare away the foolish bird. He disturbed the sleeping wrens in the eave and they flew wildly against the screen, then sailed off to the apple tree. But the pheasant was deaf to warnings and walked complacently toward his prison. In a frenzy, Dr. Pakheiser reached back to the bedside table and picked up his metal ashtray from Milan. He hurled it at the pheasant. It fell close to the quick feet and instantly the bird turned, running, this time, back over the grass through the shadow of the apple tree and disappeared in the tall weeds that grew about the abandoned boats. Freddie ran out of the cottage. The doctor fastened his screen and stepped back out of sight behind the drapery at the window, but he watched the boy whose face was contorted with fury and frustration. Tears began as he picked up the ashtray. For a second he stared at it as if he were not sure what to do with it and then, with a bawl, he flung it into the water which was at low tide and, cursing at the top of his voice, went indoors.

Dr. Pakheiser finished dressing. He knew that he was not steady enough to shave, but he washed his face and hands slowly and thoroughly, using the nail brush with unaccustomed vigor. He lighted a cigarette and sat down, aware that his delay was selfish. But his patient seemed remote, the illness unimportant. It was not until the cigarette had burned down to nothing that he got up, found his hat and went out. He stole quietly down the stairs and round the house. There was no sign of life in the back yard. From within the cottage came the sound of Mrs. Horvath's voice; she spoke loudly but in Hungarian and he understood nothing of what she said. He gained his car and he was safe. But he knew that the score was not yet settled, for as he drove away, he saw Freddie's face at the window, the strange Mongolian nose spread out as it pressed against the pane. This, finally, would be the day of reckoning.

When he came home at five that afternoon, Dr. Pakheiser found both Mrs. Horvath and Freddie in the large front bedroom downstairs. Someone had just moved out and they were making it ready for a new tenant. They were turning the mattress, but when they saw the doctor, they stopped, the great thing folded halfway over and held in their strong red hands.

Mrs. Horvath said, "Good night, Doctor. I bring you ashtray tomorrow. You lose your blue one?" He had not anticipated so devious an attack and he was nonplused. Since all three of them knew well enough that the ashtray was lying in the mud, it was absurd to carry on her game, to say, for example, that he had taken it to the office. And so he replied ambiguously, "Oh, thank you. If you have an extra one, I will be glad to have it." He started toward the stairs, but they had not finished with him yet.

Mrs. Horvath said, "Was it a good day, Doctor?"

"A busy day," he said. "But, yes, a good one, I think."

The boy, his chin upon the mound of the mattress, fixed him with the fearless eye of the insulted child and slowly said, "It wasn't a good day for me, Doctor. It was a bad day for me, wasn't it, Mom?"

His mother giggled and winked at Dr. Pakheiser. "His birds! He think of nothing but his birds. Today he don't catch one big pheasant and this evening another get out of her house and fly away."

"Oh, I'm sorry," said the doctor. "But perhaps your bird will come back. They seem so tame. They eat out of your hand, don't they?"

"That bird won't come back," said the boy. "*I* know what happened to him. That cat got him. You get a bird tame and if it gets out anybody can catch it." The cold, accusing face began to contract in a childish pucker and tears hindered the next words: "That damned cat ate my bird!" He wrenched the mattress out of his mother's hands and flung it back onto the springs and flung himself upon it, sobbing maniacally. "And if I catch that cat, I'll kill it! I'll kill it! I'll kill it!"

The doctor flushed with embarrassment at this display, unchecked by the mother who merely stood smiling beside the bed. In time, the tantrum spent itself and Freddie lay shaking, face down on the naked bed. In the quiet, Mrs. Horvath, deceptively matter-of-fact, said, "Doctor, did you read that book by the doctor of Hitler? He say Hitler don't like women, only men? You think that true, Doctor?"

He could not chart her course, begun so remotely. He stalled, took off his glasses and put them on again. She went on. "I hate Hitler, Doctor. But I do not believe all what they say. This book I buy in the drugstore for one

dollar ninety-eight cents. I think a Jew write the book
out of madness for what Hitler do to Jews."

If only he could turn his leaden flesh and carry it up
the stairs to his own room and lock the door upon these
savages! There rest, there drink his Dubonnet, there be
at home! But a score of weights held him immobile, facing the barbarous woman and he listened to her: "I hate
Hitler," she repeated. "I like Jews. But if you're mad
you don't all times tell the truth, isn't it? So this doctor
in this book I got say Hitler like men. You know? What
you think of that, Doctor?" She went on and on. Un-
skilled as were her thrusts, they were direct. And when
at last she was finished and had dismissed him (did she,
he wondered, in her marvelously malicious mind think
that perhaps *he* was the "doctor of Hitler"? Or that *he*
did not like women, only men?) he felt trampled upon.
Actually he ached and when he got to his room, he was
sure he was coming down with something. Never in all
these three years had his loneliness been so acute. It
sprained his whole body, buried his faculties so deeply
that sensation, if it came at all, was ambiguous and in-
complete. Impassively, he accepted the anonymous
voices of machines: radios, motor boats, factory whis-
tles, trains, a random bomber. They came to him thickly
insulated so that, shrill or loud as they might really be,
they did not penetrate his mind but lay, all of them together, in a humming mass on the threshold. His
thoughts faltered like sleep-burdened eyes or attached
themselves with imbecilic fixity upon one trivial object.

For a long time he studied a minute fissure in the plaster of the wall beside the window. Later, he meditated intently upon the small, dispirited American flag on a pole beside the Sikorsky plant, and when at last he broke from this trance, it was only to become absorbed in the spectacle of a fouled old fish-bucket raffishly perched on a stump at the water's edge. Once, from some remote region of the house, there came the sound of a music box tinkling over a radio and at least a hundred times he stubbornly reiterated the words he knew it heralded: "PEPSI COLA HITS THE SPOT." At last, passing his hand over his cool forehead, he closed his eyes. The sounds cohered as in delirium. He could still visualize the blackbirds and fancied them to be a deathless band of flies which refused to walk upon the glass where they could be swatted. Hearing a train screaming in the station for passengers to Boston, he tried to imagine that he stood in the Bismarckgarten waiting for the yellow tram to Mannheim, but all he could see, in his mind's eye, were the shabby girls at the flowerstall deftly plucking daffodils from the pails of water. Next, he pretended that the train he heard was the express to Munich, and this time the recollections spun out effortlessly. He had gone to Salzburg once for a fortnight at the house of a classmate, a yellow-haired boy named Heine Waffenschmidt. He remembered that in the compartment there had been two soldiers on leave who had played chess the whole journey and had gladly drunk the wine offered to them by a tipsy letter-carrier on his way to Garmisch-Parten-

kirchen to see his tubercular daughter who was dying.
The old man's blue coat glistened with age and the brass
buttons on it were so tarnished that when the light fell
on them they did not shine. *"Danke,* Papa," the soldiers
had said. Once, at the end of a game, they stretched and
yawned and told the old man what they were planning
to do. "And Papa," said one of them, "what do you
think? We have hired a café and ordered a keg of
Löwenbräu and we'll have Scotch whisky besides." Dr.
Pakheiser remembered how whenever the train stopped
at a station, the pause seemed as clearly defined as a
box; his eyes burned now as if he were looking up at
the bright blue ceiling light. It was hard to redeem
much of the two weeks in Salzburg. He had been happy,
he was quite sure, and dimly he recalled a ski tourna-
ment after which he and Heine had gone to a rathskeller
for *Glühwein.* There had been a troop of players on
their way to Danzig and one of them, an effeminate
young man, had described the jumpers he had seen that
afternoon. *"Und er geht so und so und so!"* he said,
gesturing with his hands. " *'Swar unglaublich wunder-
bar."*

The memory was flat and he rejected it. He tried to
think of his patients, but could think, instead, only of
his office where something was always wrong. The electricity unaccountably went off or the water ran rusty or
the windows got stuck. Today Miss Johnson had worn
an artificial rose in her hair and he had already been

so nervous that the sight of it had nearly sent him into a tailspin.

He had a glass of brandy which quieted his fidgeting hands. The smoke from the flat Egyptian Prettiest gave off a fragrance like sweet wood, but tonight, it did not bring back Greta. Through the open windows came sharply the sound of Mr. Horvath's voice warning his son who was clipping the hedge. "Watch out for snakes, Freddie." The shears clicked steadily; the boy was a good worker. With his glass in his hand, the doctor went to the window and stood beside it looking out. The appalling grin had come back to Freddie's face in which there were no signs of sorrow or even of anger. Once he stood up straight to rest his back from its stooping position and the big clippers dangled by their handle from his little finger.

Dr. Pakheiser went straight through the brandy and even then had not had enough to drink, so he replaced the empty decanter with the one half full of kümmel. He thought of the supper he soon would eat and he began to wonder what the Horvath family had upon their table. For some reason, he had an idea they were fond of mussels (which made him ill) and he was positive they enjoyed the displeasing flavor of celeriac in their soup. They would have chunks of fat meat; they would especially like rutabaga, watermelon, molasses, pancakes and hot tamales. Again, he wondered if they ever bathed. He had frequently seen Mrs. Horvath's wash hanging on the line in the back yard and had been certain that she

used neither soap nor hot water in her laundry. He suspected that they did not brush their teeth which were
very long and extremely black. He did not, to tell the
truth, altogether understand why the United States had
given Mr. Horvath citizenship.

The sun went down and the helicopters left the sky.
At a little before seven, the doctor heard a noise in his
room and, conscious that he was quite drunk, he allowed
his full lips to curl into a smile as he thought of the
pleasure Milenka would have if this were a mouse he
might catch for his first course. The sound came again,
a faint rustling. He thought at first it was in the closet,
but then, at its repetition, concluded that it was in the
fireplace. Rather slowly, for his hands were awkward,
he took away the flowered screen and looked in at the
bare, clean hearth. The sound continued, close beside
him. He stuck his head in the opening and listened and
it came again. There was no doubt about it, something
was trapped in the chimney. He returned to his chair in
indecision and poured out another glass of kümmel and
considered. He knew that it was Freddie's lost bird, beating its wings against the walls.

The boy had left the hedge and his shears lay atop the
formal leaves. He would be at his supper now (were
they not, at this very moment, spooning up the repellent
sauce that surrounded their mussels?) so there was still
time in which to choose between an armistice and revenge. For a few minutes the man sat still in his rocking chair, listening tensely to the desperate wings. But

presently he could endure the creature's agony no longer and he left his room, having decided to drive a bargain with the boy.

From the top of the stairs, Dr. Pakheiser could see through the window to the left of the front door. Milenka was sitting on the wall, looking archly down at the tabby who crouched in the grass. "I-yi-yi-yi, bad puss," he thought. His feet were slow on the steps and he clutched the bannister with an unnaturally moist hand. He was halfway down when Mr. Horvath came into his ken. The large man moved soundlessly around the corner of the house and stood at the edge of the lawn under a young elm tree, and in a moment, Freddie joined him, carrying a rifle. Dr. Pakheiser hesitated for the length of time it took Mr. Horvath to aim and fire and then, in order not to see the body fall off the wall, turned and went back to his room.

Late, after the Chance Vought worker had gone to the graveyard shift, Dr. Pakheiser opened the damper of the fireplace and a dead oriole fell to the hearth. He gazed abstractedly at the black and golden feathers and touched the soft body with the fire tongs. A bright apple leaf was caught under one wing. He picked the bird up carefully with a piece of newspaper and put it in a box which he found on the shelf of his closet. He carried the box downstairs and into the back yard and he floated it on the water, blue with the lights from the factory windows. He pondered if it would float to the Sound and if it did, how far it would go then. A mile on the way to Europe? Halfway? "Go, Milenka," he addressed the box which already had drifted several feet from the bank. In the cool air his head cleared a little and he felt a wonderful exhilaration as if he had been freed of a persistent pain. He ran like a young man back to the house, took the stairs two at a time and when he got to his room, he lay down without undressing and at once was fast asleep.

*Between the Porch and the Altar*

At five in the morning in February, it is darker than at midnight. The streets are empty of automobiles; the latest readers have gone to bed and the earliest risers are only just opening their eyes. The few people abroad are swift and furtive, like creatures who must quit a place before the sun shines forth. At that hour, their business seems mysterious and even shady, although they are not cutthroats or thieves but only watchmen and charwomen and night waitresses on their way home to dine at sunrise. So uncluttered are the streets, so starkly direct is the walk of the people that anyone whose custom it is to get up much later, at the normal hour, feels when he goes out that he intrudes upon a scene of bare but meaningful privacy. And a light, springing on abruptly to make a staring eye in a blackened building, may stir him with embarrassment and wonder as if this were an alarm or an esoteric signal of hostility.

It was cold and the girl was hungry. She paused in the vestibule of the apartment building and half turned to unlock the outer door again and go back to her warm bed. But as she lingered, she observed a bright blue star high over the houses opposite and the sight inexplicably gave her resolution, even though its color was so pure and frigid that it made her all the more conscious of the cold. She drew on her gloves and went out, shocked by a biting gust of wind which passed her by like a big rapid bird. She turned the corner and hurried along Sixth Avenue on her way to the first mass.

Although the star, which was now behind her, had had a decisive effect on her, it had not dispelled her apprehension and her distrust of the unfamiliar streets. While her feet were steady enough, her breath was erratic and her ears were fanciful, making her think she heard sinister noises behind the blank faces of the buildings. She looked straight ahead, fearful of what she might see in the dark doorways and even in the interiors of delicatessens and bakery shops whose cheerless windows were dimly silvered by the street-lights. And still, discomforting as it was, she took a certain pleasure in her uneasiness, feeling that even the most accidental castigation was excellent at the beginning of Lent.

On the corner of Thirteenth Street, there was a large second-hand shop whose windows she had many times studied with an incredulous amusement, so dreadful and so undesirable were the objects displayed there: funeral wreaths made of human hair, armadillo baskets, back-scratchers that looked like sets of bad teeth, ceramic vessels of an unimaginable function. The antelope with eaten ears and rubbed-off hide, the alabaster boar and the complacent Chinese philosopher made of porcelain

stared out, looking, even at five in the morning, for
someone to adopt them and give them a good home.

Within the doorway of the shop, a drunken beggar
sprawled like a lumpy rug, his feet in ruptured tennis
shoes thrust out onto the sidewalk. He was not asleep.
Under a cap set raffishly at an angle on his head, he regarded the girl's approach with an eye made visible to
her by the arc light at the intersection. Paradoxically,
her pace slowed down as her terror rose, and the man
had risen to his feet before she was abreast of him. The
smell of whisky was so strong that it was like a taste in
her mouth. He stretched forth his hand and whined,
"Lady, I'm hungry, lady."

She did not carry a purse, but in her pocket were two
dimes and a quarter. She intended to put the quarter
into the poor box and the dimes in the candle offering,
for she wished to light a candle for the repose of her
mother's soul and another for the safe-keeping of two
friends, captive in China by the Japanese. Although it
was only a fraction of a minute that she debated, a succession of images with an individual emotion attending
each revolved through her mind. She saw the poor box
in the dim vestibule of the lower church and heard her
quarter click upon the other coins. This box was stationed beside the holy water font, near by the statue of
Our Lord between whose palely gleaming feet someone
placed fresh flowers each day. Then she saw her mother
lying in the limbo of her last hours, unsightly, unconsoled, and heard the sonorous matter-of-factness of her

Protestant relatives to whom this transformation, so un-
bearable to her, was neither strange nor dreadful. It was
not that they did not grieve their kinswoman, but it was
that they had many times before known death and had
learned, through its reiteration, that it was no wonder.
She, still bedewed with baptism, had knelt and the blue
beads of her rosary slipped through her fingers until her
mother's soul abandoned its wrecked flesh. She had been,
she remembered, in the middle of the fourth decade
when her aunt, vigilant at the bedside, had whispered,
"She is gone now." And she remembered how the odor
of belladonna had obtruded so in her devotions that part
of her mind pronounced the word over and over as if it
belonged to a litany.

Then she tried to fancy her friends as they might be
in prison and could not, could only see them before their
fireplace on a winter day of the year before. She had
come to tea and had stayed on for sherry. She sat on
a maroon sofa; a little dog slept with his chin on her
arm, whimpering once in a dream. There was short-
bread to go with the wine and as she ate a piece she
realized that it was the texture rather than the taste that
made it her favorite pastry. In an easy silence that came
in the conversation, she saw her reflection in the brass
bedwarmer that hung beside the fireplace, and this
blurred travesty of her face had the power, as the star
had done this morning, to make her suddenly purpose-
ful, and she told her friends good-by that day, although
they did not leave for another week.

In the early desolation of this present year, she felt tenderness muffling her like smoke and smaller, general pictures showed themselves to her: a clean room, a forced sprig of bittersweet, her mother's silver-backed hairbrush, her friends' passport pictures.

No time at all had passed. She saw the beggar's lips part again. She could not find her voice, and one bold self chided her for her nervousness, for this was no extraordinary occurrence. On the contrary, the rarest day in New York was the one on which one was not asked for money by a fellow like this or by a senile tart or by a belligerent child. She could pass by, or she could say she had no money. But mechanically she had paused—she was not yet a craftsman in the selection of experience and her days were often a chain of pauses— and the man took advantage of her hesitance saying, with his vague face close to hers, "Lady, was you ever hungry?" Her fear of him was obliterated by an abstract but brilliant anger, for his question was beside the point, unfair, a contemptible trick. She almost spoke her indignation aloud and then her anger burnt itself out; she controlled herself stiffly like a soldier: on this grave day she should not presume to judge. And into the cold hand, she put the quarter and one of the dimes. The man muttered something but she did not hear what he said and she went on hastily. In the windows of a flower shop, she saw her shadow drift through pots of tall azaleas. When she turned the corner at Sixteenth

Street, she slowed down, for two nuns walked slowly ahead of her. Her hunger returned with savage force.

The entrance to the Jesuits' church was dark. Its black iron gates were open only a crack. A night-like and velvety blackness stood solidly between the columns on the porch of the upper church. The stone steps leading downward seemed colder than the sidewalks, and the holy water was cold. It teemed with the ripples of fingers that had been dipped there before her own, and the touch of it on her forehead was icy. Today, between the wounded feet, were dark roses. One of the sisters touched the feet and then pressed her fingers to her lips.

The mass had not begun. The girl said her prayers, but she could not concentrate, for her mind was occupied with what she would do with her last dime. Who was the neediest, she questioned: the poor, the dead, or the oppressed? Truly, she had to admit that she loved the poor less than her mother and her friends, and yet, for this very reason—for a willful sacrifice—should she not put the dime into the poor box? Then she thought, but I have given already to the poor. Lout, wastrel that he was, he was poor and it is not the duty, nor even the right, of the almsgiver to distinguish between degrees of poverty. But between her mother and her friends, how should she choose? Should one pray for someone's long life here or for someone else's shortened term in Purgatory? It occurred to her to offer her mass for her mother and light the candle for the prisoners.

This seemed like a compromise and did not satisfy her, yet there was no alternative.

Four nuns were in the pew ahead of her and, finishing their prayers, they sat back and simultaneously opened their missals. On the right hand of one, she saw a wedding ring. She had never before been close enough to a nun to notice this, and she wondered when it was that the badge of their eternal marriage was placed upon them and if they really did feel unity with God at that moment or felt, instead, hushed isolation. The words of the Gospel today were: *Lay up to yourselves treasures in heaven: where neither the rust nor the moth doth consume, and where thieves do not break through nor steal. For where thy treasure is, there is thy heart also.* The words, now that she had seen the wedding ring, seemed richer and more profoundly exciting than they had done before, and for a moment she was almost idolatrous, worshipful, almost, of the fair-skinned sisters in their tower of ivory and their house of gold. And then she recoiled, for under the coif of one she saw black stubble.

The church was full, principally of old people who slept so little that rising for the earliest mass on Ash Wednesday was no great hardship. Most of them were telling their beads and only a few had missals. An aged man behind her said his Aves aloud in a harsh, sibilant voice and his false teeth clicked on one another in a curious counterpoint to the measured whispers of his wooden beads. A bald young seminarian entered the sanctuary to light the candles on the altar. He genu-

flected gracefully and liquidly like a dancer, and the
hand with which he crossed himself was as long and
white and shapely as one painted by El Greco. He was
incongruously beautiful in his surroundings, for the
lower church was ugly and in bad taste. The statues were
gaudy, even in this shadowy light, and the crucifix was
sentimental. In all the accouterments of the sanctuary,
there was a mixture of modern leanness and Victorian
laciness. The seminarian alone seemed a product of
inspiration.

At last the bell rang and the celebrant with his altar
boys entered the sanctuary. The girl prayed that nothing
would mar the spirit of penance which she carried like
a fragile light within her; she closed her eyes to the
nun's neck and begged forgiveness for her fault-finding.
All through the mass, while she fixed her attention on
her mother—imagining her face, disembodied, hovering in a crowd of other faces in Purgatory which she
saw as an echoing marble hall—she wondered if she
had not committed an act of betrayal, both to the beggar
to whom she gave unwillingly and to the parish poor,
deprived of her offering through her cowardice. Although she knew that her confusion would be understood and unraveled by the counsel of a confessor, she
went, half dazed, to the communion rail and received,
she felt, with an imperfect heart. Afterwards, her thanksgiving was more full of petition than of gratitude: I
humbly beseech guidance and my whole heart desires
wisdom and stern purpose. Reason reiterated to her that

she had properly allocated her good will: money to the poor, a mass for the dead, a candle for the oppressed. Yet she was not assured in her heart and she prayed with a dry compulsion.

When she had received the cross of ashes on her forehead, she went directly to the altar of St. Francis Xavier at the back of the church. The cups for the candles were blood-red; the flames cast a sheen on the closed tabernacle. She knelt down to pray the saint to watch over her friends. As she stood up to take the taper to light her candle, she saw an old woman coming from the vestibule. She pretended not to see, for she recognized the old crone who was always there before the sun and the Jesuits discovered her. At later masses she begged on the sidewalk. The girl had already lighted the taper and was looking for a fresh cup when the woman reached the altar.

Blear-eyed, unctuous, crafty, she slithered to her knees. "God bless you, dearie," she began, her face touching the skirt of the girl's coat. The dime was in the pocket on that side, and it was as if the woman smelled it with her long nose or heard it with her ear beneath her sour gray hair or felt it on her furrowed cheek. It was impossible to ignore her, and the girl could think of no way to resolve this preposterous dilemma. Her hand still held the taper and her eyes still roved the tiers of candles seeking an unlighted one.

It seemed some time before the old woman spoke again. Behind them, people were moving about, unconcerned with anything but the small devotional tasks they had set themselves. Some were making the stations of the cross, some prayed at the Lady altar, others gazed meditatively at the crucifix. The bald young beadle had come again into the sanctuary and was preparing the altar for the next mass. Everything happening in the church was pious and usual, save for the squalid commerce at St. Francis' altar. The ceiling seemed oppressively low; she was reminded of a dreary train-shed.

When the woman spoke again, her voice was more eager and hopeful. She nodded toward the candles and said, "They're every one of them lit already and they won't bring the new ones round till after the eight o'clock." How well she knew the habits of this church's servants! She had probably studied them for months, huddling in shadows behind the grating that enclosed the baptismal font or in the corner where the statue of St. Ignatius stood. The girl saw that what she said was true and she blew out the taper and replaced it. But she was determined to make the offering and she stepped down to go to another altar. The old woman took hold of her coat and peered straight into her face, shamelessly. She said, "You're young and pretty, girlie." The oblique entreaty weakened her, embarrassed her movement like a web, and finally she put her hand into her pocket and took out the dime. Before the clever, metropolitan fingers had enclosed the alms, the girl had gone, running down Sixteenth Street to the corner of Sixth

Avenue. The streets were lighter now, and the big star had begun to pale. Shop-keepers were putting trash on the sidewalks; news vendors were cutting the ropes that bound the morning papers; a melancholy white horse ambled down the street dragging a milk truck after him.

When the coffee was nearly ready and her rooms were full of its fragrance, the girl looked at her forehead in the bathroom mirror and saw that the Jesuit had marked her clearly. She washed away the ashes, leaving herself alone possessed of the knowledge of her penance.

# The Bleeding Heart

Every morning and on alternate afternoons, Rose Fabrizio, a Mexican girl from the West, worked at a discreet girls' boarding school as secretary to the headmistress, a Miss Talmadge who had a sweet voice. It was sweet even when she was dictating a warm comeuppance to the laundry about its mistreatment of the school's counterpanes and bureau runners; and sweet when she was explaining the value of physical education to a recalcitrant pupil who declared that she loathed volleyball. Every day when she arrived shortly after Rose had unlocked the office and uncovered her typewriter, Miss Talmadge cried "Good morning" twice and then she said with a lilt, "How is our Westerner? Acclimated? Finding the charm of New England both within and without?" She then stepped briskly into her own office and made a great clatter with the files, rudely flung up the window no matter what the thermometer said and set to work like a whirlwind. At first Rose, who was twenty-one and uncommonly sensitive, bridled at this greeting which she believed to be subtly derisive, but now after two months, she knew that there was no feeling behind it at all; Miss Talmadge inquired, in the same sweet rapid way, quite indifferent to the answers, about the parlormaid's fiancé and the French teacher's needle-point and the riding master's brother's greenhouse. But even now, this reminder of her origin (vague as it must be in Miss Talmadge's mind, for if she imagined anything at all, she probably imagined cigar-store Indians and clumps of sage) sometimes brought on a subcutaneous prickle and distracted Rose from her shorthand so that on occasion she had fetched up with sentences that could not possibly be parsed.

Except in the vocal presence of Miss Talmadge, she *was* acclimated and she *did* find New England charming, although she was not quite sure that she had found it so both within and without, having no idea what the headmistress meant. She rejoiced in the abundance of imposing trees, in the pure style of the houses and the churches, in the venerable graveyards and in the unobtrusive shops. One was not conscious of any of the working parts of the town, not of the railroad nor of the filling stations nor of the water towers and the light-plants. Her own town, out West, had next to no trees and those were puny and half-bald. The main street there was a row of dirty doorways which led into the dirtier interiors of pool halls, drugstores where even the soda fountain bar had a flaccid look, and small restaurants and beer-parlors and hotels whose windows were decorated sometimes with sweet-potato vines growing out of jam cans painted red, and sometimes with a prospector's pick-ax and some spurious gold ore, and sometimes with

nothing more than the concupiscent but pessimistic
legend that ladies were invited or that there were booths
for them. The people here in this dignified New England town, shabby as they might be, wore hats and
gloves at all hours and on all days and they appeared
moral, self-controlled, well-bathed, and literate. The
population of her own town was largely Mexican and
was therefore, by turns, criminally quarrelsome or
grossly stupefied so that when they were not beating
one another up they stared into dusty space or lounged
in various comatose attitudes against the stock properties of the main street: the telephone poles and fire hy-
drants and hitching posts. They were swarthy and they
tended, on the whole, to be fat and to wear bright, juvenile colors. Repudiating all that, she greatly admired
the pallor of the people here and their dun dress and
their accent so that the merest soda-jerk sounded as if
he had gone to Harvard.

In this atmosphere of good breeding and adulthood,
Rose was happy half the time and altogether miserable
the rest of it, miserable, that is, with envy of the people
who had been born here of upright gentlefolk and had
been reared in mannerly calm. And Rose, although she
was full-grown and had a Bachelor of Arts degree (to
be sure she had not gone to Radcliffe and her education
had been a shabby, uninteresting affair) longed to be
adopted by a New Englander. Sometimes this longing
coupled with her loneliness—it was not to its detriment
that the town was unfriendly but quite the contrary—

fretted her so that she could neither read nor play Canfield and she sat idle and unhappy in her bed-sitting
room where the wind came down the chimney like a failing voice and now and then caused the long-handled
bedwarmer to stir on its hook, chiming against the bricks.

She had selected the very person she wished to become her foster-father, a man about sixty whom she saw
on Tuesday and Thursday and Saturday afternoons in
the town library, an incongruously modern building
dedicated to the memory of Samuel Sewell. Here Rose
read books on psychology in a western room where the
sun came amply through the windows; in this room, besides herself, there always sat a thoughtful gentleman,
wearing a lemon-yellow ascot and a sober dark blue suit.
The ascot alone would have set him down as a person
of prominence, for no one unimportant, she reasoned,
could afford to be so boldly eccentric. She did not know
what he read through the scholarly Oxford glasses which
perfectly fitted on his stately nose and were anchored
to his lapel by a black ribbon ending in a silver button.
The books were big, she knew that much, and their bind-
ings were a usual maroon. He did not take any notes (as
she did voluminously, having been so recently graduated) and he read quite slowly. He did not move all
afternoon save that at half past three he went outside
and stood on the steps to smoke a cigarette; she could
see him clearly through the window beside which she
sat reading of Pavlov's submissive dog. Either he stood
still, leaning against a half-pillar of the half-Ionic

façade with his eyes closed and his lips moving a little, or he took a turn around the little triangular yard, holding his hatless white head at a dignified backward angle. Occasionally he paused under a tree and there, ankle deep in fallen leaves from the wine-glass elm, he was lost impressively in speculation. She thought he might be a mathematician or a novelist. Often when he returned, bringing with him a final remnant of the autumn air, he looked over at Rose across the tables and gave her an amiable, perfunctory nod as if he were her busy employer passing through the office of his underlings. Once he said something to her but in so low a voice and with so noncommittal an expression on his face that she did not understand and only smiled.

Despite a heritage of headlong impulse and her practice of setting forth before the signal was given, Rose made no move to further her acquaintance with the man and, indeed, she took pains never to see him out of his context. She always left the library before he did so that she would neither be tempted to find out what he was reading, since this would give a clue to his profession, nor to discover the direction he took to go home. Earlier in the fall, before she was aware that her library habits coincided with his and before she wanted to be adopted by him, she had enjoyed walking through the woods and over the hills and beside the river. On Sundays she had always gone to the largest and the oldest cemetery and there, upon a crest of rocks which overlooked the thin, ungarnished headstones, she had thoroughly read the literary supplement of the *New York Times* and had absently considered the hedge of barberry that flourished every which way beside a brook. She had liked to imagine the furnishings of the houses she could just see opposite and to wonder what scions of Mayflower families lived in them and were about to order tea. But now on Sunday, she stayed in her room, long as the day seemed, for it would in no way serve her purpose, she thought sensibly, to be caught spying on the library-man if he should come some time to pay his respects to someone's bones, those of his wife, perhaps, or a beloved daughter dead in early womanhood.

And before this, she had gone to dinner once or twice a week to an inn a mile out of the town on a byroad. This inn had the mark of Henry Ford upon it and so had the diners who disputed facts involved in the American Revolution and who exclaimed over the hasty-pudding. The landlord, a lethargic man from Bangor, sat in a chimney corner smoking an authentic pipe and the cook was said to be descended from King Philip on the maternal side. Rose did not think it probable that the man in the yellow ascot would ever come to a place like this since the atmosphere of his own dining room would be, if anything, even more bona fide. But she did not wish to run any risk, for, just as she did not want to know what books he read (he might be proved by them to be in his second childhood) and did not want to see him laying flowers upon his daughter's grave (for it might not be a daughter at all but only some old aunt by marriage) so she did not want to see him eating lest she discover that he followed an idiosyncratic diet and therefore had a constitutional disease.

All this abstention and the restiveness that accompanied it made her days and evenings monotonous and she became very much aware of the drawbacks of her room which until now she had found—at least by comparison with the room at home which she shared with two younger sisters both of whom walked in their sleep and one of whom gnashed her teeth—ideal. She lived on the ground floor of a double house that stood on a corner and was shaped like a wedge so that the front doors were on different streets. Her room, at Number 8 Patriot Road, was flush with what she thought must be the parlor at Number 6 Faneuil Lane and through the wood and plaster she sometimes heard throttled voices, heavy footsteps, and the indignant squawk of a mistuned radio. But she never heard a sound in Number 8. She was the only lodger on the first floor, but upstairs there were several meek and apparitional figures whom she met in the mildewed hall as she went to and from the bathroom. The landlady lived across the entry-way from Rose and was visible only on Wednesday evening when she came to collect the rent and present the clean towels. Generally this transaction was performed as a dumb show and without smiles. The telephone seldom rang and the doorbell never. Besides this rather sepulchral air, the house was chilly and the lamps in Rose's room were poor.

Her feeling toward the silence of Number 8 and the

sounds, low and distorted as they were, of Number 6, passed through several stages between the middle of October and the Thanksgiving holiday. At first the quiet of her own house pleased her because she could read with such concentration and the noises of 6 irritated her when they were loud enough to intrude upon her page, yet not quite loud enough to be properly identified. Then, she was disturbed and next annoyed by the silence and felt that it was unnatural, while she was grateful for the indications through the wall that there was life just yonder. And, again, she would be strained and unsettled, waiting for the noises and unable to make use of the interstices of silence between them. She never saw the tenants of the other house, but she had an idea what sort they might be, for frequently there was an electric car in front, looking like a large, abandoned toy. The driver of it, she was certain, would be a brisk old lady with no nonsense about her and she came to believe, groundlessly, that there were two such old ladies, sisters, perhaps, or friends since boarding school days at Lausanne. One must be either rather fat or else somewhat lame and wear special shoes, for nothing else could account for the heavy tread Rose sometimes heard. Once, on a Sunday afternoon, out of a clear blue sky she wondered if the man in the yellow ascot ever called at Number 6 and she snubbed the thought, snubbed the peculiarly awful possibility that he might be there at this very moment.

On Thanksgiving Day, she went to the inn outside the

town for midday dinner. The library-man was there and the moment she saw him, dressed as usual, she knew that she had secretly expected him, for she was not at all surprised. He was sitting at a table near the fireplace engaged in conversation with the landlord and simultaneously reading the menu. A bright fire burned in the hearth and his fresh skin shone in the light like a leaf turned golden and it appeared to have a leaf's smooth texture. He sat very straight in his chair and while he waited for the soup, he closed his eyes and calmly smiled as he listened to the landlord who was apparently telling a long joke. He looked as if he might be sitting for his portrait and, indeed, he would have been a distinguished subject for a painter who did accurate "likenesses" of college presidents and notable physicians, for his face had admirable qualities of mellowness and deep, pacific wisdom and irony and casualness. He was in no hurry. He waited for his dinner with his eyes closed, not having to be occupied with looking round the room at the other diners and at the Currier and Ives prints on the walls and all the antique furniture which one might buy if one were able. Rose's own young and impatient mind immediately pranced away from him and dwelt, in quick succession, upon the brindle cat who was balancing for no earthly reason on the newel post; upon the lemon tree in the bay window, fed like an animal to produce fruit of a dreadful size; two quiet brown-eyed children who sat silent at a table with two thin old women, holding their hands between courses

in an attitude of prayer. Fleetly it struck her that these
two might be her neighbors and at that very moment, as
if she had been directed by a voice, she looked out the
window at the far driveway and saw the electric car,
its square top grizzled with frost. It must be that the
children were with their aged great-aunts for the day
and she thought it must be a doubtful pleasure to them
all since the four mute mouths bore an illegible expression.

Rose did not look at her foster-father save when her
eyes fell on him by accident. Once she caught him looking at her over a piled fork and in his surprise, he let
some of the stuffing fall off. Every inch of her skin felt
roasted and her hands shook so that for a moment she
dared not try to lift her water glass although her mouth
was dry. And later when his salad came, she looked
again and he distinctly winked at her as he tossed the
cloves of tomato and the water cress. It was not a plain-
spoken wink at all and it made her nervous. She hurried
through her meal in order that she might leave before
he did because, besides the ambiguous gambit of his eye,
she was inadmissibly afraid that *he*, not the old ladies,
might enter the electric car. She grappled hard with her
suspicions about him and imperatively pointed out to
herself that this stately aristocrat lived in a handsome
house and that he had naturally given his housekeeper
and his cook the day off and because the air was fine
and sharp, had liked to walk a mile to his dinner. She
could not help feeling that it was strange he had not

been invited anywhere, for surely a man of his position, whatever it was, would have friends in the town. Perhaps he despised the sentimental fanfare of holidays. Next year, after his adoption of her was a legal fact, she imagined that on Thanksgiving, Christmas, and Easter they would dine alone and afterward would play backgammon. Yet already she was visited with a nettlesome problem: should she play badly so that he would have the pleasure of winning or cleverly so that he would praise her? She rather hoped that he did not have a violin or any whimsical hobbies like collecting Revolutionary artifacts or going for bird-walks.

Rose did not wait for her dessert and on her way out she glanced quickly at the coats hung on the pegs in the hall. She recognized his immediately; it was black with a beaver lining and although it was quite worn, it still was very rich and serviceable. His derby was there too and a tartan muffler. Fearing the road along which, at any moment, the electric car might pass, she struck into the woods and walked home along the pale, thick river. She found a nickel and a fresh-water mussel shell and she came upon a beached canoe, withering in the dry fall. She passed behind the girls' school and glanced at the windows of the dormitory with their starched dimity curtains. The little girls had all gone home to their fathers for the holiday. She was very lonely here beside the river and she began to walk fast, counting her footsteps to forestall her melancholy, but then she slowed down again as she realized that she would be

just as lonely in her room. Until now she had been content with seeing the man in the library and had even
been a little proud in a queer way that he had a life
quite secret, quite independent of the alternate afternoons in the reading room and that what she did at
other times was equally unimaginable to him. But now
beside the woeful river, she was almost frightened to
think of him just as she had almost been frightened as
a child when everyone had left the church after the last
mass and she had wondered what happened then,
whether the plaster saints came to life and if God
emerged, full-bodied, from the wafers in the ciborium.

Rose did not know, until she was actually within her
room again, shadowy with dusk and musty with the old
upholstery of the buckling wicker chairs, that there had
been another reason why she had not liked to come
back: now she was face to face with the knowledge that
she had seen the driver of the electric car who was, therefore, one of the authors of the noises in the other house.
The car had got there before she did. The very moment
she stepped across her threshold onto the distempered
carpet with its muddy oak leaves, the sounds came,
feebly ill-natured, straight to her anticipating ears.
There were no new sounds, no children's voices.

All that afternoon, while she was thinking of the man
as he sat in his own library (the Samuel Sewell was
closed today) in one of the white clapboard houses in
the side streets of the town, the dulled hubbub went on
beyond the wall. At first she paid little heed; she was

thinking of the chintz wing chair he might be sitting in
with his feet on a brass fender before a fire. And at first
the sounds were unobtrusive. But toward dark, they became more insistent and she grew fully conscious of
them. Although she could not hear words nor could she
tell what sort of movements were being made, she was
entirely alert, straining to read this trifling mystery.
After a little, she was able to separate some of the noises
and she heard a door open and close and a telephone
ring and a clock strike and outside, in the street, she
heard a boy irrelevantly cry, "Richard?" and she heard
something bump over an uncarpeted floor. But above—
or rather beneath, for it was little more than a jerky
hum—the other sounds, there was a voice complaining,
directly on the other side of the wall; it was a venomous
and senile whimper which went on and on. It seemed
to be uttering short curses with just time for a breath
in between the tenth, perhaps, and the eleventh. Presently there was another opening and closing of the door
and a second voice, a man's voice, spoke. There was, as
well, a rattle of metal and now Rose constructed a picture: someone was ill and someone else was bringing a
tray to the sick-bed. But the important fact was that she
must revise her general notion of the household: it included a man. Yet why could it not be a doctor, summoned hastily because one of the old ladies had eaten
unwisely at the inn? She regretted that she had not
scrutinized her neighbors more closely to see if they
bore any marks of frailty in the color of the skin or the

look about the nose. She sighed and went to the window to pull down the shade for it had grown dark, and once again the electric car served her, for here it came, a silent, absurd box, round the corner and on its way toward the Mill Dam. "They have gone for the prescription," she said happily, and she saw a peaked spinster lying in a bed, another peaked one operating the simple machinery of the car. And she assured herself that the driver must, indeed must, be one of the children's great-aunts for no man in his right mind would be seen in such a thing in this day and age.

When she had pulled the bottle-green blinds and turned on her two lamps, no brighter than candle flames, she was momentarily disgusted with herself for spending so much time conjecturing on unseen and unknown people. She was as bad as her mother who could search a whole evening through for the inner meanings of a neighbor's greeting when they had not been on speaking terms for weeks or the impertinence of a salesgirl in the five and ten. So she tried to forget about the other house and to go back to the man in the yellow ascot but he was suddenly gone altogether and instead of him she could only see her real father, Joseph Fabrizio, who would be having a holiday today like everyone else and who, stupid and cynical, would be shambling about the house out West where even the hopvines at the windows were limp and unclean. Her father wore a black coat-sweater from J. C. Penney's and a spotty gray cap and Army store pants and miner's shoes studded with cleats that tore up the linoleum and made a brash racket. The putrefied smell of sugar beets clung to him constantly even after a bath which he took only once in a month of Sundays. She did not know one good thing about her father except that when she was very small she had been delighted to hear him sing "Juanita" and "Valencia" in a tenor voice for which he was admired by two or three people in the town; and one time when he must have been as drunk as a monkey, he brought her a box of Cheese-bits and a copy of *Sweetheart Stories* when she had the pinkeye. Although as far back as she could remember, she had been driven to get away, far away and never go home again, she was often resentful that he never wrote to her and that he had not been at all sorry when she had gone away. As a matter of fact, he had not even seen her off on the bus and her mother did not know where he was. Her mother said, looking vaguely up and down the street and nodding to several acquaintances, "Well, I'll tell him good-by for you," and handed her a lunch in a Honey Kist bread wrapper. The simple and humiliating fact was that he cared so little that he had clean forgotten.

The memories of her father, each one of which was uglier than the one before, made her so cross and jumpy that she knew she must quiet herself and she sat down to read *Self Reliance* which she had always found very soothing because it was so sedately dull. But she could pay attention to it even less than usual and the pattern of sounds next door presently was repeated: the telephone, the opening and closing of the door, the sound of china and silver on a tray. She was irritated and when

she returned to Emerson, exhorting him to lull her, the
voice would give her no peace but went on in its protracted peeve, hovering like a gnat over every word on
the page. Finally she grew really angry and she knocked
sharply on the wall. There was an immediate silence and
then a most terrible and much louder sound: it was a
laugh! And such a laugh as she had never heard in her
life for it was as thin as a needle and unlike the speech,
it did not quaver. For a moment she was afraid and she
stepped away as if there were real danger, and then she
was even angrier than before and her thoughts went
quickly down this ladder of unreason, "If my father
had not been a low person and if he had loved me, I
would not have grown up in poverty and I would not
have hated him so much that I had to go away from
home to the first job that came along, this mean one
that pays so little that I must live in a dark, depressing
room where the walls are so thin that the sound of sickness comes through and for no reason at all I am laughed
at by a cruel person who does not even know me." And
she envisaged her father as he had probably been that
day she had boarded the orange bus; fat and foul-
tongued he would have been shooting Cowboy at the
pool hall where they had spittoons since most of the
patrons, including (God damn him) her father, chewed
tobacco.

It was no longer possible for Rose to stay in her room in
the evenings because of the busy personalities so near,

and after dinner she went back to the Samuel Sewell. The overhead light was poor and made her eyes smart and she missed not sitting in her wrapper and her slippers. She was impatient with the spinster's prolonged illness and she saw no reason why she was not taken to the hospital. Sometimes they went on for years that way, just clinging to the ragged edge of nothing, getting more and more querulous and bothersome. Miss Talmadge noticed that Rose was distraught and when she asked and Rose said that she was dissatisfied with her room, Miss Talmadge objected with vehement sweetness, "But it is a quaint room! It is a lovely, lovely, lovely room!" and began instantly to dictate a stunning letter to the parent of a pupil who, in a tantrum over nothing at all, had deliberately broken a hockey stick belonging to the school.

One morning just before the Christmas holiday, Miss Talmadge asked, in her pink voice, if Rose would run an errand for her in the afternoon. The girls of the fourth form wished to send a potted plant to someone who was ill, a former matron. Rose was not surprised at all when she heard that the address was Number 6 Fanueil Lane. So important was this illness with which she lived that it did not occur to her that there was another invalid in the town and Miss Talmadge, never dreaming that the retired matron was the reason she did not like her room, said, with pointless cheer, "It will be so handy for you."

She accepted the commission with the greatest re-

luctance, not only because she wanted the occupants of
the other house to remain anonymous but because, as
well, she had a horror of being near old people and she
remembered a time when the fifth grade had gone to
sing Christmas carols at the old people's home. There
had been a smell of senility in the long room with its
glaring linoleum and Mission benches where the old
people sat fiddling with their neckties or with pieces of
holly purloined from the dining room decorations. The
last song was "We Three Kings" and by this time Rose
was so sick that she only moved her lips, not making
any sound. When it was over and they stood for a moment, dumb and immobile, until the teacher came to
herd them away, a terribly, terribly old man rose to
his feet and cried, "Damned brats! Clear them damned
brats out p.d.q." He had bicycle clips on his elee-
mosynary plus-fours.

She had never actually passed the other house and
she was surprised to find that its façade was altogether
different from that of Number 8 Patriot Road. The paint
was a darker shade of red and instead of two bay windows it had only one, just to the right of the off-center
door. In the windows at Number 8, the landlady kept ferns
and cactuses but there was nothing at all alive in those of
Number 6 and there were no curtains. There was only a
solitary tuberculosis seal from the year before pasted in
the lowest middle pane. Instead of a neat brass letter-slot,
there was a raveling raffia basket which hung on a ham-
mock-hook to hold the mail and there was no knocker

but a bell instead, the kind you rang by turning an embossed iron handle. She turned it and heard a tinkle and
instantly a voice very near her cried thinly, "Just a minute!" Rose could not tell where it came from but she
waited in discomfort, feeling that she was being looked
at from some vantage point no more than a foot away.
Still, no one came. It was snowing and the big soft flakes
dissolved in beautiful splashes on the glazed green paper
that wrapped the bleeding-heart. She rang again, and
again, immediately, the voice encouragingly said, "Just
a minute!" It was a high and genderless voice and was,
she thought, the same one that had laughed at her when
she had knocked on the wall. She was despondent here
in the twilight snowstorm and her fingers clutching the
pot were growing numb. The voice broke its promise for
the second time; several minutes passed and nothing
happened. She would try once more and if still no one
came, she would leave the plant on the doorstep even
though it might freeze. Each moment she hated her role
more, no matter what its outcome was to be. It would
be worse than ever now to hear the sounds through the
wall if she had the misfortune actually to see the interior of the house (how dreadful if she had to go into
the sickroom itself!) and it would be almost as bad if
the door was never opened and whoever it was that bade
her wait a minute saw her leave and enter Number 8.
Her comings and goings would thereafter be observed;
or, even if they weren't, she would think they were and

now, besides the sounds, she would be rattled by hypothetical eyes spying upon her.

She was about to ring for the last time when out of
the corner of her eye, she saw the electric car coming
cautiously down the gentle slope of the street. Now
there was no escaping. The great-aunt driving the car
and the bodiless procrastinator behind the door would
catch her there with the bleeding-heart and make her
explain herself. "Just a minute!" The voice, speaking
this time of its own accord and not in answer to the
bell, startled her and the plant slipped in her hands.
The car disappeared in a driveway behind the house and
in a little while a distant door opened and closed and
Rose firmly rang the bell. This time the voice laughed
mockingly up and down an untrue scale and she was in
no doubt at all that it was the same one that had sneered
at her knock.

The mysterious house behind the black door was
seized with spasms. Someone screamed, "Tea!" and a
stove was madly shaken down. Heavy footsteps crossed
a room and a man's voice, roared, "What? What do you
say?" "Tea! Toast!" the screamed reply rang clear and
the "s" in the toast was prolonged with hatred. "Give a
person a chance to turn around, Mother!" said the man
and the laughing voice near Rose chuckled high in its
throat and mimicked itself, "Just a minute!" and then
mimicked the deep voice of the man, "Just a minute!"
She would have set the present down and run for dear

life, but she was too late, for a light came dimly on in the front hall and feet approached the door.

"Well!" said the man in the yellow ascot with the same comforting smile he gave her in the library when he came in from smoking. He held the door wide open so that she saw a tall spooky staircase and a room to the right where chairs were arranged in a circle as if for a funeral or a clergyman's tea. Rose took a step forward and held out the bleeding-heart to him, unable to say a word.

"Well!" he said again. "What's this? A posy for my poor sick mother?" He, for his part, was not in the least discomfited by this meeting. It was clear that he recognized her but he was not surprised; it was almost as if he had expected her all along. Now that she was up close, she saw that the ascot was made of diapered foulard but she saw, as well, that it was not clean and had the uncleanliness that accumulates over a period of weeks. She wondered if it hid something repulsive like a goiter or a birthmark or if it were some sort of fascist insignia and he was cat's-paw to a band of crooks.

"Yes," she said, as bashful as a child. "It is a plant from the school."

From the left came the scream again, beside itself with rage, "Tea! Toast! Me!" The man, as if to himself, said, "Bring my tea and toast to me," and then smiling and looking directly at Rose with active brown eyes, he explained, "My mother has lost her verbs and adjectives. In fact, she has lost all parts of speech ex-

cept her nouns and pronouns, a very interesting phenomenon. Come in, please," and he put his hand under
her elbow with gallant pressure. There was nothing she
could do and she stepped inside the vestibule which had
a sweet smell like the taste of Neccos.

"Where shall I put it?" Rose asked.

"Oh, we'll take it right in to Mother, don't you think?
What kind is it? A geranium, I hope."

"A bleeding-heart."

"Oh," he said scowling. "Well, we'll have to make the
best of it." He tucked her arm in his and bent down toward her. "She likes either geraniums or cut flowers.
She has forgotten the names of all the others."

Now that she was so close to him she discovered that
it was he who smelled of Neccos and that actually the
hall smelled of ordure. There was a rustling like that
of stiff silk and the man said, "Excuse me just a minute," and right beside them but still invisible the voice
malevolently aped him. He shut the door and there she
saw a parrot in a cage on a marble-topped bureau. It
regarded her with wicked eyes like a patient maniac.

"I'll bet Waldo here had you buffaloed, didn't he?"
said the man with a laugh as he opened the cage and
the parrot stepped out on to his wrist with a haughty
mutter. "He's a great old bird."

"Hours!" shrieked the voice of the invalid and the
man translated for the smug bird, "You have been gone
for hours."

Rose, while she could not claim to be really surprised

herself, could not adjust herself to the man's unhesitating acceptance of the situation as if they had planned it together some days before. He indicated that she was to precede him down the corridor as if this were the most natural thing in the world, and they went, all three of them, down the slightly veering hall where ghostly pictures hung and on the way the man said, like a guide, "As you see, we live very simply, Mother and I. The room to your right is the parlor which we seldom use in winter. Perhaps you observed the portrait on the far wall of that room? An illustrious ancestor. Upstairs there are four bedrooms besides yours truly's. Linen closet, of course, and ample attic space." They paused at a door and he said, secretly as if the parrot were eavesdropping, "I have seen you in the library, you know, Rose." He said her name in a way that the greenest schoolgirl could not have misconstrued and she trembled from head to foot and had to grasp the plant tightly or it would have fallen. His breathing was a little heavy and the parrot, eying Rose in the twilight of the hall, gave forth a glottal giggle full of wisdom.

All the low furniture in the invalid woman's room was painted white except for the narrow bed which was blackish-brown and looked like a catafalque. The bones of the flagging body on it jutted up under a royal purple counterpane. At first only the head and shoulders of the ancient woman showed, but when the small red eyes, witlessly mean with age, saw the parrot, she drew forth a huge piebald hand and her tongue labored on her lip as she said, "Him me."

"Quite like a child," said her son tolerantly as he handed over the parrot which settled down on her wrist. "The young lady here, Miss Rose, has brought you a plant, Mother. She says it's from the school."

The old woman's fingernails were painted a morbid red and one of the fingers stroked the parrot's stout yellow talons. Although the woman did not look at her, she said, "Roses. Gratitude."

"No, Mother, not roses. I said this young lady's name was Miss Rose. She has brought a bleeding-heart." He added in an exasperated aside, "Not that it matters a hoot in hell what kind of any old thing it is."

The invalid covered Rose with an ambiguous glance and said, "I her."

"I her," repeated her son. "I don't know what she means." He began to take the paper off the plant and growled, "I surely hope she likes it. She surely should. Very thoughtful of the school to my way of thinking."

"I her," repeated the old woman in a louder voice and the man flushed. Obviously this could signify anything: "I hate her," "I want her to go," or "I have never seen her before." It was a cul-de-sac that could not very well be ignored because she said it over and over and presently Waldo joined with his one sentence and they chanted antiphonally, "I her," "Just a minute," "I her," "Just a minute." While these two obscene creatures on the bed were making a spectacle of themselves, the man was clumsily trying to get the string off the flower-pot and nudging Rose every now and again although he did not need to. There was an awful odor in the room, both medicinal and decayed, and everything looked soiled and moist. The shape of the room and the situation of the furniture were the same as in Rose's room as if in a planned parody.

The man got the knot untied and slipped the paper off and his mother said to the parrot, "Silence," and to her son, "I her bell."

"Of course!" cried the man with relief. "I heard her ring the bell?" And the woman nodded her head up and down with a delighted smile on the thin crescent of her mouth.

He put the bleeding-heart on the low white table beside the bed where a Bible lay, conventional and new, and some sticky bottles of medicine and some revolting gobbets of cotton. The other old hand with veins as thick as pencils came staggering out of the bed to pluck a blossom from the plant which it held out for the parrot. The fingernails were the same color as the little flower which disappeared in Waldo's greedy bill.

"Roses. Waldo."

"Yes, Mother," said the man soothingly, "Roses for Waldo." On the wall over the bed hung a sampler that said, "LOOK UPWARD NOT DOWN."

Rose finally found her voice and she said urgently, "I must go." But the man detained her with a soft pat on her arm. "But you haven't had your tea. You must have tea with Mother." Mother was plucking the flowers and feeding them to Waldo very rapidly for one of her years and debility. After each gobble, Waldo ducked his head with villainous coquetry.

"I'm sorry," said Rose, "but I really must go."

He was looking with some consternation at his mother. "I say, you don't think a bleeding-heart is toxic, do you? I wouldn't like anything to happen to Waldo."

"I don't know," she said miserably, and to the woman on the bed she said, "Good-by. I am glad to have met you," although this was a double lie for she was not glad and there had been no proper meeting.

"Oh, you must have tea!" cried the man and he fingered his yellow ascot nervously as if he could not bear to have her leave. "You must! It isn't often that Mother and I have such a pretty guest." She shivered and buttoned the top button of her coat. "It will only take a minute," he wheedled. "It's on the tray and I just plug in the electric kettle thing and we're all set." He gave himself a private smile and said, "All set and rarin' to go."

She was about to be very firm and cutting if necessary to this tiresome old child by whom she had been so foolishly taken in at the library, but she thought of Miss Talmadge and was afraid if she were discourteous there might be trouble. It could not last long and he could not do anything improper to her in front of his mother and the parrot whose sagacious gaze missed nothing. So she gave in and he drew a rocking chair to the center of the room and beside it he put a bench. "The tray goes here," he said, "and you can pour." And then he left the room, walking out backwards to unnerve her all the more.

The ten minutes he was gone were for Rose a bizarre and separate experience. The old woman and the parrot clucked at one another over the sinister meal of bleedinghearts and but for this there was silence in the darkening room. She was forced to accept the reality of the afternoon, that the man in the yellow ascot lived here and that he drove the electric car and that in no particular did he resemble her image of her foster-father. And it was quite possible to accept it now, but she was apprehensive of the evening to come and the next afternoon when she would meet him again in the Samuel Sewell. There were only two flowers left on the plant and for some reason she hoped that tea would be here before they were gone. She glanced toward the bed; the headboard was just opposite her desk and she knew that she could never again write there with the picture in her mind of the old woman feeding the evil bird. A good deal in her quiet life would be changed. She doubted if she would ever go again to the library on the customary afternoons, for example. She would be free, it is true, to walk once again in the parts of the town and the country she had enjoyed before but this gain was offset by the knowledge that there was no mystery left: she knew exactly where the man lived and, moreover, to her regret, she knew *how* he lived.

The next to the last blossom was gone and then the last was gone and the feeding hand retired under the covers. The old woman looked at Waldo and at Rose and said, "You him." She pretended neither to hear nor to see but stared at the sampler which had a border of pine-cones. A foot surreptitiously moved under the counterpane and Waldo walked off his mistress' hand so that Rose, nauseated, saw that he had not eaten the bleeding-hearts at all, but had only mauled them and then had dropped them onto the bed where they lay in a heap like bloody matter. The command was repeated but she heard her host coming back and she got up to open the door for him. She said, "I think your mother wanted me to take the parrot."

"Oh, did she?" he asked with interest. "That shows she likes you. Yes, sir, that shows you've made a big hit with Mother."

"But I don't like birds," she said.

"Really? How extraordinary! I had a very charming Brazilian oriole to whom I was much attached. Waldo killed her, I never was just sure how."

On the tray were a plate of English muffins and a jar of peanut butter and one of marmalade and a store-bought pound cake and a dish of pickled peaches. There were a can of evaporated milk and a tin of bouillon cubes. This last he picked up, mouthing the words, "This is what she thinks is tea. Isn't allowed tea. A stimulant." Waldo laughed.

It took a long time to prepare the meal. A good deal

of furniture had to be moved before the kettle could be plugged in; then he had to go back to the kitchen for spoons which he had forgotten and then for some plates for the pickled peaches. Then he stopped everything when he saw the mess Waldo had made with the flowers and for a moment Rose thought he was going to lose his temper. "Pest!" he said sharply and gave Waldo a baleful look. When everything was ready, the old woman said "Radio" so the lamp had to be unplugged and the radio plugged in and candles had to be lit. The kettle made the radio splutter and creak and Waldo, the everlasting Mr. Fixit, stared at the box and said patiently, "Just a minute." But at last everything was ready and Rose began to pour the tea while the man spread peanut butter on the English muffins. The old woman sucked the bouillon and gave a sip to Waldo now and then.

"I wish she wouldn't do that," said the man, preoccupied with the muffins. "It gives him an intestinal condition."

Rose said politely," How old is Waldo?"

"Forty-eight," he said. "Quite a character. He used to say some other things. 'I think you're rather foolish,' was one and 'Go by-by, Aunt Louisa' was another, but he's lost everything but 'Just a minute.' "

"It is remarkable," said Rose, referring to the habit in this household of mislaying language.

"Yes," he mused, giving her a muffin in his hand. "Yes, Waldo's quite a character. He keeps Mother company. If it weren't for Waldo, I'd never get to have my little afternoons off at the library."

Because there was something in his voice that was not altogether trustworthy, she said, "What does he eat?"

"A special food for parrots," he said. "Called 'Polly's Perfect Preparation.' But he likes fruit too. The trouble with fruit, though, is that it gives him that intestinal condition I alluded to."

Mother finished her bouillon with a hoarse swallow and said, "Time toast."

"Right you are, Mother. Time for toast," and handed her a muffin with marmalade. Returning, he said *sotto voce*, "Time for toast and tea for two, what? Do you often eat at the inn?"

"Oh, no, almost never. Do you?"

"No. Thanksgiving, Christmas, Easter, Patriots' Day, that's all. Not that the cuisine is not to my liking. But I am rather tied here to my poor sick mother. That is to say, I generally dine *en famille*." A note of woe came into his voice: "*En famille* with Waldo."

She could not think of any comment to make on this very sad state of affairs and so she said, "What delicious peanut butter." In point of fact, it was dry and tasteless and the muffin was cold and rubbery. As for the tea, *it* could not be described. She promised herself that she would eat the whole muffin and drink the whole cup of tea and then she would go even if it meant being rude.

"*Is* it delicious peanut butter? Oh, thank you," he

said joyfully and from the bed the old woman clamored, "Gratitude!"

The man asked her how she liked Miss Talmadge and if she were ever homesick for the West and if she did not find her room at Number 8 rather chilly when the wind came off the river. He said he imagined she found the fare at the Minute Man café pretty much the same old thing from day to day; swordfish, canned peas, boiled potatoes. It was a little cold for sitting in the cemetery on Sunday afternoon nowadays, wasn't it?

"Lonesome, aren't you, little lady?" he said and Waldo warned from the footboard of the bed, "Just a minute."

She drank the last of the sour tea and returned the cup to the tray. She drew on her gloves and stood up. "Thank you so much for the tea," she said, "it was most kind of you."

The old woman beckoned to her and said, "Time."

"Yes, I know. It's time for me to go." She tried to smile warmly.

"No, no," cried her son anxiously, "she means there's plenty of time."

But Rose would not be detained any longer and she moved toward the door. He was immediately beside her, following her down the hall as long and as dark as a tunnel. Halfway down Waldo came bustling after them and walked between them, laughing busily. The man held Rose's elbow tightly as if by the pressure of his fingers he could communicate the desperate state of his loneliness. "You can't imagine how awful it is," he confided urgently. "Today you only saw her company manners, but you should hear the things she says to me when we're alone." His voice was full of tears. "Rose! Rose, we're near neighbors. Strictly speaking we live in the same house, Rose. Won't you come again?"

"I'll try," she said without any pity at all.

"When?"

"I don't know."

"Tomorrow? Oh, no, tomorrow we meet in the library, don't we? What do you read there?"

She was remote and academic. "I am doing some research work."

"That's wonderful. I knew you were cultured. I went to Harvard. I dare say you've heard of that little old college down Cambridge way?"

He was such a terrible mixture of unattractive qualities that she did not know how his face managed to be so aristocratically handsome. They were at the door now and she put her hand out toward the knob, but he was ahead of her. "Permit me, Rose," he said. "Please greet Miss Talmadge for my mother and me, but don't tell her what happened to the bleeding-heart." He grasped her hand in both of his and squeezed it warmly and looking deep into her eyes, he whispered, "The Samuel Sewell tomorrow."

She ran down the steps and he called after her, "Rose! My name is Mr. Benson!"

She heard him close the door and at the corner she

paused in the snowfall, senseless with misery. She could *not* sleep another night in that room but she had nowhere to go. Tears for her homeless self went down her cheeks with the snowflakes and she let a little sound escape her, the murmur of an unhappy child. And then, because there was nothing else to do, she opened the front door of Number 8 and went into her room. She turned the radio on very loud and got a program of jazz played on an organ and deafened to any other possible sound, she began to play solitaire, violently slapping the cards down on the table. In this futile tantrum with the cards, she bent a corner of the Queen of Hearts and this reminded her of her father's custom of spending whole winter evenings cleaning a deck of cards with a jackknife. A jackknife which he used, as well, to slice off a plug of chewing tobacco, to trim his fingernails and, in the spring, to dig embedded woodticks out of his skin.

When she came back from her dinner of swordfish at the Minute Man, she found a note on the rug just inside the door which said:

My dear Rose,

If you would care to go to the picture show tonight in Acton, I am at your disposal and wish you would telephone me. My name is in the book. I could come to your door or you could come to mine. Mrs. Morton Ripley is coming to call on Mother. I do not know when another opportunity will offer so hope you will not refuse.

Awaiting your communication via telephone,

I am,

Lucius Benson

There was no sound from the room beyond the wall but the silence was an uneasy one and she shuddered thinking of what might be going on in there. Waldo and his mistress were capable of any sort of monstrous tableau if the demonstration this afternoon with the bleeding-heart had not been unusual. She thought of going to the priest to ask for his advice or to the policeman for his protection. In any case, she could not stay here and after a minute of debate she let herself out quietly and went down the street and into the Mill Dam on her way to the library. But she had only just got to the triangular square of lawn in front of it when the electric car eased up alongside her and Mr. Benson leaned across and opened the door.

"Here, here," he gaily cried. "This is no way to treat your Dutch uncle. Climb in! Hop right in, Rosie O'Grady, and off we'll go to the picture show."

"Mr. Benson," she began, giving his derby a hard look, "I can't go to the movies with you tonight."

"Nonsense," he said. "Stuff and nonsense. Hop in, dear, we'll be in time for the newsreel. Good gracious, Rosie, what are you afraid of? Do you mean to say that you're afraid of a harmless old codger, old enough to be your father?"

"No, Mr. Benson," she said, "I'm not afraid of you." And it was true, she was not afraid, she was only displeased. "But I won't go to the movies."

"Just think of me as your father," he said. "Why don't you call me that as a matter of fact? I mean, not

'Father' but one of the more familiar things like 'Daddy'?"

It was not at all likely, she thought, that this was taking place. It was much too improbable that she was talking under an arc lamp in a snowfall to an elderly roué in an electric car who had invited her to call him Daddy.

"If you won't come with me," he said rather testily, "then I will come into the library and read."

She was at the end of her tether. No longer scared, certainly not respectful of his age, no longer polite for Miss Talmadge's sake, she burst out, "Oh, go to grass," and she scuffled up the snowy path.

"Let me tell you about my Brazilian oriole," he called desperately through the quiet storm. "Waldo killed it out of pure spite! I preferred it to Waldo and Waldo killed it out of spite!"

Rose went on up the path.

"Rose!"

She heard him come running after her but she was not afraid, for the library was brightly lighted. She stopped when he was abreast of her and stamped her foot. "Go away, Mr. Benson," she said.

His head fell forward dejectedly and his beaver-lined coat which was not buttoned hung loosely on him as if he had suddenly shriveled. He was a die-hard. "Oh, Rose," he said, "I assure you I mean no harm." He touched the yellow ascot with the palm of his hand and said, "The most unsightly wen you ever saw. All I am

asking is a little pity." He began to undo the scarf as
she mounted the steps. When she was within the storm
doors, she looked back and saw him standing there in
the snow with his neck bare and his arms spread out,
his palms upward in supplication. He had flung his head
back and his derby had fallen to the ground; he wore
the yellow ascot on his left arm like a maniple. Just behind him, the electric car cast an absolutely square
shadow on the white ground.

*The Interior Castle*

Pansy Vanneman, injured in an automobile accident, often woke up before dawn when the night noises of the hospital still came, in hushed hurry, through her half-open door. By day, when the nurses talked audibly with the internes, laughed without inhibition, and took no pains to soften their footsteps on the resounding composition floors, the routine of the hospital seemed as bland and commonplace as that of a bank or a factory. But in the dark hours, the whispering and the quickly stilled clatter of glasses and basins, the moans of patients whose morphine was wearing off, the soft squeak of a stretcher as it rolled past in its way from the emergency ward—these suggested agony and death. Thus, on the first morning, Pansy had faltered to consciousness long before daylight and had found herself in a ward from every bed of which, it seemed to her, came the bewildered protest of someone about to die. A caged light burned on the floor beside the bed next to hers. Her neighbor was dying and a priest was administering Extreme Unction. He was stout and elderly and he suffered from asthma so that the struggle of his breathing, so close to her, was the basic pattern and all the other sounds were superimposed upon it. Two middle-aged men in overcoats knelt on the floor beside the high bed. In a foreign tongue, the half-gone woman babbled against the hissing and sighing of the Latin prayers. She played with her rosary as if it were a toy: she tried, and failed, to put it into her mouth.

Pansy felt horror, but she felt no pity. An hour or so later, when the white ceiling lights were turned on and everything—faces, counterpanes, and the hands that groped upon them—was transformed into a uniform gray sordor, the woman was wheeled away in her bed to die somewhere else, in privacy. Pansy did not quite take this in, although she stared for a long time at the new, empty bed that had replaced the other.

The next morning, when she again woke up before the light, this time in a private room, she recalled the woman with such sorrow that she might have been a friend. Simultaneously, she mourned the driver of the taxicab in which she had been injured, for he had died at about noon the day before. She had been told this as she lay on a stretcher in the corridor, waiting to be taken to the X-ray room; an interne, passing by, had paused and smiled down at her and had said, "Your cab-driver is dead. You were lucky."

Six weeks after the accident, she woke one morning just as daylight was showing on the windows as a murky smear. It was a minute or two before she realized why she was so reluctant to be awake, why her uneasiness amounted almost to alarm. Then she remembered that her nose was to be operated on today. She lay straight and motionless under the seersucker counterpane. Her blood-red eyes in her darned face stared through the window and saw a frozen river and leafless elm trees and a grizzled esplanade where dogs danced on the ends of leashes, their bundled-up owners stumbling after them, half blind with sleepiness and cold. Warm as the hospital room was, it did not prevent Pansy from knowing, as keenly as though she were one of the walkers, how very cold it was outside. Each twig of a nearby tree was stark. Cold red brick buildings nudged the low-lying sky which was pale and inert like a punctured sac.

In six weeks, the scene had varied little: there was promise in the skies neither of sun nor of snow; no red sunsets marked these days. The trees could neither die nor leaf out again. Pansy could not remember another season in her life so constant, when the very minutes themselves were suffused with the winter pallor as they dropped from the moon-faced clock in the corridor. Likewise, her room accomplished no alterations from day to day. On the glass-topped bureau stood two potted plants telegraphed by faraway well-wishers. They did not fade, and if a leaf turned brown and fell, it soon was replaced; so did the blossoms renew themselves. The roots, like the skies and like the bare trees, seemed zealously determined to maintain a status quo. The bedside table, covered every day with a clean white towel, though the one removed was always immaculate, was furnished sparsely with a water glass, a bent drinking

tube, a sweating pitcher, and a stack of paper handkerchiefs. There were a few letters in the drawer, a hairbrush, a pencil, and some postal cards on which, from
time to time, she wrote brief messages to relatives and
friends: "Dr. Nash says that my reflexes are shipshape
(*sic*) and Dr. Rivers says the frontal fracture has all
but healed and that the occipital is coming along nicely.
Dr. Nicholas, the nose doctor, promises to operate as
soon as Dr. Rivers gives him the go-ahead sign (*sic*)."

The bed itself was never rumpled. Once fretful and
now convalescent, Miss Vanneman might have been expected to toss or to turn the pillows or to unmoor the
counterpane; but hour after hour and day after day she
lay at full length and would not even suffer the nurses
to raise the head-piece of the adjustable bed. So perfect
and stubborn was her body's immobility that it was as
if the room and the landscape, mortified by the ice,
were extensions of herself. Her resolute quiescence and
her disinclination to talk, the one seeming somehow to
proceed from the other, resembled, so the nurses said, a
final coma. And they observed, in pitying indignation,
that she might as *well* be dead for all the interest she
took in life. Amongst themselves they scolded her for
what they thought a moral weakness: an automobile
accident, no matter how serious, was not reason enough
for anyone to give up the will to live or to be happy.
She had not—to come down bluntly to the facts—had
the decency to be grateful that it was the driver of the
cab and not she who had died. (And how dreadfully

the man had died!) She was twenty-five years old and she came from a distant city. These were really the only facts known about her. Evidently she had not been here long, for she had no visitors, a lack which was at first sadly moving to the nurses but which became to them a source of unreasonable annoyance: had anyone the right to live so one-dimensionally? It was impossible to laugh at her, for she said nothing absurd; her demands could not be complained of because they did not exist; she could not be hated for a sharp tongue nor for a supercilious one; she could not be admired for bravery or for wit or for interest in her fellow creatures. She was believed to be a frightful snob.

Pansy, for her part, took a secret and mischievous pleasure in the bewilderment of her attendants and the more they courted her with offers of magazines, crossword puzzles, and a radio that she could rent from the hospital, the farther she retired from them into herself and into the world which she had created in her long hours here and which no one could ever penetrate nor imagine. Sometimes she did not even answer the nurses' questions; as they rubbed her back with alcohol and steadily discoursed, she was as remote from them as if she were miles away. She did not think that she lived on a higher plane than that of the nurses and the doctors but that she lived on a different one and that at this particular time—this time of exploration and habituation—she had no extra strength to spend on making herself known to them. All she had been before and all the

memories she might have brought out to disturb the
monotony of, say, the morning bath, and all that the
past meant to the future when she would leave the hospital, were of no present consequence to her. Not even
in her thoughts did she employ more than a minimum
of memory. And when she did remember, it was in flat
pictures, rigorously independent of one another: she
saw her thin, poetic mother who grew thinner and more
poetic in her canvas deck-chair at Saranac reading *Lalla
Rookh.* She saw herself in an inappropriate pink hat
drinking iced tea in a garden so oppressive with the
smell of phlox that the tea itself tasted of it. She recalled an afternoon in autumn in Vermont when she had
heard three dogs' voices in the north woods and she
could tell, by the characteristic minor key struck three
times at intervals, like bells from several churches, that
they had treed something: the eastern sky was pink and
the trees on the horizon looked like some eccentric vas-
cular system meticulously drawn on colored paper.

What Pansy thought of all the time was her own
brain. Not only the brain as the seat of consciousness,
but the physical organ itself which she envisaged, romantically, now as a jewel, now as a flower, now as a
light in a glass, now as an envelope of rosy vellum
containing other envelopes, one within the other, diminishing infinitely. It was always pink and always fragile,
always deeply interior and invaluable. She believed
that she had reached the innermost chamber of knowledge and that perhaps her knowledge was the same as

the saint's achievement of pure love. It was only convention, she thought, that made one say "sacred heart" and
not "sacred brain."

Often, but never articulately, the color pink troubled
her and the picture of herself in the wrong hat hung
steadfastly before her mind's eye. None of the other
girls had worn hats and since autumn had come early
that year, they were dressed in green and rusty brown
and dark yellow. Poor Pansy wore a white eyelet frock
with a lacing of black ribbon around the square neck.
When she came through the arch, overhung with bittersweet, and saw that they had not yet heard her, she
almost turned back, but Mr. Oliver was there and she
was in love with him. She was in love with him though
he was ten years older than she and had never shown
any interest in her beyond asking her once, quite fatu-
ously but in an intimate voice, if the yodeling of the
little boy who peddled clams did not make her wish to
visit Switzerland. Actually, there was more to this question than met the eye, for some days later Pansy learned
that Mr. Oliver, who was immensely rich, kept an apartment in Geneva. In the garden that day, he spoke to her
only once. He said, "My dear, you look exactly like
something out of Katherine Mansfield," and immediately turned and within her hearing asked Beatrice Sher-
burne to dine with him that night at the Country Club.
Afterward, Pansy went down to the sea and threw the
beautiful hat onto the full tide and saw it vanish in the
wake of a trawler. Thereafter, when she heard the clam

boy coming down the road, she locked the door and when the knocking had stopped and her mother called down from her chaise longue, "Who was it, dearie?" she replied, "A salesman."

It was only the fact that the hat had been pink that worried her. The rest of the memory was trivial, for she knew that she could never again love anything as ecstatically as she loved the spirit of Pansy Vanneman, enclosed within her head.

But her study was not without distraction, and she fought two adversaries: pain and Dr. Nicholas. Against Dr. Nicholas, she defended herself valorously and in fear; but pain, the pain, that is, that was independent of his instruments, she sometimes forced upon herself adventurously like a child scaring himself in a graveyard.

Dr. Nicholas greatly admired her crushed and splintered nose which he daily probed and peered at, exclaiming that he had never seen anything like it. His shapely hands ached for their knives; he was impatient with the skull-fracture man's cautious delay. He spoke of "our" nose and said "we" would be a new person when we could breathe again. His own nose was magnificent. Not even his own brilliant surgery could have improved upon it nor could a first-rate sculptor have duplicated its direct downward line which permitted only the least curvature inward toward the end; nor the delicately rounded lateral declivities; nor the thin-walled, perfectly matched nostrils.

Miss Vanneman did not doubt his humaneness nor

his talent—he was a celebrated man—but she questioned whether he had imagination. Immediately beyond the prongs of his speculum lay her treasure whose price he, no more than the nurses, could estimate. She believed he could not destroy it, but she feared that he might maim it: might leave a scratch on one of the brilliant facets of the jewel, bruise a petal of the flower, smudge the glass where the light burned, blot the envelopes, and that then she would die or would go mad. While she did not question that in either eventuality her brain would after a time redeem its original impeccability, she did not quite yet wish to enter upon either kind of eternity, for she was not certain that she could carry with her her knowledge as well as its receptacle.

Blunderer that he was, Dr. Nicholas was an honorable enemy, not like the demon, pain, which skulked in a thousand guises within her head, and which often she recklessly willed to attack her and then drove back in terror. After the rout, sweat streamed from her face and soaked the neck of the coarse hospital shirt. To be sure, it came usually of its own accord, running like a wild fire through all the convolutions to fill with flame the small sockets and ravines and then, at last, to withdraw, leaving behind a throbbing and an echo. On these occasions, she was as helpless as a tree in a wind. But at the other times when, by closing her eyes and rolling up the eyeballs in such a way that she fancied she looked directly on the place where her brain was, the pain woke sluggishly and came toward her at a snail's pace. Then, bit by bit, it gained speed. Sometimes it faltered back, subsided altogether, and then it rushed like a tidal wave driven by a hurricane, lashing and roaring until she lifted her hands from the counterpane, crushed her broken teeth into her swollen lip, stared in panic at the soothing walls with her ruby eyes, stretched out her legs until she felt their bones must snap. Each cove, each narrow inlet, every living bay was flooded and the frail brain, a little hat-shaped boat, was washed from its mooring and set adrift. The skull was as vast as the world and the brain was as small as a seashell.

Then came calm weather and the safe journey home. She kept vigil for a while, though, and did not close her eyes, but gazing pacifically at the trees, conceived of the pain as the guardian of her treasure who would not let her see it; that was why she was handled so savagely whenever she turned her eyes inward. Once this watch was interrupted: by chance she looked into the corridor and saw a shaggy mop slink past the door, followed by a senile porter. A pair of ancient eyes, as rheumy as an old dog's, stared uncritically in at her and a toothless mouth formed a brutish word. She was so surprised that she immediately closed her eyes to shut out the shape of the word and the pain dug up the unmapped regions of her head with mattocks, ludicrously huge. It was the familiar pain, but this time, even as she endured it, she observed with detachment that its effect upon her was less than that of its contents, the by-products, for example, of temporal confusion and the bizarre misapplication of the style of one sensation to another. At the moment, for example, although her brain reiterated to her that *it* was being assailed, she was stroking her right wrist with her left hand as though to assuage the ache, long since dispelled, of the sprain in the joint. Some minutes after she had opened her eyes and left off soothing her wrist, she lay rigid experiencing the sequel to the pain, an ideal terror. For, as before on several occasions, she was overwhelmed with the knowledge that the pain had been consummated in the vessel of her mind and for the moment the vessel was unbeautiful: she thought, quailing, of those plastic folds as palpable as the fingers of locked hands containing in their very cells, their fissures, their repulsive hemispheres, the mind, the soul, the inscrutable intelligence.

The porter, then, like the pink hat and like her mother and the hounds' voices, loitered with her.

## II

Dr. Nicholas came at nine o'clock to prepare her for the operation. With him came an entourage of white-frocked acolytes, and one of them wheeled in a wagon on which lay knives and scissors and pincers, cans of swabs and gauze. In the midst of these was a bowl of liquid whose rich purple color made it seem strange like the brew of an alchemist.

"All set?" the surgeon asked her, smiling. "A little nervous, what? I don't blame you. I've often said I'd rather break a leg than have a submucous resection."

Pansy thought for a moment he was going to touch his nose. His approach to her was roundabout. He moved through the yellow light shed by the globe in the ceiling which gave his forehead a liquid gloss; he paused by the bureau and touched a blossom of the cyclamen; he looked out the window and said, to no one and to all, "I couldn't start my car this morning. Came in a cab." Then he came forward. As he came, he removed a speculum from the pocket of his short-sleeved coat and like a cat, inquiring of the nature of a surface with its paws, he put out his hand toward her and drew it back, gently murmuring, "You must not be afraid, my dear. There is no danger, you know. Do you think for a minute I would operate if there were?"

Dr. Nicholas, young, brilliant, and handsome, was an aristocrat, a husband, a father, a clubman, a Christian, a kind counselor, and a trustee of his preparatory school. Like many of the medical profession, even those whose specialty was centered on the organ of the basest sense, he interested himself in the psychology of his patients: in several instances, for example, he had found that severe attacks of sinusitis were coincident with emotional crises. Miss Vanneman more than ordinarily captured his fancy since her skull had been fractured and her behavior throughout had been so extraordinary that he felt he was observing at first hand some of the results of shock, that incommensurable element, which frequently were too subtle to see. There was, for example, the matter of her complete passivity during a lumbar puncture, reports of which were written down in her history and were enlarged upon for him by Dr. Rivers' interne who had been in charge. Except for a tremor in her throat and a deepening of pallor, there were no signs at all that she was aware of what was happening to her. She made no sound, did not close her eyes nor clench her fists. She had had several punctures; her only reaction had been to the very first one, the morning after she had been brought in. When the interne explained to her that he was going to drain off cerebrospinal fluid which was pressing against her brain, she exclaimed, "My God!" but it was not an exclamation of fear. The young man had been unable to name what it was he had heard in her voice; he could only say that it had not been fear as he had observed it in other patients.

Dr. Nicholas wondered about her. There was no way of guessing whether she had always had a nature of so tolerant and undemanding a complexion. It gave him a melancholy pleasure to think that before her accident she had been high-spirited and loquacious; he was moved to think that perhaps she had been a beauty and that when she had first seen her face in the looking glass she had lost all joy in herself. It was very difficult to tell what the face had been, for it was so bruised and swollen, so hacked-up and lopsided. The black stitches the length of the nose, across the saddle, across the cheekbone, showed that there would be unsightly scars. He had ventured once to give her the name of a plastic surgeon but she had only replied with a vague, refusing smile. He had hoisted a manly shoulder and said, "You're the doctor."

Much as he pondered, coming to no conclusions, about what went on inside that pitiable skull, he was, of course, far more interested in the nose, deranged so badly that it would require his topmost skill to restore its functions to it. He would be obliged not only to make a submucous resection, a simple run-of-the-mill operation, but to remove the vomer, always a delicate task but further complicated in this case by the proximity of the bone to the frontal fracture line which conceivably was not entirely closed. If it were not and he operated too soon and if a cold germ then found its way into the opening, his patient would be carried off by meningitis in the twinkling of an eye. He wondered if she knew in what potential danger she lay; he desired to assure her that he had brought his craft to its nearest perfection and that she had nothing to fear of him, but feeling that she was perhaps both ignorant and unimaginative and that such consolation would create a fear rather than dispel one, he held his tongue and came nearer to the bed.

Watching him, Pansy could already feel the prongs of his pliers opening her nostrils for the insertion of his fine probers. The pain he caused her with his instruments was of a different kind from that which she felt unaided: it was a naked, clean, and vivid pain that made her faint and ill and made her wish to die. Once she had fainted as he ruthlessly explored and after she was brought around, he continued until he had finished his investigation. The memory of this outrage had afterward several times made her cry.

This morning she looked at him and listened to him with hatred. Fixing her eyes upon the middle of his high, protuberant brow, she imagined the clutter behind it and she despised its obtuse imperfection. In his bland unawareness, this nobody, this nose-bigot, was about to play with fire and she wished him ill.

He said, "I can't blame you. No, I expect you're not looking forward to our little party. But you'll be glad to be able to breathe again."

He stationed his lieutenants. The interne stood opposite him on the left side of the bed. The surgical nurse wheeled the wagon within easy reach of his hands and stood beside it. Another nurse stood at the foot of the bed. A third drew the shades at the windows and attached a blinding light that shone down on the patient hotly, and then she left the room, softly closing the door. Pansy stared at the silver ribbon tied in a great bow round the green crepe paper of one of the flower pots. It made her realize for the first time that one of the days she had lain here had been Christmas, but she had no time to consider this strange and thrilling fact, for Dr. Nicholas was genially explaining his anesthetic. He would soak packs of gauze in the purple fluid, a cocaine solution, and he would place them then in her nostrils, leaving them there for an hour. He warned her that the packing would be disagreeable (he did not say "pain-

ful") but that it would be well worth a few minutes of
discomfort not to be in the least sick after the operation.
He asked her if she were ready and when she nodded
her head, he adjusted the mirror on his forehead and
began.

At the first touch of his speculum, Pansy's fingers mechanically bent to the palms of her hands and she stiffened. He said, "A pack, Miss Kennedy," and Pansy
closed her eyes. There was a rush of plunging pain as
he drove the sodden gobbet of gauze high up into her
nose and something bitter burned in her throat so that
she retched. The doctor paused a moment and the surgical nurse wiped Pansy's mouth. He returned to her
with another pack, pushing it with his bodkin doggedly
until it lodged against the first. Stop! Stop! cried all her
nerves, wailing along the surface of her skin. The coats
that covered them were torn off and they shuddered like
naked people screaming, Stop! Stop! But Dr. Nicholas
did not hear. Time and again he came back with a fresh
pack and did not pause at all until one nostril was finished. She opened her eyes and saw him wipe the sweat
off his forehead and saw the dark interne bending over
her, fascinated. Miss Kennedy bathed her temples in ice
water and Dr. Nicholas said, "There. It won't be much
longer. I'll tell them to send you some coffee, though
I'm afraid you won't be able to taste it. Ever drink coffee with chicory in it? I have no use for it."

She snatched at his irrelevancy and, though she had
never tasted chicory, she said severely, "I love it."

Dr. Nicholas chuckled. "De gustibus. Ready? A pack, Miss Kennedy."

The second nostril was harder to pack since the other side was now distended and this passage was anyhow much narrower, as narrow, he had once remarked, as that in the nose of an infant. In such pain as passed all language and even the farthest fetched analogies, she turned her eyes inward thinking that under the obscuring cloak of the surgeon's pain, she could see her brain without the knowledge of its keeper. But Dr. Nicholas and his aides would give her no peace. They surrounded her with their murmuring and their foot-shuffling and the rustling of their starched uniforms, and her eyelids continually flew back in embarrassment and mistrust. She was claimed entirely by this present, meaningless pain and suddenly and sharply she forgot what she had meant to do. She was aware of nothing but her ascent to the summit of something; what it was she did not know, whether it was a tower or a peak or Jacob's ladder. Now she was an abstract word, now she was a theorem of geometry, now she was a kite flying, a top spinning, a prism flashing, a kaleidoscope turning.

But none of the others in the room could see inside when the surgeon was finished, the nurse at the foot of the bed said, "Now you must take a look in the mirror. It's simply too comical." And they all laughed intimately like old, fast friends. She smiled politely and looked at her reflection: over the gruesomely fattened snout, her scarlet eyes stared in fixed reproach upon her upturned lips, gray with bruises. But even in its smile of betrayal, the mouth itself was puzzled: it reminded her that something had been left behind, but she could not recall what it was. She was hollowed out and was as dry as a white bone.

### III

They strapped her ankles to the operating table and put leather nooses round her wrists. Over her head was a mirror with a thousand facets in which she saw a thousand travesties of her face. At her right side was the table, shrouded in white, where lay the glittering blades of the many knives, thrusting out fitful rays of light. All the cloth was frosty; everything was white or silver and as cold as snow. Dr. Nicholas, a tall snowman with silver eyes and silver fingernails, came into the room soundlessly for he walked on layers and layers of snow that deadened his footsteps; behind him came the interne, a smaller snowman, less impressively proportioned. At the foot of the table, a snow figure put her frozen hands upon Pansy's helpless feet. The doctor plucked the packs from the cold, numb nose. His laugh was like a cry on a bitter, still night: "I will show you now," he called across the expanse of snow, "that you can feel nothing." The pincers bit at nothing, snapped at the air and cracked a nerveless icicle. Pansy called back and heard her own voice echo: "I feel nothing."

Here the walls were gray, not tan. Suddenly the face of the nurse at the foot of the table broke apart and

Pansy first thought it was in grief. But it was a smile and she said, "Did you enjoy your coffee?" Down the gray corridors of the maze, the words rippled, ran like mice, birds, broken beads: Did you enjoy your coffee? your coffee? your coffee? Similarly once in another room that also had gray walls, the same voice had said, "Shall I give her some whisky?" She was overcome with gratitude that this young woman (how pretty she was with her white hair and her white face and her china-blue eyes!) had been with her that first night and was with her now.

In the great stillness of the winter, the operation began. The knives carved snow. Pansy was happy. She had been given a hypnotic just before they came to fetch her and she would have gone to sleep had she not enjoyed so much this trickery of Dr. Nicholas' whom now she tenderly loved.

There was a clock in the operating room and from time to time she looked at it. An hour passed. The snow-man's face was melting; drops of water hung from his fine nose, but his silver eyes were as bright as ever. Her love was returned, she knew: he loved her nose exactly as she loved his knives. She looked at her face in the domed mirror and saw how the blood had streaked her lily-white cheeks and had stained her shroud. She returned to the private song: Did you enjoy your coffee? your coffee?

At the half-hour, a murmur, anguine and slumbrous, came to her and only when she had repeated the words twice did they engrave their meaning upon her. Dr. Nicholas said, "Stand back now, nurse. I'm at this girl's brain and I don't want my elbow jogged." Instantly Pansy was alive. Her strapped ankles arched angrily; her wrists strained against their bracelets. She jerked her head and she felt the pain flare; she had made the knife slip.

"Be still!" cried the surgeon. "Be quiet, please!"

He had made her remember what it was she had lost when he had rammed his gauze into her nose: she bustled like a housewife to shut the door. She thought, I must hurry before the robbers come. It would be like the time Mother left the cellar door open and the robber came and took, of all things, the terrarium.

Dr. Nicholas was whispering to her. He said, in the voice of a lover, "If you can stand it five minutes more, I can perform the second operation now and you won't have to go through this again. What do you say?"

She did not reply. It took her several seconds to remember why it was her mother had set such store by the terrarium and then it came to her that the bishop's widow had brought her an herb from Palestine to put in it.

The interne said, "You don't want to have your nose packed again, do you?"

The surgical nurse said, "She's a good patient, isn't she, sir?"

"Never had a better," replied Dr. Nicholas. "But

don't call me 'sir.' You must be a Canadian to call me 'sir.' "

The nurse at the foot of the bed said, "I'll order some more coffee for you."

"How about it, Miss Vanneman?" said the doctor. "Shall I go ahead?"

She debated. Once she had finally fled the hospital and fled Dr. Nicholas, nothing could compel her to come back. Still, she knew that the time would come when she could no longer live in seclusion, she must go into the world again and must be equipped to live in it; she banally acknowledged that she must be able to breathe. And finally, though the world to which she would return remained unreal, she gave the surgeon her permission.

He had now to penetrate regions that were not anesthetized and this he told her frankly, but he said that there was no danger at all. He apologized for the slip of the tongue he had made: in point of fact, he had not been near her brain, it was only a figure of speech. He began. The knives ground and carved and curried and scoured the wounds they made; the scissors clipped hard gristle and the scalpels chipped off bone. It was as if a tangle of tiny nerves were being cut dexterously, one by one; the pain writhed spirally and came to her who was a pink bird and sat on the top of a cone. The pain was a pyramid made of a diamond; it was an intense light; it was the hottest fire, the coldest chill, the highest peak, the fastest force, the furthest reach, the newest

time. It possessed nothing of her but its one infinitesimal
scene: beyond the screen as thin as gossamer, the brain
trembled for its life, hearing the knives hunting like
wolves outside, sniffing and snapping. Mercy! Mercy!
cried the scalped nerves.

At last, miraculously, she turned her eyes inward
tranquilly. Dr. Nicholas had said, "The worst is over.
I am going to work on the floor of your nose," and at
his signal she closed her eyes and this time and this
time alone, she saw her brain lying in a shell-pink satin
case. It was a pink pearl, no bigger than a needle's eye,
but it was so beautiful and so pure that its smallness
made no difference. Anyhow, as she watched, it grew.
It grew larger and larger until it was an enormous bubble that contained the surgeon and the whole room within
its rosy luster. In a long ago summer, she had often
been absorbed by the spectacle of flocks of yellow birds
that visited a cedar tree and she remembered that everything that summer had been some shade of yellow. One
year of childhood, her mother had frequently taken her
to have tea with an aged schoolmistress upon whose
mantelpiece there was a herd of ivory elephants; that
had been the white year. There was a green spring when
early in April she had seen a grass snake on a boulder,
but the very summer that followed was violet, for vetch
took her mother's garden. She saw a swatch of blue
tulle lying in a raffia basket on the front porch of Uncle
Marion's brown house. Never before had the world
been pink, whatever else it had been. Or had it been,

one other time? She could not be sure and she did not care. Of one thing she was certain: never had the world enclosed her before and never had the quiet been so smooth.

For only a moment the busybodies left her to her ecstasy and then, impatient and gossiping, they forced their way inside, slashed at her resisting trance with questions and congratulations, with statements of fact and jokes. "Later," she said to them dumbly. "Later on, perhaps. I am busy now." But their voices would not go away. They touched her, too, washing her face with cloths so cold they stung, stroking her wrists with firm, antiseptic fingers. The surgeon, squeezing her arm with avuncular pride, said, "Good girl," as if she were a bright dog that had retrieved a bone. Her silent mind abused him: "You are a thief," it said, "you are heartless and you should be put to death." But he was leaving, adjusting his coat with an air of vainglory, and the interne, abject with admiration, followed him from the operating room smiling like a silly boy.

Shortly after they took her back to her room, the weather changed, not for the better. Momentarily the sun emerged from its concealing murk, but in a few minutes the snow came with a wind that promised a blizzard. There was great pain, but since it could not serve her, she rejected it and she lay as if in a hammock in a pause of bitterness. She closed her eyes, shutting herself up within her treasureless head.

*A Modest Proposal*

The celebrated trade winds of the Caribbean had, unseasonably, ceased to blow, and over the island a horrid stillness tarried. The ships in the glassy harbor appeared becalmed, and nothing moved except the golden lizards slipping over the pink walls and scuttering through the purple bougainvillaea, whose burdened branches touched the borders of the patio. The puny cats that ate the lizards slept stupefied under the hibiscus hedges. Once, a man-o'-war bird sailed across the yellow sky; once, a bushy burro strayed up the hill through the tall, hissing guinea grass and, pausing, gazed aloft with an expression of babyish melancholy; now and then, the wood doves sang sadly in the turpentine trees behind Captain Sundstrom's house.

The Captain's guests, who had been swimming and sunning all morning at his beach below and then had eaten his protracted Danish lunch of multitudinous hors d'oeuvres and an aspic of fish and a ragout of kid and salads and pancakes, now sat on the gallery drinking gin-and-Schweppes. Their conversation dealt largely with the extraordinary weather, and the residents of the island were at pains to assure the visitors that this un-

wholesome, breathless pause did not presage a hurricane, for it was far too early in the year. Their host predicted that a rain would follow on the heels of the calm
and fill the cisterns to the brim. At times, the tone of the
talk was chauvinistic; the islanders asked the outlanders
to agree with them that, unpleasant as this might be, it
was nothing like the villainous summer heat of Washington or New York. Here, at any rate, one dressed in sensible décolletage—the Captain's eyes browsed over the
bare shoulders of his ladies—and did not shorten one's
life by keeping up the winter's fidgets in the summertime. Why people who were not obliged to live in the
North did, he could not understand. It was a form of
masochism, was it not, frankly, to condemn oneself
needlessly to the tantrums of a capricious climate? Tem-
perate Zone, indeed! There was no temperance north of
Key West. The visitors civilly granted that their lives
were not ideal, they were politely envious of the calm
and leisure here, and some of them committed themselves to the extent of asking about the prices of real
estate.

If the talk digressed from the weather, it went to
other local matters: to the municipal politics, which were
forever a bear garden; to the dear or the damnable
peccadilloes of absent friends; to servant-robbers from
the States; to the revenue the merchants and restaura-
teurs had acquired in their shops and bars when the last
cruise ship was in, full to her gunwhales of spendthrift
boobs. And they talked of the divorcées-to-be who lit-

tered the terraces and lounges of the hotels, idling through their six weeks' quarantine, with nothing in the world to do but bathe in the sun and the sea, and drink, and haunt the shops for tax-free bargains in French perfume. They were spoken of as invalids; they were said to be here for "the cure." Some of them did look ill and shocked, as if, at times, they could not remember why they had come.

It was made plain that the divorcées who were among the gathering today were different from the rest; *they* were not bores about the husbands they were chucking; they did not flirt with married men, or get too drunk, or try anything fancy with the natives (a noteworthy woman from Utica, some months before, had brought a station wagon with her and daily could be seen driving along the country roads with a high-school boy as black as your hat beside her); and they fitted so well into the life of the island that the islanders would like to have them settle here or, at least, come back to pay a visit. Mrs. Baumgartner, a delicious blonde whose husband had beaten her with a ski pole in the railroad station at Boise, Idaho (she told the story very amusingly but it was evident that the man had been a beast), and who meant to marry again the moment she legally could, announced that she intended to return here for her honeymoon. Captain Sundstrom reasonably proposed that she not go back to the States at all but wait here until the proper time had passed and then send for her new husband. It would be droll if the same judge who had set

her free performed the ceremony. Crowing concupis-
cently, the Captain invited her to be his house guest until
that time. A lumbering fourth-generation Dane, and now
an American citizen, he had a face like a boar; the nares
of his snout were as broad as a native's and his lips
were as thick and as smooth. By his own profession to
every woman he met, he was a gourmet and a sybarite.
He liked the flavor of colonial argot and would tell her,
"My bed and board are first-chop," as he slowly winked
a humid blue eye. He had never married, because he
had known that his would be the experience of his
charming guests; it was a nuisance, wasn't it, to assign
six weeks of one's life to the correction of a damn-fool
mistake? Who could fail to agree that his was the perfect life, here on a hillside out of the town, with so magnificent a view that it was no trouble at all to lure the
beauties to enjoy his hospitality. Mufti for the Captain
today consisted solely of linen trunks with a print of
crimson salamanders; below them and above them his
furred flesh wrapped his mammoth bones in coils. At
the beach that morning, he had endlessly regretted that
there were no French bathing suits, and privily he had
told Sophie Otis that he hoped that before she left, he
would have the opportunity of seeing her in high-heeled
shoes and black stockings.

To Mrs. Otis, who had left the rest of the party and
was sitting just below the gallery on a stone bench in
the garden in front of the house, this two-dimensional
and too pellucid world seemed all the world; it was not

possible to envisage another landscape, even when she
closed her eyes and called to mind the sober countryside
of Massachusetts under snow, for the tropics trespassed,
overran, and spoiled the image with their heavy, heady
smells and their wanton colors. She could not gain the
decorous smell of pine forests when the smell of night-
blooming cereus was so arrogant in her memory; it had
clung and cloyed since the evening before, like a mouth-
ful of bad candy. Nor was it possible to imagine another time than this very afternoon, and it was as if the
clocks, like the winds, had been arrested, and all en-
deavour were ended and all passion were a *fait accom-
pli,* for nothing could strive or love in a torpor so in-
sentient. She found it hard to understand Mrs. Baumgartner's energy, which could perpetrate a plan so involving of the heart. She herself was nearly at the end
of her exile and in another week would go, but while she
had counted the days like a child before Christmas, now
she could not project herself beyond the present anesthesia and felt that the exile had only just begun and
that she was doomed forever to remain within the immobile upheaval of this hot, lonesome Sunday sleep,
with the voices of strangers thrumming behind her and
no other living thing visible or audible in the expanse
of arid hills and in the reach of bright-blue sea. It was
fitting, she concluded, that one come to such a place as
this to repudiate struggle and to resume the earlier,
easier indolence of lovelessness.

On the ground beside her lay, face down, a ruined

head of Pan, knocked off its pedestal by a storm that
had passed here long ago. A bay leaf was impaled on
one of the horns and part of the randy, sinful grin was
visible, but the eyes addressed the ground and the scattered blue blossoms from the lignum vitae tree above.
Prurient and impotent, immortalized in its romantically
promiscuous corruption, the shard was like the signature of the garden's owner, who now, sprawled in a long
planter's chair, was telling those who had not heard of
it the grisly little contretemps that had taken place the
night before aboard the Danish freighter that still lay
in the harbor. Twelve hours before she entered, a member of her crew, a Liberian, had fallen from the mast he
was painting and had died at once, of a fractured skull.
Although it was the custom of the island to bury the
dead, untreated, within twenty-four hours, the health authorities, under pressure from the ship's captain, agreed,
at last, to embalm the body, to be shipped back to Africa
by plane.

"But then they found," said Captain Sundstrom,
"that the nigger's head was such a mess that the em-
balming fluid wouldn't stay in, so they had to plant the
bugger, after all. We haven't got enough of our own
coons, we have to take care of this stray jigaboo from
Liberia, what?" He appealed to little Mrs. Fairweather,
a high-principled girl in her middle twenties, who had
fanatically learned tolerance in college, and who now
rose to his bait, as she could always be counted on to do,

and all but screamed her protest at his use of the words "nigger" and "coon" and "jigaboo."

"Now, now," said the Captain, taking her small ringless hand, "you're much too pretty to preachify." She snatched away her hand and glared at him with hatred and misery; she was the most unhappy of all the divorcées, because it had been her husband's idea, and not hers, that she come here. She spent most of her time knitting Argyle socks for him, in spite of everything, the tears falling among the network of bobbins. She took the current pair out of her straw beach bag now, and her needles began to set up a quiet, desperate racket. Half pitying, half amused, the company glanced at her a moment and then began their talk again, going on to other cases of emergency burials and other cases of violent death on these high seas.

Mrs. Otis had brought the Captain's binoculars to the garden with her, and she turned away from the people on the porch to survey the hills, where nothing grew but bush and, here and there, a grove of the gray, leafless trees they called cedars, whose pink blossoms were shaped like horns and smelled like nutmeg; they did what they could, the cedar flowers, to animate the terrain, but it was little enough, although sometimes, from a distance, they looked beautifully like a shower of apple blossoms. She peered beyond the termination of the land, toward the countless islands and cays of the Atlantic, crouching like cats on the unnatural sea. They

were intractably dry, and yet there was a sense everywhere of lives gathering fleshily and quietly, of an incessant, somnolent feeding, of a brutish instinct cleverer
than any human thought. Some weeks before, from a
high elevation on another island, through another pair
of glasses, she had found the great mound of the island
of Jost Van Dykes and had just made out its two settle-
ments and its long, thin beaches, and she had found, as
well, a separate house, halfway up the island's steep
ascent, set in a waste as sheer as a rain catchment, where
only one tree grew. And the tree was as neat and simple as
a child's drawing. She had quickly put the glasses down,
feeling almost faint at the thought of the terrible and
absolute simplicity with which a life would have to be
led in a place so wanting in shadow and in hiding places,
fixed so nakedly to the old, juiceless, unloving land.
Remembering that strident nightmare, she turned now to
the evidences on the gallery of the prudent tricks and
the solacing subterfuges of civilization; even here, as in
the cities of their former days, the expatriates had managed to escape the aged, wickedly sagacious earth. See
how, with optimism, gin, jokes, and lechery, they could
deny even this satanic calm and heat!

Mr. Robertson, the liquor merchant, was explaining
the activities of the peacetime Army here to a Coca-
Cola salesman who had stopped off for a few days on
the island en route from Haiti to the Argentine. Robertson, a former rumrunner and Captain Sundstrom's best
friend, was as skinny as one of the island cats, and his

skeleton was crooked and his flesh was cold. His eyes, through inappropriate pince-nez, mirrored no intellect at all but only a nasty appetite. He was a heliophobe and could never let the sun touch him anywhere, and so, in this country of brown skins and black ones, he always looked like a newcomer from the North and, with that fungous flesh, like an invalid who had left his hospital bed too soon. On the beach that morning, he had worn a hat with a visor and had sat under an enormous umbrella and had further fended off the sun by holding before his face a partially eviscerated copy of *Esquire*. In spite of his looks, he was a spark as ardent as the Captain, and lately, while his wife had been ailing, he had cut rather a wide swath, he claimed; all day he had giggled gratefully at his friends' charges that he had been stalking the native Negro women and the pert little French tarts from Cha Cha Town.

Rumor had it, he told the salesman, that a laboratory was presently to be set up on an outlying cay for the investigation of the possible values of biological warfare. The noxious vapors would be carried out to sea. (To kill the fancy, flashy fish weaving through the coral reefs, wondered Mrs. Otis, half listening.) Captain Sundstrom, who was connected with the project, turned again to Mrs. Fairweather, a born victim, and prefacing his sally with a long chuckle, he said, "We're hunting for a virus that will kill off all the niggers but won't hurt anybody else. We call it 'coon bane.'" One of the kitchen boys had just come out onto the gallery with a fresh bucket of

ice, but there was no expression at all on his long, incurious face, not even when Mrs. Fairweather, actually
crying now, sobbed, "Hush!" The Coca-Cola man, in
violent embarrassment, began at once to tell the company the story of an encounter he had had in Port-au-
Prince with an octoroon midget from North Carolina
named Sells Floto, but his heart was not in it, and it was
clear that his garrulity was tolerated only out of good
manners.

Mrs. Otis picked up the binoculars again and found
the beach. For some time, she watched a pair of pelicans
that sat on the tideless water, preposterously permanent, like buoys, until their greed came on them and
they rose heavily, flapped seaward for a while, then
dived, like people, with an inexpert splash, and came
up with a fish to fling into their ridiculous beaks. The
wide-leaved sea grapes along the ivory shingle were
turning brown and yellow, a note of impossible autumn
beside that bay, where the shimmer of summer was everlasting. Mrs. Otis shifted her focus to the grove of coconut palms that grew to the north of the curve of the
ocean, and almost at once, as if they had been waiting
for her, there appeared, at the debouchment of one of
the avenues, a parade of five naked Negro children
leading a little horse exactly the color of themselves.
The smallest child walked at the head of the line and
the tallest held the bridle. But a middle-sized one was
in command, and when they had gained the beach, he
broke the orderly procession and himself took the bridle

and led the horse right up to Captain Sundstrom's blue cabaña. If her ears had not been aided by her eyes, Mrs. Otis thought she would not have heard the distant cries and the distant neigh, but the sounds came to her clearly and softly across the stunted trees. The children reconnoitered for a while, looking this way and that, now stepping off the distance between the cabaña and the water, now running like sandpipers toward the coconut grove and back again. Then the smallest and the tallest, helped by the others, mounted the horse; it was a lengthy process, because the helpers had to spin and prance about to relieve their excitement, and sometimes they forgot themselves altogether for an absent-minded minute and ran to peer through the cracks of the closed-up cabaña; then they returned to the business at hand with refreshed attention. When the riders were seated, one of the smaller children ran back to the grove and returned with a switch, which he handed up to the tall child. The horse, at the touch of the goad, lifted his head and whinnied and then charged into the water, spilling his cargo, only to be caught promptly and mounted by two others who had run out in his wake. They, in their turn, were thrown. Again and again, they tried and failed to ride him more than a few yards, until, at last, the middle-sized ruler managed to stick and to ride out all the way to the reef and back again. The cheers were like the cries of sea birds. The champion rested, lying flat on the sand before the cabaña, and for a while the others lay around him like the spokes of a wheel, while the horse shuddered and stomped.

On the gallery, the Captain had noticed the children. "Cheeky little beggars, muckering around on my beach, but I'll let them have it. I'm a freethinker, what?" he said; then, turning to Mrs. Fairweather, "I'm going to give you a fat little blackamoor to take back with you, to remind you of our island paradise, what?"

Mr. Robertson said, "Don't let him rile you, honey. For all his big talk, he's softer about them than you are." He leaned over to sink his fist into the Captain's thigh. "Get me?" he cried.

The Captain laughed and slapped his leg. "The whole thing's a lie, that's what it is, you outlaw!"

"It's a lie if the gospel truth's a lie," said Robertson. Mrs. Fairweather did not look up from her knitting, even though he was as close to her as if he meant to bite or kiss her. "Listen, kiddo, when I first knew him, he used to be all the time saying what he wanted most of all in the world to do was eat broiled pickaninny. All the time thinking of his stomach. So one day I said to him, 'All right, damn it, you damned well *will* one of these fine days!' "

Mrs. Baumgartner gasped, and one of the other women said, "Oh, really, Rob, you're such a fool. Everyone knows that our slogan here is 'Live and let live.' "

But Robertson wanted to tell his story and went on despite them. He said, "Well, sir, a little while after I made that historic declaration, there was a fire in Pollyberg, just below my house, and I moseyed down to have a look-see."

"Let's not talk about fires!" cried Mrs. Baumgartner. "I was in a most frightful one in Albany and had to go down a ladder in my nightie."

Captain Sundstrom whistled and blew her a noisy kiss.

"They had got it under control by the time I got there, and everyone had left," pursued the liquor merchant. "I took a look in the front door and I smelled the best goddamned smell I ever smelled in my life, just possibly barring the smell of roasting duck. 'Here's Sundstrom's dinner,' I said to myself, and, sure enough, I poked around a little and found a perfectly cooked baby—around ten and a half pounds, I'd say."

The Coca-Cola salesman, who, all along, had kept a worried eye on Mrs. Fairweather, leaped into Robertson's pause for breath and announced that he knew a man who had his shoes made of alligator wallets from Rio.

Robertson glanced at him coldly, ignored the interruption, and went on speaking directly to Mrs. Fairweather. "It was charred on the outside, naturally, but I knew it was bound to be sweet and tender inside. So I took him home and called up this soldier of fortune here and told him to come along for dinner. I heated the toddler up and put him on a platter and garnished him with parsley and one thing or another, and you never saw a tastier dish in your life."

The Coca-Cola man, turning pale, stood up and said, "What's the matter with you people here? You ought to shoot yourself for telling a story like that."

But Robertson said to Mrs. Fairweather, "And what do you think he did after all the trouble I'd gone to? Refused to eat any of it, the sentimentalist! And *he* called *me* a cannibal!"

Robertson and the Captain lay back in their chairs and laughed until they coughed, but there was not a sound from anyone else and the islanders looked uneasily from one visitor to another; when their reproachful eyes fell on their host or on his friend, their look said, "There are limits."

Suddenly, Mrs. Fairweather threw a glass on the stone floor and it exploded like a shot. Somewhere in the house, a dog let out a howl of terror at the sound, and the kitchen boy came running. He ran, cringing, sidewise like a land crab, and the Captain, seeing him, hollered, "Now, damn you, what do *you* want? Have you been eavesdropping?"

"No, mon," said the boy, flinching. There was no way of knowing by his illegible face whether he told the truth or not. He ran back faster than he had come, as if he were pursued. The Captain stood up to make a new drink for Mrs. Fairweather, to whom speech and mobility seemed unlikely ever to return; she sat staring at the fragments of glass glinting at her feet, as if she had reached the climax of some terrible pain.

"Oh, this heat!" said Mrs. Baumgartner, and fanned herself gracefully with her straw hat.

Something had alarmed the children on the beach below, and Mrs. Otis, turning to look at them again, saw them abruptly immobilized; then, as silently and as swiftly as sharks, they led the horse away and disappeared into the palm grove, leaving no traces of themselves behind. Until she saw them go, she had not been aware that the skies were darkening, and she wondered how long ago the transformation had begun. Now, from miles away, there rolled up a thunderclap, and, as always in the tropics, the rain came abruptly, battling the trees and lashing the vines, beheading the flowers, crashing onto the tin roofs, and belaboring the jalousies of Captain Sundstrom's pretty house. Blue blossoms showered the head of Pan. Wrapping the field glasses in her sash to protect them from the rain, Mrs. Otis returned to the gallery, and when the boy brought out a towel to her—for in those few minutes she had got soaked to the skin—she observed that he wore a miraculous medal under his open shirt. She looked into his eyes and thought, Angels and ministers of grace defend you. The gaze she met humbled her, for its sagacious patience showed that he knew his amulet protected him against an improbable world. His was all the sufferance and suffering of little children. In his ambiguous tribulation, he sympathized with her, and with great dignity he received the towel, heavy with rain, when she had dried herself.

"See?" said Captain Sundstrom to his guests, with a gesture toward the storm. "We told you this heat was only an interlude." And feeling that the long drinks were beginning to pall, he set about making a shaker of Martinis.

*Children Are Bored on Sunday*

Through the wide doorway between two of the painting galleries, Emma saw Alfred Eisenburg standing before "The Three Miracles of Zenobius," his lean, equine face ashen and sorrowing, his gaunt frame looking undernourished, and dressed in a way that showed he was poorer this year than he had been last. Emma herself had been hunting for the Botticelli all afternoon, sidetracked first by a Mantegna she had forgotten, and then by a follower of Hieronymus Bosch, and distracted, in an English room as she was passing through, by the hot invective of two ladies who were lodged (so they bitterly reminded one another) in an outrageous and expensive mare's-nest at a hotel on Madison. Emma liked Alfred, and once, at a party in some other year, she had flirted with him slightly for seven or eight minutes. It had been spring, and even into that modern apartment, wherever it had been, while the cunning guests, on their guard and highly civilized, learnedly disputed on aesthetic and political subjects, the feeling of spring had boldly invaded, adding its nameless, sentimental sensations to all the others of the buffeted heart; one did not know and never had, even in the devouring

raptures of adolescence, whether this was a feeling of
tension or of solution—whether one flew or drowned.

In another year, she would have been pleased to run
into Alfred here in the Metropolitan on a cold Sunday,
when the galleries were thronged with out-of-towners
and with people who dutifully did something self-edu-
cating on the day of rest. But this year she was hiding
from just such people as Alfred Eisenburg, and she
turned quickly to go back the way she had come, past
the Constables and Raeburns. As she turned, she came
face to face with Salvador Dali, whose sudden countenance, with its unlikely mustache and its histrionic
eyes, familiar from the photographs in public places,
momentarily stopped her dead, for she did not immediately recognize him and, still surprised by seeing Eisenburg, took him also to be someone she knew. She shuddered and then realized that he was merely famous, and
she penetrated the heart of a guided tour and proceeded
safely through the rooms until she came to the balcony
that overlooks the medieval armor, and there she
paused, watching two youths of high-school age examine
the joints of an equestrian's shell.

She paused because she could not decide what to look
at now that she had been denied the Botticelli. She wondered, rather crossly, why Alfred Eisenburg was looking
at it and why, indeed, he was here at all. She feared
that her afternoon, begun in such a burst of courage,
would not be what it might have been; for this second's
glimpse of him—who had no bearing on her life—might

very well divert her from the pictures, not only because
she was reminded of her ignorance of painting by the
presence of someone who was (she assumed) versed in
it but because her eyesight was now bound to be im-
paired by memory and conjecture, by the irrelevant
mind-portraits of innumerable people who belonged to
Eisenburg's milieu. And almost at once, as she had predicted, the air separating her from the schoolboys below
was populated with the images of composers, of painters, of writers who pronounced judgments, in their individual argot, on Hindemith, Ernst, Sartre, on Bee-
thoven, Rubens, Baudelaire, on Stalin and Freud and
Kierkegaard, on Toynbee, Frazer, Thoreau, Franco,
Salazar, Roosevelt, Maimonides, Racine, Wallace, Picasso, Henry Luce, Monsignor Sheen, the Atomic Energy
Commission, and the movie industry. And she saw herself moving, shaky with apprehensions and Martinis, and
with the belligerence of a child who feels himself
laughed at, through the apartments of Alfred Eisenburg's friends, where the shelves were filled with everyone from Aristophanes to Ring Lardner, where the walls
were hung with reproductions of Seurat, Titian, Vermeer, and Klee, and where the record cabinets began
with Palestrina and ended with Copland.

These cocktail parties were a modus vivendi in themselves for which a new philosophy, a new ethic, and a
new etiquette had had to be devised. They were neither
work nor play, and yet they were not at all beside the
point but were, on the contrary, quite indispensable to

the spiritual life of the artists who went to them. It was
possible for Emma to see these occasions objectively,
after these many months of abstention from them, but it
was still not possible to understand them, for they were
so special a case, and so unlike any parties she had
known at home. The gossip was different, for one thing,
because it was stylized, creative (integrating the whole
of the garrotted, absent friend), and all its details were
precise and all its conceits were Jamesian, and all its
practitioners sorrowfully saw themselves in the role of
Pontius Pilate, that hero of the untoward circumstance.
(It has to be done, though we don't want to do it; 'tis a
pity she's a whore, when no one writes more intelligent
verse than she.) There was, too, the matter of the drinks,
which were much worse than those served by anyone else,
and much more plentiful. They dispensed with the frip-
peries of olives in Martinis and cherries in Manhattans
(God forbid! They had no sweet teeth), and half the
time there was no ice, and when there was, it was as
likely as not to be suspect shavings got from a bed for
shad at the corner fish store. Other species, so one heard,
went off to dinner after cocktail parties certainly no
later than half past eight, but no one ever left a party
given by an Olympian until ten, at the earliest, and
then groups went out together, stalling and squabbling
at the door, angrily unable to come to a decision about
where to eat, although they seldom ate once they got
there but, with the greatest formality imaginable, ordered several rounds of cocktails, as if they had not had

a drink in a month of Sundays. But the most surprising thing of all about these parties was that every now and again, in the middle of the urgent, general conversation, this cream of the enlightened was horribly curdled, and an argument would end, quite literally, in a bloody nose or a black eye. Emma was always astounded when this happened and continued to think that these outbursts did not arise out of hatred or jealousy but out of some quite unaccountable quirk, almost a reflex, almost something physical. She never quite believed her eyes—that is, was never altogether convinced that they were really beating one another up. It seemed, rather, that this was only a deliberate and perfectly honest demonstration of what might have happened often if they had not so diligently dedicated themselves to their intellects. Although she had seen them do it, she did not and could not believe that city people clipped each other's jaws, for, to Emma, urban equaled urbane, and ichor ran in these Augustans' veins.

As she looked down now from her balcony at the atrocious iron clothes below, it occurred to her that Alfred Eisenburg had been just such a first-generation metropolitan boy as these two who half knelt in lithe and eager attitudes to study the glittering splints of a knight's skirt. It was a kind of childhood she could not imagine and from the thought of which she turned away in secret, shameful pity. She had been really stunned when she first came to New York to find that almost no one

she met had gluttonously read Dickens, as she had, beginning at the age of ten, and because she was only
twenty when she arrived in the city and unacquainted
with the varieties of cultural experience, she had acquired the idea, which she was never able to shake entirely loose, that these New York natives had been deprived of this and many other innocent pleasures because they had lived in apartments and not in two- or
three-story houses. (In the early years in New York,
she had known someone who had not heard a cat purr
until he was twenty-five and went to a houseparty on
Fire Island.) They had played hide-and-seek dodging
behind ash cans instead of lilac bushes and in and out
of the entries of apartment houses instead of up alleys
densely lined with hollyhocks. But who was she to pa-
tronize and pity them? Her own childhood, rich as it
seemed to her on reflection, had not equipped her to
read, or to see, or to listen, as theirs had done; she envied them and despised them at the same time, and at
the same time she feared and admired them. As their
attitude implicitly accused her, before she beat her retreat, she never looked for meanings, she never saw the
literary-historical symbolism of the cocktail party but
went on, despite all testimony to the contrary, believing
it to be an occasion for getting drunk. She never listened, their manner delicately explained, and when she
talked she was always lamentably off key; often and
often she had been stared at and had been told, "It's
not the same thing at all."

Emma shuddered, scrutinizing this nature of hers, which they all had scorned, as if it were some harmless but sickening reptile. Noticing how cold the marble railing was under her hands, she felt that her self-blame was surely justified; she came to the Metropolitan Museum not to attend to the masterpieces but to remember cocktail parties where she had drunk too much and had seen Alfred Eisenburg, and to watch schoolboys, and to make experience out of the accidental contact of the palms of her hands with a cold bit of marble. What was there to do? One thing, anyhow, was clear and that was that today's excursion into the world had been premature; her solitude must continue for a while, and perhaps it would never end. If the sight of someone so peripheral, so uninvolving, as Alfred Eisenburg could scare her so badly, what would a cocktail party do? She almost fainted at the thought of it, she almost fell headlong, and the boys, abandoning the coat of mail, dizzied her by their progress toward an emblazoned tabard.

In so many words, she wasn't fit to be seen. Although she was no longer mutilated, she was still unkempt; her pretensions needed brushing; her ambiguities needed to be cleaned; her evasions would have to be completely overhauled before she could face again the terrifying learning of someone like Alfred Eisenburg, a learning whose components cohered into a central personality that was called "intellectual." She imagined that even the boys down there had opinions on everything political and artistic and metaphysical and scientific, and because she remained, in spite of all her opportunities, as green as grass, she was certain they had got their head start because they had grown up in apartments, where there was nothing else to do but educate themselves. This being an intellectual was not the same thing as dilettantism; it was a calling in itself. For example, Emma did not even know whether Eisenburg was a painter, a writer, a composer, a sculptor, or something entirely different. When, seeing him with the composers, she had thought he was one of them; when, the next time she met him, at a studio party, she decided he must be a painter; and when, on subsequent occasions, everything had pointed toward his being a writer, she had relied altogether on circumstantial evidence and not on anything he had said or done. There was no reason to suppose that he had not looked upon her as the same sort of variable and it made their anonymity to one another complete. Without the testimony of an impartial third person, neither she nor Eisenburg would ever know the other's actual trade. But his specialty did not matter, for his larger designation was that of "the intellectual," just as the man who confines his talents to the nose and throat is still a doctor. It was, in the light of this, all the more extraordinary that they had had that lightning-paced flirtation at a party.

Extraordinary, because Emma could not look upon herself as an intellectual. Her private antonym of this noun was "rube," and to her regret—the regret that had caused her finally to disappear from Alfred's group—

she was not even a bona-fide rube. In her store clothes, so to speak, she was often taken for an intellectual, for she had, poor girl, gone to college and had never been quite the same since. She would not dare, for instance, go up to Eisenburg now and say that what she most liked in the Botticelli were the human and compassionate eyes of the centurions' horses, which reminded her of the eyes of her own Great-Uncle Graham, whom she had adored as a child. Nor would she admit that she was delighted with a Crivelli Madonna because the peaches in the background looked exactly like marzipan, or that Goya's little red boy inspired in her only the pressing desire to go out immediately in search of a plump cat to stroke. While she knew that feelings like these were not really punishable, she had not perfected the art of tossing them off; she was no flirt. She was a bounty jumper in the war between Great-Uncle Graham's farm and New York City, and liable to court-martial on one side and death on the other. Neither staunchly primitive nor confidently *au courant,* she rarely knew where she was at. And this was her Achilles' heel: her identity was always mistaken, and she was thought to be an intellectual who, however, had not made the grade. It was no use now to cry that she was not, that she was a simon-pure rube; not a soul would believe her. She knew, deeply and with horror, that she was thought merely stupid.

It was possible to be highly successful as a rube among the Olympians, and she had seen it done. Someone calling himself Nahum Mothersill had done it brilliantly, but she often wondered whether his name had not helped him, and, in fact, she had sometimes wondered whether that had been his real name. If she had been called, let us say, Hyacinth Derryberry, she believed she might have been able, as Mothersill had been, to ask who Ezra Pound was. (This struck her suddenly as a very important point; it was endearing, really, not to know who Pound was, but it was only embarrassing to know who he was but not to have read the "Cantos.") How different it would have been if education had not meddled with her rustic nature! Her education had never dissuaded her from her convictions, but certainly it had ruined the looks of her mind—painted the poor thing up until it looked like a mean, hypocritical, promiscuous malcontent, a craven and apologetic fancy woman. Thus she continued secretly to believe (but *never* to confess) that the apple Eve had eaten tasted exactly like those she had eaten when she was a child visiting on her Great-Uncle Graham's farm, and that Newton's observation was no news in spite of all the hue and cry. Half the apples she had eaten had fallen out of the tree, whose branches she had shaken for this very purpose, and the Apple Experience included both the descent of the fruit and the consumption of it, and Eve and Newton and Emma understood one another perfectly in this particular of reality.

Emma started. The Metropolitan boys, who, however bright they were, would be boys, now caused some steely article of dress to clank, and she instantly quit the balcony, as if this unseemly noise would attract the crowd's attention and bring everyone, including Eisenburg, to see what had happened. She scuttered like a quarry through the sightseers until she found an empty seat in front of Rembrandt's famous frump, "The Noble Slav" —it was this kind of thing, this fundamental apathy to most of Rembrandt, that made life in New York such hell for Emma—and there, upon the plum velours, she realized with surprise that Alfred Eisenburg's had been the last familiar face she had seen before she had closed the door of her tomb.

In September, it had been her custom to spend several hours of each day walking in a straight line, stopping only for traffic lights and outlaw taxicabs, in the hope that she would be tired enough to sleep at night. At five o'clock—and gradually it became more often four o'clock and then half past three—she would go into a bar, where, while she drank, she seemed to be reading the information offered by the *Sun* on "Where to Dine." Actually she had ceased to dine long since; every few days, with effort, she inserted thin wafers of food into her repelled mouth, flushing the frightful stuff down with enormous drafts of magical, purifying, fulfilling applejack diluted with tepid water from the tap. One weighty day, under a sky that grimly withheld the rain, as if to punish the whole city, she had started out from Ninetieth Street and had kept going down Madison and was thinking, as she passed the chancery of St. Patrick's, that it must be nearly time and that she needed only to

turn east on Fiftieth Street to the New Weston, where
the bar was cool, and dark to an almost absurd degree.
And then she was hailed. She turned quickly, looking
in all directions until she saw Eisenburg approaching,
removing a gray pellet of gum from his mouth as he
came. They were both remarkably shy and, at the time,
she had thought they were so because this was the first
time they had met since their brief and blameless flirtation. (How curious it was that she could scrape off the
accretions of the months that had followed and could
remember how she had felt on that spring night—as
trembling, as expectant, as altogether young as if they
had sat together underneath a blooming apple tree.)
But now, knowing that her own embarrassment had come
from something else, she thought that perhaps his had,
too, and she connected his awkwardness on that September day with a report she had had, embedded in a
bulletin on everyone, from her sole communicant, since
her retreat, with the Olympian world. This informant
had run into Alfred at a party and had said that he
was having a very bad time of it with a divorce, with
poverty, with a tempest that had carried off his job, and,
at last, with a psychoanalyst, whose fees he could not
possibly afford. Perhaps the nightmare had been well
under way when they had met beside the chancery.
Without alcohol and without the company of other people, they had had to be shy or their suffering would
have shown in all its humiliating dishabille. Would it
be true still if they should inescapably meet this afternoon in an Early Flemish room?

Suddenly, on this common level, in this state of social displacement, Emma wished to hunt for Alfred and
urgently tell him that she hoped it had not been as bad
for him as it had been for her. But naturally she was
not so naive, and she got up and went purposefully to
look at two Holbeins. They pleased her, as Holbeins
always did. The damage, though, was done, and she
did not really see the pictures; Eisenburg's hypothetical
suffering and her own real suffering blurred the clean
lines and muddied the lucid colors. Between herself and
the canvases swam the months of spreading, cancerous
distrust, of anger that made her seasick, of grief that
shook her like an influenza chill, of the physical afflic-
tions by which the poor victimized spirit sought vainly
to wreck the arrogantly healthy flesh.

Even that one glance at his face, seen from a distance
through the lowing crowd, told her, now that she had
repeated it to her mind's eye, that his cheeks were
drawn and his skin was gray (no soap and water can
ever clean away the grimy look of the sick at heart)
and his stance was tired. She wanted them to go together to some hopelessly disreputable bar and to console one another in the most maudlin fashion over a
lengthy succession of powerful drinks of whisky, to
compare their illnesses, to marry their invalid souls for
these few hours of painful communion, and to babble
with rapture that they were at last, for a little while,
no longer alone. Only thus, as sick people, could they
marry. In any other terms, it would be a *mésalliance*,
doomed to divorce from the start, for rubes and intel-

lectuals must stick to their own class. If only it could take place—this honeymoon of the cripples, this nuptial consummation of the abandoned—while drinking the delicious amber whisky in a joint with a juke box, a stout barkeep, and a handful of tottering derelicts; if it could take place, would it be possible to prevent him from marring it all by talking of secondary matters? That is, of art and neurosis, art and politics, art and science, art and religion? Could he lay off the fashions of the day and leave his learning in his private entrepôt? Could he, that is, see the apple fall and not run madly to break the news to Newton and ask him what on earth it was all about? Could he, for her sake (for the sake of this pathetic rube all but weeping for her own pathos in the Metropolitan Museum), forget the whole dispute and, believing his eyes for a change, admit that the earth was flat?

It was useless for her now to try to see the paintings. She went, full of intentions, to the Van Eyck diptych and looked for a long time at the souls in Hell, kept there by the implacable, impartial, and genderless angel who stood upon its closing mouth. She looked, in renewed astonishment, at Jo Davidson's pink, wrinkled, embalmed head of Jules Bache, which sat, a trinket on a fluted pedestal, before a Flemish tapestry. But she was really conscious of nothing but her desire to leave the museum in the company of Alfred Eisenburg, her cousin-german in the territory of despair.

So she had to give up, two hours before the closing

time, although she had meant to stay until the end, and
she made her way to the central stairs, which she descended slowly, in disappointment, enviously observing
the people who were going up, carrying collapsible canvas stools on which they would sit, losing themselves
in their contemplation of the pictures. Salvador Dali
passed her, going quickly down. At the telephone booths,
she hesitated, so sharply lonely that she almost looked
for her address book, and she did take out a coin, but
she put it back and pressed forlornly forward against
the incoming tide. Suddenly, at the storm doors, she
heard a whistle and she turned sharply, knowing that it
would be Eisenburg, as, of course, it was, and he wore
an incongruous smile upon his long, El Greco face. He
took her hand and gravely asked her where she had
been all this year and how she happened to be here, of
all places, of all days. Emma replied distractedly, looking at his seedy clothes, his shaggy hair, the green cast
of his white skin, his deep black eyes, in which all the
feelings were disheveled, tattered, and held together
only by the merest faith that change *had* to come. His
hand was warm and her own seemed to cling to it and
all their mutual necessity seemed centered here in their
clasped hands. And there was no doubt about it; he had
heard of her collapse and he saw in her face that she
had heard of his. Their recognition of each other was
instantaneous and absolute, for they cunningly saw that
they were children and that, if they wished, they were
free for the rest of this winter Sunday to play together,

quite naked, quite innocent. "What a day it is! What a place!" said Alfred Eisenburg. "Can I buy you a drink, Emma? Have you time?"

She did not accept at once; she guardedly inquired where they could go from here, for it was an unlikely neighborhood for the sort of place she wanted. But they were *en rapport*, and he, wanting to avoid the grownups as much as she, said they would go across to Lexington. He needed a drink after an afternoon like this—didn't she? Oh, Lord, yes, she did, and she did not question what he meant by "an afternoon like this" but said that she would be delighted to go, even though they would have to walk on eggs all the way from the Museum to the place where the bottle was, the peace pipe on Lexington. Actually, there was nothing to fear; even if they had heard catcalls, or if someone had hooted at them, "Intellectual loves Rube!" they would have been impervious, for the heart carved in the bark of the apple tree would contain the names Emma and Alfred, and there were no perquisites to such a conjugation. To her own heart, which was shaped exactly like a valentine, there came a winglike palpitation, a delicate exigency, and all the fragrance of all the flowery springtime love affairs that ever were seemed waiting for them in the whisky bottle. To mingle their pain, their handshake had promised them, was to produce a separate entity, like a child that could shift for itself, and they scrambled hastily toward this profound and pastoral experience.

# The

## MOUNTAIN

## LION

A Novel

TO CAL AND TO DICK

*A friend loveth at all times, and a
brother is born for adversity.*

PROVERBS XVII, 17.

# CHAPTER ONE

RALPH WAS TEN AND MOLLY WAS EIGHT WHEN THEY HAD scarlet fever. It left them with some sort of glandular disorder which was not malignant, but which kept them half poisoned most of the time and caused them, frequently, to have such bad nosebleeds that they had to be sent home from school. It nearly always happened that their nosebleeds came at the same time. Ralph, bleeding profusely, would stumble into the corridor to find Molly coming out of the third-grade room, a handkerchief held in a sodden bunch at her nose. Their mother could not bear the sight of blood and her distress, on seeing them straggle up the driveway, never lessened even when these midday homecomings had become a habit. Each time, she implored them to telephone her so that she could send Miguel, the foreman, in the car. But they never did, for they liked the walk home, feeling all the way a pleasant superiority to their sisters, Leah and Rachel, who were still cooped up in school with nothing at all to do but chew paraffin on the sly.

In the September following their illness and on the day Grandpa Kenyon, their mother's stepfather, was to arrive for his annual visit, they met with gushing noses outside the art supply room and seeing Miss Holihan through the open door at the paper cutter with a sheaf of manila paper, they walked on tiptoe, giggling silently until they reached the stairs and then they ran. Once outside in the empty schoolyard, they congratulated each other; Molly would not have to draw an apple on Miss Holihan's paper and Ralph would miss both Palmer Method and singing. Actually, they would gain nothing by getting home some hours before the school bus since Grandpa's train did not get into Los Angeles until the middle of the afternoon and then it was another hour before Miguel brought him up the driveway in the Willys Knight. So they dawdled more slowly than usual, not certain that they would find anything to absorb them at home, but certain, on the other hand, that their mother, fussing and chattering as she always did when they had company, would be as cross as sixty when she saw them.

It was a narrow, winding country road they walked along. On either side ran clear small ditches, making a mouth-like sound. Now and again they stopped and dipped their handkerchiefs and wiped the blood off their hands and arms. On their right was an orange grove from which, at all seasons of the year, came a heavy fragrance and where they sometimes saw flocks of such bright, unusual birds that they thought they must have flown up from the South Seas or westward from Japan. Some of the little pyramidal trees were always in bloom and some were always bearing fruit. There was a man on a ladder in the grove today and he turned when he heard them coming. He took off his hat and wiped his forehead on the sleeve of his black shirt and called, "Hello, you kiddoes," but as he was a Mexican, they

4

did not reply and scuttered on, terrified, until they no longer heard his derisive laugh.

Next they passed Mr. Vogelman's huge clean dairy. Mr. Vogelman was a fat German who wore a white coverall and who had once been stoned by a group of second-graders when they learned what the Huns had done to the Belgians. Their mothers, fearing that he might take his revenge by treating the milk with tuberculosis germs, had written him an apology. But as the demonstration had taken place on Hallowe'en, Mr. Vogelman had misconstrued it and did not understand the letter at all. He had Guernseys whose hides gleamed in the sun like a metal, not so yellow as a banana and not so blue as milk, but something in between. Today there was a new calf near the fence, its fawn-like face wearing a look of melancholy surprise when it saw the human children staring. Its outraged mother bellowed at them, her great black nostrils hugely dilated, and they ran away for, although they would never have admitted it, they were afraid of cows. They knew a joke about a cow which they had read in *The American Boy,* and when they were safely beyond the pasture, they recited it as a dialogue:

*Ralph:* What are shoes made of?
*Molly:* Hide.
*Ralph:* Hide? Why should I hide?
*Molly:* Hide! Hide! The cow's outside!
*Ralph:* Oh, let the old cow come in. I'm not afraid.

They laughed so hard that they had to sit down in the road holding their stomachs and the laughter made their noses bleed twice as fast so that, convulsed and aching, they dabbed desperately with their handkerchiefs, screaming with pain, "Oh! Oh!" Finally, when they were sobered, Ralph said, "I

5

guess I'll tell that joke to Grandpa," and Molly said, "Me too." Of late, Ralph had had moments of irritation with her: often, when he had finished telling a joke or a fact, she would repeat exactly what he had said immediately afterward so that there was no time for people either to laugh or to marvel. And not only that, but she had countless times told his dreams, pretending that they were her own. He did not want the joke about the cow to fall flat and so, after a reluctant pause, he agreed to let her tell it with him as they had recited it just now. It was not as long as one of the darky pieces Leah and Rachel spoke together, but it was so much funnier that they were sure Grandpa could not fail to laugh in that big, roaring way of his, slapping his knee and saying, "By George, that's a good one."

They proceeded, thinking of Grandpa, joyfully scuffing the white dust of the road until their oxfords were all powdery, even the shoelaces. Next to the dairy was a deep, dry arroyo called "the Wash." It had been hollowed out by a flood that had come in the spring of the year Leah was three, but they had so often heard the details of its devastation that they were certain their impressions came from memory and not from their mother's and her friends' talk when there was nothing new to discuss and they had to return to the thrills of the past. Mr. Fawcett had gone across a raging creek on a horse named Babe, long since dead, to rescue an aged woman whose house was later washed away. He brought her home flung over his saddle like a gunny sack of feed and gave her artificial respiration on the kitchen floor. Thousands and thousands of finches came out of the pouring rain to perch on the front porch; there were so many Father said it looked like a regular bird sanctuary;

6

Fuschia was baking a cherry pie and Father asked her if she wanted four and twenty finches to put in it. A grapefruit tree came floating right down the driveway, roots and all, and Father planted it beside the solar tank. Every year it bore one grapefruit, which was smaller than a golf ball and almost as hard.

On the floor of the Wash, Ralph and Molly could find bright-colored stones, pink and green and yellow and blue. After a heavy rain, there was sometimes fool's gold in the puddles. Strange harsh shallow-rooted flowers grew all over the steep slopes and clumps of mallow that yielded bitter milk. There was one place where the mud dried and cracked into wedges like pieces of pie and when Molly was very small, she thought that this was where the sandwiches lived. All mystery and evil came from the Wash. Those smooth colored stones they gathered were really stolen jewels and the thief was a coal-black Skalawag who slept in the daytime in Mr. Vogelman's cornbin but kept watch at night. They did not venture down into the Wash when they had nosebleeds because the Skalawag could smell blood, no matter how far away he was, and he would get up and come legging it after them. So they passed it quickly with sidelong glances. Last autumn, when they had taken Grandpa Kenyon to see the Wash, he had said, "Well, now, that's something like it. There's too damn much green in this here California. But that dried-up little old crick bed down there makes me think of a place that *is* a place." He swept his black eyes round the scene and breathed shallowly as if the sweetness of the orange blossoms offended him and he said, "To think there ain't any winter here! Why, I'd as lief go to hell in a handbasket as not to see the first snow fly."

The children were a little angry and shy and sensing this he explained to them—though they did not understand what he meant—that Nature here offered a man no real challenge. "You take that place of mine in the Panhandle. Nature ain't any ornrier anywhere in the world than she is right there, but she's a blooming belle of a fighter." When he had bought the land, there had not been a drop of water on the whole forty-five thousand acres of it, not a stream, not a pond. Everyone said he was a boob to buy it. But he turned in and bought it anyhow and then he took a little forked switch of holly and he chose a place on a rise just to the west of where he meant to build his house. He stood there with his holly wand, holding a fork of it in either hand. By and by, the rod bent down: where she showed him, there was a deep clear spring that had never yet gone dry.

The Wash, after that, had a new meaning for Ralph and Molly and they came to believe that the Skalawag was so watchful because he feared someone might come with a divining rod and once water was found, all his gems would be washed away. And now, too, whenever they went past, they thought of Grandpa's ranch in the Panhandle and Ralph, sighing, would say, "Golly *Moses,* I'd like to go out West." For they believed Grandpa Kenyon when he told them that California was not the West but was a separate thing like Florida and Washington, D. C.

For example, out West you would not find such falderal as Miss Runyon went in for. Miss Runyon lived next to the Wash in a little white house with green shutters and begonia in all the windows and Molly had loved it before Grandpa called it "a devil of a note." The flower garden came straight down to the road and standing among the

8

beds of phlox and bachelor's buttons and oxalis were all sorts of curious creatures: a huge green frog, three brownies, a duck and four ducklings, two bluebirds as big as cats, a little Dutch girl in a sunbonnet, and a totem pole. There was a sign over the front door of the house which said "Dew Drop Inn." Next to the house was a doghouse built exactly like Dew Drop Inn and over its door was a sign that said "Dun Rovin" because Miss Runyon's sheep dog was named Rover. Under the eaves on the front porch was a bird house built like the other two but its name was not so ingenious: it was simply called "Jennie Wren, Her House."

Miss Runyon was the postmistress and was known as a character. She drove an automobile herself which she called "Mac"—short for "Machine" which she humorously pronounced "MacHeinie." She ate neither meat nor spices, for she was a follower of Dr. Kellogg. She occasionally invited the Fawcetts to a picnic supper on her lawn and served them hamburgers which were really made of Grape Nuts agglutinated with imitation calves'-foot jelly. She always came on Sunday afternoon to read their paper and made no secret of the fact that she liked the funnies as well as any child, reading them with the same unamused absorption that Ralph and Molly and Leah and Rachel did. Once she said that she was tired to death of Elmer Tuggle and his everlasting baseball mitt; Happy Hooligan was her favorite. In spite of her aggressive good nature, she was very timid and could not sleep alone in a house, so she had living with her a little Japanese woman named Mrs. Haisan. If ever Mrs. Haisan had to be away, Leah and Rachel went there to sleep, although they never wanted to, for the first time they stayed with her, she suddenly looked up from *McCall's* in the middle of the evening and said tensely, "Hark! I heard a human swallow!" Ralph and Molly thought it was likely that it had been the Skalawag swallowing and the possibilities of *what* he had been swallowing were so numerous and terrifying that they could not hear the word without trembling.

It was thought, jestingly, by Mrs. Follansbee, the pastor's wife, that Miss Runyon had set her cap for Mr. Kenyon, part of this supposition being based on the rhyming of the two names; and it was true that several times during his visits she had invited them all to come and take "pot luck" with her but they never went, for as Mrs. Fawcett said in the bosom of her family, "I am sure I don't know what a hearty eater like Mr. Kenyon would do if he had to have an evening meal of cereal, I don't care how she disguised it."

Ralph thought perhaps he could tell Grandpa a funny story about Miss Runyon, not a true one but one in which he just used her name, and he stood leaning upon the picket fence, pondering and allowing his nose to drip on the palings so that two of them looked like spears that had struck home. Or maybe he could tell one about Mrs. Haisan. Mrs. Haisan had two children about his and Molly's age who lived with their aunt, a tiny little thing who was Mrs. Fawcett's washerwoman. Their names were Maisol and Maisako and one of them had been born on the Fourth of July and the other on April Fool's Day. One terrible day they had come with Hana and had made Ralph and Molly go down to the watermelon patch with them and not only had they cut up an unripe watermelon with a putty knife but they had said things and hinted at others so awful that Ralph and

Molly had to fight them. They won very easily, of course, because the Jap kids were much smaller.

Ralph could not think of a single joke except the one about the cow. He thumbed his nose at Miss Runyon's house and chanted, "Runyon todunyon tianigo sunyon, tee-legged, tie-legged, bowlegged Runyon!" And then, seizing his sister by the hand, he ran like the wind because simultaneously Mrs. Haisan had appeared at the door of Dew Drop Inn and Rover at his door, and while Rover was as harmless as a ladybug and Mrs. Haisan more than likely had only wanted to give them a candied kumquat, it was pleasanter to think that they were rushing out in anger like the Skala-wag, and as soon as the house was no longer in sight, Ralph knelt down and put his ear to the road and jumping up cried, "Hey! They're a-gainin' on us!" and they did not stop running until they had turned down their own road.

When they had gone a hundred steps, they could see the palm trees that marked the boundary of their land. On this last stretch, Molly always thought for some reason of Redondo Beach where they went for a few weeks at the end of the summer. Looking up into the blank blue sky, she could feel that she was barefoot in the hot sand, hunting starfish and sand dollars, hearing the cries of the frightened ladies to their wading children who petulantly cried back that the waves were not high. The thought of the beach made her restlessly nostalgic and sometimes made her whimper, because she always remembered a feeling of queer and somehow pleasant horror when once a gull had winked at her and she had seen that his lower eyelid moved and not the upper one. But today she did not cry: Ralph was too gay, she knew, to comfort her and that was the only pleasure in crying, to be embraced by him and breathe in his acrid smell of leather braces and serge and to feel, shuddering, the touch of his warty hands on her face. It was always possible for her to will herself not to think sadly of the beach but to think instead of her dead father, of whom she had no memories but only the knowledge that he was up in the sky with Jesus and would miraculously recognize her when she came to heaven even though she had not been born when he died. This was the most thrilling thought she ever had and it had made her almost delirious ever since the day she and Ralph agreed not to die until he was ninety-nine and she was ninety-seven so that when they got up there they would look much older than their father who had died at the age of thirty-six.

As soon as they turned in the drive, Ralph began the game of Dead Horse. He said, "I saw a dead horse lying in the road." Molly answered, "I one it," and they went on: "I two it." "I three it." Just as they got to the side of the front porch, Ralph cried out, "I eight it," and Molly screamed hysterically, "Mother! Ralph ate a dead horse *again!*" But their mother was not sitting on the front porch as she usually was, and they looked at each other in numb embarrassment.

They should have known that she would be in the kitchen, preparing for Grandpa. Now they could hear her bustling across the front hall in her French-heeled slippers, anticipating what she would see and crying, "Oh, I declare I just don't know!" And then she stood in the screen door, arms akimbo at her small waist in her pearl-gray skirt, unable to decide whether to be angry or worried, too upset for a moment to utter a word. The children waited on the bottom step like well-mannered dogs and their mother, seeing their humility, chose to be anxious and flew down the steps, embracing them but carefully so that she would not stain her white smocked shirtwaist. She smelled of orris root and gingerbread and the children, sniffing, sensed the arrival of company even more than they had when they saw Miguel drive out this morning to meet the train. He had gone early to shop for delicacies in the Los Angeles markets; among other things, they were going to have black cherries and Turkish Delight.

"Oh, the poor chicks!" she cried, her blue eyes quickly full of tears. "Oh, dearies, *why* didn't you telephone? *Why* must you aggravate your mother?"

Molly said, "If we had telephoned it would have been silly because Miguel isn't here and neither is the car and even if the car was here it would still be silly because nobody but Miguel can drive it."

Molly's logic always made Mrs. Fawcett angry and now she drove them into the house and upstairs to the bathroom, ejaculating unfinished sentences: "I simply never . . . !" "No matter how hard I try . . . !" "Today of all days in the year . . . !"

The nosebleeds almost always stopped as soon as they got home, a phenomenon that obscurely vexed Mrs. Fawcett, and once she had spoken of it in their presence to Mr. Follansbee, who had replied, with a catarrhal chuckle, "Well, you know, Rose, that puts me in mind of my sainted mother who was stone deaf *except* when she wanted to hear something." Neither Ralph nor Molly had any idea what he meant but they caught an undertone of ridicule in his voice, and fearing and hating him, they went up to Ralph's room where each of them printed "Rev. Follansbee" seven times

13

on sheets of drawing paper and then burned the papers in the gilt Buddha incense burner.

Washed and dressed in their company clothes, they went outdoors and sat under the umbrella tree playing mumbly-peg, hurriedly concealing the knife when their mother came to the door to call some warning about their clean clothes or getting too much sunlight. Mumbly-peg was forbidden as everything was that was attended by the least possibility of danger, for Grandfather Bonney, their real grandfather, had died of blood poisoning. José, the gardener, was trimming the palm trees, and as he deftly wielded his banana knife he sang songs which they knew were bad although they could not understand a word of them since he sang in Spanish. They knew, because he was a bad man. Once Rachel had dreamed that he pursued her on a bicycle without holding his hands on the handlebars, that same banana knife between his teeth, one hand brandishing a monkey wrench and the other the Civil War saber that had belonged to Great-uncle Harry Fawcett, about whom not another fact was known. And once José had called Ralph a son-of-a-gun and threatened to burn his eyes out with a red-hot poker if he took any more berries off the bittersweet for his pea shooter.

Budge, the kindly cat, lay sleeping on the rim of the frog pond, and the only kitten that had been spared her out of her last litter gazed fixedly down into the slimy green water. Mrs. Fawcett, who did not like animals even in their own place, believed that Budge had brought the scarlet fever germs to Ralph and Molly, for goodness only knew what sort of houses she visited in her search for food and tomcats, and she would have had her destroyed if Ralph had not heard her talking with Miguel under his windows one morning when he was thought to be asleep. Weak with fever, he tottered to the window and called down the stern promise that if Budge were not still on the place when he got well, he would leave at once for the Panhandle and would never come back in a thousand million years. There were times when Mrs. Fawcett feared for the reason of her two younger children: they had natures of such cold determination that she trembled to think what they might do if they were crossed in a matter very close to their hearts. She could never imagine where they had got this streak, certainly not from her side of the family, and although Mr. Fawcett had by no means been a mollycoddle, he had been very mild-mannered and had always been able to see the other fellow's side of an argument. Budge remained. And then the astonishing Molly had literally read her mother's mind one evening. Mrs. Fawcett was looking at Budge asleep on the hearth and Molly said, "If anything ever happens to Budge, like poison or something, I'm going to set the pumphouse on fire."

From the cool-looking house—the dark green blinds were drawn to keep out the sun, though the turquoise berry was so dense it admitted little light—came the dulled sounds of Mrs. Fawcett and Fuschia as they made the dinner. They had been cooking for two days. They had made pineapple upside-down cake, boiled dressing, potato salad, beet pickles, baked beans, brown bread, sugar cookies, lady fingers, Sally Lunn, and temperance punch. Fuschia had brought in the new Schmierkäse that had been swinging for three days in its muslin bag in the icehouse and she had got six bottles of grape juice from the preserve closet to put in the refrigerator.

Ralph and Molly, the afternoon before, had cracked a bowl full of last year's walnuts from their own grove and today Fuschia had glazed the whole meats and put the broken ones into penuche. The duck was in the oven, baking in a bath of orange juice. Before school, Leah and Rachel had polished the Bonney silver and had laid out the morning-glory tablecloth.

The afternoon seemed to have no end to it and yet the children were not really impatient to have it pass, for look-ing forward to Grandpa was in some ways as pleasant as having him there in the house. The sun appeared to remain in exactly the same position and the shadow of the umbrella tree to be unalterable. The bees, restless in the blossoms of the lippia lawn, and the humming birds, lancing the tur-quoise berries, worked at top speed as though eternity were not time enough to accomplish all they had to do. Mrs. Fawcett and Fuschia were forever softly banging things and chirping in muted screams, and José was forever at his palm trees. It was very quiet. The Mexicans harvesting the wal-nuts in the grove were silent. Once a dog began to bark and stopped so suddenly it was as if someone had seized his jaws and held them together. "That's Schöneshund," said Ralph. Schöneshund was a mean and hideous mastiff owned by the German family next door and Mrs. Fawcett was never willing to allow that the name had been chosen ironically; she preferred to think that the Freudenburgs simply did not know any better, for they were not "our sort." "If I could not have a carpet in my parlor," she said, "I would have some sort of inexpensive grass rug, or I would leave the floors bare. I certainly would not have linoleum." Ralph, identifying Schöneshund's bark today, wondered suddenly if Grandpa had any dogs on any of his ranches and he regretted that in the years past he had asked the old man so few questions that he knew very little about him. The two weeks he was here were always so short. Too many new impressions were crowded into the dazzling days, the smells of school that he had forgotten during the summer, the frightening complexities of the new arithmetic book, the surprise of finding in his lunchbox a hard-boiled egg colored magenta with beet-pickle juice, and over it all, the wonder of the rich old man who was different from anyone else in the world. Always before he had been too unbearably excited to plan a way to catch one of these bright hours, but he promised himself that this year he would gather facts to think about in the winter: the kinds and the names of Grandpa's dogs for one thing, whether he had ever been to a prize fight, if he had always had a beard, the name of the town in England where he had been born, and how many silver dollars he could carry in his money belt at one time.

The sun, in time, brutalized even José, and he stopped singing and worked more slowly. The children's game was languid and they had given it up long before the school bus came and Leah and Rachel trudged down the driveway, swinging their schoolbags in one hand and their lunchboxes in the other. They were cross at Ralph and Molly for coming home early and did not speak but went directly into the house and appeared half an hour later, bathed and dressed in the new Scotch plaid tissue gingham dresses that Aunt Kathleen had sent them from Marshall Field's. They came out to pick dahlias for the parlor and for the table. They walked past without looking at their sister and brother.

Rachel said, "I *was* going to give Molly my extra Cashmere Bouquet just out of the kindness of my heart, but I'm not going to now." And Leah said, "I know. I was going to give Ralph my Colgate's shaving soap, but now I wouldn't give either of them anything but a swift kick." Ralph and Molly ignored them, but when they had gone on, Ralph, looking after them with scorn, said, "If I didn't have anything better to do than send for free samples, I'd go jump in the lake." And Molly, agreeing (she and Ralph sent for gun catalogues and booklets on things like "How to Care for Your Glenwood Parlor Burner"), said in a whisper, "Do you think they're going to be sassy to Grandpa?"

"I guess they'd better not," said Ralph. "If they do you and I will make them a pie-bed that'll be so tight they'll both break both their legs."

Leah and Rachel, almost young ladies, had, along with many other people and many habits, outgrown the soiled and rumpled old gentleman and looked with the same disfavor their mother did upon his table manners, his rough and ungrammatical speech, his clothes, and his profession, even though it had netted him three million dollars. He had four cattle ranches: one in Missouri, where he lived, one in Oklahoma, one in Texas, and one in the mountains of Colorado which his son, Claude, Mrs. Fawcett's half-brother, ran for him. How Leah and Rachel could imagine their mother's distress when her mother married this second husband! What a contrast he was to Grandfather Bonney, that noble person in the portrait over the fireplace in the parlor! And how different the life must have been for her and her sisters on his ranch in the northern part of the state when they had been used to the hustle and gaiety of St. Louis!

Last September, when Grandpa left, Leah, watching the car go down the drive, put her arm around her mother's waist and said, "I could simply *cry* for you, Mother, when I think how you must have missed St. Louis." Mrs. Fawcett, who was wonderfully plucky, smiled fondly down upon her perceptive child and answered, "Well, dear, you know we can't have everything in this life." From that time onward, the two older children heaped upon the absent Mr. Kenyon an articulate and savage ridicule, commingled with resentment which was at once aimless and precocious: shortly after he had left the Colorado ranch last October, he had gone to Europe, as he frequently did in the winter, and while heretofore these casual trips all over the world had been something to admire and to refer to in conversations with other children who had no such traveled relatives, the girls this year were angry, realizing fully for the first time that their mother had never been abroad. And their anger was inflamed when Mrs. Fawcett from time to time remarked that often in the years she had lived in his house, taking charge of his child, he had taken these long journeys, not giving a thought to her. And you can imagine what those lonesome winters in the country were like for a girl who had been brought up in the city!

But Ralph and Molly, in a smaller world, would rather go to reform school than live in St. Louis. The one time they had been there they had been in tears half the time at all the poor old men selling shoelaces and lengths of elastic and at all the homeless dogs with sore eyes and limping legs; the smell of smoke and the horrid noises and the terrifying pace of the trolleys had almost made them sick. Their mother, introducing them to Mrs. Waite, their hostess, had said, "And these are my two little country bumpkins. They already want to go home. Can you feature it?" They had not really wanted to go home; they had wanted to go visit Grandpa Kenyon, but their mother wouldn't let them, falsely declaring that they would be bored to death for there would be nothing there to do. There was certainly nothing to do in St. Louis and all summer long Mrs. Fawcett and Mrs. Waite had had whispered conversations about Fatty Arbuckle so that Ralph and Molly were in a temper the whole time because, when they asked, the ladies only said, "Little pitchers have big ears."

At Grandpa's place they could have done what they pleased. Their mother didn't know anything. She said that she knew from experience that there was nothing to do. Had she not spent her boarding school holidays there with Aunt Rowena and Aunt Kathleen? All those long, still summers when there was nothing to distract their thoughts from the heat! The immense lawn, going down to the river, was bare of trees so that one had an unobstructed view of the Mississippi: one of the Bonney girls' few amusements was to watch the barges and the steamers going down toward Hannibal. Sometimes the sound of a banjo was carried to them on the motionless air, making Rowena, the least controlled of the three, so restless that she would cry, "Oh, why doesn't something *happen!*" Behind the house was an apple orchard, kept as formally as a garden, and in the center of it was a clearing with a little summer-house where they sometimes sat through the airless afternoons, fanning themselves with palm leaves, homesick for St. Louis. It was ten miles to the nearest town, and once you got there there was nothing to look at or to buy and no one at all congenial to call on. Aunt Rowena and Aunt Kathleen amused themselves by riding horseback and driving the buckboard, but their sister Rose would not join them. She would not because Grandfather Bonney's blood poisoning had been the result of a scratch from a nail in the railing of a paddock when he was watching her take her first jump, and ever afterward, feeling that she had been the cause of his far too early death, she vowed she would have nothing to do with horses.

If the Bonney girls had not all been great readers, they would have been half out of their minds with boredom. Fortunately, Mrs. Bonney had brought a good part of the library along from St. Louis and they almost put their eyes out reading Mrs. Gaskell, Dickens, and E. P. Roe. In some ways, the very worst thing of all was the conversation at mealtime. If the girls had been given half a chance, they might have elevated the tone of it by discussing the books they were reading, but there was never any opportunity. They *could* not take an interest in the talk of cattle and hogs after the cultured life they had led with their own father! And that was all Mr. Kenyon talked about; their mother talked right along with him, seeming to be really keen on hearing how many steers were being shipped to Chicago and how many bulls were being sold off the Texas ranch and how much feed would have to be bought for the Colorado place over and above the timothy that would be put up in the harvest. Table talk in St. Louis had been quite a different matter. Grandfather Bonney, who had owned a button factory, never brought his business home; he would say that he wanted to "forget the cares that infest the day" and besides that he had great respect for conversation as an art and once a year, on New Year's Day, he read selections from Boswell's *Journal of a Tour to the Hebrides*. He directed the talk at his table as adroitly and interestingly as a professional forum leader. He would start the ball rolling by saying something like this: "Today I was just wondering how much you girls know about Apollo. Do you realize how often he figures in poems, pictures, and statues?" And that would lead to a very enlightening discussion from which the girls derived far more facts than they ever would have done in a cut-and-dried schoolroom class. They talked of everything under the sun, often examining such concepts as "justice," "charity," and "truth." Some of Mrs. Fawcett's most cherished values had been developed at that table.

In the late spring of Rose Bonney's last year in boarding school, two years after her father's death and a year after her mother's unseemly second marriage, her mother bore Mr. Kenyon a son. She was then past forty—she had been much younger than her first husband—and to her daughters there seemed something shameful in this middle-aged childbed. Shameful and obscurely disloyal to their dead father. Five months later, she died a lingering death. Mr. Kenyon, so unimaginative in his innocence, thought that he was honoring Rose in asking her, her mother's eldest survivor, to keep house for him and rear the baby, Claude. It was not, of course, that he was the least bit stingy and did not want to hire a nurse and a housekeeper, for of course he did that anyway. Poor soul, he really thought Rose would like to do it. Can you imagine anyone understanding girls so little? But how could she refuse? Well, she just couldn't. Thus for ten years she buried herself alive, ten years of stupefaction enlivened only by the weddings of her two sisters on which

Mr. Kenyon had spent nearly a fortune. (Grandfather Bonney would have done it for half as much and with twice as much dash.) In all that time, she felt so little intimacy with him that she never called him anything but "Mr. Kenyon" and she never called the child by any name at all, just "you" and "he."

And then at last, when she was twenty-nine and nearly hopeless, she had been released from her prison by Mr. Bruce Fawcett, who had taken her to California to a house very much like the one she had known in St. Louis and all the niceties were restored to her that her father had taught her constituted reality. Mr. Fawcett, the children gathered, had been similar to Grandfather Bonney, although he had been a fainter and imperfect copy, lacking the vitality of the original. (For example, his jokes were never quoted and the children doubted if he had ever made any.) She had brought all the treasures that had been in the storage house these many years and those she had kept in Mr. Kenyon's house: the portrait of her father, his books, and the man himself, a heap of dust in a graceful urn whose handles were shaped like flat-headed snakes and whose top ended in a little knob shaped like a water lily.

Both Mr. Kenyon and his stepdaughter dreaded his annual visit, but they looked upon it as a duty which they would not have dreamed of shirking. He set forth from home on the first day of August, visiting first his Oklahoma place, then his Longhorn ranch in the Panhandle, and after a short trip to Mexico to buy presents for the children, he came on to Covina. Once the courteous preliminaries were over, Grandpa seemed to enjoy his stay, for he was fond of the children, especially of Ralph and Molly whose coloring was that of their grandmother and their half-uncle and, curiously enough, of himself. But Mrs. Fawcett enjoyed none of it, and for the whole two weeks was so flustered that when he left she always went to bed for three or four days with a prolonged sick headache.

To the children, this visit was a season as special and separate as Christmas or Easter, and days before he came they conjectured what surprises he would bring them this time in his big shabby grip, crammed with stiff socks and dirty shirts and scraps of useless paper with the writing worn off. All other visitors wrapped up their presents in tissue paper and tied them with ribbon, but Grandpa just handed them out the way he had got them, sometimes loosely wrapped in a crumpled piece of cheese paper. These gifts were not the sort of souvenirs the children saw in the boardwalk shops at Redondo Beach nor were they like the presents their aunts brought: toys for Ralph and Molly, hair ribbons and round combs for Leah and Rachel. Grandpa brought them heavy, hand-made objects, rings and knives and boxes, and Ralph, ever since he could remember, had loved to hold something small but solid in the palm of his hand. Once Grandpa had given him a miniature contour-globe made of Mexican silver. It was his favorite belonging.

Mrs. Fawcett, while she did not conceal her regret that he was coming, made as extensive preparations for him as if he were someone like Aunt Rowena or Aunt Kathleen whom she really welcomed, and for a week beforehand she threw the house into a turmoil of cleaning and arranging and putting away and getting out, not failing to remind the household from time to time that it was singularly obtuse in Mr. Kenyon to come at the very busiest time of year

24

when there was canning to do and when the nuts were being gathered. But there was no help for it: one of the precepts she had learned at her father's table was: "Never be near with your hospitality." Conventions, as a result, had grown up around these visits, so that just as they associated turkey with Thanksgiving and ham with Easter, the Fawcetts thought of duck and wild rice, of Sally Lunn and fig preserves as the only possible fare on the night of Mr. Kenyon's arrival. And on the last Sunday of the visit, Mr. and Mrs. Follansbee came to a buffet supper served on the front porch at which they had chicken pie and hot biscuits with salmon-berry jam. This supper was invariably a fiasco, but Mrs. Fawcett, an incorrigible ritualist, repeated it year after year. Mr. Follansbee was a voluble man, given to telling anecdotes which usually involved a passage from Scripture or from Shakespeare, and he embarrassed Mr. Kenyon, reducing him to a glassy-eyed stupor which Mrs. Fawcett earnestly strove to end by asking him questions about people in Missouri of whom she had no desire to hear nor he to speak. More often than not, he had a seizure of yawning, almost like a spell of some kind, and he yawned exactly like a dog, making a noise at the end that sounded like a thwarted howl.

Except for this one evening, Mr. Kenyon's visit was not interrupted by any social occasions, and he was only that one time required to dress in what he called his "store clothes." Mr. Follansbee, who had known her father, was the only man Mrs. Fawcett met, so to say, in the drawing room, and it would have been quite unthinkable for all concerned to invite any of the ladies of her various circles to be introduced to her stepfather. There existed between the two a cool formality as if they actually had been estranged in some way and did not simply dislike one another; Ralph knew instinctively that it had always been like that and this was one of the reasons his mother perplexed him. She was quite smiling and flirtatious with Mr. Follansbee, almost as silly as Leah and Rachel, but with Mr. Kenyon in whose very own house she had lived for years and years she acted like an impatient schoolteacher. And Mr. Kenyon, for his part, seemed shy and gawky. But there was no such aloofness between him and the younger children. He was amiably talkative with them and treated them as if they were men of about his age. They spent the hours with him after school, rambling till suppertime through the orderly avenues between the lines of English walnut trees. He had been everywhere in the world and had hunted every animal indigenous to the North American continent: deer, antelope, moose, caribou, big-horn, and every game bird you could name. He had caught wild horses in Nevada and had tamed them "into the gentlest little benches a man ever saw." He had killed rattlers as long as a man is tall; he had eaten alligator and said it tasted like chicken. Two things he never had been partial to were possum and beaver tails, though some people counted them great delicacies. The old colored cook at Claude's place would as lief eat beaver tails three times a day.

It was natural, Ralph supposed, for girls not to be so interested in hunting as he was, but that did not give Leah and Rachel any right to say, as they had been doing all this year, that Grandpa made his stories up. They were obviously all true and Molly, who was very smart, believed them. He thought he had never really liked his older sisters, that he had always suspected they were not what Mrs. Fawcett called "true blue," and that this turning against Grandpa proved that he had been right.

Now, in the garden behind him and Molly, they were talking in low voices. They had many secrets and were in love with two brothers named George and Kenneth Taliafero whom Ralph and Molly detested because they put bay rum on their hair and they called Ralph "hot water Fawcett" and Molly "cold water Fawcett." Now and again the girls' golden hair appeared over the tops of the tall flowers, as bright as the petals. They wore plaid hair ribbons to match their dresses. Leah's was blue and Rachel's was red. Their hair was as soft as down, and when it was washed and Mrs. Fawcett was brushing it, it crackled with electricity. She was ever so proud of it and said crossly, *"Oh,* this pesky stuff!" They were very pretty girls. Their mother carefully protected their fair skin from sunburn and freckles and it was uniformly the color of milk. There was a blue vein in Leah's high forehead which made her look delicate. Their faces were oval and narrow and somehow old-fashioned like the tintypes and sepia photographs of their mother and aunts when they were young ladies. Their bones were small and in time they would be prettily padded as Mrs. Fawcett's were. In addition to their winning faces, they had what the members of the Sorosis called "the poise of ladies of thirty," so completely at ease were they when they passed the cakes at tea or played duets, never having to be coaxed. Mr. and Mrs. Follansbee, who were childless, were devoted to them in a way Mrs. Fawcett found quite touching and sad. After church, when he shook hands with her, the minister often said, "Rose, if you ever get tired of these two little ladies of

27

quality, you know where you can bring them." Leah and Rachel kept this love alive by calling on them frequently and drinking cambric tea and by making presents for them at Christmas and Easter, sending them Valentines and making them May baskets. In return, the Follansbees gave them tokens of piety, small New Testaments, packets of Bible scenes, and books of a moral flavor. Ralph and Molly, for their part, wouldn't have been seen at a dog fight with either of the Follansbees.

It was hard to believe that the two girls had had the same father and mother as Ralph and Molly, who were shy and sometimes impudent out of embarrassment. Since their illness, moreover, they had been thin, pallid, and runny-nosed. From some obscure ancestor they had inherited bad, uneven teeth and nearsighted eyes so that they had to wear braces and spectacles. Their skin and hair and eyes were dark and the truth of it was they always looked a little dirty. They were small for their age but they had large bones, and it was predicted with pity that they would shoot up suddenly in that dreadful ungainly way so many children do, going then through several years of coltishness, painful to behold. They were so self-conscious that they could not sit on a chair without looking as if they perched on a precarious cliff, and if they were suddenly addressed by a strange elder, they swallowed in the middle of their words and tears came to their eyes, steaming their glasses. They were always getting cut and bruised and bumped, and this seemed so inconsiderate (of course it wasn't at all, the poor youngsters couldn't help it, but it *was* peculiar) when Mrs. Fawcett felt the way she did about injuries which could so easily turn into lockjaw. Last year Molly had run a sewing-machine needle

28

straight through her index finger and Mrs. Fawcett had fainted clean away. This had seemed to all Mrs. Fawcett's friends not only a deliberate accident but one brought on by the most reprehensible circumstances, for Molly was making a quilt on the machine, not to be outdone by Leah and Rachel who were sewing their pieces together by hand in the regular way.

At home Ralph and Molly were hot-tempered and rebellious, but elsewhere were so easily intimidated that the enemies among their contemporaries called them cowards. And while Leah and Rachel had dozens of fast friends and were invited to innumerable slumber parties and donkey parties every year, Ralph and Molly had none but one another and at Valentine's they had to stuff the boxes in each other's room at school or they would not have got any at all. In some ways the most disturbing thing about them was their precocity. Mrs. Follansbee, who was discomforted by intellect in anyone, said that their reading excesses were very likely the result (not the cause) of their having to put on eyeglasses at such an early age: first they *looked* studious and then they *were* studious. Their tastes, in point of fact, were not in advance of their years, and they really preferred Howard Pyle to Dickens though they did make rather a show of themselves by memorizing the scene in which David Copperfield gets drunk and entangles himself in Steerforth's curtains. Their reputation really derived from their ability to say off the alphabetical syllables on the backs of the *Encyclopaedia Britannica,* no volume of which they had ever opened except "Ref to Sai" where Ralph, with great disappointment, had read the article on Reproduction.

There was only one thing about Molly he did not like,

Ralph decided, and that was the way she copied him. It was natural for her to want to be a boy (who *wouldn't!*) but he knew for a fact she couldn't be. Last week, he had had to speak sharply to her about wearing one of his outgrown Boy Scout shirts: he was glad enough for her to have it, but she had not taken the "Be Prepared" thing off the pocket and he had to come out and say brutally, "Having that on a girl is like dragging the American flag in the dirt." He wished she would not tag along with him and Grandpa. How splendid it would be, he thought, if only the two of them went walking together! How fine if he could tell the cow joke by himself! He lay back on the lawn, crushing the little lippia blossoms, feeling her eyes follow every movement he made. And then, as he had known she would do, she lay back too.

The day seemed strange to him, the very air unusual. It did not possess quite the quality of a dream, but it lay beyond him as the days had done when he had scarlet fever and all the noises on the first floor had been thin and ephemeral. He remembered that late one night he had seen the sky glow suddenly with heat lightning and he called to Molly through the door that connected their rooms, "Heat lightning for the sky is the same thing as scarlet fever for us." Sick as she was, she clapped her hands and cried back, "Oh, Ralph, you always think of things!" He would have asked her now if she, too, felt funny, but he was afraid that if he shared it with her the feeling would leave him and so he lay in his selfish speechlessness pursuing the red globules that sped downward behind his closed eyes.

"Hey," said Molly and abruptly sat up again.

30

"Straw's cheaper," said Ralph automatically. He wished she wouldn't talk.

"No, listen. I've made another poem."

He opened his eyes in astonishment and looked at her. She was twisting her head around with excitement and he realized that she had not been thinking the same thoughts he had at all and that perhaps she had not even been looking at him when he lay back. Once Grandpa had said that Molly was "a deep one" and Ralph almost thought this was true. He had said it because she insisted that she had learned Braille in kindergarten, and though people would explain to her that what she was thinking of was the beads on a frame which you moved about to learn to count, she replied, "I said I learned Braille and I mean it."

"Will you listen to my poem?" she said pleadingly.

"How long is it?" Ralph did not care for poetry.

"It's real little." And then, without waiting for him to say "All right" she went on. "It's called 'Gravel,'" she said, "and this is it:

Gravel, gravel on the ground
Lying there so safe and sound,
Why is it you look so dead?
Is it because you have no head?"

"Say it again," said Ralph, puzzled now. And when she had repeated it, he said, "It doesn't make any sense. Gravel doesn't have a head."

"That's what I said. 'Is it because you have no *head?*'"

"Well, I don't know what you're talking about."

"You're merely jealous because you can't write poems yourself," said Molly, close to tears. She took her handker-

31

chief out of the pocket of her middy and snuffled into it and beginning to cry, she said, "Now you've gone and made me have another nosebleed."

He did not even open his eyes. He knew that she didn't have a nosebleed and he was so tired of her poems that he was just not going to make any effort to understand this one or to praise it. But neither did he want her to have a mad on him because that would spoil Grandpa's arrival and so he said, "Why don't you go write it down on a piece of paper and then maybe I can get the drift of it?" It was true that he never could hear things as well as he could see them and until just this year he had always thought that the song was "O Beautiful for Spacious Guys."

"I will! I will!" cried Molly and she ran to the house, chanting her poem.

Now, with her gone, he was completely at peace. The unusual feeling came over him again and he held on to it. It was almost as if he were clutching his broad mold-colored geography book to his chest. Later, Ralph felt he had had, on that long afternoon, some prescience of what would happen when Grandpa Kenyon finally came, but probably he had not and it was only desire that made him remember those hours as peculiar and significant, though they were without event.

# CHAPTER TWO

A T FIVE, THE CHILDREN WERE SITTING IN A STRAIGHT ROW ON
the railing of the porch like cats on a fence. There was
a temporary truce between the two older and the two
younger, but they were not friendly enough to talk.
Although Leah and Rachel for a week had groaned to think
of the arrival of "that old hobo," they were as greedy as ever
for the presents which he would take out of the rank gray
bundles in his grip. When finally they heard the car slow
down at the opening of the driveway, all four of them began
to giggle aimlessly and to pound their heels against the up-
rights of the railing. They did not move until he was actually
on the porch, watching his descent from the car spellbound.

He was a big old man, stoop-shouldered and bowlegged.
He looked like a massive, slow-footed bear as he heaved himself out of the car which seemed dwarfed just as Miguel,
that long, lithe man, seemed small and somehow womanly.
Grandpa stood for a moment with his legs wide apart, looking around the yard, glancing at the house and the garden
as if to make sure that he had come to the right place, and
then he took his grip from Miguel and came stomping up
the path, peering at the children over his spectacles. As he

passed a clump of turquoise berry, he tapped a sprig lightly with his shillelagh and Ralph, tense with excitement, wondered why and then wondered why he had wondered: why had he suddenly begun to notice all these pointless little things? Then, when Grandpa was actually on the porch and was setting down his bag, the boy observed nothing more and abandoned himself to the joy of shaking the strong, toughened hand—it was inconceivable that Mr. Kenyon had ever kissed anyone. Ralph was always the last to greet him and Grandpa always said, "Well, sir, I'm here again." It was true that if one of the girls had been the last to shake his hand, he still would have said "sir," but Ralph, in establishing this rite, felt personally, privately addressed, man to man.

He pushed his black hat back on his forehead and they could see the sweat running down to his whiskery eyebrows. He sat down in a wicker basket chair and took off his boots and then opened his grip and got out the soft-soled moccasins which had been made for him by a Cherokee named Daniel Standing-Deer. He would wear these all the rest of his visit, even on the night the Follansbees came. As he tugged at his boots, he said genially, "By the Lord Harry, it's as hot as Tophet."

Ralph was always surprised at Grandpa's clothes even though they did not vary from year to year. It was that no other man he had ever known dressed with such unconcern, with such a deliberate second-hand look. His store clothes were a suit of scratchy gray material, cut without relationship to his measurements. The trousers were too short and the cuffs were three inches wide, and beneath them stuck out his tremendous black boots with rawhide laces and his cattle brand, a bar and a K, burned into the leg of the left one. The coat was long and the pockets were so misshapen from the things he carried that they looked like panniers on a donkey. He carried a watch which he called a "turnip," and a jackknife with four blades, a collapsible tin cup, two pipes, a fly-book, a compass, a good-luck scarab, a collection of bolts and nuts and screws and the coins of foreign countries, and a plump brown leather notebook in which he kept his accounts and in which Ralph had one time seen an old entry, headed "Dodge City," which read:

> Mo. steers sold $6,000
> Purchase 1 pr. shoes $1.75
> Purchase 1 rum for Borchard $.10
> Purchase 1 rum for self $.10

Grandpa's vests were his only fancy in the matter of clothes. He had a great many of them and while they were all cut alike, coming almost to his beard, they were a variety of colors and patterns. His finest was made of black velveteen with silver buttons, in the center of each of which was a small turquoise. This vanity had taken root in him many years before when Jesse James and his boys rode into his yard in Missouri one night and asked for quarters. "I can't go any farther," said Jesse. "If you haven't got a bed, you can hang me on a nail." Jesse James had worn a waistcoat of dark green velveteen with large mother-of-pearl buttons which matched the handles of his side arms. Today Grandpa wore a vest of gray doeskin faced with printed challis, as delicate and feminine as the most stylish dress goods.

He tugged and mumbled, preoccupied and at last got one boot off and then the other, then deeply sighed as though the job had been a hard one. He winked at Ralph and said, "Those are damned fine boots, son, but on a hot day like this they try a man's feet." Leah went into the house to call their mother and to take Grandpa's boots to his room and Rachel sat down on the top step, humming "A Capital Ship for an Ocean Trip," hoping that she would be asked to sing out loud for she had a gifted voice. But Grandpa ignored her and turning to Ralph and Molly, scrutinized them fixedly, seeing for the first time the change in them since last autumn. "By Jupiter, you two are poor," he said. "What in the world has laid aholt of you?"

Rachel explained as if the younger children were mutes. "Oh, they had scarlet fever last March. Leah and I didn't though because Mother sent us to Aunt Kathleen's. Don't you love Aunt Kathleen's house, Grandpa? The way it's right on Lake Michigan?"

Grandpa looked at her politely: "I never was to that house that I recall," he said and then turning to Ralph and Molly, "Well, I declare that's a hell of a note. I reckon I'll have to take you back to Claude's place with me and let that coon of his fatten you up. You ain't any use this way."

"We don't *hurt* anywhere," said Ralph anxiously and Mr. Kenyon laughed, showing the glossy coral gums of his false teeth.

Mrs. Fawcett came out, chattering like a bird. "It's so good to see you, Mr. Kenyon! My, you must be hot and tired after that pesky train! Won't you rest here on the porch where it's cool before you go up, and I'll bring you a glass of nice cold punch. Molly, dear, do you think you can run in and ask Fuschia to get the punch out of the icebox? And tell her to put in a nice big piece of ice? And tell her to be *sure* to wash it first? And then bring out some glasses and we'll all have a good cool drink."

Molly started to the door but Grandpa stopped her. "Just bring your grandpa a small tumbler. I have in my valise here a quart bottle of Bourbon drinking whisky which I had the good fortune to purchase in El Paso at a king's ransom. I think that'll do more for what ails me than your punch, Rose, no offense intended."

Ralph trembled all over with delight and dread. Once he had seen a bottle of dark red wine on a shelf in Miguel's house, but he had never seen whisky nor had he ever seen anyone drink. Mrs. Fawcett bit her lip and flushed. Grandfather Bonney had never used spirits but took a glass of claret or port now and again on special occasions and if he had lived to see the Volstead Act passed, he would have forgone even that.

"Just as you like, Mr. Kenyon," she said, her cheeks still bright and her eyes blinking with indignation. "I only thought you would like something *cool*. In that case perhaps we'd better go inside."

"Why?" demanded Ralph.

"Because I say so," she replied tightly.

Leah giggled. "Goody-goody Mother! She means Miss Runyon might go past and see Grandpa's bottle of you-know-what and tell the policeman on him. But if she did see it, Mother, we could say Grandpa sprained his ankle and was putting Sloan's liniment on it." She and Rachel laughed and lovingly ran their fingers through their fine hair.

"Dammit, Rose," said Grandpa, "I'm tired, and if it don't make a world of difference to you, I'll take the liberty of drinking my whisky right here."

Mrs. Fawcett took her defeat in silence, but it was clear that she thought this beginning indicated an even more trying visit than usual. She rolled down the bamboo screen on the south side of the house so that the Freudenburgs (who went right on making beer in spite of the new law) would not see Mr. Kenyon's bottle and wrongly think she had given her approval or, even worse, that she was sharing it with him. She said brightly, "Now tell me all your news, Mr. Kenyon. I'm on pins and needles to hear about everyone back home. I was just saying to Fuschia that good as her duck smelled what I was really hungry for was news."

Grandpa reported that a Dr. Taylor had been operated on for kidney stones and was not expected to live; indeed, since he had been away for five weeks and had had little word from Missouri, it was possible that the old gentleman was already dead. Mrs. Fawcett said, "You remember Dr. Taylor, don't you, girls? He and Mrs. Taylor gave us those nice little salt spoons you like so much. Isn't it too bad he's not well?" Leah and Rachel were moved and Rachel said, "Poor Mrs. Taylor. When you write her, Mother, will you give her my love and tell her I keep my best hankies in the darling case she sent me?"

Ralph, sitting on the arm of Grandpa Kenyon's chair, hesitated a moment and then plunged, "Ain't Dr. Taylor the one you told me was crooked as a dog's hind leg?"

"Ralph!" cried Leah. "You awful little Hun! And you said 'ain't' too!"

An unhappy, beating silence fell, ended finally by Molly's return, and the conversation set forth again, a plodding drudge. Grandpa, never interested in these chronicles of deaths and marriages and illnesses which he dutifully recited for his stepdaughter, seemed even more bored than usual, more inaccurate with names and more uncertain of his facts. He said that someone called Geneva Whatyoumaycallit had had erysipelas and it had disfigured her almost beyond recognition, but as he could neither remember her last name nor where she lived, the news was not thrilling but only tantalizing. He said that on second thoughts she might as easily have been named Mildred and he was not at all sure she didn't live in Oklahoma. One Maude Pease had asked him to tell Rose how much she had appreciated the metal casserole of candy she had sent as an anniversary present. (Leah said: "Mother, is that the one that had the alfresco wedding?" She brought this up whenever she could and it always made Ralph and Molly furious because they never could remember what "alfresco" meant.) The family on the place next to his had had a run of bad luck with their wheat—had rust—and had had to sell their automobile. He said then, "I can't make out what you want to keep that bus of yours for, Rose. Why don't you get a new one? By George, a man of any size feels like a galoot in that tom-fool outfit of yours."

Mrs. Fawcett winced; she could not bear the word "bus" and did not any better like "flivver." She herself always spoke with dignity of "the machine." The Willys Knight had been extremely expensive and, although rumors had come to her that it was out of style, she had great affection for it. She replied exuberantly to Mr. Kenyon that she did not know what she would do without his advice, that it was one of the things she had wanted to talk over with him, and that she also hoped he would take a look at the shaft in the pumphouse in the morning for she felt that it needed to be replaced, even though Miguel said it was sound.

Ralph stared listlessly at a small tear in the knee of Grandpa's trousers and wanted to ask him what countries he had gone to last winter. But it was a convention that he never spoke of his travels in Mrs. Fawcett's presence. He had been to Siam, to Borneo, India, Spain, Sweden, and even to such out-of-the-way places as Lithuania and the Shetland Islands. A trip to Sydney or to southern Mexico was no more to him than a trip to Riverside to the Fawcetts. Once he had written a picture postal card to Ralph from Melbourne saying that he was bringing him a monkey, but Mrs. Fawcett had replied for her son, requiring him not to. The boy never forgave her and sulked whenever he recalled it. Mrs. Fawcett had remarked acidly that it was typical of Mr. Kenyon to select the one sort of pet that could not be housebroken. He had gone by steamer to Alaska and there had seen the northern lights and had gone out in a sealing vessel in the Bering Strait: before they even spotted the seals there had been a thundering great storm and the whole crew had nearly lost their lives; the waves were as high as the Fawcetts' pump-house and the downside of them was as steep as Mt. Baldy. The noise of the gale had had the tongue of Hades in it.

Now and again Mr. Kenyon looked at Ralph and smiled and patted his knee with a thick, out-of-shape hand. He looked rather like an Indian with his strong cheekbones, his lank black hair and his sun-stained skin and his humped nose, but of course no Indian ever had a beard like Grandpa's: it was as thick as the top of the umbrella tree. He finished his second tumbler of whisky and put the glass on the table. Spreading his hands out on his knees, he looked at his stepdaughter and said, "Rose, you had ought to be ashamed of the looks of these two. You hadn't ought to hold out on them the way you do: you had ought to send them to Claude of a summer."

"But, Mr. Kenyon! What do you mean! Why, they're much too delicate to be away from me and Dr. Haskell!"

This was a controversy that was repeated annually. Mr. Kenyon, whose scorn for Mrs. Fawcett's picayune walnut grove was boundless, saw no reason at all why the children should not summer in the Colorado mountains and each year he offered to pay their train fare; he felt it particularly unjust that she did not at least send the boy who ought to be learning the ways of a man.

"This Dr. Haskell," said Mr. Kenyon contemptuously, "is he the only sawbones in the world?"

"Oh, I didn't mean it that way, Mr. Kenyon, I surely didn't. I daresay Claude has a very fine physician up there in the mountains. I only meant that they're such babies . . . they need a mother's care. I just don't know . . . with all those horses and cows there, just danger everywhere."

Ralph, knowing beforehand that nothing would come of this argument, wondered if he might not now tell the joke about the cow since his mother had mentioned cows, but she hastened on. "You know how I have always felt about horses, Mr. Kenyon."

He replied, "Rose, there's not a damned thing on God's green earth I know any better than that. But it don't make sense that you should want to turn in and spook this boy as well."

Mrs. Fawcett blushed and vigorously fanned herself with

a palm leaf, though the breeze was cool. "I want only one thing, Mr. Kenyon: I want him to be a gentleman."

The flame died in Grandpa and he said wearily, "I don't aim to judge in the matter of gentlemen but my son Claude is a fine man."

Mrs. Fawcett put her fan down suddenly and sat up straight. "Mr. Kenyon, I think perhaps we had better discuss this some other time. You were going to tell me about Roberta Wagner's fire. How did it start?"

"Oh, a kerosene lamp or some damned thing or other in the barn."

Reluctantly he allowed himself to be steered back into tame channels, but presently there came a long pause. He could think of no more facts and Mrs. Fawcett was out of questions. They were all so bored! The children waited impatiently for their mother to go in to speak to Fuschia, for this was the signal for Grandpa to give them their presents. But because she revered custom, she would not move until it was really necessary; she did not want the dirty, tippling old roughneck to think he was not welcome, not even when she was so angry with him that she could cry.

Grandpa filled his glass for the third time. Ralph got off the arm of his chair and moved to the railing of the porch where he sat with his hands under him. "Grandpa," he said, "have you got any dogs?" The old man put his glass down on the round wicker table while he corked the bottle. Then, without warning, his head fell forward on his chest, his hat slid off and lay, crown upward, on the floor, and the bottle rolled unbroken to the railing, directly under Ralph's feet. His hands relaxed and lay over the arms of the chair; his breath came unevenly and deeply like wind through his loosely opened lips, and his eyes appeared quite blind though they were open. There was a moment of quiet so long and so pure that it seemed like an hour of dreamless sleep, and Ralph was again reminded of the scarlet fever days when the neat, still hours had been in a row like boxes. He stared intently at the long unkempt hairs in Grandpa's eyebrows and at the coppery gloss of his beard. The old feet, swollen, lay turned on the ankles and the boy saw that the moccasins were not completely on and that the heels, in white cotton socks, stuck out. In one there was a careful darn. He realized that he did not know the name of Grandpa's housekeeper, though he did know that Uncle Claude's was named Mrs. Brotherman.

Then Mrs. Fawcett cried, "José! Fuschia! Quick!" José, still holding his banana knife, came silently across the lippia lawn, the grin now gone from his face. Ralph was sent to telephone for Dr. Haskell and Molly went with him into their father's den. Leah and Rachel had run sobbing in terror to the garden.

Ralph and Molly stayed in the study until they heard José and Fuschia help Grandpa up the steps. There were gasps and moans and curses and the sound of those old helpless feet pad-padding up in the soft slippers. Then they heard the door to the guest room close, and still, for some time, they did not stir.

Unable to understand this unmanly collapse, this strange dissolving of a rock, Ralph fled the thought of it and viewed his father's study, wishing he were alive. This room was kept as he had always kept it, but there was no clue to what

43

sort of man he had been. Its simple and business-like furnishings had no idiosyncrasies and there was little to distinguish it from Dr. Haskell's waiting room. There were no pictures on the walls and the only books in the shelves were government tracts on the growing of walnuts and a set of dusty, yellow-leaved volumes called "Letters and Messages of the Presidents." On the desk there was a surveyor's telescope in a black box and an arrowhead in an abalone shell. The only article that had, so far as he knew, any history at all was the serape on the black leather lounge: his mother had smuggled it in from Tia Juana on her bustle. This had been the only act of daring in her life and Ralph admired her for it, but today he realized that he was tired of the story and he wondered what his father had been doing all the time she was having her perilous adventure with the customs inspector. The man had faded away like smoke. Even Leah, who had been six when he died, recalled almost nothing of him, and the few impressions she did have grew paler and paler until she could no longer give definite answers to any of the other children's questions but would say vaguely, "I *think* he used to say 'jiminy crickets' but I'm not sure." What was truly amazing was that the old woman he had saved in the flood was still alive!

"Oh, I'm lonesome," Ralph said to himself, and then, against his will, he saw Grandpa again, slumping in the wicker chair, and again he wondered why he had tapped the turquoise berry with his stick. And now, clear-headed, he turned on Molly in a cold, exhilarated anger and said, "Why do you always have to follow me?" He went out to the porch and sat motionless in the swing, hearing his sister sobbing and heaving about on the lounge. José had left his

44

cruel curved knife on the round table beside Grandpa's little glass of whisky which he had not got to drink.

It was the last time they saw Grandpa Kenyon until, five days later, he was brought down to the parlor, dead, where he waited two more days until Uncle Claude came to bury him.

The children did not go to school for the three days between Grandpa's death and the funeral. Mrs. Fawcett felt that this was a necessary gesture of respect to the dead man, but it was an unhappy time for the children. Leah and Rachel sorted and arranged their free samples and quarreled with one another saying. "Move *over,* what do you think I am anyway?" and Ralph and Molly roamed silently from room to room trying to think of something to do. "Why don't you settle down with a book?" said their mother. They talked, dispiritedly, in Pig Latin about Molly's poem which Ralph still could not understand. The house was quiet and dark and the Mexicans in the grove were afraid to raise their voices above a whisper. All that time, Fuschia was canning and making piccalilli and the whole house smelled deliciously of mace and dill, and yet it could not obscure the fragrance of all the flowers that lay in the parlor with Grandpa. Ralph was acutely conscious of all the smells, and he was able at last to name what it was that had been so distinct in the odor that clung to the old man: he had smelled like a raisin.

Mr. Follansbee came twice in the evening to call. The second time he left a leather-bound book of solemn aphorisms called "some Starbeams of Solace," which Mrs. Fawcett read frequently with moist eyes. In his sermon at the

45

funeral, the pastor spoke of Grandpa as a man whose "many interests and travels destined him for an active rather than a contemplative life," but since it took all kinds to make the world, there was no reason to suppose that the Lord would look on him with disfavor. "Among men, too," he said, "there are the Marthas as well as the Marys." By way of gratitude, Mrs. Fawcett, enriched by her stepfather's will, subscribed a thousand dollars toward a central heating unit for the church. She would have liked to have a stained-glass window put in in his memory, but she was by no means certain that Mr. Kenyon had believed in God.

The night after Grandpa died, Miss Runyon brought some roses, and because Fuschia was busy with the dishes and Leah and Rachel wanted to listen to the ladies talk and Molly was in bed with hiccups after getting too much sun, Ralph was sent to the parlor with them. Only one lamp was burning, the smallest one of all. It stood on a round marble-topped table at the foot of the coffin and it scarcely illuminated Grandpa's face at all. Although there seemed to be no opening in the room, the flame was unsteady and shifted behind the thin china shade with its design of tulips against a pale green ground. There were flowers everywhere, brought by all the neighbors, not in tribute to Mr. Kenyon since none of them had known him, but in sympathy with Mrs. Fawcett in whose house this had unreasonably happened. It had been one of his orders, repeated throughout his lifetime, that he be buried wherever he died, for he had no use for pomp and thought that the transportation of a corpse from one part of the world to another was wasteful of money and of time. Mrs. Fawcett would gladly have accompanied the casket back to Missouri or even to England,

46

and in her first telegram to Claude had said so, but he wired back: "Must bury him like he said."

Ralph tried not to look at the body which, even though it had shrunk in death, made everything else look small as if the importance of its metamorphosis had taken on a physical dimension. He put the vase of roses down on the library table where the Bible lay open and as he did so, a petal fell off onto the finely printed page. Simultaneously the tip of a spray of fern in a tall vase of carnations brushed against his cheek, startling him with its subtle touch. He turned quickly as if he had been spoken to and looked full into the dead man's face. He now could see the big hooked nose jutting up and casting a shadow of itself on the satin pillow, and could see the dead white wrinkled eyelids under the ragged brows. Someone had brushed his beard and his square, corrugated fingernails had been cleaned. Ralph put the palm of his hand on Grandpa's cold cheek, feeling the formation of the bones. He was neither afraid nor disgusted: the skin under his fingers was as smooth and meaningless as the fallen rose petal. But then, when he had taken away his hand and had stepped back, he was frightened exactly as he had been frightened last summer when he went onto a submarine in San Diego with Uncle Ernest and he had looked through a periscope; it was so far, what you looked at, and so watery and so strange.

In the days just past, when Grandpa had been dying, the mystery had been withheld from all the children. Rather, it had been obscured by the bustling, the quiet coming and going of Dr. Haskell and of well-wishing neighbors with napkin-covered offerings of custards and broths (the Freudenburgs had sent, of all things, some spiced dumplings!)

and the ringing of the telephone, and Miguel's innumerable trips to town to fetch medicine and to send telegrams. The guest room was at the back, in an ell, a part of the house Ralph rarely went into since besides this room there were only his mother's sewing room, the linen closet and a storage cubby; yet in these past days he had been drawn to it, bewitched by the silence, and sometimes for an hour had stood in the sewing room, tossing a bobbin of blue silk thread up in the air and catching it again, trying to hear something through the wall, hearing nothing but the night-like silence, the silence that muted the hurried commotion of the errands and the calls.

Now that everything had ceased, it was possible to look back and to realize that the soft sounds and the agitation had been only trifles superimposed upon a great, unviolent force. Grandpa was like a big river, he thought, but one that had dried up and was gone forever into the ocean. He could take in the finality of this, but he could not understand how the drying up had happened: it had been too quick. He had just been sitting there corking the whisky bottle; Ralph had just asked him if he had any dogs.

Ralph understood that Grandfather Bonney had been dying for some time, in excruciating pain, and he knew that he should be glad—as his mother had said a dozen times—that Grandpa had not suffered at all. No matter how hard he tried, though, and no matter how often he heard the story of Grandfather Bonney's tragic ending, he could not feel really sad as Leah and Rachel did, nor did he wish as they did that he had known the gentleman whose portrait he now looked at in the fluttering light. Beneath the gold-framed picture, on the mantel which was black marble and

had been taken from the house in St. Louis, stood Grandfather Bonney's christening cup and the Florentine urn
which held his ashes. Between his Alpha and Omega stood
a multitude of small mementoes of the intervening years:
a silver snuff box embossed with a salamander; a miniature
Venus de Milo made of brass which he had used as a paper
weight; a gold stamp box with his name engraved on it in
German script; a red leather jewel case which held the studs
and the cuff links, the tie pins and the Masonic ring which
Ralph, who was named for him, would get when he was
grown.

Everything in the face and bearing of Grandfather Bonney
showed that he was truly the character in his daughter's
legend, that is, that he had been a scholar and a gentleman.
He was plump and bald, but fat had not obscured the vigor
of his face. His gray eyes intelligently searched those of his
beholder and in them resided a great self-possession which
appeared also in his luxuriously full lips shining as though
he had licked them, which were closed and unsmiling above
the faintly grizzled and elegantly kempt Imperial. He wore
a pink carnation in the lapel of his morning coat; a silk
hat and a gold-headed stick, a black Chesterfield and a pair
of white gloves lay on the hassock beside his chair. He was
so spruced up that the children could never get over the idea
that he had not just come from a funeral at which he had
been a pallbearer, but Mrs. Fawcett assured them that this
was the way he had dressed on the most ordinary occasions.
He sat at a large round table laden with gold-clasped books,
the same books which were now on the same table in the
bay window, opposite the fireplace. The one that was open
under his hand—a finger pointed to the middle of the right

page—was Tennyson's *Collected Works*. The chances were strong, said Mrs. Fawcett, that the poem he pointed to was "Break, Break, Break" which he had liked especially. Still, it was hard to believe that he had been reading and had suddenly been moved so much by a passage that he had stopped to meditate upon it, for there was no softening of reflection about the lines of his mouth and eyes: they were tense as if he had just come to a decision and intended to abide by it sternly. The picture had been painted when he was in his prime, in his middle fifties. It was very soon after that that he had died.

Leah and Rachel and Ralph and Molly could not remember a time when they had not known that Grandfather Bonney had personally met Grover Cleveland at the Democratic Convention in 1888. He had himself been a Republican and had always voted a straight ticket, but all the same, he never had anything harsh to say of Mr. Cleveland although he was naturally glad that Mr. Harrison had won the election. This connection of her grandfather with the history of the United States had led the eldest child, Leah, to several confusions which she had passed on to each of the others in turn. Chief of these was that President Cleveland, wrongheaded as he might have been, was second in importance only to George Washington. They believed that during his administration the capital had been Cleveland, Ohio. They could not place Abraham Lincoln in time but they could easily do so in space, for Uncle Ernest, their Aunt Kathleen's husband, had gone to the University of Nebraska where, but for a fluke, he would have graduated *summa cum laude*.

Furthermore, because in the delirium of his last illness, Grandfather Bonney had several times spoken of his meeting with Cleveland, they associated the President with blood poisoning and with profuse perspiration and Molly could never hear his name without immediately seeing in her mind's eye a brown custard cup in which her mother had burned sugar to dispel the fetor of the sickroom. Similarly they linked Tennyson with their grandfather, for his last articulate words, spoken to Aunt Kathleen as she was arranging his pillows, were, "It's no use, Kate. I am at the crossing of the bar." Each of the children envisaged this trinity, the poet, the President, and the grandfather, in a different way: Ralph saw them fat, hatless, wearing morning coats, walking abreast along an endless beach, eternally nearing a sand bar. Leah saw them sitting at a round table drinking coffee out of mustache cups while in the distance a band played "When You and I Were Young, Maggie." Through Rachel's mind, they marched in single file down the central aisle of the First Presbyterian Church with such calm and ceremony that they made Mr. Follansbee seem remarkably rustic. Molly, who was often ill, saw them lying all three in one enormous bed with a moon like a jack-o'-lantern shining in on their big rosy faces through a dormer window.

Ralph, glancing from Grandpa Kenyon's dead face to Grandfather Bonney's living one, felt lonely and beset, knowing with unwilling shame that he should mourn them equally because, in a sense, he really knew Grandfather Bonney better than he had ever known his successor. For example, he knew all about his grandfather's fox terrier who had been named Liliolukilani and had been as sharp as a tack: she could pray and she could jump through a hoop and she knew commands both in English and in German.

Ralph could see the man as clearly as he could call up the image of Mr. Follansbee. What a sport he had been! How full of jokes and pranks! He had always been the merriest one of all at skating parties (to tease the girls he once wore a fascinator to a skating party!) and at wiener roasts, at formal balls and informal Sunday evening chafing-dish suppers. He had had gallant manners with ladies, preserving such customs as kissing their hands and paying them compliments which always contained a word or two of French. What young lady did not delight in having him say to her, "Mademoiselle's frock is truly *distingue*"? Besides being chivalrous, he could play tricks that were a scream and afterward he would say, "Forgive me, ladies and gentlemen, but I felt an uncontrollable desire to tickle my risibles." Once he had put burnt cork all over his face and had pretended to be a darky and his imitation was so good that everyone had been taken in for at least five minutes. Another time, he had sneaked up under an open window one dark summer night and when there was a pause in the conversation, he suddenly said, in a spooky voice, "Boo!" and Mrs. Bonney and the girls had nearly jumped out of their skins. At breakfast he would ask a visitor if she wanted onions in her cocoa and he would say it with such a straight face, she wouldn't know what to answer. Once, though, he had been beaten at this game, for a perky friend of Rowena's had answered back quick as a wink, "Not on your tintype, Mr. Smarty," and Grandfather had laughed until the tears came to his eyes. He had always been up to some frolic like that. Now it would be a joke on one of the colored servants (he loved to tease the old colored cook who was *just* as superstitious), now a lark down the river on a steamer to Memphis, now an outlandish slide mixed up with the scenes of Venice in the stereoptican: suddenly you would see a pair of flannel underdrawers flying from the middle dome of St. Marks! He used to say that "one is only as old as one feels" and he never felt old, not even at the last of his life.

The boy felt neither fear nor sorrow for either man. He felt only this unkind solitude that waited for him like a surly dog. In a brief foreknowledge of maturity, he thought how curious it was that it had been possible for them all to eat three times a day the same as ever: they had actually eaten the duck and Sally Lunn the night Grandpa was, as they said, "taken," and Leah had not bothered to take away his place so that it was still there, opposite Mother, the emptiest space Ralph had ever seen. Even now, after dark, alone in a room with a dead person, he was not afraid, and he was able to notice little, useless things like the dust rag Fuschia had left behind on the bookcase beside the vase of cattails. He remembered that his mother had said that just before Grandfather Bonney died she had been in her bedroom looking out the window at a bright red kite that had got stuck in the topmost branches of a eucalyptus tree, and when Kathleen came in to say, "He is going, Rose," she had, even as she hurried along the passage, said to herself, "I wonder if that kite belongs to one of the Van Buskirk children."

The ladies were in the dining room talking. He could not hear what they said, but he could imagine the shape of their mouths and the kind of thing they would be repeating over and over again in that strange belief all grown-ups seemed to have that no one heard the first time. His mother would explain, with pressing urgency, why Mr. Kenyon was to be

53

buried in the Covina cemetery although he had only come here for short visits; Miss Runyon, boisterous and inquisitive, would be inquiring about Uncle Claude who was coming tomorrow; his mother would be apologizing for her half-brother just as she had always apologized for her stepfather. At some point she would say, "First my father, then my husband, and now Mr. Kenyon. But I have my son."

Someone was at the door and he trembled violently; if one of those women came in, he thought, he would throw himself on Grandpa's dead white face and die. But it was only Molly, slinking in like a little ailing cat, snuffling and coming toward him with her hands outstretched as if she were blind. There was a sour smell about her and he knew she must have been sick as she generally was when she had hiccups. "I'm scared," she said, taking his hand. "I don't want him to be dead, Ralph. I don't *want* him to be!" They lay down on the floor beside the coffin, sobbing in each other's arms, but making scarcely any noise lest the ladies and their sisters hear them.

# CHAPTER THREE

JUST AS FIVE DAYS BEFORE WHEN THEY HAD WAITED FOR Grandpa Kenyon, Ralph and Molly lay on the lippia lawn, waiting for their uncle. An airplane flew across the sky. Its pilot was stunting and as they watched, breathlessly, he took a nose dive. "The big fool!" cried Ralph. "He's going to hit the pumphouse!" And then he smiled as he saw the plane cleverly climb up again. It occurred to him with pain that Grandpa Kenyon, who loved all unusual experience, had died before he had ever gone up in an airplane. Nor had he ever got to see the racing fellow, Barney Oldfield, of whom he had often spoken with admiration.

What would next September be like without him? Associated as he had been with the renewal of crowded days after the tranquil ennui of the summer, he had seemed to the children, after he had gone, half legendary like a figure known only in his identification with a particular place or a particular day of the year. He was a sort of god of September, surrounded by the gold, autumnal light. What Ralph missed most already was the early-morning ceremony in which he alone participated with Grandpa. The old man kept his usual hours when he visited in Covina and always got up before daylight to make his own breakfast. The fragrance of the coffee he made was so manly and stimulating that Ralph could reproduce the sensation of it at will throughout the day and could therefore daydream under the most adverse schoolroom conditions. Ralph, creeping downstairs in his stocking feet lest he awaken his mother and sisters, would find Grandpa Kenyon sitting by the stove in the half-light, his black hat pushed back from his forehead and his glasses midway down his nose. He would be waiting for the griddle to heat up for his flapjacks, but the coffee would be made already and the kitchen would be full of its strong, rather rancid smell. They did not speak to one another until the meal was over and Grandpa had lighted his pipe; at this point, he always took off his hat, Ralph could never guess why. At these times he told no stories but instead talked with homesickness of the chores that were now proceeding on his ranches: just about now in Texas the whole outfit would be fixing to go up to the range and cut out the beeves to be shipped to Panama; in Colorado, where they kept lazier hours, the old colored woman, Magdalene, would be calling the men to breakfast. As he stated these facts, he kept his eye on his watch. When the second hand had completed its circuit, he would say, "She's settin' the coffee pot down by Claude." Ralph discerned contempt in Grandpa's glance through the window at the tidy grove with its toy-like trees where the Mexicans would not come for two hours yet, and when he heard the milkman come, he sometimes grew angry, thumping his fist on the table and shouting at the boy, "Lord God Almighty, she could keep *one* cow anyway. She had ought to be ashamed." She was not ashamed but Ralph was, and once he declared

56

that he would not touch milk again until she got a cow. Her reply was a familiar and irrefutable one: "Our sort of people don't have cows."

Ralph wondered if, after all, Grandpa would have liked the joke about the cow. He wondered, too, if he dared tell it to Uncle Claude or if this would seem unbecoming on the day of the funeral. Uncle Claude. Uncle Claude. Uncle Claude. He said the name over and over to himself but it brought no picture to his mind. He could not imagine what Grandpa's son would be like and because he could not, the thought of meeting him made him shy.

At the same time that he became aware that Molly was crying and had been for some time, he saw the car coming round the bend in the lane where the blue cedars grew and with no plan at all in his mind he jumped to his feet and ran at top speed across the lawn and past the solar tank. As he ran, he thought: Now I pass the garden and Leah and Rachel haven't seen me. Now I am passing the solar tank. Now I am passing the den and in the den I am passing the deer-head and the deer-head hasn't seen me. Now the pantry and Mother isn't there and Fuschia isn't there. And now I am safe. He ran to the pumphouse and climbed the ladder as quickly as a mouse. Once on top, he squatted on his heels on the round roof. His heart pounded as deeply as the pump pulsed below him. He had no idea why he had not wanted to see his uncle. It was as if he had got to control himself by a complete physical escape, by exposing himself to the perfectly empty sky and by enclosing himself in this perfectly round small area where shapes and colors were of the simplest: the sanctuary was round, its floor was black, the sky was blue, and he was alone.

57

He would not look down but he could hear voices. His mother said, "Dear Claude. It is a sorrowful time for all of us."

If the air had not been so still, Ralph would not have heard the man's reply for his voice was so soft. It was so soft and sad that Ralph thought he must be sitting on the steps with his head between his hands in anguish. He said, "Can I see Mr. Kenyon, ma'am?"

The boy saw his uncle all by himself, casting his shadow on a white desert, on the terribly unearthly stretch of land he had seen from the train the summer they had gone to St. Louis. There had been miles and miles of nothing but sand until finally the train passed a giant pear cactus and Mrs. Fawcett, in an explanatory voice, had said, "You know, that little bit of shade would mean a great deal to someone who got stranded here."

Mr. Follansbee and his wife came to luncheon after the funeral. Mr. Follansbee sat at Mrs. Fawcett's right and told jokes which the children and Uncle Claude did not understand, although Leah and Rachel pretended to. He was an unpleasant-looking man with a small upturned chin and a large, down-turned nose and his whole face was thin and malign. Mrs. Fawcett said he had a "typical Yankee face," but Ralph could never reconcile this with the song "Yankee Doodle" which was, he thought, about a man something like Santa Claus. Molly had decided, though, that if Uncle Sam were clean-shaven, he would probably look a good deal like the minister. He wore a morning coat; Mrs. Follansbee, like Mrs. Fawcett, was dressed in black. Each child wore a sign of mourning: Ralph wore black knickerbockers and black stockings and the three little girls wore black Windsor ties at the necks of their middy blouses. In this decent gathering, Uncle Claude was a gaudy incongruity. His suit was chocolate brown, his shirt was a rich deep blue, and his tie was scarlet; there was no black about him save for his black hair and his black eyes. His whole color scheme was like that of a rooster. He was a younger and slighter version of Grandpa. His jawbones were broad and his cheekbones high, but his chin was rather small and Ralph realized with a shock that probably Grandpa's had been too and that was why he wore a beard. Uncle Claude's shoulders were massive, bullish, and his arms hung forward from them in an animal heaviness, terminating in the biggest hands the boy had ever seen. These hands, whose fingers had been enlarged and discolored as his father's had been, were long but were so wide that on the damask tablecloth and handling the coin-silver spoons, they looked scarcely like hands at all but slabs of meat with the rind still on. Leah and Rachel, scornful of his cheap ugly suit (it looked like the one the Watkins man wore), had said that he looked simple-minded and they hoped they would not have to sit next to him at the funeral. It was that his face was so innocent; he did not seem to know what had happened to him, and this house, these little girls, the appointments of this table were not in his line. You could tell he wished he had not come; but he was not simple-minded.

He had hardly spoken at all since his arrival. After he had seen his father, he had gone to the guest room and had remained there until it was time to leave for the service. Molly, hugging the trunk of the umbrella tree, had seen him standing at the oriel in the upstairs hall, looking down when the men came to fetch away the coffin to take it to the church. His silence had infected the others, and even Mrs. Fawcett's tongue had been stilled on the drive to the cemetery and home again. But now that all was over, she believed a lighter tone should prevail to efface, if possible, the sorrowful reason for their gathering together. The talk, therefore, at the luncheon table was jovial and irrelevant. Mr. Follansbee started it by telling a story about an earnest young lady, the daughter of a remote cousin of Mrs. Follansbee's, who had been sent to them with a letter of introduction for a short visit before she entered a boarding school in Pasadena.

"Oh, Rose, you will like this, I know," he said. "I can just imagine your good father in a similar position." To Uncle Claude, he explained, "I, an immigrant to California like everyone else—these four little Fawcetts are the only California natives of my acquaintance, ha, ha—and in the dim dark past I had the honor of hearing Mrs. Fawcett's father hold forth on cultural subjects far into many a night. I must confess that sometimes, for me, the midnight oil gave off soporific fumes but—ha, ha—as that most learned gentleman would have said himself, *aliquando bonus dormitat Homerus,* that is, 'even good Homer sometimes nods.'" Claude Kenyon, flanked by Ralph and Molly, looked bashfully at his plate of jellied soup and did not even pretend to smile. The preacher, with a hint of exasperation in his face, but none in his deep oratorical voice, continued, "This good lass came with loads of luggage, all of it as heavy as lead. Full of books, do you see. As pretty as a picture she was, and no earthly reason for her to be smart as well—look there at Leah and Rachel pricking up their ears! Yet she *was* smart, but the

60

pity of it was that she wasn't really bright. You call that a paradox? Well, I have a funny sort of little old mind and I maintain a person can be intellectual and not be intelligent. But don't let me make a sermon right here! On to the story! Well, sir, the first night the pretty little slip of a thing was with us, we were taking our coffee in the library, a custom I have not been able to outgrow even after many years in this new-fangled nation of California, and lo and behold and *mirabile dictu,* milady says to me, very seriously, very soberly, 'Mr. Follansbee, have you ever read Shakespeare?' "

Mrs. Fawcett, who had been ready from the beginning of the anecdote, now laughed until she had to wipe her eyes. Mrs. Follansbee, who had been present and could not be expected to react quite as she had done at the time, was milder. Leah and Rachel covered their mouths with their napkins, through which came peals of laughter. But the minister had expected this applause and did not so much as glance at any of them but fixed his eyes on Uncle Claude with a look of malicious amusement. When Uncle Claude blushed, his skin took on an apoplectic blue and Ralph, who had not been able even to grin, shuddered when he looked at him.

When there had been enough laughter, Mr. Follansbee, still looking at Claude, said, "Sir, I envy you your snowy winters. I miss them here in California. Back in Missouri, on snowy nights, I used to go through the historical plays. Read them and reread them to my great edification. I imagine you do much the same thing. I expect when you're snowbound the time may hang heavy on your hands. Literature is a great medicine: it takes us out of ourselves."

Claude put his spoon down clumsily and it made a loud

clatter on the plate under his soup cup. His ashamed eyes lifted waveringly to the minister's as he sighed. And then he said, "I couldn't rightly say I find the time hanging heavy. I have a sight of cows to feed."

"All the same," cried Mrs. Fawcett, frantically embarrassed, "I expect you manage to find the time to read! Mr. Follansbee, Claude was the most precocious youngster you ever saw, and who should be a better judge of that than I? Why, he was reading *Lorna Doone* when he was just a little bit of a thing!" This profession fell flat, but she barely paused. "Don't you remember the many many times we used to go out to the summer-house and read Tennyson aloud? How you loved *The Idylls of the King!*"

For several minutes she talked rapidly and distractedly about Tennyson, Claude's early love for him, her own love for him, her father's love for him. She did not relinquish the conversation until it was at a safe distance from the question of how Uncle Claude passed the time on a winter evening. Later on she confided in her children that she had been on tenterhooks for fear Claude would tell them what he did read. For she assumed that his tastes would be like those of his father who had never been seen reading a book and who had never mentioned any but the novels of Gaboriau which certainly could not be called "classics." As far as the ancient languages went, these might have been the Dark Ages for all Mr. Kenyon had known of them, and Mrs. Fawcett suspected that his son had not known what *mirabile dictu* meant.

Mr. Follansbee experimented with another gambit. His hobby was taxidermy and his house, which smelled of mud, was full of stuffed skunks, raccoons, woodpeckers, bluebirds and cottontails, the corpses being brought to him by his obedient flock, some of whom felt that for a minister the pastime was unduly skittish. He asked Uncle Claude if he had any interest in the subject and when Uncle Claude replied that he had never thought about it one way or the other, Mr. Follansbee said, "I'm just like a boy about it, as my long-suffering better half will testify. Why, yesterday I got a new batch of supplies and I stopped work right in the middle of my sermon to open the parcel. They had made a rather comical mistake. I had written for eyes of a vulture and they sent instead the eyes of the extinct auk."

Molly spoke for the first time. She closed her eyes and chanted, "A is for auk who lives in the wet, B is for blackbird with wings of jet." And Uncle Claude turned to her and smiled.

But Mrs. Fawcett, to whom actually the minister's handling of dead animals was extremely repugnant, told her not to interrupt and she asked what on earth he had done since obviously one could not substitute an auk's eyes for a vulture's eyes. He answered that he had sent them back and would, until the "genuine article" arrived, work on a gopher which Kenneth Taliafero had brought him. At this mention of her lover's name, Rachel giggled. Mr. Follansbee reached across the table and delicately pulled her hair. *Oh, stop it!* thought Ralph.

The meal progressed as if the silent outlander were not there. Leah and Rachel, interrogated by the minister, showed their wares boldly. Yes, indeed, they surely *were* glad they were going to boarding school next year in New Haven where they would have an opportunity to study French and music, but most of all to study elocution under someone of more gumption than the rather ungifted and certainly homely Mrs. Sawhill to whom they went on Saturday afternoon after their dancing lesson with the equally uninspired but less plain Miss Lanier. Both the minister and his wife laughed happily when Rachel, speaking of Mrs. Sawhill, said, "And I never can keep my mind on the piece I'm speaking because she mouths the words and I'm afraid her false teeth are going to fall right out because they do wobble so." Leah, not to be outdone, said of Miss Lanier, "Yes, but that's not half as bad as in ballet when she takes off her slipper and rubs her *bunion.*" It was said that Mrs. Fawcett was brave to let her little girls go all the way across the country even though Aunt Rowena would be near them to keep an eye on them. It was observed by the girls that they were already homesick.

Molly bubbled her water and said, "A child in my grade has the itch."

"Molly," said her mother, vigorously shaking her head. "Shame on you." Everyone ignored the impossible child.

A hideous accident attended the serving of the dessert. Uncle Claude had failed to remove his finger bowl from his plate and when Fuschia brought around the raspberry ice, he put his portion into the water, splashing it on the table. Leah and Rachel could not contain themselves any longer and burst into laughter. To double his humiliation the others chose pointedly to pay no attention to the calamity and Mrs. Fawcett, in a flash of venomous discourtesy, said, "I declare I do not understand why these girls can suddenly laugh their heads off at nothing at all."

Ralph felt physically sick and was afraid that if the meal did not end quickly he might disgrace himself right there at the table. Never had he so passionately despised Mr. Follansbee's cruel, smug face, his pince-nez on a black ribbon, the effeminate white piping of his vest. Grandpa Kenyon had, next to merchants, disliked clergymen more than any other people, and Ralph agreed with him, for he was sure they were all like Mr. Follansbee. Grandpa's shillelagh had been sent to him from Cork by his brother who was a clergyman and who "had undertaken to preach the Gospel English style to those poor backward natives." By the way he said it, the children knew that he did not think the Irish were poor and backward at all and that he was really making fun of his brother. He had another brother who was also a clergyman, a missionary in China, and his sister Nan was an Anglican nun. Mrs. Fawcett always told him, before the Follansbees came to the buffet supper, that it would perhaps be just as well for him not to mention his brothers and sisters as Mr. Follansbee had very decided opinions on anything the least bit Romish. She was afraid he was secretly displeased that her land adjoined that of the Freudenburgs who were Romans and went in for all kinds of superstitions like fish on Friday and statues of the virgin on top of the piano. Ralph wondered if Schöneshund had to eat fish on Friday too. Probably they gave him potatoes instead.

The horrible pastor looked at Ralph and for some reason winked his light green, reptilian eye. The boy trembled and looked away and this time glanced with ardent loathing at Mrs. Follansbee's round puffy face whose vulgar snub nose complemented her husband's downward curving one. He particularly hated her nose because she had chronic catarrh and tried, because of it, to identify herself with him and Molly who were similarly afflicted. While she was therefore ostensibly becoming their contemporary, she spoke of their kinship in baby talk and in the loud voice ladies used in addressing servants and foreigners. The only thing that could be said in her favor was that she did not talk as much as her husband. Otherwise, she was just as bad, and Ralph wished both of them would get bubonic plague.

"Who has the itch?" he suddenly asked Molly.

"Ralph!" cried Mrs. Fawcett. "This is not to be discussed at the table."

But Molly said, "Beulah. The one that stole my nickel."

"That will be enough, Molly," said Mrs. Fawcett. She dipped her fingers into the crystal bowl of water and dried them on her napkin and everyone did the same except Uncle Claude who could not wash in his dessert. Ralph's nausea and resentment ebbed. In a moment it would be over. There would only be two more meals and the Follansbees wouldn't be at those. While he wanted Uncle Claude to like him, he was glad that he was leaving the next day so that Leah and Rachel would stop giggling at his wrong clothes and his table manners and his language. He was determined not to let him go, though, without explaining to him that he and Molly were different from the rest of the family. And there was another thing: there were the presents Grandpa had not given them, so now they would really be Uncle Claude's presents. But how could he ask for them? Again he wondered if he could tell the joke about the cow, but it did not seem quite right; Uncle Claude seemed too serious even though he had smiled at Molly when she recited the alphabet thing.

After lunch it was suggested that Uncle Claude would like to take a nap for he had really had no rest at all since he left home. The fact that he had unaccountably come all the way from Denver by day coach was not alluded to before the Follansbees. The minister, who was the host in any house he entered, thought a game of Twenty Questions would be as decorous an amusement as any; Mrs. Fawcett, agreeing, said that afterward Leah and Rachel could recite their new Scottish dialogue. They sauntered slowly to the parlor, Molly and Ralph and Uncle Claude at the rear. As Uncle Claude turned toward the stairs he said, "If that Beulah stole your nickel, it serves her right to have the itch."

Most of the flowers had been taken out of the parlor and laid on Grandpa's grave, but the air was still heavy with fragrance. The room was altered. Although nothing had been moved or added, it was not the same place it had been before, and Ralph could not imagine the ladies of the Sorosis sitting here eating ice cream in tiny bites off the tip end of their spoons and talking, giving prices, of the January white sales in Los Angeles. But no one else appeared aware of the transformation. They all picked their chairs and settled down and looked around as if nothing at all had happened, as if the long old dead man had not been here just a few hours before. For a little while no one spoke: it was as if they were all consciously digesting their lunch. They heard Uncle Claude move down the ell, quietly like a dog. It was warm so Mrs. Fawcett took off her black broadcloth jacket. She wore a pink crepe-de-Chine guimpe through which showed the deep lace yoke of her camisole, and at her throat she wore a cameo brooch which Grandpa Kenyon had given her as an engagement present. She did not especially like it, finding it too large to be really refined, but she had often worn it during his visits.

"Well," said Mr. Follansbee at last. Ralph, closing his eyes, could believe that they were in church and that Mr. Follansbee was standing before the pulpit while the deacons, Mr. Brewster and Mr. Prater, sat behind him, monumental, bald, inexorably dull, looking very much like Grandfather Bonney. The sermon presently would begin; his voice always trailed dramatically down at the end of every sentence during the last twenty minutes so that you were deceived a hundred times, thinking he was nearly through. He was not quite ready for his flock to play Twenty Questions. Instead, looking up at the portrait, he made an astonishing statement. He said, "Well, Ralph, my boy, it wouldn't be hard to imagine *him* as the President of the United States, would it?"

Ralph was too dumfounded to reply and Leah said, "It certainly wouldn't, Mr. Follansbee. Why do you suppose he never was?"

Mrs. Fawcett touched her point-lace handkerchief to her eyes. There promised to be a scene of sadness and memory but Rachel, who had been seized all day with the giggles, prevented it by giggling, burying her head in Leah's shoulder, and saying in a stage whisper, "Imagine Grandpa Kenyon as the President, though!" Leah said, laughing, "Now you just stop it, you horrid girl." But Rachel could not stop and she went on conjecturing how the Senate would like it when Mr. Kenyon said, "By the Lord Harry," and how funny he would look in a top hat like Mr. Harding's. The grown-ups pretended not to hear, but they were smiling all the same at the wicked, witty little girl. Ralph and Molly, side by side on a hassock, kept a glum silence until at last Ralph said bitterly, "Nobody but a boob would want to be the President."

It was the first time in his life that he had ever shown temper in the presence of anyone but his immediate family, and it gave him a feeling of lunatic power. Rachel looked slapped. His mother, most likely deep in a dream of boating parties on the Potomac and picnics on the White House lawn, looked at him reproachfully. The minister, unaccustomed to having his speculations rejected, arranged his cunning, vulpine face to give him his comeuppance, but Ralph got ahead of him. He said: "Did you know that Grandpa Kenyon killed a man once, Mr. Follansbee?"

Mrs. Fawcett said, "You poor silly it! You should never take any of Mr. Kenyon's stories seriously. He was only telling you a western yarn, Ralphie boy."

Mr. Follansbee could scarcely conceal his curiosity, but he said, "They are the salt of the earth, those tale-tellers. The farther they get from the truth, the better the tale."

"Oh, no, this wasn't a made-up one," insisted Ralph. "Grandpa really did kill a man. Probably more than one, I guess, but I only know just about this one."

The man folded his hands and slightly teetered on his chair and said indulgently, "Let's hear this true confession, laddie."

"Oh! Do you think it's right?" asked Mrs. Follansbee and her pop eyes strayed to the place where the coffin had so recently been. "Don't you think it seems a little disrespectful?" But her husband, quoting in his brief homily from "Some Starbeams of Solace," assured them all that the deceased would have enjoyed this himself.

Ralph began with self-assurance, but it waned as he went on. He could not tell the tale as Grandpa told it: he himself was shocked and disbelieving and could not recapture the feeling of wonder he had known that day the year before when he and Molly and Grandpa had sat together under a tree in the grove. He had been telling them that when he had been in Texas the week before he had had to take measures about some sheep that had got into his pastures and that he had not a bit liked to blow those little lambs to glory, one in particular that he would have liked to bring to Molly. Ralph immediately saw the lamb that Jesus carried in the Bible picture, one awkward leg hanging over His arm. Molly said, "Then why *did* you blow the lamb to glory, Grandpa?" And the old man answered, "Well, I'll tell you, Molly. I'd rather kill the sheep than kill the shepherd."

He stopped to light his pipe. They were far from the nut gatherers now, at the north end of the grove where the trees had been stripped and the ground gleaned. There was an acrid smell everywhere of the splitting hulls and the bleaching acids.

Ralph said, "Did you ever kill a shepherd?"

"Yes, sir," said Grandpa. "I own I did."

As he told his story, Ralph could see him, a young man, riding like the wind through the dark Texas night, his money belt full of silver and gold, his twin revolvers ready to be drawn. Months before he and his outfit had driven a shipment of steers to Dodge City and he was coming back home again. He had left the train at Amarillo and had come horseback the remaining fourteen miles. "My horse was called Pearl," he said, "and she was a dandy piece of jewelry." He had been in sight of his place and had seen a light in the bunkhouse, down in the hollow, some way off yet, when a couple of men had charged him suddenly, riding at a lope out from the shadows of a thicket of screwbean. There was no moon but the night was clear and he was able to tell who they were by the starlight. They were brothers by the name of MacNeill, not good Scotch, as the name sounded, but half-breed Creeks, murderous and thieving. There had been ill will between them and Kenyon for a long time, for they had used his land to pasture their flocks and if he or any of his men caught a MacNeill sheep there, they disposed of it after giving the boys good warning. In retaliation, the skalawags rustled his cattle. The pattern was an endless circle. As they came on him tonight—they must have heard somehow that he would be riding in alone and with tolerable money on his person—they fired into the air to frighten Pearl, for they were that underhanded: they wanted to unseat him and have him on the ground at their mercy. Grandpa did not wait to find out what their business was and he stuck to his saddle as if he were nailed to it, though his mare leaped in terror. He shot the taller of the two cleanly through the heart and the other turned yellow and rode off the way he had come, not even dismounting to pay his respects to his dead brother. Ralph remembered that, when he had finished, Molly had asked if in the morning the two ravens of the ballad Grandpa sometimes sang had come to pluck out the man's bonny blue eyes.

The way Grandpa had told it, it had taken a long while, fifteen minutes or more, but Ralph, half crying, took only two or three, and at the end he realized that he did not believe a word of it. Leah pursed her lips. "I don't think it's nice to make up stories about killing people. I think it's awful."

Ralph turned on her and with the maniac laugh he and Molly had invented, shouted, "You mean because Mother killed Grandfather Bonney?"

But suddenly a mocking bird, in this broad daylight, began to sing. Mrs. Fawcett clasped her hands together and said "Oh!" as if the sound hurt her. Her large diamond ring, in the gesture, came into a ray of sunlight and two green needles shot out from the stone. Then Mr. Follansbee was across the room in one stride, shaking Ralph's shoulder. "You little cad," he said between his teeth, "you get down on your knees and beg your mother's pardon. On your *knees.*"

For a moment he defied the minister by remaining motionless, but the long bony hand on his shoulder propelled him off the hassock and at last he knelt, not feeling sorry, feeling nothing but rage, as painful as a deep cut. He could not utter a word, though this delay was agonizing, and they were all watching him and they were all waiting. He could hear Mr. Follansbee breathing heavily. Then Molly, half under her breath, said "I wish you were a fairy, Mr. Follansbee." Rachel giggled, but Mr. Follansbee did not think this was funny and he snarled, "What's this? Why do you wish I were a fairy, young lady?" And Molly whispered with deadly hatred, "So you'd vanish."

And now he could speak. Now, with this ally beside him, kneeling and clutching his hand, he could tell the lie: "I'm sorry, Mother. Please forgive me, Mother." Molly said it after him in that queer, hoarse whisper in which she had insulted Mr. Follansbee.

Mrs. Fawcett patted his head, but she said firmly, "You may leave the room, Ralph." Molly did not get off so lightly. Mrs. Fawcett slapped her face, not hard, but so that it made a sound. "Mr. Follansbee will never want to come to our house again after this terrible thing you have said. You may go ask Fuschia to lock you in the closet."

Ralph did not go to his room which was directly over the parlor but to Molly's. On the little white desk under the window she had laid out the presents from Grandpa Kenyon in the order in which he had given them to her: a doll made of straw with a sombero that could be taken off; a suède bookmark with a burned-in design of yucca; a pair of bearskin slippers which were now too small; a totem pole, three inches high which listed like the leaning tower of Pisa; a jewel box made of fragrant lemon wood and carved all over with squash blossoms; a beaded belt. Ralph touched them, one by one, and thought of his sister standing in the dark in the coat closet which smelled of naphtha and of buttons. His anger had given way to fear, to the fear of the sermon Mr. Follansbee would preach next Sunday, two days away. They always sat in the very front so that there was no escaping his darting eyes and you had to pay attention every minute, even when you had a hangnail or something like that to play with.

There was a copy of "Gravel" on Molly's desk and he read it again and *still* it didn't make any sense to him. There was also a letter which she had written to their cousin Mildred whom she did not like at all but to whom she wrote once a week because Mildred had sent her some stationery for her birthday. Ralph read it even though he knew it was against the law to read other people's mail.

Dear Mildred.

How are you? I am fine and hope you are the same. How are you getting along in school? Do you think long devision is hard? I do.

The Snake and the File

A snake one day crept into a blake-smiths shop and chaunced to knock against a steel file. This hurt the snake slightly, and, flying into a rage, he at once bit the file as hard as he could. The hard steel file cut the snake mouth, but when he saw the blood he though it was the file that bled, and so he bit it again and again until he had damage his own mouth very badly.

When we try to hurt other people we are much more likely to get hurt ourself.

Isn't that a funny story?

I guess that is all I can say so I will close your cousin.

Molly F.

He put the letter down, baffled. Molly was going crazy, he decided, and the thought made him nervous. If it were true, that was all the more reason he should get to be Uncle Claude's best friend, because if they had to take her to an asylum, he certainly wouldn't stay around here with those women; he would have to go to Colorado. He wanted to go into Uncle Claude's room, but he might be asleep and if Ralph woke him up, he might be angry; on the other hand if he were just sitting there, thinking of Grandpa, perhaps he would be glad to have company. He debated, looking at Molly's presents. Soon he heard them all go out to the front porch and almost immediately Leah and Rachel began their recitation. Now and again the grown-ups laughed and then, when they had quieted down, the girls went on.

74

It was about a girl and a boy named Jock and Jean and at the end of it, they would sing "Comin' Through the Rye." He felt suddenly that he could not bear to hear the song which always reminded him of the time Miss Runyon had come over to play Snap with them and at the end of the evening sang that song in a trembly voice and to make it all the more terrible, there was a piece of fudge on her front tooth. Hearing more laughter from the porch, he got up and went down the corridor to the ell.

Ralph was surprised to see that the door of the guest room was open and Uncle Claude was lying in the middle of the double bed flat on his back with his arms straight at his sides. He had taken off his bright orange oxfords and his coat so that Ralph could see the black and green horsehair belt; it had a design like a snake's back. The shades were drawn. Grandpa's grip was still on the luggage stand and Uncle Claude's small Boston bag, unopened, stood in the middle of the floor. A cigarette was burning in the pin tray on the dresser.

As he stepped across the threshold, Ralph was uneasy and he would have gone back to Molly's room if his uncle had not heard him and jerked up on his elbow.

"Your door was open," he said.

"You can close it now," said Uncle Claude.

Ralph hesitated, his hand wetly grasping the doorknob. "With me outside or in?" he asked.

"Suit yourself."

He went into the room and closed the door. Something inside him twitched like a cat's tail and he was afraid he might have a nosebleed. Fuschia and Miguel were having their lunch in the kitchen directly below the guest room and he heard a soft and urgent conversation. It was possible here only to hear the voices on the front porch as an uneven murmur; he was sure Uncle Claude had not heard what had happened in the parlor. Desperately he looked around the room: "Oh! Can I bring you your cigarette, Uncle Claude?"

His uncle got up and went over to the bureau and brushed his hair with two military brushes that had belonged to Ralph's father. He wore his hair parted in the middle and slicked down on either side. He ground out the cigarette and lighted a fresh one and then he sat down in the white rocking chair by the window and said, "Is this the room where he died?"

"Oh, yes," said Ralph. "Don't you see his grip still here?"

"I know," said Uncle Claude. "I thought maybe your mother just put it here to make me feel at home."

He was scrutinizing Ralph now and Ralph knew what he saw: a thin, sallow creature with his knickers hanging down to the middle of his spindling legs, hideous braces on hideous teeth, glasses that made him look ninety-nine years old. He felt that he must quickly speak before his uncle passed judgment on him and denied him permanently, but he could think of nothing to say. It would be unkind to tell him what it had been like when Grandpa had had his attack; it would be useless to apologize for his sisters and his mother and Mr. and Mrs. Follansbee; what was there to say? Finally, in a thin, singsong voice he told Uncle Claude the joke about the cow, realizing with each word that it was not a bit funny, just as he had known a little while ago that Grandpa's story about the MacNeills was not true. He did not even finish telling it, and when his voice trailed off, Uncle Claude did not even pay any attention so that Ralph knew he had not been listening.

After a long while, Uncle Claude said, "My father thought a lot of you. He was always saying he wished you'd come to visit me on my place." Then, with a smile which disarmed Ralph so that he nearly cried, he added, "But I guess you wasn't of the same mind."

"My mother . . ." Ralph began.

"Oh, well, hell," said Uncle Claude. He had a funny way of smoking. He drew so deeply that the ember took great bites in the paper. Ralph remembered evenings when Grandpa had sat on the porch smoking and the glow in the bowl of his pipe went on and off like a firefly. Uncle Claude said, "She never got over that about horses, did she? She would of kept me off 'em if she'd of had her way. But Mr. Kenyon was stronger minded than her."

"Well, I guess she worried, you know, about riding a horse and Grandfather getting the infection while he was watching her." He made his voice tentative. He did not really wish to be disloyal and so he said, "I don't really think she killed him, though, do you?"

"Jesus," said Uncle Claude. He sounded tired. In a minute he said, "What do you do around here to keep busy?"

There was very little they did that would interest Uncle Claude. They were not allowed to climb trees because splinters had been known to get into the bloodstream and travel to the heart. They did not have bicycles and they were not allowed to build things (the very thought of a nail brought tears to their mother's splendid blue eyes) nor to have roller skates or wagons. The girls played jacks and had all sorts of silly different kinds of games called "Dropsies" and "Allsies" and "Cart before the horse." He did not think that Uncle Claude would be interested in knowing that the most exciting thing he and Molly did was to watch Miguel harness the team; if Star and Swanee offered any resistance and tossed their heads, the Mexican slapped them on the nose with his gloves or gave them a wallop on the rump. He was not in the least afraid, even when they neighed at him angrily and their velvety lips rolled up, showing green teeth and a line of grass-stained foam on the underjaw.

And Ralph was sure that Uncle Claude did not want to hear about their indoor pastimes. They had sets of water colors and boxes of plasticine and Mrs. Fawcett guided their fingers so expertly and so patiently that the results made everyone believe the children were unusually gifted. In the evenings and on rainy afternoons she played games with them. They played "Lotto" and "Authors" and "Parchesi" and "I Spy," all of which Grandfather Bonney had enjoyed. Sometimes she read aloud to them from *The Little Shepherd of Kingdom Come, Sevenoaks,* and *The Old Curiosity Shop.* When it was cool enough for a fire in the fireplace, they popped corn over the flames while the Edison played records of Grandfather Bonney's favorite songs: "The Green Hills of Home," "All Through the Night," "Old Black Joe," and "I Dreamt That I Dwelt in Marble Halls." All of them, by the time they were six, could recite "The Brook" and "The Chambered Nautilus," and often they said them in unison, standing in a row in front of the bay window, their mother smiling proudly at them when she looked up from her crocheting. Leah and Rachel embroidered dresser scarves and tops for pincushions and talked in a grown-up way with their mother about clothes, to his and Molly's embarrassment. Once Mrs. Fawcett had said, "I am making some curtains for Molly's sitting room," and held up a pair of bloomers, right in front of Ralph.

Ralph could not possibly tell Uncle Claude what a sissy life he had to lead. But he had to say something and so, doubtfully, he began, "Well, Molly and I got sick last year—that's why we're so funny looking but Dr. Haskell says we'll outgrow it. I didn't used to look like this. . . ."

Uncle Claude said nothing, and there was no possible way to tell what he was thinking for he did not smile or frown or have any kind of look on his face at all.

"Anyway, we are too skinny or something to do anything much. We play mumbly-peg a lot . . . we do a lot of things. I'm in the Yosemite Patrol. I'm going to tie knots at the Jamboree next spring."

Why had Uncle Claude asked if he wasn't going to listen? He went back to the bed and lay down in the same position Ralph had found him in.

"Don't you feel well, Uncle Claude?"

"I don't know."

"Did you ever hunt savage animals, Uncle Claude?"

"You mean like tigers?" he said. "Or do you mean like deer?"

"Either kind," said Ralph.

Uncle Claude narrowed his eyes reflectively. "I get me a deer now and again, but a man couldn't call a deer a savage animal. I never seen a bear or a mountain lion. The chances are they might put up a fight if you didn't hunt them just according to Hoyle."

"Is a mountain lion really savage?" said Ralph.

"Why, son, if you was a setting hen, he'd tear you limb from limb," said Uncle Claude and laughed.

A fat autumn fly thumped and fretted against the screen.

"Uncle Claude?" He put his hand out and touched the handle of Grandpa's grip. "Uncle Claude, I think that maybe there's something that belongs to me in here."

Uncle Claude did not open his eyes but he smiled and said, "Sure, help yourself."

The catches sprung back easily and the mouth of the grip gaped wide, showing the familiar gray wads of clothing, a suit of winter underwear, nearly black around the neck, a few blue work shirts, a pair of denim overalls. Ralph took out everything and shook it and looked in the pockets and in the toes of the socks, but there were no presents. He came finally to the bottom where Grandpa's big blue-black revolver lay, and though he again shook each garment as he put it back in, he found nothing but Grandpa's own belongings. So what had happened? Had he felt bad in Texas, too bad to go to Mexico? You would think that in that case he would at least have brought some rattles off a rattlesnake. It was incredible and it gave him a creepy feeling, knowing that this autumn they had been far from Grandpa's thoughts. And now he could not make Uncle Claude include him in *his* thoughts: he wondered suddenly if anyone in the world were thinking about him, Ralph Fawcett, at this moment. If anyone was, it was Molly sitting on top of the galoshes in the closet. For some reason he thought of the crazy pilot banking his plane like a hawk and he said to himself, "Pilot, whoever you are, I am thinking about you."

"Do you want to hear something funny, Uncle Claude?"

Uncle Claude shrugged his shoulders. "I'd just as soon."

"Well, the other day, I went to get some brown sugar and I put a whole lot of it in my mouth and it wasn't brown sugar at all. I'll give you three guesses what it was."

"Corn meal," said Uncle Claude.

"No, no. I mean it looked like brown sugar all right."

Uncle Claude next guessed dried milk and oatmeal even though Ralph had explained that it had *looked* like brown sugar.

"It was nitrate fertilizer that Miguel had got to put on the four-o'clocks!"

Uncle Claude chuckled. At last Ralph had won. Pleased as he was, he was a little disquieted because this had happened to Molly, not to himself, so he quickly said, "But don't tell anybody because it would make Mother mad."

"I won't breathe it to a living soul," said Uncle Claude. "You know it's a funny thing. At lunch I was just thinking about the time Mr. Kenyon got this here impetigo and then your sister said Beulah had the itch."

Why, he was wonderful! He didn't talk like the usual kind of grown-up at all. Ralph thought he was probably sincerely glad that Beulah got what she deserved for stealing Molly's nickel. He said, "I like you, Uncle Claude."

Uncle Claude stretched out his hand, beckoning to him. "I like you, too, Ralph." Then he lay down beside his uncle, careful not to touch him. They lay there for a long time, dozing and waking. In all that time, Uncle Claude did not say a word, but twice he put his hand on the boy's thin shoulder. For the first time in days Ralph was free of the

81

smell of flowers. Uncle Claude had a smell something like Grandpa's but it was younger and had less raisin in it, perhaps because he smoked cigarettes and his father had smoked a pipe.

Soon after they heard Mr. Follansbee cranking his car and driving off, Uncle Claude sat up and yawned and said, "You come on out next summer to my place and bring What'shername along."

"Well, I don't know if Molly can come. I think maybe something is going to happen to her."

"Like what? Is she going to have her adenoids out?"

"No. They're already out. I mean . . . well, Uncle Claude, strictly speaking, I think Molly's going crazy." Then he recited "Gravel" which he had read so many times that he knew it by heart.

Uncle Claude laughed but he was puzzled too and he said, "I wouldn't worry if I was you. I always did think that the folks that wrote poems were bughouse but harmless. No, you bring her along."

Ralph sucked at a wart on the heel of his hand, at first refusing the daydream, but he could not hold out against it and he allowed it to overtake him and to crowd from his mind all else: Grandpa's neverness, the sermon next Sunday, the darkness of the coat closet, the embarrassment of the meal they soon would eat.

When his mother called to him from the foot of the stairs, he left his shoes where he had put them, right beside the orange oxfords. But once again, when he had closed the door, the smell of flowers greeted him like an ocean wave. He moved toward his mother, toward Leah and Rachel,

82

toward the portrait in the parlor. She called again sharply, "Ralph! How many times must I ask you to come downstairs."

"Hush," he whispered, leaning over the banister. "Don't you know Grandpa's dead?"

# CHAPTER FOUR

THE BIG DINING ROOM WAS DIM BECAUSE A HOP VINE GREW over the windows. The foreman, the six hands, Mrs. Brotherman and her daughter, Winifred, Uncle Claude, and the Fawcett children all sat at one long narrow table which was covered with mottled red linoleum. In one corner of the room stood a gun cabinet which looked like an upended coffin and showed, in this half-light, the blue glint of a dozen barrels. On the long wall behind Uncle Claude, casting an enormous shadow of itself, was the head of a bighorn. The horns, like white half-moons, curled rakishly away from the stupid and dignified face; it did not look dead but only despondent, unlike the head of the doe in Mr. Fawcett's den which Mr. Follansbee had once said looked more embalmed than stuffed. Ralph realized that this was the first dining room he had ever seen in which there was not a still life of fruits or fish or a rare roast of beef. From this eccentric omission, he proceeded to observe other peculiarities: the knives and forks did not match and the dishes did not all have the same design; the spoons were in a tumbler in the middle of the table.

The men ate quickly and efficiently, bending their heads

low over their plates and not straightening up even when they spoke. The girl, Winifred, who sat nearest the kitchen door, kept a close vigil on the dishes and took them away the moment she saw they were empty and brought them back refilled. The food was strange and Ralph and Molly ate with mistrust. There was strong, tough meat which Uncle Claude told them was "buckskin." Too tongue-tied to ask what he meant by that, they listened for a clue and finally got it when Mrs. Brotherman made the chance remark that this was the last of the deer. There were string beans cooked until they were almost brown and there was fried mush with gravy. At either end of the table stood a quart can of strawberry jam and the men took out tablespoonfuls of it and ate it with their forks. Globules of cream floated on the top of Ralph's glass of milk and he could not drink it. Before each plate was a smaller plate with the dessert, a fried pie which was shaped like a rubber heel.

No one took any heed of the newcomers; perhaps they were as shy of the children as the children were of them, and Ralph and Molly endeavored to be as silent and small as possible and did not look around save when the talk was general and the speakers were off their guard. Ralph's first impression was that all these men were the same size and shape and color, that they were all large, spare, and red-brown, and this, in general, was true, but as the meal progressed, he saw that one of them was very blond, that another was handsome and had auburn hair, that a third had a flattened nose like a prize fighter's. Similarly, their voices had at first seemed indistinguishable from one another but in time he heard variations in the timbre and even, slightly, in the accents.

The talk was endless but it seemed to be made up almost altogether of non sequiturs. The men did not interrupt one another, but they did not listen. Questions were answered, but were usually reshaped to fit a statement that was uppermost in the speaker's mind. At the very beginning of the meal, Uncle Claude asked Homer Armitage, the foreman, if he thought it might not be a good idea to put in a strip of electric fence along the pasture where he kept one of his prize bulls, and Homer replied, "I never was a man for electric fence. If the current goes off, where are you? Old man Terry put some in once but I don't know if it was ever worth the money or not. Don't remember ever hearing anything more about it, only just that he put it in. I seen old man Terry today and he said he seen elk sign half a mile this side Wolf Forks. He said it was as clean as a whistle, and I aim to go up there this coming Sunday if the weather's good."

Uncle Claude and Homer retired into silence, the one to think of electric fence, the other of his hunting trip. Then one of the hands, who was named Dump, said, in the direction of Homer who was now bowed over his plate, "Bernard Tobey's got his still up there to Wolf Forks."

The man next to him said, "I knew Bernard Tobey in Glenwood. He was a barber there. I guess he got tired of drinking bay rum."

"Some people like Tobey and some don't," said Dump. "One that don't is Agnew Prescott. Those two hate each other like poison and have for a dog's age."

"Kenyon," said another man, "did you hear that Prescott took his bulls out to Denver last night?"

"No, I never heard that," said Uncle Claude. "I ain't tak-

ing any of mine till fall. I'm studying on whether I ought
to sell Advance Anxiety."

Homer exclaimed with surprise and alarm, "Why, you
must be touched! Why, my God, he's the best bull you ever
had on this place."

Uncle Claude said, "You may be right. I reckon I won't
sell him. I wonder if it wouldn't be kind of a good idea
to put up a strip of electric fence around that pasture where
I got him."

They had all been to a horse sale that afternoon, but each
man made a different report. None of them had seen the
same people or the same horses and none had heard the
same bids, so that it sounded as if there had been eight different auctions in eight different places. And yet each knew
what the others were talking about. Homer, who had not
known that the blue-eyed stallion had been sold to a dude
for seven thousand dollars—though, from Uncle Claude's
account, this must have been the high note of the afternoon
—said, "You mean that ugly old paint that Bill Prescott sold
to Roger Campbell here awhile back? You mean that colt
that was that little wild mare's, that one B. F. Ward got in
Idaho?" They all knew the names and the lineage of all the
horses in the country and they spoke of them as if they were
people in the way, Ralph thought, fishermen would speak
of boats. They talked of Ruth, the cow pony whose master
had once hitched her up with a team horse when his other
team horse had lost a shoe; of Poncho, a dandy little chestnut who had thrown Prescott once when he was three sheets
to the wind; of Meadowlark who was herself an ugly piece
of business but had foaled two good colts.

The children were tired from the long, halting journey

over the mountains from Denver where they had parted from their tearful mother. The train had not been like any they had ever been on before. Instead of little rooms with white towels on the backs of the seats and a little shelf by the window where the porter put the glasses of lemonade, there were just rows of bronze-green seats which were straight up and down and so hard you felt after a while your bones were going to come right through. The windows were dirty and the car was full of smoke. All the towns they passed through, pausing for a long time while freight was unloaded, were exactly the same. The buildings along the wooden walks had high square façades and on them, in faded letters, were printed "Livery," "Odd Fellows' Hall," "Assayor's Office." Undernourished dogs meandered about the streets looking for food in the ruts they already knew by heart. There seemed to be no trees in any of the towns, though the great shaggy mountains beyond were densely forested. The train had labored up and up, going right through the mountains, through tunnels too many to count. They spoke very little but each was conscious of the other's misgivings, and they did not eat any of the Martha Washington candy their mother had bought for them. Once Molly almost cried when they had stopped at a town called Blackriver and a man with a bandanna around his neck looked right in the window at them and then turned and spit tobacco juice at a cat. She felt the same surprise and anxiety as she had one morning when she woke up and saw a grasshopper on her pillow, looking at her.

They were bedazzled by the mountains and the ranch. They had not bargained for anything on so large a scale; it seemed beyond their compassing and they had already begun to withdraw. Ralph looked at the guns in the cabinet, so much bigger than he had imagined them to be from the catalogues, and now, while the whole point of coming had been to learn how to ride horseback, he was afraid. For months he and Molly had planned how they would defy their mother's injunctions ("If there is a Shetland pony there, you may ride that if someone is with you," she had said. A Shetland pony, indeed!) and how they would disobey Mrs. Brotherman who, through frequent letters, had promised that she would exercise the most stringent discipline to keep the children away from guns and horses. The moment they had met the sad, mild-mannered housekeeper, they had known that she could easily be shaken from her resolution and this, in itself, was enough to cloud their passion. Yet, though they no longer felt daring but on the contrary were afraid, there was no waning of their determination. They knew, both of them, that they would try to escape, would invent headaches, would have nosebleeds, would hide behind books, but they would not, in the end, successfully evade Uncle Claude; they were bound to learn.

It was the presence of the genteel Mrs. Brotherman that had finally persuaded Mrs. Fawcett to allow Ralph and Molly to come to the ranch. They had given her no peace after Claude had left and had had tantrums whenever she suggested the alternatives of Puget Sound or Lake Tahoe, and then, when Dr. Haskell said he thought the mountain air might be good for their catarrh, she finally wrote to her half-brother, inquiring whether he had any trustworthy womenfolk in his house who could watch out for the children's baths and clean underwear and health. She put faith in Mrs. Brotherman because she was from Salem, Massachusetts, and Grandfather Bonney had been born in Boston. Besides this, Mrs. Brotherman was herself a mother and a widow and could be expected, therefore, to be more responsible than a spinster or a woman with a husband.

Ralph and Molly had been prepared to dislike and mutiny against the housekeeper. They saw her as a stout, ill-natured and red-faced woman with all the power and habits of a school principal, so that this afternoon they had been astonished and almost disappointed to find her a fragile, dispirited gentlewoman who appeared to find everything in the world immeasurably sad and who spoke mostly in the past tense. She did not say, "I think you will want to wash before supper," but "I thought you would want to wash." She was the widow of a Swedenborgian minister who had come West to die in the sun of tuberculosis. After his death, she had not gone East again because her daughter was said to have a "tendency." Winifred was fourteen, a tall and lovely girl who did not look in the least delicate. She was very brown and clear-eyed; she had thick dark hair which she wore short and which lay in tight little curls all over her head. She had her own horse, a sorrel gelding named Noel since he had been Grandpa Kenyon's Christmas present to her the year she was twelve. Grandpa Kenyon had given her silver mountings for the bridle and a crop made of snakeskin.

Winifred was the first of the household they had met. They had stood, begrimed with train smoke, miserable, already homesick, in the shadow of a cottonwood tree while Uncle Claude got their suitcases out of the back of the car. The ride from the station to the Bar K had been difficult; Uncle Claude had three times inquired after the health of their mother and sisters, twice had said he was glad to see them, and this, together with the children's monosyllabic replies, had constituted their conversation. Now, in the shade of the summery tree, they felt doomed to failure. Unable to take in the huge, snaggle-toothed mountain ranges that completely encircled the valley where the ranch lay, alarmed by the rapid rushing sound of the river which they could not see, frightened by the steady commotion of animal noises— cows bellowing, horses neighing, dogs barking, birds screaming—they had been glad to fix their attention on one single thing, the girl who came riding her horse across the bridge which spanned a slough to the west of the house. She dismounted quickly and looped the reins around the hitching post across the lane from where they stood and when she started forward Uncle Claude told them about Noel, as if this would establish a bond between her and Ralph and Molly. But the gleaming horse, stamping his delicate foot and flicking his handsome tail, made the presents Grandpa had given them seem paltry and perfunctory. However, Ralph remembered that Grandpa had wanted to bring him a monkey from Australia. So, in a moment, he shook hands with Winifred, noticing as he did so, with a shock of pleasure, that her blue jeans were stained with dung, and he thought with contempt of Leah and Rachel who had never got their clothes dirty in their lives.

"I'm mighty pleased to meet you," she said and smiled showing small, even teeth. Ralph and Molly were taken aback by her words and her slow, uninflected speech. They had been taught that the expression she had used was vulgar. You were supposed to say "How do you do."

Molly said loudly, "Who are you?"

The girl looked startled but she smiled again and said, "I'm Winifred Brotherman. I know who you are."

"I don't suppose you write poetry, do you?" said Molly. Ralph wished she would stop that kind of talk. She had recited "Gravel" to the conductor just as the train pulled out of Los Angeles and although he had smiled and said the poem was fine and dandy, it had been perfectly clear that he had not thought much of it.

"Why, no," said Winifred. "I reckon I don't. I've got to go now and get the cows."

She mounted and rode off, over the river this time. Ralph hoped that Molly and Winifred would be friends so that he could spend all his time with Uncle Claude, and when he had finished his unpacking he went into her room and said, "I think Winifred's peachy, don't you?" Molly replied, "She has Nell Brinkley hair," and said no more.

Now, watching Winifred as she moved from the kitchen to the dining room on silent moccasins, Ralph admired her and glancing sidelong, he saw that Molly, too, followed her with fascinated eyes. Suddenly a wave of pity for his sister came over him and he impulsively touched her hand which rested in her lap. His pity was focused on her clothes: she wore a flowered batiste dress with a full skirt, smocked at the waist and at the neck and the prettiness of it made even more ridiculous her thin, freckled arms, her ugly little face framed by black hair with which, Mrs. Fawcett often remarked, nothing could be done. Molly, at the touch of his hand, turned and looked him full in the face and smiled wistfully. Ralph met her eyes only for a moment and then looked away, looked at Uncle Claude and saw that he was watching them inquisitively; he read the look as a question of his worth or of his manliness, and abruptly, despite all these lean, red-faced strangers who, now that the meal was over were thoroughly picking their teeth, he said, "Uncle Claude, when are you going to teach me how to ride horseback?"

Mrs. Brotherman, putting her napkin in a bamboo napkin ring, gazed vaguely at the hop vines. His uncle smiled. It was again that winning, bone-enfeebling smile whose memory he had kept since last September; he was as friendly as a child and he said, "Is first thing tomorrow morning soon enough?" Then he got up and led the way into the living room, patting Ralph's shoulder as he went by. The others followed him in single file, all with a slouching gait as if they would otherwise be unsteady on their high-heeled boots. Ralph longed to join them but Mrs. Brotherman, in her unhappy way, said she was sure he and Molly were tired and should go to bed at once and Ralph realized that he was, indeed, so tired that he could hardly bear to think of going up the stairs and getting undressed.

Before he went to bed, he had a conference with Molly who came into his room and sat on a bench, hugging her knees. She had taken off her glasses and she looked like a black-eyed rabbit.

"Whoever heard of calling an animal Advance Anxiety?" she said.

"I thought of that, too," said Ralph. "But what would you do if you were a man and your name was Dump?"

"I would dump it."

"No, you would have to lump it."

They laughed, delighted with one another. Ralph had decided that Molly was not going crazy after all, although

93

there had been a period of a month during the winter when she thought she was going to be kidnapped and had worn a Hallowe'en mask in the school bus every day. She was just different from other people, he supposed. He liked her when they were alone, but she embarrassed him in public because she said such peculiar things. For instance, she said to Mrs. Brotherman this afternoon, "Do you have any opinion on the false Armistice?" and when Mrs. Brotherman said no, she really had not, Molly had said, "Oh, of course you don't live in California so you wouldn't have seen the Los Angeles *Gazette.*" What she was talking about was the old newspaper they had with the one word PEACE printed in letters four inches high on the front page, but how was Mrs. Brotherman to know?

"Do you like it here?" said Ralph.

"I don't know. I'll tell you later. I don't like the food, I must say. String beans are the bane of my existence."

"I liked the buckskin."

Molly frowned and said nothing for a moment and then she said, "You know, I don't think I'll learn to ride horseback tomorrow. I think I'll wait for a few days as I have an idea for a short story about an amateur kidnapper."

How he regretted his headlong contract with Uncle Claude! He heard a horse snorting in the pasture right under his windows and his hands turned as cold as ice.

"Darn you," he said angrily to Molly, "darn you to heck. You *always* make up an excuse." He knew he was quite unreasonable; Molly had said nothing about learning to ride, but it seemed so unfair that she could always get out of anything by saying she wanted to write something. "All right for you," he said, "if you don't come tomorrow, you can't ever come anywhere with me again."

"My literature is more important to me than you are, Ralph Fawcett," she said coldly and left the room, pausing in the doorway to make donkeys' ears and say "Hee haw."

For the first weeks of this first visit to Uncle Claude, Ralph and Molly were not happy and most of the time they were afraid. The landscape itself was frightening. Above timberline the snow was thick in the deep gashes; to the north were two long glaciers which sometimes shone pink through the haze; this pinkness came from bacteria which inhabited the glacier snow, and when he learned this Ralph was curiously disgusted, he did not know why. Below timberline and above the dry sagebrush of the foothills, the forests of conifers were dense, their dark blue-green here and there interrupted by a small grove of golden aspens or a bright upland meadow where Winifred often went to gather columbines. The mountains were at once remote—their summits were often enshrouded by clouds—and oppressively confining. The children had been used to summers at the seashore and the sea, even in a storm, was something that could be taken in at one glance; its evils, however, were quite hidden, so that sharks and sting-rays, hurricanes and calms seemed only legendary and needed not be reckoned in their impressions; and even when they went out in a glass-bottomed boat and saw the fish all golden and green and huge, looking up at the passengers, they did not feel any of this was real but was only like a movie.

But the mountains wore peril conspicuously on their horny faces. Through Uncle Claude's field glasses they could look

95

directly at the ledge from which a packhorse had slipped and fallen to her dreadful, screaming death. They knew the place where a bold dude had frozen in midsummer, having lost his way in a cloud when he was scaling an arête. The foothills were alive with rattlesnakes. At dawn the coyotes wakened them and through their windows they could see the small, shadowy sneak-thieves on the rim of the hill to the south of the house; the howling had a cold and beggarly sound, sometimes intolerably like an outraged human voice.

The house, spacious and rambling, made of white brick, faced north upon the fast stream called the Caribou River which cut the pasture land in half. On its banks grew cottonwoods and weeping willow trees, and dense amongst them, chokecherry and sarvis berry bushes. Here beavers made their clever dams and here hoot owls warned at night: there was no place that was not alive with something. A bridge led to the pasture on the other side of the river where the milk cows grazed and where there were cattails five feet high and where often the children saw blue herons. To the west was a broad, treeless field of timothy, bound on one side by the slough that ran along the red road; its west fence was parallel to the railroad track where the slow mixed train went past in the early evening, ringing its lonesome bell. The foothills leading to the summer range were to the south and the view of them was cut off through the lower windows of the house by a line of eight Lombardy poplars. Between the house and the road was the pasture, and the barn and the many sheds lay to the east.

Everything and all the people, with the exception of Mrs. Brotherman, made Ralph think of Grandpa, and he had the feeling that the old man's other ranches (which now

Uncle Claude would visit once a year in September) were similar, save that this was the only one in the mountains. The men were skillful, good-humored, hard, living within the present time and on a large scale. When they got drunk on a Saturday night, they did so with abandon, behaving exactly as drunk people in the movies did. Their lawlessness seemed natural. It seemed altogether reasonable that they hunted at all times except during the open season when, as Uncle Claude said, "there was too much danger of getting shot at by them dudes from Denver." The revenue officers and the game wardens intimidated no one; strangers to the country, they could not police all the hundreds of hiding places for stills in the mountains, nor could they catch the poachers who wanted wild meat and proposed to have it.

Ralph thought of the house in Covina with all its flurry of little objects, little vases and boxes on little gilt tables and whatnots hanging in the corners; and then thought of the big, bare rooms of the ranch where the furniture was heavy and solid as if it were nailed to the floor and the only small things were catalogues from L. L. Bean and Montgomery Ward, boxes of buckshot, fly-books, odd bits of leather and metal which had no use but which remained undisturbed, week after week, on the mantelpiece and the tables. He thought of the delicate food they had at home and then of the sage hen and puffballs and head cheese they had here, and Ralph felt that when Grandpa left them he must always have gone away hungry.

But the most amazing contrast of all was between Fuschia and Magdalene. Fuschia was young and pretty and good-natured but full of respect so that she called them "Miss Molly" and "Mr. Ralph." But Magdalene! She was the first

Negro besides Pullman porters they had ever seen up close. Molly was so frightened when the old woman took her hand in her skinny black one with its pink palm like a monkey's that she wanted to go home at once. Magdalene seemed hundreds of years old, so old that if she lived another century or two, she would not look any different. Her skin was not yellowish to show that she had white blood; it was rather as if it had faded to a bluish gray. Her lips were purple and they had so many lines that they looked like narrow grosgrain ribbons; her brown eyes were as mean and watchful as a chipmunk's, and the scraggly fuzz on her little head looked like dirty snow. She was not in the least kind; she was always smoldering with an inward rage or a vile amusement over something sexual or something unfortunate, and she spoke chiefly in obscene or blasphemous expletives. But she was wonderfully wise. She knew when it was going to rain and when someone was going to get sick and when a cow was going to get through a fence. Her wisdom was something antediluvian and cosmic and the almanac she went by dated back a million years before the fall of man. She was, Molly thought, the wife of the Skalawag at the Wash. She had her own little cabin between the barn and the bunkhouse and she raised white rabbits in a hutch beside it. No one ever saw the interior of it, but the children imagined that it must smell frightful, for not only were the rabbits so near, but she cooked strange things on her stove, things like beaver tails and the lungs and testicles of freshly butchered calves.

Up on a hillside, a mile behind the barn, Magdalene kept some goats of her own, milking them every morning before sunrise and again in the evening while the others were finishing their supper. One afternoon Ralph met her coming around the corner of the corral, carrying a dead and bleeding goat slung over her shoulder. In her free hand, she carried a small hatchet, bright with thick neck blood. Ralph asked her why she had killed her goat and she replied, "I was hongry, that's why, you lil ole June bug, so I went out and botched 'im on the haid." Uncle Claude could not remember where Grandpa Kenyon had found her, and she would never tell the children where she had lived before. When once they asked her where she had been raised, she said, "I wa'n't *raised*. A cow-bird laid me in the sagebrush and the sun hatched me out." They did know that she had two sons, named Salem and Jordan and a daughter named Psalmetta. Once Jordan sent her a bottle of Ben Hur perfume and while she laughed like a lunatic with contempt, she poured it all over herself and the kitchen reeked. It smelled like the cheap chocolates with pink fillings they got in Covina, four for a penny.

Magdalene's territory was the kitchen and she never went into the other part of the house, for besides bringing the food to the table, Winifred made the beds and did the cleaning. Magdalene did not like to have anyone fussing in her kitchen. She did not mind the men hanging up their chaps there or even having a cup of coffee in the middle of the morning if they were working around near the house; and she suffered Ralph and Molly to poke into the cupboards and watch her make pies so long as they did not ask for anything to eat, although occasionally she would give them bits of raw potato, always with the remark, "Knew a horse died of 'em." But she would not stand for Mrs. Brotherman, whom she called "Miz Bo-Bo" or "Miz Budmanny," or

Winifred to hover over her, and if, in the morning, she discovered that after she had gone to her cabin for the night someone had made fudge with her sugar in her pan on her stove, she swore a blue streak half the day through.

Molly got the idea that she looked like Magdalene and for some time thought that she was probably her daughter. She had never been at all certain about the circumstances of her infancy for Leah had told her that for the first years of her life she had been only the size of a talcum powder can and they had kept her on the mantel beside Grandfather Bonney's ashes. This was, of course, a big fat lie, but all the same there were some peculiar things about those early years. For example, she clearly remembered riding an elephant and the more she looked at her, the more certain she became that Magdalene had been the driver. But she did not ask her about it because Negroes were essentially the same as Mexicans and if you did not keep your distance from them there would be the dickens to pay. But she watched her and listened to her and in her diary she referred to her as "Mrs. Skalawag."

The one part of the ranch that was anything like home was Mrs. Brotherman's sitting room directly above the parlor. Mrs. Brotherman and her room always smelled of apples, giving the children a feeling of perennial Hallowe'en. Everywhere there were small baskets and bowls on the tables and hanging shelves, full of McIntoshes and winesaps and of Golden Grimes. As vivid as the smell, almost, was the sense of oldness in the room, coming from the furniture and the oddments and coming, as well, from Mrs. Brotherman's Boston accent and her strange syntax. Close as they lived to the Brothermans—the Fawcetts' rooms were across the hall

—they were invited so seldom into the sitting room that it always held an air of foreignness for them, and because they never got so used to it that they could take it for granted, the fruity fragrance always surprised them. So also did the coolness and the furniture which sat upon a dim cabbage-rose carpet, between walls on whose yellow paper were tidy rows of dark green laurel wreathes which cast oblique and questionable shadows. In the center of the room there was a large round table with a single stout leg. It was covered with a blue velours and the four corners hung straight to the floor, weighted and decorated with wiry gold tassels. On the table was an armadillo sewing basket which Ralph found so revolting that if Mrs. Brotherman asked him to fetch her scissors from it, he shuddered. There was a music box on the table which played first "O Mistress Mine" and then "Why Does Azure Deck the Sky?" There was a bust of Socrates on a shelf and a picture of George Washington over the fireplace. There were two wing chairs covered in chintz with tatted antimacassars on the arms and the backs, and there was a terrarium with a peaked roof in which grew brake fern, partridge berry, and wintergreen. She had a silver candle snuffer and a glazed bowl holding aromatic pine cones, a Van Briggle vase of everlastings, and a souvenir sofa pillow from the Garden of the Gods. There was nothing chipped or marred or stained or dusty; only time had altered the looks of things by draining away the colors as it had drained them away from Mrs. Brotherman's cheeks and hair and eyes. She was as secretive almost as Magdalene about her past life, but once, in a thin burst of expansiveness, she told them that before Winifred was born, she and Mr. Brotherman had gone to Manitou Springs for two weeks, and she showed them a photograph of herself and her husband, sitting on a rock, holding up two folding cups of mineral water. In the background was a cement pop bottle ten feet high. They both looked bleakly into the eyes of the camera. The children could tell by the looks of the narrow-faced and wasted man that he had been as sad as his wife; they concluded that she had been born that way and it was not her widowhood alone that had cast her into eternal twilight. They often spent hours with her helping her weed in her flower garden which was famous for its roses; she dried the petals for potpourri and gave them to the ladies who sometimes came to call in the hot afternoons to visit with her in her sitting room and drink iced tea and eat gingersnaps.

They liked Winifred more and more, although at the very beginning they had been in doubt about her because she had taken them swimming in the pool behind the barn and had said she was going in without her suit. But she didn't, of course, and after a while they realized she had only been teasing. They started a detective agency and found clues all through the foothills; they believed that Dump was running a gambling den in a gulch and they collected a great deal of evidence against him, but he outsmarted them all summer long.

Ralph could not make up his mind about Uncle Claude. One thing was certain, he was not as nice as Grandpa. He laughed unkindly at their blunders and told about them at the table. Once poor Molly asked who milked all the cows up on the range and he laughed so hard he made her cry. Mrs. Brotherman explained to her that this was a breeding ranch, not a dairy farm, but she was unconsoled and hated Uncle Claude for three days.

And still, he would occasionally give Ralph a friendly push or invite him to ride along with him in the pick-up to town, and when he did this he smiled with the same sort of generosity in his mobile face as Grandpa used to. The trips to town, though, were never a success. The sun was always so glaring on the asphalt that Uncle Claude was too preoccupied with his driving to talk, so Ralph stared at the fields where the whitefaced Herefords grazed and at the dreary, unpainted farmhouses that stood here and there along the road, unprotected by any tree, bleak and dusty in a grassless field. Then, on the way back, Uncle Claude was wrapped up in remembering what news he had heard in town and the purchases he had made, and while he was talkative enough then, Ralph was really not interested in learning that Bernard Tobey's horse had the sweeny or that Shorty Peterson had hired a Mormon kid who had been baptized a hundred and twenty-five times or that Roger Campbell, always as independent as a hog on ice, had refused to give back Claude's hackamore, maintaining that possession was nine-tenths of the law.

There were times when it seemed to Ralph that Uncle Claude was somehow trying to get even with his mother. Every time he took them riding, he would say, laughing as he got into his saddle, "I reckon your mother would have a set of dishes if she could see you now." It both thrilled and frightened them to think what she really would do, probably send them to the penitentiary. He and Molly rode only the oldest and safest horses, but something always went wrong. Uncle Claude told them that a horse had a sixth sense which could judge whether his rider was afraid and would, out of pure orneriness and show-off, play tricks on him if he were. So that the old white horse Eye-Opener whom Molly rode would pretend that he was half blind and would deliberately stumble into gopher holes so that she pitched forward, clinging desperately to the pommel with a flushed face and wide, staring eyes. And Studebaker, the black Ralph rode, refused to wade the streams. "Give him your spurs!" Uncle Claude would cry and Ralph would tentatively push his heels into the horse's flanks. "Harder! Give him something to think about!" So that Ralph would dig harder, driven by shame, mortally afraid of being thrown into the water. Then Studebaker, snorting, would fling back his head and rear so that Ralph had to rivet himself to the saddle to keep from falling; but he did not, like Molly, grasp the horn, for Winifred had told him that this was something only dudes did.

Although, more and more often, he enjoyed the rides through the ripe meadows and along the red roads, beside the river where the sarvis berry brushed its cinnamon-smelling flowers against his face, into the cow pasture as the sun was setting, Ralph did not outgrow his uneasiness at being so high off the ground and being dependent on so capricious an intelligence as that which lay in the long black head. And when he began to saddle his horse himself, it was hard to keep back the tears when he put the bit in Studebaker's enormous mouth with its enormous square teeth and yellow-green tongue. Uncle Claude occasionally praised him and his confidence grew, but he was so mean to Molly ("You set on that bench like a sack of potatoes," he would say to her) that she seldom went with them but stayed at home to help in the garden or to write. She was now writing an article for *Good Housekeeping* called "My Summer at the Bar K."

In the latter days of June a series of tragic accidents took place, following one another as if by a spiteful plan. A horse, frightened by the backfiring of a car, stumbled and fell on the rain-slick highway, breaking his leg and crushing the foot of his rider, Homer Armitage. Nauseated with pain, Armitage roused himself enough to shoot the horse and then lay half an hour in the road until a passing motorist found him. The men at the Bar K carried the dead horse in a truck up to the place where the coyotes gathered most often after they had robbed the henhouse, and they poisoned the meat with cyanide. Later, a magpie brought a chunk of the meat down into the yard where Uncle Claude's favorite dog, a beagle, found it, ate it, and died in convulsions. Ralph never forgot his uncle's rage when Magdalene brought him the news at dinner. He got up and went at once to the gun cabinet and then strode through the kitchen. Dump said, "I reckon he'll pick off a magpie. A man cain't blame him." Everyone was silent, waiting for the shot.

There was only one report from the .22, but Uncle Claude did not come back to his dinner, and someone said he had probably gone to bury the dog. When the meal was over, Ralph went out into the yard and there, beside the milk house, he saw nine magpies standing in a circle round a tenth which was dead. They were scolding in unison, their harsh, hawk-like voices clawing at the noontime quiet. Their impeccable feathers, coal-black and snow-white, gave them the look of professional mourners, formally attired. Ralph approached, but they did not fly away; instead, two turned and faced him, shrieking abuse and hopping with anger. Their racket continued until one of the men came out of the house and tramped through their circle to pick up the dead bird and fling it with disgust into the slough, crying back to the others, "Shut up, ya goddam buzzards." They left the ground then, but for a long while afterward sat in a neat row on the fence, remembering from time to time to mourn raucously.

Uncle Claude was mending fence today, Ralph knew, and after a decent time had elapsed, he got on Studebaker and set out for the farthest pasture, up behind the barn. He had hesitated as he mounted, partly because he had never ridden so far alone before, partly because he was not sure that he should intrude upon his uncle's sorrow, just as he had not been sure after Grandpa's funeral. But he thought that since the circumstances were so similar, they might again reach the same kind of amiable understanding they had done the other time.

It was hot in the sun and he had forgotten to bring his hat; the glare on the meadows was as blinding as if it shone on tin. There was a violet heat haze hiding the tops of the mountains toward which he rode. He was stupefied by the silence and by his solitude and by the even trotting of his horse who, today, behaved himself and even forded the river at the shallows with hardly any persuasion though Ralph, for an unseen audience, gave him his spurs and felt the rowels spin lightly against the tough flesh. Only once was he afraid, for it occurred to him that Uncle Claude might have finished the fence this morning and was mending somewhere else; the possibility of not fulfilling his mission made him uneasily self-conscious; he would feel like a sap when people asked him at supper where he'd been and he would have to say, "Oh, I just went for a ride," for no one here did anything without an end in view.

He ascended a ridge and then, across a wide field of alfalfa, he saw Falcon, his uncle's horse, cropping peaceably near the fence. Falcon, a young palomino and the handsomest horse on the place, was sought after by all the other horses, but he had singled out Studebaker as his particular friend and in the early evening, as soon as they were unsaddled, they trotted up the lane together and then went running up the road to disappear in the foothills. When they were pastured with other horses, they were stand-offish and if one of them came too near, Studebaker would rear up and kick the air with his hind legs.

Studebaker, catching sight of Falcon, neighed, his whole body shuddering with vibrations and then, though Ralph tightened the lines, he broke into a lope and then into a run. Ralph was claimed by the wildest terror he had ever known. The hot wind stung his cheeks and ears and his feet, flexing in the stirrups, his knees, hugging the horse, ached so intolerably he could have screamed with pain. Blinded by the speed and by the sun he could not see his uncle but he did see Falcon, huge, blond, his creamy mane waving, come running toward them, whinnying passionately. In his quick agony Ralph scanned the field in vain and screamed his uncle's name. Instantly from some place he could not determine, his uncle shouted "Falcon!" and the palomino slowed down with a final, disappointed whinny. But Studebaker paid no heed and raced on. Then Uncle Claude, appearing suddenly from nowhere, came running bare-headed across the field, hollering words Ralph could not understand, and when he was fifty feet from them, Studebaker changed his gait to a gallop, but swerved suddenly to avoid the man and in doing so, reared, not high but so abruptly and surprisingly that Ralph's feet flew out of the stirrups, his sweaty hands turned loose the lines and he went crashing down into the sweet, gentle clover, his glasses falling off to lie unharmed beside his nose. He closed his eyes and listened to the hooves retreating and the lunatic neighs saluting and responding, listened to his uncle approaching him on running feet: "You damned little numskull, are you hurt?"

He did not know whether he was hurt and he did not care now that he was safe on the ground, but the annoyance in Uncle Claude's voice wounded him. Uncle Claude knelt down beside him and Ralph opened his eyes. The sunburned, sharp-boned face was, when Ralph first looked at it, so stern that he thought, "Now he will send me back to Covina." But then the look gave way to that rare smile and Uncle Claude said, "You better see if you're hurt. You can't trust that fool bench when he's around my horse."

Ralph sat up cautiously and pulled up his Levis. His legs were not hurt except for a big bruise on his left knee. His elbow was skinned and there was a bump on his left temple, but these were his only injuries. He was giddy, though, and the meadow swam like fishes under the high sun; then he realized that his glasses had fallen off and he groped for them with both hands as if he could not see at all.

Uncle Claude found them for him and handing them over, said, "What's the matter with your eyes that you have to wear those things?"

"I don't know. I've always worn them ever since I had scarlet fever. The nosebleeds come from that, too."

"Will you always have to wear them?" There was a curious eagerness in his voice. This was the first really personal question he had ever asked Ralph.

He replied, "I don't know. Dr. Haskell never said."

Both he and Molly had grown so used to their glasses that they did not even mind particularly being called "Four Eyes" by other children; indeed, there were times when they took pleasure in their weakness which distinguished them from others and which served, as well, as an excuse for not playing baseball or pom-pom-pull-away at which, before scarlet fever, they had been so poor that they were the last to be chosen on a team.

"Well, you look a whole hell of a lot better without them," said Uncle Claude.

"Thank you," said Ralph, although he realized it had been what his mother would have called "a left-handed compliment."

"What did you come up here for anyway?"

"I came to see if I could help you bury Juanita," he said.

"Well, that was nice," said Uncle Claude and Ralph, once more unsure of himself—despite the smile—thought he used the word "nice" contemptuously. "It wasn't much of a job. She was a little dog."

"Ken Burkhardt threw the magpie you shot into the slough."

"Did he now?" said Uncle Claude, but he was preoccupied; Ralph could not get through. He remembered a time when he and Grandpa were in the grove one Sunday morning; for some reason he had not had to go to Sunday school and he was exuberant with a holiday feeling, but he could not make Grandpa talk to him. He asked for a story but the old man refused, not crossly but distractedly. Ralph had felt compelled to force him to talk and so he began to ask questions: Was it true that if you swallowed a lemon seed a lemon tree would grow in your stomach? Did he like Post Toasties? Had he ever seen a buffalo, not in a zoo? Did he not think that monkeys looked a lot like people? Did he have very many dreams? At first Grandpa had answered briefly, but not unkindly, but then suddenly he jabbed the ferrule of his shillelagh into the ground and said sharply, "Dammit, lad, can't you see I've got something on my mind?"

Today he felt that same compulsion, even when he remembered how hot and faint he had been after Grandpa's rebuke, and seeing his uncle light a cigarette and lie down full length in the alfalfa, covering his eyes with his handkerchief, he said, "Where did you bury her?"

"Yonder," said Uncle Claude vaguely motioning toward the river. "By the shallows."

"Oh! I must have passed the place."

There was a silence. Studebaker and Falcon had calmed down now and were cropping side by side in the middle of the meadow. It was not really silent; there was a steady undercurrent of the noises of the land, but they were so closely woven together that only a sudden sound, like the short singing of a meadowlark, made you realize that everywhere there was a humming and a rustling. And then, the separate sound, the song or a splashing in the river, was like a bright daub on a dun fabric.

Ralph said, "Are you going to get a new dog?"

"Sure, I'll get me a new dog. I'll miss that little old hound but I'm not a fellow that goes to the mope-house over a dog."

"What is a mope-house, Uncle Claude?"

"It's a place where the niggers go and mope when somebody dies."

Uncle Claude grew rather talkative after that. He told Ralph that there were towns in Oklahoma where only Negroes lived and at the outskirts there were signs saying "White man, get out of this town before sundown." He said Ralph could come along with him this fall when he went to look at Grandpa's ranches; he'd be glad to have company.

"I haven't finished school yet," said Ralph. "I don't think I'll go on past the seventh grade. How far did you go?"

"Eighth. I wouldn't of gone that far if it hadn't been for your mother. Mr. Kenyon used to tell her and tell her that you couldn't make a silk purse out of a sow's ear but she didn't believe him. I reckon she believes him now, all right, after the way that preacher showed me up that day."

"I'll tell you something funny, Uncle Claude, about that day." And he told what Molly had said to Mr. Follansbee. Uncle Claude laughed so that his belt buckle hopped up and down on his stomach like a jumping bean. "That Molly!" he cried. "She's a caution."

"Do you like her?" said Ralph.

"Sure I like her. Sometimes she's too many for me but she's as funny as a crutch. Sometimes I don't think she is on purpose." He sat up, laughed again, and said, "Come on and help me mend this outfit. Just as quick as I get one stretch mended then she busts out in a new place. Beats me."

All afternoon Ralph worked like a grown man, holding

the posts steady while Uncle Claude nailed on the barbed wire. He was happy at first but gradually he got cross from the heat; the smell of alfalfa became cloying; a dozen times he asked his uncle what time it was. He was depressed at the thought of having to mount that crazy Studebaker again. Uncle Claude had said, when they were working on the first post, "A fall like that one don't amount to anything, but the first time it happens to you, you feel kind of worried." Ralph had replied, "Oh, I wasn't scared!" He wanted the time to pass quickly so that he would be safe at home again, but when he thought of the moment of getting into the saddle, he trembled all over and wished the sun would never set.

But when the time came, he was not afraid. Claude had something of a time catching Falcon who took it into his head to run around in circles like a trick horse, but he was outwitted at last and Uncle Claude led him to where Studebaker stood, for once oblivious of his friend. They were almost like people who were temporarily not on speaking terms. Ralph mounted and realized intuitively that he was in complete control of his horse. He spurred him at the river and Studebaker leaped forward at the pricking and then, when he had crossed the water, resumed a steady gait. Uncle Claude pointed out the place where he had buried Juanita and said, "I don't know why I wasted a bullet on a magpie. A dead magpie ain't going to bring back my dog." He said he would bring Ralph up here at dusk one day and see if they could catch the beaver that was damming up the west slough that ran off from the river at a right angle. He went on then to talk of hunting trips he had made and hunting trips he would like to make. This year he would miss his expedition to the Bear's Ears because he would have to make the rounds of the ranches. At the Bear's Ears, he hunted elk and deer and it was there that he had got the bighorn whose head hung in the dining room.

Two things he had never seen were bears and mountain lions. To be sure, they weren't anything a man would want to eat, but he'd like to see them anyhow. About fifteen years ago, before Uncle Claude came here, there had been a raft of mountain lions in this country, but they seemed to be all gone now. At least no one he knew had ever seen one.

"What do they look like?" said Ralph.

"How should I know? I just got through saying I never seen one."

"Well, I'd like to see one." He wished he would be hiking by himself in the mountains one day and suddenly come on a lion's den. He would shoot the mother and the cubs and then take Uncle Claude up to see. He could just hear Uncle Claude suck in his breath and say, "Well, I'll be a son-of-a-gun."

# CHAPTER FIVE

O N A WINTER SUNDAY AFTERNOON WHEN RALPH WAS FOUR-teen, the Follansbees had come to call and he and Molly were sitting in their Sunday clothes and Sunday solemnity on the hassock in the bay window. Looking at the portrait of his Grandfather Bonney, Ralph read into his face vacuity and self-pride; he saw the plump hands as indolent and useless and believed that in a handclasp they would be flaccid. He understood now why Grandpa Kenyon, when he had used the word "merchant," had uttered it like a curse. He decided that the world was made up of two groups of people. The first he called "Kenyon men" and this included those who, like Uncle Claude, knew the habits of animals and subjected themselves to the government of the seasons and who, with age, became neither fat and bald like Grandfather Bonney nor bony and ragged like Mr. Follansbee. The other group he called "Bonney merchants" and this included everyone he had ever known with the exception of the people at the Bar K, Grandpa, and Molly. The fundamental distinction between the two groups was, he thought, their attitude toward horses and, vice versa, the attitude of horses toward them.

For four years now Ralph and Molly had divided their year between the men and the merchants. Their lives were like those of the children of divorced parents who spend a season of each year with their father and the bulk of it with their mother and who feel themselves thus split in half and sometimes find their memories confused, so that they cannot be sure what books have been read, which ideas acquired, which sounds and shapes perceived in the two separate households. Their own relationship was likewise a double one. At the ranch, they all but ignored one another, but in Covina, alone with their mother now that Leah and Rachel were away at boarding school, they were still close friends.

Their estrangement at the ranch had begun on a day late in August in the very first summer they went to Uncle Claude's, a day on which Ralph's whole life had been changed. Uncle Claude had taken him and Molly and Winifred up to the nearest of the glaciers. They went horseback as far as they could, a little below timberline, then hobbled the horses at an abandoned mine and climbed the rest of the way. Uncle Claude's clowning Newfoundland, Walter, charged into every pool they came to and slunk out, shuddering and coughing. Claude and Winifred were skilled and tireless mountaineers and the two of them went straight up without stopping, leaving Ralph and Molly far behind. When the children finally got to the top, weary, cold, hungry, and exasperated, they almost cried to see that the others had not waited for them there but had gone on and had climbed a cluster of rocks near by. They were sitting on the topmost one, side by side, and they laughed down and waved, turning then to one another to say something the children could not hear. Ralph was too depressed and too tired to take any interest in the vast slide of ice to which he had been looking forward for weeks, nor in the strawberry snow at the head of the glacier. Warm with resentment of Uncle Claude's desertion, he glanced around him casually and then joined Molly who had begun to pluck the waxy yellow orchids growing profusely there, for they had promised to take a bouquet to Mrs. Brotherman. Actually he was less angry than perplexed, for he did not understand why Uncle Claude should prefer the company of a girl to his nor, on the other hand, why Winifred should desert a child for a grown-up. Suddenly it occurred to him, stunning him, that Winifred was really not a child but was as old as Leah. This realization made him feel colder and tireder than ever and he would have lain down amongst the flowers if this would not have appeared an act of weakness to the sitters on the rock. He looked at his weedy sister with dislike as she crouched on her heels, plucking the lilies all around her, and when she looked up at him, her large humble eyes fondling his face with lonely love, he wanted to cry out with despair because hers was really the only love he had and he found it nothing but a burden and a tribulation. She kept a diary in which she recorded everything he said and everything he did and she insisted on reading each entry to him before they went to bed. At first he had been flattered but now he was only embarrassed. She was especially rhetorical on the subject of his shooting at which, if the truth were known, he was quite inferior. Molly would not learn to shoot, and she did not like to touch a gun even when it was unloaded, for their mother had frequently warned them that it was the unloaded ones that always went off. But she went on about Ralph's handling of his .22, under the tutelage of Winifred, as if he were a champion. His first game was only a portly pack rat which had got into the potato cellar on the side of the hill, but later on he shot two jackrabbits and a sage hen. Molly wrote in her diary that he had shot three Rocky Mountain laughing hyenas.

For the most part she did not pester him much but hung around Winifred on whom she had a crush. But he was always conscious of her, always nagged by the suspicion that she felt left out. Half the time, though, it was he who was left out like right now when Winifred had stolen Uncle Claude.

Later, after they had eaten their lunches of salmon sandwiches and Baby Ruths, Uncle Claude offered to let Ralph look through his binoculars to see if he could spot any automobiles on Cuthbert Pass, and when he took off his glasses, Uncle Claude said, "Why don't you leave them things off all the time?"

And Ralph obeyed. He began by not wearing his glasses for an hour at a time and then for two hours and then for whole days except when he went out to shoot. It caused him at first to have hammering headaches and they, in turn, made him eventually vomit and then writhe miserably on the settle in Mrs. Brotherman's sitting room with a damp washcloth over his forehead. But he persisted, and within a few weeks his headaches came infrequently and he was able to see almost as well as he had done with his glasses. Molly tried it too, but in vain: her eyes were much worse than his and without her glasses she was as blind as a mole. After that, everything happened. For example, Uncle Claude took him one day to a deep wet-weather branch where a cow was calving and at the moment he saw the horrible little

117

hoof appear, he felt a painful exultation and he tried to remember what Maisol and Maisako had said that day in the watermelon patch. He was not in the least embarrassed, only filled with wonder at the bewildered wet calf that was finally born and immediately stood up although it was so small and weak it swayed piteously under its mother's big rosy tongue. But when he told Molly about it, she stuck her fingers in her ears and screamed at him, "You're a liar! You're a dirty liar!" and her nose began to bleed.

And Uncle Claude always let him help with the butchering when he was doing it himself. He would shoot the steer through the skull and then would fling his pistol to the ground and run to slit the creature's throat. He stood back after that while the blood gushed out and waited until the reflexes stopped and the dainty legs ceased kicking. Most of the process was sickening, but there was one part he liked and this was the skinning of the carcass after it was strung up. The tight hide came off like an eggshell under his sharp knife and he was always surprised that there was no blood at all and that when the hide was off, nothing showed but another skin of white fat. It looked like someone in winter underwear. He turned his head aside when Uncle Claude commenced to draw it, for the blue guts were hot and steamy and as they slithered out, they stank like a backhouse. Sometimes, by accident, the knife went into the stomach and then green grass came bulging out, fetid and slimy like the stuff around the stems of zinnias that had been too long in water. Ralph carried the tongue and the liver in a pail to the kitchen and the bloodthirsty old Negro woman looked on them as greedily as a scavenger bird.

For four summers now Ralph had been his uncle's constant companion. Occasionally they went into town in the early evening to visit one of Uncle Claude's friends. They would sit around the kitchen table drinking iced tea or sometimes home brew; Ralph had Coca Cola or Orange Crush which Uncle Claude would buy at the drugstore on the way. They talked of murders, of hunting, of horses, of dudes. Some nights, though, Uncle Claude went in alone, not telling anyone what he was going to do, and deeply and secretly Ralph suspected that he was going to a particular street whose nature he would not allow himself to imagine. It was a street one block long and on either side of it were small white one-room houses; at the end of the block there was a larger house made of red brick where lived a woman named Dago Mary who one day had called out to Ralph as he was hurrying by at dusk to meet Uncle Claude at the post office and had asked him to run down to the drug store to get her a package of Luckies and an ammonia coke. He had not even refused; he had run on, his heart pounding. Often, on those nights when Uncle Claude had set forth mysteriously, Ralph thought of how, before he had seen the birth of the calf, he had been like Molly, savagely refusing the knowledge of such things, but now, bad as he knew it all to be, it sometimes gave him a warm feeling like cocoa on a cold night.

Winifred did not like him and he did not know why. In the very first year he had tried to win her by praise, by telling her jokes, by teaching her Boy Scout knots, but she was always aloof with him. And then one day, they had a real falling-out. They had gone hunting and he had shot a prairie dog but she had not hit anything. They sat down to rest on a knoll near the river and Ralph, on an impulse, asked her if she had ever heard about the time Grandpa Kenyon had killed a man. He had assumed, in his possessiveness of Grandpa, that she would not possibly know and his question was rhetorical, holding the expectation of her astonishment and eagerness to hear the story. He even forgot for a moment that Molly knew and that Leah and Rachel and the Follansbees did; he felt that he was offering Winifred a new and precious gift, so that he was completely taken aback when she said she had known it before Ralph was "dry behind the ears." She spoke with such ferocity that he blushed deeply. Molly turned on Winifred, enraged. "He was not your grandfather! He was *ours!*" Winifred jumped up, her eyes blazing, and she said, "He was as much mine as he was yours. He wasn't any *kin* to you, you dirty little snobs!"

Recalling this now as he looked at the portrait, he wondered if there were not some kind of operation you could have to drain off the Bonney blood in you. You could then have a transfusion from Uncle Claude. The terrible danger was that he might get fat like his mother; it was awful that she had named him for Grandfather Bonney and that she kept saying all the time that she wanted him to be exactly like him when he grew up. Sometimes he really hated her just as he had moments of intense hatred for Mr. Follansbee when, listening to the sermon, he knew that he did not believe in God. Especially he hated his mother when he hurt her feelings and she cried. The tears did not move him, nor was he taken in when she blubbered that he was all she had left in the world, but he could not bear the display: her pretty face became dropsical and red and she made piping

120

noises like a fretful kitten. She was a Bonney merchant, through and through.

Ralph handled the symbols of his life delicately like superstitions. Round Grandfather Bonney's portrait and urn he walked with care lest he arouse his ghost, and when, on the anniversary of Grandpa Kenyon's death, he went with his sister and his mother to lay flowers on the gravestone, fixed his attention on the impersonal junipers that hugged the slopes of the low mound and refused himself the memory either of the living man or of the corpse in the parlor. For he believed that if he did not allow even his most hidden mind to prefer one dead man above the other, Grandfather Bonney would not creep forth to haunt and discolor his days at Uncle Claude's where his whole existence betrayed his mother. She knew, to be sure, that he rode and shot and was around dangerous machinery and she cried a good deal over this and there was always a wretched scene in Denver when she saw them off on the train to the Bar K. But she was secretly glad to be rid of her volatile two in the summer and to bask in the sunny dispositions and pretty faces of her two older children.

Today, in the damp twilight, Ralph seemed unable to escape the man in the portrait and he was filled with a terrible physical disgust. Momentarily he closed his eyes and allowed the voices to seep into his mind. His mother was speaking of him and she was saying, "You know, Mr. Follansbee, the single disappointment in my father's life was that he had not studied law at Harvard. It is my dearest wish that Ralph will."

Mr. Follansbee, who had a "digestive condition," belched slightly and perfunctorily sought pardon. He said, "An excellent plan, Rose. And how about it, sonny, how do you feel?" He did not expect an answer; he was a rhetorician and cared little for give and take. He made a speech as if he were in the pulpit, scattering Latin phrases where they fell and bringing in such subsidiary matters as a friend named Dr. Lucius Kennedy who lived in Somerville, a felicitous conversation he had held with a Mr. James Brooks on a bench in the Boston Common, and a Pasadena lawyer of high reputation who had been discovered recently to be the owner of a still in the neighborhood of Carson City. He concluded, addressing Ralph directly, that it would be an ungrateful son who did not grant his mother's dearest wish. He pointed to the portrait and said, "Emulate *him,* my boy. For he was a man among men, a man whose motto was the single word 'Honesty.'" Ever since the scene in this room on the day of Grandpa's funeral, Mr. Follansbee had been spitefully on the look-out for ways to nettle him and Molly. He would refer obliquely to "tall tales," to Paul Bunyan and Baron von Munchausen and pinching Molly's sallow cheek would say, "Hello, hello, my pretty little fairy. Take care you don't fly away."

Now he spoke of the fine blood that ran in Ralph's veins (it was as if he had read his mind!) and went on to speak of the love that bound a son to his mother. Ralph's embarrassment—the preacher ruthlessly kept his eye upon him— was so febrile and agitated that he could not keep his feet and hands still and they danced foolishly. He tried in vain to envisage Uncle Claude, but could see, in his mind's eye, nothing but his mother, bending over him anxiously as he lay sick of scarlet fever, the neck of her gray silk blouse open so that her breasts showed. And then, once, her image was replaced by that of Grandfather Bonney, Tennyson, and President Cleveland plodding arm in arm toward the sand bar.

When Mr. Follansbee had paused, Mrs. Fawcett said, "I know many things may happen in these years before he is ready to go to college, but I do not feel that anyone has ever suffered by taking the longer view of things. Besides it is not much more than two years. When the time comes, I will sell this place and we will go East to live."

"Not me," said Molly.

Mrs. Fawcett smiled. "Molly doesn't want to do anything anyone else does."

"The rugged individualist," said Mr. Follansbee with a chuckle. "Well, Molly, what do you want to do?"

It was, Ralph knew, all she could do to keep from sticking out her tongue. "I want to stay here with Grandpa," she said.

They all were shocked. The depths of this child were unfathomable and Mrs. Fawcett at times was really afraid of her. Somehow time did not soften her, did not make her have thoughts and feelings like other children. Now Ralph, although he was still unusually sensitive and in some ways eccentric, had normal interests—much as she wished the object of his admiration had been someone of more culture and refinement than Claude Kenyon, Mrs. Fawcett was bound to admit that it was right for him to enjoy the company of a grown man—and, moreover, he was beginning to look . . . well, to put it bluntly, to look like a human being. But poor Molly, although she had shot up and was taller than any of her schoolmates, looked just the same as she had done when she was eight. And the things she said!

Mrs. Fawcett faltered, "Molly, dear, you mustn't say things that make us sad." Molly stared at her and curled her lip. Mrs. Follansbee rescued them, asking in her domestic voice, what sort of house Mrs. Fawcett would buy in the East. She said she would settle somewhere in Connecticut, near Aunt Rowena, and that in the winter she would rent a house in Cambridge so that Ralph would not have to lead the irregular life of the dormitories. It was planned, parenthetically, that Molly would go to a boarding school in the vicinity of Boston and would then go either to Radcliffe or to Wellesley. Mrs. Fawcett said, "I should like *one* of my daughters to be a college woman, and the other two give me no hope—they write of nothing but beaux."

It was time for tea and Mrs. Fawcett rose to wheel in the table from the dining room. As she passed her son, she stooped and kissed the top of his head and with a small, sweet-smelling hand, patted his cheek. And then, as a sop to her conscience, she ran her fingers through Molly's hair. The preacher and his wife smiled benignly on the scene, exchanged the sorrowful glances of the childless, and the man belched, the woman sighed. In the few minutes that Mrs. Fawcett was gone from the room, the Follansbees changed their pious, general tone and inquired of Molly and Ralph lightly and condescendingly—Mrs. Follansbee speaking in a very loud voice—whether they did not keenly look forward to going to college.

Molly said, "We're not going to college, neither one of us, and we decided that before you were born."

Mr. Follansbee humorously clucked his tongue. "And what do you Methuselahs intend to do?"

She said, "We will get married and stay right here with

124

Grandpa." And then she turned to her brother and said, "Won't we?" She would never believe him when he told her that marriage was not what she thought it was. The first summer at the ranch she had wanted to marry Studebaker and a long time ago she had told everyone at school that she was engaged to Schöneshund. The Follansbees looked at her with horror and Ralph whispered in her ear, "Don't say anything more. I'll tell you why later."

There was always a long, uncomfortable pause when the water was coming to a boil over the spirit lamp, and no one seemed to be able to think of anything to say. Today, as always, there was an expectant hush and Mr. Follansbee's stomach made a noise like a querulous voice. Disgust overwhelmed Ralph. Would they never take their awful Bonney bodies away?

He took a drink of his tea and said, "The milk is sour, Mother."

"Nonsense," she replied. "I poured it into the pitcher myself. Mr. Vogelman brought it this morning."

He drank again and repeated, "It's sour, I say."

Sour spit flowed from behind his jaws into his mouth and he swallowed desperately. He tried to think of something else but he could think only of milk and of its smell. Shaking like an old man, he returned his cup to the tea wagon and said, "May I be excused? I am going to be sick."

"The milk is fresh," insisted his mother. "Sit down, son. It is very rude to behave this way."

"My brother will be sick," said Molly dully, stating a fact. He put both hands over his mouth and ran to the door. His illness lay in small pools of froth on the carpet and all the way up the stairs to the bathroom. When he had finished being sick, he went to his room and lay down on the bed with his eyes open, watching the green sky darken and the rosy clouds divide, assume new shapes, then disappear from sight. He did not know what had happened to benumb him in this way, and he knew that the milk had not been sour. But he felt as disabled as he had done when his tonsils were removed and the ether mask had been fitted over his nose. He had never forgotten the blue, spicy smell; now, six years later, he could remember it accurately and he gagged again.

He could take no pleasure in thinking of the Bar K. Next summer would bring him closer to the end of these summers, nearer to New England, a cloudy abstraction no more imaginable than the world of sleep. He knew that his mother would not let him go back, once she settled in Connecticut. He could not bear the thought of not seeing Uncle Claude again and the ranch itself and the mountains which both he and Molly loved as if they owned them. Sometimes he went swimming naked in the cold, amber pool of the Caribou behind the barn. (How long ago it seemed that he and Molly had been horrified when Winifred had said she was going in without her suit!) Alone in this rustling, humming wilderness, he pretended that he was an Indian. Later, coming back to the house, he paused on the ridge to the west of the barn and surveying the buildings and the pastures, he imagined himself as Uncle Claude's partner, saw himself riding in a caboose to Mexico with carloads of stock in front of him, saw their consultations in the office on what to buy and what to sell. In time, growing taller and filling out, people would take him for Kenyon's brother, Grandpa's younger son. Often he went climbing with Molly and Winifred. They hunted for beaver dams, filling their pockets, for no reason at all, with the chips of wood that littered the ground around the fallen trees. They found sweet piñon seeds which covered their hands with pitch that smelled like medicine. Winifred had taught them how to climb without getting winded and to go up the chimneys of the pinnacled red rocks, their hands on either wall, their rubber-soled shoes squealing at their pressure against the narrow footholds. Each time they went into the mountains, something unusual happened: they would come upon a ranger's saddled horse, cropping in a field of columbine, an old man panning for gold in a stream. Once they found an empty whisky bottle covered over with pine needles in a place so far from everything that they could not imagine what sort of person had put it there. From a favorite cliff they looked down into the valley and could see the pretentious dude camp west of Uncle Claude's, set in a barren waste of scrub oak and sage. A cattle train, puffing out a clean-lined cloud of white smoke, burrowed through the red banks like a mole, disappeared, and sent back a faint, protesting valedictory. There was always the possibility that they might see a mountain lion; they never did, but often they saw eagles.

The very life would be crushed out of him if he were deprived of all this! Of late, he had been wild with all sorts of angers and with an anxiety which he could not name but which pestered him continually so that he could not keep his mind on reading and sometimes he could not even pay attention to the movies. Sometimes he loathed his physical being for the alterations that were taking place in it: when his voice cracked, he wanted to die of shame, and when Molly laughed at him, he was abjectly humiliated.

He was filling out now; he had lost his pallor and his eyes, quite strong, were clear. He would have taken pleasure in his appearance if it were not for Molly with her ugly face and her lankiness and the slouching, round-shouldered gait which she had developed and which caused her enemies to call her "the crab." There was something wrong with her and while he still loved her, he wished oftener and oftener that she did not exist.

The sky darkened suddenly and in a few minutes it began to rain. The calm sound of it in the turquoise berries outside his window soothed him. He lay as still as a stone. He thought: there was something preying on Grandpa Kenyon's mind that day—perhaps he knew he was going to die —and that was why he had absent-mindedly tapped the turquoise berry with his shillelagh. That was the sort of meaningless thing you did when you had a great worry.

As soon as Ralph left the room, Molly returned her cup to the tea wagon and said, "If you will pardon me, this is the pause in the day's occupation which is known as the children's hour."

Mrs. Fawcett shook her head and sighed, "She's simply not happy unless she can be with Ralph. If he's asleep, don't wake him."

Mr. and Mrs. Follansbee said, "Good-bye, Molly," and Molly said, "So long," so that she had to come back and curtsy and say it properly. She stepped around Ralph's sickness which the grown-ups had chosen to ignore. It was just spit and it was already sinking into the carpet.

She had no intention of going to Ralph's room. It had been perfectly clear that he was not going to marry her

128

and she suspected that he was going to marry Uncle Claude. She went down the hall to the kitchen. It wore its Sunday-afternoon look of lifeless cleanliness. Fuschia did not prepare their supper on Sunday night but left a pot of soup to bubble slowly on the back of the stove. This was all they had except toast and peanut butter and a chocolate drop a piece. The funny papers were on top of the refrigerator and she read "Out Our Way." It was very funny today. The two kids and their father were out cleaning the backyard and getting terribly dirty. They had to pass the living room door to get upstairs to the bathroom to wash and the mother was having company. So they took a sheet off the line and the father said they would all get under it and it would just look like a white flash going past the door, but it didn't work because they got mixed up and went *in* the door instead of *past* it. She laughed for a moment and then, looking in the mirror over the sink, she said, scarcely moving her lips, "Ha. Ha. Tee. Hee."

Molly let herself out the back door without a sound. Budge, who was old now and insensate, lay on the top step, unmindful of the rain, but she did no more than look at her and murmur, "Hi, purr-cat."

She went to the shed where the bleaching vats stood ready for the next year's harvest. There was a chemical smell here and this, together with the murkiness and the drizzle against the window panes, made her think of *Dr. Jekyll and Mr. Hyde* and she proceeded as if she were walking in her sleep. She went directly to the beakers of acid on their racks which Miguel had warned her and Ralph against since they were tiny children, pulling out their stoppers to show the sour blue vapor emerging from the hidden heat.

One drop of it, he said, on the bare skin would hurt like a red-hot poker and he put an eye dropper of it on an old piece of canvas to show them how quickly it would eat through any substance. Miguel had taken a correspondence course in chemistry and the shed looked almost like a laboratory with test tubes everywhere stained purple and green and bile color; there was a Bunsen burner and a collection of beakers of bizarre and attractive shapes. He experimented with all kinds of things; once he had let Molly and Ralph watch when he combined his spit with something and it turned bright green. Ralph asked him if the acid would burn off warts, but Miguel said no.

There was a test tube marked $H_2SO_4$ which Molly knew was the most dangerous of them all. That was what was used to make the walnuts pale. She took the small flat cork out and smelled the nasty smell. Then she held her left hand over a basin and poured the contents on it. At first it did not hurt at all; it stung a little like the liquid soap in the basement at school, but that same blue smoke came up from her hand and almost at once big puffy blisters came out, as white and opaque as mushrooms, and there was a new and terrible smell. The smell, not the blisters, alarmed her and sent her plunging to the sink where there was a cold water tap. But the more water she allowed to flow over her hand, the bigger the blisters got and when she took her hand away and sniffed at it, the smell was worse than ever. Then she began to cry, not with pain but with terror at this odor of her destruction and she stood in despair in the shadowy room, full of the sound of rain.

She ran out of the shed as if she were being chased and

back through the kitchen sobbing, "Mother Mother! I have hurt myself!"

Ralph was in the kitchen cutting himself a piece of raisin bread so she knew he had not been very sick, and when he heard her, he stumbled out, dropping the knife on the floor.

"Look," she moaned, "look what happened to me."

The pain was not severe; it was the knowledge that the acid was *eating* her, the way the Follansbees were eating cake, the way Ralph had been about to eat the raisin bread, and in this revulsion she paid no attention to her brother who was saying, "What *is* it, Molly? What did you *do?*"

She sat down at the table and put her head on her right arm and stretched out her left arm in front of her so that Ralph could look at the burn and she wept with pity. Ralph stared and impatiently repeated, "What *is* it?" until finally she was able to say, "Miguel's acid," and then he went crying along the corridor to the parlor as she lifted up her head and screamed, "Help! Help!"

Molly lay on the lounge in her father's den and refused to answer any of their questions. Through her half-open eyes she saw them standing in a row beside her: her mother was wearing a pink dress with an accordion-pleated skirt and her cheeks were as pink as the cloth with passion as she insisted, "Tell Mother, my baby. Mother is not cross with her little girl," but Molly knew that this was a lie for she heard the anger in her voice as clearly as she saw it in Mr. Follansbee's eyes which were green like the cases of fish in the aquarium. He stood at the foot of the lounge, looking from time to time at his watch. He had promised Mrs. Fawcett that he would stay until the doctor came, but he was nervous for fear he would not have proper time for his supper before Epworth League. Mrs. Follansbee, who had declared herself to be "chilled to the marrow," sniffed into her handkerchief and often repeated that the best thing in the world for burns was butter. Molly thought slyly: then the acid would eat the butter; the acid would have a buttered hand sandwich. Ralph stood at the head of the lounge and she could not see him but every so often he stroked her forehead and said, "It won't hurt in a little while."

At last they heard Dr. Haskell's car in the drive and Molly said, "I don't want you to stay in here."

"Young lady," began Mr. Follansbee, but Mrs. Fawcett checked him with a wave of the hand and said, "Yes, sweetheart, if you are sure you won't be afraid."

"Ralph can stay," she said and Mrs. Fawcett looked at Mr. Follansbee and said, "You see?" and then they left the room.

Both Molly and Ralph had always been fond of Dr. Haskell who did not take their mother seriously and who had a nice angular face and curly red hair. When they had scarlet fever, he brought Molly a brown candy reindeer and Ralph a bear. He drew up a chair and glancing at Molly's hand said, "Molly, you give me a pain in the neck. I was just sitting down to my supper and I was going to have waffles."

"I can't stand waffles," said Molly, and Dr. Haskell laughed.

"Now tell me what you did this time," he said, picking up her hand and touching the blisters lightly with his finger.

She could have told the truth without embarrassment, that she had done it on purpose to punish Ralph, but while she liked Dr. Haskell, she did not entirely trust him. Once he had told Mrs. Fawcett that she and Ralph were "nervous" and their mother was stricter than ever after that, saying, "I think you need a little rest. We don't want to get tired out and then be nervous, do we?" The word "nervous" came to be as disgusting to her as "body." So now, if she told the truth, she had no assurance that Dr. Haskell would not tattle—for that matter she was no longer even sure of Ralph, and she said, "I went out to the shed to see if I could find my art gum."

Ralph said quickly and suspiciously, "Why would it be in the shed?"

"I thought maybe Miguel had borrowed it." Now she was disquieted and her heart beat strongly. "I was looking around there but it was dark as a pocket and all of a sudden I knocked over a little bottle of stuff and it went all over my hand."

Dr. Haskell went to the door and called across the hall, asking for a basin of hot water. Coming back, he said quite matter-of-factly, "And the cork was out of the bottle?"

"Yes," said Molly. "Yes, it was."

The doctor clucked his tongue. "That is very careless of Miguel. We must speak to your mother about it."

"Oh, no!" she cried. "Oh, please don't! Miguel would knock my block off. It wasn't his fault."

The doctor's smiling glance went straight through her and he said, "This time, then, I won't. But if it should happen again, Molly . . ." And his smile went off like a street light.

133

"What did you do then?" asked Ralph.

Molly, remembering the basin where some of the acid would still be lying, remembering the cork which had just been sitting there beside the rack of test tubes, was afraid now and her hand began to hurt dreadfully. She whimpered, "I put my hand under the water faucet, but it didn't do any good."

"I guess not," said Dr. Haskell.

Mrs. Fawcett, returning with the basin which steamed into her face, asked, "It isn't serious, is it, Doctor? I cannot tell you how often and often I have warned them about the acids."

Dr. Haskell said, "It isn't too serious. There is danger of infection, though, if we are not careful."

"Infection!" cried Mrs. Fawcett, stumbling from the room, her hand pressed to her bosom, and Molly's heart said, "Goody! Goody!"

For some weeks it seemed possible that Molly might lose her hand. She wore upon it a cast of paraffin, for Dr. Haskell was afraid that if air got to the wound and a scab formed, the acid would continue to eat its insidious way through the flesh. In time it began to have so unpleasant a smell that she lay in bed with her arm stretched out, her head turned to the wall and a sachet of lavender pinned to her pillow. The pain was never great, but she was obsessed with the horror of being consumed alive.

She did not go to school for a few days and as this was a time of cold rain, she stayed indoors reading *Bleak House*. It was not like being sick, for she did not have to stay in bed but could go wherever she liked in the house. Sometimes she sat in the parlor and sometimes in the guest room, but usually she sat in her father's den. People rarely came in there except to use the telephone so she would not be bothered in the middle of a paragraph by someone saying, "How do you feel, Molly girl?" or "Would you like some Ovaltine?" People were always looking at her and she knew none of them believed it was an accident. Ralph hadn't, from the beginning, and the night it happened Ralph came into her room and whispered, "If you have to do dumb things, I don't see why you have to be so dumb about it. I went and got the cork."

"I did it to punish you," she said.

"What did I do to you?"

"You said we were not going to get married and stay here."

"Molly!" he said irritably and then, more kindly, "I never said that."

But though she asked him every day if they were going to get married, he always somehow changed the subject. She had almost come to the conclusion that she would marry Dr. Haskell.

One day Mrs. Fawcett came into the den to sew. She had never done this before, but Molly could tell by the way she frowned as she bent over the buttons that she meant to tell her something of importance. Molly glanced at her from time to time over her book.

"Molly," she said at last, "what do you do at Uncle Claude's all the time? Do you play with other children your age?"

"Of course not," said Molly. "What do you think he lives in? A *town*?"

135

"But what do you *do?*"

"I swim. I hike. I ride Eye-Opener. I talk to Magdalene."

"Magdalene? Oh, the cook. I wouldn't talk too much to a darky if I were you, Molly."

You would, thought Molly, if you were probably a darky yourself and Magdalene's own child.

Molly said, "What do *you* do while we're gone?"

"Why, just what we always do," said Mrs. Fawcett with surprise. "Do you know, Molly, I sometimes think you and Ralph are happier with your uncle than you are at home."

"I do not believe in happiness," said Molly.

Mrs. Fawcett bit her lip. "That is a very foolish thing to say. You are a very foolish girl, Molly." She had something up her sleeve. She said two mysterious things. She said, "Well, I used to think it was wrong to let you go, but now I think it's a very good place for you at your age. There must be lots of cunning little calves and lambs and colts and so forth." Molly did not know what her age had to do with it; the colts and lambs and calves were a lot younger than she was. And the other thing was, "I hope you don't try to tag along with Ralph too much." Molly replied with falsehood, "I am with him every minute every day every week every month."

They did not talk for a while and Molly went on reading about the man who went up in spontaneous combustion from drinking too much gin. Shortly before the school bus came, Mrs. Fawcett let the cat out of the bag. She said, "Molly, I wonder if you and Ralph wouldn't like to spend a whole year with Uncle Claude?"

"Why?" said Molly. She was not at all sure she would

136

like to spend a whole year at the ranch. The public library was too far away, for one thing.

"I just wondered because, well, Molly, I may as well tell you. Now I don't want you to be disappointed because your turn will come. I am going to take Leah and Rachel around the world."

"When?" said Molly tensely, closing her book.

"As soon as Rachel has finished school. This spring." Leah had finished the year before but she was staying with Aunt Rowena so that she could enjoy the cultural opportunities of New York.

Molly, thinking of the pictures in her geography book of the Taj Mahal and the pyramids and the Rock of Gibraltar which her sappy sisters would get to see, threw *Bleak House* on the floor and stamped both her feet. "See if I care!" she howled. "You just wait till I tell Ralph!"

"There, there," said her mother. "Don't fuss, Molly. Didn't I say your time would come?"

"I'll be too old by then."

"Would you like to go to boarding school instead of to Uncle Claude's?"

"No. I want to stay here if I can't go around the world."

"But you can't, Molly dear," said Mrs. Fawcett nervously, "because the house will be sold."

She had done all this behind their backs. She wasn't content to make the far future look horrible, she had to make it start right away. Molly stared at her bandaged hand in which now and again there was a slow pain. Dr. Haskell said she was out of danger now and she was glad that she was not going to lose her hand but she was also glad that the burn would leave a bad scar. Her mother was going on talking about how necessary it was for her to take the girls around the world because she did not belong to a society to which she could present them; this was a substitute, to be sure, but she felt a very satisfactory one. As for Ralph and Molly, she thought the year in the mountains would be very character-building and she was pleased with Molly's wisdom in not wanting to go to boarding school. In public school one learned a great deal about responsibility and democracy. Fortunately Leah and Rachel had sterling characters and had not become snobs; all the same she realized now that sending them to so fashionable a school had been a dangerous experiment.

"But, Molly dear, before we go, I want to have a long talk with you about a few things."

"About what? Go ahead. Shoot."

"Not now, not yet. Goodness, Ralph is late. The roads must be bad." She put her sewing away and got up. As she left the room, she said, "We're having your favorite dessert for dinner tonight, lemon pie."

When April came and Molly looked at the spring in Covina for the last time, she was homesick as if she were only remembering the sweet orange blossoms in the Freudenburg's grove, the palm trees, the bee-filled lippia lawn, the workmen with their doe-like eyes. She visited both the graves of her father and of Grandpa Kenyon and she sat for hours in the shade of a blooming tulip tree in the cemetery. She was restless when she thought of strange children lying under her umbrella tree and strange women cracking the walnuts.

Now and again her care-worn melancholy made her suddenly self-contemptuous and she brushed it off like a spider. Once to prove to herself that she was not a crybaby, she took a still live wood mouse from a trap and drowned it in a milk bottle half full of water, rejoicing brutishly in the swimming and the squealing which became slower and fainter and at last ceased while the small speckled body swelled and the sharp teeth showed themselves in an angry grin.

Ralph was as sad and jealous as she. They often quarreled. She wondered sometimes if she liked him as well as she used to. Once they were walking home from school together when a girl on a bicycle came riding by. Her name was Ardis Westerlund and she enjoyed the distinction of having fainted several times in school. She was frail and pretty and had long yellow hair which was held in place with a round comb; her mother dressed her to look like Alice. This year she had given Ralph a Valentine and once Molly had seen them earnestly talking together by the parallel bars at recess, and when the bell rang she saw Ralph touch his fingers to his lips and blow Ardis a kiss. Today, as she went whizzing by, she cried, "I name Molly for the prettiest girl in school!"

Both Molly and Ralph halted and Molly snarled, "Why don't you stop breathing?" but Ardis Westerlund was far away, streaking past the Wash.

Ralph made a convulsive gesture to take Molly's hand, but she brushed him off and said in a cold, level voice, "I know I'm ugly. I know everybody hates me. I wish I were dead." Unappealing, unloving, she continued to stand motionless in the bright sunshine. She knew the light made even yellower her yellow skin with its hundreds of shining bronze freckles. She could see herself as clearly as if she looked in a mirror. A blue Indian-head jumper hung on her slackly; her ruffled organdy blouse was mussed and soiled from the long day at school; one knobby knee was covered with a scab from a wound of two weeks before; one of the ear pieces of her glasses was bound with adhesive tape. Molly was not only ugly, she had a homemade look, a look of having been put together by an inexperienced hand.

She closed her eyes and teetered. Ralph shook her, "Come along, Molly, we've got to get home."

"I haven't got a home," she said and she let go her school-bag so that its books and pencils and loose-leaf notepaper scattered in the dust at her feet.

"Listen, Molly . . ."

"Go away. I wish they had had to cut my hand off."

"All right!" he cried and his voice rose to a shout. "All right! Why don't *you* stop breathing?"

Molly smiled a particular smile that always made him crazy-mad. He spat at her feet and yelled, "I hate you. Damn you, I hate you! Stay here all night for all I care!" When he had gone, running down the road, she picked up her books and her papers and wiped the dusty pencils off on her skirt.

# CHAPTER SIX

M RS. FAWCETT AND HER ELDER DAUGHTERS, ON THEIR WAY West from Rachel's commencement, met Ralph and Molly late in June in Denver. As in former years when only their mother had been with the children, they stayed at the Brown Palace hotel. While Leah and Rachel and Mrs. Fawcett were shopping and Molly was at the Museum of Natural History, Ralph sat in the lobby where one looked up past gallery after gallery to a fretted dome, and he imagined the days of the gold and silver harvest when towns sprang up in the mountains to exist for a few opulent years and then to be abandoned. The train that took them to the Bar K passed through several of these ghost towns: the sagging, rotten, tall Victorian houses, windowless and with the porches maimed, still wore traces of their original elegance, and there was something deeply mournful in the sight of a cupola whose gingerbread remained intact but which listed like a hat on a drunk man's head. Patches of gilt still clung to the pillars of the boarded-up opera houses; the saloons and gambling dens, as haggard as death itself, still wore their flush names: The Golden Horn, The Gold Nugget, The Silver Dollar, The Silver

Moon. The mouths of old mines yawned blackly beside the pyramids of ore. Grass grew in the streets, all the houses were tenantless, and even the trees looked dead.

The Brown Palace had been part of those days, and while it was as flamboyant as ever with its profusion of marble, of tall rubber plants, of gilt-framed mirrors and of frescoes, it failed to recall the life of the Eldorado as clearly as did the derelict opera houses. It seemed like any hotel in Los Angeles, and the businessmen who sat in the modern leather lounge chairs, smoking good cigars, were pale-faced and stout, not Westerners. Only occasionally did ranchers, unmistakable by their gait and their hewn faces under tall buff hats, amble through the lobby like restless dogs; uneasy in their city clothes they picked the chairs behind the rubber plants so that they would not be seen. The others, the buyers and the sugar merchants, were often in the company of women who were too young to be their wives and Ralph, against his will, was pleased by this just as he was pleased that his mother and Leah and Rachel were the objects of admiring, libidinous stares when they came into the dining room.

On the eve of their departure, the family gathered in Mrs. Fawcett's bedroom for a farewell visit. Mrs. Fawcett talked of her grief at leaving her two babies behind, but brightly promised that they would have their trip around the world in that most far-off future "some day." She was grateful for her own bravery in being thus able to face a year without them, but said she knew that it was for their own good. "It will be very good for you to be on your own. Grandfather Bonney used to say, 'Solitude is the greatest tonic in the world. Loneliness is the poison put into solitude by

142

weaklings and cads.' And I know you aren't either of *those*. Molly, you must ask Winifred to use the fine-comb on your hair after you wash it. And when we come back—you'll see how quickly the time passes—we will all be together in a lovely new home in Connecticut."

Molly, who had been captious for days, said, "How many times must I explain to you that it is incorrect to use the word 'home' in that way? You mean 'house.' "

Mrs. Fawcett smiled patiently. "Very well, my dear, *house* since you know so much more than your mother. May I continue what I was saying when you interrupted me?"

"Molly, you are becoming an intellectual snob," said Rachel, taking out a gold and white Coty's compact she had got for graduation.

"*Becoming?*" said Molly. "I have been one ever since I was nothing going on one."

Ralph, while he was in entire agreement with Molly on the distinction between "house" and "home" and had, in fact, suggested it to her in the first place, hated the smirk on her thin ill-natured mouth and hated the unblinking vigil of her nearsighted eyes. This disconcerting stare often caused people to falter nervously in their speech or to flush, and frequently, in front of company, her mother scolded her, "Molly dear, you must *not* stare. It is very much like pointing." And in school these eyes, missing nothing, intimidated her teachers, already intimidated by her intelligence and her talent for writing themes of a savagely satiric nature. Everyone said that she had the brains of the family, but as Mrs. Fawcett was not interested in brains, she thought this a handicap rather than otherwise and often told Molly that there were other things in life besides books. But, thought Ralph, what else could there be for that scrawny, round-shouldered tall thing, misanthropic at the age of twelve? It was curious that she bore so close a resemblance to him. She had the same coarse, straight, black hair, the same heavy eyebrows, and the same prominent nose that looked as solid and unbreakable as a stone. But in a girl such ruggedness was not handsome as it was in him and Uncle Claude, and nothing could be done to improve the features nor, probably, would she have permitted any alterations even if they had been possible, for she took a vindictive pleasure in her plainness. She would stand before the mirror in the hall and when someone passed by would point to her reflection and say, "Admit I'm prettier than Mary Pickford."

Looking at his older sisters with their fine, tender faces, their shining hair, their dresses of flowered pongee, catching their clean, delicious smell of soap and talcum powder, he wished Molly had never been born. He was still contemptuous of the others, but he was so conscious of their beauty that sometimes he desired, to his horror, to put his lips on their smooth white necks or on the long green veins in their arms. They had been completely oblivious of Ralph and Molly and had talked about esoteric things like "the Winter Carnival" and "the Yale-Harvard game," "the sixth-form dance at St. George's" and "Olivia's coming-out."

Mrs. Fawcett's voice went chattering on, joined sometimes by Leah's or Rachel's (once Rachel said, "But, Mummy, I think it will be too *poky* not to stay in Paris for at *least* two months." Ralph and Molly exchanged glances and each formed the word "Mummy" soundlessly.) It was hot.

Ralph's pants stuck to the varnished chair and he drank water slowly out of a sweating hotel pitcher. He gazed greedily at his sisters and the desire to kiss them became almost irresistable so that he had to blind himself from time to time by staring into the blazing ceiling light. Then, suddenly, he thought of Winifred Brotherman and in an instant, he was floundering in his first real love. For a few minutes he sat motionless; then, from somewhere in the hotel, a jazz band began to play "The Sweetheart of Sigma Chi." The woodwinds, grieving their hearts out, the dancers he imagined with their eyes closed, the dimmed lights he saw, the smell of the girls' perfumed hair and of the boys' breath sweet with gin, made him tremble like a tree. He thought of her as he had seen her once last summer, lying on the lawn, a bottle of Coca Cola, half drunk, forgotten in her hand. The sun seemed to darken her skin as he watched and her curls looked molded out of metal. He had been pleased to look at her, and now he understood why he had stood so long at his window looking down at her, keeping Uncle Claude waiting for the knife to skin a beaver.

On the pretext of a headache from the movie they had gone to in the afternoon, he went to his own room across the hall and lay in the darkness with his hands crossed on his chest. The music here was louder than it had been in his mother's room. Each time the tempo changed, the scene in his mind changed. With the fox trots he imagined them dancing, although he did not know how to dance; with the waltzes he saw them sitting in Uncle Claude's car in the darkness, outside the dance hall or driving up Cuthbert Pass until they came to an unfrequented road where they would park the car to kiss for hours. This was nothing like what he had felt for Ardis. That had been a sweet and nebulous romance and its only incidents were that once she had given him a Valentine and had blushed and said that someone else must have signed her name and once he had blown her a kiss. They had loved in their silences and in their sidelong glances exchanged in study hall. It gave him a sense of almost conjugal comfort to know that Winifred was three years older than himself. It did not occur to him that she might already be spoken for; he felt that this was not a sudden miracle but that it had been prepared for since he was a little boy and it must, therefore, have been simultaneously prepared for in her. How curious it was that in all these years he had barely been aware of her! How curious that she had seemed to dislike him!

Toward eleven o'clock there was an intermission, and when the music ceased, his mind wandered perversely to Leah's high, cool forehead, and as if he were already married and already unfaithful to his wife, he exultantly felt her enclosed in his arms while he first put his lips and then the tip of his tongue upon the small blue vein which marked it like an artist's signature. Then, when the music began again and he returned to Winifred, he fashioned out of his sister and out of memories of girls in movies and girls in books the rival to whom he would allude in his first days with her. He wished to miss nothing and when he remembered, at first with pain, that she would be away at college, he rejoiced that there would be love letters and that she would come home for the Christmas holidays and then in the spring. He whirled round and round in his rapid love; it pricked him on the breastbone like a needle.

He wanted to be shut up in a small space to think about it. He wanted to grab it and eat it like an apple so that nobody else could have it.

At the train, Mrs. Fawcett and Leah and Rachel all cried, for departures and railroad stations required sorrow and they honored ceremony. They had brought farewell presents. Mrs. Fawcett's and Rachel's were boxes of candy, but Leah gave them nothing except an envelope which she pressed into Molly's hand, telling her not to open it until the train left. Kissing them all good-bye, Ralph felt a twinge of envy of the boat they would sail on but he did not fail, as Molly stubbornly did, to wish them a bon voyage when his mother said, "Now aren't you going to wish us a bon voyage?" He and Molly waved from the observation platform until they could no longer see three separate figures but only a single clump, and then they went back to the rusty green seat where their presents were. They opened the envelope first. On a sheet of thin Japanese writing paper with a heading of two ladies drinking tea, Leah had written:

Dearest Molly girl and Ralphie boy,
Mother made me *promise* not to tell but she can't do anything now since by the time you read this I will be on my way to China!!!!!! On the third finger of my left hand, I am now the proud wearer of a diamond ring! Mother is quite silly (don't we all know it!!!!) and says I cannot announce my engagement for a whole year and that's why I have to go around the darned old world. Of course she's the limit, but I must say I am looking forward to the Taj Mahal not to mention the Holy Land. Garden of Eden, here I come, right back where I started from. (Apologies to California.) If you are good and don't breathe this to a

soul, I'll bring you back a whole trunkful of presents and will write you every day about what we have seen and the adventures we have had.

I will hang my close on this line,

Loads of love,

Leah

P.S. The Donor of the Famous Engagement Ring is named Robert Appleton and he is a senior at Dartmouth. I'd give anything to see your faces when you read this.

Molly went over the letter, sentence by sentence, devastatingly, and when she came to the parody of "California, here I come," she put her hand over her mouth and said, "Hasten, Jason, bring the basin, ulp! Too late, bring the mop." Recently she had been very much attached to the word "bourgeois," and she used it as if it were the most venomous in the language. She had once said to her mother that she thought the Sorosis was "as bourgeois as all outdoors," and of Ardis Westerland, once she had recovered from the shock of her insult, she said, "Why should I bother about that lousy bourgeois stick-in-the-mud?" So now Leah's letter, Leah herself, and the trip around the world were, she said, the most bourgeois things she had ever heard of in her life. "Bonney Bourgeois," she said with finality.

Ralph was deeply disturbed by the effect of the letter on himself, feeling somehow cheated and, furthermore, he was ashamed that Leah, engaged to be married, was the very figure he had meant to use to rouse Winifred's romantic jealousy. He felt, as well, a terrified guilt as though he had despoiled his own sister, and now, to make everything even more sinful, her letter, a clear confession of a relationship with a boy, tempted him again to think of her high

forehead and again to imagine his lips upon it. The wickedness fluttered round him like a moth-miller which he could
not catch.

As a safeguard against betraying himself, he changed the
subject quickly and said, "Will I be glad to see old Studebaker!"

And Molly said, "Will I be glad to see Eye-Opener!"

Now they were really glad to be going to the ranch and
they talked with amiable venom of their mother and sisters
and said that, among other blessings, they would not have
to hear Mr. Follansbee again as long as they lived. They
planned and remembered, and then Ralph, looking in a
pause at Molly's hand which was still puffy and blue,
pointed to it and said, "Why did you do that?" But Molly
said, "I'm through talking now," and opened *Les Misérables*
so that Ralph had to contemplate once more his evil
thoughts.

At the end of ten miles he was already tired and Molly
was deep in her book, leaving it only now and again to
goggle at the open box of candy on the seat beside her
and, with maddening regularity, to select a gum drop. The
journey always made Ralph homesick, not for people or
for a place, but for cleanliness and comfort and orderly
houses. For always on the train were the most pathetic
travelers in the world. Not the ranchers, returning from
Denver or Omaha, rumpled but still well dressed; and not
the rodeo riders on their way from Pendleton to Frontier
Days in Cheyenne; nor the dudes in their mottled silk
shirts and ten gallon Stetsons, but the others who belonged
in no classification. Each year there was always a group
consisting of a gaunt young woman and three or four small

children who ate graham crackers out of an oiled paper parcel and whined nasally. Years of hard work and bad food had given the women a canine look in the mouth and eyes; their skin was brown and old; if their teeth had been replaced, the false ones were gold, but generally there were only spaces where they had rotted and fallen out. The groups varied little, but they could not always have been the same one, for the children were the same size. The mother's hair was always reddish brown and hung about her sunken face like dirty strings, but her children were tow-headed and their eyebrows were too light to see. Sometimes they had skin diseases or birthmarks or Hutchinson's teeth. If another passenger struck up a conversation with the mother, the car usually learned that they had been to Denver to a doctor and the complaint was always something dangerous like mastoid or rheumatic fever. They would get off some hours before Ralph and Molly did at a bleak, treeless town where a mustard-colored depot and a mustard-colored water tower glared in the sun, and where small cottages and outhouses with drooping doors straggled up the dry sides of the foothills. The halts were so long that it was often possible to watch the whole progress of the woman and her children up the dirt road onto the porch of the house itself. They moved so slowly they did not seem to be glad to be at home at all. The scene gave Ralph great thirst, and when the train moved on again, he would go to the back of the car and drink cup after cup of tepid water.

This time the woman wore a tall, tan hat which sat on her head like a pail; it was spotted with mildew. Her dress was a sleeveless evening frock of azure georgette and its scalloped skirt was longer in the back than in the front.

A flower made of orange crinoline with spiny, life-like pistils was pinned to her shoulder, and she wore a choker of pink beads. As the train mounted to the high country and it grew chilly, she put on a black satin coat with a neckpiece that looked like toasted cotton. She smoked cigarettes in a carved bone holder and ground them out on the floor of the car with the heel of her tennis shoe.

There were only two children this time, a little girl of about three and a boy a little older. They stared vacantly with pale blue eyes at their fellow-passengers and ate Cracker-Jack with their mouths open, forgetting what they were doing and allowing the boxes to fall from their laps, spilling their contents everywhere. They were silent for the most part, but now and again, for no visible reason, they wailed loudly as if they were in pain and then stopped as abruptly as they had begun. They absent-mindedly plucked at the tussocks of their mother's collar and she told them, without any feeling, to "lay offn' me."

He tried to read *The Girl of the Limberlost* and could not. He worked at the crossword puzzle in the Denver *Post* but gave up when he came to "the soubriquet of Ferdinand II." He endeavored and in vain to feel the rapture of last night and he even hummed to himself some of the songs they had played: "Glow Worm," "Sleepy-Time Gal," "I'm Looking Over a Four Leaf Clover." He fled from Leah's face but it gained upon him and was before his mind's eye, doll-like and china-white. The train, the slowest on earth, seemed to rocket up the peaks and hurtle down the valleys and through the long tunnels, taking him, at this mad rate, miles away from Leah, miles on the way to Winifred whom now he was bound in conscience to love in order to purge from his heart the unholy image of his sister.

At noon they went into the forward car where there was a small buffet at one end. An amiable Negro sold dry ham sandwiches and coffee of a strange buttery flavor. Opposite Ralph and Molly, sitting with a table between them, were four ranchers, drinking whisky out of Lily cups. Farther up the car was a sandy-haired little man with a small, spiteful mouth and blue pop eyes. He wore a cerise silk neckerchief and a black and yellow braided belt; his Levis were stiff and new and he had turned up the cuffs to show his black boots with curlicues burned into the tops of them. He had a bottle too, but he did not fool with a Lily cup; instead he put the bottle to his mouth and gurgled loudly. Molly continued to read as she ate, having made the statement when they came in that Napoleon was a man she wished she had known platonically. Ralph gazed out the window at the deep gorge of the Wolf River, full and foaming from the big thaws. The train slowed down so much for a steep grade that he saw a fat woodchuck calmly eating something on a rock at the edge of the track-bed. They came then into a brilliant valley, checkered with neat fields, and here the river was deeper and was the color of dark, dim gold.

A large Germanic man who smoked a pipe said, when they stopped at Peacetown and he had scrutinized the landscape, "Don't Luke Fisher live up there? Yonder, I'm talking about, past them cottonwoods? Seems to me like he does."

His companions first agreed, then doubted, then denied, and it was established finally that Fisher lived twenty-seven miles to the east. But this did not dissuade the speaker, as it would not have done a man at Uncle Claude's table, from talking further of Luke Fisher. "He done mighty well with them kids after his wife died, that's one thing you can say for him. All of them but the oldest boy and that one, Milton, turned out ornery as a bobcat. You ever hear about the time he was working for Roger Campbell and turned loose a stallion with the saddle horses? You know the stallion I mean? He was an ugly bastard of a paint with one blue eye. Campbell bought him off Prescott and sold him to some blooded dude here a while back for seven thousand dollars. Well, this here Milton—Milt, they called him—was wrangling Campbell's horses up there one summer. Campbell used to have a whole hell of a lot more dudes than he's got now, don't ask me why because I don't know. Anyway, I guess this Milt got aholt of a bottle of rotgut whisky and drank it one Saturday night because the next Sunday morning when the dudes went out to get on their horses, there wasn't anything in the world in the corral but that ball-face stallion kicking the bejesus out of every goddam bench on the place. Campbell had some good horses too. Bought a colt off him myself once, pretty near the finest horse I ever had. Ken Burkhardt's got her now down to Kenyon's place."

It was not unusual for Ralph to hear his uncle's name in these conversations. Indeed, he could not remember a time when Uncle Claude had not come up in connection with something or other and it gave him a sense of security and pride. His name was as well known here, as much taken for granted, as that of President Hoover. Sometimes he and Molly talked loudly to establish their identity so that

153

the men would speak to them, but they never did, although usually they knew who the children were, and when they got off at White Woman, someone would look out the window and say, "Well, there's Kenyon's pick-up, so the kids won't have to walk home."

Between swallows, the solitary man cut his nails with a jackknife and whistled tunelessly between his teeth. He finished his whisky as they sat there, and when he had tucked the bottle away under the seat, he smiled at the men across the aisle. His smile was only a physical adjustment of his lips; it was like the grin of a panting dog. He spoke with a Texas accent, and he said, "I don't like to horn in on you boys if you're discussing something private, but I was studying on maybe one of you all having an extra bottle of corn whisky that I could buy off you. I aimed to stock up better than I done, but I'm a stranger to Denver and only got just this one pint. Hadn't stocked up on the password was my trouble." There was a pause during which he did not close his mouth. The four men shrewdly sized him up, and although it was clear that they did not approve of him, one of them nevertheless fetched down his valise from the luggage rack and got out an unlabeled pint bottle. The Texan handed him three silver dollars and the man pocketed them wordlessly.

The stranger drank and then, to the men who had not taken their eyes off him, he said, "Well, no offense intended, but that ain't worth three dollars and it ain't worth two. If a man felt right free, he might give six bits for it. By Jesus, they got us coming and going between the goddam government and the goddam bootleggers."

His listeners' faces were expressionless. Presently, the tall Germanic man said, "Where you from?"

"Well, Mister, as of seventy-five hours forty-five minutes ago, I'm from San Fernando Hospital, San Anton'. I laid on a bed for six holy months. Broke my leg bulldogging a steer on Christmas day."

He had recovered now and was on his way to Laramie to put on an exhibition for a millionaire and his pals who had hinted of Madison Square Garden. "Can you feature a rodeo indoors?" he said. "I can't, but, Momma dear! I *can* feature the cash in them New York dudes' jeans." He had never been through this country before, he said, but in Reno once last November he had met a man from here. He had met him at a gambling table and he would swear on a stack of Bibles that he had never seen a man with such luck. "I can't call his name, though I'd remember if I heard it. But anyway, that man had the most gorgeous luck I ever saw in my born days. He won him one hundred twenty-five dollars before he said quit, and if I'd of been in his place, I would of gone on. But then, I always was a sucker."

It was agreed, finally, that the lucky gambler was Homer Armitage and the details of his fortunate career were reported, how, at Spit-in-the-Ocean, he had bluffed his way into a twenty-dollar pot, had never been known to lose a cent at Stud, and was the one man in ten thousand that could make a slot machine pay off. The stranger said, "He cheats, don't he?" and grinned.

The four men sat up straight and the one who had given him the whisky said, "You had ought to watch the way

155

you talk, Mister. Homer Armitage don't cheat and you're among his friends."

Molly looked up from her book and laughing noiselessly, said, "Ride 'em, cowboy." Ralph, who until then had seen nothing amusing in the native's defense of a fellow-citizen against an outlander, scowled, annoyed that, as usual, she was twice as quick-witted as he even though she had appeared to be absorbed in her book.

After that the Texan drank in silence, sucking his bottle like a baby, and the others did not speak to him again, but went on talking of Homer. When his luck at cards had been exhausted, one of them said, "Hear Armitage bought a quarter interest in Kenyon's place. If the man's got money to do that, I don't see why he don't get his own place. It ain't any good working for somebody else."

"Kenyon ain't bad to work for," said another. "He pays his men good."

A yellow-haired and cross-eyed man said, "Hear Kenyon's going to get married."

"You don't say? Who to?"

"I haven't got the foggiest. Just something my wife picked up and told me. She didn't know either. I asked her."

"Well, it's time. It ain't that girl of Kennedy's, is it? The one that has the school up to the Forks?"

"Christ, no. She's Harmon Tucker's girl."

"Well, I'll be damned. I wonder who it is."

Molly closed her book and leaning across the empty plates and cups, whispered, "Did you hear that? Do you know what I think? I think Uncle Claude is going to marry Magdalene."

He did not bother to be irritated with her. The thought

156

was immediately in his mind that Uncle Claude was going to marry Winifred, and now the blustering passion of last night returned. Imperfectly, as if he looked through waves of heat, he saw his sister's forehead furrow with surprise and then smooth out again as her lips curled in a smile whose intention he could not grasp. He thought: what has given me away? But Molly said nothing and prepared to go back to the other car. For one interminable moment he sat still. The train was picking up speed, for they were coming down off Booth Pass. Between this and Cuthbert there was a ride of three more hours during which they would pass through fourteen tunnels, one of which, the longest, they were rushing toward now. This was the part of the journey he and Molly had always looked forward to. Sometimes they saw a man standing in a niche at the side, the pale light from the lamp on his cap giving his grimy face a corpse-like luminosity. Once a bat had flown against the very window at Molly's elbow.

As Ralph lurched through the buffet car, he heard the train hoot, protracting its note of warning so long that he knew they were almost at the mouth of the tunnel. By the time he had passed through the vestibule, the lamps in the car were turned on. They were not powerful and the blackness of the tunnel, even at its entrance, was so complete that the light was crepuscular. Coal smoke, forced back from the locomotive, seeped through the door of the observation platform. His mouth already tasted foully of sulphur. He made his way toward Molly. The woman with the children leaned out into the aisle as he passed by and she said in a flat voice, "You got a match?" He flushed in the dimness as he shook his head, ashamed that he did not smoke. He saw that she wore no wedding ring.

He sat down beside Molly, although the seat in front was pushed back so that they could be opposite one another. Partly he did not wish her to read any further in his face and partly he wanted to feel her near by. He thought of her as if she were the last foothold beneath which the world fell away in a chasm: it would be so easy to lose his footing, relax his fingerholds, and plunge downward to wedge his bones in a socket of rocks. Vile fogs baffled him and vileness was below him. Molly, alone, he thought, did not urge him to corruption.

For the moment he was protected by her elbow and her knee which touched his, and by the sexless odor of her new white shirt which she wore with a pair of black sateen gym bloomers. He saw the tunnel as an apotheosis of his own black, sinful mind which had incestuously coveted Leah (he trembled to think of Mr. Robert Appleton) and the girl who might well be his aunt-by-marriage, the mind that had observed with delight that the mother of the seedy children had no wedding ring. He urged the train to make haste. Once out in the bright green meadows of the valley he thought he would be safe from the thoughts that swarmed about him like a dream of reptiles. As long as Molly was here beside him, though, he could hang on.

And then he knew he had been wrong, that he was not safe; he was weakening and ready to fall, and now he actually slumped down in the seat so that his shoulders were on a level with Molly's and he said, in the lowest voice, "Molly, tell me all the dirty words you know."

He heard himself almost with relief. Before there was

time for Molly to move away or to utter a cry, they had emerged into the light which streamed like glory through the dirty window panes. The sun was high and the fields shimmered. Round them, for miles, as far as the eye could see, were the violet mountains, clean-lined, clear of haze. The eye could not detect a single impurity in all the scene.

Ralph's childhood and his sister's expired at that moment of the train's entrance into the surcharged valley. It was a paradox, for now they should be going into a tunnel with no end, now that they had heard the devil speak.

# CHAPTER SEVEN

WHEN THEY CAME INTO THE LONG LIVING ROOM LATE IN the afternoon, Mrs. Brotherman was waiting for them as she had always done in former years. She sat, thinner, sadder, more pearly than ever, beside a table where she had put a bowl of apples and a pitcher of cider. These days of early June were still cool in the mountains when the sun was setting, so there was a fire in the hearth and the housekeeper, whose aging blood was pale, leaned toward it with a wan, inadmissible hunger. Ralph recalled the gritty heat in Denver: it had been as recently as last night that, sweating in the hotel bedroom, he had listened gluttonously to the music of the jazz band which was itself suffused with summer heat and moistness. The room had been cleaned that day and it shone dustlessly in the light from the fire and the light from the setting sun that burned through the windows. All the catalogues and the magazines of western stories were stacked up neatly and there was a feminine order in the arrangement of sacks of Bull Durham, boxes of cartridges, and tins of pipe tobacco on the big varnished table, an order Uncle Claude, seeming almost driven by necessity, at once demolished by seeking cigarette papers with a planless hand.

Familiar smells came to Ralph faintly after he had been greeted by Mrs. Brotherman and had sat down for a ceremonious moment of silence. There were the smell of fat meat cooking in beans, the smell of the apples and of the pitch in the spitting pine logs; over them all was the nameless smell of the house itself whose elements comprised leather, saddle soap, oily ramrods, dogs and drying hides. With the well-known smells came the sounds of a cow bellowing for the calf that had been butchered that morning; the team horses, turned loose, neighing as they ran foolishly in circles round their pasture; the barking of dogs on distant farms; the clatter of milk buckets down at the barn; the obstreperous arrival of the tractor across the bridge over the big slough.

He could taste the apples in the cider and he wondered if wine really tasted of grapes. Often in the past summers Uncle Claude had given him a glass of Dago red, but it had only tasted thick and faintly sour. He had liked, though, to sit in this room with him and the other men on special evenings—Saturdays or when it was storming—and watch them pass the gallon jug back and forth as they filled their teacups, bragging that they were getting as tight as ticks, although Ralph could see no difference in them.

Uncle Claude now stood with one leg flung over the end of the table, rolling a cigarette. His hat was pushed back and a lock of black hair lay on his forehead like a leech. He had not shaved and the small blue spines made his jaw look sunken. Although he was otherwise unaltered, this detail made Ralph quickly alert to him, not as his uncle nor as the man's man, drinking bootleg wine, but as an almost anonymous man, old enough both to have a heavy beard and to marry a girl. Indeed, he had never known how very old Uncle Claude was until today, on the way from the station, Molly had asked him and he had told her that he was thirty-six. "You're the same age as my father," she had said. Further, Ralph observed that if he himself had been looking for the cigarette papers, he would not have messed up the other things and he wondered if there would ever be a time in his life when he could be untidy without being self-conscious about it. At this moment of resentment, as if he had spoken his futile envy aloud, Uncle Claude said, "Where's Winifred?" Ralph was sure he heard a note of possessiveness in his uncle's voice and that when Mrs. Brotherman's reply came, he saw a flush under the stubble. "She went to see *The Scarlet Pimpernel* with one of her beaux." Molly gave Ralph a rapid, spiteful glance and then looked at her feet, smiling with dreadful secrets. It seemed to him that something was going to happen and there came to his mind, quite inexplicably, the idea that an arrow was going to be shot from an unseen bow the length of the room to imbed itself in the neck of the antelope on the south wall. But the charged moment ended when Mrs. Brotherman, refilling Molly's cider glass, said humbly, "How nice for your sisters and your mother to go all the way around the world. I expect they will have wonderful tales to tell when they get home."

"I suppose so," said Molly, "if you happen to like that sort of hogwash and soul-butter. I happen not to be the type."

Uncle Claude laughed. "Hogwash and soul-butter, that's a new one. Where'd you get that one?"

Molly said, "In a book I read when I was a child. A book by Samuel Clemens."

"Listen to Grandma," said Uncle Claude.

Ralph was quite unable, even though he concentrated so hard that his head began to ache, to feel any emotion at all over Mrs. Brotherman's announcement that Winifred was at the movies with a beau. And not just "her *beau*" but "one of her *beaux*." The word had a fusty, old-fashioned sound and made him think of his mother who would say, "When I went to a taffy-pull with a beau," or "a beau of mine gave me the souvenir spoon from the Alamo." All that really took his fancy was the fact that Winifred was seeing *The Scarlet Pimpernel* which had, to his regret, been scheduled in Covina for the week after they left. He wished somehow to convey his indifference to Molly, but she sat, incommunicable, enclosed within herself, staring at the flames as she munched her apple, an enemy to both the fire and the fruit. It was barely possible that he had misread her smile in the buffet car, and in this case, silence was the only possible policy.

Uncle Claude and Mrs. Brotherman asked them questions about who had bought the walnut grove, the name of the ship on which the travelers were sailing, whether Mrs. Fawcett had spoken to the caretaker about Grandpa's grave. Molly replied in pig-like monosyllables, watching Ralph as he politely filled in and then, in his turn, inquired after Homer Armitage who, for some inscrutable reason, was taking a correspondence course in shorthand and who had not, as the man on the train declared, bought an interest

163

in the Bar K; and after Magdalene who had made more than a hundred dollars last winter by trapping skunks; and after the men to whom, it appeared, nothing at all had happened.

"When's the wedding?" said Molly at length, biting an apple seed between her front teeth.

"What wedding?" said Uncle Claude.

"Yours and Magdalene's."

"Molly!" cried Mrs. Brotherman, horrified.

Uncle Claude looked at her as if they were exactly the same age. "If you don't watch out, they're going to put you in the booby hatch. I never seen anybody in my life with such damn crazy ideas."

"Well, if you're not going to marry Magdalene, who are you going to marry? Me?"

"Shut up, Molly," said Ralph, beside himself with embarrassment, and then, to Uncle Claude, he explained what they had heard on the train.

"Well, I'll be," said Uncle Claude, pleased. "It don't happen to be true but I'm obliged to those boys for thinking I'm a ladies' man, which I am as far from being as Molly is from having good sense."

"Then you *aren't* going to get married?" said Ralph with an eagerness he could not suppress.

"You bet I'm not," said Uncle Claude.

Molly said crossly, "Why isn't there any salt for the apples?" and glared balefully at Ralph.

It was only a question of minutes, he thought, before the grown-ups would begin to suspect that some issue had been raised between him and Molly, even though neither was quick to observe such things, Uncle Claude because he wore his own feelings clearly on his face and expected everyone else to do likewise, and Mrs. Brotherman because she had imposed on all the world a smooth, unruffled sadness in which all events were exactly the same. She returned with a melancholy warmth to the world cruise and asked Molly if she were not proud of the travelers.

"Why?" said Molly. "Why in the world would I be proud of them? I could have gone too if I had wanted to, and now I'm sorry I didn't."

"Why, Molly," said Mrs. Brotherman. "Why, Molly, what a thing to say. Your uncle will think you aren't happy here."

"I'm not," said Molly.

Uncle Claude colored and Molly, fearless and level-headed, looked from him to Ralph and back again, disliking them both. It was true, of course, that she had never been close to Uncle Claude and had held a grudge against him for ending her companionship with Ralph; but if a word of criticism were spoken against him in Covina, she was savagely defensive, principally because he was Grandpa Kenyon's son and Grandpa Kenyon continued in her rapt memory as the only hero of her life. Today, in her fault-finding gaze, there was something besides this old resentment, but Ralph could not put his finger on it.

Mrs. Brotherman was distressed and said, "Oh, dearie, you are worn out from the journey. Have another apple, do." Molly took the apple, her third, and slumped down in her chair to eat it in small bites like a squirrel, mumbling once, "I prefer bananas, of course," and then subsiding into a vigilant silence. Everyone but this forthright monster was embarrassed; black-haired, studiously misshapen, noisily nibbling, she tyrannized them into a gawky silence and then suddenly she kicked Ralph sharply on the shin. It made him gulp with pain but he said nothing although he could feel the very skin draw tight over his cheeks.

Uncle Claude looked curiously at them both and said, "Did you two have a scrap somewhere along the line?"

"No," said Molly shortly and returned to her apple. Anyone else would have been fighting back tears, but Molly's tantrum was controlled and dry-eyed.

"Then what's eating on you?" Often Uncle Claude did not, as Mrs. Fawcett would have said, "know when to let well enough alone."

"None of your beeswax, Mr. Kenyon," she said, "and that's that."

Uncle Claude was furious. For a moment Ralph thought he was going to pull her hair or twist her arms behind her back, and he did take a step toward her, but checked himself and pretended he had only moved nearer the fireplace to throw his cigarette away and then, ignoring her entirely, he said to Ralph, "Come on up to the gallery. I want to show you something."

The gallery ran the length of the short wall of the room. Most of the space was taken up by the poker table and the chairs, but at one end there was a sort of alcove, called "the office," with a rolltop desk where Uncle Claude kept the registration papers of his pedigreed bulls and all sorts of other documents of an important historical nature, such things as land grants, dark yellow with age, signed by Buchanan and Lincoln, a trap-shooting certificate belonging to Homer Armitage and Uncle Claude's birth certificate in which his middle name was written down as "None." Over this desk, obscured by the shadows of a lodgepole pine which grew close to the house and thrust its needles against the window screen, was a picture of Ralph's grandmother. It was a journeyman portrait with a background of a blue lake in the distance and nearer at hand an ailanthus tree in flower. She wore a lace cap over her brown hair which hung in ringlets to her shoulders, and in her hand she held a white silk fan. Mrs. Bonney-Kenyon had a firm Scotch face with narrow lips and a small thin nose which ever so slightly tilted up. None of her children or her grandchildren bore any resemblance to her at all, but this, really, was no wonder, since both her husbands had been such powerful characters. Ralph could not tell whether she looked humorless or beaten or whether the unhappy look in her hazel eyes, set close together, came from embarrassment at the anachronistic curls which beset her plain face. As he came up the stairs behind Uncle Claude, he glanced in at her and he was struck with terror, thinking of how she had died giving birth to the man ahead of him.

They went to the window opposite the poker table and Uncle Claude pointed out to a bull in a small pasture by himself. He had a hairball in his jaw the size of a grapefruit. The vet had not been able to come to operate yet and the beast suffered noisily. As they watched, he faunched up the grassy ground around him and then, bellowing with pain and fury, rubbed the great tumor against the trunk of a poplar tree. He seemed to stare directly into their eyes with hatred as if they were responsible for his torment. There was something horrible in the spectacle and Ralph was absorbed by it. His uncle, likewise, seemed half hypnotized, and in this brief time of their brutal preoccupation, their companionship was so complete that it almost frightened Ralph; it was as though he had set forth on an adventure whose terms were so inexorable that he could not possibly change his mind and go back, as if they were on a boat in the middle of a landless sea. He looked at the heavy, small-chinned face in which, as the dark clear eyes studied the sick bull, there was a certain ponderous stupidity, a sort of virile opacity, an undeviating dedication to the sickness and health and the breeding of animals. The bull, by acquiring this infirmity, had temporarily become a nothing since he could not perform his function as a sire. It was almost as if he had made a fool of himself, for surely the smile that came and went in Uncle Claude's face was a mocking one. While this discovery appalled him, he was determined never to be degraded in the man's eyes as the bull had degraded himself, as Molly had done, simply by being the kind of person she was, bookish and unhealthy. Even so, he was mixed in his feeling about Uncle Claude and his resolution was the result not of a refreshed admiration but of the desire to go unnoticed by having no shortcomings. Because his own masculinity was, in its articulation, so ugly, and he could therefore take no pleasure in himself, neither could he respect it in anyone else, and he was sorry now that he had heard Uncle Claude use dirty words to Magdalene. Was it possible that even Grandpa had been like that? He quickly thrust away the dishonorable thought.

Mrs. Brotherman, in her sighing monotone, was telling Molly about the bad luck she had had last winter with her house plants. Several times Molly said something in reply, but Ralph could not catch her words which she uttered as softly as a secret. Poor Molly, so unflower-like, should have been interested in something like minerals, but she loved flowers, and at times, when her writing was not going well, thought that she would be a nursery man. Mrs. Fawcett always sent Leah and Rachel for the delphiniums and the roses, but Molly picked the marigold and the calendula. They would come across the lippia lawn, Leah and Rachel in front, carrying dozens of full-faced roses whose gentle petals touched their perfect little chins, and Molly following behind with her sidelong lope, clutching the hairy stems of the harsh, scentless orange flowers. But Mrs. Brotherman, leaving the winter's woe to talk instead of her summer hopes, included Molly in her gardening plans and once Ralph heard his sister say, without a bit of cynicism, "Do you think we can *ever* have a rambler, Mrs. Brotherman?"

Suddenly Uncle Claude put his hand on Ralph's shoulder and said, "I'm mighty glad you've come to stay a while this time," and Ralph, while he did not move, felt himself grow cold with withdrawal and with something like distrust for the enthusiasm in his uncle's voice, so boy-like that it actually cracked. For right now he did not want any attention paid to him at all. But when Uncle Claude went on, he realized to his relief that it was not he that had so inspired the man, but the tale he now commenced to tell him.

"Don't you know how I've always said I wanted to get me a mountain lion?" he said. "Don't you know that? Well, I'm on the trail of one now."

He paused and smiled, waiting to be questioned and Ralph cried, "Where?"

Uncle Claude had seen the lion in the foothills before you got to Garland Peak. He had seen her only once early in April and had gone back time after time to have another glimpse of her or of her mate. He had been so bent on having her hide that he had wasted a lot of hunting time just fooling around looking for her and he hadn't got a piece of game this year, though there had been plenty to be had and the boys had stocked up well. She was about as big as a good-sized dog, he said, and she looked for all the world like an overgrown house cat. He thought about her so much that he had given her a name; he called her Goldilocks because, running the way she had in the sunlight, she had been as blonde as a movie star. He had told the boys, including Homer, that he would fire any one of them that drew a bead on her because if anyone got her, it was going to be him. Old Magdalene had ragged him a God's plenty, saying that *she* was going to catch the lion with fresh kid meat. No one had quite understood why he was so all-fired crazy to get her and he could not quite make it out himself. "But you know, every now and again a man will get a bug like this and there's no more rest for him." Sometimes he would go up and spend the whole day, packing his lunch along with him, and by sundown he would be cursing her, talking to her image as if she were a person.

He had decided that he was going to let Ralph hunt her too. They were never to hunt alone and were, when they separated, to keep within hailing distance of one another. This singular honor made Ralph feel as if he were actually rising in the air and he warmly thanked Uncle Claude while, deceitfully and unsportingly, he resolved that it would be *he,* not the man, who got the lion. For a few minutes his joy was immediate and unspoiled, and then it was smashed and he remembered again what he had said to Molly in the tunnel, for through the quiet—all other noises were suspended for this new sound—came the roaring of a car, tearing along the road with the cut-out open, and he could see it, a scarlet Model A roadster with the top down as it appeared and disappeared in the lacy sarvis berry that grew along the bank. He knew at once that this was Winifred and her beau, and when the car came fully into view and turned in at the lane with a brash squeal and he saw the girl (*his* girl!) sitting beside a boy in a porkpie hat, he was overcome by the most painful sensation he had ever known and thought he was going to become too limp to stand up straight. And yet, in spite of his consuming daze, he had the presence of mind to look quickly at his uncle and to see, with another emotion that he could not name, that nothing had registered in his face at all, that he did not even glance at the car but turned to look at the sick bull again, saying, "Laid up thisaway, that bastard is losing me money right and left."

The car now passed out of sight, drawing up to the front of the house. Its engine was suddenly raced and then it idled like a loud whisper. Molly and Mrs. Brotherman continued their secret conversation about the roses and Uncle Claude muttered to himself about the bull. Only Ralph was conscious of the laughter of the boy and girl which, high, prolonged, gasping, was immodest and exciting and he felt himself to be in extreme danger. At last there was an antiphonal good-bye which, lacking the greed of the laughter, rang out mournfully over the yellow valley and the sudden car went back up the lane like a clowning dog.

He heard her come through the screen door and he turned jerkily, leaning against the railing of the gallery.

Uncle Claude did not stir. Winifred raised her hand in salutation to him, smiled widely, and said, "Hi, chum," and then went to Molly and kissed her after the manner of cousins and grown-up women friends. She was plump now and so mature and feminine that Ralph could not recognize in her the shooting companion of earlier summers, that rather negative and taciturn person who, without playing a role, had seemed like another boy. Now she was a positive creature, self-assured, beautiful and glowing with an interior smile. She threw her polo coat over the back of a chair and sat down on the milking stool before the hearth. She was wearing a white dress, sleeveless and low in the back and low at the neck, and her flesh looked as brown as Fuschia's against it. He could not remember ever having seen her in anything but blue jeans and a faded work shirt; she was shorter than he remembered. There was, somehow, a settled look about her; she had a tender, untroubled, and vacuous gaze, and it would have been impossible for any-one to tell what she was smiling at.

He was uncertain. As soon as he no longer heard the red car, he was no longer jealous. And when he saw her sitting there, as native to the stool as a cat, he felt nothing at all, but the void was not painful; rather it was like a great soothing boredom. He turned to Uncle Claude and said, "What'll we hunt her with? A thirty-thirty?"

But Molly drowned out his uncle's reply with a sudden laugh. Her voice was deep for a girl and her laugh was slow and muffled but, though now she laughed her same laugh, it seemed to Ralph it had in it some of the same immodesty Winifred's had when she lingered with the boy, and in panic he thought, "She has *told!*" He knew this to be untrue, but the pleasure of the hour—scattered as it had been and filled in the interstices with embarrassment and guilt—was gone. Darkness was beginning and he felt friendless, separate, unclean. Again he tasted the sulphur at the back of his jaws and again he saw the woman in the train and her claw-like, ringless hand.

After supper Molly refused to play Continental Rummy because there was too much danger of having to speak to Ralph, and she went directly upstairs to take a bath. She drew the bolt and turned the key in the lock as well and she pulled down the window shade even though there was nothing outside but night. She was very dirty from the train. Dirt had seeped through her basketball shoes and her feet were a sight. Her arms were uniformly gray, beginning at her wrists and going up to her elbows which felt like dried-up biscuits. She had washed her hands before supper so that she appeared to be wearing a pair of pinkish gloves. Molly enjoyed being this dirty; when you were not black or at least gray, bathing seemed wasteful and self-indulgent just as did making your bed if you had not mussed up the covers much. But if you were properly dirty and could take a long, large bath, it was fun.

She had brought to the bathroom with her a Boston bag which she kept locked and hidden away on the topmost shelf of her closet. It contained green bathsalts and violet bathsalts of so inferior a quality that no matter how hot the water was, they did not melt but lay, as sharp and shining as quartz on the bottom of the tub so that it was necessary to sweep a place clean with her hand before she got in. Even so, they gave off a sweet fragrance and she could imagine that she was in a garden. Besides the bathsalts, there were a cake of soap in the form of a yellow rose, a can of Armand's talcum powder, a bottle of Hind's Honey and Almond, a jar of Daggett and Ramsdell vanishing creaming, a bottle of Glostora shampoo, a jar of Dr. Scholl's foot balm, a jar of freckle remover, some scissors, a nail file, a toothbrush, some dental floss, a comb, a brush, a buffer, a chamois skin, and a pearl-handled corn parer. Covering them all was a maroon bathing suit.

She hung a towel over the back of the chair and moved the chair in front of the keyhole to thwart any Peeping Tom. Then she stood on the chair and took off her blouse and her gym pants and threw her wrapper around her shoulders while she took off her undervest and bloomers and got into the bathing suit. She sat on the chair waiting for the tub to fill, thinking of nothing, for there would be plenty of time once she was in the bath. It was unlikely that any of them would come up and try the knob because they were all sitting around the table in the gallery, all but Mrs. Brotherman who spent her evenings, and always had, crocheting a bedspread for Winifred for when she got married. They would be sitting there, those illiterate men, scratching themselves and getting the ends of their cigarettes wet and saying things like "he don't" and "you was" and "those kind" and if the subject came up, pronouncing "apricot" with a short "a." As likely as not, if Winifred had decided not to play, they would drink whisky and wine which, as everyone knew, was nine-tenths fusel oil and the chances of going blind on it were ninety-nine out of a hundred. However, they were quite unimportant to her.

174

Under the roar of the hot water, she said, "*I* should ish-kibibble if they all commit suicide."

She turned off the water and got into the tub, but she had run in too much cold and had to get out again and run in some more hot, for Molly never sat in the bathtub while the water was running: a slender snake might come right through the faucet. At the thought of snakes, she shivered all over and remembered every single encounter she had had with them, beginning with the very earliest when she was four and was too little to go to school. She was waiting one day under the umbrella tree for the bus to bring home her sisters and her brother. When she heard it coming, she walked across the lippia lawn to the patch of clover and there she stepped on a coiled-up snake which uncoiled under her bare foot and slithered off. She had stood there, unable to move but screaming at the top of her voice until Miguel came running and picked her up. She had never known whether it was the feeling of the snake under her foot or the smell of Miguel's sweaty shirt that made her throw up over his shoulder as he carried her to the house. "Aren't you ashamed," said her mother. "Why, it was nothing but a harmless garter snake." Ralph found it and killed it with a rock and took Molly out to see, but the sight of it, even dead, only made her scream again until he had to carry her piggy-back to the porch so that she would not have to step on the ground. There was another time when she and Ralph, acting out "The Little Swiss Twins," had taken a lunch of cheese and crackers to the Wash and all of a sudden Molly discovered that she was sitting right beside a bright green grass snake. This time Ralph was not kind to her. When she screamed, he slapped her face and said, "Oh, you make me sick, you big fat baby." The worst of all had happened right here, the first summer, although a real snake was not involved. She had been reading *The World Almanac* one day in the leather chair in Uncle Claude's office and had taken a horse hair out of a tear in the arm to play with in her mouth because she had forgotten to bring a match and quite unexpectedly she had swallowed it. She went down to the kitchen to ask Magdalene what to do and Magdalene said she must quickly drink a glass of water or it would turn into a bull snake in her stomach and eat up everything she ate so that she would die of starvation; Magdalene had known at least eleven people that this had happened to. She rushed to the sink and Magdalene said, "That's hard water. That ain't no good for what ails you." So she ran upstairs to Mrs. Brotherman to say that she had better get right back to Covina so that Dr. Haskell could operate on her and Mrs. Brotherman told her that Magdalene had made the whole thing up. She returned to the kitchen and said, "You're a nigger," and Magdalene replied, "You're pore white trash."

Mrs. Fawcett said she would outgrow this fear as soon as she was able to distinguish between the harmless snakes and the poisonous ones, but Molly knew this was not true because she did not even like to look at the pictures of them in the illustrated part at the back of the Unabridged. It enraged her to be told that they were useful because they ate destructive insects, and when Leah and Rachel said that if she had any sense of beauty at all, she would see that their colors and patterns were wonderful, she replied, "Who cares about a sense of beauty? I'd a whole lot rather have a sense of *proportion,* you conceited Elsie Dinsmores."

Molly lay soaking in her bathing suit so long that her skin became white and ridged. Every now and again, she got out and stood dripping on the rag rug while she ran more hot water in. She washed her hair in the bath water and let it drip down her back, the drops crawling like flies. Lying full length sometimes she let her feet and hands float to the surface and saw that they looked like something drowned; she thought of the flood when her father had brought the old woman into the kitchen. The only other thing Molly knew about the old woman was that it was said that when she was a child she had lived in a goiter belt, so now she had to drink iodine in her water.

She looked at her long feet which she allowed slowly to sink again. But for the most part, she was not conscious of her body (she was never conscious of it as a *body* and had never spoken this word aloud and almost died when one of her sisters would jokingly say, "Don't touch my body"; Molly thought of herself as a long wooden box with a mind inside) but of what had happened that afternoon in the train and she went over the whole scene time after time, each time redeeming the brilliant hatred that had spread over her exactly like bath water. Often she had hated Ralph but she had always got over it. She hated him for a month once because, when she showed him a picture in tempera of a New England kitchen, he had laughed so hard that he spit and made the red and white checked seat on the rocking chair run. Once he had brought her a little horseshoe magnet and told her that the teachers had voted to give it to her as a reward for being so diligent in collateral reading, and when she went to thank Miss Bandy,

Miss Bandy said, "Why, Molly, I think this is just something out of a Cracker-Jack box."

But while she would never forget these injuries, they no longer made her feel as if she were going to have a nosebleed. This new outrage, though, was a horse of quite a different color, and she vowed several times, raising her right arm out of the water, that she would hate Ralph Fawcett for the rest of her life. She was not certain yet how she would show him that she was his permanent enemy, but she was in no hurry to decide. For the time being she could simply lie here in the tub, safe behind a locked door, and contemplate the thing he had done, so terrible, so blackly wicked that it was thrilling. It was sharply pleasant, too, to think that she could now add Ralph's name to her list of unforgivable people, a list that included almost everyone. There were some doubtful cases (she was not completely sure about Winifred and Uncle Claude), but there were only two people who were purely forgivable and these were her father and Grandpa Kenyon. She did not forgive her father simply because she had never known him, or Grandpa just because he was dead; after all, Grandfather Bonney was a foremost unforgivable and even Grandmother Bonney was a doubtful. She often wondered, proudly, why she hated people. Sometimes she could figure back to the moment the feeling began. For example, she had hated Pinky Freudenburg beginning one day when she had stayed in at recess to work on her long division and he had stayed in too; she had gone to the pencil sharpener and he had sneaked up behind her and kissed her on the cheek and at that exact same moment, a front tooth fell out onto her tongue. She had liked Pinky until then because he made up dances to illustrate her poems besides others which he made up on his own. There was a "Pineapple Dance" and a "Ten-Cent-Store Dance" and a "Mashed Potato Dance." They were all rather alike but very exciting to watch, and Molly was sorry that she had to put her handkerchief over her eyes every time he did one of them in the playground. She had known, too, the moment Grandfather Bonney had become unforgivable. It was the day Ralph threw up in the living room and she poured the acid on her hand. She had looked at the portrait just before Ralph said the milk was sour and had thought "I h. that man," and had known that this would be true forever and ever. But she could not remember when she had begun to hate her mother and Leah and Rachel. As for the Follansbees, of course, she had hated them before she was born.

It occurred to her as her fingers grew more swollen and furrowed that she hated them all for the same reason, but she could not decide what the reason was. You could say, Because they were all fat. But this was not true of Mr. Follansbee and it was not true of Ralph and strictly speaking it was not true of Leah and Rachel although they talked in whispers of corselets. But fatness did have something to do with it. There was something fat about the way Mr. Follansbee belched and the question Ralph had asked her had been fat. She remembered, closing her eyes to see precisely the horrible image, the day early in April when the Follansbees had gone with them one Sunday to Redondo Beach, and Mrs. Follansbee had come out of the bathhouse in a bright red swimming suit. Her thin, knock-kneed legs were traced with thickened varicose veins; her stomach was soft and pendulous and made Molly think of a cake

that had run over the side of the pan. But Mr. Follansbee
was every bit as bad in his emaciated half-nakedness; his
spindling legs, covered all over with black hair, came out
of long, loose trunks with a white band around the edge
and his arms were hairy too, but his neck was as white as
a fish. She would not go in swimming with them but sat
on the beach, writing her name and grade in school in the
sand with a piece of driftwood. Her mother came once,
dripping and glistening, to sit beside her and plead with her
to "be a good sport," and she looked at the dimples in her
mother's pink knees and hoped she would get bitten by
a crab. Ralph had been embarrassed that day, too, and when
they had their picture taken against a fake background of
the ocean with sea gulls painted on the canvas, both children had refused to be in it and Ralph had muttered, "I
wouldn't be in a picture with those ginks if you gave me
the Statue of Liberty." But it was clear that no one could
be trusted, Ralph least of all. He had always hated the right
ones before and now he had become one of them. It did
seem a shame, really, that he had turned out so badly. He
had told her in so many words that the day he got sick
over the tea it had happened because he had seen through
Grandfather Bonney, and they had been best friends for
a month or so after that, marveling that it had come to
them at the same time.

After a long while she pulled up the stopper and let the
water run out, slipping down her sides, tickling a little,
and deep in her throat she imitated the sound it made as
it gurgled down the drain. If she ever got fat, she thought,
or ever said anything fat, she would lock herself in a bathroom and stay there until she died. Often she thought how

comfortably you could live in a bathroom. You could put a piece of beaver board on top of the tub and use it as a bed. In the daytime you could have a cretonne spread on it so that it would look like a divan. You could use the you-know-what as a chair and the lavatory as a table. You wouldn't have to have anything else but some canned corn and marshmallows, and if you got tired of those, you could let a basket out of the window with a slip of paper saying, "Send up some hot tamales" or some hard-boiled eggs or whatever you particularly wanted at the time.

But she doubted if she would ever get fat enough to have to live in a bathroom. She looked at her thin upper arm and gave it a monkey-bite. There were too many simple ways to avoid it as well as the drastic one of getting a tapeworm. She did profoundly hope, though, that Ralph would get fatter than Tweedledum and Tweedledee put together, and she put both her fists in her eyes, thinking with rapture of how tightly his pants would fit over his seat and his shirt would just barely button over his awful stomach. His cheeks would get so fat they would nearly cover up his eyes. All this time she, Molly Fawcett, would be getting thinner and thinner until she was practically famous for it, and when the time came, she was going to drop the fat name of Molly and be called Clara after Aunt Clara, Father's sister, of whom there was a full-length portrait in the album. Aunt Clara had been as straight up and down as a yardstick and she had enormous stick-out teeth. In the picture she wore a straight black skirt and a straight black jacket, black gloves, black shoes, and a black hat with a wide brim so that all you could see of her was her crooked nose and her great big teeth resting on her lower lip. Molly often stood before the mirror holding her teeth out and saying "Clara? Clara?" as if she were calling to her in the grave, calling to tell her that she would try to look just like her. Otherwise, Aunt Clara had not been very admirable as she had died having a tumor removed, and Mrs. Fawcett, in telling this, would say, "Why, girls, it was such a big tumor that everyone thought she was in a certain condition." She would lift her eyes questioningly and Rachel and Leah would wisely nod. Molly would not have dreamed of asking what the condition was, but she supposed it had something to do with all that tommyrot with which people were constantly trying to ruin her life.

Finally the last of the water was gone and she stood up, putting one foot on the rim of the tub and drying it and then standing on the rug while she dried the other. She gently moved the chair and tried the knob in case anyone had picked the lock while the water was making so much racket and then, taking off the bathing suit, she dried herself and bound her stomach with a piece of outing flannel. She wrapped it so hard and pinned it so tight that it gave her a pain and she had to lie down on the floor to get her slippers because she could not bend over. Then she put on her long-sleeved, high-necked pajamas, and the night-cap she had made over her drenched hair. It was her desire to have tuberculosis, and at the ranch, where she was not supervised, she often went to bed with her hair soaking. She had tried for years to find out where Winifred kept her toothbrush.

She packed up the Boston bag again, having used out of it only the soap and the bathsalts, and let herself out. The voices of the card players came twanging up the stairwell and there were no lights showing under any of the doors save Mrs. Brotherman's and she got to her room without being seen. If she had been seen by anyone, she didn't care who, in her wrapper on this particular night, she would simply have dissolved like a slug with salt poured on it. When she got to her room, she pushed the washstand against the door and she didn't care who heard her. If they did, they did not bother; they bothered about very little around this place and this was one of the few good things about it.

When she had hung her bathing suit up in the window, she got into bed and took up her diary which she kept under her mattress. She wrote:

Ralph has gone beyond the pale. I am his permanent enemy and do not know whether I will ever speak to him again as he has literally beat a rivet of hatred into my heart by a remark he passed on the train today. I am not sure about Winifred this year. She is too fat but she told me a good joke and for the first time in a month of Sundays it was funny enough for me to laugh at.

WINIFRED'S JOKE

You call someone up on the telephone and say, "Are you the lady who washes?" and the other person says, "No," so you say, "Why, you dirty thing," and hang up.

I am not sure about Winifred, as beforesaid, because she told me that she had been to the show with her steady and when I asked what she meant by a steady she said the boy you were dippy about and was dippy about you.

But getting back to the subject of my former brother, what he did is so devilish I could like Leah by comparison in spite of the letter she wrote that made her sound non compus mentis. I will not mention the subject of this letter nor will I write down what Ralph said to me in the train, but I can assure you, Molly, that they were plenty bad. I intend to read all of Sir Walter Scott, Dickens, Stevenson, and James Fenimore Cooper while I am here so that I won't have to have anything to do with R.F. He and Uncle Claude were talking about hunting a mountain lion. I can think of nothing more boresome personally. Uncle Claude looks very old. Naturally. He is thirty-six. I am not sure that I tolerate him. He didn't know what I meant when I said "hogwash and soul-butter" and I am perfectly certain he didn't know that Mark Twain's real name was Samuel Clemens. There are only two I am sure about, Mrs. Brotherman and Magdalene. Mrs. Brotherman will let me do the roses with her, but I do not know whether they will be any good because I read on the train in the Denver *Post* that the aphids are going to be very bad this year. I have not as yet conversed with Magdalene, but she said she had a rabbit foot for me which is said to bring good luck.

Resolution: think all the time about Ralph getting fat. Tomorrow I must look at the pictures of the stout men's underwear in the catalogue and decide which one I want him to be.

# CHAPTER EIGHT

In former years, ever since he had seen the calf being born, Ralph had been excited to a point of ecstasy by the robust and perpetual birth of the farm creatures. He had trembled all over at the sight of a mare being carried away in a truck to the stud farm and he had been on hand at every calving. He regretted always that the lambing came in the spring before he got there. Molly, of course, had steadfastly held her ground, and once, two years before, when he had tried to explain to her the difference between a stallion and a gelding, they had had a serious quarrel. She would not be shaken from the belief that they were simply two different breeds of horses. He had not, in any conscious way, really connected his knowledge with people, as now he did, to his shame and sorrow, wondering, with especial revulsion, about the Follansbees. He found himself compelled to study the faces of the men at the dinner table and to look with stunned amazement at Mrs. Brotherman.

Now, this summer, he took no pleasure in the colts and in the sucking calves, and he was glad that his horse and his uncle's had a pure masculine friendship and that they ran away from Winifred's mare whenever she came near

185

them. Winifred herself made him shy and uneasy but he was not in love with her; yet he thought, in a cloudy way, that if he had not committed the crime in the tunnel, he would have been.

For a time there was little, indeed, that he took pleasure in. When, now and again, he lost himself in some small enjoyment, his guilt started and the world was spoiled. He was obsessed with the phrase "the bowels of the earth" and imagined blackened intestines spilling forth from the carcass of a gigantic steer strung up on a pulley as high as a mountain, butchered out by a knife as long as a train. Wakeful at night, he lay with his head under the pillow to shut out the brilliant starlight; he was alert to every sound, hearing Molly, who despised him, turning and grumbling in her sleep; the owls cautioning in the cottonwoods; the men coming home late from White Woman. On these cool nights, full of the clean, unripe smells of June, he could not summon any daydream. For now he aspired to be nothing but what he had been before the evening at the Brown Palace, and he could not even pretend to be that person again because Molly knew his secret, nasty nature. Not even his favorite and foolproof image would come, that of himself as Uncle Claude's partner. If he did not become Uncle Claude's partner, what would happen to him? He had no variety of ambitions as had Molly who, in the course of a week, would plan to be a salesman for the *Book of Knowledge,* a grocer, a government walnut inspector, a trolley conductor in Tia Juana; of course her real vocation was writing and these were to be only sidelines.

Ralph was troubled by the loss of his desire to enter Uncle Claude's world completely. He had continued, against his will, to remember how he had looked at the sick bull and he thought, "If anything happened to a *person*, he'd be the same way." How was this possible, though, when Grandpa Kenyon's death had broken him up in pieces like a plate? Perhaps it was not death that annoyed and disgusted him but only the circumstances leading to death, and Ralph remembered that he had not asked a single question about Grandpa's attack or his three-day illness.

He would brood for a while about Uncle Claude and then brood about Molly. In time he invented a reason, abstruse and clever, for his defection in the tunnel. He said that something, some dark creature like the Skalawag, had cast a spell over him and he had been powerless to break from it. The fact that Molly had been the victim was pure chance; he could as easily have abused the anonymous woman in her dispirited party dress. At times he could almost believe that he had said, "*It* told me to ask you to say all the dirty words you know." But this was little consolation, for he could never explain it to Molly; he could never refer to what had happened in the slightest way, even though she herself mercilessly used the words "tunnel" and "dirty" so often and with such contriving that he felt sure someone would one day remark it. She never spoke to him except to say something unkind. Once she clapped her hand over her mouth and through her fingers gasped, "Oh, my gosh, for a minute you looked just like Grandfather Bonney." And another time she said to Winifred, "You know it runs in our family to be fat. It's bad enough for a woman to be fat but don't you think fat men are terrible?" And she had looked at him as if she wanted him to get fat.

187

There was no escaping his anxieties, and plagued as he was by them, he sought solitude, but Uncle Claude, who could not bear to be alone, frustrated him, insisting that he go mending fence, hiring the hay crew, fishing before daylight. Ralph found himself hiding when he heard his uncle call. He would hide in the barn in a grain bin or behind the skins in the slaughter shed, his heart trying to burst out of his shirt and his mouth as dry as paper. Often, on butchering days, he went off to town right after breakfast, hitching a ride on the highway to spend the whole day lounging with the high school loungers in the doorway of the old livery stable or in the booths of the drug store. Sometimes a tangle of hysterical girls would come sweeping down the main street, shrieking, into the booths with porcelain-topped tables. It was a prolonged giggle there in the drug store, a battle of wits with the boys who sat in separate booths and courted them by tossing over wet straws and wadded-up paper napkins. Occasionally Winifred and John Fulbright, the boy with the scarlet car, sat in the very last booth, silent and bedazzled.

Uncle Claude was puzzled by this desertion and he said, "I can't make out what's got into you. Why, I thought you was going to turn into an A Number One butcher," and Ralph could only reply, lightly, "I don't rightly know why I'm off it myself." He began even to resent the fact that he was obliged to speak like Uncle Claude in order not to sound impolite.

They were leaning one afternoon against the railing of the corral, their hats over their eyes to keep out the sun. Ken Burkhardt and Dump were hog-tying the sick bull, and the vet, a fat, dapper little man in green gabardine trousers and a pink silk shirt, was sorting his instruments beside the gate. Ralph had not wanted to come, but Uncle Claude had insisted. "It's part of your education," he had said. The bull was thrashing and bellowing and Ralph, certain that he was too much for just two men, did not put his foot up on the railing but stood alert, ready to run.

When the operation began and the knife went in, he had to keep his jaws closed tight and he shut his eyes, swaying sickly. There was a smell which hit them in a hot wave, and the bull made a wailing screaming sound that went splintering though his skull. He dared not look but kept his eyes fixed on the green ball and the two red arabesques that floated behind his eyelids. While all this was going on, while the poor beast was being cut up like a piece of food, Uncle Claude said, "We'll go fishing tomorrow up to the Hell Hole."

He felt no anger, but he was determined not to go, and he said, "I am sorry, Uncle Claude, I can't."

But Uncle Claude only said, "You be up by four. It ain't any good if you wait longer than that."

"I can't go," said Ralph. "I'm going to do something else tomorrow."

"My eye," said his uncle.

"I am. I'm going to play pool."

"At four in the morning? Where you going to play it? In the swimming pool?" He poked Ralph in the ribs, laughing at his joke. Ralph moved away irritably. The bull roared and the vet said good-naturedly, "Take it easy, old man, we're comin' right along here."

"I can't go fishing tomorrow, Uncle Claude," said Ralph stubbornly.

189

His uncle said, "Well, I ain't going fishing to the Hell Hole alone and I ain't going to take your sister, so it looks like I'm taking you."

"Looky here," cried Ralph, "looky here, not you and not anybody else is going to tell *me* what to do, goddamit to hell." He left the corral, walking in enormous strides back to the house, immediately remorseful, his pride receding. He knew—and even when he had had his tantrum he had known—that Uncle Claude did not want to impose his will upon him, he just wanted company, and when you came right down to it, a man couldn't deny another man that. So he would go as he had known all along he would go and as Uncle Claude had known.

Never had there been such weather. It was clear and hot in the day and cool at night. Curds of bruised clouds hung motionless in the sky. If rain came, it came as a spectacular storm, beginning with brilliant lightning and thunder which sometimes stuttered far away in the distant ranges and sometimes was so close at hand that it sounded like blasting at the very base of Garland Peak. The rain followed with a push like the heavy wings of an eagle, obscuring the mountains, the timothy fields, and the outbuildings. During the storm, everyone sat moody and damp in the parlor, stubbornly listening to the radio over which came nothing but an outraged cackling and, at great intervals, a thin wisp of song. Uncle Claude paced the floor restlessly. He hated rain just as he hated illness or anything else that kept him indoors.

Very late on one of these days of storm, a man stopped by, riding at the head of a string of twenty blooded horses.

He asked for quarters for the night. Uncle Claude, who never turned anyone away nor asked a stranger what his business was, said he could sleep in the bunkhouse and his horses could shift for themselves in the cow pasture. It was nearly as dark as night when Ralph and Uncle Claude rode out with him to lead the horses, but now and again the sky was split with lightning; the frightened neighing of the horses and behind that sound the thunder seemed unreal, like something in a western movie. Ralph experimented; he spurred Studebaker to a run and standing up in his stirrups he screamed but he could not hear his own voice, he could only feel it in his throat.

The stranger, by his very coming, elevated everyone's spirits. Uncle Claude built up the fire and he said to Ralph, "Go tell that coon to pack up a jug of Dago out of the cellar." But Ralph went himself although Magdalene argued, saying that she didn't want him "amessin' around in my spuds and my engerns and my conserves." He was so excited by the storm and the stranger and the twenty horses that he could not remember, once he was down there, what he had come for. He turned the flashlight over the shelves and a pack rat ran with a glittering eye behind a crock. When the light fell on the jugs of wine, he remembered, and instead of taking just one, he took two.

Warmed by the fire, freed by the wine, the man talked volubly, and all the other men and Ralph and Winifred sat around him listening and laughing as if they were outcasts to whom at last a visitor from the world had come. He told them that he was riding to Vernal, Utah, to take his horses to a gambler (he pronounced it "gambular") to whom he had lost them on a bet. Uncle Claude said, "That's a long ride, Mister. Would you do better to put them in some boxcars?" The man had a long, lopsided chin and rheumy eyes. He laughed and replied, "He took my fare as well as my riding horses."

The lights went off and they had to eat supper by kerosene lamps. They did not come on again that night, but the fire was bright all evening and they crouched around it, some of them sitting on the floor like Indians. Molly was learning to play the ukulele and she sat in the darkness on the gallery, plucking the unresonant strings and singing softly over and over again, "My dog has fleas." The stranger would not tell them what the bet had been for which there had been such high stakes, and all of them passionate with curiosity and with the wine and the howling storm that did not abate for more than a minute all evening, questioned him time and again, sometimes impatiently, sometimes uneasily. Now and again he looked quickly over his shoulder, but this was only meant to tantalize them for afterward he laughed in their faces.

Ralph drank several glasses of the wine and the effect of it was as odd and elusive as the atmosphere which the stranger had imparted to the evening. He was by turns drowsy and keenly awake. Winifred sat crosslegged in front of the fire on a deerskin, saying nothing at all, but looking up with an abstracted smile at the stranger sometimes and at Uncle Claude who was the company's principal spokesman. It was one of the few nights since Ralph and Molly had come that she had stayed at home, and the men had teased her about it at supper, saying they guessed her boy friend was no great shakes if he let a little thing like rain keep him away. Her mother gently remonstrated, "Winifred has better sense than to make herself sick by going out in the rain," and the man who had started the raillery mumbled an apology, recalling her "tendency."

For the space of this long evening, secure in the darkness from questioning eyes, safe from Molly whose meaningless plinking was as steady as the rain, Ralph allowed himself to think of Winifred and a guiltless desire ruffled warmly over him. It was hardly possible, he thought, that she and John Fulbright did not kiss. Often he heard them coming down the lane at midnight, coasting quietly, and then there was an interval of a quarter of an hour or more before the car went away and he heard Winifred coming up the stairs so softly she must have walked in her stocking feet. She was not like the other girls who were boisterous and brash, liking to walk loudly in their high heels across the drug store's tiled floor and, in the booths, suddenly begin to sing. They were loud-mouthed and posturing and could perpetrate their tomfoolery for hours together. But Winifred was demure, soft-spoken and almost pensive, and always upon her lips was that enchanting, mysterious smile. Ralph had heard in the town that she was a very good dancer and he marveled that she had this skill as well as the masculine ones of riding and shooting. When he first heard this, he said to her, "I have a t.l. for you." She said, inadequately, "Homer says you are the best help irrigating he ever had." When he told her what he had heard, she said nothing and was not at all embarrassed, as if this were her simple due. Molly who, according to her custom, had been lurking unseen in the room, sidled forward, *The Pathfinder* folded over her thumb, and said, "What I heard is of far more import than that. I heard you could read Latin at sight." Winifred frowned and cast down her eyes as if her character had somehow been impugned.

Winifred stirred, and looking around at Ralph, she said, "Where are they now?" so that with surprise he realized that she, too, had not been listening to the men.

"Where are who?" he said.

"Your mother and Leah and Rachel."

Everyone listened as he said, "I don't know. The last letter was from Hong Kong."

The stranger peered at him closely. "Well, I'll be. So your folks are in Hong Kong. I was there once and I seen one of them mongooses kill a cobra snake."

The ukulele immediately stopped and Molly, out of the darkness, said, "I doubt that. The mongoose is native to India." Her voice was firm and clear and its effect upon the stranger was so prompt that sweat came out on his forehead, glittering in the firelight, and his hand trembled so that some of the wine spilled on his khaki Army and Navy store pants. He did not dispute that voice, like the voice of conscience there in the pitch blackness, but he replied quickly and nervously, "By golly, that's right. I must of been thinking of Bagdad." Molly laughed derisively and began to play again.

The men wanted to hear of the stranger's world travels, but he would not tell. The most they could get out of him was an account of an opium den he had been taken to in the San Francisco Chinatown.

Ralph thought, half enviously, of his mother and sisters. All summer plump letters and picture postal cards came to him and Molly from Yokohama, Tokyo, Shanghai, Canton. They gave the cards and envelopes to Magdalene who kept them on a shelf in the kitchen in a Roi-Tan cigar box which until then had only held an announcement of Grandpa Kenyon's funeral and the business card of a Watkins man named Edward P. Ottolengui. Leah and Rachel, in their letters, alternated between a formal essay style ("You will next want to know about the peculiar vehicle they have here which is called a 'rickshaw' and is the equivalent of the American taxicab") and a gushing coquetry ("our nice new suitcases have been just ruined by all the awful stickers the hotels put on them"), but Mrs. Fawcett always wrote in the same way; her tone was a combination of the sisters' two styles, half educational, half jocular. She wrote, "Luncheon has become a 'movable feast' for us since we never can tell what adventure is going to o'ertake us in the forenoon to keep us from our victuals. And, my dears, the victuals when we finally do get to them are just as strange. I'm afraid my persnickety Molly would have to change her habits if she came here. We have become very partial to bean sprouts! (How is Uncle Claude's garden, by the way? I hope you are both helping Mrs. B. in it, for that is a very nice way to show your gratitude to C.K.) What would the Orient do without bean sprouts and rice, I often wonder, but I dare say there is no danger of at least the rice giving out, as from every train window you see nothing but fields upon fields of it, dotted all over with coolies in their picturesque hats like those on the postal Leah sent you yesterday."

It was not the nonsense of the letters that disturbed him. Indeed, he was rather relieved to find that traveling had no effect upon his mother's silliness. What made him dread the daily mail was that each letter contained a passage on that happy future when the family would be reunited in Connecticut. There was an implication of ponderous finality in this reunion. Between the lines, he read that she would bury Uncle Claude as completely as she had buried Grandpa, and while this year he was often discontented and often wished to be elsewhere, whenever he thought of his mother and of Connecticut, he clung with passionate devotion to his uncle and to Colorado. He was, at these times, like someone who has been told that his lover will die soon and who, unable to conceive the metamorphosis of his habits and thoughts after her death, becomes the closer bound to the necessity of this love so that when the hour comes and she is gone, he feels that he has not been prepared at all. Such, he brooded, was the shape of the earth that the farther away the world-travelers went, the closer they came to the Atlantic seaboard and to their inexorable plans. In a short few months from now, his father's gravestone and Grandpa Kenyon's would be separated from him by the whole width of the continent, but Grandfather Bonney, portable, ubiquitous, reposing for the summer in a safety deposit vault, would always be at hand. And so, always at hand, would be Molly who could ruin him, blow up his world if she chose. He knew, but for no reason he could name, that she would do nothing so long as they were here, but in that bare wasteland where they were to live under the shadow of the trinity of fat men, he must guard himself against her weapon.

In the middle of the evening, Uncle Claude complained restlessly that the rain was getting on his nerves and that the wine was not doing him any good. Suddenly in the room there was a sense of fear and Ralph saw Dump look furtively at the stranger. The man, mean-mouthed and nasty-eyed, sat with his chair tilted against the fireplace. He had got over the nervousness Molly had caused him and had for some time been asking about the hunting in these parts. At first the men talked enthusiastically, blandly and casually interrupting one another, but bit by bit they withdrew and one by one fell silent. Uncle Claude for a while did not sense their dim suspicions, and having the floor to himself, told story after story. Then he said that he had not done much hunting this spring himself as he had in years past, but he told how many pounds of elk and deer the other boys had brought in, most of it hanging up out there in the icehouse this very minute. He recounted their adventures as if they had been his own.

"But you say you ain't got none of this meat yourself?" said the stranger. "How come?"

This was a question he had wanted to be asked and he smiled. "I'll tell you. Along here in April I was scouting around in the foothills having a look for a good fat beaver and one day I seen . . ." He paused. Now his men's distrust had made itself known to him. It was almost as if they were shaking their heads at him and even Winifred sat up straight, tense and waiting. He finished, "I seen something that took my fancy."

"And what in the world was that?" said the man. He let his chair down slowly and leaned forward, holding his wine glass in both hands.

"Well, that's a question I don't feel called to answer," said Uncle Claude.

Ralph was perplexed. He knew that what had stilled the men's tongues was that they had begun to wonder if the

stranger were the Law in disguise and had come to collect
evidence against them to settle their score with the game
authorities. But why had they not wanted him to know
that there was a mountain lion on Garland Peak? There
was no bounty on them. Perhaps it was no more than a
cumulative resentment of the man who had drawn their
secrets out of them but refused to tell what the bet was
that he had lost.

Hearing the thunder once again burst in the mountains,
the thought of the lion enraptured him and he wondered
where she was and if she were asleep now in her den. They
had looked for her day after day but had never seen her,
though twice they were sure they found the prints of her
paws in the squelchy ground near the beaver dam. Then he
knew that the reason Uncle Claude had not named Goldilocks by name was that she was his own property, his and
Ralph's. The other men could know because they could be
trusted not to hunt her. But you could not trust this ugly
man who now, laughing out of his uneven mouth, said,
"I wouldn't think you'd have to go to the mountains to
hunt that kind of game. What's the matter with the little
lady settin' here? Settin' right here with all us big grown
men?"

Uncle Claude slowly turned his eyes to Winifred who had
not even seemed to hear and he said reproachfully, "That's
no way to talk." He sounded hurt like a misunderstood
child. "I was talking about something else."

Soon after this, they all went to bed. Ralph lay for a
long time listening to the rain and to the frequent thunder.
Often the lightning shot like a flare through the curtains
and illuminated the posts of his bed which ended in carved

pineapples. There was too much noise outside for him to hear Molly in the next room, and for the first time in weeks he did not think of her, but only of Uncle Claude whom now he thought he understood. He had never grown up and his hunt for Goldilocks was a childhood game; his men indulged and protected him like an innocent. They wanted him to be happy and so they wanted him to have the mountain lion.

The day dawned in a dry brightness. But the stranger was gone before sun-up, leaving no trace but the marks of his horses' hooves in the mud of the lane. The sheriff came at noon with a posse and gave Uncle Claude a proper dressing down. "So, though he don't account for himself and he's drivin' twenty thoroughbreds, you don't catch on. By God, Kenyon, you must of got dropped on the head when you was a baby. And so must of your whole outfit here." He tapped his forehead with his finger and said, "To let." But all of them, including the sheriff and the mock-angry men who rode with him, were delighted that the stranger had been a thief. The Bar K outfit, at dinner that day, said they had known it all along. "I knew it from the start," said Dump. "I never let on but just played into his hand to watch the show. I knew from the start he wasn't no Law, he was an *out*law."

From that time forward, the summer was a rush of pleasure. In late July there was a forest fire in the mountains to the north and the unhealthy sun, remote behind the smoke, was as small and lusterless as a withered orange. People twenty miles away from the burning trees coughed and their eyes watered. All the men from the Bar K went to

199

help fight it. They rapidly dug trenches in the soft ground, slippery with pine needles. Ralph's hands were blistered by the handle of his quick ax and his face was swollen with the heat. After twelve hours, when the fire was under control and there was nothing now but smoldering in the underbrush, Ralph and Homer Armitage and Uncle Claude went to the ranger's look-out where Ralph had his first drink of whisky. He did not enjoy the experience; he was hot already and the liquor set him ablaze. It was just dawn and he had had nothing to eat since the evening before. At first the light-headedness was pleasant; his ears rang as though he were holding shells to them and he heard the men talking as if from a far and golden distance. But in the next stage he was heavy-limbed and heavy-eyed and it was thus that he began the long walk home. He had to calculate each step before he took it lest he fall down. The other men had gone on ahead, and by the time they got home there was no one in the house but the womenfolk who were sitting at the table in the dining room drinking coffee and waiting to hear about the fire.

Ralph did not want to eat; he wanted only to lie full length on his bed and sleep, but he forced himself to lift his coffee cup with a sore hand to his parched lips and he ate part of a fried egg though it sickened him. He was aware that Molly was watching him, but he was too weary to care, and when finally, unable to sit up any longer, he excused himself and she said, half under her breath, "So you drink, too, Ralph Fawcett," he was not in the least afraid of her. He said crossly, "So's your old man," and joggled the back of her chair.

At haying, a whole new gallery of people came, Mormons

and people from Oklahoma with outlandish ways. A family named Prevost came to live in the house. The man was clumsy and once, out of simple awkwardness, fell off his rick. The woman, in unbroken silence, helped Magdalene with the cooking. They had brought with them a tow-headed girl of nine named Darling and a boy of three named Gasper. They had come on foot, carrying a shuck mattress and a couple of laundry bags which bulged with everything they owned in the world. They were from Muskogee and had accents so grotesque that not even Molly, an able mimic, could copy them. Although Uncle Claude offered them two rooms on the third floor, they preferred a small back bedroom downstairs off the kitchen, and they all slept in the same big brass bed. When their eldest daughter, Opal, lost her job in a café in town (a circumstance enshrouded in mystery) and came to stay with her parents, they still remained in one room. And then, in the last week of the harvest, three of Mr. Prevost's cousins, two women and a man, drove by to spend the night, and all of them slept in the same small room, eight of them together, six of them grown.

The cousins had come in a tall green Reo, as rusty and sorry as something left to perish on a dump. They left the next day at sundown, not even waiting for supper, taking the Prevosts with them. The Reo made loud gusty sounds and the driver, a dreary man they had called Cheesie, played the fool with the clutch so that the car shook back and forth in a paroxysm and with a racking cough until it died in the lane while the curious horses watched, hanging their long heads over the fence. Cheesie and Mr. Prevost got out and lifted up the hood and tinkered for a long while until

Ralph, who was watching from the porch, went to tell his uncle that they needed help. They worked uselessly until dark. The mute women, once the light was gone, got out of the car and built a fire in the middle of the road. Gasper and Darling went to the slough with a pan and they brought it back full of water and Mrs. Prevost made coffee, crouching over the small blaze like an unhappy gypsy woman. Uncle Claude gave the Reo a push with the pick-up over the bridge, but Cheesie had not understood his instructions and instead of turning down the road, he kept on straight ahead so that the Reo plowed up into the sage and stopped there, hugging the hillside for dear life.

They did not debate at all what they should do. The uncomplaining women and children stamped out the fire and joined the men and in the darkness they set out on foot, carrying their laundry bags, disappearing in the luminous sarvis berry. The Reo remained there, but the Prevosts, seen once in a strong light, were never seen again. The car disintegrated almost as one watched. The doors swung open and the hinges loosened until they all but fell. The tires collapsed; the running boards sagged and the top, on which the magpies impertinently sat, acquired blisters and dents. Whenever he looked at the car, Ralph remembered Opal, a yellow-haired girl with acne all over her face, who had spoken to him only once and had said, "Did you know my daddy used to raise goats?" Her dead voice was full of damaged pride; she had not asked a question but had stated a vanished fact. The Prevosts, like the downcast women of the train, existed lifelessly like the senile Reo in which the former animation, now quite gone, was unwilled.

When the quiet autumn came, inching redly over the

202

valley, and Winifred had gone to college and Uncle Claude had left for Missouri, Ralph roamed through the days like a sleeper, barely conscious of anything but the irrational feeling that if he could only figure out the way, he could make the world break open at his feet, even in spite of Molly.

# CHAPTER NINE

IN THE WINTER, MOLLY WOULD GO ON SATURDAY MORNING up to the summit of Garland Peak where by chance one day, turning over a stone, she had found it red with hibernating ladybugs. No one at the ranch or at school had ever heard of this phenomenon and the president of the Nature Lore society, a boy of fifteen, told her it was something that ought to interest the people at the agricultural college. Accordingly, she sent the entymology department thousands of them, packing them into matchboxes and wrapping them carefully in heavy brown paper. She got no acknowledgment at all except for one typed postal card without a signature which notified her that her parcel—it was the eighth—had arrived. She was not at all disheartened and continued weekly to gather the sleeping bugs, sure that an investigation was under way and that in time her name would be mentioned in a monograph in a scientific journal. She went even on the coldest days when the snowdrifts were deep and the pine needles in the glades were ossified with ice. The shapes of the high blue trees were obscured by the snow that encumbered their branches and they looked like formless ghosts. Sometimes the wind came fiercely down the trackless slopes, blowing sharp pellets into her face. On the upland meadows the sun was blinding, and walking there was difficult because the crust was thin and the soft piles of snow beneath were deep.

Garland Peak had always been her favorite to climb. It was one of the lowest in the first range, lying to the north and west of the ranch. In the summer she went up the face if it, but since this involved scaling three chimneys, she had to change her route when the storms came and was obliged to approach it indirectly, first climbing half way up a higher peak and then cutting across a mesa, down a gulch, and up the opposite bank to the northern base. The ascent was not an easy one at any time of year, but it was worth all the fatigue. From the summit she commanded a view of the entire valley, of the range as far as the eye could see, and of Cuthbert Pass beyond which, disappearing finally in a gauzy blue, were the highest mountains of all, the Arrowheads, which seemed as far away as the end of the world. In the summer the mesa below was like a sheet of rusted metal with densely growing Indian paintbrush, and there was a part of it where columbines grew at the edge of a stream in which, down near the gulch where it broadened out just before it joined another stream, there was the largest beaver dam in all the hills around. In earlier summers, when Winifred or Ralph had gone with her, they had often seen deer grazing among the blue flowers, but she had never seen anything, not so much as a rabbit when she was alone.

She had been here in the fall when the aspens shone like money among the conifers on all the foothills and the high fields were dark green with the first shoots of winter wheat.

The hay had been up for weeks by then and the stubble in the meadow was short and even and had an itchy, barbered look. The highway, a narrow glitter, went between red banks until it vanished midway up Cuthbert at a pyramidal stone called the King's Tower. At that time, through Uncle Claude's field glasses which she took surreptitiously from his desk (Grandmother Bonney's eyes, each time she did this, seemed to follow her), she had been able to see the cattle moving down from the summer range, their white faces bobbing up and down like buoys as they ran; it was hard to see the bodies behind them for the soil up there was almost as red as their hides. She could clearly see Uncle Claude's place. One day she heard a shot ring out and she could see Homer running across the yard to a flapping turkey. She knew it was Homer by his black shirt. Another time she saw Mrs. Brotherman moving about in the kitchen garden and Molly, spying on her, said aloud, "Miz Budmanny's at the muskmelons."

Until she had found the ladybugs, Molly had gone to the mountain to be undisturbed at her writing. She carried her materials with her in a small knapsack on her back: three notebooks with glossy blue covers on the inside of which was printed the multiplication table and information about weights and measures; a pocket dictionary; pencils and a pocket knife to sharpen them with; a safety-match box full of paper clips and one of rubber bands; and, though she had no use for it, several sheets of carbon paper. She had found an ideal glade for her study. It was very small and surrounded so densely by trees and chokecherry that they were almost like walls, and right in the middle, as if planned for her, was a big flat rock.

The first thing she had written there was a long humorous ballad called "The Fierce Mexican" which she was able to admire for several weeks, rereading it nightly when she was in bed, but she turned upon it finally with such loathing that she tore it up into tiny little pieces and tried to forget it, but she could not. The imperfection of the rhyme of "Mexican" and "Mohican" stuck to her mind like paste. She had quit writing poetry after that and had simultaneously begun a detective novel called "The Mystery of the Portland Vase" and a short story about a leper colony. The novel was not successful because it was too short. Furthermore, the reading public would have immediately found her out because the article in the Sunday supplement of the Denver *Post* from which she had got the idea had said that the vase had just been found and had been put under lock and key in the British Museum, about which she knew nothing. But she was well pleased with the short story and thought of submitting it to the *Scholastic Magazine*. The hero was a man named Lord Garnsborough who had so wasted away that all that was left of him was one tooth; he and his close friend, Launfal Hottentot, who was all gone but the lobe of his right ear, traveled about together in a glass cage, visiting people in worse conditions than they. An especially pitiful case was that of Malachi Strattonbottle who had nothing left but a small spitcurl of oleaginous hair.

Now in the winter she wrote in her bedroom in the evenings and on Sundays and she kept a meticulously detailed account in a separate notebook of what she had seen on her ladybug trips. The ladybug place was very near her studio and she always looked in; completely covered in snow, it was as if it lay under dust sheets waiting her return in the spring. In some ways the view from Cuthbert was more exciting at this season than at any other. On a clear day it was possible to see the men on the ricks in the pastures, pitching down feed to the herd which appeared to be hundreds of small red blocks on the glaring snow, as small as her ladybugs. The Caribou was frozen solid and all the trees on either side of it were bare. Molly loved the snow. When she had seen her first snowfall, she pretended to have a sore throat and did not go to school that day but stayed in bed, watching the snow flurry in imperfect circles over the poplar trees.

Both Ralph and Uncle Claude thought Molly's enterprise was absurd and they said they imagined her boxes of ladybugs had given rise to all sorts of jokes in the laboratory. Uncle Claude said she called to mind a cranky friend of Grandpa's who had shot magpies for three weeks and had tried to sell the feathers to a veterans' hospital to use for burning out the sickroom smells. She did not care a red cent for the opinion of either one of them on this or on any other subject. She rarely talked to them, but now and again if she particularly did not want to talk to Mrs. Brotherman about plants—she was rather outgrowing her interest in them as a result of Mrs. Brotherman's preoccupation this winter with snakeroot which Molly found singularly unattractive—and if she had finished a book and did not want to start another, she would play Double Canfield with one of them or Casino with both. They were so stupid and slow-witted that there was no sport in playing with them, but it was fairly fun to watch them make mistakes.

It seemed to Molly when she was alone in the mountains

that she had been by herself for years now, really ever since Grandpa had died. It was as if Ralph and her mother and sisters were no blood kin to her at all, as if nobody ever had been except her father and Grandpa Kenyon who was really only what you called "a connection." She was entirely solitary at school which she disliked this year. She disliked the harsh mountain voices of the children and the teachers and the smell of winter clothes, and she hated riding Eye-Opener over the river and then two miles into town every morning when the sun was just barely up and then back in the late afternoon when it was already going down and the light on the snow-covered meadows was blue. The children in her grade were so backward that she had to be given extra work to occupy her and she made notebooks of advertisements clipped from magazines showing different types of "Houses," "Landscapes," and "Occupations." The motto for the Occupations notebook was "Give us, Oh, give us the man who sings at his work." When she was not unhappy, she was bored. The only things that really gave her pleasure were the ladybugs, her writing, and her plans for a horrible life for Ralph. She became so obsessed with the idea that he would turn into Grandfather Bonney that she almost believed that he looked like him already and on the flyleaf of her diary she drew a farcical facsimile of the portrait under which she wrote "Ralph Bonney, Jr."

Every Saturday she took her Brownie along. She did not have much luck with photography and in her pictures the sky took up more space than anything else and trees and buildings tended to be diagonal. But she hoped that she would one day see Goldilocks and could take her picture.

Uncle Claude and Ralph, timid of the snowy slopes ("Typical! Typical!" exulted her scornful heart), had left off their hunt and said they would find her in the spring. But just as always before, she never saw a living thing when she was alone.

And then, the very day they came with her, they caught sight of the mountain lion. On the Saturday before Christmas Uncle Claude decided that they must have a Christmas tree. They said they would go to Garland with Molly and on the way down would cut a big fir, and they took a sled along, leaving it at the foot.

There had been a big snowfall on Thursday and there had been no thaw. The sun was warm on the slopes and mesas and brilliant in the branches of the evergreens, but the air was cold and the wind was raw in the unprotected clearings. Uncle Claude said it might drop to twenty below that night. They had got the ladybugs—Uncle Claude scraped them up with his hunting knife to Molly's exasperation for she used a spatula which seemed more humane and also more scientific—and had started down. Uncle Claude was the first to get to the opposite bank of the gulch and just as Ralph and Molly began the ascent, he turned around and motioned them to come quietly. It was an easy climb and the path was deep in snow so that they made no sound. Once Molly broke off an ice-covered twig on a chokecherry bush but the noise was slight. Their uncle stood absolutely still, watching something. He had moved into the cover of a small deformed scrub oak laden with snow and he beckoned them to join him. They stepped carefully in his boot-prints, not seeing yet what he did. Then, when they were beside him, he pointed to the east side of the mesa and there they saw the mountain lion standing still with her head up, facing them, her long tail twitching. She was honey-colored all over save for her face which was darker, a sort of yellow-brown. They had a perfect view of her, for the mesa there was bare of anything and the sun illuminated her so clearly that it was as if they saw her close up. She allowed them to look at her for only a few seconds and then she bounded across the place where the columbines grew in summer and disappeared among the trees. Her flight was lovely: her wastless grace and her speed did not make Molly think immediately of her fear but of her power. When you saw a running deer, you were conscious only of its instinct to flee danger. The lion had sensed peril and yet they, the watchers, sensed peril in her, under her tawny hide, in the way her tail had moved against the glint of the snow, in the way she streaked across the flat land. Molly shivered to think she might now have climbed a tree like a tame cat and might be sitting there observing them with large green eyes.

"Goddamn," said Uncle Claude. "This would be the day we'd see her when we never brought our guns." His face, in the snow glare, did not show so much disappointment as anger, as if he really hated the mountain lion and wanted to kill her for that reason and not for the sport of it. Ralph did not say a word but continued to look at the place where she had been, smiling a secret smile. She was afraid and thought she could never come here again. The lion grew to huge proportions in her reflection. She imagined its claws, its teeth, the way it would hiss. She remembered a lioness in the zoo at Balboa Park who had stopped in her prowling now and then to lift her lips and grumble deeply; she had not reminded Molly at all of a cat with those heavy dewlaps and puppy-like paws, and it seemed incredible to her that their pansy-faced Budge belonged to the same species, though Leah and Rachel and Aunt Kathleen kept insisting that she see the close resemblance. Afterward, Molly often had a dream that she was being chased mile after mile through the streets of San Diego by the lioness who almost overtook her at every mailbox.

When they started down, she twice looked back over her shoulder and she kept close to Ralph. When they got home, she did not wait to help take the tree off the sled but went straight into the house, feeling unsafe until then. Mrs. Brotherman was in the living room putting up the holly wreaths and when Molly came in to warm her hands at the fire, she said, "A friend just sent me a box of Delicious apples and I do think they're quite the best I ever tasted. Let me finish this one wreath and then we'll go upstairs and have one." Molly looked at the scar on her hand and then she thought again of the golden cat and her fear left; in its place there came a soft, inexplicable sadness. On the way down, her arm had once brushed against her brother's and remembering this, she felt weak.

The warmth of Mrs. Brotherman's sitting room and the smell of the apples, the sight of the widow watering a pot of begonia with a small sprinkling can, the bright winter sunlight through the dimity curtains made Molly even sadder. She was full of wishes. She wished that she had yellow hair like Leah's and Rachel's and the lion's. She wished she could go to London and become a famous writer. She wished she did not have to wear glasses; she wished she were only four feet five.

Mrs. Brotherman, blowing up the fire with a pair of small red bellows, said, "I am always sad at Chistmas here, although your uncle does everything he can to make it a happy season." The statement must have come at the end of a long string of thoughts, but in that even, toneless voice there was no clue to their nature, whether Christmas made her conscious of her widowhood or whether she longed to be a child or longed to be in Salem. Molly was embarrassed and quickly said, "Oh, I forgot to tell you. We saw Goldilocks."

Mrs. Brotherman sat on a bench before the fire, clutching her hands together in her lap, and even though Molly could only see her profile, she saw fear arrive in the twilit face and remain there. Then, turning, she said, "There is nothing here but danger and there never has been, but this is the worst yet. I had hoped Mr. Kenyon had been mistaken."

"Oh, a mountain lion isn't dangerous," said Molly, courageous in the presence of this adult cowardice. "They're just as afraid of people as deer are."

"Perhaps. But I will feel safer when it is dead. I hope you will not go back there. If the men must go, they must, but it's not right for a girl to be alone in the mountains with a lion loose."

Molly threw her apple core into the fire and heard it hiss briefly. She, too, would not feel safe until the beautiful animal was dead. She would never be unafraid at Garland again because in the back of her mind she would always know that the big cat might be watching her from the crotch of a tree or from behind a rock.

213

She left the sitting room and went to her bedroom where she wrapped up the last of the ladybugs she would ever send. She could not keep her mind on anything; it kept darting around like a darning needle and she did not know what was the matter with her. If only she had yellow hair, she thought, she would be an entirely different kind of person; she would not be cross all the time. At the very thought of her crossness, she began to grow very angry and it became clear to her that Ralph and Uncle Claude had gone with her today, knowing they would see Goldilocks, just in order to spoil her ladybug project. They had *known* that she never saw any wild animals when she was alone and they had come today deliberately so that everything would be ruined. There had been absolutely no reason for them not just to stay at the foot and cut down their idiotic Christmas tree. She personally would have nothing to do with the tree as she thought the whole idea of it was too sentimental for words. In fact, she thought Christmas itself was bourgeois and she had never got anything she wanted but just things like a patent-leather hatbox or yarn flowers that you were supposed to pin on your coat, as if you ever *would*. There was going to be a piece of mistletoe hung in the door between the dining room and the living room and the thought of it gave her gooseflesh because she remembered once in Covina Mr. Follansbee had kissed Miss Runyon and Miss Runyon had squealed and said, "Of all things! Aren't you the foxy grandpa!" And besides that, Uncle Claude had bought a lot of grain alcohol and rotgut (*rotgut!* People ought to be put in jail for using words like that) and kept saying that they would all "get stinko and then I'm gonna trim every jack man of you at

Red Dog." It was not hard to imagine. They would all pile up to the gallery and clank their silver dollars together, acting as if they were in a movie.

And Winifred was coming home. She was coming on the evening train tonight, in fact, and there was no doubt at all that she had acquired insufferable airs. Molly knew because she had got a letter from her in which she sounded exactly like Leah and Rachel. "My sorority sisters are griped because I am the only pledge who has already got dated up for the Junior Prom." Molly had replied, "Personally, I have never heard of a Junior Prom. Possibly you are thinking of Promenade. I thought you went to college to study Cicero's essays and I must say, Winifred, that you do not sound as if you are making much effort to be an outstanding *bas bleu.*" It had been a severe measure, but one thing no one could ever say about Molly Fawcett was that she was wishy-washy. Decisively she got out her diary and added Winifred's name to the list of unforgivables and then, because he had wrecked the ladybug business, she also put down "Claude (Club-Foot) Kenyon." Recently she had learned that Claude meant "lame," and she had decided to put a new character in the story about the leper colony called Claude Binks who only had one toenail left.

She lit the incense in the gilt incense Buddha burner which she had brought from Covina and very briefly prayed that the mountain lion would either clear out of the hills or would step into a skunk trap; she hoped neither Ralph nor Uncle Claude would get her. Molly had not decided yet whether she would be a Catholic or a Buddhist but she had narrowed the choice down to these two as she certainly had no intention of being either a Presbyterian or a Christian Scientist. Magdalene had told her about the Holy Rollers, but Molly did not think they were her style. Her final decision depended on what would make Mr. Follansbee the maddest, and now she sat down at the table and wrote him a letter, frankly asking him. She also wrote a letter to President Hoover and one to Henry Ford. They were identical and read:

Dear Gentleman:
I have been apprized of your outstanding munificence with regard to helping people along the highway of life and so I wonder if you have any typewriters that you don't need. I am very needful of one myself and if you could see your way clear to sending me one, I will be very grateful.

I think what you have done for other people is wonderful and hope it will come to pass that I will have first-hand knowledge anent this.

Respectfully yours,
Molly Fawcett

P.S. There is no Railway Express here so you will have to send it by freight.

These were quite useless, she knew. She had already asked ten other people of lesser importance—including Dr. Haskell—and had got only one reply (except for a comic postal from the doctor on which he wrote "If at first you don't succeed, try, try again," and so she had) and that was from Spencer Penrose's secretary saying that Mr. Penrose was out of town, was, in fact, in India, but would attend to her letter when he got back. Of course the blatherskite never did, and he had been in Colorado Springs for two months now and she had not heard a word from him. Furthermore, she had read in the Denver *Post* that he had bought an

216

elephant to bring back to the Broadmoor (what for? thought Molly) which seemed really unfair considering how badly she needed a typewriter and how much cheaper they were than elephants.

She sealed her letters and then stood in front of the mirror with her teeth sticking out. "Clara? Clara?" she said. Then, without leaving the bureau but leaning on one elbow, she reached for her diary and her pencil and to the list of unforgivables she added her own name. She burst into tears and cried until she was hungry, and all the time she cried she watched herself in the mirror, getting uglier and uglier until she looked like an Airedale.

Easter came late that year. The pasque flowers were already paling on the mesas and the cactus was in bloom, smelling like melons. This time of year was full of wonders. Even the howling of the coyotes had a queer charm for Ralph, and after they had ceased, the meadowlarks sang freshly for an hour or so. The light lying on the meadows just at dawn and then again just before dark was a singular ominous yellow, giving to trees and to animals a submarine remoteness and ambiguity of outline. But then in the broadlight and then when the night came the shapes were separated. There was always a haze on the far mountains and sometimes it bedimmed Garland Peak. The evenings were cool and light; through the open windows came the smell of the first new leaves of the hop vines and the upturned dirt of the flower garden. There were clear, nocturnal sounds from the direction of the Caribou where the Negroes from the mines fished in the dusk and then when night came built fires on the river bank to fry their trout and to drink whisky and sing spirituals amongst the weeping willow trees.

Ralph dreamed of the mountain lion and thought, "Oh, if I don't get her, I will *die!*" He saw himself standing where they had stood before Christmas, taking perfect aim, shooting her through her proud head with its wary eyes, and then running across the mesa to stroke her soft saffron flanks and paws. Ralph had always loved cats and when Budge had died this spring of old age, he had been wretched for days, mourning the lost purr and the quiet feet. He would not skin the mountain lion, he decided, if he got her, but would have her stuffed and keep her in his room all his life. If he had to go to college, he would take her along with him. He wished that Uncle Claude were not so keen as he, for he felt, somehow, that he had more right to Goldilocks: he wanted her because he loved her, but Uncle Claude wanted her only because she was something rare. Besides, Uncle Claude would be here forever and could get another, but this was Ralph's last chance. Sometimes, indeed, he forgot that he was not her only hunter, and at such times he seemed to sink into a golden bath of joy.

They saw the mountain lion on Easter Sunday. This time she was beside the stream, nearer the gulch than the place where she had vanished before, close to the beaver dam. They had only a momentary glimpse of her and then she leaped away and was out of sight before they could even raise their rifles. They ran to the place where she had been and found that she had left her food, too startled by their voices to carry it off. A half-eaten woodchuck lay beside a tree stump, its entrails chewed but its silly head intact and twisted to a sheepish angle. It had been mauled and slobbered on and its grizzled hair was clotted. There was blood on some of the chips of wood left by the beavers when they had gnawed down the tree.

Uncle Claude, frustrated, angry, moved around the stump, examining everything as if he expected to find a clue which would lead him to her den. Sighing, he said, "Blast the yellow bitch."

And Ralph, feeling himself on the verge of tears, said desolately, "What'll we do now?"

"Go home, I reckon," said Uncle Claude, "but by damn, I'm going to get me my cat yet."

Ralph kept the edge out of his voice but his heart was rapid. He said, "You mean, I'm going to get *me my* cat."

Uncle Claude glanced sidelong at him but said nothing and they started down the creek bank. The creek was swollen from the thaws and there were places where the water sprayed like a geyser in the hollows between the rocks. Between two boulders at a widening, Ralph saw the points of a set of antlers sticking up out of the water and he waded in, not bothering to take off his shoes. But what he found was not just one set of antlers: he found the skulls of two deer with horns so tightly interlocked that he could not get them apart. They were wedged in between the rocks and he had trouble getting them loose. The water was cold and insistently flicked up his pants legs and once he lost his footing and slipped on a rock. When he came out with his trophy, he found Uncle Claude sitting on a patch of grass smoking, watching Ralph without the least interest.

"What'll you do with them now you got them?" he said.

Ralph did not immediately answer, but tried again to

get the horns apart. His heart constricted when he conjured up what must have taken place: the two bucks charging one another and then, by lunatic accident, being joined as one, toppling into the water to drown, still struggling to get free. But it was not so much the violence of this wilderness death that made him quiver; it was his uncle's indifference, the same indifference he had seen when he had looked at the sick bull. His passion for Goldilocks went over him like an ocean wave, for he was determined that she, at least, would be killed not out of this cold calm of Uncle Claude's but out of his own love for her golden hide.

Uncle Claude repeated, "What'll you do with them?"

"Why, I'll take them to Magdalene as a present," he said. "Or, no, I'll take them to Molly."

Uncle Claude laughed shortly. "You'd better take Molly a box of candy to sweeten her disposition. What's the matter with that kid anyway?"

Ralph took in his breath sharply. "Search me," he said.

Later, when he took the antlers up to Molly's room, he found her lying on her bed with the counterpane over her head. She pulled it down and stared at his present with terrible woe but without scorn. They exchanged, at last, after these months, a look of understanding and Molly said, "Thanks, Ralph. I'll shoot them with my Brownie."

Finally school was over. On the night of commencement, he sat in the hot auditorium where the June bugs bumbled foolishly against the window screens and the teachers sat among the baskets of gladioli and the potted rubber plants on the stage, listening to a boy in glasses deliver the valedictory. His voice broke twice, rising to a plaintive scream once on the word "emperor" and once on "romance." He used phrases like "elegiac cadences" and "poetic counterpoint" and he said that Vergil had been born to "the purple of classical literature." When he came to the end, he begged permission to finish with the lines of a "devotee of Roman literature more mellifluous than myself, *id est,* Alfred Lord Tennyson," and he recited *Frater Ave Atque Vale.* Ralph immediately saw the portrait of Grandfather Bonney and he was clutched by terror at the shortness of the time. He felt that his mother and sisters, who were now in Venice, were speeding, were about to overtake him, and there was no time to lose for he *must* have Goldilocks before they came. He looked for Molly who was to receive an eighth-grade diploma. She was sitting three rows away from him and when the boy had finished, she turned round and looked directly at her brother, puffing out her cheeks to look like a fat person.

The day after that they took the car, Ralph, Winifred, and Molly. Winifred drove and they went as far up Garland as the red road went. She and Molly climbed the face but Ralph could not manage the chimneys with his gun and went around the other way. Uncle Claude had taken a mare to stud and he had told them that when he got through, he would come looking for them in the hills and he would pack some food along so that they could cook out.

Ralph met them at the stream. Red dust had come off on their hands when they climbed the chimneys and they washed it off in the cold water, letting the fool's gold run through their fingers. All three of them lay down, crushing harebells, and looked straight upward. A chicken hawk lazily banked and coasted across the sky; behind them, in the forest, the chipmunks and the bluejays sent up their absent-minded racket against the wind which was always present in the pine trees like a voice. Hearing it, Ralph wished he were at the foot of a tree in the strange and smoky shade and were lying on the pinkish-brown pine needles; but the high, hot sun was too excellent to leave. Winifred held her arm over her eyes and Ralph noticed the tiny golden hairs on her wrists and on the backs of her hands. She was not going back to college next year; she was going to marry John Fulbright on the first of July and they were going to the eastern part of the state to start a truck farm. Mrs. Brotherman, too, was leaving the Bar K, now that her daughter was grown; she was going back to Salem. Ralph was sure that the odor of apples would cling to her rooms. He thought how lonely his uncle would be next winter and was sorry for him. The winter was an idle time for him and in this year Ralph had seen that idleness aged him. He did little of the feeding himself because, some years before, he had ridden into town without chaps, had been delayed, and coming back after the sun had gone down and when the thermometer registered twenty-five below, he had frozen both his legs and he was afraid thereafter of freezing them again. He hunted a little, emptied his traps, and took care of his beaver and ermine hides, gave a hand with the milking and gathered the eggs for Magdalene. The rest of the time he spent at his desk, studying the histories of his bulls and writing letters on lined paper with an indelible pencil to his foremen on the other ranches; playing a kind of Solitaire called "Once in a Blue Moon"; and reading books like *The Count of Monte Cristo, Graustark,* and *Beau Ideal.* Ralph pitied him so much at this moment that he almost wished Uncle Claude would get Goldilocks, but his generosity was brief-lived. Where was she now? How wonderful she must be in this hot sun!

The smoke from Winifred's cigarette went straight up and then opened out into a horn like a blue lily. Ralph thought somnolently: the lilies of the field are numbered. He saw in his mind's eye that wide, bare plateau at the glacier where the yellow orchids grew. Now, years after their expedition there, he thought how curious it was that he and Molly had not been tempted to eat the strawberry snow, for it had looked as delicious as sherbet. That was the day his friendship with Uncle Claude had begun and the day on which he had abandoned Molly. It had begun in a look of recognition.

He fell into a lazy meditation. He wondered if Montreux where the travelers were going next was similar to this and if the Alps were as tall as the Rocky Mountains; he wondered if their hotel would be like the Brown Palace. He pretended that he lay on the thick carpet in the center of the lobby looking up at the dome as if it were a motion-picture screen. He saw ladies in taffeta dresses and small velvet toques, mitts and pointed satin slippers, saw the gambling tables where the croupiers used heavy shovels because the money was all in gold bricks. In those days, the ladies had bathed in champagne in gold-plated tubs. Everything that presented itself to him was gold: the bark on the palm trees in Covina, the whisky in the glass that Grandpa had left when he went upstairs to die, Leah's hair above the tall chrysanthemums, the clasps on Grandfather Bonney's books. He did not will any of these images but they came in a stately promenade. There was a small gold brooch of two

223

clasped hands in his mother's button box and in the same box was a tarnished heart-shaped locket on a fine chain. He remembered Jesus' halo on the cards given out at Sunday school, the gilt star of Bethlehem on the Christmas tree, his Tenderfoot pin.

Once they heard a freight train going out and once, from somewhere miles away, a blast of dynamite. Contented as he was with this present time, he was idly trying to think what it reminded him of and when at last, opening his eyes, he saw the chicken hawk again, he remembered the airplane those long years ago when he and Molly had lain on the lippia lawn, waiting for Uncle Claude to come and bury Grandpa.

He said, "Molly, do you remember the airplane that day of Grandpa Kenyon's funeral?" His voice sounded submerged and hesitant to him and he found he was trembling for her answer. She paused a long time and then, leaning across Winifred, she looked straight at him and said, "All I remember in the whole wide world is that I hate you and I hope you will get fat."

Winifred laughed. "You've got the worst temper in the county."

"I beg to differ," said Molly. "It is the worst in the state, in the United States, in North America, in the Western Hemisphere, in the world, in the universe." She said this rapidly, letting her voice rise powerfully.

"All right, be a bad sport," said Ralph wearily and closed his eyes again.

"You'd be a bad sport, too," she said to Winifred, "if you knew what he said to me."

"Molly!" he cried and sat up straight.

224

"What did he say?" asked Winifred, amused.

"Molly, if you tell, I'll . . ."

"You'll what?" She looked at him coldly. Then she stretched out her long thin arm and pointed in the direction of Cuthbert Pass and said, "If we had the field glasses, we could see the tunnel from here."

"What did Ralph say to you, Molly?" insisted Winifred.

"Oh, I don't intend to tell *you*, Winifred Brotherman. By the by, don't you think Ralph is getting fat?"

He jumped to his feet and picked up his gun. "I'm going now," he said tightly.

"What for?" Molly smiled at him teasingly, twirling a harebell between her fingers.

"Cat fur to make kitten breeches," he snapped and then was annoyed with himself for using the childhood joke.

"That is a very good pun, I'm sorry to say," said Molly. "I surely don't think you knew you were making it as I have never known anyone more unfurnished in the upper story."

He did not know what she was talking about; he did not understand the pun he had made. Striding through the harebells, he enjoyed the feeling of crushing the blue flowers under his feet. Winifred called after him, "Good luck," but he did not turn back. He could not have any luck, for even if he saw Goldilocks, he couldn't shoot until Uncle Claude came. He went downstream toward the beaver dam, making too much noise at first in his irritation with Molly and then treading lightly on the mossy, resilient ground. He passed the place where he had found the antlers and thought how wrong he had been the day he had given them to Molly and had thought they had understood one another again. He felt suddenly that he was going along this stream for the last time.

Molly had spoiled everything and he could not even care about Goldilocks. Damn her, he said, damn her. It was only Goldilocks that had made him able to forget the tunnel. Now she had wrecked it all. It was possible that even now she was telling Winifred, but on second thoughts, this seemed unlikely: she was too smart; she would save up and use it when the right time came. She was always saving up something and always had; she saved her candy at Christmas until everyone else had finished and then, a day or so later, she brought all hers out and ate it in front of them and wouldn't give them a crumb of it. And she saved up all the jokes she heard and the things people had said and other people's dreams so that she had the reputation of being interesting, although no one could stand her because she was so sarcastic. She would, for instance, take the pun he had made and pretend it was her own.

He sat down finally on a lichen-covered rock beside the beaver dam. One day late in October he had come here by himself, not to hunt for Goldilocks but to escape Uncle Claude who had wanted him to go to look at the winter wheat. The day had been cold with a wind and a chill that crept along the skin, not quite penetrating. The sky was heavy and the leaves were all fallen and were all brown. The skinny trees were already gray with winter and the ferns underfoot crumbled, making a faint sound. He had seen a weasel and had thought how in just a little while its coat would turn white and it would be an ermine.

At the very moment he remembered the weasel, a salamander, black and orange, streaked through the fern brake

226

beside his rock, making him think of Grandfather Bonney's snuff box. Was there anything in the world, he wondered, that did not make you think of something else? From the snuff box he went on to the night Miss Runyon had brought the flowers and he and Molly had sobbed silently for Grandpa on the floor beside his coffin. Nothing had ever been really right since then, but why? He perfectly saw the old man and perfectly heard him sing:

> Oh, we'll sit on his white hause bane,
> And I'll pyke out his bonney blue e'en,
> Wi' a lock o' his gowden hair,
> We'll theek our nest when it blaws bare.

"I'll never be happy again," he said softly and aloud. Neither would Molly, but Molly did not want to be happy and she wanted him to be as wretched as she. If she told his mother, if his mother gave him a moral lecture often using the expression "not quite nice," he would leave home. He would not just threaten, he really would join the Navy.

The decision made him feel better and he got up. He moved around the beaver dam, looking alertly through the trees. Just beyond this black silent pool there was a little glade he knew of with a flat rock in the center of it like a table. He thought he heard someone across the dam and stopped to listen, but he concluded that it had only been a bird rustling. It had occurred to him that it might be Uncle Claude, but he realized that he could not have got back from the stud farm so soon. Quiet as it was, there was, as always in the forest, a feeling of life near by and when, softly moving aside a branch of chokecherry, he saw Goldilocks in the glade beside the flat rock feeding on a jackrabbit, he was not surprised. He had been certain, this last moment, that he would find her there. She delicately moved the rabbit with her paw and then savagely ripped it with her teeth. He stood, holding his breath, utterly motionless for a minute, debating, but he could not hold out against the temptation: Uncle Claude would have to forgive him; if he didn't, Ralph would go away.

As he raised his rifle, he heard another sound but this time from the direction of the face of the mountain. Goldilocks heard it too and lifted her heavy head; before she could find him with her topaz eyes, he shot and immediately he was stone blind. His blindness lasted for an exploded moment and when he was able to see again, to see the tumbled yellow body on the bright grass, he realized that he had not been blind but deaf, for there had been another gun, another shot a split second after his.

Uncle Claude came charging through the brush, hollering like an Indian. "By God, we done it! By Jesus Christ, we both done it." And he ran to the lion, throwing his gun on the ground. She had fallen toward Ralph on her wounded side and no blood was visible. Uncle Claude turned her over to look for the wounds and Ralph stepped forward.

"She's so little," said Ralph softly, as if Goldilocks were not dead but only asleep. "Why, she isn't any bigger than a dog. She isn't as *big*."

But what mattered was whose bullet had killed her. They looked together eagerly, pushing back the hair with their hands. Ralph was surprised to find how short and harsh it was. There was only one bullet hole, and it was not in the place where Ralph had aimed. He was sick with

228

failure, sick and furious with his uncle for coming so quietly and winning so easily.

Uncle Claude said, "No man alive can judge which one of us got her. I reckon we'll have to call it a corporation."

There was a sound in the chokecherry bushes beyond them, opposite where Ralph had stood to shoot. It was a sound that could come only from a human throat. It was a bubbling of blood. Uncle Claude and Ralph stood up and looked at one another in an agony of terror and for a moment they could not move but stood, hatless, the sun blazing down upon them and upon the lion at their feet.

"Somebody . . ."

Uncle Claude, bending almost in two at the waist, ran across the clearing and Ralph followed, his body a flame of pain. Molly lay beside a rotten log, a wound like a burst fruit in her forehead. Her glasses lay in fragments on her cheeks and the frame, torn from one ear, stuck up at a raffish angle. The elastic had come out of one leg of her gym bloomers and it hung down to her shin. The sound in her throat stopped. Uncle Claude knelt down beside her, but Ralph stood some paces away. He could as clearly see the life leave her as you could see fire leave burnt-out wood. It receded like a tide, lifted like a fog.

When Uncle Claude stood up, Ralph began to scream. He threw back his head and with his mouth as wide as it would open he let the sound flow out of him, burning up the mountains. Then he was too hoarse to scream any longer and he threw himself down on the ground and pounded the pine needles with his fists and with his feet, moaning, "I didn't see her! I didn't hear her! I didn't kill her!"

Uncle Claude came to him and seized him by the shoulder roughly and made him stand up. "Cut it out," he said sharply. "Get the hell out of here and go get somebody."

He stood with his arms hanging at his sides and said, "I didn't know she was there."

"Goddamit, I know *that*. Shove, now. Go on. *Get* somebody."

In a minute, he thought, just let me have a minute. He knelt down beside his sister and touched the blood on her forehead, stroked her cheeks, felt of her sodden hair. "Molly," he said. "Molly girl." He kissed her blood-salty lips as if like a dog he could lick her wound and heal it. Uncle Claude kicked him in the ribs and said, "When I say shove, I mean shove."

He had to go then. He stumbled across the clearing trying not to look at Goldilocks. At the head of the beaver dam he saw Winifred running toward him and knew that she had heard his screams. He stopped and waited for her, sitting again on the rock where he had seen the salamander. He pulled from its sheath a stalk of upland bearded barley and bit its succulent stem and chewed. There was neither a past nor a future to his life in this single, yellow minute.

When she came panting up, he said, "Go on through the clearing. They're on the other side," and though her face questioned him, she ran on without a word.

For a long time, he sat there muttering like a crazy man: Molly, Molly, Molly, Molly. He said it until they came back, Winifred carrying the guns and Uncle Claude carrying his dead sister with her ruined head. They had tied a handkerchief around her forehead so that you could not see the hole but the blood had soaked through; relaxed like that in Uncle Claude's arms, she looked like a tall, slim monkey.

By the time they got her down to the car, the sun was setting. Directly, Ralph thought, there would be that evil yellow light. Uncle Claude and Winifred sat in front and Ralph sat in the back beside Molly, whom they had propped up like a person. He looked straight ahead, watching the road being devoured by the car like an endless red noodle.

Magdalene was in the front yard picking mint and Uncle Claude called to her to come and help. She came to the car and looked in at Molly. There was no emotion at all on her pleated black face, but as soon as she spoke, Ralph was able to collapse. She said, "Lord Jesus. The pore little old piece of white trash."

# BOSTON

# ADVENTURE

A Novel

*FOR FRANK PARKER*

# BOOK ONE
## HOTEL BARSTOW

# CHAPTER ONE

Because we were very poor and could not buy another bed, I used to sleep on a pallet made of old coats and comforters in the same room with my mother and father. When I played wishing games or said "Star light, star bright," my first wish always was that I might have a room of my own, and the one I imagined was Miss Pride's at the Hotel Barstow which I sometimes had to clean when my mother, the chambermaid, was not feeling well. I knew its details so thoroughly that I had only to say to myself the words "Miss Pride's room" and at once my feet stood on the tawny rug with its huge faded peonies, and before me was the window seat covered with flat, flowered cushions, at one end of which was a folded afghan, at the other, three big soft pillows on which cherubs floated amongst blue daisies, holding up in their dimpled hands a misty picture of a castle. And I could gaze through the windows which overlooked the bay. On a clear morning, looking across the green, excited water, littered with dories and lobster-pots and buoys, I could see Boston and its State House dome, gleaming like a golden blister.

Often at night, I pretended that I was sleeping in the big brass bed, under the fringed white counterpane, my head upon the inflexible bolster. Turning over, I imagined I could hear the rattling of the loose balls which decorated the foot-rail and which, when I tucked in the sheets, gave the Spartan bed, with its hard mattress and thin blankets, a kind of saucy vitality. Suddenly, as if it were borne on a wind, there came to me the fresh, acrid odor of Miss Pride's costly soap which she kept in a large carton under the bed. She was part owner of a soap factory, I had heard, and so, of course, it cost her nothing.

Some nights, though, my vanities were driven off, and I could not hold in my mind a picture of the room nor could I summon up the rich old lady. For on those nights, I lay terrified at the sound of my parents' quarreling voices. I mocked the deep breathing they expected of me, but the air would not go down into my lungs and was caught like a hiccough in my throat. There was a raw-edged blade of pain straight through my chest to my backbone as though fear had laid back the sheath of my nerves. Anxious for morning, I lay on my back staring at the invisible ceiling or cautiously I turned over on my side, making out the contours of the sagging bed where my mother and father were enormously sprawled out and humped up, hissing their fury at one another. Until I was about ten years old, though, my distress did not continue after their voices had ceased and, exhausted as much by being an audience as they were by being the actors, I would fall asleep at once. It was not until then, the summer of my tenth year, that I learned, in what terms of childhood I cannot remember, that peace was to be desired above all things. The upraised voices, the bitter blasphemies, the profound outcries of hatred carried through the day. If at the end of it there was a silent night, I lay awake for a long time waiting for the storm to break, and in the morning got up fretful for my vigil.

Our poverty was my mother's excuse for perpetuating the old anger. Although she had never been anything but poor, for her life in Russia before she married had been a tale of privation and suffering, still she had dreams of what it was like to be rich and, as she accused him, my father had promised her the finest of goods when he asked her to marry him. And what had she instead, she demanded. A two-room house in a fishermen's village where the sand seeped in the doorways and across the window sills, where the winter winds gained access through the cracks in the walls, and where in the summer time the heat descended from the low beaverboard ceilings in a steady, unmerciful blast. And had she to eat the fowl, the caviar, the strawberries and melons and pears he had promised? Our fare was no better than the poorest peasant's: day-old bread, *pokhlyobka,* side meat, and on great occasions, eggs. And did Shura Korf have a servant girl to go to the wine-cellar and fetch up champagne, Malaga, Rhine wines and Scotch whiskey, vodka and kümmel? Perhaps four times a year my father bought a bottle of corn whiskey from a bootlegger, and in the sordid kitchen they drank it

4

in hot toddies which neither pleased their palates nor elevated their spirits and made them waken the following day with headaches, biliousness, and intermittent vertigo. Where were the yellow dresses, the summerhouse and the island in the lake, the solid silver samovar and the little black dog and the chestnut mare? What a brazen liar he had been! He was not the clever, ambitious man he had said he was when on the boat, caressing her as they leaned against the rail of the third-class deck, he had told her how he would have a great shoe business in the United States, selling only shoes made by hand and of the best leather money could buy. Why, he had declared he would have ten workmen under him! He would have commissions from the millionaires of New York City and Washington and Boston!

But see how it was instead: after ten years he was a nothing, a nobody. He *repaired* boots for the poor fishermen; he did not make them for the millionaires. He had not made a single pair for anyone but her, himself, and me.

My father, his pride lacerated, his shame festering would, at this point, retaliate. He would call on God as witness to his wife's failure to observe the laws of marriage: she did not honor him nor love him nor obey, but had made for herself a stifling little box of a life where she did nothing but slothfully brood and cry because she had no yellow dress. What man on earth would *want* to work for a creature like that?

I remember one of these quarrels especially well, not because it was different from any of the others, but because of what followed it on the next day. It was in September, the week before the Hotel Barstow was to close for the season, and I was awake, sorrowing that Miss Pride would soon go back to Boston and that all winter long I would have nothing to do but go to school. My father had gone off to the Coast Guard house where he often spent the summer evenings, playing checkers and drinking home-brew with the men off duty. I was always glad when he went, for usually it meant that my mother would be asleep by the time he came in. But tonight she was restless and several times she spoke to me, "I can't sleep. Sonia, are you awake, darling?" I did not answer and I heard her turn over, sigh, and murmur to herself, "Too hot." It was always either too hot or too cold for her, and not even in the spring or the autumn would she admit that the temperature was pleasant. She would present her perspiring face to my father, or, in December, would hold out her blue hands and say, "You want to kill me!"

For some time I had been living with Miss Pride, first in her room at the Hotel and then in her unknown Boston house and I was either half-asleep or else so preoccupied with my thoughts that I did not hear my father come in and it was only when I heard my mother whisper, "I hate you! Christ God, I hate you!" that I realized he had got into bed and that the close room was full of his breath.

"Let me alone," said my father. "I'm drunk."

But my mother repeated her malediction over and over as if neither he nor she would ever realize its full meaning. After a while, my father howled wearily, "Then go away, for the love of God!" He turned over and the bed springs gave a prolonged creak. My mother, though, knew that he was not asleep, and she began to talk in a monotone, marshaling the injustices she had suffered her whole life long until their perpetrators thronged the room. She began, as was her custom, with the beastliness at hand: "He tells his wife to go away. First he promises her he will be rich and give her a fur cape and French perfume and a hothouse with a gardener to grow white grapes. And then, in a little bit, he tells her to go away out by herself in America where she don't know how to talk to beg. He wants this wife of his to be a beggar! You wish it was winter, don't you, *mein Herr?* So you could send me to the snow without shoes, me and my little girl. Well, sir, wait till the first cold weather and drive us out then. It won't be the first time for me. The child, she knows the words to beg with."

"You speak English," said my father.

She paid no attention. The past was advancing slowly upon her. I knew, because in the quiet I heard her sighing and I heard her rubbing her hands together as she always did when she was thinking of Russia. "It will not be the first time a man drove me into the snow."

"Shura!" implored my father. "Don't tell me again! I will go tomorrow to Boston for work if only you'll go to sleep now."

Heedless of him, she began. Under the night's still heat, her voice flowed like a deep, unbending river as for the millionth time, using

6

the familiar words and images, she recounted the disasters of her childhood. It was a tale so fantastic that not even I, a little girl, could believe it. Yet it was one so horrible that to scoff at it would have been inhuman. In the pauses I listened but could not hear my father's breathing and I knew that he was wide awake, counting off each episode as it fell from her lips and calculating how many more were still to come before the end. As she mourned on, the heat was dispelled and the cold of Moscow's winter streets invaded the bedroom. As clearly as a few minutes before I had seen Miss Pride's afghan and pillows, now I could see nothing but crusted snow, a little cold, yellow sun, and the blue faces of poor people freezing in the gateways and the alleys.

When she was nine or ten years old, her mother died. Her father, who was a tailor and a libertine and a brute, commenced to drink heavily at the funeral dinner and continued to stay drunk for a week. It was in January and it was bitterly cold. The seven children, whom their father and his rioting friends drove away from the stove, kept warm only by hugging one another while the revelers, warm as toast with vodka and the stove heat, poked fun at the shivering little bodies and the chattering teeth and the bright red noses. One day, Constantin Ivanovitch Korf began to malign his dead wife, calling her in one breath a whore and a pious old crone, though she was neither but only a good hard-working creature who had come to the city from the farm and perhaps had died of years of homesickness.

Here came a hiatus in the narrative and I knew that my father, like myself, was mouthing the words that were to follow. She brought out: "The Russians are always homesick people." It was a minute or two before she went on, and in the firm enclosure of the silence, I seemed myself to ail like a Russian and a hot cloud grazed my eyelids.

"There was a yellow-haired German milliner who sat on his lap and pulled at his beard. *Fräulein* Lili, she called herself. I suppose she had no real parents and that was why she had no family names. She would sit there plucking the old goat's beard and call him, 'Constantin, my little bear.' Ah, it was sickening!"

His grief had flown away like a sparrow and he shouted for a song from *Fräulein* Lili. One of the children whimpered, whether from

7

sorrow or shame or cold no one knew, but whatever its cause, the outburst was contagious and directly all the children were sobbing and wailing. You would have thought Constantin Ivanovitch would be too drunk to hear or care. But he flung the woman from his lap and stood up, his feet wide apart, shaking his fist at his sons and daughters. He shouted that he was through with his brats, they could freeze that night for all of him. Then he advanced and together they rose, holding up their little arms as if to thwart the blows from his hairy hands. They turned and made for the door as he followed, slapping their backsides until they were across the threshold. The door was shut. The bolt was drawn. Immediately the milliner began to sing:

> Till with age my hair starts graying,
> Till my locks have ceased to curl,
> Let me live in joy and gladness,
> Let me love a pretty girl!
> Let me live my life in joy and gladness,
> Let me love a pretty girl!

The children scattered, knowing that no one would take them all in together. Whether my mother wandered by herself for hours or for days, she was not sure, she said, for such cold as the cold of Moscow tyrannizes over the light and the dark; the sun is like one poor candle in a vast hall, or else, shining forth with a rowdy blaze, it burns and the kindled snow sears the eye. But at the end of whatever time it was, she was taken into the house of a witch, so-called because of her profession: for a price, she mutilated men who wished to escape military service. She cut off their fingers or their toes or broke the arches of their feet. This Luibka was a dried and wrinkled old prune of a woman with a cackling voice and a bright, shrewd eye and hands which, even in idleness, crooked as though they held a knife.

"*You* would have come to Luibka, Hermann Marburg," she accused my father. "*You* would be too lazy and cowardly to be a soldier."

"I served my time," he replied dully.

"In Germany, yes, where everything is soft. But you would have come to Luibka in Russia where the food is scarce and the soldiers' boots are no good."

The witch was not a bad woman, my mother insisted, but was only the innocent slave of the wicked men who patronized her. The customers might cuff and kick the little girl who washed the knives and handed up the cloths, but the old woman never raised a finger against her and never spoke so much as a single word of reproof. And still, though she had enough to eat and a dry place to sleep, there came a time when the witch's kindness was not enough to stop my mother's ears to the screams nor to close her eyes to the bloody blades and the anxious hound who sprang from his corner whenever a gobbet of flesh fell to the sawdust-covered floor. She was already a tall girl, about fourteen years old, when she left Luibka; and she was so comely that once she set about it, she had no trouble in finding work. She became a waitress in an officers' tavern. From two o'clock in the afternoon until two in the morning, she brought the gentlemen dinners and tea and suppers with champagne as well as the occasional glass of vodka and Löwenbräu beer, imported from Munich, the specialty of the house.

In many ways, my mother felt she had advanced considerably in the world for she was supplied with a pair of handsome uniforms and she was allowed to feed on delicacies, and her tips, because she was beautiful, were by no means trifling. And yet, with all her good fortune, there were times when she would sooner have been handmaiden to Luibka, for the officers made such impertinent overtures to her that she could scarcely sleep at night for shame. Once, in her second year, a cossack whose advances she had rebuffed slapped her face in a drunken fury and his companions jeered her and to him they cried, "Touché!" A few days later, she fell ill of a mysterious fever. She recalled that two old nuns, friends of the landlady of the tavern, came to see her sometimes in the afternoons and stroked her hot forehead with their cold white fingers. When she told them that her sickness had been brought on by a ruffian's spitefulness, they exchanged a glance and, smiling benignly down on her, they said perhaps God would call her to a convent.

All the officers were angry with Shura when she was well and went back to work, and as she served their dinners, they twisted her arms or dug their nails into her hands or stepped on her feet, and she was afraid to cry out lest she be discharged if the master learned

9

how much his clients hated her. Once, as she was going home to her room a few streets away, a soldier followed and pushed her under the wheels of a cab; she was not hurt badly, but her face was cut and her whole body was one great bruise.

In her seventeenth year, she had saved enough money out of her tips and wages to set forth into the world. It was on the boat which brought her to America that she met my father. A week after they disembarked they were married. How great had been her hopes the day she left Moscow! Her fellow waitresses, clinging to her, sobbing with envy, had sworn that she would be rich. Disentangling herself and mounting the steps to the train she laughed and called to them over her shoulder, "Your turn will come. Come to a picnic on my island, my dears!" And how close to fulfillment had seemed those hopes when the fair-haired German boy, tall, well-dressed, smelling of expensive cologne, had promised her that fine house, that immense wardrobe, those journeys to Paris and to Shanghai and to the Panama Canal. Each night, as the old boat rocked and groaned through stormy water, he shouted his promises over the racket of the wind and the protesting timbers.

"What do I have?" she groaned. "Nothing. No dresses, nothing but slops to eat. Ah, Hermann Marburg, I hate you from the bottom of my soul!"

My father, now that the long, sad tale was done, had had enough. He laughed at her, and that laugh, made up of all the scorn of devils and all the resentment of the damned, made me half sick to death with fright and I was glad for the darkness so that I could not see his genial face askew and scarlet, for the sound could not help corrupting what it issued from.

"Hush!" said my mother. "You'll wake up Sonia."

But he only laughed the harder, gasping and choking as though this glee were a convulsion beyond his control. Then, quieted, in a solemn, even voice, he said, "The child should never have been born."

His words concluded the scene. Worn out, they went to sleep. Over and over, until my eyes closed, I imagined the day on which my parents would die and Miss Pride would come to take me to live at the Hotel, if they died in the summer, or in Boston, if in the winter. Or I watched the waves part and saw a dry path laid for me between the water's furniture and then I stepped forward off the beach and walked across to the first wharf in Boston harbor. I could hear the calm waves washing the rocks and the shore and although my mind was far away, I could hear their undertone, gentle and melancholy, reiterating endlessly my father's words: the child should never have been born.

## 2

On the following morning, both my parents slept late, and I was on edge, fearful that my mother would not be on time at the Hotel or that a customer would come to my father's cobbling shop at the rear of the house and finding the place closed would leave and not return. My worry made my fingers all impatient thumbs and the fire would not start for me. Through a shimmering veil of tears, particulars of the room, aglow with morning sunshine, were distorted in a dream-like beauty: the stains of the dark blue sink under the window were invisible and it appeared, with the glittering waterdrops that depended from its brassy taps, patinated with green, like some old and precious vessel. The crimson geraniums on the sill above were blurred in a tropical splendor. As the kindling caught, my eyes cleared, winking away the transformation of the sink and seeing once again its preposterously graceful legs and its drain-board bristling with sodden splinters. I counted slowly to sixty before I lifted the stove-lid again to see the progress of the fire, and as I counted, stared at the two pictures which hung one above the other over the table. The lower one was a barn-yard scene of russet hens and two majestic roosters avidly pecking at the foot of a pile of manure while beyond them there loomed a red barn from which stared out a thoughtful cow. The higher picture represented two little girls in white dresses and white satin slippers playing with five white puppies under the supervision of the snow-white mother dog.

When the kindling had caught, I dropped in a few lumps of coal, then waited until I had counted two hundred before I closed the damper. I gazed at one object until I had counted fifty and then shifted my eyes to another. We had three hard chairs with imitation leather seats adorned with lions' heads in bas-relief; a bright red step-ladder; a footstool made of a cheese box; a pea-green washstand where stood a pitcher and bowl, discarded by the Hotel Barstow. Long ago, when he had bought the house, my father had put shelves up against one wall which were called "the book shelves" although they contained only a German translation of *Riders of the Purple Sage,* a Bible, my schoolbooks and a very old copy of *Harper's Magazine* in which I had one time read a bewildering advertisement: "Everyone wants a gold tooth. Now you too can have one by sending only ten cents (10¢) for a complete Dento-Kit." The shelves were crowded with pliers, hammers, Mason jars full of bacon grease as old as myself, an empty caviar can which my mother fondled now and again in memory of the day, ages ago, when she had eaten its contents; broken pipes, broken knives, shattered sea-shells, a landing net, a wooden snake, a gauze bag filled with venerable headache pills.

Just as I lifted the stove-lid for the third time, the door to the bedroom burst open and my parents tumbled out, shouting at me to put the kettle on for tea and to run unlock the shop and to run to the Hotel to say Mamma was not well today and I would do for her. These tousled, foolish creatures seemed not the same at all as those hobgoblins who had rollicked and bawled in their temper tantrum the night before. My father, while he rubbed his eyes with one hand, patted my cheek with the other and said, *"Good* morning, *Fräulein.* Look sharp, there. Today is the day we get rich all of a sudden, *ni't wahr?"* My mother did not hear him, for she was running water at the tap for her perfunctory toilet.

My father gave me then a purposeless wink and nodded toward the box of corn flakes on the table. "Esel von Hexensee hasn't eaten his hay yet." This was my favorite joke. Out in the shop, in the dark little room that smelled of pipe smoke and leather, he made up stories, pretending that I was a boy named Fritz or a donkey named Esel von Hexensee, and if I were the latter, he would fit a saddle to my back and two Concord grape baskets for panniers and drive me up the Zugspitz for some droll, pious purpose such as taking hot soup to Fritz who had fainted from the altitude. The games delighted me and when he was tired of playing, I would beg him to go on. "Na," he would say, suddenly sober. "I am stiff from beating that *Dumm-*

*kopf* Esel," and picking me up like a cat, he would put me out of the shop and bolt the door behind me.

I drank a cup of tea that had not brewed long enough, swallowed a few spoonfuls of corn flakes and ran out of the house towards the road leading to the Hotel. The fishermen were untying their boats and calling greetings to one another. Their wives stood on the doorsteps complaining to their neighbors that it looked like "another scorcher." Mrs. Henderson, who lived next door to us, cried something to me but I did not hear what she said and I ran on, flinging back, with no thought of its meaning, "I know it!"

We did not live far from the Hotel, perhaps no more than a quarter of a mile, but because after the cluster of fishermen's cottages there were no houses at all on either side of the curving white road, it seemed a long and tedious distance. Here there were no shade trees to interrupt the glare of the sand and the dry flowers that straggled half-heartedly along the road were too dwarfed even to cast a shadow. It was a relief to take a turning and then, from a slight rise, to see the big white frame Hotel with its bright flower beds and its verandas where hung baskets of fern and ivy.

The Hotel Barstow was the sort of place which never changes and then, with very age, it falls and the site is used for a new structure. Such a day was impossible to imagine. Anyone who had lived there assumed that the stuffed hoot-owls and the Wilson snipes and the herons would go on forever patiently standing on one leg in hoary moss or placidly sitting on unseen eggs behind their glass cases in the dining-room, that until the end of time the same old ladies, musty-smelling and enfeebled, would be offered cream-of-wheat as the first entrée on the evening menu. Forever, too, the same sort of pert, plump man would stand behind the curved desk in the lobby, fetching down keys and mail and inquiring after his guests' health.

Miss Pride, an early riser, was drilling on the beach, unwithered in spite of the sun which was already very warm. The clerk, Mr. Hagethorn, called from the veranda, "Well, Miss Pride, is it hot enough for you today?"

Unsmilingly she replied, "I observe no change from yesterday. Has the mercury risen?" Even in midsummer, she always wore black broadcloth suits and an olive beaver hat. She apparently suffered neither from the heat nor from the cold, for she did not shiver or perspire, and she was never heard to discuss the temperature.

I slackened my pace in order to hold her in my vision: straight as a gun-barrel, she carried her lengthy shadow up and down the golden sand; or she rested it, squarely facing Boston, looking with her formidable eyes into the very conscience of her care-taker who was probably loafing on the job. I had heard someone say of my mother, "She is beautiful except in one thing, her eyes are too large." I believed, therefore, that Miss Pride was beautiful for hers were very small. They were eyes more like a bird's than any other creature's: that is, such was their intensity and their sharp change of direction (they never wandered, but rather, disconnected their focus from one point of concentration and abruptly fixed it upon the next) that they gave the impression of being flat to the skull or slightly convex, that they had a container more like a plate than a socket. They were "on" her head rather than "in" it. I suppose in her passport they were called "gray" or "hazel," but to me they were "cold gold" and were like the yellow haze that followed sundown when the shine of the sand was gone.

I hesitated a moment in the hope that she might turn and greet me. A sigh, involuntary and profound, ruffled up through my lips and when it had passed, I ran to the back of the Hotel. Without explaining to the head chambermaid that my mother was ill, I snatched a mop and a broom and a dust-cloth from the closet off the kitchen and ran up the backstairs two at a time. For I wanted to repeat the strange experience I had once had of regarding Miss Pride through the windows of her very own bedroom. She was still on the beach when I stole to the central window. Now a few bathers had come for an early dip and Miss Pride was plowing up and down through the sand, fixing them with her clear, indifferent eyes as though, without loss of dignity to herself, her gaze could penetrate them to their very giblets. As I watched her, taking in with admiration each detail of her immaculate attire and her proud carriage, I heard, from the adjoining room, embedded in a yawn, the waking squeal of Mrs. McKenzie, a garrulous and motherly old woman whom I had always disliked. Her room was no pleasure to clean: her bed was strewn with corsets and short-sleeved nightdresses, and on her bedside table,

I often found drying apple cores which I removed gingerly, having in my mind an image of her with her sparse hair unpinned sitting up in bed cropping with her large false teeth. Upon the bureau, amongst sticky bottles of vile black syrups and tonics and jars of fetid salve, there lay her bunion plasters and her ropes of brown hair which she sometimes arranged in a lofty cone on top of her head. Usually she was in the room when I entered and she saluted me with disgusting moonshine as "mother's little helper" or asked me if my "beauteous mamma" was sick.

Now in Miss Pride's room, there was never anything amiss. Perhaps once or twice a summer, I found a bottle of imported wine or whiskey on her writing desk; this was the only medicine she took and she took it regularly in small quantities. On the bureau, the china hair receiver did not receive a wisp of hair, and there were neither spots nor foreign objects upon the white linen runner. A hat-pin holder, sprouting long, knobbed needles, two cut-glass cologne bottles, and a black glove-box, shaped like a small casket, were reflected in the clear swinging mirror. Though I should have loved to dearly, I had not the courage to investigate the drawers which were always neatly shut, but I was sure that they were in scrupulous order. The other old ladies, almost without exception, allowed the feet of stockings and the straps of camisoles to stream from each gaping tier like so many dispirited banners.

As I watched, Miss Pride ascended the steps that led from the Hotel beach, and I knew that now she would enter the dining-room and, after she had eaten one boiled egg and one slice of toast, she would examine the newspaper over her coffee while all about her, her coevals would be prattling of their sound sleep or their insomnia, depending on how the dinner of the night before had affected them. It seemed to me that Miss Pride looked up and saw me even though my face was hidden by the marquisette curtains and my body was behind the heavy drapery. I backed away from the window and began to run the oiled mop over the edges of the floor which the rug did not cover. While I worked, I heard Mrs. McKenzie thrashing about in the bed and rise finally, stumbling over her shoes, bumping against the furniture and repeating her vociferous yawn. The sound of the bed rolling across the floor, as I pulled it out to make it, roused her to rap on the wall and cry, "Good morning, Mrs. Marburg! I've been a lazybones again today!"

I did not answer. There was something in the tone of her voice, a quality of dampness—as though the words themselves were kisses from unminded lips—which embarrassed me. She called again, "Yoo, hoo, Mrs. Marburg!"

"It's Sonie," I grudgingly gave out.

"Oh. Well, Sonie, I'll be out of my room in three shakes of a lamb's tail and then you can come get me straight."

"Yes, ma'am."

"Get yourself a lemon drop, dear!"

Presently I heard her door open and close and heard her toil down the stairs, one dropsical foot at a time. I now worked rapidly, brushing my cloth over the bedside table, the writing desk, and the bureau, plumping up the cherub pillows and setting the bolster precisely at the head of the bed. When I had finished, I stood for a few minutes before the mirror and, as I had done many times before, pulled out the stoppers of the bottles and inhaled their clean, alcoholic fragrance. I opened the black box and gazed upon the white silk button gloves, the yellowing white kid and black chamois ones, amongst which were scattered single cuff-links, broken bone buttons, a mysterious, star-shaped brooch and three edible beads. My brief survey finished, I sat down before the desk and though I touched nothing, I took in everything: the brass letter opener with its carved wood scabbard, the matching ink-pot and pen and the dark green blotter in a brown leather holder, the calendar which gave the date, September 7, 1925. A week from today she would leave. All winter she would live in a house I had not seen and could not imagine, a house of which I knew nothing except that it was on the celebrated Beacon Hill, perhaps close by the luminous dome of the State House. My sorrow was reinforced when I saw a stamped letter, addressed in her careful hand to her niece, Miss Hopestill Mather, Camp Pocahontas, Southport, Maine. For, if I could not envisage the house which stole her away from me each autumn, I knew exactly what the little girl looked like who lived with her. Once, the summer before, when she was ten years old and I was nine, she had been brought by a small nervous woman, Mrs. Brooks, her second cousin, to have luncheon at the

Hotel. She had been so self-assured, carried her head with such a grown-up dignity that she seemed advanced in her teens. I, who that day had been charged with filling the water glasses, stared from the sideboard at her bright red hair, caught at the left temple by a green ribbon and falling down her back, long and straight, over a white batiste dress, printed with tiny yellow flowers. As I passed by Miss Pride's table on my way to Mrs. Prather, I heard her say, "How absurd, Auntie! You ought to know the counselors are all stupid." And later, when I had returned to my post where, sick with envy of her voice and her cultured language I felt my face color and the pulse in my forehead leap, she signaled me with her white hand, calling, "Waitress! Water, please."

I could linger no more in Miss Pride's room, but cleverly I omitted to put clean towels on the rack beside the wash-stand in order that I might return after my other work was done, this afternoon when she had gone for a drive.

It was nearly luncheon time when I came into the lobby to dust the albums on the brocade covers of the round tables, and all the old ladies were spryly exercising the rocking chairs on the veranda, having a chat about relatives with diabetes and friends with Bright's Disease, and talking of their own improper pains, their bizarre sensations in the region of the gall-bladder, and their physicians who were either "very understanding" or obscurely "unsatisfactory."

"I love cucumbers," Mrs. Prather was saying, "but they don't love me."

Mrs. McKenzie replied, "I'm the same way with seedy things. They give me heart-burn and of course they clog the colon."

I drew back my hand with horror from the golden callosities of the "worked" covers on the albums for, smooth and round, they resembled human organs as I recalled them from the colored diagrams in my hygiene book.

A voice I did not know well inquired, "Has the Hotel Barstow always had a restricted clientele?"

"No, indeed!" cried Mrs. McKenzie. "About three years ago, a new manager came, a really vulgar person whom I'm perfectly certain was a Jew although his name was Mr. Watkins. And by the time I arrived—I came a little late that year—the Hotel was swarming with uninvestigated guests. I dare say we won't forget Mr. Johnson in a hurry, will we?"

The story of Mr. Johnson, one of the veranda favorites, was retold for the newcomer. From what walk of life he had come was impossible for anyone to tell. But he was no gentleman as a child could see in the first glance at his reversible silk shirts, his diamond tie-pin, his bright orange oxfords and his loud, checked jacket. He teased the old ladies by putting a bottle of bootleg whiskey on his table in the dining-room in imitation of their phials of medicine. "Oh, my hair hurts so," he would say and take a drink. He carried a walking stick, although he was neither a cripple nor a great walker, and the other guests thought it was probably hollow and contained a rapier.

"I've heard of such a thing, you know," said Mrs. McKenzie. "When my poor sister was in Wiesbaden taking the baths for her arthritis which nothing on earth would cure—how much money she spent I couldn't tell you and she must have suffered twenty years—there was a man living in a pension a block away who was proved beyond a shadow of a doubt to have a rapier in his stick."

"But now," pursued the unfamiliar voice, "now your manager is discreet?"

"Oh, Mr. Hagethorn is the soul of caution. He caters solely to those of us who have been coming here for at least twenty years. We call ourselves the Barstow family."

Mr. Hagethorn, pleased with the compliment that had come to his attentive pink ears, bawled in authority, "Sonie, clean up around the ferns there. Don't dawdle." The ferns and several potted palms made a little triangular garden in the far corner of the lobby, and as I made my way towards them, I perceived Miss Pride, sitting erect on a straight chair, half hidden by the foliage. This was her reading hour. Today she held *The Atlantic Monthly* directly in front of her. Her thin lips were set in concentration beneath her short, sharp nose with its contracted nares. She did not look up when I knelt down, three feet away from her and began to brush the fallen fronds into a dust-pan. I kept my eye on her and presently I saw a frown invade her high forehead. I did not know if she had come to a word she did not understand or if she were annoyed with the chatter that came through the screen door. Evidently the old ladies were now scrutiniz-

18

ing the fashionable young people on the beach who had drifted down from the smarter hotels and who were clad in bathing costumes that exposed long, sun-browned legs. "I just don't know," said someone, "I just don't know. Are we advancing? Or are we going back to paganism? I don't say it's immoral to expose the legs to the public eye: I say it's not fastidious. Why, our chambermaid, Mrs. Marburg, has more modesty than those young ladies out there who, you can rest assured, either have come out or will come out at the Chilton Club."

Even at this mention of my mother and although she must have known that I was beside her, Miss Pride did not look at me. Her frown deepened; reluctantly she closed her magazine just as the only male guest of the Hotel, Mr. Brock, slipped quietly through two pots of fern, carrying with him a folding chair which he set down beside hers. What impressed me in that moment was that the frown, which had lasted two or three minutes, showed that she had known of his approach long before I either heard or saw him.

"Good morning! I hope I am not disturbing you at your devotions?" The chuckle following his remark was not returned and Miss Pride only said, "Good morning."

Mr. Brock was a soft-spoken and scholarly old man who, although he had come from New York, called himself "a professional Bostonian." He was the victim of a delusion which he propounded, whenever he had the opportunity, to myself, my mother, the Mexican gardener, Gonzales, to Mr. Hagethorn, to the waitresses. He believed that of all languages, only the English was capable of vulgarity, and he claimed that bad American books were transformed by translation into promising, if not brilliant, prose. He had made a collection of such translations, having E. P. Roe, for example, rendered into French and the Elsie Dinsmore books into Spanish. He had given my father his copy of *Riders of the Purple Sage* and my father, although he was totally indifferent to Mr. Brock's thesis, so thoroughly enjoyed the book for its adventure that the old man danced for joy, sure that this was the proof of the pudding.

Now he produced a leather-bound book from his brief-case and handing it to Miss Pride, said, "I sought you out to show you my latest find. This is *Bob, Son of Battle* in German or *Old Bob, der graue hund von Kenmuir* and it is enchanting. Would you care to read it?"

"No, Mr. Brock, I would not," said Miss Pride sternly. "I do not share your enthusiasm for foreign languages. And as for dog-books I had no use for them in my girlhood and feel quite sure I would find them even less to my taste now that I have passed beyond the age for juvenile literature."

He was not rebuffed. "I admire your linguistic singleness, Miss Pride, since in you I am sure it is the result of strong nationalistic convictions. Alas, we are not all by opinion or antecedents eligible for membership in the English Speaking Union."

"I am not a member of the English Speaking Union," she returned. "But in any case your remark is, to use a foreign phrase, a *non sequitur.*"

Mr. Brock, receiving the book which she extended, allowed his disappointment to show briefly in his foolish old face and then, catching sight of me, he cried, "Now here is someone whose father will appreciate the book." In a voice a little lower but not intended to be inaudible to me, he added, "Did you realize that this child's father is an educated man?"

"I believe I haven't had the pleasure of knowing him." Miss Pride took me in, perhaps for the first time since I had been coming to the Hotel, and I felt that in her rapid but comprehensive examination of my face and person she had discerned everything about me, that she knew I had once broken my collarbone, that I did poorly in arithmetic and singing and well in reading, and that brushing my teeth had not yet become habitual with me.

"Yes," Mr. Brock went on, "Hermann Marburg, the Chichester cobbler, is an educated man. A graduate of the *gymnasium* of Würzburg, Germany, and, except for an ineffacable accent which I myself find appealing, has been completely bilingual since the age of eleven, and partially trilingual—his third language, of course, being French —since the age of fifteen."

Miss Pride did not seem impressed but rather than humiliate me, as I assumed, said nothing. "I have had several illuminating conversations with Mr. Marburg, sometimes in German, sometimes in English. I neglected to mention, by the way, that through his wife he has also picked up quite a considerable Russian vocabulary. Now a graduate of a *gymnasium*, Miss Pride, as you are perhaps not aware, is, if anything better educated than a candidate for an American baccalaureate degree. Yet the *gymnasium* is the counterpart of our preparatory school!"

"What do they learn?" inquired Miss Pride, frankly dubious.

"Having been something of a Latinist myself at Mr. Greenough's, naturally I admire Mr. Marburg's firm classical foundation. I must admit his Latin is less literary than ecclesiastical, for he was trained by the Franciscans, but it *is*, nevertheless, good, sound Latin. In addition he knows history. Oh, he knows his history *well*, Miss Pride! Roman and the French Revolution are his specialties. And then, although he's a modest man, I have no doubt in the world he could put many of our Harvard men to shame in the field of philosophy. Literature he is not so keen on although he did drop the remark that he had at one time been a great admirer of Goethe. Now there is a man who has the perspicacity to see what I mean when I say that in his language *Riders of the Purple Sage* is a superb piece of craftsmanship."

Miss Pride had had enough. She rose and her face, shaded by the wide brim of her hat, represented the pure substance of scorn. "You will forgive me, Mr. Brock, for finding your crotchet fantastic. It is my cantankerous opinion, sir, that you do not believe this nonsense yourself, but that you wish to disguise your appetite for rubbish. Not to put too fine a point on it, how could you, without the aid of some such camouflage, indulge yourself in Elsie Dinsmore at the age of seventy-two?"

Mortally wounded, he gave her a wan smile. "Your wit is all that it is said to be, ma'am."

Less coldly but with the same firmness she went on, "What interests me about this Mr. Marburg is, does he make his shoes well? Does he know *that* craft, Mr. Brock, as well as his Latin?"

"Oh, I have no idea. I never discuss business with him."

Miss Pride was looking at my feet, shod in a pair of white moccasins which my father had made. I was ashamed that they were so dirty and that my socks were ragged. She turned at the announcement of luncheon, but I did not fail to hear her say to Mr. Brock as they crossed the lobby, "I gather that he knows his business and has little of it."

After Audrey, the headwaitress, and I had set the tables for dinner, I went upstairs with Miss Pride's fresh towels. The corridor was quiet, for all the guests were napping. I could hear, through the wall by Miss Pride's bed, the faint popping of air in Mrs. McKenzie's nose as she slept deeply. Immediately I took my post at the windows and in about a quarter of an hour, I saw Miss Pride go down the wooden stairs of the porch, pinching the hand-rail with her gloved fingers. Then she waited on the lawn for her high, black limousine. Once I had seen in it vases for flowers on the sides, hanging like pictures in a house. I believed she had other decorative furnishings in the back seat as, perhaps, a needlepoint footstool and a writing board. What if she even had a tea table and at a suitable hour and place, ordered the car to be stopped and then served herself tea! I would dwell on this enchanting thought sometimes as long as half an hour, seeing with an overwhelming happiness the actual seeds of the strawberry jam.

Here came the car! Slipping round the corner of the Hotel, its long black snout caught the rays of the sun which shot fitfully into my eyes. It stopped and Mac, the chauffeur, stepped out. He was a thin, sharp, silvery young man who, in his gray livery, looked like an upright rat. He suffered from some strange distemper that caused his feet to swell, but though the valetudinarians of the veranda perpetually foretold Miss Pride's doom when the man while driving should die at the wheel (for they were enough acquainted with his symptoms to know that foot swelling indicated a rheumatic heart for which there was *no cure*), she kept him on and about twice a week was handed into the car by his lean, gray paws which, since they went out and withdrew so quickly, seemed to abhor their contact with the desiccated elbow that they briefly cupped.

"Well, Mac," came her voice, "I trust we are all in order. I must run in to Pinckney Street today."

So that was the name of it: Pinckney Street. I repeated the words to myself and the house where she lived all winter now seemed less strange because it was not merely in Boston but was in a specific street with a specific number of houses. Henceforth my daydreams would not begin with the vague condition, "When I live in Boston with Miss Pride," but with, "When I live on Pinckney Street."

"Oh, but before we go," she said, her foot on the running board, "I want you to take me to the shoemaker here. A Mr. Marburg."

The car drove off and I sank into the chair at the writing desk, faint with a conflict. For the joy I felt in Miss Pride's going to call on my father was scotched by my shame of our shabby shop, my father's untidiness, and my mother's loquacity. Nor did I know whether she was seeking him out as Mr. Brock did, because he was educated, or if she was going to him on business, to have him half-sole her Ground Grippers. If her intention were the latter, now, at this very moment, I must relinquish my ambition to be her young and well-beloved friend.

The letter to her niece was gone from the writing desk and in its place was one addressed to herself and postmarked London. I was less moved by the foreign stamp and the strange, thin paper of the envelope than I was by what next caught my eye: it was my own name, Marburg, written on a memorandum pad together with the legends: "Call Breckenridge at three" and "flue in the upstairs sitting-room." That meant, then, that there was also a *downstairs* sitting-room so that the house was surely big enough to accommodate me as well as Hopestill Mather and Miss Pride. Perhaps even now she was saying to my father that although she realized he was a good man and well educated, she believed he owed it to me to give me a better home which she herself was willing to provide.

While I was meditating, I was interrupted by Mrs. McKenzie. She took very short naps and I heard her suffocated scream. I was afraid she might sense my presence in the room next to hers and summon me to eat a lemon drop or send me to the village to fetch her a bottle of Moxie. I tiptoed out of the room and through the Hotel and then stood in the back yard hesitating. For I could not decide whether to go directly home and present myself in the shop where the interview would probably take place—unless my mother's curiosity were aroused at the sight of the black car and she insisted that they sit in the kitchen—or to go down to the Point and wait there until it should be over, passing the time in watching the sailboats and the barges going out from Boston harbor. But as I debated, I saw two old ladies round the corner of the Hotel with walking sticks and parasols, and I heard one of them say, "It's not far. The view is gorgeous and at this time of day, we'll have the whole Point to ourselves."

In order that my mother might not intercept me, I took the road on the bay side of the peninsula, approaching the shop from the rear. I stood on tiptoe outside the window and I saw, enveloped in the shadows, Miss Pride seated primly on a stool beside the wheels and shoe stands, while my father knelt, taking the measurements of her right foot. This foot, short and narrow, wore a tan silk stocking with heavy cotton reinforcements at the toe and heel, and I was momentarily shocked at the sight, for I had assumed that every article of her clothing, down to her underwear, would be black.

"I understand that you are a friend of one of my fellow-lodgers, Mr. Brock," she was saying.

"He comes sometimes. He is a scholar, I suppose."

Miss Pride smiled. They were both silent as he removed her other shoe and began to measure the left foot. I wondered what she thought of this large shaggy man who always looked unkempt and would have even if he had fastidiously groomed himself. He was the opposite, in this respect, of my mother who never looked dirty or untidy though she was both, and to a far greater degree than he. He was a tall man and the muscles of his youth had not yet been overlaid by flesh, but, at thirty-three, had begun to sag a little as though they were preparing themselves for a permanent relaxation. His thick, yellow hair looked like a palm thatch and now, as he bent over and it fell forward from his skull, I felt that I could lift up a flap of it and clip it at a single root like the midrib of a leaf. His face was broad and red and its hollows were scooped out cleanly so that, although it was full, the shape of the skeleton was clearly visible. His chin was cleft and his lips, whose usual attitude was one of curving downward, were quiet and contemplative and seemed not to belong to the chilled blue eyes which were those of a decisive man. Today, because of the heat, he was dressed like a boy and when he stood up to get something from the work table which required him to turn in my direc-

24

tion, I saw to my embarrassment that his white, short-sleeved shirt was torn at the shoulder, revealing a segment of skin, browned by the sun on the days he had gone bathing. His hair seemed fairer than usual and at the temples it was almost white.

Miss Pride, who had been leaning over his bent back, withdrew as he stood up, and she said, "I expect a good pair of shoes, Mr. Marburg. Your price is steep, but I have every confidence in German workmanship."

He did not rise to her compliment but gave only the smile which politeness demanded. I fairly danced with impatience in the sand at his unresponsive face and at the impudence which had made him charge her a high price when he should, I thought, have done the work free and presented her as a gift the finest pair of shoes he could make. Ah, if she had come to call on *me,* not my father, how I would have entertained her! I would have made her a pot of tea and run to the village for a lemon and half a dozen jellied doughnuts. And I would have listened carefully to every word she said and nodded my head in constant agreement as she talked.

Although she saw that he was disinclined to talk (he could so easily, with the opening she had given him, explain that he had not always been a poor, shabby man, but that in Germany, he had been of a well-to-do family), she persevered. "You learned your trade in Germany, did you not?"

"Oh, yes!" In his voice, there was an impulsive note which, combined with my sudden apprehension of a half-empty whiskey bottle on the shelf over the door, alarmed me, and I was afraid that he might begin to calendar, not the events of his past life, but its errors. For when he had been drinking, he became neither rebellious nor self-pitying as did my mother, but he brooded, morosely accusing himself of heartless infidelities to the traditions of the Catholic church, of his family, and of his country. My mother believed herself to be persecuted by everyone she had ever known—with the exception of Luibka, myself, and a few neighbor women—but he knew, and was powerless to rectify the fault, that all his torture came from his own flabby will which swung him like a pendulum between apathy and fretful indecision. I could see through the clouded

25

windowpane that he was preoccupied with some tangential thought as he wrote down the specifications of Miss Pride's feet in his note-book, and I was in mortal terror that he was going to tell her how long it had been since his last confession. When he did speak again, it was not in self-accusation, but it was from a point far removed from her question.

He said, "But even so, they don't know good shoes from bad here."

"If by 'here' you mean Chichester," returned Miss Pride, "I'm certain you're right. And while they might know skill when they saw it, these poor fishermen could not pay for it. But I beg to differ with you if by 'here' you mean something larger. Don't you think, Mr. Marburg, that in Boston, *we* know the real thing?"

The light which flickered in my father's face was quickly extin-guished. "It's too late for *that*," he said.

"You are an obdurate man, sir. My father used to liken your countrymen to our own Puritans. Therein, he said, lay the greatness of the nation. I must confess Papa and I never saw eye to eye on your 'greatness' for even as a young lady, I was displeased with your romancing and your 'earth-spirit' but I can see that some of you are hard-headed. If you were not, how could you work so cleverly?" She paused, watching my father closely as though she were waiting for a reply or a confirmation, but neither was forthcoming. She went on. "If you came to Boston, you would be out of the doldrums. I recol-lect the governess to the child of one of my friends. When she came, poor *Fräulein* Ströck, she was timorous and wistful, for she had been for some time in an establishment in the middle west where her gifts —a little too Prussian for my liking—were not appreciated in the least. But she had not been with us, with Boston, that is, for a month before she had blossomed into what she had been born to be, a first-rate disciplinarian. I believe you will find we have our feet on the ground and that we need no divining rods to find our treasures."

My father, no more than I, did not know what to make of her lec-ture. Had I been inside with them, I would have inquired how many children were under Miss Ströck's charge or why it was that she was too Prussian to please Miss Pride entirely. My disappointment in my father's indifference and in the gesture he made of passing his hand before his face as if he were befogged, was converted into anger as I realized that he did not intend to make any sort of comment at all. Surely he, a grown-up man with an education so proudly advertised by Mr. Brock, could select something out of that subtle speech as a point of departure! How stupid and contrary of him not to ask, at least, if Miss Pride had ever been to Germany. Why, I, a little girl, could do that much!

But Miss Pride, to my astonishment, did not appear annoyed. With a grace which obviated the need for a transition, she said, "If I am pleased with my shoes, I shall want you to make more for me. I shall be anxious to put you in the way of further commissions. Surely you won't refuse."

"No," he said, but there was neither gratitude nor excitement in his voice. "If I am nothing else, I am a workman who does his work."

She stood up. "Now when the shoes are finished, you may mail them to me at this address." Taking a leather case from her handbag, she extracted a card from it. "I must say there is something about your shop I like. It strikes me as what I spoke of before: the real thing. Nothing is so close to my heart as that, sir: the real thing. And if you had known my father, you would see I came by my passion honestly."

"I hope you will be satisfied with the shoes," said my father. "But you must not expect too much. My hands are not as clever as they used to be. I am, you see, no longer a shoemaker, I am a shoe-fixer."

Miss Pride gave him her hand. "It's time you changed. Good-by."

He stood stupidly in the center of the room and did not open the door for her, did not, indeed, bid her good-by. When she had gone and the motor of her car started up, he sat down on the stool she had just occupied and putting his hands over his face, the fingers so tightly interlocked that their knuckles whitened, he groaned with some profound, enigmatic misery, and I stepped softly away from the window, perplexed that she who could cause me only happiness had caused him only pain. As I went toward the house, I was gradually infected by his terrible sorrow and felt my face grow feverish, recalling his words last night: the child should never have been born.

27

In the kitchen, I ran my fingers over the cold stove. My mother was sitting in a chair beside the sink and she drew me down to kiss me. "Who do you love, little Sonie girl?" she said, gazing at me with her great black eyes. And while I answered her as she desired me to, my mind was telling me the truth: "Miss Pride, not you, Mamma."

# CHAPTER TWO

During the two years that my father supplied Miss Pride, her niece, and a couple of her friends with shoes, there were frequent conferences on the advisability of buying me a bed. But because the plans were always projected when my parents were drinking a bottle of whiskey and the morning found them oblivious of everything but their malaise, I continued to sleep on my pallet, made a little longer now to accommodate my increased height. Our prosperity was manifested in very little beyond a regular Saturday night pint of liquor. We did have a cerise rayon bedspread, a piebald linoleum for the kitchen floor, an eccentric shower-bath crowded into the minute closet we called the "bathroom," and I had a red coat with an astrakhan collar. But my mother had none of the things she longed for, and if my father, when he was drinking, offered to buy her a yellow dress, she refused, saying sadly that she did not want pretty clothes unless she had an estate with a lake where, on its island, she would be hostess at summer picnics. My father would commend her good sense and tell her, in a foxy whisper, as if for the first time, that he was "laying away a little something" and in a few years his savings would accomplish everything her heart desired.

When there was no whiskey to provide a recess in their old war, they sang two different tunes. My father cried that he was enslaved to Miss Pride whom he had come to detest, for he believed that her patronage of him was an alms-deed. "Four pairs of shoes in one winter for an ugly old woman!" he exploded. "Maybe she sells them at a profit. She can't wear out my shoes so quick!" He was displeased, too, that all his transactions with her were conducted by mail, as if she counted herself too good to come to his shop. When she ordered a new pair of shoes for her niece, she sent a careful drawing of the girl's feet together with the height of the arches. And when the

29

sandals or the moccasins or dancing pumps were delivered, he received a curt note of thanks which was folded around the check. Time and again he declared, "I will make no more for them." But he could never resist new, costly leather and he always took the work.

My mother, on the other hand, deplored his failure to exploit his Boston customers and said, with considerable truth, that if we moved across the bay to the city and opened up a shop there, we would really become rich. Then I could have as many pairs of shoes as Hopestill Mather and she could be driven about in a black car like Miss Pride's. But nothing could avail against my father's indolent pessimism, and he went on living in our poor little village precariously, like someone who, being exposed to the cold, finally quits the struggle to keep awake and sinks into what he knows is his last sleep.

For myself, I was torn between gratitude to Miss Pride for noticing us at all, for affixing her signature to letters to my father—letters bearing her address on Pinckney Street—and the knowledge that her relationship with us would never be anything but commercial. Nevertheless, my reveries of life in Boston persisted, became, indeed, as my experience widened, more specific and in a sense more real than my existence in Chichester. In the wintertime at school, I was known as a daydreamer and often my teacher would hustle me out of Miss Pride's house with a mocking rebuke that made the whole class laugh: "Tell us what is so interesting that you can't remember the capital of Rhode Island, Sonie." At home, depending on the tempers of my parents, I was called "bright" or "stupid" or "silly" or "older than my age." Confined during the day by school-room walls where hung Sir Galahad and "The Stag at Eve," George Washington and President Wilson and Kipling's "If," plied by unanswerable questions, required to sing "I am a little *blue* bird" in reply to the teacher's full, contralto query, "Who is a little *blue* bird?", I would gradually float away, leaving my body behind, still sitting at the stained red desk. As I vanished, I would see the teacher jump to attention, gather her forces and in a moment overtake me, but not before I had slipped into Miss Pride's drawing-room, wearing a brown velvet dress and a yellow bone round-comb in my hair.

At night, bound by the narrow walls of our kitchen, I was not always absorbed in my book about girls at boarding school whose clever mothers had sewed for months before their departure, making silk dresses and dark wool jumpers, warm wrappers, innumerable muslin guimpes, had crocheted fascinators and had bought blue merino stockings. Although I envied the fortunate creatures, my own life which I plotted in a variety of patterns was richer. My hair became blond; my name was Antoinette de la Mar. "Soon after Antoinette or Toni, as her chums called her, went to live in the Pride mansion on Pinckney Street, a handsome Harvard student named Andrew Eliot Cabot Lodge fell passionately in love with her. But as she had already decided not to marry anybody, she spurned him with a few kind but firm words. That night he shot himself, but he did not die and she nursed him back to health. She had many suitors but she lived only for Miss Pride who adored her and often had her do a toe-dance for her visitors who were often foreign kings and queens. They would say, 'I say, Antoinette de la Mar has it all over Denishawn. Why, Denishawn could never whirl on one toe that long.' "

My mother, who spent nearly every winter evening playing Patience (she always cheated, to my indignation, and as other disrespectful children in a fury curse their mothers, I would howl at mine, "You cheat at cards!"), would notice that for an hour I had not turned a page in my book. "Are you asleep, booby?" she would scold. "Are you asleep sitting up like a little cow?"

If my father raised his eyes from *Riders of the Purple Sage*, quaintly called *Das Gesetz der Mormonen*, to join our quarrel, perhaps to accuse me harshly of thinking of boys, my mother would instantly come to my defense and would commence to belabor him with vituperation. When they had finished the skirmish, my father would lift the red felt cozy off the white china coffee-pot and drink from a thick cup. He would then return to his book and my mother to her cards as she remarked, *"He* gets the fine pot for his coffee but Shura Korf has to keep her tea in a tin can." Perhaps he would ignore her, or would say, pointing to his chest, "The pot is *mine*. It is a *coffee* pot. Why don't you drink coffee?"

If she were in the mood for it, my mother would burst into tears and weep, "I hate you, ah, God, I hate you!" The real battle would then begin. They would threaten to kill each other or to kill themselves; they would wish damnation to each other's immortal souls;

and each would blame the other for behaving badly in front of me. *"Lieber Gott!"* my father would groan, pressing the knuckles of his big red hands into his eyes. "What will become of my baby girl?"

My mother, clasping her hands together as if in prayer, would return, "She is safe with me! I will kill you if you hurt one single hair of her precious head!"

The outburst would be followed by a lamentation on my father's part as my mother sank into a brooding silence. He would draw me close to him and run his fingers through my hair and tell me he was sorry that he had neglected me. Sometimes he apologized because he had not reared me as a Catholic and he would go out to the shop, bringing back a catechism. But we made no progress. Our minds wandered from the questions, mine to Boston or to the last movie I had seen, and his to his boyhood. He would talk for a long time, but to himself. "Sonie, my patron is Bonaventure, but how I have forgotten him like all the other saints! It is the irony that he should be my saint · because he hated idleness. Brother Sebastian, one of the friars who taught us, brought my brother up short and myself a few years later. For we did not like to be shoemakers like our father and our grandfather and our great grandfather. Friedrich would have nothing to do with the trade. He would go to Paris, to the Sorbonne, to study literature, he said, and philosophy. And I, I would go to Berlin to study the law. But Brother Sebastian knew it wasn't in us. He made us not ashamed of shoe-making. He would quote Saint Bonaventure: 'You, Friedrich, and you, Hermann, are amongst those to whom the Lord has given the grace to labor.' I would pray to my saint night and morning, to cure my sloth! It was a monstrous state. *Monstruosum quemdam statum inter contemplativam et activam.* See! It comes back."

In his excitement, he would take both my hands in his and cry, "My Latin is not gone, Sonie! I will teach you. Have we a book? A grammar? Well, then, tomorrow we must buy one."

But by the next day he would have forgotten. The catechism went back to the shop where for the next month it would lie untouched. Saint Bonaventure, Brother Sebastian, and indeed God, would be shelved like the little book. My father's face would resume its mask.

While I, glad that I had escaped his instructions, happily pursued Miss de la Mar's career.

In my twelfth year, hardly a night passed from September until November that I was not unhinged from my sleep by my parents' voices. Something, I knew not what, had brewed between them a hotter rancor than ever before. I was propelled by their curses into consciousness and seemed driven into a socket in the dark from which there was no outlet. My bounded brain was as unalterable as a ball and it could neither veer in flight nor proceed to understanding: solid and of one material, terror, it lay in a minute cavern whose walls were fashioned from the rhetoric and the darkness. The daylight, freeing the sounds of boats and trains, the voices of fishermen and children, discovering the diverse landscape and the harmless countenances of my sleeping parents, repealed the fast laws that had held me to a rapt and aboriginal response and gave me the relief of wild tears. As soon as I had dressed, I would run to the porch of the Hotel Barstow as to a shrine and there, all alone and out of earshot of anyone, I cried until I could cry no more and until the reason for my grief had become obscured by the cold and my hunger. Often at this hour, the fog lay on Boston; I would be unable to see the State House dome and unable to visualize Pinckney Street. At last I would get up and start towards school, slowly at first because my legs were cramped, then faster until I was running through the mist. I usually arrived out of breath, a little late. Among the teachers it was a great joke that when I was asked why I had been crying, I would reply, "Oh, no, I wasn't crying. I didn't sleep well last night." They would say, "How imitative children are at this age! Don't you know exactly what has happened? One of her parents often says at breakfast, 'I didn't get a wink of sleep last night' and the child has picked it up."

On a morning in November, when the snow had fallen, I was crouched in a corner of the steps of the veranda, my face muffled in the harsh curls of my astrakhan collar. Today it was not foggy, but my view gave me no pleasure for the sky was leaden and the angry bay was deserted by all the boats. Last night my father had laughed, it must have been for half an hour and then, as if something had broken in him, shattered like a glass, he had begun to sob. I could hear his heavy body trembling on the creaking bed, and the weeping claw at his throat. And because each morning that was the way I cried, I knew his stomach ached and his nose was full. Not a sound came from my mother. In the intervals between the plunges of his agony, I could hear him whisper, *"Verzeihung!"* How far away he seemed! As I peered upward through the darkness at the dim white block which was the bed, I could not feel that the person weeping, as no man should do, was my father. Rather, it was the figure of a nightmare which crudely represented him. And yet I knew I was awake, for nothing was distorted as in a dream. Quaking upon the clattering springs, the figure was like a caged beast that had broken down in its futile struggle to escape. Downwards it plummeted into some unknown and pitch-black chasm of despair, but rose again in a brief respite to breathe that one word, *"Verzeihung!"* Twice, thinking I could stand it no longer, I started up to go to him and to lay my hand on his arm. But I thought then of how I was enraged at such a gesture when I was crying, and I lay back, mouthing the words, "Please don't cry, dear Papa." Why did my mother not comfort him? Once I heard her sigh and thought perhaps that was the prelude to some speech. But she said nothing and my father wept on, for hours it seemed to me.

The snow had begun to fall in the night and by morning it was thick on the ground. My father's face, in a deep sleep, was ashen and his eyelids were distended, the golden lashes stuck together. An arm was curled about his head. The woman who lay beside him, as motionless as he, appeared the soul of innocence as the gray light, filtering through the holes in the green blinds, exposed her white skin and her red lips and the black hair, unpinned and spread like a fan upon the pillow. She lay straight, her arms at her sides, as if she were dead.

This morning I did not and I could not cry. It was as though my father had done all the crying that could be done. Against my will, I continued to review his terrible collapse. What could it mean, I wondered, in a grown man? And would it happen again? Once he had broken the rules of a man's behavior, would he cry as often as I did?

I was startled at the sound of someone's boots on the gravel path at the side of the Hotel and before I could get to my feet, Gonzales, the gardener, was standing before me. He had always frightened me, for no reason that I could discover. He had the mildest of pink mouths under a thin, romantic mustache, and large bovine eyes beneath a low, protuberant brow. I disliked the way in the kitchen, in the summer time, he would steal up on me in his sneakers and put a soft finger on the back of my neck so suddenly that goose-flesh covered me and my heart pranced in surprise.

"What do I see?" he said, laughing, showing his teeth which were so small that the gum was visible above them. "What is the matter with *Señorita* Marburg? You tell Gonzales your troubles, honey."

He sat down on the step and put his arm around me. There was a strong assorted odor about him of something oily and something acrid, of garlic and of bootleg beer. He put his lips close to my ear, lifting up the edge of my tam. "Tell, Gonzales, honey."

Too frightened to move or to cry out, I trembled in his embrace as he continued his unwelcome consolations. "There, there. If you don't watch out your face will freeze that way, sweetheart. Don't you want to tell your Uncle Jesus what's the trouble?"

"Is your name Jesus?" I asked him, my admiration for a moment making me forget both my misery and his rank smell.

He said "Yes," softly, like a lover, and hugged me closer to him. "If I was my own master like your daddy, I would make a lot of Novenas. But me, Jesus, I don't have the time."

In the summer, he always greeted me with some such pious announcement. He would remind me that my father was in a state of mortal sin because he had not been to confession or mass for seven or eight years, and he would ask me if I did not long to be baptized. He himself, with his eight children, received the Blessed Sacrament every morning at the six o'clock service and on Sundays entertained the priest, Father Mulcahy, at breakfast after the eleven o'clock mass. Once he had come to my father's shop, beseeching him to deliver himself up to the mercy of God. His big brown eyes had been full of tears. But my father had only confounded him by saying, "I know my own mind. I am no boy."

I said nothing in reply. He released me, lowered his head, and dangling his hands between his outspread knees, murmured, "Always remember, *Señorita,* that you and your poor father are in my prayers."

"Thank you, Mr. Gonzales," I said and slipped over on the step. "I've got to go to school now."

"Yes!" he cried, slapping his knee. "And I to work must go. I'm afraid to look in the pit. I'm as sure as my name is Jesus Francisco Gonzales that the hydrangeas were frozen last night." He stood up and started down the path, but pausing at the corner of the porch he faced me once more. "How is your mother, sweetheart?" I answered that she was well enough, only a little tired, for I was remembering how soundly she slept when I left the house.

The Mexican winked at me. "Tired of carrying the little one?"

"What?"

"I mean your little brother or sister or whichever it is Our Savior intends it to be."

"I don't know . . ." I began, but he cupped his hands round his plump lips and whispered loudly, "Your mother is going to have a baby, *muchacha.*"

## 2

When I came home from school that afternoon, my mother was not in her accustomed place beside the stove, a most surprising fact, for she was a creature of tenacious habit, and had, since I could remember, taken up her place there an hour before sundown to idle over a glass of strong and bitter tea. She would rise, as I entered, and embrace me as if I were an intimate friend for whose visit she had been impatiently waiting, and then, drawing me to a chair beside hers, she would rub my cold hands between hers and say, "Oh, Sonie, how cold you are! Oh, the darling little hands all red!"

Often at this hour, I found neighbor women seated round about her, going over in exhaustive detail the difficulties of maintaining a household when there was no money to pay the high prices of food. I wondered if these women were as gloomy in their own houses as they were in ours, or if my mother's winter melancholy was contagious to them as it was to my father and myself. Strangely enough, when the heaviness of the bad weather skies had invaded our kitchen, she cast off the dark colors she had worn all summer and stepped

36

forward, as lively as a bird, in a costume like a ballerina's. But her full skirt, the length of a peasant's dress, which was made of black challis and printed with bright pink flowers and fantastic pea-green leaves, her scarlet flannel blouse with tarnished German silver buttons, and her high blue leather boots, laced with tan hide, were not an antidote to her perverse mopes but seemed rather to be the excuse for them. Mrs. Henderson would come in and say, "How gay you look, Mrs. Marburg! Why, I can warm my hands at *you*." But my mother, in a voice bleaker than any winter wind along the beach, would answer, "It is the red that fools you. But look at the boots. Now *they're* the color my hands used to be all day long in Moscow, even in the house, and they were so stiff I couldn't hold so much as a wine glass by its little tiny stem." Sometimes, out of spite, she would then slip her arms into the sleeves of a blue Beacon-cloth bathrobe whose skirt hung to the floor; a high, pointed hood was attached to the back of the neck. It belonged to my father, and the sleeves were so long that the unfilled portions of them flapped like seals' flippers as she gestured with her invisible hands. Had it not been for her face, she would have looked like a monk of some outlandish order.

Softly I opened the door to the bedroom. She was lying there, either asleep or else so deep in thought that she did not hear me on the threshold. The dark green blinds were down, but the light of the sunset, coming through the holes and falling on her immobile face, gave it an even incandescence like that which comes through the hand when it is held up to a bright light. Her body was covered with an army blanket and though the room was cold, one bare white foot dangled over the side of the bed. I could see my breath. The windows did not anywhere quite fit their frames and we had failed to stop up many of the cracks in the walls, either through laziness or through the conviction that it would do no good.

There was only one other article of furniture in the room besides the bed, a tall combination wardrobe and bureau with a sliver of flawed mirror at the top, in a frame carved with the same ornate roses that decorated the feet. My father, I suppose because it was solid and perhaps reminded him of something at home, admired the *schrank* as he called it, and each spring he spent one entire day polishing it with salt and olive oil. Today, to my surprise, I saw that the two pots of geraniums stood on the top, blocking out the mirror. Their transfer from the sunny kitchen window was stranger to me even than the sight of my mother lying in bed before we had had our supper. Was she, I wondered, going to have the baby now?

Presently I tiptoed out and went to my father's shop. He was not working. He was sitting on the bench before the monkey stove, his head in his hands.

"Papa?"

He did not look up, but he thrust forth his long arm in welcome. "Hello, Sonie girl. Didn't you eat anything yet today?"

"I guess not."

"Why didn't you come home at noon?"

"Oh, I don't know. I guess I wasn't hungry, Papa. I guess I had an apple. What's the matter with Mamma?"

"She's tired maybe." Now he turned his face toward me and I saw that his blue eyes were troubled, but they showed no signs of their storm of last night. He smiled and with two hard fingers that smelled of tallow, he tweaked my nose. "I know what you want, Gretchen von Hexensee, you want to look at the tintypes."

They were not really tintypes, but the word amused him. I fetched the fat album from the high shelf above the window. It lay with his fat little *Messbuch* and a few fine leather-bound volumes of Schiller, Leibnitz, Cicero, Goethe, Mommsen, and Balzac. The books were not worn. Probably my father had never read them. They were mostly gifts from his schoolmates on the day of his commencement from the *gymnasium* and were inscribed in a bewildering handwriting, the same that I saw on the occasional letter which came to him from Würzburg.

Together we looked at the photographs in which my relatives genially smiled forth, all with my father's eyes. My grandparents sat side by side on a plush settle with a high, carved back. Their fat arms were intertwined and they stared directly into the camera. Their round faces were frank and innocent and benign, and their sober, old-fashioned clothes—my grandfather wore a long collar with a full ascot, a black coat with wide satin lapels and upon his knees he balanced a gleaming top hat, while my grandmother, with a black lace jabot at her stout old neck, was dressed in a striped jacket with leg-

o'-mutton sleeves and a deep pointed bodice which met a black skirt
—advertised them as people of respectability. Both of them were
dead. One of the letters that had come to my father had been from
his brother, Christian, announcing that they had died within half a
year of one another.

My favorite picture was one of my cousin Peter taken when he was
about five years old. His wide eyes stared at the photographer's in-
corporeal birdie and his lips were opened in perplexity. He was a
bewitching little boy with fair hair, matted in curls tight to his skull;
his solid body was encased in leather breeches, a jacket decorated
with hearts, and tasseled socks. In his hands he ferociously clutched
a hat with an improbably long feather.

"Some day, when we are rich," my father said, "we will go to see
that boy. Shall we take our Packard car with us and honk outside of
Fransiskanerstrasse *zwei und zwanzig?* Or should we not take it and
walk from the station as calm as you please?"

I debated for a moment. "Let's take the Packard car," I said.

"I don't know when it would be that we would go."

"If Miss Pride keeps on buying shoes, we'll get rich."

"She only feels sorry for me, and I don't like that. No, in America
they don't know a good boot from a bad."

"Then why don't we go to Germany, Pa?"

When he answered, he looked away from me. He moved to the
window and stood looking out at the last glow of the sun on Boston.
"I would be ashamed," he said. "How am I going to explain to my
brothers and friends that I never had my child baptized?"

Whereas it embarrassed me to have Gonzales talk about his sins
of omission, it frightened me to hear my father speak of them. Once,
at Christmas time, he had made a *crèche* for me, carving out a youthful Mary and the doe-eyed animals and three Teutonic wise-men and
the faceless Christ-child with a boyish rapture. I was delighted with
it until, once it had been brought from the shop into the house, I
saw that my mother had no interest in it and that my father had lost
his. It was as if some ungovernable force in her was determined to
extinguish every joy her husband might have. In his frustration and
furious disappointment, he abruptly seized the platform and dashed
it to the floor so that all the figures were broken and the frame was

splintered. He stared down at the fragments, his hands hanging loosely at his sides. He said nothing, but in a moment he took his hat from the shelf and went out. Hours later, when he came back, totally drunk, he sat in the kitchen for a long time, laughing his in-human laugh. In the morning I found him sleeping with his head on the table. For a week thereafter, whenever we were alone together, he invited me to look on him as the most obstinate of all sinners, and while I was not certain what he meant, I would rack my brains for a pretext to escape him, for I was mortally afraid.

He had pressed his cheek against the windowpane and when he spoke, a cloud formed on the glass. "Or how confess it to a priest?" he inquired. "Or anything else?"

There was no sound in the room but the spanking of a live coal against the purple sides of the monkey stove. And my father was motionless, with his eyes and his lips closed. Perhaps he had cried last night out of fear of his sins and the punishment God would deal to him. And what were his sins? He did not tell lies and he did not steal and he was not a murderer. It was true that he spent a good deal of time carousing with the Coast Guards, but so did the fishermen. What, then, had he done that tormented him so, even now when there were no outward signs of it beyond the pallid weariness of his face and the tension of his pose? I would have asked and my lips parted, but something hindered me from intruding upon his mys-terious meditations and I said, my voice cracking, "I guess I better go help Mamma."

"*Ja,* you better." He sighed so that his whole lengthy frame shiv-ered, and he turned to me with a willful smile which did not fool me, for the corners of his mouth twitched and would have turned down but for the effort he expended on their upward curve. "Don't you expect me for supper. I have some business." With this, he took down his sheep-lined mackinaw and his hunter's cap, put a pipe and tin of tobacco in his pocket and drew on a pair of mittens.

"Are you going to the Coast Guard?" I asked him.

"Curiosity killed the cat," he said waggishly but, like his smile, his jollity was forced and did not take me in.

"Where are you going, Pa?"

Suddenly irritated, he pushed me towards the door. "Shut up

now," he snapped. "Go along to the house and mind your own business."

I watched from the kitchen windows until he had disappeared round the bend of the road, and then I stole out and followed. Over the crusted ruts for a mile I ran, ducking behind cottages and sheds when I feared he might turn around. At this hour the village was usually deserted save for the men going in and out of the pool hall in the splattered window of which a sign futilely proclaimed, "Ladies Invited." I had expected my father to turn in there, but he went on, passed the large, shadowy general store about which, even in winter and when the door was closed, there hung an odor of fish and fishermen and a rich, sweet smell which came either from raisins or chewing tobacco. I glanced across the street at the Bijou where the obfuscated films which wavered before our eyes like dispirited ectoplasm bore no more relationship to entertainment than the lusterless exterior bore to any jewel known to man. It was closed now and the torn sign advertising "Ben Hur" was streaked from melted snow. These, with a few churches, a little library, and a post-office made up our business district. On one side, overlooking the sea, was the Coast Guard house, on the other, overlooking the bay, was a small white hospital, enveloped for a quarter of a mile on all sides by a pall of mortal silence. Midway between the village and the hospital was the school, so newly built that its yellow-brick walls had not yet been relieved by shrubs and ivy. As I lingered in the doorway of the store until my father should be a safe distance ahead of me (he had paused to knock out his pipe), I was visited by a longing to see Marblehead, Salem, and Boston, and I was as weakened by the feeling as though I had seen them and something in the winter evening had made me nostalgic. And then I conceived the stubborn notion that the crisis which my father was passing through would end in a change of residence. Perhaps even now he was headed for the Marblehead bus stop and when he came home, he would have news of a house and a shop to which we would immediately move.

It was with a flush of anger that I saw, in a few minutes, what his destination was: the Catholic church, a small white building with a

*41*

high green spire. It was called "The Chapel of the Little Flower." I followed him.

My schoolmates had told me, in frightened whispers, that Catholics prayed the dead out of Purgatory, whatever that might be, and I fancied my father kneeling before a High Necromancer, chanting in an unknown language. I had heard that priests were ghosts and since they had no substance, could never marry. Someone said they could change from one thing to another: "They can look like anything they want, like a billy goat if they want." There was something impressive to me in the sight of my father starting out to Mass on Sunday, wearing his suit and his polished boots, and carrying the *Messbuch* with its bright ribbons. Impressive and a little scandalous, even though I knew he never got as far as the church porch, but instead took another road which led to the Coast Guard house where he would spend an hour playing checkers.

A few parishioners were kneeling in the front pews of the darkened chapel, and now and again the door to the confessional swung open; I could hear the wicket slide and presently another penitent entered the box. There was a murmur, caught by a silence, and broken at last by the faint, sibilant Latin of the absolution. Those who had been cleansed slipped into the kneeling benches to say their penance, and as their lips mouthed the words of the prayers, their eyes were fixed upon a shining golden object on the altar: it looked like a child's drawing of the sun, for from the round white center, a thousand rays of gold shot out, glittering in the red light cast by the vigil lamp which swung very gently at the end of a long iron chain. My eyes grew accustomed to the shadows and I saw my father at the altar rail, far to one side, his head buried in his arms. Each time someone emerged from the confessional, I expected him to go in, but he did not stir. It was cold in the church and I shivered, leaned up against the side of the pew, and hugged my knees. It seemed to me a long time that I waited for the terrifying moment when my father would become a part of the esoteric game. At least five people went into the closet with their sins and came out purged of them. The last light of the day perished from the stained glass windows. Now only two people besides my father and myself remained.

Presently, the Irish priest came out, a tall, red-haired young man.

round-shouldered and near-sighted, with a face ravaged by boredom and eczema, but not an unpleasant face and in no way similar to my picture which had represented him as lithe and swart, wearing a mustache and pointed beard over which darted bright evil eyes. He passed close by my father as he went into the vestry, but my father, deep in his prayer, did not look up, and only after the door had closed behind the priest did he rise and hasten out, looking straight ahead so that he did not see me. But when the swinging doors had shut upon him, I heard a voice in the vestibule intercept him: "Thank God, man! You've come back by the grace of God! The new one will have a better chance than Sonie." It was Gonzales. There was the sound of a match being struck, and my father replied, "You fool busybody." The outer door opened and banged to, forcing a blast of cold air into the church. Gonzales went down the central aisle, genuflected at the altar, and went to the right where he knelt before a statue of a woman saint in a brown robe who held roses in her hands. He crossed himself and began to pray audibly. I ran from the church appalled, for there was a presence there, not of God nor of angels, but of something human, yet shockingly bodiless, and I felt as I had done the time I had dreamed that I was dead and the only thing left of me was the knowledge, suspended in a ball of solitude, that I was dead.

The house was as it had been when I came in from school. My father was not there and the shop was dark, and my mother, still lying in bed, had not changed her position. I spread a piece of bread with margarine and sprinkled it with sugar and I ate, sitting on the floor by the stove, as in the light from the fire through the isinglass I read a book lent to me by a schoolmate called *Frances and the Irrepressibles at Buena Vista Farm*. The thick pages were glossy and each one bore an actual photograph of a character or a whole group of them together, posing in the costumes they had worn at a mock wedding or at the minstrel show they had ingeniously produced. A child cannot sustain his moods for long, and I, after a few minutes of inattention, became completely absorbed in the adventures of these wealthy, carefree, and urbane children. They were all upright and considerate with the one exception of a rotten little boy named

Dickey Doolittle who one had no doubt would come all right in the end under the influence of his companions. They all lived in Wisconsin on a farm where fresh diversions presented themselves every day and where in the neighborhood, chicken thieves, Indian caves, buried treasure, and watermelon patches were to be had for the asking.

The door opened and my father, in an ugly temper, scolded me: "Now you'll go blind. What is the meaning of this, young lady?" When he found that the mantle of the Coleman lamp was burned out, he cursed savagely and ordered me to fetch a new one from the top shelf. As I did so, a pipe clattered to the floor and broke in two. It was one he never used, but he kept it as a curio, for its bowl was porcelain and baked into it was a picture of the cathedral at Worms.

"Now damn you!" he screamed. "Now give me the mantle from your damned butter fingers!"

He slapped me on the side of the head with his open hand and there was a sudden ache in my opposite ear. Then he turned away and as he adjusted the mantle, he growled, "What is the use? They make me come into a dark house and then they break my things. They should go to jail." When the white light flared up, I saw him move the red felt cozy and look at a heap of bits of white china, all that was left of his coffee pot.

"*I* didn't do it!" I cried. "I never did!"

"I know it," he said. "Your mother did it. She picked it up and threw it at the stove." Our eyes turned together and saw, beneath the oven door, two or three white glittering splinters amongst the ashes. I could not imagine so violent a gesture in my lazy mother. Her only weapon was her tireless voice. There must have been a quarrel of unprecedented savagery while I was at school, and I was glad that I had not come home at lunch time but instead had eaten an apple and a fig-Newton given to me by the Hendersons.

"Well?" shouted my father. "Well, where is my supper?"

"You said not to expect you, Papa. You said you weren't coming home."

"I did *not*." He spouted like a child and stamped his foot.

My mother did not come out, and my father was angry with me for cutting his bread too thin and burning the bacon, and when I asked him what I should put the coffee into now that the pot was broken, he pounded the table with both his fists so that the cutlery bounced, and then he put his head down until his forehead was in his greasy plate and shouted, *"Confiteor Deo omnipotenti, Beatae Mariae, semper Virgini . . ."* but he could not go on. He rolled over until his face was pointed upward to the ceiling and he wailed, *"Gott! Gott, warum hast Du mich verlassen!"*

"Papa, do you want some cheese?"

"Cheese? Yes, that's the remedy! Give your father a spoonful of cheese and that will get him out of hell!" He took me by both arms and shook me until my dizzied eyes began to hurt. "We're fit for nothing!" His eyes, afire and yet still as cold as ice, looked upon me with such hatred and so terrible a threat that I commenced to cry. My chin lifted and my eyes narrowed and when he shook me again, the tears fell out. I could not stop and though, when he released me, I covered my mouth with my hand, the sound escaped me and the warm tears welled up as freely as water from a drinking fountain. He let me go and stepped back, aghast. Cruelly, yet out of the necessity to justify myself, I sobbed, "I don't care! You cried last night!"

Twice he told me to be quiet and when I could not, being now at the mercy of my gulping, he drove me into a corner of the room, out of the circle of the lamplight and there, beside the dark blue sink, I huddled against the wall, bawling softly as my stopped-up nose bubbled and a faint interior disturbance in my skull made me think my brains were rattling.

He pushed back the dishes and settled down at the table to read, still so distracted that by mistake, he opened *Frances and the Irrepressibles* and for some moments stared stupidly at the pictures of little girls in hair ribbons and white party dresses and high button shoes before he realized, with an outburst of wounded dignity, that this was not *Riders of the Purple Sage.*

Just as he had thought I deliberately broke his pipe, now he thought I had mischievously substituted my book for his, not only to insult him with its childishness but to remind him that he could not read English well and that I could. He strode across the room and plucked me to my feet. "I've had enough of your monkey business." He turned me around and hit me four or five times on the backside. I did not cry out but my tears continued to fall and I felt giddy as the blows stung me through my thin skirt. The action satisfied him and he drew his chair to the fire and began to read. I collapsed once more into my corner, pondering how I could avenge myself.

Probably from his frequent readings of this book, my father longed to see the west and one time, some years before, when he had made a little extra money carrying trunks at the Hotel, he bought a fine yellow hide and made a pair of cowboy boots which he sometimes wore on Sunday. As he read, I could tell by the pleasure that illuminated his face and caused him now and then to chuckle deeply in his throat, that he was far away from me and that the world in which he rode a pinto cow-pony or a roan mare contained no blubbering, angry child nor any sullen, pregnant woman. Once he paused and swung an invisible lariat over his head, leaned forward on his horse's neck as to its flanks he pressed spurs with tied rowels. A little later, he whipped a revolver from his holster and aimed at the empty caviar can. Then, conscious once more of where he was, he kicked the stove in vexation and scratched his head.

As I crouched in my corner, I felt thin drafts of bitter air coming through the cracks in the wall and I thought of the hard, dirty snow outside and of the wind that came across the bay whipping granules of sand into the faces and onto the legs of walkers. I thought of my mother, when she was about my age, being cast out into the brutal night, and it came to me with a shock that that incredible man who dandled the German milliner on his knee was my own grandfather. I tried to imagine him and succeeded only in calling up an image of my father as he might be when he was old. This person I brought into the room and allowed to approach me and to send me away as he had sent away my mother and my aunts and uncles, and I tried to imagine what it would feel like to be exiled from one's own house. I was intent upon my painful fancy; I had closed my eyes and the cold from the window seemed more acute. The vision of my father-grandfather seemed actually to take on flesh and spirit.

A harsh and sudden voice spoke out: "Sonie, get to bed."

I had thought my father had forgotten that I was still in the room; his unexpected command, though its intention was disciplinary rather than unkind, thrilled me as if it were the completion of the scene behind my closed eyelids. For a moment I was not sure whether I had heard him say, "Get to bed," and not what I had expected the grandfather to say, "Get out." Whether it was the confusion in my mind or merely the shock of hearing words after so intense a silence, I do not know, but I burst into fresh tears, so stormily this time it was as though I had been storing them up and had only waited for a trifle to start the avalanche. My baffled father stood up and peered at me in my dark corner. He came towards me uncertainly, but I could not tell whether he was angry or remorseful. "Now, Sonie, now, girl. Come out of your corner." I did not stir.

"Come, *Mädchen*," he wheedled and I knew, because he used that tender word, that he was not cross. Perhaps he regretted his harshness and had realized my innocence. Still, I did not move, and he continued to come closer. He crouched down on the floor beside me. "There. There." He followed the dirty meanders of the tears on my cheeks with his forefinger. "Maybe they'll freeze there like icicles, *ni't?* The kids at school will call you a cry baby girl." Grieved at his mistake and not trying to make up for it by caresses, as my mother would have done, he had a dignity which I was bound to admire, and at last I smiled at him. "*Jawohl!*" he cried in genuine pleasure and then, in imitation of the friendly rancher of the Saturday night movies, he awkwardly offered me his hand and said, "Put 'er there, pardner!"

The cold from the windows laid metallic ribbons across my back. I was sickened to think of my aunts and uncles trudging, whimpering, in the Russian night, and in a glow of relief at my better fortune, I grasped the extended hand. In a meditative way, with his head bowed, my father began to finger my hand, pressing the ball of his into the hollow of my palm, lacing our fingers together, feeling the knuckles.

"Sonie," he said after a time. "What is it you want to do when you grow up?"

I could not tell him that my only ambition was to live with Miss Pride, for I did not want him to know that I preferred her to himself. But I said, "I guess I want to live in Boston."

*47*

"Boston? Is that all you want to do? Why, I thought you wanted to be a school teacher at least."

"Oh, no!"

"I guess I haven't done anything right. You should want to be a school teacher, I think. How far are you in your Latin now?"

"We don't start Latin till the eighth grade," I told him and then, because I saw how curiously he looked at me, I added, "I'm in the seventh now."

"It would be a comfort for a man to know what he used to know," he mused. Then, to include me he said with a spurt of good spirits, "I'll tell you what we'll do, Sonie, we'll go west some day to Cheyenne, Wyoming. Wouldn't you like to ride a little wild horse?"

I said I would in much sincerity, but because I was unschooled in both the scenery and the customs of the west, I did not immediately seat myself astride a horse or envisage Cheyenne, but instead, heard Miss Pride say to a friend, as I entered the drawing room, *Here* is our cow girl. You know she and her father own several thousand wild roan stallions."

"I could make us some boots." He said that undoubtedly there was a place for a man like him who could make leather things. Cowboys were particular about their clothes, he had heard; that is, not dandified, but they liked expensive wool shirts and Stetson hats and since they hadn't for the most part any family to support, they could spend all their wages on clothes and *Schnaps*. He dwelt for a long time on their emancipation and prosperity; sometimes, for variety, he called them "the punchers" until I became quite breathless and pleaded to go at once.

I returned him from his rapture. He looked down at me through the sad gloom. "Well, now, *Mädchen,* when will you be ready to go?"

"Now!" It did not occur to me that we could not go the moment we had agreed on our destination, for, being altogether unacquainted with travel, I was not aware that it cost anything. I supposed, moreover, that if we needed money for our dinner on the train (I already saw myself eating a pork chop and as many bananas as I wanted) he, like Betty Brunson's father, the dentist, could "sell a bond." For this, I believed was the prerogative of a father. Whenever anyone

*48*

said, "I wish I had a ukulele," or "I wish I had a solid gold barrette," Betty would reply, "Why don't you ask your father to sell a bond? Daddy always does." I had always had the vague idea that my father's bonds would be German and therefore less easily disposed of but that in an emergency he could market them.

"I am thinking," he said with a sigh, "that it might be better if I went on first and got things lined up, you might say, and then sent for you. By that time I would have the corral built and have you a nice little palomino horse. It's a long way out there. You would get sleepy."

"How far?"

"Maybe as far as two thousand miles. I expect it's five days or so on the train. A long, long way, Sonie girl."

"I want to go with you, Papa. Now."

He stiffened and stood up. My mother was standing in the doorway of the bedroom, her shadow so long it fell the length of the room and, making a right angle turn at the juncture, continued up the wall. She was pale and her staring eyes seemed uncommonly large. It seemed to me that they were never so beautiful as when she was angry. The whites of them were immaculate, not marked, as most eyes are, with shabby red tendrils, and the iris was so dark the pupil was nearly invisible, but in the sun or in the lamplight as tonight, an amber ray appeared intermittently in the iris, ending in the profound depths of that rich center. When my parents drank together, my father would gaze into her face and murmur, *"Die wunderschönen Augen! Die magischen Augen!"* Tonight, in her sickness or in her despair or her fury, whatever it was that had driven her out to us, these eyes seemed, because of their wonderful and awful size, to be holding back their lids with effort.

Her black hair, pouched with white combs into a pompadour, hung to her waist and swung heavily with the movement of her body; it shone like a blue-jay's feathers. She stroked one hand with the other and in the hush we could hear the muted hissing of the skin being rubbed. On her right forearm, I saw that there was a long scratch that had been painted with iodine.

My parents stood as if entranced, each waiting for the other to speak. If only they would now be merciful, embrace, speak softly!

How could my mother, so beautiful a woman, create so much un-happiness for us all? For she was beautiful and her beauty was as holy a kind as that of the statue in the church before which Gonzales had been praying. Her rosiness, her clear skin, the sheen of her hair, her calm eyes, made the old ladies at the Hotel Barstow say of her, "She is the image of a saint." The line of the hair on her high fore-head was almost straight as though a child, drawing a picture and unable to trace in it the actual irregularities of his model, had simpli-fied, had tidied up. The planes of the face were clean and the silken flesh shrank shallowly beneath the cheekbone and became pallid or golden as the light struck it. She was a tall woman, with a graceful, lethargic carriage. Her hands were her only blemish, for they were always red and scaly with the cleaning powders she used in the sum-mer to clean the bathtubs, and in the winter they were chapped. Her fingers were torn with cracks in the tips or hangnails or cuts from knives or gouges from bedsprings. They were always cold as though too much blood had flowed out of their rents, and I supposed that was why she continually rubbed them.

"It is no use, Shura," my father said at last. His voice was even and formal.

At his words, she bent her head down on her breast. The hair tumbled about her like a veil and at the base of her skull, the scalp was visible between cords of the hair heavily tossed forward. She moaned, "But you must not take Sonia away from me!" She flung back her head again and I saw that not even now was her face dis-torted by her feelings. Not even her mouth, filter of anger, bitter-ness, sorrow, became less charming, and the sweetness of its shape, the texture of its dark red flesh seemed to abate her passion, making it something strapped and aimless.

"If I go, I will take nothing but my body and my soul."

"Soul!" She spat on the floor before her bare feet. "Does a man have a soul that cuts his wife?" She held out her scratched arm. "Sonia, look! What do you think of a father like that, eh?"

"Why do you lie before the girl? She knows I never laid my hands on you. Tell her that you broke my china coffee pot and nagged me until I was crazy!"

50

"I hate you. Ah, I would hate any man that cried tears like a woman."

"And I hate you, Shura, with all my heart. You've ruined everything for me and I've had enough."

For the briefest moment, alarm showed in my mother's face, but then she smiled. "And so have I. If it weren't for Sonia . . ."

"Even for Sonie I've had enough now. From the beginning it is all wrong."

My mother's insistence flagged before the determination in his voice and she could not accuse him of any specific thing, but only said, complacently, "Thank God, she's a little girl. And by the grace of the Holy Ghost, there will be another little girl. I'll call her little Luibka."

"So, Luibka!" He laughed like a lunatic. "So we will call the witch's daughter after the old hell-cat. But what if the little whore in your belly turns out to be little Ivan instead? Little, little, little Russian woman, little God damn you to a little tiny Russian hell!"

"Hush! Before the child!"

His raging voice did not alter in pitch as, wheeling upon me, he commanded, "Pray for yourself, Sonie! Sonie . . ." He faltered and then, calmed, he took my mother's arm. "Put on your shoes, Shura, and come to the shop."

My jaws were sour and my mouth was full of saliva which escaped and wavered on my lips. When they had gone out, I moaned, and still, while my misery did not lessen, I saw myself slipping out of the house and running up the road to the Hotel. I would go through the basement and creep up the dark stairs and through the kitchen, the dining room, the lobby, up the staircase and through the corridor until I came to the door of Miss Pride's room. I would lie on the window seat with her afghan over me and my head in the plump pillows and there I would go to sleep. Perhaps I would find the furniture covered with ghost-clothes as I had once seen them so dressed in the lobby when I peered through the cracks of the boarding at the window. I would be delighted if the hat-pin holder were covered with a dust-shroud, and if the cherubs were dressed for winter. But I remembered, sadly, that there would be nothing in the room, for before she went away, Miss Pride always locked her belongings in the closet and handed the key to the manager. Well, then, what I must do was go to Mr. Henderson next door and ask him to take me across the bay in his boat. If I came to her, late at night, without a coat, she could not refuse to let me in. "I was expecting you," said Miss Pride to Antoinette de la Mar as the latter sank down on the green velour davenport in the elegant drawing-room, "and so I have some sandwiches and a big pot of cocoa ready for you. Will you take one marshmallow or two?"

I was awakening for a long time, climbing the waves of my sleep and relapsing, dreaming and knowing that I dreamed. A cat had laid five hen's eggs which Betty Brunson advised me to name "Frances Irrepressible." The purr of the mother cat shaped into words, "Sonia, are you awake?" Beside me was my mother's lax, warm body, and through my half-opened eyes, I saw that her scratched arm lay across my chest. I was afraid she might kiss me and I pretended that I was still asleep.

"Sonia?" she inquired again.

The room was dark so that I was not sure it was day until through the thin walls I heard Mr. Henderson's voice. "Sarah!" he called. "*Oh*, Sarah! Bring me the gaff like a good girl," and I knew that he was going out to his lobster pots. Immediately afterward, the bells of the Catholic church rang eight o'clock and my mother sat up, as though the sound had alarmed her. She tested the temperature of the room by exhaling her breath in little puffs and saw, by the vapor issuing from her mouth, that it was keenly cold. Before she got out of bed, she shivered into her blue wrapper and drew on her stockings. I opened my eyes and asked, "Why am I in the bed, Mamma?"

She smiled. "Because your father went off somewhere last night. We are all alone, darling."

"Did he go in the *storm?*"

She nodded, but her thoughts were not on him. "You lie there till the fire is going," she said. "Maybe you won't go to school today? I'll make you a boiled egg for breakfast!" The prospect of so unusual a festivity brought a dancing light into her eyes, and with a liveliness I had never seen in her before, she moved about the room, stroking the velvety leaves of the geraniums which still stood on the bureau.

"He said he was going to put them into the stove because his pot got broken," she said as she took the flowers down. "But I hid them in time."

I lay still after she had left the room, listening to her shaking down the ashes and drawing water for the tea. I remembered, as from a dim former life, that some time in the night I had staggered, bloated with sleep, upon my mother's arm into the bedroom and I had flung out protesting arms and had muttered, "Leave me be," as she took off my middy blouse and undid the waist from my skirt.

I had never dreamed that the bed was so soft. The blankets and pillows were like loving, hugging arms, and I closed my eyes again, wishing that now I had it all to myself I might stay in it the whole morning. Directly I heard the Hendersons joining the Kadish children on the road to school. "Where's Sonie?" said one of them, and when there was no answer I was certain that they were whispering amongst themselves. Probably the Kadishes had heard the quarrel last night, for our houses were only a few yards apart. But I was not yet wide awake enough to be conscious of shame, and careless of all but this snug bed, I burrowed deeper into the blankets like a hibernating animal and thought of how, presently, I would break my boiled egg over a piece of bread and salt and pepper it while a cup of tea at the side of my plate steamed into my face.

# CHAPTER THREE

My father had taken nothing with him: no clothes but those he wore, no tools, not even an extra pipe. Through the years of his absence, I used sometimes to wonder, as I looked at the kitchen shelves or at the traps in his shop, if he had not had time to collect his things together, if he had wanted to be on his way before the violence of his decision capitulated and left him still obliged to go but to go now without the desire; or if he had taken nothing in the intention of beginning anew, as unencumbered as possible, free both of the nuisance of carrying his belongings and of the reminders implicit in them of the life he had left behind.

His empty-handedness struck both my mother and me as evidence that he would come back, for he had a strong sense of possession, obvious from the clutter in his shop. He had brought from Germany four great boxes besides numerous small ones. These had never been opened because, being a poor man and unable to make new acquisitions, he did not want to wear out what he had. He saved everything for a "rainy day" but even when he was deluged with bursting clouds, he never so much as considered unlocking his treasures.

After we had had our breakfast, my mother, explaining to me that she was now in the fourth month of her pregnancy (sensing my disapproval she implored me, "Ah, good Christ, Sonia, you be nice to your poor mother!"), sent me to fetch Mrs. Henderson. She was feeling unwell and thought that the neighbor woman would prescribe something soothing to help her over the shock. She did look ill and weary and I was glad to shift the responsibility for her to someone else. Actually, I suppose, she was not in much discomfort, for as soon as Mrs. Henderson came, she brightened up and began to talk and eagerly to drink the tea into which had been poured a little rum. Mrs. Henderson was a large, good-natured woman, prematurely gray. Because of her hair and because she wore bifocal spectacles, I thought she was old, and at first had believed that she was the grandmother, not the mother of the children with whom I played. Plainly, she did not want to hear my mother's account of last evening, the preface to which greeted her the moment she stepped across the threshold. She asked me a great many questions about school, whether I was looking forward to the Christmas pageant, and if I liked Civics this year and if I did not agree that Miss Pickens, my teacher, was the sweetest woman on earth. My mother, who had no interest in my education, nodded her head now and then in bored courtesy until she could bear it no longer and wrested the conversation from us. She began to talk in a passionless monotone of what she called her "condition," and as she spoke of my father's disappearance only in relation to it, I could learn nothing new about what had happened after I fell asleep on the floor. Blushing, I went out to the shop.

For some time, I sat on the work bench gazing about me at the tools and the bottles of dye and polish and the hides hung along the walls. I intended to open my father's boxes, and it was as though I expected a new world to rise in primeval mist when I had lifted up their lids. For, knowing nothing but charm of Germany, I assumed that their contents would be charming. From my father, I had learned that castles were a natural part of the landscape of his country, that a faëry life as old as the earth whispered and flirted in the enchanted forests, that all families were large, rich and congenial and every Sunday afternoon went walking through the hills until they came to an inn tucked away in the chestnut trees. The father would point his stick and cry, "Listen, what do you say to a piece of cake, you, Hermann, you, Friedrich?" And they would all go in to drink some coffee or perhaps some red wine with a cherry *torte* or a plate of *lebkuchen*. I knew, moreover, that on the façade of my father's house in Würzburg, there were bas-reliefs of kings' heads, bunches of grapes, lyres, and goblets, and that within the house there was a big tile stove and all the sheets were pure linen.

Nearby the nail where the key of rings to the trunks hung, there was another nail from which dangled a black rosary with golden gauds, a present, he had told me, from his Aunt Therese, on the day of his confirmation. As the sheen of the beads caught my eye, I wondered if perhaps this afternoon, wherever he might be, he would go to confession. What would the father in the cubbyhole say to him? Would he tell him to come back to us? I was not sure yet that I wanted him to return. I had no feeling of loss thus far, and I could think only with joy that there would be no more quarrels at night. Perhaps now that he was gone, my mother would change, would emerge from her slovenly wrapper and her lazy ways, and would no longer spend all her time staring at the sea. (It happened that my father, from his windows, and I from Miss Pride's, looked toward Boston, but my mother, looking out the windows of our kitchen, could see only a long white stretch of sand and a few crags far off, and then the endless sea itself. It was an arresting landscape but one whose eternal monotony became maddening in time. But towards the sameness of her prospect, she was altogether indifferent.)

Into my life, moreover, my father's escape introduced a theme of mystery. Already he was, in my mind, an almost mythical figure, belonging to no category I had hitherto known outside the pages of books, for he was not merely a fugitive, he was also particularly my father whom, after a while when I was grown up, I might seek my whole life through, as I had seen daughters do at the Bijou, missing by a few minutes a reunion in a South American cabaret, a Peking tea house, an English garden party, our gondolas passing one another on the Grand Canal just as the moon was darkened by a cloud.

There were moments, to be sure, when I rebuked him for leaving us stranded with nothing but twenty-four dollars, which my high principled mother had tried, this morning, to put into the stove. But my prayers for our better fortune were today not directed towards him but towards some unknown benefactor. And when, as the day wore on, I began to miss him, I did not wish he were here with us, but wished that I were with him, as he walked along a road, smiling, his fair hair blowing, unconscious of everything but his freedom and the strength of his body.

I took the keys from their nail, pushed aside some cartons and heaps of kindling in front of one of the trunks, found the proper key and opened it. The lid resisted and the hinges faintly screeched. The odor of camphor balls rose strongly. Each article was wrapped separately in heavy brown paper. Everything was unused, but some of the cloth had rotted at the folds from lying there so long, and the paper of the brochures of cobblers' tools was brittle; the *Lederhosen* and the ski boots were stiff. I found cleated shoes, woolen underdrawers, skis, ski poles, ice skates, embroidered suspenders, hunting knives, and a rucksack. His clothes showed that he was not only a sportsman, but a gentleman as well, for amongst them were a dinner-jacket, a white silk ascot, a top hat, and a walking stick with a gold snake's head.

There were pictures of my grandparents taken at various times in their lives, tinted and contained in heavy gilt frames. Did these old people with their stern eyes and kindly mouths know, before they died, that they had a grandchild in America? Perhaps in the big shop in Würzburg, run now by my uncle Christian, there was a picture of Cousin Sonia tacked up on the wall. I could recall only one picture of myself, taken on an Easter day by Mr. Henderson. Together with his children I had posed, holding a calla lily in my hand like a scepter, and because the sun was in my eyes and I could not close my mouth for I had a cold in the head, my face drooped with stupidity. But I had worn new shoes, made by my father, and stood with one foot thrust forward; they were riding boots and at the tops, my initials, S.M., had been burnt into the leather. Perhaps even if my uncles and my Cousin Peter did not care for my face, they would see by the boots that I was their "kind."

My shoes, and nothing else, had always set me apart from other children, for they were of the finest leather and were most elegantly embellished. As I saw this morning how shabby my boots were, touched the thin spots on the soles that would soon be worn quite through, and remembered that I could no longer wear my summer sandals for my feet had grown too large, I was sorry that Papa had gone away. For if the other children had been surprised at this incongruous note in my raggedness, they had admired it. Even Betty Brunson, the wealthy dentist's daughter, had begged her mother for shoes like mine. And the band of horrid boys who, when I had pigtails, teased me for them and teased me even more when they were cut off and my ugly "bob" was fashioned to the uncompromising lines of a cereal bowl: they, too, had looked with envy on my red-brown boots of this year, laced with rough yellow thongs and equipped on the outside with pockets in which I carried a small, dull hunting knife, salvaged from the kitchen shelves, and an eight-inch celluloid ruler.

I looked again through Papa's effects, in the hope of finding some bauble that I had overlooked which would distinguish me as much as my shoes had done. There was nothing but the rosary, and although I was tempted to slip it around my neck, superstition checked me. In my ignorance, I thought its magic properties might operate to my destruction.

The sun was high and the piled snow was melting. I heard the Henderson children coming home for dinner, and I knew it was time for me to leave the shop which I already thought of as my own. I looked back one more time for a treasure, and now, not amongst the things spilled over the sides of the boxes, but on the work table, I saw a pair of slippers my father had made for Hopestill Mather. They were sandals with a strap up the center, through which passed another strap, fastened at the side with a gold buckle, and they had been dyed green, the color of the first leaves in the spring. One was unfinished: the sole had not been trimmed and jagged spears of thick leather stood out on all sides. But the sole of the other was so smooth and polished that it felt like satin to my cheek. I supposed she would have a green dress, made of taffeta or chiffon, and that in her hair she would wear a green ribbon like the one she had worn at luncheon that day with her aunt. I could see these little slippers dancing across a ballroom and I could smell the child who wore them: she would smell of Miss Pride's soap and of the sharp lily-of-the-valley cologne in the cut-glass bottle. I could see no one else at the party and even her partner was no more than a black mist. But the girl, with her yellow eyes and her white skin, her head flung back so that the bright hair fell far down, was as real as the soft sandals I held in my hands, and I hated her. I took off my boots and my lisle stockings and sat down to try on the finished shoe. It did not fit. My foot was too long and so broad that it would not even go into the vamp although I struggled and pulled until I was sweating. Angrily, I flung it into a corner of the room where, in the smudged shadows, it gleamed like a wet leaf. Her hands would be small too! Half the

58

width, half the length of mine, white as her face, smooth as the sole of the slipper, her hands would be covered with rings and bracelets, set with green jewels. And her room in her aunt's house on Pinckney Street would have a green carpet and pale green walls and a green satin counterpane for the little green bed.

I ruined the slipper with the crude sole. Both straps I cut in two with a pair of heavy shears and I dipped my thumb in machine oil to deface the surface of the kid. I pulled off the buckle with a pair of pliers and I drove a long nail through the heel and into the wood of the work table so that it was pinned there. And then, leaving the contents of my father's boxes in disorder on the floor, I went out, glancing backwards once at Hopestill Mather's absurd shoe.

Mrs. Henderson had prepared a meal for us: a cabbage soup, made according to my mother's instructions, was simmering on the stove and beans were heating in the oven. She had brought a loaf of fresh brown bread, a glass of apple jelly, and a nicely colored pat of margarine. My mother had been asleep and she looked rosy and rested. When I helped her into the kitchen—for she said with entreaty in her eyes, "My condition makes me feel funny"—and put pillows at her back, brought the table near so that she would not have to stir about, I felt a momentary affection and kissed her lightly on the forehead. I told her that I thought we might sell my father's clothes and his ski equipment. Since they were foreign, I believed they would fetch a high price, and I fancied a sign which I would put up over the door of the shop: "Miss Sonia Marburg's Sports Goods Shoppe."

"Sell them? My God, you are talking crazy! He would kill you if you sold any of his trash. Kill you till there'd be nothing left of you."

"But perhaps he's not coming back," I said.

"I'll take another plate of *pokhlyobka*. Mrs. H. is a saint from head to toe." As she dawdled with the spoon, she went on, "He'll come back, you'll see, darling. I won't say when, not knowing where he went, but he'll come back and I know that. And if he finds his wool drawers sold, there's no telling what kind of way he'll kill us. I was saying to Mrs. Henderson that what I think he did was go to

59

Boston to get a gun. For us, you know, sweetheart. And so tonight I am going to keep a lamp on and if they see it go out they'll hurry over to save us."

This transformation of my father into a murderer made me laugh aloud and when I covered up my giggle with a cough, she remembered that he had, she had always suspected, "sores on his lungs" because he coughed so much, and a pity it was he couldn't have kept his hands off me. Though my cough was purely voluntary and though I had never known my father to be ill, the remark distressed me and it was not for years after that that I was completely free of the notion that I had or might develop tuberculosis. She spoke of it from time to time, occasionally giving me garish accounts of his hemorrhages when his face turned blue and his eyes all but dropped from their sockets and blood spilled out from his lips as freely as wine from a bottle.

In vain I tried to convince her that it was only right we should sell the things in the shop. I said he would want us to, that, granted he was a bad man, he was not so bad as to want us to starve. After she had several times repeated in agitated whispers that he would be back that night to shoot us, she fell into her old, familiar placid grief, believed he would never return, and that I, poor, thin child, must make our living. "And the Hotel not open until summer time," she mourned, turning her eyes to the sand, the crags, and the ocean. "And Luibka coming. You must go to your teacher, darling, and tell her what a fix we're in." I asked her if I might have one of the dollars my father had left so that I could buy something at the store for our supper. She did not answer. Her elbow rested on the edge of the blue sink and she stared through the leaves of the geraniums, restored to their proper place.

2

On my way to school for the afternoon session, I thought considerably of my father. If he had left us at a different time of year, I think perhaps I would have been more casual. If it had been spring, the illimitable activities which the warm weather provided would have allowed me to set the catastrophe aside to think about when nothing appealed more strongly to me. For once April had come and my summer sandals were on my feet and my heavy sweater had been laid away with bags of tobacco to keep off the moths, I became a furious engine, liking to pursue, with an imaginary bow and arrow, an imaginary deer whose wild hooves carried me on a windy chase to the Point and back. In the fresh evenings, I played Run-Sheep-Run with the Henderson children and their cousins from Marblehead. Sometimes, hiding in a pack, feeling the hot breath of my fellows upon my neck and arms as we hunched up together under the shoulder of a rock or under the branches of a spreading bush, I would try to imagine another occupation: "What if I were doing arithmetic at home?" but the question would sink under my intentness and I could not, try as I might, conjure up a picture of myself in any other circumstances.

One spring, a disaster had befallen me. I had a pitiful little cat of which I was fond. It was ridden with fleas that it hunted with its sharp teeth, seizing bits of its hide ferociously enough to draw blood. And its ears were bald with mange which had also thinned the hair of its neck so that pink skin showed through. In its misery, it never purred, but under my petting turned up milky, half-shut eyes in a sort of stupid gratitude. It had been a charming kitten, though, and I hoped through some benevolence of nature it would be restored to its original state. And then, it was killed by Gonzales' bulldog when it still ailed. I saw the dreadful slaughter: the dog's eyes popping as he rent and strangled the creature, spittle mingling with blood, and I heard the cat's single wail of entreaty. Yet, although as a witness I was nauseated, once the cat was underground in a shoe box filled with petunias from Mrs. Henderson's flower boxes, my tears dried, my faintness passed and all that evening, as though nothing had happened, I exuberantly played Kick-the-Can. But then, months later, after the summer was over and the early evenings were too dark and cold for outdoor games, I felt my loss and besought my father to kill the bulldog and, for good measure, Gonzales too. He replied that it was "good riddance." Not only was my only companion for these winter nights gone from me forever, but my bereavement was mocked. My mother, hearing my lamentation, added to my sorrow such a weight of depressing generalizations on death and cruelty that the cat assumed a tragic stature and I thought I should never forget to mourn.

Now it was still winter when my father left, and in the desolation of the beach, I felt the desolation that would fall upon our house. The thought came to me that perhaps he would never walk along this road again and that he was therefore, in a sense, no longer alive, just as on foggy days when I could not see the State House dome, it was as though there were no Boston but that the city had dematerialized in the mist. A little wind, cold and wet with salt water, blew freshly into my face. I stooped to tighten the lace of my boot and as I did so, I felt that I had done this same thing before, but although I troubled my memory, I could not recall the other time. Afterwards and for many years, whenever I thought of my father, I saw him as though I were kneeling in the sand looking up at him on a gray winter day, our hair curling in the wind. Because my hands were cold and the lace was damp, the knot was not easy to tie. As I bent over, the smell of wetted leather came to me. When the odors, as distinct as on the day he left, came back at certain, sudden times throughout the years, with them always came the evasive feeling that every gesture I made and every particular in the landscape had been copied from some earlier day.

The fear that I might be taunted for my father's desertion rose to make me walk more slowly. I hoped to arrive after the others had already gone into the building. But immediately afterward, I quickened my pace at the thought of being stared at if I were tardy. I could hear the cries of children playing in the yard, mingled with the thud of balls being caught by the big boys of the eighth grade, and with the whizz and whine of swings where the younger children were pumping up. Then, when I had reached the gate and poked my head about one of the big cement columns which advertised the name, "Chichester Public School," and the date of erection of the building, and saw my boisterous schoolmates, I was urged forward by the desire to be hailed by them and was held back by the fear that I would not be and that my deficiencies, so mysterious to me and so apparent to them, would be more laughable today than ever. (I was always or nearly always the last to be chosen on a team, and I was convinced that the snub was directed against something less fundamental than simply my awkwardness in catching a ball or my inability to run without falling down on my face.) I expected to be greeted with a volley of catcalls which would proclaim my poor father's delinquency and would not spare my hair-cut. But my advance to the front door, although it was observed, did not disrupt the games.

Betty Brunson, who rarely addressed me, was embracing a young elm tree near the door and swinging round it, her head appearing now on one side, now on another. "Hi, Sonie Marburg, whatcha going to do this aft?"

"Oh, I don't know," I stammered.

"It so happens," she said, "that I happen to be going to New York. My father happens to be buying a car in New York City, New York."

A week ago, or yesterday, her voice would have been supercilious, for she would have been poking fun at me for being poor. But today, through a wonder of wonders to which I had no clue, she was *including* me as if her news and even her father's car were to be shared with me in the casual, communistic spirit that inspires the friendship of children. Heretofore, she had found space in the circle of her father's reflected glory for only two others, Esther and Ruby Beeler who were, strangely enough, even more impoverished than I. They, who had been pale, insipid waifs, bloomed under the patronage, became hearty extroverts with bold grins on their pinched little faces and roses in their cheeks which came, not from an amplified diet, but from happiness at being chosen. My first thought today was that they had offended Betty and that she was replacing them with the first person to come along. Her round face, with bright blue eyes and an obtuse nose, was framed by yellow, marcelled hair and the waves were held in place by tortoise-shell barrettes studded with rubies. She wore a coat of lambskin and a hat to match and from her pocket protruded fur-lined capeskin gloves. Without preamble, she began to relate the events of a "keen" Sunday she had recently spent with her highfaluting relatives in Boston. In the midst of her account, the Beelers came up. The three entwined their arms about one another and swayed round the elm tree with solemn faces as Betty listed the vegetables in the salad and the different designs on the coffee spoons.

When she had finished, she said, turning to Ruby first and then to Esther, "We know a secret, don't we, Beelers?"

Her protegées said chorally, "We *sure* do."

Their solemnity reassured me. It was very likely no secret that my father had run away, for the Hendersons and the Kadishes would have conferred and brought the tale to school. There was, in the manner of the three girls and in the circumstances of the encounter, evidence that the secret bore a relation to myself and was not in the same category as the new automobile. I assumed that it was something from which I would make either a social or a material gain: I saw myself riding in Dr. Brunson's new car, going to a Valentine party at the Brunsons' house, receiving a box of candy, a charm bracelet, a round comb or a bottle of perfume from Betty, and, finally, achieving the summit of the improbable whose ascent is so easy when we are lifted up by the wings of our dreams, I imagined going to a "slumber party" at the house of Betty's surgeon uncle in Boston. Betty and Betty's life became the Alpha and Omega: I aspired to her small, snobbish sorority that fed on Tootsie Rolls and licorice wands, and whose insignia, provided by her father, was a Roi-Tan cigar label worn on the middle finger of the left hand.

The girls, or, as I now thought of them, "my friends" would not tell me, but continued to repeat in singsong, "We know a secret and we *sure* won't tell," until finally Betty, using her father's language nonchalantly, remarked, "Oh, by the by, old girl, I almost forgot. Pickens wants a word with you." Ruby, who was dazzled by her friend's recherché speech, but not too dazzled to follow with what, in her social stratum she believed was as debonair, said, "Ain't it the truth." Betty gave me a push. "Well, ta-ta till after school," she said and they retreated, walking backwards, their smiles giving way to brief glares of consternation as they almost lost their balance.

So Pickens (I dropped the "Miss" in my private thoughts, out of respect to Betty Brunson), I surmised, was in on the secret. This I did not relish, for it was to her that my mother had insisted I appeal for help. "Just tell her that your rascal papa left you and your mamma is in a condition. You beg her, Sonie, there's a good girl. You cry and say, 'Oh, Miss Whatyoumaycallit, I am *so* hungry, and we haven't no money, no food, nor fire and not a thing.'" Of course no child could say anything of the kind. I had made up my mind to speak to Miss Pickens about customers for my sporting-goods shop, to make it clearly understood that I was launched already on a commercial enterprise of which the mechanism needed only the turn of a switch—the turn she would execute—to start producing a livelihood for me. In my determined independence, I thought of offering her a commission "per head" for any customer she brought me, a trick of business I had heard of through friends of my mother who paid taxi-drivers for touting rooms which they wished to let in the summer. My offer would demote Miss Pickens automatically from any position of benefactress. She was not a warm-hearted person but she was very sentimental and she viewed all successes as well as all misfortunes through tears which misted her spectacles but seldom acquired enough body to fall.

Miss Pickens was young but she already bore the marks of spinsterhood. Her fine chestnut hair was sparse at the temples and she vainly tried to hide her baldness with an absurd pompadour, bolstered up with a transformation, or, as we preferred, in our beastly way, to call it, a "rat" which sometimes became dislodged and hung spiritlessly down her cheek until she could repair herself in the teachers' rest-room. In her choice of clothes, she seemed to aim deliberately for the most unbecoming; she was perversely fond of chartreuse, mauve, and tan, which influenced and increased her sallowness. And so great was her belief in the ensemble that she wore everything to match exactly, including her stockings and gloves, even if she had to dye them, with the result that she resembled a caterpillar whose cocoon matches the leaf on which it is spun. Her medicine fetish was as persistent as any old lady's at the Hotel. During arithmetic in the morning, she ate a whole cake of yeast; at recess she measured out ten drops of belladonna from a bottle labeled "Poison!" and in the afternoon, stirred up a glass of psyllium seed which, mixed with water, looked like a thin brown mucus and repelled us all. No child had a crush on Miss Pickens, although I had at first been attracted by her cold, cultured voice and her elevated vocabulary which contained such words as "literally" and "intolerable" and "indefatigable," but her mannerisms quickly began to irritate me and I joined mine to the general growl, "Aw, she thinks she's smart." Her tear-clouded, octagonal glasses had given her the reputation of meaning well among the parents, who met all the teachers annually at the P.T.A. clambake. My mother was fond of relating how moved Miss Pickens had been when she told her of the time I broke my collarbone at the age of four by falling off the roof of the shop. "A person would think," my mother said, "that it was her own collarbone or her own child and happening right now instead of eight years ago." But really Miss Pickens' tears were trumped up. When Lottie Cummings' mother died, our teacher was blinded when she first interviewed the child but made no move to comfort her, only made her cry the harder by calling her "My poor, poor little girl." And after that, Lottie, who at the age of thirteen weighed 135 pounds, complained to her that the other children had commenced to tease her again now they felt the interval of mourning was over, but Miss Pickens did not restrain us in any way.

The building was empty save for a few teachers clustered about the radiator far down the corridor. As I opened the heavy storm doors and my nostrils were greeted by the familiar but always new odors of school—varnish, floor oil, felt erasers full of chalk—I experienced the feelings of light-headedness and pleasure I always did after I had been ill and then was well enough to go outdoors again. For it seemed ages ago, not yesterday, that I had entered here. I advanced, hunting signs of change, and found them everywhere: the old freckles on the drinking fountain I had never seen before, the ancient chains on the cloudy transoms, a green, crazed flower-pot which must have stood for fifteen years in the corner of a window sill above the stairs. And there was added to the heavy atmosphere a smell that was new to me, yet one I must have smelled daily for seven years: the smell of wet paper towels that filled the wastebasket beside the drinking fountain. It was so strong that the varnish, oil, and erasers were all but obliterated.

Miss Pickens, who had been humming "Comin' through the Rye" and supplying the percussion by tapping the gauge of the radiator with her long foot encased in a "health shoe," broke off her song and detached herself from the group of teachers to come toward me, her arms extended. I halted, suddenly trembling, like a person armed to defend himself against wild animals, but on meeting one face to face

66

is immediately turned to stone. I quickly went into the seventh-grade room and scurried to my seat, laying my head on the desk, my arms folded on top, with the ostrich's belief that I was perfectly concealed, even though I could see her through an aperture of my intertwined arms, swaying through the aisle, the frolicsome tails of her beige chiffon scarf floating above the inkwells. She sat down in Rosalie Kadish's seat opposite me where there always hung an aura of onions which combined now with the teacher's smell of yeast, sachet, and a slight mildew.

"I understand," she said in her clear, uplifted voice, "that your father literally flew the coop. It was a naughty and intolerable thing to do. But every cloud has a . . . ?"

"Silver lining," I promptly supplied.

"Exactly. For one thing we won't ever drink beer at noon again and be sleepy in our sewing lesson, will we?"

Her sweetness curdled at the allusion. It was true. Whenever my father had the money, he brought home several bottles of beer from an old man who lived behind the Presbyterian church and carried on a paltry bootlegging business. I always begged for a glass, but my father, more through greed than prudence, refused me more than a cupful which he poured into my soup. However, this was enough, having it as I did in the middle of the day when I was already drowsy from the morning in school and the long walk home, and having it in combination with heavy food, to make me thick-witted and often Miss Pickens found me *lit*erally asleep," a state at any time deplorable, but in my case magnified enormously since its cause was immoral, barbarous, and illegal. "To spoil good soup!" she fretted. Once, after I had committed some monstrous blunder in buttonholing, she called on my father and charged him with rearing me to be a drunkard. My father shrugged his shoulders and pretended not to understand her: *"Bitte, sprechen Sie Deutsch, gnädiges Fräulein?"* he said with a troubled face. She left, defeated and unfriendly, and had thereafter a chillness towards me which accounted, as much as my dreaminess, for my low grade in Deportment.

I said I supposed I would not drink beer again and the prospect saddened me. My teacher then laid a damp hand on mine and said, "There, there, it's hard, poor child, but we mustn't cry," and though she was not, of course, referring to the beer, I decided that my life would be unendurable without it. "We" had had until now no urge to cry, but her words, so mushy and stale and yet so tender and personal, started up a torrent of tears, and each time my inquisitive tongue received a drop, I was reminded, bitterly, of the way my father had put salt in his beer. I suffered her to lay her moist fingers on my head and arms and to come quite close to me in an embrace in which all the unhealthy odors she dispensed rose and eddied about me at the slightest movement on the part of either one of us.

"We must be *brave* and not be a burden to Mother who is bringing a baby into the world just for *us*," and then, to distract me, she said, in a fun-loving way, "I'll tell you what: I'll bet you a dollar to a doughnut it's a boy." When I agreed with a sobbing "Okay," she went on to tell me that as luck would have it, Betty Brunson's mother was also expecting the stork very soon, and she had been saying only the other day how much she would like to find a girl to help with the housework, and Miss Pickens had said to herself, "Why, I know just the girl. My Sonie Marburg is very capable and works at the Hotel in the summer so she must know how things are done, dishes and so on. I wouldn't be a bit surprised if she wouldn't love to work in that nice shiny new house where her chum Betty lives."

I lifted panic-stricken eyes to my teacher and dropped them at once. The shock had stopped my tears. I could not become a servant in Betty's house when she was about to admit me into her circle! Such a job, possible anywhere else and even attractive (for, in spite of my intention to refuse, I saw what I might gain in the way of petit larceny of sugar lumps and birthday candles and other staples which would never be missed), would cancel all those social engagements which had practically been proposed to me on the school ground just a few minutes ago. It was only after my stammered reply that my mother needed me at home, when Miss Pickens said, "Why, Betty thought it would be lovely. She'll be *so* disappointed," that I realized this was the secret. Everything had been ill-timed, and I, in my uncircumspect cockiness, had been caught in a trap.

Miss Pickens was stubborn and set before me arguments that I could not refute. I saw that the sooner I resigned myself the better, for my commercial pipe-dream could avail me nothing now that the teacher, essential to its working out, was set upon the new plan which, in her surpassing conventionality, she regarded as great good luck for me. She, being comfortably off herself, had no patience with pride in the poor as she often told us, apropos of tales she had read in the newspapers. Nevertheless, urged by desperation, I told her what I had intended to do.

Her befogged eyeglasses glared at me. "I'm surprised at you, Sonia. I didn't think you were a *silly* girl. You've been reading silly books instead of good books, suitable for your age group." ("Age group" was the sort of expression that had once fascinated me. She had learned her "Education" well and had not forgotten it, so that she sprinkled her speech with its vocabulary with a serene disregard for the class or age of her interlocutor. She had baffled Mr. Henderson by telling him that one of his children had no "community urge.") "Nothing, you poor silly child, could be less feasible than a sporting-goods shop in Chichester. There is only one sporting man in town so far as I know, that Dr. Galbraith at the hospital. And he, of course, goes in only for riding equipment. But I have a friend" (by a faint glow that simmered in her face I knew she meant a man friend) "who likes winter sports and if your father's skis are any good, it is quite possible I may be able to arrange a sale for you."

She obviously doubted the quality of my father's paraphernalia, and I said, "They're very expensive."

"Well, we'll see about that part of it. Don't you worry. I'll do my bit for you if you'll be sensible and go work for Mrs. Brunson."

I was gradually persuaded; rather, one self, already installed in the Brunson kitchen and reaching out a hand toward the sugar canister, was persuaded. Miss Pickens was pleased with my change of heart. "And now," she said, rising and plucking me by the shoulder, "now we must get rid of our tears, isn't that right? Hurry along, the bell's about to ring." And she hustled me down the corridor toward the teachers' rest-room. There was a recrudescence of my disappointment and I felt that I could not face Betty again today. I told Miss Pickens I felt a little sick and had a headache, couldn't I please go home?

"Certainly not," she said severely, but then, seeing how woebegone I was, she relented and in a burst of kindliness, even suggested that I wait in the lavatory until the other children had assembled in the classrooms so that I might leave the building without being seen. I was surprised that the teachers' rest-room smelled like ours and had the same gray enameled doors to the toilets. Only on great occasions of illness or accidents were children admitted to the room. Once, in the year before, some privileged little girl told us that as she was recovering from a nose-bleed, she had seen a cigarette butt on the floor, stained with lipstick. We tried to detect signs of guilt in all the teachers' faces, and could not, but the worldly Beelers said, "Oh, piffle, you dumb-bells. They *all* do it, but they flush them down the toilet."

I thought, as I sat on a backless couch, waiting to hear the last column of children march up the stairs and into the classrooms, that if only circumstances had not conspired against us, Betty and I, fast friends, might have taken up smoking.

# 3

To my mother, my father's desertion was like an eternally renewing spring from which she hourly drew accusations and complaints, and she shared her poisoned, enervating drink with anyone who would partake. Her companions in misery were poor neighbor women who, alternately pitying and envying, welcomed our misfortune as a distraction from their own worries. Mrs. Kadish, a thin, pinched, crotchety woman, the wife of a ferryboat engineer and the mother of six famished children, often came to call. She sat prissily erect, her hands folded tightly in her lap, nodding her long, hard head which was topped by a coil of graying hair. When she was not speaking, she pursed her lips in permanent displeasure, and when she did speak, it was in a high, nasal key, not loud, but like a distant scream.

As I came in one afternoon, she was saying, "I was on my feet at five A.M. this morning and I'm telling you, I've been on the go ever since. It's pick up! Wash up! Sew up! Rinse out! till a person could drop down senseless. You was saying, Mrs. Marburg, that it's hard if the man goes off and leaves the woman, but to my mind it's six of one and half a dozen of the other. If you don't have a grown man around, you don't have to cook so much and do up all them work shirts. Kadish could leave tomorrow and I wouldn't hardly notice only for the little dab of money he brings in."

"He hasn't left you yet, sweetheart," said my mother. "It's not the money. It's the *shame*. My God! You'd think this here wasn't his child not born yet and he went off to punish me. I know *you* don't think so, Mrs. Kadish, darling, nor Mrs. Henderson nor two or three other Chichester ladies, but what about the *other* people?"

Mrs. Kadish did not regard it a likely suspicion though it interested her. "You mean maybe they think you you-know? Oh, no, I don't *think* so. Why, Mrs. Marburg, nobody would say you was that type lady."

My mother began on a new tack: "Well, then, maybe they say *he* was the bad one and went off with one of those women from Marblehead, and maybe that's true, Mrs. Kadish, who knows? I'm no fool and I used to see them last summer wobbling down the beach by the gentlemen's house in dresses no longer than your camisole." The "gentlemen" were the Coast Guards, so known because one of them, five years before, had gone to Harvard.

"You're not telling me news," returned her friend. "But I wouldn't think that a family man like Mr. Marburg would take up with that type."

"Whatever people say—if they blame it on drink or on the other thing or something else besides—it's all a shame. But what can you do with Hermann Marburg? He is a *German,* dear."

Her voice fell upon the word "German" in such a way that the emphasis was ambiguous: either a German was infamous beyond pardon or pitiable beyond hope. Mrs. Kadish, after this statement, perused my face for a time. "German," she intoned. "And you, Mrs. Marburg, what was you saying was your nationality?"

"I am a Russian," said my mother without pride and without deprecation but with a kind of finality which set "Russian" distinctly apart from "German" as though it was perhaps not ultimately the best thing to be but was at least comprehensible. I could have corrected her: Russians, to the children at school, were utterly improbable though all that was known about them was that they had ludicrous names. A favorite sport was to tease me by saying: "Hisky, Sonivitch, have you got your geographysky home-workski vitch?" In a way, I was flattered by this, for it had replaced Pig-Latin and was known as Sonie-Latin. On the other hand, Germans were perfectly credible and, because of their reputation for cutting off the hands of sleeping children and of being sired by Kaiser Bill, they enjoyed a certain prestige. Sometimes, the three or four of us in the lower grades who knew a little German were bribed to sing, in a secret place, *"Stille Nacht, Heilige Nacht"* and the eyes of our audience grew more enraptured with each evil word.

"Rooshun," brooded Mrs. Kadish in her piercing voice. "So your kid is half Rooshun and half German—half Hun, as they say. Well, mine are bad enough: half Jew and half American. But not so bad as that." I felt a rush of shame which my distaste for her smelly children did not intercept. "But I don't doubt," she added in the same shrill note of lamentation, "but what she's a bright little slip."

"Bright!" cried my mother. "She's full of brains as big as an apple, that little thing is. And helpful, my God! Well, she's everything in the world you could want, Mrs. Kadish. Come here, Sonia girl, let me show Mrs. K. how long your eyelashes are," and she gathered me to her, pulling my hair as she held up my head for our neighbor's admiration.

"Tchk, tchk," said Mrs. Kadish. "She'll be pretty. She won't have no trouble getting herself a man, you know what I mean?"

"There's where you're wrong," replied my mother. "Not but she couldn't have any man in the world for the asking even now and only twelve going on thirteen, but what kind of a mother would I be to let an angel like her be treated the way my poor self has been?"

"You wait and see," warned Mrs. Kadish. "The time will come and whoosh! she's gone. But I wouldn't be thinking so far ahead, Mrs. Marburg. I must say I don't agree with you that she could get a man right now at her time of life. To my way of thinking she looks poorly. My Nathan might take her, along about sixteen or seventeen."

My mother gave a foolish laugh. "Your Nathan! Well, pardon *me*, Mrs. Kadish, but no thank you. I don't mean anything by that only I couldn't do without her." She pressed my head into her breast until I could scarcely breathe, but I had the strength to pull away from her and turn aside, my cheeks blazing. I did not know, indeed,

72

what she would do without me, but I knew well enough what I would do without her. Right now, I thought bitterly, I would be *playing* with Betty Brunson instead of being on my way to her house to *work*. I murmured that I must go, that I would be late, for the sun was already going down.

"Poor baby," said my mother, stroking my hand. "She is her mother's staff of life."

"Would you mind telling me, Sonie," said Mrs. Kadish with a wily leer, "just what them Brunsons pay you?"

I told her they gave me three dollars a week. "Well, I'll be!" she exclaimed. "They're real free, ain't they? If you ask me, that's pure charity or pure show-off, I don't know which. Three dollars! And pretty soft, I expect?"

"Soft!" burst out my mother. "Soft! She slaves herself to the bone!"

Mrs. Kadish's curiosity was not satisfied. "You live high on three dollars a week now, and I'm not saying that isn't dandy, I'd just like to know how you do it. Now, me, I have close to ten a week and I can't hardly make both ends meet."

"We have a golden egg," said my mother proudly. "But we don't touch it only now and then."

"A golden egg?" queried the neighbor. "How's that?"

I was infuriated with my mother. She was talking about our "nest" egg as Miss Pickens had called it, the fifty dollars her friend had paid us for my father's skis, poles, boots, and leather shorts. I had wanted to keep our wealth a secret for I was sure it would be stolen as we had no good hiding place for it. Miss Pickens had advised me to take it to the bank in Marblehead, but I was afraid to go so far alone with that much money on my person, and we had put it between the leaves of my father's Bible, so close to Mrs. Kadish at this very moment that she could stretch out her hand without moving from her chair and take it all.

"You know the teacher, Miss Pickens?" whispered my mother. Her friend nodded, leaning forward. "She brought a man here and he bought all Hermann's trash for fifty dollars."

"No!" Mrs. Kadish's lips curled into a smile of disbelief. "May I inquire what this here trash was?"

I said, quoting the purchaser, a sickly young man who had resembled Miss Pickens and who had scarcely been able to contain himself at the sight of my father's belongings, "Four pairs of Bavarian skis and poles covered with plaited leather and four pairs of genuine Salzburg *Lederhosen* and galluses to match."

"Galluses?"

"I don't know the English word," I said.

The woman looked at me with respect. "Nathan knows some foreign words, too. Fifty dollars. I'm glad for you, I surely am. No telling what will happen. Sonie might get appendicitis and have to have them out. That fifty dollars would come in handy." She rose to leave and my mother extended her hand, fingers pointing downward as though she expected it to be kissed. "You come again, sweetheart, I'm always here in the afternoon."

"Some pregnant women crave dill pickles," said Mrs. Kadish. "I'll bring along four or five when I come next time. I was always crazy for them myself."

When she had gone I put out my mother's supper for her: a plate of cole slaw, a loaf of rye bread, a dish of Liederkranz, and a casserole of beans that had been heating. She looked with displeasure on the meal. "If only I could have one small cucumber in a dish of sour cream, I wouldn't ask for anything else in the world." We had been through the cucumber argument many times before.

"Oh, Mamma!" I cried. "You *know* they don't have them at this time of year."

But, as always before, she either did not hear or did not believe me. "A cucumber is a little thing to ask. If I could have just *one,* just a small withered one in just a little bit of sour cream, ah, ah, I could bear all the rest!"

She did not move from her chair beside the stove, and knowing that she would only eat when the notion struck her, I went out. But I did not go at once in the direction of the Brunsons' house where I had long since been due. Instead, I ran across to the Kadishes' house where a light was burning. Through the uncurtained window, I could see the children gathered about a round table in the kitchen, each of the six intent upon some project, piling up matches or painting with water colors or cleaning a comb, but not too absorbed to chatter now and then and to dart their black eyes about the table with a controlled ferocity as though they all hated one another but knew that they must stick together. All of them came from the same mold: the same crisp black hair glittered under the lamplight; their faces wore sharp, shrewd expressions, the upper half seeming to be drawn down by the weight of the nose, loosening then below the nostrils into soft lips and little chins.

Nathan, the oldest, a boy of fourteen, sat near the window reading, and as the lamp was directly shining upon him, brightly illuminating his face, I was able to study the birthmark on his cheek. It was probably because of this shocking purple disfigurement that he was so ill-tempered and also so precocious. He was as sensitive as if his mark were a raw sore, continually being rubbed against or hit. It extended from the cheekbone, over the eyelid and the low forehead, to the hairline, appearing the more brilliant because of the dead pallor it interrupted. His lips were pouted in profound misanthropy and he seemed, for all his concentration, to detest his book, for his forehead was drawn into a scowl and his erect body wore an air of unwillingness. I knew by hearsay as well as by the ever meditative look upon his face and by the constant presence of a book under his arm that he was learned. He did not read *The Boy Scouts in Arizona* or the *Motor Boat Boys,* but instead, lives of Napoleon and histories of Rome and the Waverley novels. He had greatly admired my father, and often on Sunday afternoons had come to the door, inviting him to take a walk. My father never refused him, and it was on these expeditions round Chichester that Nathan had learned the foreign words of which his mother was so proud. Tonight it was *Quo Vadis* that he had propped up against a sugar bowl.

I respected his scholarship, but in my lassitude felt no urge to emulate him. I sometimes wished that we were friends so that I might absorb his culture through our association. But I did nothing to make myself commendable to him, nor could I have, for he was a formidable critic of everyone and especially of girls. A foolish girl of his age had once cried out in derision, "Cranberry Kadish is my ideal of a perfect man, like fun!" "Her ideal," said Nathan with a contempt that far surpassed hers, "I suppose she means Platonic ideal because I wouldn't touch her with a ten-foot pole." The girl blushed and said, "You know what I *meant*. I meant 'idea.'" But her correction was too late and as she fretted over the failure of her arrow to kill, he regarded her with a triumphant sneer that twitched at his birthmark.

Tonight, made thoughtful by my mother's conversation with his mother, and, restless in my trap, I wished more than ever that Nathan were my "best friend" and that we took walks together in the evening, confiding in one another our sorrows and our ambitions. The desire for his companionship was tantamount to a betrayal of my mother who for so many years and so diligently had schooled me in the treacheries of men, although I believed she assumed that I would marry in spite of her warnings, would profit by none of her precepts, but by my experience would confirm what she had told me. And I, although it was my intention to remain unmarried (more in imitation of Miss Pride than to escape the pitfalls my mother had described to me), had a quite reasonable curiosity to know what were the manifestations of a man's descent from Satan. The marred Jewish boy, at his sullen labors, roused in me a strange new ravening and I all but tapped on the window glass as a sign that he was to come out to speak to me. As quickly, the impulse waned and I turned to go. But as I did so, I resolved hereafter to come each night about this time and take up my brief, secret vigil. I was light-headed as I went on my way and I felt a little sick. Each time his image returned to my mind, my throat thickened and my footsteps faltered. But though it was novel and mysterious, my disquietude made me happy and I began to sing one of my mother's songs:

> Far from where the men were reaping,
> Soon my weary self was sleeping;
> Slept and then waked—oh,
> Slept and then waked.

> Thus as I the time was whiling,
> Came a fellow, started smiling,
> Courting me, too—oh,
> Courting me, too.

> Long my mother waited, wondered,
> Long my sister waited, pondered
> Where I might be—oh,
> Where I might be.

Night came down upon the stubble.
Women have all kinds of trouble!
Woman's sad lot! Oh,
Woman's sad lot!

My installation in the Brunsons' house had been a disappointment, for I was in many ways farther removed from Betty than before. And so it was that I plucked the sting from my evenings there by silently communing with Nathan Kadish through the lamplit window.

At the Brunsons', as in my own house, the central figure was a pregnant woman, the very blazing personification of indecency, and Betty, quite unlike myself who found my mother daily more distasteful, adored hers increasingly, though I forgave her for she believed that her mother was going to a hospital to buy a baby from the supply kept there in a large ice-chest. The myth had been so fully developed in her mind that she was convinced the child had been specifically planned as a birthday present for her. It could not be a surprise since sometimes babies spoiled and you could never tell when there was to be a shortage. The Beelers, thoroughly sophisticated, left off their vain instructions when she told them sternly not to *dare* say anything nasty about her mother ever again. "But lookit how fat she's getting!" said Esther. "Look here," snapped Betty, "my Uncle Harry told my mother she *had* to get fatter, and if you don't like it, you can go jump in the lake."

The presence of the Beelers in the house was a sharp thorn in my side, for while I was confined to the kitchen, except when my chores took me into other rooms, they roamed at will throughout the house, obstreperous, dirty, and either through preoccupation with their absurd hilarity or through snobbery, they ignored me. I pondered how Betty, with her fastidious ways, could possibly find them preferable to me. They had warts and they did not wash. Yet, while I was paring vegetables, the three of them sat in the parlor playing Old Maid or came into the kitchen to blow soap bubbles or raced about in the upstairs, howling and giggling in some aimless game. I was not ashamed, though, as soon as they left the house. I was pleased to wear a starched white apron over a black sateen uniform when I brought in the soup and then served the dinner. The dark, round table glittered with silver and pink glass. The centerpiece was a bunch of crystal grapes on an oblong mirror. The Brunsons always ate by candlelight; the radio played soft "dinner music," "Roses of Picardy," "The Bells of Saint Mary's," and "The Blue Danube." They had elegant table manners, holding their left hands in their laps, breaking bread into small pieces before they buttered it, and making not a sound in their throats as they drank water.

My duties were very slight and Mrs. Kadish's accusation that I was overpaid was quite true. The reason was not, however, that Mrs. Brunson was a spendthrift, but that the cook, Maudie, shocked by my pallor and emaciation, did all my work while she kept me in the pantry eating beef sandwiches and doughnuts, and drinking eggnog. Maudie was not a native of New England, but had come here from Idaho because she had always wanted to see "the spreading chestnut tree and Plymouth rock and that old bridge where they disappointed the British." And so, when her husband was thrown by a "spooked" horse and died of a skull fracture, and her two sons had got married, she set out with her insurance money to see what she called "the old country." She was a horsy, red-cheeked, raw-boned woman, nearly six feet tall. On her day off, she lounged in a one-room house not far from the Brunsons', drinking whiskey and reading magazines called *Lariat, West,* and *Rio Grande Romances.* The combination of the liquor and literature produced in her a virulent homesickness which was contagious to her cronies—all men—so that her shack rocked with sighs toward evening when the men had gathered after work, as Maudie, in a plaintive, guttural voice, "My whiskey tenor," she called it, told anecdotes of horses, cattle, and bears, for all of whom she was lonesome. "Why don't you go back, Maudie?" the men would ask. "Oh, hell," she would reply, "it wouldn't be the same. My husband's dead and that dear old bench that throwed him is dead, and without them two Idaho'd be an ornery outfit. She was a little strawberry roan by the name of Skylark and she loved him like another horse and he loved her like another human. I often say it's good they went together." She would relapse into a dreamy silence. The men were deeply touched.

During the week she was never sad. She sang a great deal, but she had a very small repertoire. I think she knew only "Home on the Range," "I'll Build a Coffin of Pine," "Holy, Holy, Holy," and the obscene verses of "Frankie and Johnny," and she had only one tune to which she fitted all the words, like square pegs in round holes, as Dr. Brunson said. Finally she was asked to stop. She did, but the moment the kitchen door banged to and she was on her way home, her voice came thundering back to us.

She called onions "engerns" and told me to "pack them spuds to the dudes," and if Mrs. Brunson scolded her, she said with a laugh, "The old heifer's on the prod agin." I memorized her expressions and used them in imaginary conversations with men in ten-gallon hats as I rode the range or hog-tied the steers or branded the calves. Under the influence of Maudie's magazines, which I pored over far into the night after my mother had gone to bed, I began to write a story: "On a cold November morning," I wrote with a blue pencil on manila drawing paper, "you might have seen, if you had been on the sharp lookout, a shabbily dressed man standing in a dark door-way on the main street of Boise, Idaho. Over his left hip was a bulge and that was a shiny black single-action Colt .44 meant to kill Buck Johnson, steely blue-eyed foreman of the Lazy S 4 later in the day. The party in the doorway was a tough customer and his name was Scrub Maxwell. The men of Boise, who were every last one of them square-shooters, hated Scrub's innards, for he was a cattle rustler and a scalawag in more ways than one." There followed a series of un-connected adventures, including stampedes, the discovery of wolves in the chuck-wagon, the puncturing of the bellies of "five million head of pure-bred Hereford white-face cows and bulls as well as calves, heifers and steers that had the bloat off Indian paintbrush." Miss Pickens, to whom I unwisely showed my story, deplored this intellectual climate as much as she had my postprandial snoozes when my father had given me beer, and my compositions, all upon the same subject, that is, the heroism of the young sheriff, Sonny Mar-burn, came back marked in a vehement red pencil. And when I wrote in an examination that "st." was the abbreviation for "steer" she held me up to the class as an outrageous example of the idle mind.

Maudie left as soon as the Brunsons had begun their dessert and I stayed on to serve the coffee and to wash the dishes. It was strange, rather than embarrassing, to serve Betty and to find her eyes always elsewhere than on me, and after dinner to see her hidden behind a magazine in a corner of the sofa while I cleared her parents' coffee cups away and brought in the ice-water. But later, when I was washing the dishes, she came into the kitchen and sat on a high green stool, talking with me, telling me the plots of movies she had seen, reporting on her Saturdays in Boston which were filled with visits to the dentist ("My daddy wouldn't hurt me for the world," she said, "so I have to go to Dr. Harrison on the Bay State Road."), with music and dancing lessons, fittings at the dressmaker, excursions to Schrafft's for hot chocolate with tons of whipped cream, and visits to her Uncle Harry's house on Beacon Hill. Or she told me about the decorations in her bedroom, as if I had never seen them, had not, on Saturday when she was away and it was my day to clean the upstairs, fondled and pawed the porcelain shepherdesses that supported the lamps on her dressing table, their crooks bursting incongruously into parasols. I had gazed, awed, at the glassy photographs lining the walls, of Bebe Daniels, Clara Bow, Ramon Navarro, Janet Gaynor, Richard Barthelmess, inscribed with grandiloquent scrawls to "Betty." I had looked through the windows of the doll-house where a whole family was engaged in ossified enterprises: a baby with a rosy backside lay face down in a cradle; a fat old grandmother stood in the bathroom, intently studying the tub as if she wanted to make sure how things looked before she left the house—she wore a hat and a fur-trimmed coat and carried a folded umbrella in one hand and a knitting bag in the other. A mother stood squarely in the center of the kitchen, a china broom lying flat at her feet; and on the roof, the father of the establishment was always emerging from the chimney where he was presumably making repairs; his legs, up to the waist, were invisible from the top but could be seen dangling through the ceiling of the dining-room, his heels nearly touching the rare roast beef (so life-like there were smudges of blood on the platter) and the golden banana which dwarfed the meat, these two dishes being the sole fare of the family from the beginning of my acquaintance with them until the end of it. Two children, a boy and a girl, stood facing each other at opposite ends of the parlor, doing nothing. I was charmed by the tiny kitchen stove with a door that really opened, the delicate round gilt table in the vestibule which showed, through its glass top, a bright blue butterfly with folded wings resting on a shasta daisy, and with the perfect little Christmas tree that stood in the sun parlor, everlastingly green, its bangles and loops of tinsel and tiny Santas proclaiming that to this happy, paralyzed family, Christmas was every day.

I liked to look at Betty's collection of tortoise-shell round combs, her barrettes and her grosgrain hair-ribbons, her party dresses with artificial roses at the shoulder, her splendidly equipped writing desk with lavender and pink note paper, a brand new set of Prang's non-poisonous water-colors, red sealing wax, a gold pen and pencil engraved with her name, and a soft, white leather-bound New Testament with many colored place ribbons given her, it said on the fly-leaf, by her loving mother two years before when she had been an angel in a Sunday School pageant. The inscription impressed me: "From your loving mother, Mrs. Robert Killigrew Brunson."

Occasionally, when I had washed the dish towels and had swept the kitchen floor, Mrs. Brunson would call out to her daughter, "Go on and make the popcorn if you want to, angel face." I would stay on then sometimes until ten o'clock if the Brunsons, absorbed in magazines, forgot to send Betty to bed, and as we ate the buttery popcorn (made in an electric drum with a wooden handle which one turned round and round) she might digress from her own affairs to talk about people and things that I knew.

Once she said, "I don't know how you stand living next to those awful Kadish simps, chum. Honestly, they're lousy. Cranberry makes me sick to the stomach to look at him. My mother wouldn't let me go with them for anything. Do you want to know something? They're *Jews*."

I was ashamed of my passion for Nathan and I said in defense, but meekly, "My father was a Catholic."

"Oh, that's different," she soothed me. "Daddy says you don't have to be a Catholic just because your daddy is. I mean, that's silly. I mean, well, after all, I'm not a Mason, am I, just because Daddy is?"

Despite her cordiality, there was a note of reserve in her voice as if my heritage had been discussed and rationalized and not merely accepted. "Anyhow," she went on, "Daddy has some good friends that are Catholics, but he won't have anything to do with a Jew."

A little later, on an evening when the Brunsons were entertaining, I learned how I was regarded in the household. Someone remarked on my extreme youth, and Mrs. Brunson replied, "But she's a jewel even so. You see, she was practically born in the pantry of the Hotel here and was trained before I got her." Dr. Brunson, a rash democrat, said, "She's good company for Betty, too." But his wife snapped irritably, "That's beside the point, Bob."

Betty, in our kitchen conversations, had not a trace of the haughtiness with which she had hitherto behaved towards me at school. At the same time, she gave me clearly to understand that our lives would never run parallel. She was to go to a finishing school and afterwards would come out in Boston at a double début with her cousin Frances Barker, the daughter of Mrs. Brunson's wealthy and successful surgeon brother.

One evening in March, Mrs. Brunson suddenly cried out during the salad course. We all—all but Betty—knew that her labor had begun several weeks before it should have. In their prudish way, her parents had planned to spare Betty any demonstrations like this and had hoped to have her installed in New York with a distant relative. In the tumult of getting Mrs. Brunson off to the hospital, the child was all but ignored, her father only casting instructions over his shoulder to Maudie to stay all night in the house and to me to keep Betty company as long as I could. Yet even in his agitation, he recollected her innocence and shouted loudly from the vestibule that he would telephone from Boston as soon as they had selected a baby. She was perplexed by the abrupt departure and a little annoyed since her mind had been made up to receive the baby after her trip to New York, but far from suspecting that she had been misled, she thought her mother had been informed (presumably by telepathy) that a particularly choice specimen was available and that if she wanted it she must make haste to be the first bidder. This delicacy was hard to understand, for in every other way the Brunsons were extremely common or, as they put it, "broad-minded." I, whose rearing had been far from gentle, had been told that it was unseemly to discuss any adventure remotely connected with the bathroom at the table, but any of the Brunsons might say, without a hint of embarrassment (although, because they always laughed, it was clear that they were somewhat self-conscious), "There isn't any more toilet paper."

Maudie, Betty, and I put up a card table in the parlor and Maudie taught us how to play five-draw, deuces wild. In the midst of the game, she brought us some hot chocolate and said, "Well, boys, let's lay off for five-ten minutes." Betty's mind had not been on the game and she was glad for the recess.

"Maudie," she said, "do you think Mummy is terribly beautiful?"

"Shucks. Of course she is. *You* know that and you're just fishing."

"I want to be just like her when I grow up."

"Don't you worry," said Maudie with a wry smile and a wink to me, "you will be. You're the spittin' image of her now."

"I love her dresses!" cried her daughter in a rhapsody.

Mrs. Brunson dressed flamboyantly, even when she was pregnant, wearing, in the evening, flowered chiffon dresses that trailed the floor behind and barely covered her knees in front and black satin afternoon dresses touched up with rhinestone gimcracks. She always wore high heels. From her rather large, powdered ears depended tarnished bangles. Her blond hair, lighter than Betty's, dipped and rose in hard permanent waves that framed a puffy face with orange lips and an orange circle on either cheekbone, eyebrows like peaked black thread and a beak of a pink nose.

Maudie and I agreed that not only was she the handsomest, she was also the best dressed woman in Chichester.

"Mummy has style," said Betty smugly.

"Yeah," replied Maudie with a chuckle. "You mean the way she talks." Betty nodded. Her mother did have a certain style but it was not the kind that prejudiced anyone in her favor. Her everyday language was a mixture of slang and profanity. For years she said "for crying out loud" with an occasional variation, "for crying in the beer," and something that pleased her was "the cat's pajamas." But if she was annoyed with her husband, Maudie, a trades person or myself, she used a fastidious vocabulary and an elegantly sarcastic tone. "My good man, I scarcely mean to imply that *all* your meat is inferior," she said once over the telephone to the butcher, "but the cut you have sent me is *effroyable*," pronouncing the "effroy" to rhyme with "cloy."

Betty, after a moment's silence, inquired of the cook, "Maudie, when you got your boys, did they come right off the cake of ice or were they down on the shelves underneath?"

"Honey, I never got my boys that way. I got 'em like the cows git calves."

The little girl was startled. The Beelers had used dogs for illustration. She had believed that they were insulting her parents and indirectly calling them liars by stating as fact something contradictory to what she had been taught. Now she was disturbed in her ivory tower to find Maudie, an old woman and a mother, addicted to the same heresy. She asked for a fuller explanation.

"Well," Maudie began, "I ain't saying it's the same with everybody. Maybe we just tackle it this here way in Idaho." She talked with an impersonal candor as Betty's lips began to tremble and tears to falter from her eyes. When Maudie finished, "And I think it's a mighty shame you never knew about it before. Why, dearie, my boy Horace went to his first bulling when he was four years old," Betty burst into sobs and buried her face in the woman's bosom. "It spoils everything!" she cried. *"Everything!"*

"Now looky here," said Maudie, "you just quit that favoring yourself. Do you see Sonie Marburg bawling?"

But Betty sobbed on and on until finally she drooped with fatigue and Maudie carried her upstairs to bed.

The telephone did not ring that night, and it was only the next day that we learned what had happened. Dr. Brunson came back to Chichester and, harried, cruelly disappointed, he made no allowances for Betty's innocence, but announced forthrightly that the baby had been stillborn. A week or so later, Mrs. Brunson came home from the hospital and, quarrelsome in her convalescence, she discharged Maudie with the declaration, "This is an upper-class household, my good woman, and here we do not discuss certain facts, or, to put it in plain English, sex." But she was obliged to re-hire her when she could find no other cook. She made neither an explanation nor an apology to Betty; moreover, Dr. Brunson decided at the last moment that he could not take her with him to New York to buy the new automobile, and on her birthday she sat in the kitchen on the high green stool with Maudie and me, blowing out the candles and wistfully beseeching me to share my mother's baby with her.

# CHAPTER FOUR

I had grown stiff from kneeling on the floor of the shop, my head pressed against the splintery work-bench. My hands were blue with cold for the fire in the monkey stove which I had built earlier had died. I must have been there a very long time. It was still some hours before dawn when my mother had jostled my arm and told me to run for Mrs. Henderson and now, from the looks of the shadows, it must be nearly noon. I had alternated a game of Patience with a prayer all morning long, for Mrs. Henderson, a pious woman, had enjoined me to implore of God my mother's safe delivery, and she must have known my mother very well for she had added that I should pray also that the baby be a girl. Now and then I had made a plea for myself, asking for the fulfillment of the wish I now wished every evening on the first star: "Let me go live on Pinckney Street." From time to time, carried away with speculations on the *décor* of Miss Pride's sitting room, I quit my devotions and went to the window, pretending that I saw there not the bay but the Charles River and that the ungainly dories were the sculls of Harvard crews whose existence I had learned of through Betty.

Hopestill Mather's slippers were where I had put them on the day my father disappeared: one, soiled now to a greenish gray, sat forlornly in the corner while the other was pinned to the work table. Miss Pride had written about them. I had opened the letter, addressed to "Hermann Marburg, Esq.," and read her request that the slippers be sent at once and that my father begin to make her a pair of "stout brown walking shoes." She expressed her surprise that my father was doing his work with less than his usual speed, but went on to say that his tardiness would be of no consequence if only the slippers were delivered on such and such a date. I assumed that on that day, a month before Christmas, Hopestill Mather would be going to a party. Several times I made an attempt to write to Miss Pride, explaining why they would never arrive, but I tore up each letter when I had finished it, and it was only after a second and much sharper note came from Pinckney Street that I at last sent off my apologies: "My father," I wrote, "has gone west and will never come back to Chichester again. He went to Cheyenne, Wyoming, to his cattle ranch. I am sorry about the dancing slippers, but he never finished them before he left and he said for me to tell you that he was sorry. He would have written you himself but at the last minute he had so much business to attend to that he did not have time. Yours truly, Sonia Marburg." A reply came by the return mail: "My dear Sonia: It was very thoughtful of you to write to me. I regret that your father has left Massachusetts. With best wishes, sincerely yours, Lucy Pride."

Even though the envelope had been addressed to me and this was the first letter I had ever received in my life, and even though its author was the one person whom I had never dared dream would write to me, I had been disquieted by it. It was not the brevity that disappointed me so much as it was the finality which was twofold in its implication: it told me that my father would never return (when I had written the word "never" to her, I had only half believed in it) and that now he was gone, she would have no further business with our household. And still, though her meaning was so clear it made my heart ache, so old and habitual were my aspirations that I did not cease to plan my life with her on Pinckney Street. And now, as I was awaiting the birth of my mother's baby, I was so far removed from the present time and Chichester that each moment of delay was a moment of bliss. A sound recalled me: I was still in tatters, the room was the reeking shack, the March wind through the cracks of the walls had set my teeth to clattering. Someone was tapping on the window and I turned.

"Come along, child, open the door!" It was Mrs. Henderson's sister from Marblehead who was visiting in Chichester that day. I unbolted the door and met her greedy face which nosed into mine, seeking my feelings. "Is it a girl?" I asked.

"It's not anything yet, sweetie, but it will be one or the other in a minute and your mother wants you there."

"I'll wait till it happens and then I'll come in," I said.

"No, you come along with me now. She's carrying on bad and wants you near."

Indeed, I could hear her carrying on, and while my feet were wooden, I knew at the same time that something must be done to hush her, and so I followed slowly, deliberately shutting off from my mind what was taking place in the house and instead calculating the number of steps from the shop to the back door. There were thirty-seven. I had never failed to count them when I went to the shop or when I returned and I never failed to forget how many there were.

Mrs. Henderson's sister ran her fingers through my hair as I opened the screen door for her. "How old are you?" she asked me. I told her that I was twelve. "Such pretty hair!" she said, but her face said, "To go through this and only twelve years old!"

The air in the kitchen was solid with heat and even the March cold we brought in with us was immediately absorbed. The stove raged and the ebullient pots danced on the iron lids; roasted and sealed into the atmosphere was the smell of carbolic acid and, I thought, of yeast. Seeking the sources of the odors, I saw in the wide window-ledge, beside the geraniums, a shallow bowl over the sides of which swelled an unbaked loaf of bread, and I wondered vaguely which of the two ladies had left my mother's side to make it.

The house was suddenly quiet. The door to the bedroom was closed, and beyond it I could hear nothing save the rustle of cloth and a splash of water. Mrs. Henderson's sister, her finger upon her lips, motioned me to the door, but I told her, "I'll go if she calls." The woman, who was not at all like her sister but was small and pretty and wore a velvety brown mole on her cheek like a beauty mark, hesitated and asked me if I were hungry. When I said I was not, she suggested that we play "Twenty Questions." I replied that I would rather just sit and wait. She felt then that she had done her duty and, relieved, hurried into the bedroom and its fascinating business.

My mother did not call for me, but now and then in the long hour when the obese and sweating dough held my gaze and my thoughts never came to life but labored futilely, I heard her groan and heard Mrs. Henderson speak kindly to her as she persuaded the child from its hull. Both the ladies had said to me when they arrived separately in the morning that they loved nothing so much as a tiny baby. I thought of Mrs. Brunson who still kept to her bed. Her pudgy fingers were always quarreling in a box of chocolate creams, trying to find one "fit to eat. My Gawd!" Now Betty, who had set her hopes on a baby, must content herself with her father's Packard sedan, with presents he had brought her from New York: a fire-opal ring, an angora cape, a rock garden in a glass sphere. For the least of these, I would have traded my mother's baby.

At last I heard the cry of a child, and I sprang to my feet. Mrs. Henderson was intently slapping the skinny backside of the wailing baby boy who looked like a brick-red fish and nothing human. His black hair did not grow from his skull but lay close like a mat pasted on, and his poor head which seemed all out of shape, curiously dented and noded, lolled over the midwife's wrist as though his neck had been wrung. When he was bathed and oiled and swaddled in a blanket, Mrs. Henderson carried him to the bedside and with a scoop of the blanket, framed the pitiful face from whose crimson mouth issued a ceaseless protest. My mother turned away with a groan. "Oh, take it away! Oh, leave me be!"

The neighbor woman, her kindly mouth half open with anxiety and surprise, whispered to her sister, "Poor dear, she's all worn out. Look, would you, he has his mother's hair and eyes," and she turned her bundle to me. I could see no eyes among the furrows of the ancient, vociferous face. But I pitied the improbable thing and against my will felt drawn toward it and asked if I might see its hands and feet, for I wondered if they, like the useless bud of a nose, had been executed as amateurishly. Indeed, no! Several authors had collaborated on the composition of this creature. The novice hand that had created the nose which possessed only one property common to noses, that is, two large nostrils, had not been the same one which, with so grim and un-Christian a humor, had made the long, prehensile feet with all five toes the same length, flexing and straightening as though a jungle vine to swing on were just outside their reach.

"Somebody's pleased with her little brother, that's not hard to see," said Mrs. Henderson's sister with a giggle as she held out a finger for the gruesome foot to grip. Brother! I felt with this prodigy only the most general fraternity: we breathed and were flesh. And yet, immediately the words were out, a leaven commenced to resolve my wonder into the emotion the woman had assumed in me and my pity became protective. Almost as soon as my instinct to mother him matured, there came to me the more complicated feeling of love, so that I longed to hold him myself and to kiss his bawling, cockled face, and to bestow upon him all the tender services that were the right of anything so supremely helpless.

He was, said Mrs. Henderson to her sister, a "puny one," and the sister, feeling his feet and skinny legs, agreed, although she said she had seen punier. My mother, who lay with her eyes closed, scarcely moved her lips when she said, "If it's true he's puny like you say, maybe he won't live forever."

The midwife cried, "Oh, perhaps he's a little small, but he's healthy as you please. Just look at these fine hands and feet. Why, he has lovely bones, Mrs. Marburg!" But my mother had no wish to feel her son's well-shaped feet. Her hands curled as though protecting themselves from contact with the baby and only when he was taken from the room did her long, scarred fingers lie straight upon the coverlet.

Thinking she would fall asleep, I started to follow the women into the kitchen, but she called me back, piteously begging me not to leave her, and when I had gone to the bedside, she grasped my hand and would not let it go. From under the lids of her still closed eyes, a few tears seeped out. I was shocked at the sight of them and felt my throat grow thick.

"Come closer," she said softly. "I want to tell you something and I don't want the ladies to hear." I knelt at the side of the bed and she put her lips to my ear. "You're only a little girl," she whispered, "but you're not too little to learn something. Your papa won't come back now because somebody has taken his place. Listen to me: he prayed for a boy!"

"Oh, Mamma!" I cried. "It's just a little baby!"

The poor red parcel wailed in the kitchen and Mrs. Henderson cooed, "There, there. Isn't it a squirmer though!"

"Everybody's a baby once, darling," continued my mother. "That

90

don't mean they don't get cruel by and by. I'm afraid of it, Sonia!"

But there was fear neither in her face nor in her voice as she lay back upon her pillows. I stood up. "Can't I open a window, Mamma?" I asked. "It's hot in here." It was not hot but it was close with a strange odor.

"Yes," she said with a sigh. "Open the window and let me get some air. Even though the sea air is bad for a person. I should live in the mountains."

I drew up the green blind, opened the window, and stood there breathing in the moist cold. The sun was bright as gold on the sand. My mother talked on. "There is nothing here but sand! In the mountains I would have a garden with melons and radishes and cucumbers. My God, I would have flowers! I love flowers, Sonia girl. Maybe you might buy me some? Fifty cents out of the golden egg wouldn't hurt, would it, to get your mother some *tsvetiki?*"

"I'll get you some," I said. "Maybe when Mr. Henderson goes to Marblehead he can bring them back. Is it violets you want, Mamma?"

"No, it's roses I want. Little yellow ones, Sonie." She stretched out her hands to me but withdrew them as I went to her. "Do you remember what was the name he said for a boy that night he left?"

I did remember. "Ivan."

"Yes, that was it. We'll call him that. Ivan." She pronounced it like a curse in order that without delay the child might shoulder the double burden of her hatred for him and her hatred for his father who had used the name to taunt her.

## 2

Until the Hotel Barstow opened and Miss Pride had come back and the Brunsons had gone to Provincetown, I was completely absorbed in my brother, and my daydreams of Boston came to me only at intervals. And still, though my love for him was so despotic that I could not imagine loving anyone else so much, I realized, the first time I saw Miss Pride at her regular place in the dining-room, that he had not, after all, won my whole heart. One of the waitresses had cut her finger, and I was sent in with the dessert, a bowl of canned peaches and a thin slice of chocolate cake. Miss Pride had been reading a letter but when I served her, she looked up.

"How d'you do, Sonia? Are you taking your mother's place to-day?"

"Yes, ma'am. I'll be here in her place all summer."

"Oh, indeed? Does she have other work?"

"No, ma'am. Mamma isn't very well this summer." Her eyes demanded the nature of my mother's illness, and I faltered, "She had a baby on the twenty-first of March."

"Mm." Then, as though she had given me as much time as she could spare, she turned again to her letter. I thought I had heard a note of disapproval in her voice and I regretted that I had not said my mother had broken her arm.

A few days later, she came into her room as I was dusting the bureau and, handing me a parcel wrapped in blue tissue paper, said, "I didn't know whether the baby was a boy or a girl, so I brought a little thing that would do for either." She left the room at once, before I had even time to thank her. My hands trembled as I untied the white satin ribbon around the little box. I was sure she had given Ivan a silver spoon. Instead, from a nest of white paper, I lifted out a bright yellow celluloid rattle made in the shape of a gourd. Still pasted to the neck was a sticker giving the name of a Marblehead novelty shop and the price, "15¢." My disappointment lay heavily on my heart until it was lightened by a remark my mother made when she looked at it. "Now that's what I call *lady*like," she said, shaking the rattle for her own amusement. "It shows she don't think we're poor or anyway she don't want us to know that she knows we're poor. If she had given us something useful, I would be mad." Mrs. Brunson, she went on to say, was not ladylike, because she frequently reminded me of my poverty by giving me Betty's out-grown dresses and sweaters. Until now I had not perceived the insult at the core of her generosity and had been only grateful. Mrs. Henderson, who was calling on my mother, eyed the rattle and said nothing. "Isn't that right, Mrs. Henderson?"

"I don't know but what it is, Mrs. Marburg," replied our neighbor in a voice of restraint. "As the saying is, it's not the gift but the spirit in which it is given."

During this summer of my thirteenth year, I was in the dining-room regularly, and because I often served Miss Pride's table and carefully attended whatever she said, I learned a great deal about her. I had been in the habit of thinking that she had come to the Hotel Barstow all her life, but I learned that a long time before she had spent every summer in Europe. Travel had left no mark upon her. When she spoke of France or Italy or Germany or England, it was to condemn the train service and the touts who "sprang out of the ground, especially in the Latin countries, selling everything regurgitated by the ocean and everything exported by the Japanese." She would say, "They hang too many pictures on one wall in the galleries. The Uffizi is a tiresome junk-shop." And I could see her marching through Europe without surprise, taken in by nothing.

Occasionally Miss Pride's lawyer, a Mr. Breckenridge, came to luncheon and I heard them talking of taxes and dividends. Once she said, "When you get back to town, I'd be obliged if you'd give Barton a ring and tell him I want to sell my Sears Roebuck. I'm going in for public utilities." I was deeply impressed by her State Street argot, a few phrases of which I had heard Dr. Brunson use to his friends. But Dr. Brunson could never have said, with such casual yet unfeigned interest, "By the way, what did the pound do in the Bourse yesterday?"

Even more than by her familiarity with high finance, I was stirred by her intellectual life. For years without fail, she had set aside two hours of each day, from eleven until one, when she sat erectly in a corner of the lobby reading *The Atlantic Monthly, Harper's Magazine,* and the novels of Trollope, Henry James, Thackeray, and William Dean Howells. When I was enchanted by a book and did not put it down for several hours together or when, in the winter time at school, I found myself in arithmetic lesson dreaming of being free to read, I was ashamed of my intemperance, remembering Miss Pride. I wondered if she would not be flattered if I dropped an intelligent remark now and again which would reveal that I had read what she had. Consequently I borrowed *The Awkward Age,* by Henry James, from the public library. The title appealed to me for I had heard Mrs. Henderson say of her daughter, Sarah, that she was at "the awkward age." After a tormenting evening of poring over the completely unintelligible sentences of the novel, I returned it early in the morning of the next day and I did not try again to read Miss Pride's favorite authors, but contented myself with attracting her attention in more modest ways. I made her a pen-wiper out of the top of a black cotton stocking and delivered it with a bunch of black-eyed Susans. She thanked me graciously. "You are very thoughtful," she said. "I will think of you every time I wipe my pen." Emboldened, I invited her to come see my little brother of whose appearance I was very proud, but she declined. "Some other day, my dear," she said. I never had the courage to ask her again, for I felt that she was not really interested in Ivan. I told her once that he had prickly heat. She shuddered. "Oh, mercy! How dreadful!" It had not seemed dreadful to me, but only uncomfortable for my little brother. Later on I realized that by "dreadful" she had meant "unattractive."

. I was pained that summer by an episode in which she figured. Gonzales' little boy, Emmanuel, had clever hands and often painted water colors of flowers and waves and bright blue birds, and this year he had begun to carve things out of soap. One day he came proudly into the kitchen with a little madonna he had made. Everyone marveled at the folds of her gown, the delicacy of her halo, and the perfection of her tiny, snubbed nose. Audrey, the headwaitress, said that the figure must be exhibited in the dining-room to the guests at luncheon. Emmanuel's protests were taken as modesty, and so that day, the little Virgin was passed around from table to table and was universally admired. At last it was placed before Miss Pride who examined it carefully and did not smile; with a frown of annoyance, she lifted it to her nose and sniffed. "This is my soap," she said sharply. A silence fell upon the dining room and Audrey blushed as Miss Pride handed the figure back and waved her away. Some days later, I heard Mrs. McKenzie tell Mrs. Prather that Gonzales had paid Miss Pride ten cents for the cake of soap his son had stolen from the box under her bed.

The old ladies, with whom Miss Pride never associated, gossiped about her incessantly when she was out of the Hotel, and it was through them that I heard tales of Hopestill Mather, so discrediting that they afforded me the greatest joy. Mrs. McKenzie had heard from the mother of one of Hopestill's schoolmates that she had so hot a temper not one of the mistresses could discipline her, that she deliberately chewed gum in chapel, had spoken of God as "the old boy," and of the Apostles as "the whole gang." Miss Pride, it was said, obviously had no affection for her and only tolerated her in the house during the brief vacations at Christmas and Easter. In the summer, she was sent to camp in Maine.

"I pity the little thing," said Mrs. McKenzie in a low voice. "It can't be a natural life, you know. I've heard that her father wasn't all he should have been. Bad blood shows up, try as you may to conceal it. But fancy the high-spirited child spending her holidays in that gloomy old house on Pinckney Street! As I understand it, she hasn't any other close relatives. The line is dying out, and I do believe our friend is the last of the Prides."

If I were Hopestill Mather, I would never permit my dear aunt to send me away to boarding school. I would prevail upon her to let me go to a day-school in the neighborhood so that I might sit across from her each day at tea and on certain nights have dinner with her. On Sunday I would go, dressed soberly like her, to church. After the service (and I supposed we would sit in her own hired pew) we would walk around the basin of the Charles, no matter what the weather was, and then would lunch together at a long table, being sparing of our helpings.

Occasionally I heard Miss Pride speak of her niece to friends who came to the Hotel. I recollect one conversation I heard when Mrs. Brooks, who had brought Hopestill to the Hotel some years before, had come to spend the night. Miss Pride said, "I sometimes wish I had never seen the child, Josie. Yesterday I had a most unfavorable letter from one of the counselors. She's a born trouble-maker, you know. What will she be at twenty? It's not only bravado—one can't begrudge a child a measure of that. It's a deep rebelliousness against everything fitting and proper."

"You exaggerate, Lucy," replied Mrs. Brooks. "You can't get her father out of your mind. Amy says all the girls like her. Isn't that the important thing, after all, at her age?"

"I don't believe Amy said that, Josie," said Miss Pride, peering deeply into her cousin's skull. "Did she now, truly? No, I won't make you answer, for I know what's what. But anyhow, it's not what she does now that worries me, it is what she will do when she has, so to speak, reached the age of discretion. For I am as certain as I am that you are sitting here with me that with her it will be *in*discretion. The counselor wrote me that she had been caught smoking. At fifteen, Josie! And that she had tried to run off from camp in a baker's truck. I won't have you telling me that these are only a child's pranks. There is something loose in her character. Her holiday tantrums are blood-curdling! If she were not a child, she would have apoplexy, I'm quite sure—her face turns as blue as the sky."

Mrs. Brooks stretched out a consoling hand. "Lucy, you will never change. We can't all have your self-control, my dear! Why, Amy, your affectionate Amy Brooks, has her temper too. It's Hope's lovely red hair, as the superstition goes. But don't suppose I don't sympathize with you."

"I must confess her hair endears her to me."

"It should. She looks more like you every year."

As I was removing the plates, Miss Pride said, "By the way, Josie, remind me to show you the pen-wiper this child made for me. Isn't she clever to be a chambermaid and seamstress when she's only thirteen?"

Mrs. Brooks smiled at me and I noticed that her left eye twitched as she did so. "I should say! I expect my Amy and your Hope could learn a great many useful things from her. Is your father a fisherman?"

"Her father is a *fuyard*," said Miss Pride. She explained to me that she had told Mrs. Brooks that my father was a cobbler and added, "You don't know French, do you, Sonie? It's German you know, isn't it?"

"Yes, ma'am. In German it's *Schuhmacher*."

Whether Miss Pride appreciated my pen-wiper or whether she compared me, to my advantage, to her niece, I could not tell, but at any rate, she was increasingly cordial to me that summer. She sent me on errands to her room when she was waiting for Mac or settling down to her reading in the lobby. "Run upstairs and bring me a handkerchief, my dear," she would say, and the "my dear" or "my good child" made me think my case was not an altogether hopeless one. And when she left in September, she gave me a sealing wax kit in token of her approval of the way I made her bed. The wax was rather old and did not go on smoothly and the "S" of the seal was backwards. But I did not care. On the fly-leaf of each of my school books I dripped the blood-red taper and impressed my initials in the molten mound. So that just as each time Miss Pride wiped her pen she remembered me, I remembered her whenever I opened a book.

## 3

My brother Ivan would have granted my mother's wish and died soon after his birth if it had not been for the constant ministrations of Mrs. Henderson, who was both a generous and a sharp-eyed woman. If her attitude had been preponderantly the first when the baby was born, it was the second that for five winters and summers kept her in daily communication with our household. For she was one of those people we call "good." There was in her not the impulse to intrude, but to embrace, not to scatter kindness but to mend with it, and to do so not in the light of this or that principle, but because love was her nature. Mrs. Henderson's reputation was widespread in Chichester and had even reached the Hotel Barstow. Once, in the third summer of Ivan's life, I heard Mrs. Prather saying to a young relative, "I'm far more tolerant of the Catholics than most of my friends, but I can't agree with them that everyone must go through Purgatory—oh, *I* shall, I'm a sinner, but I've known people so pure I'm certain it's the good Lord's intention they should go straight to Heaven."

The girl looked doubtful. "I don't believe you do know such a person—at any rate it can't be anyone I've ever seen in your house."

"No, she has never been in my house. But you know her if you've ever had any sewing or mending done when you've visited here. I mean Mrs. Henderson who lives on this road up about a quarter of a mile."

"Oh, yes, I've been there. But how do you know? Surely you haven't struck up a friendship with her!"

"There was no need. Her goodness is as plain as the nose on your face." And she went on to describe the serene household, equipped with children whose manners imitated their mother's and with a husband who, whatever he might be outside the house, behaved in that atmosphere as commendably as one of his own children.

The girl was still unsatisfied. "You have given me no proof. What has your seamstress *done?*" There was a silence. Mrs. Henderson's advocate could not publish the chief reason for her immediate assumption into Heaven when I was near-by. But when, glancing back at the table from another part of the dining-room where my duties had carried me, I needed not to hear the words issuing so eagerly from her lips: she was, I knew, recounting our "story."

No doubt Mrs. Prather, who was a sentimental woman, exaggerated our benefactress's virtues. Mrs. Henderson was a "natural" and was to be envied and respected as are all people to whom being good seems the easiest part of life. A more sensitive person, one more dedicated to *doing* good, would have had, as I believe she did not, periods of despair at my mother's indifference to her services, Ivan's malicious ingratitude, and my own mercurial humors. She was as patient and dependable as a devoted dog who suffers his master to pull his tail and play all kinds of humiliating tricks on him without once growing angry. If, finding her at our house on my return from school, I saw that her finger was bound up with court plaster, I did not learn from her what the injury was, but rather from Ivan who had done the mischief himself with his sharp little teeth while she was fitting a new suit of clothes on him. And when he planted himself in her path as she was crossing over to our house with a plate of hot food and cried some unpleasantness which he put in the slang he had learned from me and the Kadishes, calling her a "lousy drip" or a "crazy dope" or a "dumb bunny," she only chuckled and with her powerful hands set him aside like a hurdle made of tissue paper.

She dressed my brother in the clothes her own children had outgrown and cut them down, taking great pains to make them fit his puny body properly. In the early years, she had been his faithful nursemaid, had, when she was too busy and I was at work or at school, charged her eldest daughter, Sarah, with his care. Between them they had fed and bathed and aired him and taught him to walk and talk. If they had failed to teach him manners (as my mother accused them—she had long since forgotten that she had any responsibility towards him herself), it was not their fault. They had tried to make him learn to say "thank you" and "please" but since in his own home there was no occasion for such delicacy, they had been unsuccessful.

If Mrs. Henderson deplored my mother's apathy, she never revealed it. Indeed, she treated her much as she did Ivan, receiving with composure the most outrageous insults, the most preposterous complaints with which my mother besieged her. She had once, soon after Ivan was born, made an appeal to her: "It's not my business, Mrs. Marburg, but I was wondering if you couldn't get a place now. There are jobs to be had for the asking in Marblehead and Lynn."

My mother stared uncomprehendingly. "And may I ask what Sonie would do if I was gone all day long and nobody was here to have a piping hot dinner for her?" Mrs. Henderson, who knew that I always prepared our evening meal before I reported at the Brunsons' in the winter and at the Hotel in the summer, sighed. "The child worries me. She don't look strong. I've a good mind to put her on Josephine's tonic."

Even though, since there was a shortage of help, my mother had been offered a slight raise in salary at the Hotel, she steadfastly refused to go back. She spoke of her "disgrace" and said that she could never face respectable people again. "Respectable people" became, in time, all the world but Mrs. Henderson and myself. If another neighbor—Mrs. Kadish or Mrs. Radcliffe whose society she had heretofore enjoyed—came to call, she bolted the door and slipped into the bedroom where she stood trembling until the knocking stopped. But if she were surprised out of a daydream and looked up to find a caller outside the screen door, she put her finger to her lips and motioned towards the bedroom. "Sh! The child, he's sleeping." The visitor, who as likely as not had seen Sarah Henderson sitting with the baby on the beach, put down her offering—a pot of soup or a bowl of pudding—and smiled and went away and finally, wiser after a few more rebuffs, did not come back.

Although my mother had never particularly liked her neighbors and had rarely returned calls, she had always had sufficient relations with the women of Chichester to remain something like them, and had gone abroad enough to realize that the world was larger than her

99

kitchen. Her walks now became shorter. She no longer, in the summer evenings, sat on the little step beside the door, star-gazing and dreaming of Moscow. Nothing would have induced her to go to the village, for she was afraid of being ridiculed. Once, when a Fuller brush man came and offered to give her, without charge, a toothbrush with black bristles, she believed that the whole community, in the person of this representative, was teasing her for not brushing her teeth. Thereafter, when peddlers came, she pretended to be a deafmute and gesticulated at them with a look of hopeless regret on her dreamy face. Her voluntary imprisonment gradually became complete, and for four years, after my brother's first birthday, she never crossed the sill of our door, save on a series of winter evenings in the last of those years.

One day, when my brother was about three, Mrs. Henderson came to sit awhile and as she sat, worked at some embroidery for a table runner. It represented a green straw basket from which radiated a bouquet of larkspur and daisies of unlikely colors, these being the satellites to a rose, three times their stature and as big as a plate in diameter. In the void of muslin on all sides of the design, single pansies, petunias, and bachelor's buttons came fortuitously to life under Mrs. Henderson's needle. My mother watched, entranced, and as the neighbor filled in a petunia's corolla, she bent over the work excitedly. "Oh, how magical!" she cried. "Could I ever make those beautiful posies?" Mrs. Henderson assured her that she could, and laying aside her table runner, she took up a piece of plain cloth and gave my mother a lesson in the elementals of fancy-work, demonstrating the "lazy daisy" and the French knot and the feather-stitch. My mother was impatient to try her own hand and when she had finally got a needle threaded and her hoops fitted together, began to copy the stitches. They came out all askew and unrelated; her French knots were rough burls and her draggle-tailed lazy daisies exposed their unkempt framework which should have been on the underside. But she was not in the least disheartened and long after Mrs. Henderson had gone, she continued to practice, admonishing herself, "Ah, Shura, you're clumsy. All thumbs and butter fingers."

The following morning, I found she had got up hours before me, had had her breakfast, and had even washed her dishes and now was back at work on her embroidery. I was sure she would be tired of it by afternoon, but as it turned out, I quite underestimated my mother's patience with herself. From that day onward she stuck to her late calling with the tenacity, the absorption, and the humility of an artist. When I could not buy cloth for her to embellish, she set to work on her own petticoat or on my winter underdrawers or on the kitchen curtains. Once, being without anything at all and having a great urge to execute some oak leaves and acorns, she ripped open one of our pillows, letting the feathers fly where they would, with the result that for weeks we inhaled down. The ticking, when it was re-stuffed, was still so roomy that what feathers I had salvaged assembled at one end or the other but never spread out evenly. She was so proud of the leaves and acorns which were, to be sure, done in remarkable verisimilitude but interested me less than almost any other of her creations, that she made a new pillow cover to protect them which had the same design, and as it turned out well—better, she felt, than the original—it too required a protector, also bearing the same design, and so on, until it appeared that our pillow was to have as many skins as an onion. And no doubt it would have if Mrs. Henderson had not providentially given us for Christmas a very elaborate pillow case, adorned with hollyhocks, which my mother felt was just the thing to cover all her precious acorns. She would gaze at the pillow and say, "You would never guess what's underneath!"

I thought that her activity should be functional and once suggested that we try to sell some of her work. She greeted the proposal with surprise but acquiesced and pulled out from under the bed one of the boxes that had contained skis and was now used as her treasure chest. She could not make a choice: this was the only spray of lilac she had ever made, that was her most successful poplar tree, the dish towel half-covered with a cerise posy had been made in honor of my birthday. She could not part with anything. As our house was becoming overcrowded with her heaps of decorated rags, I at length persuaded her to use the shop as a storeroom, and finding that once the things were out of sight she forgot about them, I advertised them at the Hotel the next summer among the help. Though I realized no money, I sometimes had the luck to exchange a pin-cushion bearing a Russian monogram in cross-stitch for a dozen eggs or a pot-holder in the form of a purple rooster for a pat of butter or a pair of old shoes. Some of her work I still have: a flour sack, smocked in scarlet silk which she gave me one Christmas. She could assign to it no purpose but said she knew I would like "the red." When this poor thing, its banal legend GOLDEN GRAIN showing through the smocking as G L D E R I N , turns up as I straighten my bureau drawers, Chichester's long winters return, sprouting their evergreen leaves and everlasting flowers in the snow and the wind.

After the first rapture of fancy-work had spent itself and she merely burned with a steady, sober flame which only now and again flared forth, as in the case of the oak leaves, she found several supplementary diversions which never lasted but which she undertook when she had nothing to embroider. Thus, on four evenings running one winter, I was commissioned to take dictation from her. I wrote long lists of all manner of things: the names of the guests at the Hotel as far back as she could remember, the nations of the world, kinds of flowers and fruit and fish, the days of the week, and the months of the year. And as she dictated, she drew from memory the designs she had worked in her colored thread, covering page after page of a composition book with likenesses of cosmos and bumblebees. She complained that her memory was bad and she wanted the names of things preserved for her. Even though she could not read my lists, the very paper was reassuring; looking at it, she said, she knew that she had the key to things, even though she could not find the door.

During the same winter that she employed me as amanuensis, she fell one day to musing on the wicker furniture on the Hotel porch, one piece of which, a rocking chair, had been given us by the manager when it had reached a state of total dilapidation. It was quite useless, but Mamma had dressed it up with a cushion and a tidy each saying "Hotel Barstow" which I had lettered for her and which she had filled in with lavender feather-stitching on yellow Indianhead. She inquired of me if the Hotel chairs were ever cleaned and when I told her I doubted it, at least that I had never been told to do anything with them except to move them into the sun or out of it, she was scandalized. Who knew but what that Mrs. McKenzie, who was always nibbling, had lodged an apple core or nutshells between the cushion and the frame? She began to explore the crevices of our rocking chair with a hairpin and brought up a quantity of lint and poked out to the floor a good deal of fine sand.

"There!" she cried triumphantly. "What did I tell you?"

All day she worked at the chair and when I came home from the Brunsons' that evening, I found a shocking monument of dirt on the floor which she had patiently dislodged. She was wearing a coat and a scarf on her head and she told me that she had a little business to attend to, would I accompany her and be so good as to find some candles? Since she was, I saw, bent on going and bent also on not divulging where or why or for how long, I agreed, and took Ivan to Mrs. Henderson's where he directly disrupted the tranquillity of the house with his evil howls, clinging to me as though I were the last familiar spar in that sea of piety and kindness. He bit my leg, at once to declare his ownership and his dependence. One of the little girls, Josephine, offered him a cookie which he threw to the floor in a fury. Unruffled, she picked it up and tried him with a balloon which pleased him slightly. "Now, then, aren't you ashamed of yourself!" I said and shook him by the elbow. But Mrs. Henderson pulled my brother to her and said soothingly, "Now you run along, Sonie. He's my boy for the evening. It wasn't a nice cookie and he had the good sense to see that."

It was a fine, cold night with surfaces that split under our feet and a bare sky furnished only with a few stark stars and an austere moon that pitched, in a thousand elliptical and gouty travesties of itself, amongst the waves and whose light resurrected from the shadows shafts of earth and the roofs of sheds and exposed completely a steep incline to the water which seemed, so regular it was, to have been paved by hand with smooth, round stones. We took the road that led to the Hotel and walked fast because of the cold. My mother, companionably holding me by the hand, walked erect and seemed herself, herself of days so long ago that now they had all but slipped from memory since there was so little in her now out of which to construct her as she had been.

It was the first time in years that we had gone out together and it was this phenomenon, coupled with the vigor of her movement and vivacity of her talk about most trifling matters of the village, and the inexplicable joy in her face, that unburied for me a Christmas Eve when I was four or five years old. My parents took me to a pageant in the Sunday School rooms of the Methodist church on such a night as this. Part of the way I walked between them and part of the way my father carried me, grumbling that I was too heavy. The Christmas tree was as tall as the room and topped by a sugary star, and onto its branches had been grafted incongruous fruits: crimson bulbs and asbestos peaches and tongueless bells, all floured with snow and illumined with a hundred candles whose flames tossed whenever the door opened and closed. The people sang carols, so simple and loud that I could catch all the words, and my father, in a great tuneless voice, roared out the German to the ones he knew. Each child was given a popcorn ball and a glazed apple by a masked and padded Santa Claus. I was terrified, when I received my presents, to see, between his glove and cuff half an inch of black skin! I told Rosalie Kadish the next day and she, after conferring with her brother Nathan, informed me that underneath his fine red suit, Santa Claus was the pastor's Negro chauffeur.

All the way home from the party, my mother and father drowned the sound of the waves with Russian and German songs, interrupting one another and seeming to me, who rested half asleep against my father's shoulder, more talented than birds, for their repertoire was endless and their voices were the loudest I had ever heard. I could scarcely keep my eyes open, but I refused to be tucked into my pallet and sat in the kitchen while they drank spiced wine that simmered on the stove, giving off a fragrant steam from cloves and sticks of cinnamon. A slice of lemon floated in their glasses. My mother blew on her glass to cool it and my father suddenly seized her hand. "I wish we were on the boat again, don't you?" My mother laughed and flirted at him with her black eyes. "Go on!" she said. My father mouthed at her the words "I love you," and then they looked at me and smiled. "The sandman's got a certain party," said Mamma. I stumbled, dizzy with sleep, into the bedroom and swayed as my mother took off my clothes. When I was buried under the comforters and coats, they both knelt down beside me, their arms entwined. The sweet odor of the mulled wine was heavy on their breath. The last thing I recalled was my father turning to kiss my mother on the mouth as though their love had been refreshed by the songs, by the wine, and by the sight of me, their child, going to sleep.

My brother would never have so pleasing a recollection as this. I had tried to amuse him with the games my father played with me, but he was bored with Esel von Hexensee, and he detested Fritzie. If I read him a story, he would stamp his foot suddenly, stick his fingers in his ears and scream, "Shut *up!* I hate *Black Beauty!*" On rare occasions, if I brought him a stick of chewing gum or a jaw-breaker, he rewarded me with a pinched, reluctant smile, but an hour later, for no reason, would slip up behind me and give my hair a savage pull. He was so horrid and perverse and unresponsive that I think I should have lost my patience and whipped him if I had not known from experience and from Mrs. Henderson's tactful advice, that if I allowed my mother to see that he tormented me, her hatred would be dangerously magnified. Consequently, I suffered him to pinch and bite and scratch me, laughing if I could.

As I felt my mother's warm hand in mine, I was perplexed by the change that had come over her in the years since that happy Christmas Eve. Tonight, I found her lovable as she had been then, and as I had not found her for a long time. Each time I made a resolve to dedicate myself to loving her and making her happy, I was at once disheartened by the apathy in which I found her or, instead, by the senseless, fussy affection in which she buried me. These wards of mine were incorrigible. In both of them, the rare moments of joy and sanguine temper which I so greatly wished to protract forever, were accidental, and no matter what new order I introduced into our life, it would still be some short-lived genius of disorder that would galvanize them. Thus, for a week together, I might bring a new toy or sack of goodies each day to Ivan, sent by Maudie or Mrs. Brunson, and he would hate them all. Yet he would discover in my coat pocket a Luden's cough drop, fuzzy with lint. His eyes would dance with pleasure as he held it up to the light. "Let me have it, Sonie!" he would plead.

We were approaching the Hotel and my mother quickened her pace until she was nearly running. Reaching the porch, she went up the stairs two at a time. Then she held out her hands to me. "Why, they're not here, Sonie!" she cried. "Not one of them!"

"What aren't here?"

"The chairs, darling, all the dirty wicker chairs!"

"They're inside, in the lobby. They aren't left out during the winter, Mamma, you goose. Why, the rain and snow would ruin them."

"I suppose," she said sadly. "And I had looked forward so much . . ." She was peering through a crack in the boarding of the main door. "I can't see a thing," she said. "I don't believe they're in there." But another survey of the veranda convinced her that they were not outside. "Well, then," she went on, "the only thing to do is go in. A pretty pickle of fish."

I was about to object. My mother's absurd business might, if it were found out, cost me my job. How could we force a way into the Hotel without leaving traces? And would it not be guessed immediately that only crazy Mrs. Marburg would do such a thing, in the dead of winter, when even the most naïve burglar would realize that there would be slim pickings there? But I did not object, because I was curious about the way the Hotel looked, and had many times thought of doing just this myself, in those nights when my father was still with us, and most particularly the night he left. There was in my mother such a buoyancy, even after her first disappointment, that I was affected by it. We set about to find some entrance and at the back discovered a window with loose boards that yielded easily, and when we had rattled the frame awhile, we pushed it up and climbed inside the outer kitchen.

While from the outside, the building appeared impenetrable to light or air, within, drafts and moonlight, admitted through cracks, were everywhere. The old coal range, mammoth under a silvery hood, was lighted with a lackluster glow and it seemed, from the broken pane of its isinglass window and from the rim of its lids and its half-open damper, to expel cold air like needle-fine projectiles as we passed by. In the dining-room, the faithful birds stood obscurely behind their moonlit glass, waiting patiently through the long winter for the diners who, slowly through the years, had come to resemble them. Here was the owl that hung above the table where sat Mrs. Thompson, an obese, bedizened woman who had, in recent summers, abandoned her lorgnette as being both troublesome and ineffectual since she was half blind and vanity could hold out no longer. Now, upon her raptorial nose, she wore tremendous tortoise-shell glasses which, combined with the feathery, touched-up curls that beset her cheeks and the boned neck-piece of tawny lace that upheld her jowls, made her so like the staring owl above her that it would not have seemed altogether odd to hear a duet of solemn hoots proceeding from that corner of the room. And no less like her bird was Mrs. Holman whose table was beneath a blue heron, for she was lengthy and slim and she dressed in faded blue or gray; she swooped her graceful wings downward for the salt cellar or upward to arrest a slipping hairpin, as though she were always about to alight or about to fly off. Mrs. Prather, whose minute head, untidy as a nest, was an impudent joke upon her spreading, pyramidal body, was as ludicrous as her benumbed ptarmigan. Providentially, Miss Pride's table was in the center of the room and there was no feathered cartoon of her above her head.

There in the lobby crouched the chairs, their laps obliterated by diaphanous shouds of muslin. The covers of the round tables hung to the floor like skirts; I knew that the square humps atop the tables were the photograph albums and the paper weights in whose glass interiors were embedded pictures of a Sequoia redwood through which a man could walk, or a photogenic waterfall beneath an emerald sky, or a burro whose mouth released a balloon to hold the words: "Hee-haw! Howdy, Folks! You're looking at a Rocky Mountain Canary."

Our candles gave a gelid animation to the unshifting moonlight. The glass eyes of an antelope glinted darkly at us from above the desk and the shadow of the newel post on the main stairway swelled upon the wall like a jinn. My mother at once set to work. She uncovered a chair and set two candles on a cherry-wood milking stool, making stands of drippings. Her tools were a paring knife, a hairpin, and an awl from the shop. She was as intent as a surgeon. I watched her for a few minutes until she complained that I made her nervous and as the light was poor enough anyhow, she did not want my shadow interfering. "Run and play, sweetheart," she said. "You've made my hairpin slip through and now it's caught in a crack. Go away, do."

I glanced around, wondering if there had ever been a child who could obey her command, "Run and play," with any joy and frolic through this chilly company of ghosts without a backward glance. I lighted the third candle and proceeded to the stairway. My mother did not look up; she was humming faintly an old tune she had used to sing to me long ago.

Miss Pride's room was utterly bare. Even the mattress had been taken away and the skeleton of the bed rattled tinnily as I crossed the creaking floor. Its rug gone and its windows stripped, its cushions removed from its bare bones, the room was like a fowl plucked clean. There was no aperture in the boarding at the windows big enough for me to look through towards Boston, and in my disappointment, I tore at the wood and filled my fingers with splinters. The gesture was one almost of panic though my feeling had been disproportionate to it, but because my hands were so furious, I abruptly plunged into a welter of introspection, a train of incoherent moods. I had not thus indulged myself for a long time, for the simple reason that I had been too busy balancing my brother's humors to observe any lack in my own equilibrium.

Now, in her appalling summer room, my old longing to live with Miss Pride was revived in so weakening a way that I sank to my knees before the wooden barriers, feeling my face grow warm in spite of the cold and my eyes swell with tears that did not fall but clung to my lids. And when this first pain had gone—like the pain of a lover who visits an old rendezvous without his beloved—I dully recovered myself. The only gain there could possibly have been in this bizarre trip to the Hotel was a return of the joyous feelings I had had in the summer when I looked out these windows. And I had, without fully realizing it, expected an altogether novel sensation in seeing the dark, moon-tracked water from this hiding-place. For, although the years had brought me new and sometimes strong infatuations, knowledge had not abused the dream of my childhood. My perspective of all else might have changed, but Miss Pride and Miss Pride's room had remained unaltered, so that even now, when I was no longer a child, I had often in the summertime been healed of my anxieties over Ivan and Mamma the moment I stepped across the threshold of the room.

But tonight, in this cold nakedness, I was cheated out of my solace for I could not, with my eyes, burn a way to her in Boston. The uproar in me was brought on partly by the discrepancy between the placid vagary that was holding my mother's attention downstairs and my own tempestuous one upstairs, for, although they were equally profitless, mine had a kind of direction, and it seemed consistent with my bad luck that she was happy while I was so miserable, that she could sustain herself indefinitely on follies and unreal pageants and old woes. And my suffering was augmented when I reminded myself that I was nearly eighteen years old and in my last year of high-school and that the unplanned future was like a jumping-off place which I rapidly approached. My classmates talked confidently of college or business school or marriage and in all their talk, there was an implication that whatever they did, they would do it away from Chichester. The farther distant they set their next year's residence, the more unshakeable seemed their resolve so that I believed they would all be in Alabama or Oregon or New York and I alone would remain.

In truth, though, I had an indisposition towards all these careers. When I fumbled in my adolescent semi-sleep for what our teachers called "a way of life," there would come to me the image of Nathan Kadish who, of all the people I had ever known (excepting, of course, Miss Pride), commanded of me a profound respect. I had been in love with him for five years and all that time had carried with me a sharp recollection of the exact moment I had fallen in love, so that whenever I saw him, I could feel myself, a child, rise on tiptoe to look through the lighted window at his birthmark.

He had become, in his graceful, small-boned body and in his right profile, a coldly handsome boy. But because from one side he was beautiful, from the other, with its brilliant smear, he was more hideous even than he had been as a little boy. He had won a scholarship to Boston University where he was studying literature, but he came home for the week-ends and for holidays. Occasionally he came to call on me, late at night after my mother had gone to bed, and he talked to me with a grave, impersonal grandeur of his intellectual accomplishments.

In his Freshman year, in the first flush of rebellion against every thing he had heretofore known or longed for, he had been a member of the Communist Party and had always carried with him his membership card with the alias, Stanley Finn. He made it clear to me each time he came to call that he would not have come if he had had anything better to do; our economic system was such that he had no money, he said, to go to Marblehead to get drunk; obviously he could not endure the atmosphere of his house where all aspirations were bent towards the impedimenta of a bourgeois life, the Philco radio sets, the Frigidaires, the upholstered parlor suites. There was nothing in his conversation or in the complete indifference of his countenance to indicate that he in the least enjoyed my companionship. I listened patiently to him, understanding almost nothing of what he said. As he talked, he concealed his birthmark with his long hand. But presently he would forget. His fingers would reach for a cigarette in the pocket of his sporty checked jacket and I could see the exciting monstrosity of his left profile. Feeling that I could no longer listen to his monologue, I would suggest that we drink some coffee, and as I busied myself with the stove and the water, he would continue, unperturbed, to analyze the villainies of liberals, but I would pay no attention. Instead, I would nurse the thrilling, secret glimpse I had had of his peeled cheek. He would be saying, "I'll tell you what. If you ever come to Boston, I'll take you to a meeting of the Party. You may be our type, as a matter of fact, though I can't be sure. The most sensible laborer often turns out to be a solid individualist. Some members of the Party used to be rich; they *know* that bath tubs and evening clothes are decadent. The rest of us have to take it on faith, and of course we do. But witness the perversity of human nature: here I am, a crusader of the Revolution, and do you know that even I sometimes would like to get dressed up in tails and go to the Ritz roof? Of course if that ever did happen, I'd snap out of it in pretty short order. I imagine I wouldn't be able to take their guff and would flash my C.P. card and land up in jail."

In this year, Nathan had withdrawn from the Party although he repeatedly told me that he still upheld its principles and had only stopped going to meetings because he had other things to do. Now he fancied himself not as revolutionist but as a literary person of Paris. His resolve had been made shortly after an evening we had

*110*

spent together in my father's shop. He had asked if he might look at the books there, remembering from his boyhood that some handsome volumes had stood on the shelf above the door. He took down two, bound in red leather and heavily engraved with gold, and he said, "These are what he used to talk about. Your old man, I mean." They were *Wilhelm Meister* and *Werthers Leiden*. After that, whenever he came to see me, his manner was strangely gallant, his voice was softer, and he often used German words, uttering them with surpassing tenderness. He would go to the window and say, *"Ach, der Abendstern!"* Or he would fall into long, melancholy silences and occasionally would leave the house without a word.

Only the last Sunday he had brought me a book to read. It was called *Confessions of a Young Man*. I had not read much of it yet, but its effect on me was already marked, and I was anxious for the next week-end to come so that I might tell Nathan that I understood why it was he wanted to go to Paris. Shivering in the icy room, I thought of the book and wished that I were a young man, queer enough to keep a tame python, clever enough to educate myself at the Nouvelle Athènes where the painters and poets gathered nightly as a learned and bibulous academy. I thought how simple my actions would be if I were a great, confident pagan egoist like George Moore. Would I not, if I were a young man, leave Chichester and my foolish mother? But I was not fitted for such a life, not only because I was a girl, but because I was an ignoramus. I nearly cried aloud thinking of the sloth of all these past years that had prevented me from reading less than a tenth of what Nathan had read. Here, only two years older than I, he was a storehouse full of books. Even at my own game, he surpassed me, for he spoke and read German with twice my facility. To be educated was the privilege of our class, he had told me. That was the weapon whereby we could conquer the bourgeoisie. I did not know precisely what he meant. Whenever I dwelt upon his words, I could only imagine myself dazzling Miss Pride with my culture; I had no desire to overthrow her, only to make her welcome me.

All plans were as cold as my quaking shoulder-blades. I stood up and stamped awake a sleeping foot. Opening the door, I heard my mother caroling happily at her excavations. I called, "We've got to go now, Mamma. I'm nearly frozen."

"Why, we just got here, silly. I've only begun. Flap your arms."

When I went down, I found that she had finished one chair and was beginning on a magazine rack. She said, "If you'll help me, we'll get through faster. But it's not easy work and you're not used to it, so perhaps you'd better just sit there quiet and watch Mamma." She had, for years, spoken to me as if I were still ten years old. I watched her for a while. She had stopped singing and her lips were parted in concentration. Her eyes sparkled in the candlelight and when she withdrew a long, matted strand of lint she laughed for joy and cried, "Goody!" At last I could hold out no longer and begged for a hairpin. It was good fun and when I, too, extracted a rope of lint, I felt the same brief glow of achievement that I did when I won a game of Patience. But my enthusiasm for the business quickly died and I grumbled that I would leave Mamma alone there if she did not come home at once.

On the way back my mother enumerated the varieties of filth she had brought to light. She planned her schedule for the next night's work. With industry she believed she could finish all the chairs in less than a month. She found me quiet and suspected that I did not care. Very well, I needn't go back. She would go alone if I preferred to stay at home idling with that little black beast of a boy.

Knowing perfectly well how angry she would be if I did not mollify her, I still could not bring myself to speak. For after my fretting in Miss Pride's eviscerated room and after I had become disgusted with the explorations of my hairpin, I had concluded that my predominant feeling towards my mother was boredom. I was surprised because always before I had thought it was a mixture of rebelliousness and loyalty. I was suddenly impervious to her and did not care if she burst into tears and cried for days. I even smiled smugly in my brutal silence.

The pitch of her voice never changed, but its volume increased so that halfway between the Hotel and the Hendersons' house, she was howling abuses, not at me, for as always her madness showed its method, but at my father whose bad treatment had made me lazy, dull-witted, completely insensitive to important things. She railed to the wind for I steadfastly held my tongue. I was closer to my father because her racket had brought back those nights when she had quarreled with him. If I had broken my silence, it would have been to imitate his laugh, provoked by the devil that had taken up permanent residence in her and, anxious for a wider acquaintance, sought admission also to me.

From a little rise, we could see the Christmas tree alight in the village square, a bright triangular scar in the darkened town, and to me, a mockery of that other one, that charming, dressed-up fir whose needles' fragrance lingered still in my memory and seemed even to cling to my mother's hair as she spluttered beside me. She, too, saw the tree and stopped talking, ending a sentence with a smile. She touched my arm. "Now isn't that pretty?" she said. "It would make a nice Kodak picture."

"I was thinking I would get Ivan a Christmas tree, Mamma," I said. "Do you remember the one in the Sunday School rooms a long time ago?"

"That must have been when Hermann Marburg was still here. He used to pinch your little toes and I would tell him what a terrible thing it was to do but he would never stop."

My anger flared forth. "You mean *you* pinch Ivan's toes!" I cried.

"Sonie, you stop it. I don't know what's come over you. Did you ever *see* me pinch him?"

"Yes! No, oh, I don't know and I don't *care!*" I took her firmly by the elbow. "Look here, you've got to stop being mean to poor little Ivan. Do you hear?"

She did not answer but tried to wrest herself away and looked at me with widened, terrified eyes. "Damn you!" I cried. Because I had never cursed her before and the sensation was intoxicating, I repeated it twice until she, stricken speechless, loosed from my grasp, hurried on ahead of me. On the instant I saw her disappear from view I felt released from my responsibility to her and it occurred to me that if she were walking out of my range of vision forever, I would not have the slightest remorse.

Yet my emancipation vanished when I had reached the Henderson house. Ivan, being part and parcel of my duty towards her, required my care, and while it was too late to reform her, he was not yet damned. I must continue as before. Sarah Henderson opened the door for me. In her face, calm had been replaced by solemnity and the gesture she made of extending her hand and laying it upon mine, so gently I knew she meant me to be quiet, made me sense that disaster had befallen someone.

We entered and I saw my brother asleep on the leather sofa. At the first sight of him, I thought I had been mistaken at the door and Sarah had only intended me not to disturb his sleep. But then I saw the signature of agony in the blotches of red on his white cheeks and the blood on his lips, the saliva that bubbled up with each deep, sighing breath. The pose of his body was not like a child's but like an adult person's, drugged or unconscious. Simultaneously, I heard the voice of my heart consenting to the appeal of his collapsed flesh, and heard Mrs. Henderson telling me that he had been "seized" while he was playing. He had been in a temper that I was so slow in coming and had flung himself to the floor and kicked his heels, had been so convulsed in his rage that he was doubled up and frothing at the mouth and muttering all manner of strange things. Finally Mr. Henderson had gone for Dr. Galbraith and the doctor had said the child was epileptic.

"Will it happen again?" I asked Mrs. Henderson.

"Yes! Yes!" cried Sarah, beside herself, unmindful of her manners and of the charity in which she had been schooled by her mother. "You must take him away and never bring him here again! It's too awful!" And she ran from the room weeping. I was unnerved by the change in her and knew that what she had seen must truly have been "too awful" if it had disrupted her serenity.

Mrs. Henderson and I faced each other over the sleeping child. "If he's not excited, he won't have the fits. It's temper brings them on. Don't you mind Sarah."

Mr. Henderson, a small, sandy man, usually as easy-going as his wife, shifted his chair beside the fireplace and said, "Well, *I* mind Sarah and I mind my other children, and God save you, Sonie, but you mustn't let us see this again."

"Hush, Ross," said his wife. "Pity the poor girl and boy."

"I do! I do! Lord knows I do, but I'll do nothing more than that."

He pronounced the ultimatum without rancor, but I knew he

would never retract it. He kicked the hearth and commenced to pare an apple. A curl of red skin coiled into the coal scuttle and at last the globe of fruit was naked and white. He quartered it, leaned back, and began to eat, surveying his domain but never once permitting my brother and me to enter his ken. I stared at him with envy. There was a look of satisfaction in his stark, rusty face as though he were in command of his squads once again after an undisciplined excursion. His house, with its long-waisted, uncomfortable chairs, and the sturdy tables, more hewn than built, and the useful gimcracks—the basket for firewood, the cast-iron hearth accessories, a dun-colored cushion or two, a braided rug—the house and his sleeping children were like a standing army at its post, not hostile but prepared for hostilities, on guard at all times against intrusion. At a distance he might pity the enemy but he would fight to the death if they tried to impose their outlandish ways on his world.

He finished the apple and spat into the dying fire. "Well, tomorrow's another day," he said, and as though he shut a book, he closed his face for the night, locking in its changes of expression and its few words. Presently he left the room.

"I'm sorry," I said to Mrs. Henderson. I could think of nothing else.

She put her large arms about me. "There," she said. "You don't pay any attention. You pray, child."

# 4

For five successive nights my mother went alone to the Hotel and each time stayed past midnight. She did not know until the sixth day what had happened at the Hendersons', for Mr. Henderson and I had carried Ivan home after Mamma was asleep and in the morning, except for a clot of blood on his lip, he appeared normal. But on the sixth day, Sarah Henderson came to bring some bread to us while I was at school. Probably still under the influence of her terror and knowing too little of my mother's aversion to Ivan, she told the whole story and heightened some of the details. She was fascinated in spite of herself and was drawn to us with a morbid curiosity. If we met on the street, she paled and would have turned into the nearest shop to avoid me had she not longed to know the answer to the question she asked me each time, "Has he had another one yet?" Her myopic eyes behind rimless spectacles registered her disappointment when I told her no.

By evening of the day on which my mother first heard of Ivan's affliction, she was convinced that she had seen the fit and she described it to me in such accurate detail that I was half convinced myself. She told me how his face had turned purple and his eyes had started from his head and his voice had sounded strangled. There was a frightening eagerness in her face as she talked and when Ivan came in from the bedroom, she stretched out her arms to him and said, "Come, sweet baby boy, come, darling, come kiss your mother." Ivan stuck out his tongue and Mamma laughed as if nothing had ever pleased her half so much.

Later that evening I was studying my lessons and she was at work on a stamped bureau runner I had brought her from town in the hope that she would give up her sprees in the Hotel lobby. Ivan was quietly playing on the floor with a toy truck Mrs. Henderson had sent. Absorbed, I was not watching them, though now and again I was aware of them, for I would come to a word in *Macbeth* which I was obliged to look up in the glossary. The interruption caused my mind to slip back into the ordinary world and I looked up, taking in my surroundings with detachment. They constituted, with their other occupants, a prison escapable only through some such occupation as I was just now engaged in. My dog-eared book, bound in maroon cloth, bandaged with adhesive tape where it had been pulled apart by careless hands, was called *Literature and Life*. I had never fathomed the title.

It may have been a sound or it may have been intuition that made me turn and see my two companions hypnotically attached, their gazes joined, their large eyes directly focused and mirrored as though the reflection could burn through to the brain and destroy it, gazes of equal strength, age meaning nothing. Hatred and desperation freighted all the black eyes. But age gained. As I watched, Ivan screamed, throwing back his head which languished on its stem while his live mouth travailed in calling my name, "Sonie! Sonie!" He was purple when I reached him and gripped by a vise I could not pry apart. His teeth were clenched and his fists were clenched and his head, which the second before had been horribly agitated, was turned to one side as though fixed there forever. But before I had really taken in this petrifaction, he was violently released from it and his head, his arms, his eyelids, his legs twitched, and over his busy lips poured blood-stained foam such as I had seen drool from the jaws of the bull-dog that had killed my kitten.

"The beast!" shrieked my mother, and in her face and body, a sympathetic disquiet began, aping his, until she rose from her chair and went to the window where she stood sobbing with her forehead pressed against the glass.

He *was* a beast, the very repository of all bestiality, composed of filth and evil, as though his interior life, in the cavern of that rocking skull, were one of utter nastiness. In a moment, he passed into the third phase of the fit, a coma so profound that I might have thought him dead if I had not seen him like this at the Hendersons'. I carried him to the bedroom and put him on the army cot I had bought for him the year before. While I bathed his face, I heard the sobbing of my mother in the other room, like the sad cries of certain birds or the collision of breakers with the sand. I sat down on the floor beside the little boy, feeling no longer any disgust now that he was relaxed. In a little while my mother came in, bringing another lamp. She had unpinned her hair which rippled to her waist and glowed in the light and upon her face there was, as I saw so often, the beauty of a saint which flowers through the perpetual renewal of mercy.

"My God! What shall we do, Sonia?"

"He'll be all right in the morning," I said.

"Will he do it again?"

"He won't unless . . ." I was on the point of saying, "unless you scare him again," but I changed the syntax to the passive voice, "unless he's scared."

"But he wasn't scared tonight. How could he have been scared?" Her direct, innocent gaze did not prevent me from hearing the guile in her voice.

The next morning, before school, I took Ivan out to the shop on the pretext of giving him a present and I told him that if Mamma ever frightened him, he must run out of the house and either bolt himself into the shop or else walk down the beach and wait for me to come home from school. But he must not go to the Hendersons'.

"She don't scare me," he said sullenly. "*You* scare me, you lousy old girl," and he gave me a kick on the shin that made me wish to thrash him.

My warnings for a long time were useless. He remembered nothing of what had happened before the fit, but only that he fell asleep and awoke, inexplicably sick at the stomach, his lips and tongue sorely bitten. Gradually he began to attach these feelings to me, for I was always the first thing he saw when he came out of his coma, and he developed such a repugnance to me that when he saw me coming home in the afternoon, he hid under the bed, and it was only my gift of candy or a new lead pencil that induced him to come out. Again and again, I begged him to leave my mother when he felt nervous, and at last, after a particularly severe attack when he had emerged from the coma only to repeat the frightful process two or three times, he told me that he remembered something Mamma had done: she had been looking at him although he had his back turned to her, and when he faced her, he was afraid, he did not know why.

Then, instead of me, he began to avoid her, and sometimes he followed me all the way to the Brunsons' like a little dog and sat in the pantry without moving or making a sound until I was ready to go home. Nearly every afternoon I met him on the road, his overcoat buttoned up wrong, his pilot's helmet pulled down so far over his face that he could barely see where he was going. He refused to go to the shop, for he said Mamma came after him and looked in the windows and he could not look away when her eyes were on him.

# 5

On a Friday afternoon, early in January, a snowstorm came up. The snow fell in swift spirals, floating like gulls into the tree branches in the school-yard. The soft, circling petals smoothed away the harsh outlines of buildings and bony trees and transformed the light in the study hall. By the time school was out, the snow was several inches deep and was still falling. Mrs. Brunson was having a dinner party and had asked that I come to work immediately instead of going home as I usually did to prepare supper for my mother and Ivan. I enjoyed the evenings when the Brunsons entertained: the overheated house, immaculately clean, was redolent with the perfume of cut flowers delivered that morning from Boston, with the smell of roasting beef or turkey, of whiskey, and of cigars. Latterly, much of the management of the dinner parties had fallen to my lot since Maudie had begun to drink more and more and at the same time had lost her ability to hold her liquor. As a consequence, she often forgot essential dishes on the menu and ruined others.

The guests lingered a long time over their drinks. When the Brunsons drank, it was neither in the manner of my father and mother who had been maudlin or gay by turns, nor in the manner of Miss Pride whose indulgence at specified hours was less for pleasure than for the observation of custom. With them, it was a ritual which employed its own argot and its own paraphernalia. They drank whiskey high-balls made with ginger-ale, out of glasses decorated on the outside by a horse's head which, on the inside, underwent a sly metamorphosis into a naked woman. At the end of the third drink, Dr. Brunson would say, "Well, I guess this one can't be told in mixed company. No, no, I can't do it." But he was quickly persuaded that the ladies were not so easily embarrassed, that they themselves could tell much worse, and he would tell a story, usually with a medical background. I, passing the canapés, could not understand it, but I could not have been more shocked, for the laughter that exploded at its conclusion was as brazen and knowing as the look on the face of a small boy who has just chalked an obscene expletive on the sidewalk.

Tonight, in addition to drinks beforehand, the guests were served wine at dinner and they dallied at the table an unconscionable time. Maudie had complained early in the evening, "Somebody keeps spiking that grape juice I have to drink to keep my strength up. Why, Momma dear, that there's so all-fired potent, like the feller says, you could float a sledge-hammer on top of it," and she had staggered out of the house the moment the dessert was served. It was after ten o'clock when I got home, and I was surprised to see the light still burning in the kitchen, but more surprised, when I en-

119

tered, to find my mother idle for the first time since she had taken up fancy-work. She looked up, smiling.

"What kind of soup did they have, darling?"

"Chicken," I said, warming my hands at the stove. "It's cold, Mamma. You've let the fire go nearly out."

"It snowed hard, didn't it? A big deep snow, wasn't it? And did they have a salad?"

"Yes, and chocolate soufflé and two kinds of wine."

"Ah," said my mother. "Ah, how nice! But tell me, Sonia, sweetheart, how *deep* is the snow?"

"It's terribly deep. In some places it was up to my knees and there's a terrible wind."

"It's funny that you came home alone."

"Why? Did you expect someone?"

"Oh, no."

I was taking off my galoshes when she said, "Ivan went to meet you. It was snowing, but he didn't care about that. He only thought about seeing his precious Sonie."

"When did he go?" I cried.

"Oh, a long time ago. Just after the storm began. Here, have a little tea. You look tired."

"Which way did he go?" Though I knew I must find him at once, I could not leave for my amazement at the way she sat there, offering me a cup of tea. What would she be able to say to herself if I found him dead? And I knew, without believing it, that if I did, she would not feel the least necessity of making excuses to anyone, certainly not to herself.

She laughed uncertainly. "I don't know which way he went, but he went fast." And then, reaching out her hand to me she whispered desperately, "Let him go, for God's sake, Sonia, let him go!"

I did not answer but ran out of the house. The snow, which had let up for a little while around dinner time, was falling more thickly than ever and the loud wind drowned my voice as I stumbled down the road toward the village, calling to Ivan. Twice I thought I had found him and when I discovered that what I had seen in the distance was only a rock, I sank down with weariness and grief and would have stayed there but for the image of my brother as he might be suffering that drew me to my feet again. The versatile wind enclosed me in a live, round cloud and the next moment flattened me against a moving wall and then withdrew, leaving me in a noiseless little space where the snow fell gently and straight down. From time to time, I felt warmth slowly returning, but it never reached my feet or fingers because the wind halted it again and exploded charges of snow into my face or beleaguered me with unremitting blasts. Sometimes I plunged up to my knees in drifts as soft as pudding. I was trying to go in the direction of the Brunsons', thinking he might have found his way there, but I could distinguish no landmark to set me right. In a brief lull of the wind, I heard the angry ocean and the next moment slipped and fell into a deep pit which I recognized as being a few hundred yards from the Coast Guard house. I rested a moment and closed my eyes to the wet snowflakes and then struggled up the steep bank. A sharp stone cut into the palm of my hand and I could feel blood seeping through my rent wool mitten. I called, "Halloo! Halloo!" hoping that one of the Coast Guards would hear me. I went on, bent nearly double against the blast. Now I had lost all sense of direction: when the wind paused, I listened for the ocean but the sound came now from one place, now from another. I did not know whether I was hearing the bay or the sea. I rose up straight to call again and saw through the snow, near by, a lighted doorway, and I ran on shouting. As I drew closer I saw that the figure framed in the yellow block of light was Mrs. Henderson, shaking out a tablecloth.

"Ivan is lost!" I cried.

"Lord have mercy! Sarah, Ross, Jack, Josephine, get on your overshoes! The little Marburg boy is lost in the snow!"

The three children and the father were ready at once, as if they had been awaiting the alarm, and with no more account of the catastrophe than they had heard through the open door to the dining-room where they had been sitting round the table playing Lotto, they hurtled out the back door and into the storm while Mrs. Henderson filled a glass with rum and told me to drink it before I went out again.

"You're soaking wet," she scolded me. "You should have come here first." She tied a scarf about her head and went out after the others.

I started after her but halfway to the door shivered with mortal cold and turned back to drink the rum. It had an immediate effect on me. A bone-deep drowsiness made me nod and shake myself. I stared into the dining room from my place at the kitchen table and saw the scattered Lotto cards, the chairs pushed back, the upturned ash-tray on the floor. The alarm clock in the window sill above the sink, ticking off the minutes of my brother's absence in the furious snow, attracted my eyes and I watched the minute hand creeping so slowly it seemed not to move at all. I closed my eyes, but the measured tick-tock stayed with me. It must have been for the briefest moment that I half fell asleep while I still heard the tinny seconds clicking into the past, and when I opened my eyes again I knew that I had dreamed of being in Miss Pride's drawing-room where I had seen a box of ferns like that in the seventh-grade room at school. I had been alone. I felt I had just come in off the street, for cold enveloped me like a loose cloak. It was the selfishness of my dream that made me leap to my feet and run out the door, but just as I reached the bottom step, I heard voices near and Mr. Henderson came into sight, carrying Ivan's insensible body.

"The poor little duffer," said the man. "He was lying in the pastor's garden."

We kept him there that night, though Sarah and her father protested, sure he would have a fit immediately on regaining consciousness. I said I thought we should have a doctor, but Mrs. Henderson assured me that a doctor could do nothing that she could not do for the time being and that we would call one tomorrow if it were necessary. She made a bed for him on the sofa in the parlor and we sat up all night, for he was feverish and tossed so violently that he would have hurled himself to the floor if we had not been there to hold him back. Mrs. Henderson took up her knitting and worked nimbly at the heel of a sock. The room was unbearably hot and smelled of the camphor-oil on Ivan's chest.

"Why don't you sleep a little, Sonie?" said Mrs. Henderson.

But I refused. I felt I must be vigilant now since I had abandoned him this afternoon. "I love Ivan," I said.

"I know you do," replied the woman. "I'm sure of it."

"I couldn't bear it if anything happened to him! Do you believe me, Mrs. Henderson?"

"Indeed I do, Sonie. You mustn't feel bad about staying away this afternoon. He'll be all right, you'll see. Sonie, over there you'll find some magazines. Don't you want to look at them? I think we oughtn't talk too much for fear of waking the little boy."

Toward morning he was more peaceful and his forehead was cool. At sun-up we carried him home. My mother had been waiting up all night for me, and she was melancholy. She said nothing, only stared as we lowered Ivan to his cot.

He improved during the day although he developed a cough that troubled us and when in the afternoon he seemed to be choking with it, Mrs. Henderson sent me to the hospital for Dr. Galbraith. "Be clear with him, Sonie," she said. "It's sometimes hard for the doctor to follow what a person's saying, you know."

It was not because he was stupid but because he was an alcoholic that Dr. Galbraith could not follow. His quick speech, hampered by a hasty stammer, was deceptive. He spoke so rapidly he concealed the degeneration of his mind and appeared to be a man whose energy outdistanced his tongue, whose attention at any moment was subdivided many times, giving to each focus a degree of concentration varying with its importance. Breathless with the long run through the cold, I stood beside the desk in his sterile cell, while the doctor nervously twisted a fountain pen round and round between his plump fingers and interrupted me.

"Just a minute, you must try, you must try to control yourself."

I sensed in his voice an agitation that surpassed my own. And while he kept me there with his trivial questions which he brought out with a great struggle (he even asked my age) he only made me wilder and himself more confused, so that, in the end, when he did come, he was not in the least prepared for what he found. I had identified Ivan as the child he had seen at the Hendersons' and he thought he was being summoned to another epileptic fit. For a moment I was not sure that he would come at all. He sat staring at me, moving his lips. He had a repulsive face, flabby, blotched, and dissolute. The crescents of dark flesh under his eyes were distended and the eyes themselves were bloodshot, filmy, and of a color akin to auburn. His lips, tumid and wet, worked slowly over what his eyes saw as if, once the object were removed, he would still be able to recall it by running his tongue over his lips which had mouthed it and shaped its secret formula. He had had, I had heard, several attacks of jaundice and his skin was permanently stained to so dark a color that it resembled sunburn.

At last he rose with a convulsive jerk. "Will I need my stethoscope?"

Thinking he spoke to me, I said, "Why, I should think so, sir!"

He laughed self-consciously. "I talk to myself. It is the privilege of an old man." And abruptly he pinched my chin between his thumb and forefinger.

Ivan's illness was diagnosed as bronchitis. The doctor prescribed mustard poultices and a benzoin kettle. "Keep him well covered up and put on the mustard as hot as he can stand it. It's not a bad attack and the fever isn't high. Call me if he seems to fail, but he won't, he'll be all right, quite all right."

He left some sleeping powders with us and these we gave Ivan every eight hours so that for several days we kept him asleep save when we woke him to pour a little water or broth down his parched throat. We made a tent of an old sheet and kept a pot of benzoin bubbling on a kerosene stove beside his bed. He was never himself but muttered and groaned and stared at us without recognition. His bright cheeks blazed under my fingers as I tried to stroke away the illness that racked him, hooped his body with a cough and cast it down, gasping.

My mother remained in the kitchen, sleeping on the floor occasionally, but for the most part making feather-stitched pot-holders. As she worked, she sang Fräulein Lili's song in a soft but penetrating voice, over and over again until I begged her, bursting into tears, to cease. And when she did not, Mrs. Henderson laid her hand on mine and shook her head.

When I came home at noon and later after school and then in the evening, I could hear her before I had left the road to turn into the lane:

> Well they know without my telling
> Where she lives, for whom I long.
> Round their hoofs the snow is swirling.
> Loud the coachman sings his song.
> Round their flying hoofs the snow is swirling.
> Loud the coachman sings his song.

Or, in the night, half asleep but alert to every noise, I could hear her sorrowing, for she had changed the gay tune into a dirge:

> Hurry, horses, faster, faster!
> Quick, my flying hawks, away!
> Days and hours like these are golden—
> We must seize them while we may.
> Golden days are these and golden minutes—
> We must seize them while we may.

She never spoke to me. She might look me full in the face as if she were about to say something. Then, if I spoke, she drowned out my words with another verse of her song or, instead, repeated one line again and again with a passionate monotony:

> Hurry, horses, faster, faster!
> Hurry, horses, faster, faster!
> Hurry, horses, faster, faster!

But my little brother heard nothing. His fever was coy; each time it went down, Mrs. Henderson and I were comforted, but only for an hour or so. On the fourth day, there was no diminishing of it at all. On the contrary, it went steadily higher until it had reached 106 degrees. Mrs. Henderson said he should be taken to the hospital at once and she called out the window to Sarah to run to the village and telephone the doctor. It was late in the afternoon and I had been home from school for an hour or so. Terrified as I was by the anxious tone of the woman's voice, I was so weary that when she advised me to go into the kitchen to rest for a few minutes until the doctor came, I agreed.

My mother, her head bent over her work, was singing through smiling lips. The sun was going down. The red light glowed on her face and hair with a softness and subtlety that made it seem a property of her own being, an interior light which, passing through the many filters of her body, the tissues, bones, and muscles, was revealed, at its mellowest, upon her skin so that her face did not reflect the sunset but resembled it. Through the window I could see the sky, striped with stratus clouds of pink and deeper shades of pink, separating here and there to disclose a streak or patch of green like pale shoots and leaves amongst flowers.

Each day, I wished to prolong this hour so that I might have time to do in it all the things that were suggested to me. I wished to walk down the road to the Hotel Barstow to see the rows and rows of windows shining like solid blocks of wine-red ice, giving to the old-fashioned, quasi-baroque façade an interest which was lacking at any other time. The whole aspect of the building would be improved, for this was a benevolent kind of light which enriched the shadows with the same ruddy color it infused into the surfaces, but in such a way that there were no abrupt contrasts, only a deepening and reinforcement. It was quite unlike the light earlier in the afternoon which, cold and white, accented the dirtiness of the old paint and brutally discovered all the vulgarity of the building, the whimsical fenestration following the roof line, the tedious repetition of egg-and-dart, the ogees of the veranda, the festoons of roses looped and ribboned over the doors and windows. I should have liked, too, to look at the State House dome from Miss Pride's belvedere and to accompany with my eyes the snail-paced approach of coal-boats to Boston harbor; or to watch, from the topmost of the rocks at the Point, the fearful, reddened water which now in the winter supported few fishing and no sailboats, as if it had devoured them all but still in hunger thrashed many tails and snarled for something more to swallow.

I could not even choose between the sky and my mother's face, and my eyes roamed heavily from one to the other. Her chant, toneless, and yet indescribably sweet, went on:

> Till with age my hair starts graying,
> Till my locks have ceased to curl,
> Let me live in joy and gladness,
> Let me love a pretty girl!
> Let me live my life in joy and gladness,
> Let me love a pretty girl!

I felt that I had all the time in the world. In various versions, I posed myself the question: Is she mad? Can she sing really as carelessly as this when her son is dying? Or is it that the song hides her feelings? Her needle's movement followed the pattern of the rhythm of her voice; at the end of a line or at a rest, she would gracefully and deliberately draw out her green silk thread and let it hang in the air a moment like a sunbeam. I could not tell, afterwards, if it was one or several minutes before I realized that she was silent and had looked up from her fancy-work. She rose and crossed directly to the bedroom door. I followed her.

She went to the cot and said in a whisper, not to me nor to Mrs. Henderson but to herself, "I think he's going to die." She touched the little boy's forehead lightly with her fingertips. A shudder coursed through Ivan's thin body under the bedclothes, and my mother drew back in alarm. His stifled breathing seemed to stop and then began again, a rattling, wheezing inspiration. Forgetful of my duty towards him and even of my love, I could only look on him with horror, but I was impelled to his side where I knelt down, taking his tiny wrist between my fingers. The pulse raced under by untutored touch. His sharp little face was distorted and blue; the red lips hung and the cheeks drew in. I heard someone come to the door and, thinking it was the doctor, turned in relief, but it was only Sarah. "He advised another poultice and he's coming in half an hour."

"Oh, Lord!" cried her mother. "I don't know what to do. His poor little chest is raw where they've been." But, although she was certain that the doctor was wrong, she was obedient to his professional orders, and went to the stove to heat the mat. I followed and opened a new shaker of mustard. The sharp smell stung my nostrils; in this one whiff seemed to be embodied all the others that I had taken in in these four long days. I lunged heavily against the stove in my sudden fatigue and burned my wrist. Instinctively, I put the hurt place to my tongue and as I did so, my mother called from the bedroom, "Sonia! Hurry! I think he's dead."

As I dropped his hand, thin as a bird's foot, and turned to my mother I thought I saw, passing like a light across her face, a look of pity and regret; but perhaps I only imagined it for immediately she smiled and said, "See how peaceful he is."

Mrs. Henderson covered his face with the sheet and, turning, hid my face from him in an embrace. I could feel her bosom rising and falling tranquilly as she murmured, "There, there, the little fellow's better off now God has taken him. Just you rest a little, pet, and then you go over to my house and stay until I come." But in the other room, while she was comforting me, my mother was admitting Dr. Galbraith and I heard his voice, curiously cleared of its stammer: "What charming work you're holding there, ma'am. I had no idea my little patient's mother was an artist."

"My son is dead."

"Oh, I didn't know! It must have been only a few minutes ago."

"In there," she said. "I was just making a poultice—you see I had everything ready, when suddenly he cried out and I went to him. He died in my arms."

"God bless you."

My mother began to cry softly. "I tried!"

I did not ponder then what she meant. I leaned against Mrs. Henderson and breathed in, with the sweet, herbal odor of the benzoin, still bubbling futilely, the smell of her freshly ironed cotton dress.

"You run along, Sonie. Get Sarah to make you some lemon verbena. It'll rest you."

I did not want to leave her, for I was protected by her kindly, corseted body in its pale blue dress printed with little white flowers. The moment I released myself, I would see Ivan and know that he was dead. I was broken suddenly and I sobbed against the cotton, "Oh, Mrs. Henderson, my wrist hurts where I burned it!"

128

# CHAPTER FIVE

Over the place where Ivan's cot had been and where now there was nothing but a rag rug with four square indentations, the smell of benzoin still hovered faintly. The snow from the storm had melted and a dense fog enveloped Chichester. All day, from early morning, we had heard the solemn foghorns. My mother and I sat silent before the stove in the afternoon. Her face was overcast and I believed that when she had wailed to Dr. Galbraith, "I tried!" she had meant, "I tried to love him." For in the night, sleepless for both of us, she had murmured, "My tears are all gone, Sonie," as though all the springs of her being, save her love for me, had been drained, perhaps long before his birth.

Mr. Greeley, the undertaker, had come to take my brother's body away when I was still at the Hendersons' house. He was a man of dreadful stature and horrifying countenance which consisted of a pair of lifeless eyes set in deep, dark pits, a long nose which had deviated markedly to the left, and a set of long and murky teeth behind a walrus mustache. He relished his profession. His parlors were situated in isolation on the road towards the hospital. The yard behind his sprawling, tacky yellow house was planted with tombstones, for he was a merchant as well as an undertaker and a licensed embalmer. When Mr. Greeley learned that we had no money and that Ivan was to be buried as a pauper, he could not conceal his disapproval from my mother and Mrs. Henderson. "For a child," he reproached them, "I have such a nice choice: one sandstone group of angel, lamb, two doves, another along classical lines in which the lily *motif* is used. My real prize is waiting for a little child, a granite headstone with an all-over design of cast-iron roses." He went on to complain that a child should not be sealed into the ground without the services of either Father Mulcahy or Pastor Ferguson. The grave would be unmarked, he said, and we would never know where my brother lay.

Mrs. Henderson, repeating his words to me, assured me that he was not an unkind man but only tactless in his disappointment at being cheated out of a ceremony. But she deplored his effect upon my mother, who had become almost hysterical, had declared that she would die of shame if she could not buy the cast-iron roses for her son. And she had implored the undertaker to wait a few days before he buried the child, for we would surely be able to find some way to have a decent and proper funeral.

Exhausted, my grief still tightly coiled as the kernel to my shock at seeing him die, I was vexed and said heartlessly to the neighbor woman, "Oh, why *can't* Mamma leave well enough alone!" for I felt that now I could not bear to hear her lamentations, which I knew would be forthcoming if the gravestone had become, as I believed it had, a fixed idea.

Mrs. Henderson replied, "She will forget, Sonie. Never you fear. She's upset, poor thing, but she'll get over it."

"You don't know Mamma," I said irritably.

"Oh, I'm not so sure. Here, you take her this bit of upside-down cake and see if you can't get her to take a little nourishment."

To my surprise, my mother did not mention the funeral that evening, and in the morning when she spoke of it, I was sufficiently relaxed to feel my loneliness and to think she was right in wanting something better for Ivan than an anonymous grave in a potter's field.

We had been shown great kindness by the townspeople: they had sent us flowers and notes of sympathy and someone had brought a book of funeral hymns. Dr. Brunson, with well-meaning generosity, had personally delivered a bottle of imported brandy and had said bluffly, "I think at times like this you ought to think of the living." My mother had wanted to open the bottle at once but I had dissuaded her. These tokens of commiseration offered us only a spiritual crutch, and there was not one name signed upon the cards that I could call out and ask its owner for the price of a headstone. Not even Gonzales who, although he had neither called on us nor given us flowers, had sent one of his children with a note informing us that he would offer his mass each day that week for the repose of Ivan's soul.

That morning, I had gone to the store for a box of matches. The hush which greeted my entrance and passage between the long, brown counters was more than the ordinary respect paid to the bereft. Accompanied by intense stares and a coloring of cheeks and a withdrawal away from the aisle, it had in it an edge of doubt. And when Mr. Bennett, the store-keeper, said to me, "How is your poor mother?" and without realizing that his question was elliptical and expanded would have been, "How is your poor mother bearing up?" I replied, "Oh, she's awfully well, thank you," a murmur of voices rose behind me. I knew, although I could not catch a word of what they said, that the story of Ivan's illness was known and that this self-appointed jury which convened whenever the population of Chichester was reduced or added to was putting down his death as "peculiar."

Set into the counter there were bins of dried foods and in the glass door of one, I caught the tilted reflection of my face. I saw, to a shame that made me cringe away, that upon my lips there was a light and careless smile! Then, as though to show my judges that my sorrow had not left me so indecently soon, I turned to face them and as I did so, saw Sarah Henderson and her father at the center of a knot of people in the back of the store. Mr. Henderson averted his gaze as I looked in their direction, but Sarah met me coldly with her enlarged, near-sighted eyes. Then Mr. Henderson looked up. Encircled by the marks of sleeplessness, his eyes accused me, I thought, of bringing trouble to his household, and when, in a voice I could not control so that it was cracked and breathless, I said, "Good morning, Mr. Henderson," he did not answer. Later, remembering his silence, as wounding as ice to the bare skin, I told myself I cared nothing for his opinion. But my urgent indifference did not heal me.

A change had come over Sarah Henderson which alarmed her father and herself, and indeed her whole family, and which had begun shortly after Ivan's first fit. Whether the shock of what she had seen that night wakened what had been merely dormant, or whether her strangeness would have come about anyhow, I cannot say. At any rate, she had begun to walk in her sleep, and while she never wandered farther than the back porch, she was in dread lest she should walk down to the sea and be drowned before she could master herself. She had headaches and bad dreams and she was ill-humored. Mrs. Henderson thought new glasses would cure her headaches, and that her bad dreams came from eating indigestible sandwiches and pickles before she went to bed. And if Sarah would take a little more exercise, her disposition would improve. She had been out of school for several years and had never been able to find work; she had no talents, no interests, and no beaux. Mrs. Henderson said, "You're bound to get notions if you're idle."

But Mr. Henderson blamed Ivan. He also blamed his wife who, he thought, in going so often to our house, brought back with her some contagious and powerful virus. At last he saw nothing for it but to move away and had got a job in Maine. He was already making his preparations, and this morning in the store he had piled up several pasteboard cartons. Now I have no doubt that we did not drive him away and that the removal to Maine promised the family far more than they had ever had in Chichester. But my self-consciousness dyed everything to match its own color, and for a long time I believed that I had uprooted Mr. Henderson and had unbalanced Sarah.

The villagers recovered their voices as I stepped away from the counter with my matches. As though by way of apology to me for their silence or to indicate that they had not yet heard the news, they began to talk of things which bore no relation to the death. They commented on the fog and listed its attendant injuries to motorists and mariners, and they prophesied the immediate ruin of the United States under its existing government, exchanged receipts for salt-rising bread, and told jokes involving a judge and a colored man named Rastus. But the lively tone was betrayed by a slackening of pace as I went down the aisle toward the door, feeling the eyes of everyone upon me.

And yet, when I had been at home only a few minutes, the flowers began to arrive and the notes, composed laboriously in an embarrassment that concealed itself behind phrases like "the dear departed" and "passed on to a better world," so that I thought I had misconstrued the silence in the store, for the names of some of the people who had been there were on the cards.

We sat among the sweet carnations and daffodils and roses whose fragrance and chaste petals, some of them made even lovelier by the whorls of steam rising from our teacups, softened the edges of our predicament.

It was my mother who spoke first. "If it was summer, the ladies at the Hotel would get us a nice coffin and a pretty tombstone. Miss Pride would give us the money if it was only summer. Don't you have anything left of the golden egg?"

The golden egg had been used up years ago, but my mother could never believe it and now and again she sought it in my father's Bible, tearing the thin pages in her impatience.

I had thought of Miss Pride, but I had hoped my mother would not. The temptation to send her a letter had been strong until I remembered that often I had heard her talking to her friends of the impertinent requests she received through the mail. A young man who described himself as a "would-be writer," after paying Miss Pride and her deceased father (neither of whom he had ever known) three pages of fulsome compliments, asked her to forward him a Remington typewriter at her earliest convenience. It was his specifying the make of the machine that most appalled her, and she had sent him a lead-pencil with the note, "I regret that I cannot supply you with a Remington typewriter and hope that you will instead accept, with my best wishes, this Ticonderoga lead-pencil." But, on the other hand, I had heard that she had sent two deserving young men, of good but impoverished families, through Harvard. I thought of how, when I was a little girl, I used to dream of her coming to our house, wearing black silk gloves and carrying a funeral wreath for my dead parents. I said aloud, "I wonder if she *would*."

Pretending that I was going for a walk, I went out of the house, but instead, crossed over to the shop. It was here before Ivan's epilepsy that I had done all my reading and studying, for in the house I could never be free of interruptions. I had made my father's work table into a desk, its principal feature being a German silver inkwell embossed with doves which I had found in one of the boxes. The room was dark from the fog and I lighted a candle by whose unsteady flame I composed my letter to Miss Pride. I stated my case formally, saluting her "Dear Madam" and offering her, in exchange for the fulfillment of my "novel request" my services in the humblest part of her establishment for the rest of my life. I asked her to telegraph her reply. But if she were disinclined to forward me the money, I begged her to forget my importunity and to regard me still as her "obedient servant, Sonia Marburg."

The moment I had dropped the envelope through the brass lips of the box in the post-office, I burned with shame and had I not dreaded the curiosity of the postmaster, would have begged him to return it to me. The text of the letter now seemed at once flippant and turgid. I had been tricked into my pomposity by the corpulent silver ink-well as though its original owner had left his nineteenth-century clichés behind to mingle with the ink.

Dr. Galbraith was fitting the key to his post-box and as he withdrew a packet of mail and glanced through it, he was the object of the scrutiny of the postmaster who, leaning forward against his bars, remarked, "Well, Doc, I sure did fill your box this morning, but I guess it's mostly ads and them journals."

"Oh, yes, yes," said the doctor in his pestered way. "Thank you. It's a very interesting collection," though he was shuffling the envelopes so rapidly that he could not possibly have told where they had come from.

"You been riding a horse, Doc?"

To the doctor's fuscous cheeks arose a blush as he looked down at his clothes and then at the postmaster, who had not been in Chichester long.

"Uh, no, no, as a matter of fact, I haven't."

The doctor's innumerable costumes were all spectacular and meticulously tailored, and they gave him the air of a "sporting gentleman" of a bygone era. One thought of his "cravats," not of his neckties, and remembered their large, loose knots in the French style. He very often wore riding clothes as he did this morning, and it was said that he had once been an excellent horseman, just as it was said that he had once been an insatiable student of literature and had once "performed creditably" on the violin. Now, the only reminders of those talents were his dashing habits, his immense, unhandled library (presided over, I had heard, by busts of Dante, Pericles, Shakespeare, and Vergil under whose staring eyes he drank each night to a point of stupefaction), and the recollection of Mrs. Prather who had heard him play the solo of Dr. Joachim's Hungarian Concerto.

With his russet breeches, which descended over his handsome legs into boots so lustrous and pliant I longed to touch and crush them in my hands, he wore a checked and belted red-brown jacket and a maroon silk ascot, and upon his head, a green hat grizzled with silvery veins and proclaiming its continental origin by a *gansbart* sportively stuck in the band. It was no wonder that the old ladies at the Hotel Barstow, too old to be the object of his lascivious eyes, found him charming and said he "cut a fine figure." They admired his apparel and said that too often a physician tends to resemble his successor, the mortician. His other suits were of fine materials, all double-breasted and of a cut which did not vary through the years, yet always seemed to be at the peak of fashion. And while the colors and the patterns of the stripes or checks were conservative, the accessory trappings were of the liveliest declensions, being the racing lifeblood of the subdued carcass: neckties (or cravats) of orange silk and crimson wool, printed challis, dotted China silk, pongee, fortified linen, diapered or imprinted with arabesques or stripes or hexagons. His handkerchief and his muffler, if he wore one, matched or complemented the tie as did his socks and the band in his hat. And carrying to its uttermost his nice feeling for detail, he even had alternative spectacles which today, to go with his riding togs, were horn-rimmed, but tomorrow, with blue serge would be rimless octagons, and the next day, if the fancy struck him to dress for dinner and go into Boston, would be a pince-nez with a black ribbon and mother-of-pearl nose pieces.

Dr. Galbraith did not seem to recognize me, though once or twice he looked in my direction as I lingered in the room, studying the announcements of Civil Service examinations and the photographs of coarse, unshaven rascals with prices on their heads for the robbery of banks or the kidnapping of children. I wished to speak with him but hesitated in the presence of the postmaster who was still regarding him with the frankest inquisitiveness.

135

He was about to leave and I prepared to follow him, but the post-master, perhaps in the intention of keeping him there a little longer so that he might continue his investigation, bawled, "Doctor, what can a person do for the bloat? Seems like every meal I get all bloated up afterward."

The doctor wheeled about. "What a thing to say," he spluttered, "in front of a lady," and he motioned toward me, "whose brother has just died."

The man gaped stupidly behind his bars. "Well, bless your heart, hasn't she ever heard of the bloat? I'm real sorry to hear the bad news, but I don't see I gave her any reason to be peeved."

"Come, Miss Henderson," said Dr. Galbraith and held the door open, adding, as we passed into the fog, "What the devil is your name?"

"Marburg. The Hendersons live next door to us. Dr. Galbraith, I wonder if Mr. Greeley would let us have another day . . . you know, about my brother. My mother doesn't want him to be buried like a pauper, and I thought if you spoke to him, he might give us some more time so that we can try to find some money."

We were walking so close together that our arms kept brushing and each time I moved away from him, his hand groped out towards me for support.

"Just a minute. I can't seem to think in a fog."

We could see no more than ten feet in any direction, and I felt as if I were suspended in a gaseous sphere, for the blindness of the air made my locomotion seem rotary and almost effortless, and when the doctor softly collided with me, it seemed even more that we were going round and round in a circle, he overstepping the bounds of the outer ring while I, with difficulty, maintained my footing in the inner one.

I repeated my question to him. "Well, I don't know . . ." he said.

Beyond us, we could now and again hear voices and the distant foghorns which only isolated us the more since there could be no proof, until someone entered our shortened range of vision, that the experience was not unique for us, just as it is said that perhaps a tree, falling in a forest, makes no sound if no one hears it.

The doctor stopped me and sighed deeply. "Look here, Miss Martin, I don't believe . . . I'm not certain, but the fact is that when a cor . . . someone is buried in this way it is not . . . well, frankly, it is not embalmed. I . . . no, I regret very much that it really is an impossibility." He clasped my arm tightly with his trembling fingers.

"But we will know by noon tomorrow and it could be embalmed then, couldn't it?"

"I wouldn't worry about that if I were you, my dear. These things are . . . my poor girl, there is no *shame* in being a pauper! But if you should know by noon tomorrow, I daresay something could be arranged. I'll speak to Mr. Greeley."

I thanked him and prepared to take leave. "How is your mother?" he asked me.

"Very well, thank you, though she's terribly upset to think we may not have a funeral."

"Ah, yes, yes, it's too bad. She is an, ah, an admirable woman. What is her name again?"

"Mrs. Marburg."

"Oh, yes. She is very handsome. She isn't an American?"

"No, she's a Russian."

"Fascinating!" he cried. "She looks like a painting I used to be fond of. A madonna, you know, something of that sort, very likely by a Russian painter. Will you give her my regards?"

"Yes, Dr. Galbraith, and thank you for all you've done."

"It's nothing, my dear, nothing at all," and he grasped my arm again before I could escape our hollow ball and get into another where I was alone. When I had gone some yards beyond him, I heard him call, "Morgan, is it, or Martin? What the devil is the name again?" But I did not answer.

My mother was embroidering when I got home. Upon the chest of Ivan's outing-flannel nightshirt, she had made an enormous rose in black cotton and was now sketching a wreath of smaller roses to encircle it.

"The shroud," she explained.

I would have snatched my brother's pitiful nightshirt from her hands, but I knew, by the diligence with which she bent over her work, that if I did, I would be subjected to an endless tirade. I only said, "Listen, Mamma, you mustn't count too much on the funeral."

She looked up innocently. "But you promised the cast-iron roses, darling! Why, Sonia, I wouldn't have gone to all this trouble to make the shroud if you hadn't promised me!"

"Mamma . . ." I began, but words were useless. I drew a chair to the fire and sat brooding, my eyes fixed upon the oven door where the word "Enterprise" was elaborately printed in blue. "For God's sake, Miss Pride, help me," I thought. "If she doesn't get the cast-iron roses, what will I do?"

The fog continued into the next day so that when we got up, it was only the clock, not the appearance of the world, that told us it was morning. From six until noon, I waited for the telegram. I was no longer ashamed of my letter. I was conscious of nothing but the hours ascending to their climax, three o'clock, which was the hour Mr. Greeley had told me he would "dispose" of the body. One of the hours dragged by so slowly that each second of it was a lifetime, but the next was swiftly gone. Because, in my impatience for the message, I could not bear my mother's humming and smiling as she patiently filled in those gruesome black roses, I had gone to the shop soon after breakfast where I fidgeted with the playing cards and dreamed over *Ethan Frome*. Each time I heard a voice calling another name, not mine, I bent my head over my desk and closed my eyes in a total blankness of disappointment. Hopestill Mather's time-blackened slippers, which had remained all these years where I had put them on the day my father went away, infuriated me as they had not done in a long while. I would have slashed to ribbons what was left of them if my father's tools had not been rusted beyond use. Now, at this very moment, when grief and terror were consuming me, Hopestill was probably laughing, with her handsome head flung back, her bright mind far from death or poverty. What would she do, I wondered, on a slow, gray day like this? She would still be in bed, under a light green eiderdown. Or perhaps she was having her breakfast on a tray and in a little while would lazily get out of bed for a long, perfumed bath. Why, her allowance for a month would pay for my brother's headstone!

The time was so deliberate that I could fix my attention on nothing save the knocking at our kitchen door and even my desire for what the telegraph boy would bring became vague. My necessity was so pressing that several times I was sure I heard my mother call to me. At last, indeed, I did hear her, and I ran out. As I crossed the yard I heard, like an insistent warning, the long-held note of a fog-horn which was answered on the other side of the tongue of land by another, the two echoing and re-echoing. Then they subsided and there was a silence until a still more remote bleat sounded up the coast.

My mother was smiling radiantly and I smiled in response, sure the telegram had arrived. "It's all right, darling," she said. "You sit down and I'll tell you about it."

I glanced round the room for a yellow envelope, but I saw none. I observed that my mother had laid aside Ivan's nightshirt and was now making a basket in cross-stitch on a pot-holder.

"We have been stupid," she said. "Why, Sonie girl, the thing to do is to give our little boy an ocean burial the way the sailors do."

"In the water, do you mean, Mamma?" I cried.

"Yes. It's clean out there, and, oh, so much better than to be buried like a poor person!" She leaned forward eagerly and took my hand, saying in a whisper, "After dark, we can go tonight. No one will see us."

"But we would have to have a boat. Oh, no! No, Mamma, I can't bury little Ivan that way."

She tried to persuade me. Softly and affectionately, she described the dignity of such an act, told me how the bells and the waves would be eternal mourners for the little boy. She said the strange things that grew at the bottom of the sea would be fine flowers for his grave. If we must go out in a boat, would not Mr. Henderson take us? We three would go out, dressed in black, early in the evening. It would be ever so much nicer even than the cast-iron flowers.

Hearing once again the inconsolable moan of the foghorns, I was almost won but I did not speak.

"You run ask Mrs. Henderson," she coaxed, "and then go to the man who took him away. You fix it for me, sweetheart."

Mrs. Henderson had toward the sea the animadversion common to all the wives of Chichester mariners and fishermen. She personified it as a treacherous siren, forever discontent with her partial government over the men and striving with all manner of clever devices like storms and fog, to win full sovereignty over them. Thus, when I told her of my mother's proposal her bland face was disordered with revulsion. She recovered her voice and told me she was very sure so irregular a procedure was quite illegal, but as she was by no means an authority, we would go together to inquire of Mr. Greeley, and we set out through the fog.

It was a little after two when we were admitted to the mortuary parlors by a disheveled and grumpy housekeeper who, having been so long in the society of cadavers, seemed to have lost the use of her voice and addressed to us a solitary grunt, presumably intended as a command to us to follow her. We waited for Mr. Greeley in a small, cold room, immoderately decorated with rubber plants which had grown to a disquieting height, and furnished with seedy leather rocking-chairs. Perhaps I only imagined it, but it seemed to me that under the smell of disinfectant that pervaded the house, there was the rank odor of putrefaction, and I whispered to Mrs. Henderson, "Oh, let's go home! I'm frightened!" But the undertaker had entered the room. He greeted us with as warm a smile as his parody of a face could muster and said, "Ah, ah, then you have found a way to get the little boy a headstone. Well, I'm glad, indeed I am. I hope you'll take my jewel, my roses. He will sleep better beneath it."

"No, sir," I said. "We can't have a funeral after all. But there is something else . . . Mrs. Henderson, *you* tell him."

The woman told him my mother's plan, and as she talked he pulled the ends of his mustache, exclaiming softly, "Ridiculous! Fantastic! What on earth!" And when she had finished, he rose to his full, improbable height and declared, "One may not cast a body into the street or into a running stream, or into a hole in the ground, or make any disposition of it that might be regarded as creating a nuisance or be injurious to the health of the community. This is the law, Madam. And 'running stream' can, in this instance, refer to the water of the bay or of the ocean. Do you think that I care to be apprehended by the Boston Harbor Police? Do you think that *you* have the authority to do what you wish with this body?"

I could feel the large and abundant tears crawling down my cheeks at his impressionistic yet graphic picture of my brother's corruption. Seeing my misery, he was gentler when he spoke again and even laid his hairy hand, which wore a Masonic ring, on my jerking shoulder.

"Look here, young lady," he said, "you let me bury him now as I planned and if you get some money some day, we will disinter the body and start all over again. All right?"

I nodded my head, for I could not speak. I heard Mrs. Henderson inquire if she might at least supervise the dressing of the child for whom she had had so great an affection and heard the undertaker refuse. She took me by the elbow and I rose. "God bless him," she said, and as we left the room, Mr. Greeley's voice came to us in a clatter of enthusiasm. "I hope you will be able to get my rose piece! The best of luck to you!"

"You mustn't mind him," said Mrs. Henderson as we started home. "It's his job, and a thankless one."

"Oh, I don't blame him! I only don't want to have to tell Mamma."

"Well, then, we won't tell Mamma," said Mrs. Henderson with a trace of annoyance. "I suppose there's nothing against a white lie to give *you* a little peace of mind, Sonie."

"But she'd want to go to the grave sometime."

"Not if she thought he was buried at sea, dear."

"But she wants to go out in the boat herself, Mrs. Henderson!"

"Oh, we could change her mind with a hot toddy, I think. You mustn't suppose I don't know your mother," she said grimly. "And since we're going off to Maine directly, I'd like to think I left you without too many worries. Let her come down to the wharf, yes, and let her see you get into the boat with Ross. He'll take you out a little piece and she'll never know the difference. If she wants the poor lad to be down with the seaweed, let her think that's where he is." She was very angry. With an outraged, "I declare!" she fell silent for so long a time that I thought she had not been in earnest. The plan was, I saw, ideal, but I dared not hope it could ever be realized, for I was certain Mr. Henderson would not agree to so romantic an enterprise.

We had reached our cottage before the neighbor woman spoke again. "Sonie, you mustn't ever think I was being harsh with you a while back there. I was out of sorts with your mother for a minute, thinking as I was how you're nothing but a child yourself and put up with all these carryings-on. I'll serve my time for those mean thoughts about poor Mrs. Marburg. I do think it's best to humor her. We'll do what I said now. I'll step across to your place after supper."

That evening, about seven o'clock, my mother and Mrs. Henderson and I were waiting on the beach by the wharf. Although we could not see them, we could hear the dories dip and sway at their sodden moorings. Someone passed behind us and we could hear the hiss of his slicker and dimly we saw his lantern. My mother, wearing her bright winter dress covered with an old, rusty black cape, stood erect beside me. I was surprised to see that she was a little taller than I. Her arm was linked in mine, and through the mist I could see her long fingers on my coat sleeve. Mrs. Henderson stood on the other side of us. None of us spoke, but there was something in my mother's stance and in the way her hand, seemingly relaxed, was firm on my arm, which told me that she was profoundly excited and a stealthy glance at her parted, upward curving lips, informed me that her excitement did not come from grief. My glance, shifting, met Mrs. Henderson, who had likewise been looking at my mother, and it seemed to me that her eyes, behind her faintly glimmering spectacles, would be cold and unforgiving.

"A nice night," said my mother after a time. "Don't you think it's nice, Mrs. Henderson?"

"A little chilly," replied the woman. "I'm worried about you, Mrs. Marburg. I don't think you're dressed warm enough. As soon as he comes, we must hustle back to the house."

"Oh, yes," cried my mother. "Oh, of course we must! Did Sonia tell you what that good man said when he brought the brandy? He said, 'I think at times like these, you ought to think of the living.'"

It was some minutes before we heard Mr. Henderson call out to us. "Ready!" he cried. "Can you see, Sonie? Come straight to the end of the wharf."

I stepped forward, the two women following me until we reached the wharf, which seemed no more than a long, insubstantial shadow.

Mrs. Henderson squeezed my hand, and my mother, who had already withdrawn, called, "Dear Sonia! Dear little girl!"

"Mamma!" I cried in an abrupt, inexplicable desperation. "Mamma! Mamma! Where are you?"

"Hush!" said Mrs. Henderson.

"Are you lost?" came Mr. Henderson's imperative voice.

"She's coming, Ross!" returned his wife.

I lingered for a moment at Mrs. Henderson's side. We were both motionless. We heard my mother's feet lightly running over the wet sand, and in a little while, an eerie voice singing in the distance. Then I ran to the end of the wharf, my head down, scuffing my rubber soles to keep from falling on the slippery boards. I went down the ramp to the float where the boat was moored. As Mr. Henderson stretched out his hand to help me, a phrase of my mother's song came swelling towards us on a little wind.

"Mr. Henderson, I'm sorry . . ." I began.

But his calloused hand was full of sympathy and he muttered, "Rich or poor, a person must stand by another person."

The dories softly plopping in the water made a sound sadder even than the horns. "We'll go round the Point and out a bit," said Mr. Henderson. "I like a fog myself."

The whirr of the motor prohibited talk, and the foghorns were all but obliterated save when they were very near. To our right, until we rounded the Point, were the lights of Boston, blurred into one long line which shifted with the movement of the boat. Miss Pride and her niece would be just sitting down to dinner. I could hear Miss Pride say crisply, "I had another of those beastly begging letters today. Do they think we're made of money?"

The water was choppy around the Point and I was filled with a mixture of terror and exultation when I considered that not far from here were the high seas in whose tumultous bowels lay the bones of the dead and the timbers of shattered ships. The fog was a little lighter. Far away were dimly visible a bunch of lights and I knew that it was the steamer to New York proceeding to the Cape Cod Canal. What worlds there were on this side of Chichester! On the bay side, there was Boston, single and supreme. But here: the furious cemetery, over the residents of which one plowed in a massive ship to Europe; the fabulous New York; and to the west of New York, that variegated land so tediously described in the geography books. I supposed that bizarre as its name was, even Nebraska was real. The feeling and the taste of the spray were unaccountably thrilling, and I, forgetting the absurdity of our errand, wished that we might all night long cut through the water, our motor as loud as gunshot in our ears, and all about us the danger of death. And I knew then why Mr. Henderson had been so amenable to his wife's suggestion: he, I was sure, enjoyed the outing as much as I.

Suspended in my excitement so that for that brief time my life was one dimensional, I could not tell how long it was before Mr. Henderson cried at the top of his voice, "Now, girl, it's time to turn back!" Then I wished my brother's body *were* in the boat. Here, out at sea, I would push it into the water and the waves would move him miles away. The putrid smell, in its thick envelope of formaldehyde, which I had detected in the mortuary, returned to me and I retched as I did whenever I smelled ether. I would rather have Ivan in this vast natural grave than in the unmarked, communal earth where lay the unclaimed bodies washed upon the beaches.

I bent my head in my hands and cried because the child was dead, and I did not look up again until I knew we were going through the narrow shoals at the Point. I could see the sharp, glistening rocks and could hear the gulping of the water against their base. Since I could remember, I had been afraid of this place, for here, in a storm, a fisherman's dory had been dashed against the crags and his two children's bodies had never been found. We entered the dense fog again and made for the wharf. As he shut the motor off, Mr. Henderson said, "Well, Sonie, well, you had your ride."

I said, "Mr. Henderson, I am very grateful. I hope you don't think I'm crazy."

"You? No, I don't think you're crazy, Sonie." He was searching for something in the bottom of the boat. "Look out you don't lose your way in the fog."

"Well," I said. "Good-night, then."

"Good-night." I moved on up the ramp. "Was that your mother singing?"

"I guess so," I said.

"I never heard a thing like that before."

Though his words had perished, I now, as I reached the float, apprehended the note of fear in his voice.

I had just passed the great shadow of the Hotel when I heard footsteps somewhere near me. "Where are you?" cried a man's voice. "Here!" I called. "Are you lost?"

We approached each other, crying out at intervals, my invisible companion saying he had lost his way. We met then, and I was able to make out the indistinct contours of Nathan Kadish whose voice had been in no way familiar.

"What a hell of a thing," he said angrily. "I can't even find my way home."

"I'll lead you." We took hold of one another's hands and moved forward through the murk, he with his other hand thrust out before him as though he were brushing branches aside.

"I went to see you and your mother told me where you were. Listen, Sonie, I'm sorry."

We groped in silence. I did not know whether to tell him that the journey in the boat had been a ruse to fool my eccentric mother or to allow him to think that I had buried Ivan so that he would not know we were now technically known as paupers.

Suddenly, when our feet told us we had reached the road, he stopped and seized me. His mouth waspishly raged over my face with kisses while he held me in an embrace so disabling I could not breathe or defend myself. "Isn't it queer like this in the fog?" he whispered.

"Let me go, Nathan," I gasped.

"Come back this way. Let's sit on the Hotel porch."

We walked far apart, the fog rearing a barrier between us; we found the path leading to the Hotel, fumbled up to the top step, and sat down side by side.

"I suppose you think it's funny that I picked tonight of all nights to start making love to you. I didn't do it accidentally. I was waiting for a sign and tonight I got it when your mother said that Henderson was taking you out in his boat."

"What kind of a sign was that?" I asked him.

"Oh, that you're deep."

"But it wasn't my idea," I protested, immediately regretting my honesty. "It was Mrs. Henderson's."

"Hell," he brooded. "But you *are* deep. I couldn't be in love with a woman who wasn't. If I could, I would have been in love with your mother for her looks."

I laughed. "In love with Mamma? Why, she's middle-aged!"

"She's thirty-four, as you told me yourself."

"But, Nathan! You're nineteen."

"That doesn't cut any ice. I happen not to be in love with your mother. My interest in women does not lie entirely in their accidents but in their substance, and the substance of your mother appeals to me about as much as the substance of Mrs. Gonzales. However, the point is not that I am not in love with Shura Korf, but that I *could* be if I wanted to. I might add that I at one time conceived a major passion for a woman of forty and discontinued the affair only when she talked of divorcing her husband, a beauty-parlor operator, in order to marry me. And mind you, it was not her age that made such a marriage unappetizing to me. I am, and I acknowledge it without false modesty, extremely precocious and I have known for many years that marriage precludes love."

Recognizing the source of his position, I said, "Oh, I forgot to tell you. I've been reading *Confessions of a Young Man.*"

"By that I assume you mean to imply that I picked up my ideas about matrimony from George Moore," he said with a sneer. "The presentation of your charge is grotesquely naïve. My integrity obliges me to correct you: I am, to be sure, very similar to Moore, but the similarity antedated my reading of the *Confessions.* I have *always* been a citizen of the world, a pagan, an iconoclast, and from time immemorial my motto has been *Ars longa est.*"

"Are you going to be a writer, Nathan?"

"Of course," he replied simply and his voice was surprised that I should ask the question. "I am a satirist."

"What are you going to write? Poetry?"

"I will not choose my form until my soul is ready. My knowledge is vast but inchoate. At the moment, I am collecting experience. That is why I sought you out tonight. You interest me and when I say I love you, I am not using the word in its conventional sense. In a way, the word is almost synonymous with *curious*. I am curious to know what sort of person has emerged from that amazing combination, Hermann Marburg and Shura Korf."

"Have you found out?"

"No, but I have a clue."

I remembered, from long ago, the words of this boy's mother: "So your kid is half Rooshun and half German, half Hun as they say." I said, "Do you think I'm more like Mamma or like my father?"

"I can't tell yet. If you got to be like your father, I'd want you to live with me—for a while at least. He was the most sensitive man I ever knew."

"Did you know my father very well?"

"I know him better now than I did then, of course, because when we used to take those walks together, I didn't know as much as I do now about what had soured him. But looking back, I can see that he was crucified. Why, God! His conscience was hammering the nails in every minute of his life, and because he couldn't reason well—he didn't have much mind, you know—he figured that that eminent monument to filthy lies, the Roman Catholic Church, was right and he was wrong."

"I wonder if he ever went to confession after he left us."

I began to muse upon my father. How immediate before me were his crude bones, refined by the sunburned flesh! How directly did the wintry eyes advance! The face retired, and instead, I saw myself kneeling in the road to tie my boot lace. My loneliness was spatial and atmospheric, implanting in my heart a sadness which had not been there when the fact of his leaving stood alone. And as I saw that figure of myself in the uninhabited landscape where, in the leaden sky, the sun seemed slowly to fade rather than to sink, like a light-globe with weakening filaments, there came again that disturbing half memory which had eluded me as I knelt down and felt the salty breeze in my face.

"And that is why I love you," Nathan was saying and I realized with a start that I had not been listening to him.

"Why?"

He looked me full in the face. His eyes alone were distinct in the

*147*

misty darkness. "Which one of them were you thinking about? Your father or Ivan?"

As he spoke, six horns, one after the other, lamented Ivan with a single, prolonged moan. Nathan took my hand as the sound died. "How wonderful it is in the fog," he said, "when you can't see Chichester and you can't see Boston and *ergo,* if you have any gifts, you are, as I said, a citizen of the world."

"I'd rather be a citizen of Boston."

"You're not that stupid." His head hovered over mine, swaying down and withdrawing as if, preoccupied with his thoughts, he had started to kiss me and then had forgotten. "Really, you're not that stupid, Sonie. Don't you know you don't fit into the pattern?"

"I don't know what the pattern is."

"I don't know either, but you don't fit into *any* pattern, not any more than I do."

"Oh, but I'm not intellectual like you, Nathan."

"I should say you're not. Still, that doesn't keep you from being intelligent, does it? For instance, you don't have to know the theology of the Catholic Church to know that your father was persecuted, do you? And you don't have to know psychology to know that your mother is . . . well, to know what your mother is like."

"What did you start to say about her?"

"Nothing." But his arm pressed hard against my shoulders. "Freedom is the first thing you've got to get. Think of the *Confessions.* That was the primary requisite for him, and it's the same thing for us."

I was seduced by the memory of the Parisian apartment and in that moment, when Nathan's proximity lent me strength and when, moreover, Boston was visible only as a line of murky lights, I promised myself that I would have the best, whether that was to be had across the bay or across the ocean. I said to Nathan, "Now I know what you mean."

"Do you?" he cried. "If you do, I'm mad with joy! But you must know independently of me, you see, Sonie."

"Oh, I do. I see it quite apart from you."

And I did, because in that vague but luminous and intricate future, that tree-filled and fragrant garden, I did not see Nathan more

148

clearly than I saw any other of the witty and sensitive and handsome people. What I saw was myself, that activating principle which set my feet upon a boulevard, and simultaneously made me love, sense loss, hear, now in Chichester, a final foghorn, that law or theorem of nature for which the term "Sonia" and its variant "Sonie" had arbitrarily been chosen.

Nathan stood up. "What happens next," he said bitterly, "is that we do what everybody else does. We fall in love and then it goes bad, but that can't be helped. You are in love with me, aren't you?"

"Yes."

He ran down the steps. I could hear his feet quickly crunching the sand as he withdrew into the fog. I sat still a little while. His kisses, like echoes, were repeated on my skin. From the points where his lips had touched, sensation rayed out until my whole face throbbed. But although I felt as brilliantly branded as he was himself, I was aware, not so much of the maturation of my love for him as I was for the achievement of knowledge: the knowledge that my father had deserted me forever and that forever Ivan would be dead.

2

The fog was dispelled on the next day; all traces of the snow were gone save for small pyramidal drifts in the corners of steps and in the crotches of leafless vines on the wall of the Catholic church. And the sun, in the vivid sky, warmed the wind, disclosed again the waves and the broad, shining shingle. It was one of those days that come as a surprise in the middle of winter, like a gift sent on no anniversary, so that the pleasure takes us unaware.

Early in the morning, hunger had awakened me. But as I dressed, my desire for food faded and I felt a little sick, for I remembered, seeing the empty space where Ivan's bed had been, that last evening I had been unfaithful to him by greedily snatching at Nathan's praise and affection. I made myself a cup of tea and as I sat down to drink it, I heard the Kadishes' door slam and through the window saw my lover running, hatless, his shirt tail streaming out behind him, with a book in one hand and a cinnamon roll in the other. He did not seem ludicrous. I half rose to call out to him, but remorse arrested

149

me, and I deliberately looked away, whispering my brother's name as I bent my head: "Oh, Ivan, Ivan, Ivan," but the invocation was futile.

My mother kept to her bed all the morning and in the early afternoon she called me in. At first, when I sat down on the edge of the bed, she only stared at me. In these past months, her eyes had made me uncomfortable; I was afraid when a look from her demanded one directly from me, for it was as if she spun out a thread connecting with me which some vague superstition prevented me from breaking. If I came in from school and found her huddled into the old wrapper, staring at the oven door or gazing out the window, removed in a world as private as sleep, yet obliged by habit to make a transition back to the world that contained my presence, she would carry her stare to my face and, after a time, would see me. "I didn't hear you," she would say, for her senses were confused. Actually, she had heard me, but the sound of the door and of my footsteps were only now related to the sight of me. So now she regarded me for long minutes before she spoke. Her eyes, in another setting, might have made her look perpetually feverish, but because of her high color, they were the domestic and innocent eyes of a healthy animal. And yet there was something added to them; they, like the lines of her face, had been touched up, refined, perhaps by some ancient drop of Oriental blood. It was not hard for me to understand, seeing her this morning, how Nathan could be in love with her.

"He's drowned," she said. "You can't imagine what it looks like when they take it out of the water."

"Hush, Mamma, you go to sleep now."

But she would not be quieted. She gave me a sly smile. "Let me tell you what happened to me once, Sonie. Okay?"

"No! I don't want to hear."

"Please! It's not about Luibka, darling." Knowing that if I did not hear the story now I would be obliged to later, I sat down. She held both my hands tightly and her eyes never left my face.

On a feast day, when the summer was at its hottest, she had gone in the evening with four friends to the river to swim. They had to pass by the cemetery at the Devitschiepol convent where tents had been pitched for the feast and where *kwass* was sold at little pavilions along the paths. Each of the five girls carried a white sheet to wrap herself in when she came out of the water. On the way they had been joking, calling them their shrouds and winding sheets.

A group of Cossacks, a little drunk, were standing beside a booth, listening to a fair-haired Pole who, in a piercing, sorrowful voice, was singing this song:

> They shout the loud alarm,
> My war steeds paw the ground;
> I hear him neigh,
> O, let me go!

One of his companions cried out, "And what does the girl say to that, eh?" And so he sang again:

> Let others rush to death
> Too young and gentle, thou
> Shalt yet watch o'er our cottage home;
> Thou must not pass the Don.

Laughing, the girls went on, and one of them paraphrased the last line of the soldier's song, "Thou must not swim the Moskva." Already they could feel the cool water on their hot, dusty bodies and they hastened on through the crowds into a quiet lane that led to the river bank. One by one, as silently as fish, they slipped under the still, black surface. How good the water felt when they floated on their backs, letting their unbound hair be soaked to the roots! They called to one another: "Isn't it splendid, Dounia?" "Are you cool yet, Varenka?" "Look at Shura! She is going under the water!"

Afterwards, they sat for a while, wrapped up in their sheets, listening to the remote, enchanting voices from behind them in the town. Across the river they could see the fires of night fishermen. A trout leaped like a silver tongue. Someone began to sing the Cossack's song, but all at once broke off and cried, "We're not all here! Shura? Marfa? Dounia? It is Varenka who is missing!"

With the tails of their sheets flying behind them, they ran in their bare feet up and down the grassy bank, calling to their friend, but there was no answer save for the sleepy murmur of the river and the bumbling of the city. They called for half an hour until their throats were sore and then, crying, clutching at one another, they fled back the way they had come. The festival was as lively as ever, and the Polish soldier, drunker than he had been before so that his voice was deeper, slower, and more melancholy, was singing still as if he had never left off:

> Let others rush to death
> Too young and gentle, thou
> Shalt yet watch o'er our cottage home;
> Thou must not pass the Don.

The girls, half naked, their bare legs showing through the folds of their white wrappings, shivered though it was a hot night, ran into the church of the Virgin of Smolensk, and after they had told two nuns of the catastrophe, fell on their knees and prayed.

Days later, the body was found in shallow water and brought in by a boatman. Varenka's companions were summoned to identify the sodden, bloated parody of a human being. Faceless, livid, softened, it was a horrid spectacle. Of all the girls, Varenka had been the gayest. Only two days before, her grandfather, a rich merchant in St. Petersburg, had sent her a pair of Torjeck-leather boots and a blue silk blouse with a thousand tiny pleats. How Dounia, Marfa, Shura, Manetchka prayed for her! And yet, not one of them could remember how she had been when she was one of them, but only how she had lain dead on the counter, swollen like a fat fish, and like the fish, white, shapeless as if the bones themselves had been worn thin by the water and were no stronger than those of a halibut.

"If you had touched her, your finger would have gone in like dough, Sonie. Oh, you can't imagine!"

I was dazed, not by her dreadful story, but by the realization that she had hated Ivan so much that she had tried to make his burial the most loathesome she could conceive. It occurred to me to tell her the truth, but I was afraid of the cunning in her face.

"If I could forget about *him*. But his head keeps floating up at me. Oh, so white and ugly!"

In my astonished face, she laughed! She was laughing not with humor but with joy, like a young girl in love who can find no other expression for her rapture. And then it came to me with a shock that the song she had been singing last night as she went through the fog was the same one she had sung me this morning when she told me the story of Varenka, so that I knew it had all been planned and she had not just now recollected her friend.

I looked upon my mother with sheer fright. It was as if I looked upon naked evil in the person of that woman whose beauty so far surpassed any other I had ever seen that it was almost divine, as if she had come directly from the hand of God, but had, immediately afterward, been inhabited by a ravenous and indefatigable fiend. Or perhaps she was not alive with wickedness but was dead with it: an empty vessel, or an excellent hull holding a withered fruit. I wondered how deep she was and if my own depths of which Nathan had spoken were the same.

There was a familiar expression in her face which had taken on repose after her fit of laughing, and seeking, at last I redeemed the day Ivan had been born when her strength had rallied to give him a name. I had wondered why she had called him Ivan rather than Hermann since the latter had come to be a generic term of opprobrium to her. It was that her eccentricity, her madness, call it what you would, was shrewd. Hermann would have been too much. I had known that even in her stupor then she had hated my brother and, later throughout his lifetime, I had sometimes wondered why she had not hated him as she carried him before his birth and why she had not hated me. She had not, because she had fortified herself, long, long before, with the conviction that men were all villains and women were their innocent victims.

She had closed her eyes. "Leave me alone now, Sonia," she said wearily. "It is all over."

I stood looking down at her for a moment and I exulted in the trick Mr. Henderson and I had played upon her. Saddening as it was not to know where Ivan was buried, I was consoled by the fact that he lay in the dry ground.

Just as I closed the door behind me, I heard a car stop on the road beside our house, and stepping to the window, I saw that it was Miss Pride's and Mac was handing her out. Rattled as I was, I collected myself sufficiently to realize that it would not do to receive her in the house, for my mother might repeat to her the story of Varenka's death. I went out to meet her. She was carrying a fuchsia-colored

153

cyclamen planted in a little white pot. When she caught sight of me, she said, "My dear, am I too late?" vesting her cold voice with a gentleness I had not heard in it before, and looking at me with a genuine compassion.

"We buried him yesterday," I said.

She took my hand. "I only got your letter this morning and I came immediately."

The word "immediately" made me see her leaving her breakfast half eaten and her mail unopened and not waiting even to cancel her engagements for the day. Had I observed my picture carefully, I would have seen it was full of errors, for it was already afternoon and if she had got my letter in the morning post, she would have had ample time not only to finish her breakfast but her luncheon as well. Neither did it occur to me at once that she was not telling the truth and that she must have got my letter the day before.

"It's very kind of you, ma'am," I said. "But I'm sorry that I troubled you."

"What kind of friend would I be if you weren't free to trouble me?"

Twice as electrifying was this second shock, this designation of herself as my "friend." But strangely, my first reaction was not one of pleasure, but almost of disgust as for a few seconds she stood before me, not as that grand Bostonian to whose slightest favor I had aspired, but as a selfish old woman who, as a sop to her conscience, had brought me a potted plant. It seemed to me that she had aged remarkably since the past summer. Probably no change had taken place in her at all. It is difficult, in a wrinkled face, to compute how many new wrinkles have appeared in a year's time, or to see, in white hair, all the stages of its purification. It was, rather, that I had changed and my altered feelings had turned a spotlight upon the arthritic stiffening of her fingers from which she had removed the white gloves, the desiccation and the yellow hue of her creased skin, the protuberation of her veins, the liverish patches on her wrists, the aridity of her thin lips. But a censor in me checked me before I had disarrayed her features beyond repair, and as from her small, brisk person there emanated the sharp odor of her expensive soap, she recovered her familiar and beloved shape.

She said, "If you're not needed here, won't you drive to Boston with me and have a cup of tea? Mac will have you back in time for dinner."

I told her I must be at the Brunsons' by four o'clock. "Nonsense. No one would make you work today. What Brunson is it?" And when I told her Dr. Brunson's name, she said, "Oh, then he must be the Brunson brother-in-law of Harry Barker. I dare say he's not such an ogre that I can't beard him in his den. I'll just run on and tell him you won't be there while you're getting your things and we'll pick you up afterwards."

It struck me, as I went into the house to get my "things" (a large blue tam and a shabby leather jacket the sight of which, hanging listlessly on a nail behind the kitchen door, made me wish I had not accepted the invitation) that it was odd she had gone to the dentist and not to Mrs. Brunson. I concluded that she was afraid she might be trapped into a conversation with my mistress if she called upon her and such a conversation, entertaining as I conceived it, would cause Miss Pride severe discomfort.

My mother had fallen asleep. I put the cyclamen on the high bureau, predicting as I did so that when Mamma learned where it came from, she would remind me, as she had often done in the past, of Miss Pride's gracious gift of the rattle. (I was not disappointed. That evening when I came home, she was drinking a glass of the dentist's brandy and tenderly cupping one of the blossoms in her hand. "It's just like that man said, a person ought to think of the living. I think that Miss Pride's sweet.")

Warmed by a lap robe as soft as fur and lulled by the steady speed of the automobile, I looked through the windows with careless eyes, not paying the close attention I had always planned, to every feature of the road and the villages through which we drove. And yet I repeated to myself, "At last I am going to Boston," and the wonder of it was reinforced when Miss Pride marveled that in eighteen years I had not been farther away than Salem. Had she known, she said, she would have come to fetch me long ago. Sometime this spring she would come for me and would show me the Public Gardens when the tulips were blooming and the children were riding the swan-boats.

She inquired if I had heard recently from my father and when I told her I had heard nothing since he left, five years before, she shook her head with some unexpressed disapproval and said, "You have been very brave, my dear child."

I could not reply to the compliment and I had no wish to deny it. I said, "Did Dr. Brunson say it was all right?"

"Oh, perfectly. He's a very good-natured man. I was amused to see a placard hanging prominently in his office which read 'Terms Strictly Cash.' He appears to be more prosperous than most men of his profession in small towns."

"He has a practice in Marblehead too," I threw out.

"As a matter of fact, I have met him before and his wife, too, on several occasions. And isn't there a girl about your age? I met them under circumstances which makes it more convenient for me to be unable to place them clearly."

Inspirited by my curiosity, I asked, "Was it here or in Boston that you met them?"

"Why, it was in my own house, Sonia. They came uninvited to my open house on Christmas Eve two or three years running, and each time I was so muddled by the throngs of people, all of whom appear at those affairs more or less familiar, that I said to Dr. Barker, with whom I have a nodding acquaintance, 'One does see such remarkable people in one's own drawing-room on these Christmas Eves of ours. Can you tell me, for instance, who that blonde woman is over there by the buffet with the identical daughter? Perhaps they are friends of the accommodator.' And of course, as you've already guessed, the woman was Harry Barker's sister. But what an unconscionable snob the doctor is! He did not enlighten me. He allowed me, each year, to make the same mistake. This past year, someone standing near-by jostled my arm and led me away to inform me of my *faux pas*. I was at first outraged with Dr. Barker for disclaiming any connection with his relatives. It's not the sort of thing one does. But on second thoughts—and on looking for a second time at your employer—I forgave him, but could not resist the temptation to apologize for my mistake. I fear I made the poor man quite miserable. He greets me most perfunctorily on the street now." She smiled at her triumph, effaced the look of amusement, and said, "You are disloyal. You should not have allowed me to tell you that unfortunate story. As penalty, you must now tell me *your* opinion of Chichester's leading citizens."

"Why, they have been very good to me, ma'am."

"You speak the language that befits the grateful servant. But it was my intention today to give you a little vacation from your servitude. I wanted to have a long talk with you about that very charming man, your father, and what you remember of him, and what you think has become of him. And I wanted, even more, to know something about *you*." Placing her hand lightly on my wrist, she said, "I admired your letter. Its restraint, its language gave more pleasure to me than anything that has come in the mails in thirty years."

"Thank you, ma'am."

"Now, Sonia, for the rest of the afternoon, *do* call me not 'ma'am' but 'Miss Pride.' As I was saying—you must forgive me; I am an old woman and apt to shoot off on a tangent at any moment—this is your holiday. I want you not to speak as a servant. I want to know something about you and therefore, I wish you to begin with your opinion of the dentist's family."

I thought for a moment. "They are rather money-minded, I think. And Dr. Barker won't come to their house, although they invite him all the time. It's as though he were ashamed of them. I don't know why he should be unless it's that Mrs. Brunson wears an awful lot of lipstick and she's too fat for her dresses and for the high-heeled shoes she wears."

My companion's face showed nothing. I did not know whether her objective had been the one she had stated to me, or if she had wanted, out of sheer malice, to hear ill spoken of people so far her inferior that I was surprised she even troubled herself with thinking of them. She questioned me not only about the Brunsons' reading habits and their friends and their political and religious opinions, but also about my own, and when she had exhausted my information, said, "Now that I have your *dossier*, let me ask a final question: Would you really come to work for me without any wages?"

"Indeed I would, ma'am."

"Miss Pride, please. You don't think you could do better? You don't think you have any other talents?"

"Oh, no, I have no talents, Miss Pride. I'm very poor in school. I won't be given any honors at commencement."

She smiled. "Nor was I given any honors. But I wasn't thinking of that kind of talent. I mean the talent of character which hasn't much to do with braininess. With brains, yes, but not with braininess. That, you may as well know, I can't abide. It isn't useful to a woman and I'm not altogether sure it's useful to a man. Dr. Philip McAllister is a brainy man and he's not as sensible as he might be. Do you know him?"

I said I did not, that I had only heard his name. He was one of the house physicians at the Chichester hospital.

"He's one of my niece's beaux and a charmer. But brainy, as I say. I suppose you had Dr. Galbraith for the little boy? Between you and me, Sonia, he's a rascal. He's killed as many patients as he's cured, but then, as I often say to Philip, they all do. I am my own physician. I ventilate my house well and I take a walk every day. As a result, I'm never ill. I don't believe in any of these fads, these vitamins, allergies, neuroses. I am the most old-fashioned woman in Boston."

I told her—because I could think of nothing else to say—that I was never ill, and that I believed I had made up my mind never to be ill when I was a child and was offended by the medicine bottles of the Hotel guests. And then, when she said nothing, I asked her pointlessly if she were coming back this summer. "What made you think I would not? No, *I* don't change."

There was a momentary silence. Twice she parted her lips but thought the better of it. Then she plunged in. "You have read more than I thought you had. Not more than I should have expected you to, but more than I really like. At your age, you should concentrate on manners, my dear, not on ideas. But that can be remedied later. Will you be satisfied with a very simple explanation of why I have fetched you out of Chichester? Can you believe it is no more than that I am interested in human nature and see in you an interesting juxtaposition of class—whatever that absurd term may mean—possible only in a democracy in an advanced stage of decomposition? I mean by that: my family, on my mother's side, was established in this country by an indentured servant whose master settled in Virginia. The descendants of my ancestor, having acquired their freedom, worked north to Massachusetts. In those days, to be sure, such servitude was often little more than a convenient way to get passage to the colonies. A servant had not necessarily been a servant. In the case of my family, I don't know, for the records are full of gaps. But for the sake of argument, let us say that servants' blood runs in my veins. Yet I am, for all practical purposes, a member of the oldest American aristocracy."

Her glittering golden eyes, full on my face, commanded me to keep my mind on what she was saying, and I listened intently, nodding now and again as I did in Plane Geometry class when I did not understand a word of the instructions.

"You're no servant, Sonia. You belong to a class which no longer exists in this country, that is, the artisan class. And since so august a body of society has been demolished you must, so to speak, skip a grade. I may as well tell you that your father is the only specimen of his lamented genus I have ever had the good fortune to know, and it was a bitter day when I heard he had left us. For he left *me* as well as you and your mother, my child. I felt, 'So long as Hermann Marburg makes my shoes, I will be in touch with the reality of the past.' Ah, he did not realize his responsibility!"

As she spoke, she lifted the hem of her long coat. "You see what I wear now. Painful, hideous, expensive, flimsy! And look at your poor feet, those poor feet I used to see when you were a little girl. Then they wore shoes that had been *wrought* with devotion. I hope for your good father that he went back to his family in Würzburg."

"I hope so too, Miss Pride. But he said that night when he left that he was going out west."

"Perhaps you'll meet once again. You must forgive me if I am blunt: he was a fool. He took the indifference—they were poor, how could they help it?—of the fishermen as an index to all Americans towards good leather-work. He was like the visitor who sees only New York and carries away the impression that the United States is a hodgepodge of skyscrapers and horrible racket. Actually, if he had come to Boston as I begged him to do time and again, he would have prospered."

"I guess so. But he didn't have any energy, you know."

159

I was thinking of how he would brood on the winter evenings because Saint Bonaventure had failed him or he had failed the saint, he was not sure which. He was not altogether dead, for, corruptible as were his vows to go to Mass, they must have sprung from a recognition of his sloth which, by the creed of his hard-working family as well as by that of the church, was a deadly sin. And the fact that his reaction was overt, even though incompleted, suggested a residue, at least of the talent of remorse. Paradoxically, this very filament of remorse had served as the central thread in a great fabric of mortal sin, for, stirring him out of his house on Sunday morning, setting his feet on the road to the chapel, it languished; his contrition melted and, his mind reflecting, his will consenting, he went no further, took the other road leading to the Coast Guard house. But it had not occurred to me until now, hearing Miss Pride praise his talents, remembering how Nathan had admired his sensibilities, that my father was not a man whose misery could be mitigated by a change of environment or an increase of worldly goods or an establishment in a society. He was a robbed man, and the robber of what Miss Pride had esteemed was the very thing Nathan had loved: his sensibility, refined by what influence I could only conjecture. And this sensibility had led him away from the traditions of his religion and his work and neither the one nor the other could stand alone.

"Energy?" queried Miss Pride.

"I don't know how to say it. I only mean that I'm not sure he would have been happy just to thrive in Boston."

"Why, on the contrary, I think he would have. He was, after all, not a very complicated person. I daresay if he had just had his beer and *Wienerschnitzel* and had been able to hold up his head amongst his neighbors, he would have been completely happy."

Although I did not disagree with her, I did not, reflecting on him, think that my father had been so naïve a man, nor had he been so much the conventional comic-strip German. Miss Pride was either forgetting or ignoring my mother who was the author of a good deal of the tumult in him. Quite different, for example, from the rough kindness he showed me in the shop had been the nature I saw in the house when all the mild amusement at our jokes had faded from his face, as if he stepped from the sunlight into the shade, or as if his skin, obedient to the affections of his soul, darkened with his entering into the gloom which enveloped my mother and all she touched. Just as, at other times, in his shop, he would be gazing out the window at the bay and his heart could not fail to impart to his face some of the joy he felt in seeing the clean white sails under the blue sky and on the blue water. The impressions, altered by his heart into a desire for a life inclusive of such things, would be altered once again until in his eyes and lips there would be indications that he was deep in a radiant dream of being already part of such a life, being free, I suppose, not only of his duty towards my mother and me, but free even of the memory of it. How inevitable it seems that happiness will be the next state we come to if only we are once rid of our present sorrow! Our troubles seem to have but one axis: we forget that even though our love were returned, our debts would not willy-nilly take themselves off; that even though the headaches which plague us were cured, we should still suffer from a broken heart. Could my father, who had cried like a child and sobbed that despairing word, *Verzeihung*, be content ever with what Miss Pride imagined for him? His sin of omission, because it seemed imposed upon him by some external evil, angered him, for he had gone so far in his transgressions against the law of the church that he could no longer bear his terror of the consequences and temporarily substituted another emotion. Just so, the dipsomaniac wrests himself from the fear of his desire by changing the name of it to "need," thus to tolerate his destruction as if it were no fault of his own. It was this reasoning in hallucinations whose existence he felt obliged to prove to others that made him say, if I asked him why he had not gone to church, "Something I can't account for held me back."

Miss Pride was asking me a question. "You're finding the approach to Boston distasteful, aren't you?"

I quickly looked out. We were going through the merry slums where wanton cats sprawled full-length on the sidewalk and dirty, murderous children shot pop-guns at one another and hideously howled against the exasperated clang of the trolley-car. Bleak tenements nudged a pallid sky where Chichester's sun did not shine. Dark cafés, sunk like black eyes into the walls, advertised with winking, blood-red lights, "Beer . . . Schlitz . . . Beer . . . Schlitz."

Some distance ahead of us I saw the white column of the Customs House, and I realized with disappointment that all the way, the State House dome had been invisible, and that, because of the detours we had made, my original impression of it as dwarfing all the other buildings on the mainland, would be altered, would be perhaps forever lost. I asked Miss Pride if we drove past it.

"Oh, you shall see it, never fear. I see you've been properly brought up to respect Boston." Her voice was ironic. "But I'll let you in on a secret—I think the State House is a perfect fright."

She said there was no time today to acquaint me with Boston's points of interest (dashed by her contempt for the State House, I was just as glad) but she would show me the one thing which she had always felt was the jewel of the city. She would not care about the destruction of everything else, the First Church or the gardens or King's Chapel, if only the Granary Burying Ground were preserved.

We entered its iron-bound precincts and advanced down the central path between the splitting gravestones that tilted backwards toward the austere obelisk of Franklin and the eroded sarcophagi. The several trees of the yard, black-trunked, thickly burled, and leafless now, and the naïve death's-heads, sprouting angels' wings on the decaying wafers of rock, were dextrous accidents, for they, and the wind we heard when the noise of traffic was briefly suspended contrived to give the place an air so formidable and esoteric that I felt death, at his most facetious unsightliness, walking beside me. I understood why she had said this was the heart of the city. Walled on one side by the Athenaeum through whose back windows a solitary old Bostonian, withered and hewn, was gravely regarding us, the sparse and lowly graves of the harsh garden testified to the city's conviction of its rightness and its adamant resistance to change.

Miss Pride confessed that she was partial to graveyards and often spent a full day in the one in Concord where the famous authors were buried, and of which she was particularly fond since it accommodated many of her ancestors. She spoke of others in New Hampshire and in Maine but declared that this small antique plot where we moseyed was her "first love."

"I don't know why it is nowhere but in New England do you find a well-turned cemetery. In France, they're nondescript. There is one other graveyard that took my fancy. When I was a young lady, I one time went to New Orleans and took a side trip to a little town where some sort of pioneers, German, I believe, had been buried. (My ignorance about the rest of this country, my dear, will shock you. I'm like the woman who said she went to Los Angeles by way of Charles River Village.) It was in a grove of oaks, dripping with Spanish moss which made everything most gloomy, most Doré. I found it creepy, I must admit, but it *was* handsome."

I admired the darling of her heart but asked her why she preferred it to all the others, and she said, "Well, in some of them, the newer ones, the horticulture is rather too much and the epitaphs have certainly gone downhill. But the fact is, that the names in the others are second-rate. That is, even Mr. Emerson can't compete with Revere or Otis. Don't misunderstand me. Some of my best friends are named Emerson."

She had sent Mac on and we walked to her house down the street past the State House to which I found myself indifferent. And at the moment I released my long-cherished impression of it, I realized that my desire for Boston had never been so real as it was now as, grimy, tattered, large for my age, I strode beside this clean, tart woman, so certain of her good blood, her wit, her wealth, her position in society (so *au courant* with her ancestral history that she could call a Cabot inferior to a Prescott, like a Howard running down the House of Windsor) that she could appear on the streets of her city in any company without the slightest risk of censure. Earlier, I had told her that I was not properly dressed to go to tea. "Dressed?" she had said. "Do you call me dressed? You may be more formal in Chichester at tea time than we are in Boston, but you look dressed enough to me. The important thing is, are you warm enough?"

"Now, we turn here," she said, "and then we start going down. Our Hill is a real hill. I always say it's really much steeper than the Great Blue Hill." Indeed, with a push, one could go hurtling down the brick-paved sidewalk and never stop, but shoot into the Charles which was visible, far below, as a wedge of chilly blue, crossed now and then by a white sail. Miss Pride, sure-footed as a burro, marched briskly down, and I, joyously regarding her from the corner of my eye, kept as close to the houses as I could in order not to bump clumsily into her. Her house was not far; its front windows faced Louisburg Square and here, as if it were an oasis chosen to delight the eyes of some favored heavenly power, the sun, hidden elsewhere by the city's smoke, shone brilliantly on white doorways and their brass trimmings.

Tea was served to us in the library, a lofty room at the back of the house, chilled and dark. Through the drawn, dark red curtains, the late afternoon light barely penetrated. Miss Pride asked me if I would like to have the lamps turned on and when I replied that I liked the dimness (it was not true; I would have liked to look at everything under a searchlight), she said, "It seemed a little *triste* to me, but you, of course, are feeling a little *triste*." She had thought to have a fire today but it had turned out so warm we would only be uncomfortable—she found the room stuffy as it was. I agreed, although the damp coolness of the place filtered through the layers of my skin and set my bones to dancing.

When she went out for a moment to speak to a servant, I made a tour of the room. The middle sections of the end walls were recessed for twin fire-places with black marble frames; in either was a bed of solid, tawny ashes, the careful accumulation of years. The hearths were flanked with bookshelves reaching to the ceiling and in a far corner, near the windows, stood ladders which might be attached to a track at the baseboard and to an upper shelf so that one might investigate the high books. I was more impressed by these appurtenances than by any other in the room, for they suggested a most serious purpose and I had never dreamed of seeing anything like them in an establishment other than a public library or a shoe store. The outer wall was taken up by two long casements between which stood a Governor Winthrop secretary. On the wall above, a gentleman forthrightly speculated on the tall cabinet opposite him through whose glass doors were visible silver loving cups and brass placques standing upright in a narrow trough. I say "gentleman" because I knew at once that he could have been nothing else. The edges of his gray waistcoat were piped in white and his cutaway, the warm color of a dove's back, was striped with fine silver threads. He was a lean man and in his severe face, age had peeled the flesh almost to the skeleton, but it was evident, in the bright, flat eyes (uncannily perceptive either through the painter's skill or his model's power to project his character into the canvas) that age had not deprived the brain of its faculties; they almost spoke. He was, I knew, some relative of Miss Pride's, and I believed he was her father, for the eyes were exactly like hers and, for the sake of experiment, endowing them with life, I observed that from numerous angles, they, too, seemed to stare suddenly first at one thing and then at another. They did not *follow* me, but waited until I had reached my new destination before they apprehended me again. I was standing near the cabinet when Miss Pride came back into the room. Before me was a small table on which stood a satinwood chess-board and ivory men. Two chairs had been drawn up in readiness for a game and upon a little glass-topped stand, a decanter had been placed with two inhalers.

"Oh, do you play?" asked Miss Pride. I said I did not. "You should learn. It is the best of all games, the greatest test of intelligence. Bridge, I have no use for. My father, whom you see up there above the desk, was the foremost chess-player of Beacon Hill in his time. This room, in a sense, is dedicated to his pastimes. For in addition to being a past-master at chess, he was a great reader, as you can see from the size of his library. And here, in this cabinet are his yachting trophies. But I have tried to make the place cozy, not too much like a museum, you know, not too much like a mausoleum. After all, we have graveyards to take care of the dead, we needn't keep their ghosts in our houses."

I was curious to know who the chess-game had been set up for, and presently she enlightened me. "I must confess to a degree of vanity over my own game. My friends were corrupted some years ago by that humdrum Oriental importation, Mah Jong, and have never since been able to keep their wits about them at the chess-board. Consequently, for a long time I have had to be satisfied with playing against myself. Occasionally I get wind of a young man at Harvard College who knows a smattering and I do enjoy the combat. But a young man against an old woman is not quite pleasing. They're always anxious to finish the game so that they can start reforming me." The word "reforming" she whispered, drawing out the second syllable with an intentionally comic puckering of her lips that made me laugh and ask her what their mission was.

"My dear," she said, leading me to a fat, short sofa, upholstered in red velour which had faded in some places to a rusty pink, "don't ask me that until I have had a cup of tea." The tea had arrived just then, and I was disappointed to see that the refreshments were only rye bread spread with sweet butter and thin slices of fruit cake to which I had always had an aversion. "Will you have sugar and lemon or sugar and cream?" she asked. I told her I took nothing in my tea and I refused anything to eat. My abstention seemed to please her for she remarked, "Why, you're a perfect guest. I think it's foolish to stuff oneself at tea time on strawberry tarts and all sorts of sandwiches. In some houses it's become a regular meal. I feel we carry our Anglophilia too far sometimes, don't you? Or perhaps you think we don't go far enough?"

I had no idea what she meant. There was nothing patronizing in her voice, nothing in the least supercilious and I concluded that any young lady should be able to specify at once, and with reasons for her choice, the camp to which she belonged on the question of the American imitation of British customs (I was at least, through the help of my reading, able to grasp the meaning of the word). I was tongue-tied, but at length, when I saw her hand poised over the teapot as she waited for my answer and realized that she did not introduce subjects of conversation that one might take or leave, I brought out, "I have never been to England." The faintest of smiles pinched the corners of her eyes, and she changed the subject to literature which I had told her, on the way in, was my principal interest.

I learned that she regarded literature as utilitarian, as essential to good breeding. It was an ingredient of life like religion, and just as one believed in God and invoked Him but trafficked only with the minister, so one believed in Shakespeare but depended on *The Atlantic Monthly*. Instinctively she felt learning to be a masculine province, even though she was an advocate of equal rights. She told me how well-read her father had been, how he had been instructed by all these books that lined the walls, whether they were poetry or fiction or history, and she rather raised her voice on "poetry" as though it were remarkable that he had found it useful, and admirable that he had renounced the temptation to enjoy it, had solemnly been "instructed." In the last years of his life, he had taken up Oriental languages and for this she had the deepest respect. "Now the mastery of a language I can understand. It is as thrilling as chess, and it is useful, although poor Papa never benefited from his Japanese as he only learned it when he was too old to travel. But he had the illusion, at least, that he was getting somewhere, don't you see." Hastily, as an afterthought, she added, "My dear, you must not think for a minute I'm like that quixotic Mr. Brock at the Barstow. A foreign language is useful in a foreign country, and I suppose that if one were cast on to a desert island and had nothing to read but a French translation of Mr. Emerson, one would be justified in reading it."

The mission of the young men who played chess with her was, it appeared, to induce her to read modern poetry. She had no patience with these eccentric cubs who had demolished tradition, and she found particularly infuriating certain New Englanders who had seen fit to poke fun at their countrymen. "I see nothing intrinsically humorous in the name, *The Boston Evening Transcript,*" she said in temper, "and much as the author of its contumely is respected, I think he writes doggerel. I have never quite got his connections clear. All I know of him is that he was born in Saint Louis, even though he really was an Eliot. Times change. In the old days the people we claimed as our literary men were born in Concord or Cambridge." I asked her if she had known Amy Lowell well and she replied, "The less said about Amy Lowell, the better," so that I supposed—because I was sure Miss Pride had the pick of all Boston society—that the two had had a disagreement in which, of course, Miss Pride had been in the right. And later when she said, reverting to an earlier subject, that literary people were often "brainy" and that she did not enjoy brains when she was relaxing at her tea-table ("All things," she said, "in their places."), I decided that Miss Lowell had perhaps never been invited to the house and that their meetings had only taken place in the Athenaeum.

Poetry frankly made her uncomfortable. She had not the same aversion to music or painting, perhaps because the media of the composer and the painter were foreign to her and she did not see their creations in the context of their lives. Not so with a poet who laid his very heart at her feet, tracing upon it as upon a contour map, his unbridled passions. Some young person, child of an old friend, had one day come to tea and had brought with him the Holy Sonnets of John Donne, and in spite of her protests, had managed to read one aloud to her. It was a particularly passionate one (Miss Pride, disliking such words as "passionate" said "fantastic") ending with the couplet:

> Except you' enthrall me, never shall be free,
> Nor ever chaste, except you ravish me.

The same young man had, she understood, taken to writing poems himself, much in the insolent tone of the mocker of *The Boston Evening Transcript,* and had composed some vicious lines on the Granary Burying Ground. The young man's "case" was a mystery to her because he had not only come from a perfectly dignified family and had gone straight to Harvard from Groton and was going into the law, but also because he was directly descended from at least two of the illustrious skeletons in the yard.

I was in love with that young man who had perhaps sat on this very sofa, resplendent in a long coat and trousers of a different cloth and thick-soled shoes and a bean-shave, reading poetry in the accents of Beacon Hill's Olympians. Magnificent creature, that intellectual aristocrat, pausing between crew practice and an evening at the Porcellian Club to exhibit, in an old lady's fusty house, the fullness of his life! I at once hoped that I should one day see him here in all his gentlemanly regalia and that he had been forbidden to come again for his importunity. For equally in love was I with Miss Pride whose small, dour world was governed by one and only one principle, a principle that varied neither in time nor place, a law which forbade riot to follow on the heels of chance: John Donne might once in her house pose as a forward woman, begging, in so many words, to be seduced, but he would not behave so twice. Between those two astronomies, the young man's whose earth was plural, and Miss Pride's whose solitary world was Boston, round which the trifling planets revolved at a respectful distance, I could not choose, for both were true.

We had finished our tea. Miss Pride rose and as she moved about the room turning on the lamps, she said, "Your letter so charmed me. And as I read it—let me say that I was impressed by your calligraphy which has the purity without the flourishes of the Spencerian hand—I said to myself, 'Here is *one* person of the new generation who preserves the ideals of my own. I will, indeed, come to her aid.' I cannot tell you how much it grieves me that I was too late. My little flower, I'm afraid, was hardly a substitute. Yet, without me, you solved your problem, you were not stumped. Oh, you'll be all right! I will say quite candidly that it flatters me to think I have perhaps had some influence on the development of your character. I have, although you have perhaps not been aware of it, been closely observant of you for several years and had thought, from time to time, of making the proposition to you which you set forth in your letter, that is, that you enter my service. But when you wrote me, I knew then that that was not the ticket. My dear child, what talents you have! And a chambermaid!"

I had nothing to say in reply, but cast my eyes down at the carpet as she went on, "I was saying to my niece that if she had only kept her eyes and ears open as you have done, she would have been a singular young woman. Now I know nothing of your circumstances and little of your capacities, but I shall not lose my interest in you and since I should like to do a little something, in return for the rare pleasure your letter gave me, I have ordered *The Atlantic Monthly* for you and in the next few days will send you a box of books which I am sure you'll find profitable."

"That's very good of you, Miss Pride," I said. "I like to read."

She asked me then if I knew stenography. "What a pity," she said. "I thought they taught you that sort of thing in the public schools. I was about to say that I shall presently be looking for a secretary. The fact is, my dear, which I hope you won't breathe, that I have been thinking of writing my memoirs. Now you'll think me outrageously pretentious. I haven't a scrap of talent, as I'm quite aware, but I feel it my duty to preserve certain things, certain recollections of my father, a most praiseworthy man. But there's no time to tell you about Papa. Perhaps you wouldn't care for that sort of work anyhow."

"Oh, on the contrary," I cried. "I should like nothing better. But of course I could not leave my mother."

"No, I suppose not. One's first duty, after all, is to one's mother, or to one's father, as in my case. Well, we shall see."

The chiming of an unseen clock warned me that I must leave. Miss Pride led the way to the drawing-room to show me her Copley which she had mentioned earlier. As she opened the door, I saw, seated before the fire on a low bench, a girl with long red hair. She did not turn at the sound of the door but said, "Auntie?"

Miss Pride turned to me. "Some other day you shall see the Copley. Good-by." And without shaking hands with me, she disappeared into the drawing-room, closing the door behind her.

The word "drawing-room" had fascinated me for many years. When I first learned that Miss Pride's house was equipped with such a place, I furnished it with an erratic ensemble, elements of which I borrowed from every interior I had known or read about. It contained, among other things, a box of ferns like the one in the sixth-grade room at school. I had at first interpreted the meaning of the word as "a room where people draw pictures"; but this I rejected when I heard the expression "to draw out," and I thought that a drawing-room would be the setting for skillful conversation. When at last I learned that the word had been truncated and was actually "withdrawing," I envisaged a group of ladies cringing through a door as brutal men advanced, much in the manner of "The Rape of the Sabine Women," a brown, stained print of which hung in the classroom of the Latin and French teacher.

Today, seeing my first drawing-room, I was deeply shocked, for in that brief glimpse, I was able to take in everything. It was no larger than the library and because it was well-lighted and the other had been dark, seemed even a little smaller. It was dominated by three large rival "units": a bay window equipped with a long seat and a great many pots of foliage, a grand piano draped with a Spanish shawl, and a fire-place. Amongst, between, around these three behemoths, crouched chairs, to each of which had been assigned a companion, if not a table, at least a footstool or a standing lamp. The impression I got from the threshold was that if one wanted to reach the bay window, for example, he would have to "thread" his way through the furniture as in a crowded restaurant where the only vacant table is at the farthest end from the door.

As for a moment I stood where she had left me, I tried, quite frankly, to hear what was being said beyond the double doors. I caught only one sentence, spoken by the girl: "No, Aunt Lucy, it isn't that *you* depress me, it's the house. Otherwise, I would have dinner in tonight."

I tiptoed across the hall. I did not know what to do. My jacket and tam were nowhere to be seen, and for a terrible moment I thought Miss Pride had forgotten to tell Mac to drive me home and that I should either be obliged to wait until she came out of the drawing-room, displeased to find me still here after she had told me good-by, or that I would have to find my way back to Chichester on foot, through the evil purlieus of the city. Near-by me, I saw a table on which lay a silver plate containing calling cards. The magic names sprang forth from their immaculate plaques in the dim light of the hall: Cabot, Frothingham, Coolidge, Hunnewell, Adams, Heminway. I could feel the very breath of her eminent callers who dropped, as though it were nothing, their venerable surnames in her vestibule.

A door behind me opened and, startled, I wheeled about, still holding a card that bore the name Apthorp. I thrilled to the recollection of having seen the name in *The Education of Henry Adams* which I had read by mistake for Civics class instead of *The Americanization of Edward Bok*. To be caught thus snooping in the calling cards gave me the same feeling of terror that I had felt in grammar school when I was apprehended in the act of passing or receiving a note, and for a second, being unable to make out who was in the hall with me (for I was so confused that I saw a white apron without realizing it), I was sure that I would be turned out of the house in disgrace. But it was only the servant girl with my things to inform me that Mac was waiting.

## 3

My mother had been ill for a long time with stubborn influenza, complicated with bronchitis. For two months, with a few brief intervals, she had been stupefied by fever and by the enervating sweats which came on when her temperature fell. Her sleep was disturbed by nightmares and she would call out to me in a terror that did not leave even when I had wakened her or when she had told me her dream and I had talked soothingly to her. The dreams pursued her even in her lucid moments and she would fall to weeping because the room had taken on the appearance of the cave she had seen last night or because, superimposed upon my face, was a word of Russian written in huge black letters, or because the bed was intolerably filthy to her since a few hours ago, two colossal tomcats had relieved themselves there. I suppose her dreams tarried exceptionally long because of the fever which could construct a complete hallucination from the barest materials: a piece of lint on the counterpane could swell and shape itself into the mammoth cats, or, vice versa, the cats of the dream could be reduced to a piece of lint. Her whole life was a fantasy, whether she was awake or asleep. If by chance her mind cleared and the objects about her righted themselves, it was not because she had recovered her senses, but that pain had driven the delusions away. Then she lay gasping, pressing her hand against the place in her chest that ached and burned from her shattering cough, and what she saw then: the bleak features of her impoverished room, my face ashen from the glare of the snow-light, the snow itself outside the uncurtained windows, these things were worse than her imagined tormentors and she would tell me to draw the blinds and light a lamp, do anything to change the scene of her suffering, to divert her for a few minutes at least.

Chief of her nightmares was one in which Ivan appeared to her. Often, when I wakened her, she would mistake me for him. She would shrink away and breathe, "You're dead!" Invariably, after this exclamation, she would be seized with a violent attack of coughing which even her syrup would not soothe. I could hear the tortured rasping of her breath between the barks, and if any ease came at all, she used it up in moaning, "Oh, God! I can't breathe!" It was no doubt only coincidence that made her suffer particularly after dreaming of Ivan, but I believed, half superstitiously, that she was being punished in her own heart. She often spoke of him and of Varenka, and whenever she heard the foghorns, every muscle in her body tensed and between clenched teeth she said, "It is down where *they* are, wrapped in seaweed." Who "they" were she could not or would not tell me. And she thought his hair had grown long and that his nails had pierced through his shroud. "I can see him, Sonie," she mourned. "His little body, swish, swish with the waves, just like Varenka. Oh, Merciful Mother! Oh, *mertvoye ditya!*" The Russian words, "the dead child," were uttered with an elegiac languor, implicit in the syllables themselves.

It was partly because I was sure she would not believe me that I did not tell her where the dead child really was. Even more, though, it was because I took a cruel and perverse pleasure in what I was sure was the remorse of her inner soul. His death seemed newly accomplished each day and gradually, while at first my grief had been intermittent and like a tide had washed over me only at intervals, now it became a constant and a profound pain, reaching to the farthest corners of my heart, delivering an unpredicted blow to every delight, whether or not I had been reminded of him. Flirting, in a band of girls with a company of boys, I abruptly ceased my giggles; the isolated moment silenced the flattering insults. I could smell the strange rankness of Mr. Greeley's waiting room, could see the black roses on the little nightshirt, and I could feel in my temples the vibrations of Mr. Henderson's boat as we passed through the shoals where the water had a sinister, subterranean rhythm. Or I would waken in the night and leap from the bed, thinking he had called out. Confronted by the emptiness, my being screamed at the knowledge that he was dead.

Dr. Galbraith came once or twice a week to see my mother, although I had never summoned him. The excuse he gave me, jocularly as though I had no connection either with her or with Ivan, was that he did not want to lose another patient in our house. He gave her, I thought, too much sympathy, so that as she grew a little stronger, she declared that she was growing weaker, and when for a whole day her temperature was normal, the next day it had soared, by the aid of hot tea, to 103 degrees. Beguiled by the idea that she might have consumption, she told the doctor that her mother and father had both died of it, and she was delighted when he promised that as soon as she was well enough to go to the hospital, x-rays would be taken of her chest. In the beginning, I believed that he was deliberately leading her on and that he hoped to cure her psychotic mind as well as her infected bronchial tubes. Thus, one day when he left her bedroom, after a cursory examination and a long talk, I walked out to his car with him on the pretext of asking him how her chest sounded. But instead I told him of her cunning trick of elevating the mercury in the thermometer by immersing it in her tea. "I don't want Mamma to become a hypochondriac, sir!" I said. "Can't you help me?"

But he missed the point entirely. "The temperature may be absent altogether in a case like this," he said. "It's the sound of the râles that tells the story."

"Oh, I don't deny that she's ill," I replied. "But, Dr. Galbraith, she shouldn't put the thermometer in her tea!"

"No, she shouldn't." He laughed. "Be sure you don't give her very hot tea or the thermometer will break into smithereens and you'll have to buy a new one. Good-by! I'll drop around in four or five days. In the meantime, just follow my directions."

When even her authentic abnormal temperatures had subsided and her cough had gone almost entirely and by her color and her returning flesh I knew that she was nearly well, the doctor still did not discontinue his visits. He came only in the evenings, and sometimes called for me at the Brunsons' to drive me home, a courtesy that never suited me since he was not the kind of man who could inspire young people to chatter, and if he asked a question, the answer was always too simple, and I would reply in a monosyllable. He would inquire, for instance, if I liked Latin, and because, in his voice, Latin acquired a colossal unimportance, I could say no more than "Yes" or "No," depending on how well I had translated that day. A gluttonous boredom resided in him and its appetite was insatiable. He might look at the full moon whose reflection floated on the dark blue water and he would sigh with a vast ennui. Occasionally, he exhaled the piney odor of gin and at these times he was more animated, but he looked at me so lecherously and his talk tottered so perilously on the brink of obscenity, that I preferred his other mood. "I bet you're the kind of girl that keeps the boys at arm's length, aren't you?" Or, "What do you young people do after the picture show? You don't go home and you don't study. Or do you study nature, that is, *human* nature down at the Point?"

Some people, among them the charitable but mawkish Gonzales, declared that Dr. Galbraith had only taken to drink after his wife's death. But others, like the Hendersons, said he had always "gone pretty heavy on the bottle." He was known to have women just as he was known to be a drunkard, but he took great pains never to be seen in the company of the women and never to be seen drinking. Thus, his depravity, never demonstrated as sordid, was surrounded by an appealing aura and no one identified so dapper a "professional man" with a "drunk" or visualized him with a fancy woman. Through a wonderful stroke of luck for him, the old ladies at the Hotel knew nothing of his reputation as a voluptuary, and if they had been told that his eccentric color came from jaundice which had been brought on by many years of copious, solitary drinking, they would have said confidently, "Oh, you're quite mistaken. He goes every year to Florida and somehow manages to keep his tan twelve months at a time."

My Latin teacher, a scholarly man named Mr. Sylvester, thinking that Dr. Galbraith was a friend of my mother's (for he, like the rest of the village, had heard of these visits, but had not troubled to acquaint himself with my mother's social position so that for all he knew she could have been a well-bred woman who had seen better days) told me that I should value his society since he was a man of rare talents and had written more than a dozen musical compositions, chiefly string quartets. The information had come to Mr. Sylvester in a roundabout way and he could not even recall whether he had heard it from anyone of taste, but he was under the impression that the doctor had been first-rate. "But he gave it up for some reason, and one wonders why," said the teacher. Accordingly, partly to satisfy my curiosity and partly to stave off his discomforting badinage, I told the doctor one night what I had heard.

"Yes, as a matter of fact, I did make up two or three little things. I hadn't thought of them for years. I haven't played my fiddle since my wife died. Who told you about that?"

"Mr. Sylvester, my Latin teacher."

"Apropos of what?"

"Nothing. I suppose he knew you were taking care of Mamma."

"Oh, yes, of course. I suppose you told him your Mamma was sick

175

and that I was bringing her prescriptions and what not? Well, will you give my regards to Mr. Stuyvesant and tell him that my music is a dead soldier?" He had stopped his car beside our house and turning his fuddled face away from me, said into the fresh, windy April air, "You have brought up the past to me by what you've just said. When you are my age and can look back as many years as I can, you will remember this evening and say, 'Ah, at last I know what Dr. Galbraith felt.' Miss Moffatt, I had the most beautiful wife in the world. She was French and she was religious. My house is full of sacred objects that she bought in the by-streets of France and Italy. I have a *prie-dieu.* A Spanish crucifix dating from the thirteenth century, set in a tabernacle of Carrara marble. On my desk, a *memento mori,* a small skull carved of bone. I could never replace the least thing." He faced me again. "You forgive an old man his reminiscences, don't you?" He leaned across me to open the door, and as I stepped out, he said under his breath, "The odd thing is I have forgotten every word of French. *Madeleine,* there, I pronounce even *it* the English way."

The wistful note had left his voice and the sorrowing smile his lips by the time we had entered the house. "I'll just have a look-see at my patient," he said heartily. "She is, ah, she's valiantly combatting this pestiferous bug." Because I knew as well as he did that the combat was over and that if she wished she could get up any time and resume a normal life, I looked away from him in embarrassment. He sensed it and he said, "The peril of this kind of thing is the relapse, you know. There's the danger of tuberculosis." The last word he said in a whisper, stretching up on tiptoe as if to carry the sound completely out of reach of my mother in the next room.

"Sonia!" came her voice. "Sonia, darling, is the doctor there? I coughed some blood up this afternoon."

Dr. Galbraith's face twisted in a faked consternation.

"I don't believe it," I said sulkily.

"Coming, Mrs. Morgan!" cried the doctor. "Oh, by the way, I forgot the bouquet I brought your mother. It's still in the car. My garden is, so to speak, overflowing, and I thought I would like to share it with someone. I don't know what it will be . . . my man just snipped a few things for me. Would you be so kind as to fetch them?" He went into the bedroom, leaving the door wide open. As I left the house I heard him say, "We'll get the better of those darned old bugs yet and put some roses in your cheeks."

I was out of the house for only a few minutes, but when I came back, I found the door closed although, because the lock was defective, it had fallen slightly ajar. I heard a conversation about my mother's fancy-work. In her convalescence, she had begun to make fir trees, the decorative possibilities of which she had heretofore overlooked, and extraordinary birds which never pleased her. She would say, "I've left out something," and puzzle over the creatures, turning her hoops now to one side and now to another and never seeing that each one of their plump behinds was destitute of tail feathers. But the doctor, blind with infatuation, assured her that they were beautiful, that she was a "regular ornithologist."

"I like to see these homely virtues in a woman," he was saying in a voice that had borrowed some of the nocturnal quality of my mother's. "My own wife was a great hand at dressmaking. I still have some of her gowns in an old trunk in my attic."

"Did she die or did she light out one fine day?" asked my mother.

Shocked by her expression, he did not immediately reply. "She died," he said at last. "It makes one lonely."

"Lonely! After my Hermann went away I used to cry myself to sleep every night of the world. But that was nothing to what it's been like since little Ivan died."

"I know, I know."

"You was saying you have some of your wife's clothes. I wish to God I had some of Hermann's. But my little girl sold them all as soon as he was gone."

"We can't expect children to understand these things."

There was a long pause. I had put the flowers in a jar and thought to take them in to Mamma, but as I approached the door, I was urged by a powerful curiosity to know what was taking place in the bedroom, and I crept along the wall to peer between the hinges of the door. The doctor was bent forward, his hands palm upward lying on the counterpane. Their skin was even darker than his face and the nails were a corpse-white. The fingers were short and swollen, the skin stretched so tight it seemed about to split like the skin of

177

a sausage as it is being cooked. These clean, brassy hands played the supernumeraries in the drama of the eyes and lips, and as I watched, they curled into cups as slowly as a flower closes. Then the thumbs moved over the nails of the index fingers with voluptuous deliberation as though the contact with the smooth surface were exquisite. The left hand was raised. The man carried the source of the sensation to his mouth, passed the nail several times over the sensitive area under his lower lip.

My mother's eyes were cast down but her lashes coquettishly flickered. Her fancy-work lay at her side. The doctor wiped his shining lips with a purple handkerchief (This evening he was dressed in a gray suit and his accessories were purple. He smelled, as well, of lavender water.) as if he had been eating the face before him and its flavor had been so delicious that in his gorging he had been too enthusiastic to mind his lips. But he was not making love. In a moment, although he whispered it, he said, "Let me listen again to that right lung." I saw him push her nightdress down and explore her breast with his stethoscope, his head bent down so low he seemed to strain not to lay his face on her naked flesh. "Oh, that's so-so," he said with a laugh. "I must keep you here another week," and gazing, deeply stricken, into her eyes, he took her pulse and announced, as if it were a declaration of love, that it was still a little rapid. My mother made no response, but picked up her embroidery hoops across which, this time, was stretched a branch of honeysuckle to which a deformed humming-bird was paying a visit. Dr. Galbraith glanced down and cried, "Charming! How I would like to have some of those things in my house! Would you . . . could I . . . my dear Mrs. Marburg, would you do some table runners for me?"

"Just at present I'm rather busy," said my mother. "But perhaps I could do a few later."

"Excellent! I'm going to New York next week. I'll just pick up some stamped things there."

"My hoops are cracking."

"I'll buy you some new hoops! I'll buy you some ivory ones inlaid with gold. I dare say they have such things?"

"Why, certainly they have," said my mother. "Once I had a pair of solid gold ones with diamonds set in. That was just one of the things Hermann carried off with him." She coughed a little and the doctor bent closer to her.

"What you really need," he said with such terrible excitement that the stethoscope shook in his hand, "is mountain air. Don't you know anyone in the White Mountains or the Adirondacks that could put you up for a few weeks?"

"Ah, doctor, that's just what I've always said! The sea air is bad for me. But no, no, I don't know nobody in the mountains. I'll just die here like the child."

"Yes, yes, well, that's neither here nor there. I have made up my mind that you *must* have mountain air. I will see what I can do—come to think of it, *I* have a friend in the Adirondacks who might very well let me, that is, let you have the use of his cabin. Charming place, set in a grove of fir trees with a lake near by. The problem, of course, would be finding someone to take care of you."

"Oh, Sonie's a good mother's helper. She's a dreamy girl and goes off a little crazy now and then, but she's a sweet nurse all the same."

"I don't doubt that," said the doctor. Frustrated, unable for a moment to find his way to the fulfillment of his obvious scheme, he swore softly under his breath, apologized, and said he had just remembered an important engagement he had not kept that afternoon. Then he continued, "I don't wish to interfere in the upbringing of your daughter, Mrs. Marburg, but it seems to me that this is a very important time of her life . . . that is, in school. That is to say, from my point of view, it would be actually *dangerous* to take her out of school now, just a few months before commencement. Why, she might not get her diploma! Where would she be then? No, I think you ought to let her finish the year out. I will find you a companion myself."

My mother's eyes shone at the prospect of the mountains. It was the first time, to my knowledge, that she had ever earnestly wished to leave Chichester. I have never known anyone in whom wanderlust was so completely lacking. Perhaps she was incapable of imagining a place in America other than this seaside village, but tonight she was granted second sight. As if she were already listening to the wind through the fir trees, she murmured, "I love the mountains. They don't smell of clams."

179

"True, true! And not only that but they're healthful. Why, you'll be a new woman in a month or so. I'll just send my friend a telegram. You leave it up to me, Mrs. Marshall, I'll arrange the whole thing."

My mother did not thank him, for, completely egocentric, she was never aware that the betterment of her fortunes initiated in anyone but herself. Yet for his reward, the doctor got a flashing smile of joy which so enlivened her pale face that he could not resist the temptation to touch her and he lifted her hand which still held the hoops and yarn and kissed it. I nearly cried out, for I was not only surprised at the doctor's premature and uncircumspect advances, but I was afraid my mother would be shocked out of her placid daydream of the mountain cabin and would realize what his motives were. But either through greenness or complacency, she did not object to his caress. Barely conscious of it, in fact, she allowed her hand to lie in his until she was urged to go on with her humming bird.

The doctor rose and as he did so, his greedy eyes suddenly widened with horror as he realized that they had been talking loud enough for me to hear. "I completely forgot! I brought you some flowers. The girl went out to my car to get them . . . it's strange I didn't hear her come in."

"She came in all right," said my mother. "She'll be out there doing her lessons. She wants to be a school teacher, doctor. Won't that be a feather in my cap?"

"It certainly will!" he cried passionately. "She's a fine girl. Now I must be running along. *Au revoir.*"

I slipped back to my place at the table and opened *Literature and Life* at random; the pages fell back at *The Deserted Village*. I pretended to be so engrossed that I did not hear the doctor come up behind me and jumped, startled, when he said, "Well, now that's a coincidence I was about to tell you that the village of Chichester is soon to be deserted by its gracious citizen, your mother. I have been thinking for some time that she needed mountain air to dry up those little scoundrels in her bronchial tubes, and I've got her consent to send her off to the Adirondacks."

"That's awfully kind of you," I said. "But we have no money

even to pay her railroad fare, and I shouldn't like to let her go alone anyhow."

"But she wouldn't be alone. I would . . . that is, I intend to get a companion for her, a sort of nurse person, you know. I'll pick up someone or other in New York."

"But the money . . . we haven't any money at all."

"In questions of life and death, we cannot consider money. I understand that you intend to be a school teacher. Very well, then, when you have your post you can pay back the money I intend to advance you. No!" He raised his hand for silence. "I won't hear any objections. I *owe* this to you. I have few pleasures in life. I am a lonely man, a widower, and where I can spread happiness, I *will*. Let me, I implore you, let me send your mother to the Adirondacks in memory of my wife."

He did not look at me as he spoke but gazed about the room and finally, his eye lighting on Dr. Brunson's brandy, he seized his hat and cried, "I must get on at once. Now, Miss Marburg, I'm not taking 'no' for an answer. I'm going to drive your mother down myself. Doesn't that reassure you? I've got to run on to New York anyhow in a week or so and it will fit in perfectly. Good-by for the present. I'll look in tomorrow."

My mother was delighted with the flowers and buried her face in them. She was still flushed with her thoughts of the mountains and she talked ecstatically. "My stars, darling, imagine it! It was fate that made me start doing the fir trees. Oh, how happy I am! I've been so unhappy! You don't know how unhappy a person can be, baby girl."

"Mamma, don't go away," I said sadly. "I would be so lonesome without you."

"There! She's cross that I'm happy! She doesn't care if her mother dies. Oh, Sonia, I never thought you'd turn against me, I never did!" Tears started to her eyes and she drew up a pathetic cough. "All right, I won't go. I'll just die here. I suppose it was a whole cup of blood that came up this afternoon, but it don't matter." She caught her breath. "Give me the syrup . . . No, no, don't give it to me. I'll just go on and die now."

"Don't talk like that, Mamma," I said. "Wouldn't you like a cup of tea?" But she refused. I sat down on the edge of the bed and pulled her fancy-work toward me. "Oh, what a lovely humming-bird! You're so clever, Mamma."

Pleased, instantly reconciled to me, she caught my hand and kissed it quickly. "Do you like it, darling? What do you say I do some of them around the hem of your voile dress?"

"Well, I don't know . . ."

"No, I don't either. It might make the other little girls jealous. It might hurt their feelings. Oh, you're good, dearie, always thinking of others. You're my baby girl, aren't you?"

"Yes, Mamma. Shall I turn out the lamp now or do you want to work a little longer?"

"I'll work a bit. I'll tell you what, when I get my ivory hoops, I'll make you a blouse with tulips on it!"

As I studied, unable to concentrate, I heard her talking to herself. I thought that perhaps it was the approach of sleep that made her mutterings more and more incoherent. Several times I looked in, but she was wide awake, still multiplying the blossoms of the honeysuckle. At first she talked of the mountains and the fir trees, inquired of herself if she thought the snow would still be on the ground, said, "Yes, it will be a good thing for her. Shura, even as a child, didn't like the smell of fish. She was real unusual about it, Mrs. Henderson." She proceeded then to her work. "It's not as easy as rolling off a log to do a sandpiper, Sonie, darling. Naturally it looks easy as pie to somebody that don't know the first thing about needlework, but all the same I'm willing to make them. Do you want two on each side of the collar or just one? No, the sandpiper is not my favorite bird. Best I like peacocks, next best parrots, third best bluebird. Sandpiper is way down the list, maybe last."

Then she ceased to make sentences and though she did not raise her voice, it became intense as she uttered single nouns or strung together a group of unrelated verbs: "Run and swim and holler." After a moment, "Mrs. Purple Grackle?" she inquired. "No, Mr. Humming-bird. *Mister?* Or *Doctor* Humming-bird?"

I paid little attention to her. Gradually I forgot about the doctor's visit and I read hard at *Ode on Intimations of Immortality,* my next day's assignment. My interpretation of the poem, nevertheless, was influenced by the childish prattle that issued from the bedroom and a part of my mind (the same shallow part that put into my mouth most preposterous errors when I was translating Latin at sight, making me read "In the midst of its boughs and yearly arms spread the opaque elm tree, huge, where sat Sleep vulgarly," for *"In medio ramos annosaque brachia pandit Ulmus opaca, ingens, quam sedem Somnia vulgo"*), obeying the advice of my English teacher to bring literature into my life and vice versa, suggested to me that my mother was returning to her childhood and if her mood lasted, she might go even further and briefly visit her heavenly home.

She talked continuously, then sang a little, then imitated a drunk, "They're flying *all* around thish room. Get thosh boids out of thish room." Something clattered to the floor. "Sonie!" she screamed. "Come quick!" I ran into the bedroom. She had flung off the bedding and was sitting up straight, her hands over her face.

"Mamma!" I scolded her. "Put the covers over you. You'll catch cold again."

"There were birds in here, Sonie!"

"No, no, you only dreamed there were." I put the back of my hand to her cheek. It was blazing. "There, now, you've got yourself worked up into a fever again," I said and put the thermometer into her mouth. Troubled, I wondered if she had actually coughed blood that afternoon. I looked around for signs but saw none. Gently I drew the blankets up about her again but she cast them off, mumbling around the thermometer that I was trying to suffocate her. She did have a fever, higher than it had been since the last acute phase of her illness, but I told her that her temperature was normal. "You're just tired, Mamma. It is a little warm, I guess. Would you like a sleeping powder now?"

"Yes. And you come to bed, do, darling. I know there were birds in here. You keep watch for two hours and then wake me up and I'll keep watch. I don't want them to get tangled up in my hair. They do that! Especially the kind that are part mouse, you know the kind I mean."

"Bats?"

"Yes. I wish I had a nightcap. I know, let me wear the little boy's stocking cap."

I took the little red and white cap out of the bureau drawer. "It won't fit," I said. But she reached out her hand for it and set it on top of her head. She pulled at it but when she had let go, it immediately contracted, skimmed to the top of her head and sat there precariously. But she was satisfied: "It looks like a nightcap, anyway, don't it? It's like not letting a dog know that you're afraid and he won't bite you. I suppose it's the same with bats."

She was still restless and insisted that I sit with her a little while. First the lamp, then the darkness after I had turned it out, harried her and she turned her head this way and that, groaning and sighing until at last she fell asleep and I went to bed on the pallet. Because I was exhausted and slept dreamlessly, I was sure I had only just closed my eyes when a cock's crow and my mother's shriek came simultaneously to my mummified mind and I awoke to the grisly light of early dawn and to my mother, kneeling at my side. She had had a nightmare. She was in the house of the witch who was no longer a woman but a man; a semicircle of people stood round about an ancient hag dressed in black who writhed in death-throes on the floor. The onlookers were solemnly interested but made no move to help the woman who had been poisoned by the witch. My mother was accosted by Ivan, grown into a tall young man, and he said, "That is my Mamma. We knew it would happen at the Reds of Easter. When is it your turn?" Suddenly, looking at her hands, she saw that they were covered with a crumbling brown incrustation, green in spots with mold, and the witch, who stood near her, touched her bare foot so that more of the crusty scabs appeared. He touched her at various other places until her whole body was infected; she could not get away from him although he was not holding her; her feet were rooted to the floor. A hideous scream came from the throats of the people who watched. At last, when she was entirely covered with the vile stuff, he seized her by the arms and kissed her lips until the blood streamed from them, soaking her blouse. She saw then that he intended to lift her up and carry her to a couch, set in a vast bowl of water through which swam goldfish with enormous human eyes that devilishly winked at her. In shame and fear she begged to be released, and as he laughed at her protest and lifted her up, she screamed and wakened.

I got up and led her back to bed. She was crying now with horror at the memory of her loathsome skin and yet with relief that it had only been a dream. Her skin was cool and in spite of her tears she looked rested. I would have liked to go back to bed, for my head was throbbing from insufficient sleep and my eyes were hot, but my mother declared that she could not close her eyes again for fear the dream would go on to its dreadful climax. She asked for a lamp and while I was getting her breakfast, she commenced to work again on the proboscis of her humming-bird. "Talk to me, Sonie. You know, talk a blue streak so I'll know you're still there."

Sleepy and cross, impatient with her fancies, I talked, with an intended irony which missed its mark, of my stolid mistress, Mrs. Brunson, who slept until ten every morning, never had nightmares, was never ill, and did not depend upon her daughter for her amusement. I did not, it was true, have the slightest respect for her. She was growing stouter as the result of over-indulgence in chocolate creams and alcohol and although it never occurred to her to reduce her consumption of either, she had become extremely touchy on the subject of her expanding hips. If someone paid her the compliment, "How well you're looking, Dorothy," she interpreted it as meaning "How fat you're getting," and she would reply testily, "Same to you." I had at no time envied Betty her mother, but this morning, as I waited for the tea to brew, I wished my own mother's silliness were more like hers which did not rouse the household out of sound sleep and did not, even when she was drunk, conceive the notion that birds were flying about her bed. Moreover, Mrs. Brunson's dreams, which she was fond of telling at the dinner table since her best ones came during her afternoon nap, were of the most pedestrian variety, as banal as her speech.

"And Betty writes to her mother once a week from boarding school," I was saying, "and every time says, please send me a white bengaline evening dress or please send me twenty-five dollars to have my picture taken. And Mrs. Brunson just says okay. She's the most unselfish mother I ever knew. Mamma, are you listening?"

"Sure. That Mrs. Brunson must be lazy. Why, I wouldn't feel I was worth my weight in gold if I didn't get up till ten o'clock."

"Do you by any chance mean worth your weight in *salt?*"

185

"Toot toot toot toot toot! Somebody got out of the wrong side of bed this morning, it seems to me."

I went on with my narrative. The tempo of the Brunsons' lives slowed down as I talked until, by the time the tea was ready, the dentist and his wife had become as inactive and unfeeling as the china family in Betty's doll house.

"I can't wait all day for my breakfast," called my mother.

"It's only five-thirty. The fire won't get hot. Oh, Christmas, Mamma! Why can't you be like *other* people?" I had not intended to be harsh, but I had burned my fingers on the metal teapot as I lifted it from the stove and since I was vexed already, the little injury enraged me. No reply came from the bedroom. When I took in her tray, my mother did not look up but stared at the back of her hands. "In the dream, the bones right there felt like they were broken under the sores. It was awful! I don't know if I can eat anything, thinking about them."

Nevertheless, she lifted the teacup and drank a little. "Listen," she said, "it wasn't Luibka in the dream at all. It was a man, like I said, and he wasn't a stranger either, but for the life of me I can't think who it was. Not your father. Not Gonzales. Not Mr. Kadish. Who in the world was the nasty dog?" She named the men she knew: doddering old Mr. Brock at the Hotel, Mr. Henderson, the Fuller brush man who had given her the black tooth-brush, Mr. Greeley, her father, Nathan Kadish. The doctor did not cross her mind.

I thought of going to the hospital after school to tell the doctor that my mother could not see him that evening, and yet I reasoned that I could give him no proper excuse, that I might offend him by appearing to be suspicious of him when perhaps he was only acting out of the goodness of his heart. All day I was anxious. I could feel my forehead wrinkle into a frown that did not come from my diligent following of the text of the *Aeneid* or the *Ode*. I did not hear my name called out in the Algebra class roll and I elicited from my teacher the remark, "I must be having a hallucination. I could swear someone was sitting in Sonie Marburg's seat."

All the day I was thinking the word "insane." In telling my mother that morning of the daily life of the Brunsons, I had recalled a recent conversation between the dentist and Dr. Roberts, the only other physician of the town besides Dr. Galbraith. The doctor had just been reading of new surgery which was now employed in some cases of insanity. "The cure, to my way of thinking, is as bad as the disease. To be sure, they don't take after you with butcher knives and so on, but they become inhuman, have no feelings. The optic thalamus is put out of whack. Tell them somebody died and they'll laugh their heads off. Tell them a rattlesnake is behind their chair and they'll just grin. I'm an old-fashioned man. I believe in the good old-fashioned insane asylum." Mrs. Brunson who, when she had had too much to drink, tried always to ask intelligent questions—perhaps to prove that she could still follow the talk even though she could not hold her fork in her hand and spilled water in her lap as she lifted her glass to her lips—said, "But that would be used only for violent cases, wouldn't it? Not for the people that just say strange things and think they see pink elephants and so on?" The doctor, a man who in all things saw black or white, replied shortly, "I may be wrong, but personally, I think people who see pink elephants—unless they're stuffing you—are insane. We all have our off moments, but I don't think a healthy mind is ever off enough to see a pink elephant."

Had my mother actually seen the birds last night, I asked myself, or was she only teasing me? Perhaps it was the fever that had made her talk so strangely, so much more strangely on reflecting today than it had seemed last night. Moreover, I wondered why she had forgotten the mountain air and the pine trees in the Adirondacks this morning when she had been so enraptured at the thought of them last night. I did not want her to go! I was sure she did not need mountain air—the doctor himself, at the beginning of her illness, had told me that the idea that climate had anything to do with pulmonary diseases was nonsense—and I believed that on the contrary what she needed most, and what she would always need, was my pampering, for she was a very young child. And while I pitied Dr. Galbraith, I was not willing to sacrifice my mother to his loneliness, not even in the memory of his devout French Madeleine. Nor, on the other hand, was I any more willing to sacrifice him, poor gallant goose, to the persecutions to which Mamma had subjected my father.

Briefly I desired to tell Dr. Galbraith how she had literally driven Papa away, and when school was out, I started down the road toward the hospital. But I turned back, realizing what such a revelation would imply. It would be the grossest impertinence on my part to tell him, a physician, and presumably acquainted with mental as well as physical disorders, that my mother was insane. It struck me that perhaps I had been wrong all along, that he had no improper designs on her, that in reality the cabin in the Adirondacks was a sanitarium. I planned to talk with him that night and to beg him not to take her away.

The doctor did not call for me at the Brunsons', and as there were guests at dinner and the cocktail shaker had been refilled so often that I did not begin to serve until nearly eight, I was late in leaving for home. Maudie had gone sometime before, inviting me, as she did almost every night, to drop in "for a snort." For the first time I had been tempted. I was very fond of Maudie, even though she was tiresome, and my spirits never failed to rise in her presence so that even my boredom was curiously exuberant. I did not want to go home; there was something gruesome about the doctor, and I kept thinking of the *memento mori* on his desk in the library where he drank alone, as his servants reported in the village. And I thought of the marble tabernacle for the crucifix. When I visualized the latter, I was simultaneously reminded of the shoals, I cannot possibly say why except that the word "marble" suggested something chilled and ghostly and "tabernacle" made me think of the dark-room at school where the physics teacher developed films and where, because of the structure of the room or its position in the building, the acoustics were peculiar and the sound of feet in the hallway above was like the surge of waves.

I thought perhaps he would not come tonight or that he would have left by the time I got home. Consoled a little, as I passed by Maudie's cottage I was glad I had decided not to go to her, for from the open door, brightly lighted with a Coleman lamp, came the sound of her loud, untrue contralto harmonizing with two masculine voices in obscene excerpts from "Frankie and Johnny." The rest of the way home, I reiterated a telepathic message to the doctor, "Go home, Dr. Galbraith, go home."

But his car was beside the house. The kitchen was mobbed with flowers as though a garden had magically been planted there since I had been gone. Branches of lilac drooped over the sides of the blue sink; the table was piled with jonquils and iris; on the chairs, wrapped in wet newspapers, were sprays of syringa, forsythia, and Japanese quince. Old marmalade jars and jelly glasses were filled with lilies-of-the-valley whose little ivory bells trailed down or nestled close to their broad caressing leaves. I stood on the threshold, breathing in the sweet air. A breeze blew through the kitchen window and carried to me the whole essence of the lilac with which it had been charged as it traversed the sink. For a moment, overjoyed with his bountiful gift, I was remorseful that I had been suspicious of the doctor. His flowers showed that our pleasure was his purpose.

From the bedroom, as usual, came the voices. They were laughing tonight over some private joke and I gathered that it had to do with the cabin in the Adirondacks, for I heard the isolated words "lake" and "firewood" and "chipmunks." Evidently they had not heard me for they continued to talk as I walked about the kitchen from one group of flowers to another. Shortly the door opened and the doctor came out.

"Good evening," I said. "How lovely your flowers are!"

The doctor grinned obscenely at me and leaned against the table for support. One foot, handsomely shod in a half-boot, moved in an uncertain circle on the linoleum. The bright bronze hands tossed fretfully from their limp junctures as he said thickly and in a masterful imitation of my mother's accent, "I am *so* glad you like them, dear. They are all from my garden and they are *all* for you." His sweet breath came to me in gusts, mingling with the flowers' fragrance. Abruptly, his hands and feet were stilled and he rose to his full height, rocking slightly but apparently in command of himself again. "It's close in the bedroom," he said, still thickly but now without the accent. "I felt a little giddy for a moment. I was just about to examine your mother. It wouldn't do to fold up in the midst of that, would it? Give a patient a bad idea, make her say, 'Physician, heal thyself.' " Suspecting that he had a mission of delicacy in coming away from my mother, I asked him if he would like to wash his hands before he made his examination, and although the door to our "bathroom" was open and revealed only the toilet, its sole article of furniture besides the shower, he thanked me, said that was what he had come out for, and went in.

After I had kissed my mother in the dim bedroom—for instead of her lamp, only a single candle burned on the stool at her side—I went to open the window at her request. Just as I turned back into the room, Dr. Galbraith entered and resumed his seat at the side of the bed. I saw that more of his flowers were strewn on the floor and my mother clutched a spray of lilies-of-the-valley in her hand. She had not been working on her embroidery; there were signs of no activity at all, and to my relief, I saw that there were also no signs that the doctor had been drinking here. Beside the window was our clothes closet—a rod across which had been stretched a cretonne curtain—and I stepped back into the large shadow it cast, less out of the desire to spy than out of reluctance to pass the doctor and be required to speak to him again.

"All righty," he said. "We'll just have a look at this clogged-up ventilator and then I'll be running along. Will you just slip your nightie down over your shoulder, please?"

My mother obeyed docilely, gazing the while at her nosegay. "Isn't it sweet," she murmured, "just like little darling bells."

Dr. Galbraith ran his hand over the smooth round of her shoulder and a look of alarm fled over her face as she glanced up at him. Almost shyly he looked away and fumbled at the clasp of his stethoscope case. But he did not complete the business. "Oh, Shura!" he cried. "Let's not pretend any longer!" He slipped his arm under my mother's shoulders and drew her up to him, covering her face with long kisses as his whole body shuddered.

My mother struggled and screamed, her head flung back and her eyes dilating as the stubborn man continued to kiss her neck. "Sonia! God Almighty!" I stepped forward into the weak light but the doctor was oblivious of me. "Darling, forgive me, I frightened you." His forehead glimmered with drops of sweat which he wiped off with the back of his hand. My mother, whimpering, could not take her fascinated eyes from him while he, as if he were paralyzed, hovered over her, afraid to kiss her again, yet afraid to move lest he break the enchantment cast by her unworldly eyes.

I touched him on the shoulder, feeling nothing but the deepest commiseration for him, and he drew back from the bed. But still he could not rise and, relapsing into his violent desire for her, he grasped her stiffened hands as she shrieked again, quivering pitiably like a baffled mole dislodged from his safe tunnel. "The sores!" she howled. "Oh, oh, God! They're all over me!" He stood up and perceiving that I was beside her and that she was free of him at last, my mother turned away from us and buried her head in the pillows, and there lay murmuring.

"What the devil is she saying?"

"She's talking in Russian. She does that when she's upset."

"My God!" He strode in fury out the door and I followed him. "Well?"

"My mother has always been a little strange, Dr. Galbraith," I said, "ever since my father went away. Even before that I guess." He stood with his arms at the sides of his long gray tweed coat. He was staring bleakly at the barnyard scene above the table. "Dr. Galbraith," I went on, "there is no way I can pay you. I'm very grateful, really."

"I had never considered a fee. A doctor assumes responsibility for a patient without thinking of the money," he said impatiently.

"I'm so sorry about it all, sir! You see, I think my mother is insane."

It was the first time I had said the word aloud and it shocked me almost as much as it did him. He stared at me, absorbing the words after the sound was gone. "Insane?" he repeated. "Why, of course she is insane, but, I must confess, she hides her symptoms well. I swear, Miss Marburg, I had no proof of it until tonight."

"What shall I do?" I asked him, for it was natural for me to appeal to him since he shared my knowledge. His expression changed from disgraced rage to anxiety. "Come to my office tomorrow afternoon," he said, "and we'll discuss it. She shouldn't hear us, you know, in her excitable state. Tomorrow, promptly at four." He hurried out, businesslike, professional, hiding beneath his manner the relief he

191

must have felt in knowing that my mother had not "rejected" him since she was incapable of doing so.

When I had heard his car drive away and I went in to her, I saw the marks of her real madness in her glazed eyes that looked at me without recognition and did not move as I moved but continued to focus in the place I had just quit, and in her rigid pose which broke only when she tore the petals languidly from the doctor's flowers, and in the steady monologue in Russian that ended at last in a fitful sleep. And when, in the morning, there was no change in her and she would not eat, but pushed the tray aside, spilling the tea on the counterpane and watching it spread, I thought there was no hope. "Mamma?" I tested her, but she would not look up. I should perhaps stay with her, I thought, lest she conceive some devilish desire to hurt herself or to wander to the village in her nightdress. But because she was no longer recognizable as my mother, but was only an inhuman parody of her, I was frightened and did not want to remain in the house. A little faint, because I could not eat my breakfast, I took up my schoolbooks, locked the door behind me and started down the road.

It was a fine day; as green as leaves, the water was bifurcated by the yellow spear of the land. Our little white house and the Kadishes' blue one sagged on their shallow foundations, hiding from my backward view the Boston shore-line. Just ahead of me, Father Mulcahy sauntered slowly, reading his breviary. As I passed him, looking sideways into his raw-boned face that years in Chichester had not filled out or sweetened, it occurred to me with a wild, obscene humor that I might ask him to come exorcise my mother. I was so close to him for a moment that I could smell the wine on his mumbling lips and by leaning a little towards him could read, at the top of his book: "Die 28 Apr.—S. Pauli a Cruce." He jerked his head like a rooster and said, "God's warning."

"What? What did you say?"

"I said good morning." He looked curiously at me.

"Oh! Good morning, Father. I thought you said . . ." And I ran on, strangely exhilarated by the priest's odor, with which the air still seemed saturated, though I knew that was impossible and what I smelled now was the perfume of the lilacs blooming in all the yards.

# CHAPTER SIX

Dr. Galbraith was not in his office at four on the next afternoon, and I was told that he was ill. I did not believe it, but felt sure he was avoiding me. Nor was he there on the next day, and the nurse, refusing to tell me when he might be back, suggested that I go to Dr. Roberts. On the fourth day, having resolved that this would be the last time I should inquire for him (I thought the nurse had been given my description with the orders that on no account was I to be admitted to his office) and should then go to the other doctor, I was informed that he had died that morning, a little before noon, of a heart attack. Upon the words "heart attack" the nurse ever so discreetly placed a stress which told me that he had perhaps died of what he said but that its cause was a prolonged debauch.

The nurse behind the circular counter wheeled her swivel chair back into place before her typewriter and began sorting large yellow cards. I wanted to ask her more, but I could not think of a way to frame my questions. To be sure, the doctor's death was no more than coincidence and my mother, who all day long talked tenderly to herself in Russian and one by one ripped the petals from his fading flowers, was no more to blame for it than I, or than this imperturbable woman in the starched white cap. Though I had cared nothing for this stammering dandy and had many times wished him out of the way, I had wished him no harm, "out of the way" having meant only "out of our house." But I was shaken with something simulating the grief I had felt when I dropped my brother's hand, and my knees went weak, as I remembered that I had sometimes pitied the man. I had pictured him in his library, perfectly groomed, as if his loving toilet had been made for some honored guest, though no one ever called on him, and he sat alone, sunk in his jejune thoughts that the whiskey enshrouded. Gossip ran that in this room, the shrine of his dead wife's sacred objects, there was a bar concealed in the paneling which opened at the pressure of a button, so that in the evenings Dr. Galbraith could dispense with the services of his butler who was allowed to enter the room only in the morning to clear away the evidences of his master's lonesome spree before the parlor-maid came in to clean. I wished to ask the nurse if he had died there. Once he had told me that two malachite urns stood on his mantelpiece and that the draperies were ruby-colored brocade. Perhaps he had chosen as his shroud one of his Scotch tweed suits in which the brown was enriched with red and with it he had worn green socks and a green cravat.

"When is the funeral?" I asked, although I did not really want to know.

"I haven't the least idea," replied the nurse without looking up. "You might ask his housekeeper. All I know is that he is to be cremated."

I felt that if I moved from the counter where I rested my elbows, I would fall in my weakness. An interne who had been watching me absent-mindedly as he whirled a piece of rubber tubing round and round, pocketed his plaything and stepped to my side. Out of a mechanical kindness, he placed his hand on my shoulder and said, "Take it easy." I burst into tears, inexplicable to myself, and stumbled through the sunlit lobby, my legs enfeebled, my mind a blank. The scene detached itself from its aseptic smell and the white entourage of nurses and internes: its properties receded and I, hurtling up the road, was too alone to measure the degree of my loneliness, for I did not know where to turn for advice.

Yet, on the day following the doctor's funeral in Cambridge, I was receiving counsel from young Dr. McAllister in the same office where I had first seen Dr. Galbraith. That other day, the hygienic glare of gray walls and white wainscoting had combined with the blue shadows of snow-filled trees beyond the windows into a hard, glacial light. The old man's skin had been green as if its natural yellow hue had been mixed with the blue shadows, and his eyes, pillowed by their pendulous sacs, had ambled sensually over me while his addled brain danced in bewilderment. The tall, bony elms of the hospital courtyard had whined and rattled and then, when the wind died, a company of discursive sparrows raised their voices in the hush. The only other sign of animation to be seen from the window was a solitary pigeon promenading over the slate roof of an adjacent ward about whose red chimney wound the steam from two small exhausts.

The new occupant sat before the open windows through which, gentle and billowing, came the May day's limbering breezes and edgeless light. The world beyond was spacious and subtly illuminated; the landscape, perhaps as much as the young doctor's adroit kindness, loosed the strictures of my terror, and after my first ferocious declaration that my mother was insane, I was able to speak without a stutter.

Dr. McAllister was somewhere between twenty-five and thirty; he was spare and angular and erect and his obvious good health recommended him, whereas Dr. Galbraith's diseased complexion and unstrung manner had made him seem, from the very beginning, an uncertain ally. The tone of the young man's voice was restorative, for he was at once casual so that my story seemed automatically less calamitous than I had thought, and authoritative so that I knew I could depend upon him.

I had come to him because I had not wanted to consult Dr. Roberts, who, being a good friend of Dr. Brunson, might, despite his professional ethics, drop a few hints to the dentist. I wished, so far as possible, to keep secret this new excitement of our household. To be sure, everyone in Chichester had said for years that my mother was mad, and the children who had used to come to play up towards our house no longer came. The villagers and the shopkeepers had, after Ivan's death, stopped inquiring about her. But still, they had no proof.

It had not been easy to gain an audience with Dr. McAllister, who was a house-physician and not allowed to have private cases, and so I had written him a note, saying that Miss Pride had asked me to look him up. He had sent back the reply that he would be delighted to meet me at such-and-such an hour on Sunday afternoon at a tea-room in Marblehead. It was the hasty note of a busy man who, aware of his duty towards his friends, parcels out his leisure time with no sign of the irritation he feels that he can keep no part of his life to himself. I would have let the matter rest there had I not, on returning to my mother, found her up and dressed, carrying a basket on her arm with the intention, I was afraid, of going to the village. I had urged her to go back to bed, but my entreaties were futile for she understood nothing but Russian. I had then given her a glass of brandy (she had at least not forgotten brandy) in which I had dissolved one of the sleeping powders left over from her illness. I must say here that this ingenious trick afforded me the only amusement I had in ten days. I could not help smiling, as I pulverized the pill, at the grave necessity that had driven me to practical joking, and when she began to droop, after no more than a quarter of an hour, I laughed outright. I had then locked her in and run back to the hospital where, on a sheet torn from my loose-leaf notebook, I wrote Dr. McAllister that I had an urgent message for him from Miss Pride. A cold, dubious answer came back at once saying that he would see me in his office in a few minutes.

The doctor had been reading. When I came in, he took off his horn-rimmed spectacles, uncovering eyes which were a blue resembling the flame from certain kinds of wood or oil, a color simultaneously fierce and smoky. In his face there was a union of austerity and simplicity, coming partly from its actual architecture: the defined planes of the jaw and cheek and forehead, the thin lips, the narrow nose, and partly from his expression as he intelligently and nobly appraised me, trying to adjust me to my note.

"You have a message for me?" he said, smiling and motioning me toward a chair. "You must be a friend of Miss Pride's."

"I am, in a way," I said. "But I am really here under false pretenses, for I have no message for you. I had to see you. It's about my mother."

"I don't have a private practice," he said. "Our head, Dr. Galbraith, recently died, as perhaps you know, and his place has not yet been filled. But Dr. Roberts is in town, I'm quite sure." As though to clinch his dismissal, he withdrew his spectacles from the pocket of his white coat and opened them.

"I know that," I said. "But I don't want to go to Dr. Roberts." He waited for me to go on, but I could find no more words, and as I kept my eyes averted from him, seeing the green felt under the glass top of his desk with the harried realization that I had no idea what I was looking at, I knew what his next question was going to be, but as in the dream when our benumbed throats will not let pass a cry for help, I could summon nothing to stave it off, and when he spoke, I heard him as though his voice came from a phonograph record whose revolutions I did not know how to stop: "Look here, I don't know who you are but I don't believe you are Miss Pride's friend. All this mystery doesn't ring true. Are you quite sure it's your mother who is ill? I don't want to sound unkind, but tell me frankly, isn't it instead that you've committed an indiscretion and, to use the common expression, have got yourself knocked up?"

Because I had known that that was the way he would interpret my timidity and my lie about the message, I could not be angry with him for anything but the vulgarity of his phrase, which he had used in the intention of lowering himself to my level, but at the same time had uttered in almost audible quotation marks to assure me that he would have nothing to do with the matter, that I had come to the wrong person for an abortion.

I found my voice and said, "Oh, no, it's not that at all. It's that I think my mother is insane."

"You should have said so at once. Please forgive me, but your coming here was so unusual. Why do you think your mother is insane?"

I told him her history. As I talked, his attentive blue eyes showed me that he was marshaling recollections that my presence and my story disinterred, was giving the skeletons flesh and blood, yet was keeping me, my "case," separate like the solo part of a concerto which is enriched and surrounded by the ritornelle. To ease me, to divert me from the horror of what I told him—for one's sin or sorrow is most intolerable at the moment of confession even when we know that we are soon to be absolved or comforted—he halted me now and again with seemingly inconsequential questions or observations. He had, for example, been to Würzburg and as he spoke of it, pleased that I had caused him to remember the hotel where he had stayed which had formerly been a Franciscan monastery and still preserved an atmosphere of asceticism, he canceled out the distaste and aloofness that had been in his voice when he thought I was pregnant, and without deviating from his purpose as a physician, elevated me to his own plane as at first he had descended to mine. He was, I could tell, profoundly moved by Ivan's death and burial. He said, "Your story *is* a Russian one," and asked me if I had read Dostoievsky. I said I had not, but he led me to the place from which he surveyed the geography of my mother's mind so that I saw her not as my mother, but as a type, as the embodiment of the traits he had read about. We looked together from our vantage point and, lighted by the stories and the novels from whose context he extracted what was applicable to my mother, I saw her, for a little while, as he did.

When I had finished my account and he began to speak, he did not offer me any solution and he said he could not counsel me until he had seen my mother and had judged for himself whether her symptoms corresponded to my report of them. It was easy enough, he said, even for an experienced person to confuse hysteria with insanity, and while he did not say so, he implied that possibly because of my concern over Ivan, my own hysteria had made me exaggerate her eccentricities. "She is perhaps best off at home," he said, "where she can be guarded against excitement. If, that is, she's curable, and the chances are that she is."

"But where else could she be?"

"Perhaps I have misunderstood you." He looked away from me and briefly examined the scene from his window as though he were trying to integrate all its essentials, its colors and its forms, as if he hoped to find there the way to put his words best. "That is, I assumed in your coming to me that you wanted more than a listener. I thought you had been debating whether or not to send her to an asylum."

Chiefly, I suppose, because there was none near Chichester and I had, therefore, no actual impression of the appearance of such an establishment, an asylum had never once occurred to me. My mother's madness had been clearly separated from any other madness. And I said to Dr. McAllister. "Oh, but she isn't violent! She couldn't be put into a strait-jacket."

He laughed. "You're behind the times. We're not going to put your mother into a strait-jacket. Why, mental hospitals are no worse than this these days." He motioned toward the silent corridor. "But we needn't talk about that any more. I'll look around some evening

soon, as though I were paying a call on you, and see what's what."
He glanced down at the blue card on which he had been making
notes, to refresh his memory of my name. "We've covered every
thing now, haven't we, Miss Marburg? I would like, though, to ask
you one more question. Why was it you used Miss Pride's name instead of another? You know, you could have said Dr. Brunson sent
you."

"She spoke of you to me. I connected your name with her and
with her niece, for she said you were friends. You see, last February,
when my brother died, Miss Pride came to see me and took me into
Boston. I had tea with her . . . in the library." I had heard no more
from her. She did not come to fetch me to see the Public Gardens,
as she had promised, nor had she sent me the box of books although
*The Atlantic Monthly* came regularly. Boston had receded a little
farther each day until now, the sea again seemed the only road to
the State House whose glittering dome had once more recovered its
pure shape after my new impressions of it had shuffled off into the
past. I had thought my afternoon with Miss Pride was engraved in-
delibly on my mind, but at last I remembered clearly only the horny
black trunks of the trees in the Park Street cemetery, only the names
Franklin and Revere, and only the metallic voice of the girl saying
"Auntie?"

But the proximity of this man, to whom having tea with Miss
Pride was probably the most ordinary occurrence brought back the
objects of our common knowledge: the portrait, the chess table, the
silver platter for the calling cards. And with the objects came my
hostess's warm, albeit noncommittal, compliments. On an impulse,
I said, "Perhaps you could tell me why she invited me to come to
tea?"

"Miss Pride is a very generous woman," he said with the simplicity but lack of conviction with which, in speaking of the people
we do not like, we acknowledge their virtues that are good in themselves but can serve no purpose to us. "She is known, I believe,"
he continued, "as one of the *most* generous women in Boston. Last
year, for example, she gave five thousand dollars to the Community
Chest."

"I have admired her ever since I can remember," I told him.

"Really? Well, then, perhaps that's one of the reasons she was, as you say, so 'kind' to you. I have never had the honor to be at tea with her alone . . . and never in the library."

I could not grasp his irony. Did he mean that I *had* been singularly honored? Or had she, by shutting me up in the library, merely been taking precautions against my being seen by a chance visitor? I rose to go, dissatisfied with what the doctor had said and liking him a little less for not praising Miss Pride with the passion that I had believed must reside in the breast of anyone who knew her. He came around the desk and I observed that when he walked, his body did not bend in the slightest; his back was as straight, as inflexible as Ivan's had been a few hours after his death.

"You can count on me. But the next time you want to crash a gate, make sure you have the right password. You wouldn't have got in today if I hadn't had an inkling that your 'message' was nothing but a leg-pull."

I knew, by the pink eastern sky showing through the leafy chestnut trees, that it was time for me to be at the Brunsons'. Since my mother had been ill, I had been allowed to come an hour later but had made up for the lost time by working all day on Sunday. Mrs. Brunson was displeased with me, for I had been distracted and had done my work carelessly. Still, she had made a tentative promise to promote me to Maudie's place in the fall. Maudie had by now completely lost control of her appetite for whiskey and twice had watered Dr. Brunson's Vat 69 to his humiliation, on the second occasion, before a guest who, sipping a cocktail made from the expurgated bottle, remarked, "They certainly don't put any teeth in their whiskey any more, do they?"

In spite of knowing that I would get a dressing-down, I dallied along the way. This garden-filled and springtime world through which I moved was perfumed with the closely clustered lilac blossoms in the yards I passed, roofed over by a coral, turquoise, and violet sky. The heard, but unseen, white skirts of the sea fluttered sweetly against its boundaries. Just as Nathan's kisses in the fog had warmed my sorrow to its bloom, and my love, though contiguous, had only served to enhance its somber colors, so the young physician's accidental exhumation of Boston had, immediately afterwards, caused me to see the loveliness of Chichester to which for several months I had been indifferent. And now, stopping to bury my face in a branch of lilac in a sudden infiltration of an unobjectified but passionate happiness, the purpose of my interview seemed to me to be but a tenth part of what had been accomplished, and the least important part, as if my fear that Mamma was insane had been only an excuse to know Dr. McAllister and had been, in a sense, almost as trumped up as my "message" from Miss Pride.

He had said, "We should not rush ahead to conclusions, but you should think this over. Let us say you keep her at home, protect her for the better part of your life so that you don't marry or don't realize whatever your ambition is. Would the martyrdom be worth all that? It's the question you must answer for yourself, for salvation for one soul is perdition for another and what might send me to hell would give you grace." His lofty terms, *martyrdom, salvation, perdition, grace,* were no longer the mere names of abstract states over which I had carelessly slid my eye on the printed page, but were the components of my own future, and I said "grace" aloud, my lips stopped by the dense purple trumpets of the flower I had pressed against them. My happiness confounded me. As though it were as perishable as the crisp lilac, I allowed no thought to come near it and refused to listen to the voices within the house behind the hedge which, organ of their owners' uncertainty, talked back and forth of the likelihood of rain. But the footsteps which I heard coming behind me, I did allow to intrude upon my mind, thinking perhaps they belonged to the doctor on his way home—his home? I questioned, but could see him only behind the desk in Dr. Galbraith's office where the white marquisette curtains were inflated by the breeze. The footsteps were quick and the heel-taps rang brashly on the sidewalk. Someone called my name, but there was no need to turn, for Nathan Kadish was beside me and had put his shoulder behind mine. When I saw his face, it was the good side at which I looked.

"What have you got there?" he asked me, although all I had, as he saw perfectly well, was the branch of lilac that I had bent down to smell, but love is a child at language, speaks nonsense, asks stupid questions, makes insipid replies—"Don't you know a lilac when you see one?"—and means to convey just the opposite of impertinence.

"You don't seem surprised to see me," he said. Rather he whispered, so close to my ear that his lips almost touched me, for the voices on the porch reminded us that we were not alone here as we had been in the fog. "I never can remember," said a woman, "whether it's feed a cold and starve a fever or the other way around just like I can't remember whether a ring around the moon means good weather or a storm."

"I guess I was thinking about you," I said, although this was not true. I had been thinking not of him, but of myself in whom the blood had defecated its black humors and had left only love but love as an envelope that was as yet empty.

"You're not sore, then?" He meant: Was I not angry, then, that my last glimpse of him until now had been when, shirt-tail out, he hotfooted it for the bus to Boston without a backward glance and had not written me a letter? No, I could tell him honestly, I had not been angry. I *had* been sore; my heart had been skinned by his silence. I had learned from his mother (who believed, for the simple reason that we were neighbors and about the same age, that Nathan and I were friends, but never dreamed that when she uttered his name my skin erupted into goose-flesh) that he would not be home again until the end of the term for he had got a job working in the Brookline Economy Store and all his leisure time was occupied. But I had not failed to call at the post-office once a day for two months in the hope of some word from him. The soreness had gradually disappeared, like a headache, and though I was not conscious of my relief, I was able now to pass the post-office with indifference. But just as the headache has not really gone but has been hidden under sleep and requires only a sharp noise to cast off its covering and meddle with our nerves again, so Nathan's appearance—weeks before I had expected him—reminded me of the shame of his neglect, renewed the sensation of his kisses, and made me, as before, stretch upwards as if I stood on tiptoe to scrutinize his birthmark, sudden through the lighted window. And I knew I had not ceased to love him, that the wrappings in which I had laid away my hopes were not winding sheets, were only masquerade, out of which they came now with their sweet, young faces.

202

The dense branch swung back to the bush from my relaxed hand as five o'clock rang out from the Catholic church. "Golly, I'm late," I said.

Nathan stepped to one side and with a gallant gesture offered me the outside of the walk. He said, "I know you think it's impolite of me to walk on the inside. I do it intentionally because I do not believe in bourgeois etiquette. Probably you want to hurry because you are afraid of the bawling-out you'll get from that bourgeois ignoramus who has the egregious impudence to call you her 'servant.' I have no doubt that if I invited you to stop in at Red's café for a Budweiser draft, you would refuse. I'm not reproaching you. You're merely victimized, a helpless cog in the machinery of social corruption."

"I would stop at Red's," I said, "but it's so late already and I promised to be on time tonight. They're having company."

Nathan's full lips curled in a sneer. "Don't go into detail, I can get the picture. I can just *see* their company. Does that illiterate trollop, the daughter of the house, still infect the atmosphere with her noisome presence?"

I told him that Betty was at school in New York. "As it should be," he said, nodding gravely. "There she will learn the elegant antics of the capitalistic prostitute. Oh, lofty ideal!"

He was lagging, coming to a full stop occasionally to convey his italics or exclamation marks by kicking a paling of the white fence, and if I quickened my pace, he pulled me back by the elbow, saying, "Where's the fire? Courage!"

I was nervous and bewildered by his talk, and although when his fingers closed over my arm as he detained me, the contact softened my bones and caused me to float without exertion, I could not help being disappointed that we dwelt in worlds so far apart. "Nathan, are you a Communist again?" I asked him.

"Again? When was I not? Oh, wait a second. Do you mean am I a member of the Communist Party? Or do you mean am I a dialectical materialist? Am I a Marxist, is that what you're asking me?"

I could only shake my head at his terms.

"No, I belong to no party, faction, or school of thought. But I hate the bourgeoisie because they are the enemies of freedom. I am a revolutionist, yes; I am a nonconformist, yes. But no, I am not a Communist, I am a cosmopolitan. Sonie"—he turned to me with a serious stare—"I am going to Paris."

"When?" I asked.

"Typical," he said irritably. "Typical of an unimaginative woman to try to pin me down about *when*. Next you'll ask me where I propose to get the money and if I intend to live in the thirteenth *arrondissement*."

His irritation was transmitted to me. I was angry that from our conversation had been deleted any reference to ourselves except as we figured in the grim farce of existing Society, by the denunciation of which he made me cherish my desire to know what it was before it was annihilated utterly by the revolution. The word "society," even though I was sophisticated enough to realize that he used it in its larger sense, was reflected on my mind as "Boston Society." But while Nathan had no doubt that if, in his life-scheme, he decided to include me he could convince me of the truth of his cosmopolitanism, so I believed he would sacrifice his crotchets to my own. Each of us regarded the other as a child; each smiled inwardly and with indulgence at the other's self-deceptions. And when I said, partly to tease him, that I still admired Miss Pride, he patted my hand comfortingly as if to say all was not lost, that he himself would remove the scales from my eyes.

Now and again, I was exhilarated by what he said of Paris. "My genius will bloom in a shabby *bistro*," he said. "In the beginning, I will have only friends, rum, *bock*, and market girls. But later, having fame, I will, if I want her, have a bonafide Faubourg *duchesse*."

Without realizing that the source of my rage was jealousy of that imaginary duchess, I blurted out, "Oh, I'm *sick* of George Moore."

"Give me three reasons," he demanded.

"I'm not interested. But no one with that much conceit can be decent."

"Decent? What language they teach them in school nowadays! I suppose you think an artist ought to be a humble worm? Humble, like you? You, Sonia Marburgovna, are the most self-conceited baggage I have ever known."

"I?"

"Yes, you," he mocked me. "For example, on the night you made that melodramatic, also fraudulent, also imbecilic Lady-of-the-Lake voyage around the Point to deposit an imaginary corpse in the Atlantic Ocean, did you not later lap up for flattery what was intended as advice? Did you not, when I absent-mindedly exaggerated your nature and called you deep, believe that you really were deep?"

I blushed and did not reply. We had turned into the street where the Brunsons lived, and Nathan stopped. "I won't go any farther. As it is, I'm close enough to smell the putrefaction. Since you won't —or as you are deluded into thinking, you *can't*—go to Red's now, would you like to after you have finished cleaning up their swill?"

I had not drunk beer since my father went away, and I was curious to know what it tasted like and what its effect would be. I was elated at the thought of the evening we might spend in the dark, disreputable saloon that advertised tables for ladies. Encouraged by the beer (and bock beer was in now), perhaps we would be able to revive the mood in the fog. But when Nathan added, "Shall I call for you here or at home?" the image of my home and its drugged occupant made me catch my breath as I realized with abject shame that I had not thought of my mother since the moment Dr. McAllister, changing the subject, had asked me why I had used Miss Pride's name.

"No, I'm sorry, I can't." Too late I saw I should have said, "I can't *tonight*," but the pressure of the immediate future when my mother should awaken made me unable to look further ahead into an evening when I might be free to drink beer. I think Nathan acted not out of embarrassment but at the command of a reflex when, before I had uttered the last word of my refusal, he put his hand to the left side of his face and leaned into the shade of the elm tree under which we stood. His unilateral smile of twisted lips and one bright, malicious eye measured the altitude of his anger whose heights he had instantaneously scaled. With his right hand he tipped an imaginary hat and said, "I *beg* your pardon, moddam. No offense intended, merely a case of mistaken identity."

I started to explain to him why I could not go with him, but he raised his hand for silence. "No, really, I'm not in the least interested. I was under the impression that we had a tacit understanding, commonly known as 'friendship,' but I see I was wrong. It is just as well. Momentarily, under the influence of certain romantic symbols, I forgot that I must burn the midnight oil tonight over the misguided but well-meaning Thomas More. Please overlook my brief collapse."

"Oh, Nathan!" I cried, hoping by the tender tone of my voice to convey my despair so that he would forgive me and I might then tell him about Mamma. But I did not achieve my aim. The long white fingers of his left hand stole downwards and revealed, bit by bit, his garish cheek. "It was all right in the fog where nobody could see you, wasn't it? But it's a horse of a different color—rather, to be more exact, a *freak* of a different color—in the clear public light of our respectable village *bistro*. Come off it, lovey, you call me Cranberry behind my back, don't you?"

I was possessed by the deliberate unveiling of the birthmark and in a voice that came not from my conscious self but from the fanatical rapture with which I had secretly stared at it when I was ten years old, I said, "No, I love your birthmark."

He had not expected me even to say the word, spoken perhaps for the first time in his presence since he was a child and was the target for his contemporaries' downright jokes. My beastly declaration, a maudlin lie as he believed, brought a flush to the uncolored side of his face. As if confronting me with the tool of my crime to watch as my guilt blanched and shook me, he slowly turned his head so that his right profile was concealed by the trunk of the tree and from the dull ember which ran from his hair to his chin, the diabolical eye winked its purple lid. His limber lips were drawn to this side and from them issued a laugh in which mirth was not even pretended but which was the distance-muted entreaty of a wounded animal.

"That's a hot one," he said. "*Very* funny. Your wit, if you must know, surpasses your beauty. Let me say, however, that I have always been attracted by your hair. I observed the redolence of its natural oils in the fog. It reminded me, I don't know why, of the interior of a water-logged tennis ball. I trust you will never cut its pristine grease with that decadent commodity manufactured by your Heroine of the Barstow, that is, soap. Well, I must go home. Hark! Do I hear my doting mother calling Cranberry! *Oh,* Cranberry!"

Jauntily, his arms swinging and his metal heel-taps clicking pertly on the sidewalk, he went back down the street, but at the corner turned and called, "I say, be an old dear and burn up those letters of mine, will you?"

"What letters?" I cried.

"Oh, curses on my absent-mindedness. Here I was thinking you were Josephine." And he was gone, around the corner, his footsteps audible for a few seconds.

I reasoned, as I lingered in a breathless sickness, that if he had loved me, he would have sensed that I was in trouble, would have reviewed my words and noticed that there had been an inexplicable change between the time we met and the time we parted, and that the love so obvious in my voice when I had spoken through the flowers could not have perished within the space of ten minutes. And yet, when I considered what our relations might be after he had begged my pardon (for I had gradually progressed from a state of dazed helplessness to one of indignation and desired not to make an apology but to be tendered one by him), I was not sure that my love had not begun to wane a little after all. I was almost certain of it later, at the Brunsons', when I heard Dr. Roberts remark, "We couldn't hope to get a prize like young McAllister for this town. He's cut out for a metropolitan practice. He'll be one of your fifty-dollar-a-house-call society doctors. He's got the style all right," I had just gone through the swinging door into the kitchen to bring more wine from the ice-chest. When I heard the young man's name mentioned, my cheeks warmed and I cooled them at the rush of frosty air from the opened door as I withdrew the bottle of sauterne.

In the following weeks, I did not become indifferent. The turbulence that stormed about my memories of Nathan did not subside but I moved, so to speak, out of range of its danger by promising that I would not make the first step towards our reconciliation. And in time the cool-headedness that I feigned became actual, and once more when I looked toward Boston, the city which I imagined stretching out behind the State House did not go beyond that part of the Charles visible from the top of Pinckney Street, did not include Boston University or the Brookline Economy Store.

Dr. McAllister, after he had seen my mother two or three times, said that for the present she was well enough off at home. The first time he came, a few days after my talk with him, she was still in a state of total lethargy, but she had begun to speak English again. She was under the impression that the doctor had come to see her fancy-work and she exhibited it to him with the boredom and hauteur of a great lady who has at last summoned up the energy to pay a duty call on a dowdy friend and dispenses her good manners with an effort of will. "Thank you," she said when he complimented her on a set of table mats embroidered with yellow tulips. "It don't show up in this light but it's done well if you like tulips." Dr. McAllister said he was very fond of tulips and was surprised at my mother's indifference to them. She smiled with some lofty, secret knowledge of the flower's faults which she did not impart to us. Soon afterwards, in what I later recognized as a gauche breach of taste, I invited the doctor to drink a glass of brandy. My mother allowed her daft eyes to rove from one to the other of us. "Brandy?" she queried. "I don't know what you're talking about, Sonia. You must forgive my daughter, Mr. Whatyoumaycallit, she's always been a dreamy girl." I started to point to the shelf where the bottle stood, still half full, but the doctor shook his head at me, and my mother went on, "I had a little money here years ago and this silly child can't believe it's all used up. Mamma, where is the golden egg? she'll ask me and look in the Bible where we used to keep it. But she's a treasure all the same."

She would have gone on in an interminable eulogy of my abilities, my eyelashes, my character, had she not been silenced and rendered immobile by the returning torpor which immediately extinguished the light in her eyes and fixed her mouth. She sank to a chair and did not change her position for the half hour that the doctor lingered. Her hand, resting on the table covered with her fancy-work, could have been made of marble.

On his later visits, Dr. McAllister saw her alone, in the bedroom, and I could sometimes hear him interrupting her in the midst of what I knew, though I could not distinguish the words, was a tale of persecution. "Now, wait a minute, Mrs. Marburg, I haven't got the scene clear in my mind. Tell me what the place *looked* like." She would begin again, her voice sailing the calmed waters of her perpetual woe.

He told me that it was possible she was posing, that she was cleverer than I thought, but when I asked him what it was she could gain hereby, he could not answer to my satisfaction. "I don't know. Maybe she's afraid that now you are nearly grown you will leave her. But that mustn't alarm you, for I don't think she'd ever do anything drastic to keep you with her."

"Drastic? Why, she would never harm a hair of my head."

And he replied, "Certainly not," but his tone was so positive that paradoxically it was suspicious and a week later, when I went to the hospital to see him, I said, "The other day when you said my mother would never do anything 'drastic' to me, did you mean it?"

"I knew you would be troubled by that and I regret I said it. But the fact is that insane people—and mind you, I'm not saying she's insane—can turn against anything if they feel they're driven to a wall. For instance, when your mother discovers that you lock her in, she may be furious. That's why we must decide about the asylum soon because you won't be able to deceive her indefinitely. And that's why—that and because even suicide is not an impossibility—you'd better get rid of anything she might use against you or against herself, knives and so on."

"I can't believe it," I said. "Why, now she's not much different from what she's been for years. Now that she's started to speak English again."

"I don't doubt that. But has it ever occurred to you that for years you have been in exactly the same danger that you are now? You don't think, do you, that this has come on her overnight?"

"Oh, no," I said. "I guess I've known it for a long time. I always just thought she was queer and never was afraid until that night Dr. Galbraith came."

I could hardly bear to be in the room with her, not because I was afraid of what she might do to me, for, despite the doctor's ominous warning I remained convinced that, as I had told him, she would not "harm a hair of my head," but because she trusted me and did not know that at any moment I might lock her up behind high walls whose corridors rang with maniacal laughter and groans of the hope-less damned souls of this hell on earth. And when Dr. McAllister one day gave the place, which hitherto had existed in my mind merely as the word "asylum," a name and said we would send her to Wolfburg, it seemed to me that evening that she must be able to read my mind, obsessed with its hypocrisy. For heretofore *the* asylum had been as remote in space as her admittance there had been in time. But the articulation of the name and, further, the articulation of one that was not unfamiliar to me, forced me to open my eyes to its masonry, its approach, its gates, for this was a tangible destina-tion. Thus, we could no longer use the conventional formula, "if she is taken somewhere," but now must say, "if she is taken to Wolf-burg." Moreover, Dr. McAllister had this time used the active rather than the passive voice, had said, "We will take her," not "She will be taken," making personal the escort which had formerly been an ab-stract force. The doctor said, "Wolfburg has beautiful gardens, kept by some of the inmates." I wondered that he, in his kindness, should have built me so cruelly real a picture, going even so far as to name a particular feature of the lunatics' industry, an herb garden rivaling the famous one in Concord. But his intention was not tactless; it was just because of his frequent references to Wolfburg in the weeks that followed that I was able, when I first saw it, to enter the gate with composure and to admire that very horticulture, the first mention of which had unnerved me.

Miss Pride, either through Dr. McAllister with whom I saw she was on very good terms (even though he was too "brainy" for her liking and though his liking of her had certain reservations which he had taken no pains to conceal from me) or through her sharp eyes, knew that something was troubling me, and from the first day of her return to the Hotel, I felt her observant gaze upon me, missing nothing, as I served in the dining-room. Forbearing to make any comment when I confessed that I had not read anything in *The At-lantic Monthly* but the stories and the poems, she gave me a look so discerning that I felt any explanation was unnecessary since she ap-parently already understood why I had not been able to study out the essays. I was careful to wear an imperturbable countenance whenever she was near-by. If it happened that during the night I had slept badly and had dreamed of Ivan and had wakened to my mother's presence beside me in the bed, then had been unable to burst from the infrangible circle of my anxiety over her, I was still not so forgetful in the morning as to allow my face to relax into its natural weariness, but instead smiled and walked briskly as I took Miss Pride's dropped egg in from the kitchen. The effort that went into keeping myself upright and my eyes wide open perhaps imparted to my appearance the very rigidity I had strived for.

It was my misfortune, however, to be caught off guard several times by other guests. Mrs. Prather, for example, a woman of what are called "good intentions" had come to call on my mother at the very first of the season, for she had heard of Ivan's death through Gonzales. She was, as are all those with good intentions, democratic, as I had often heard her say. "I do not feel toward my servants as many people do," she would remark on the veranda. "I think of them as human beings, every bit as good as I am." In her humanitarian ardor, she called on us one Sunday on her way home from church, crept to the door with a soundlessness which may very likely have been calculated in spite of her charity. She caught me in tears, their cause being vague in my mind now, for I could have been brooding either over Nathan or over my mother. But I explained them to Mrs. Prather as being brought on by headaches from which I was never free. She refused to accept my reason and, offering me a handkerchief which she carried in a tatted pouch and smelled faintly of scent and, as if I were five years old, producing a lemon drop from a paper bag in her pocket, she begged me to tell her "all about it." I stuck to my guns and she asked then to see my mother, but I replied that she was in mourning and did not wish to speak with anyone.

After this visit, I sometimes overheard my name spoken on the veranda and I was said to be "looking badly." The voices were lowered as the ladies explained why I did. Some believed that I was anemic; others thought that my mother was ill and that my pallor came from staying up with her at night. No one suspected her of being mad, but they delighted in talking about Ivan whose epilepsy had been reported to them in as much detail as he could recollect, by

Gonzales when he drove them from the station. A number of them said that the disease was hereditary and either through loyalty to their sex or through expostulation of my father whom they had never ceased to discuss, they designated him as its transmitter. They were opposed by the group who maintained that epilepsy was acquired after a blow on the head or an attack of scarlet fever.

Miss Pride, of course, took no part in these discussions, but possibly in the intention of showing the other guests that she had an interest in me far more generous than theirs, which was merely clinical, conversed with me as I served her. Far from elevating her in their estimation, her gesture was deprecated as bad taste and disservice to myself. "She won't go to heaven by bending over backwards to that child, pretending to be a Little Sister of the Poor, when she wouldn't part with a red cent of her precious money," it was said vindictively. "My word! You can't get credit for *talk!*" The old ladies were more displeased with Miss Pride this summer than ever, for the young Dr. McAllister was a frequent guest at her table and it was so arranged that it was never possible for anyone else to engage him in conversation. What if he *was* a personal friend of hers? Were not physicians, in a sense, public property? Consequently, since Dr. Galbraith, whose death was long and solemnly lamented, could not be consulted over the soup and since his successor never came to the Hotel for meals, Miss Pride's monopoly of the market was found intolerable. Finally someone hit upon the hypothesis that she had paid for his education and had offered to set him up in practice, the bribery being motivated by her desire to marry off her troublesome niece to him.

It was quite true that the chief interest in common between Miss Pride and Philip McAllister was Hopestill, proof of which required only the most casual eavesdropping. But it was also true that Miss Pride had known the young man's family for many years and had moved in the same feminine circles as his mother, who had gone that summer to London, and his grandmother. Dr. McAllister's father, a retired Unitarian minister, used sometimes to come to see his son and always made a point of lunching at the Hotel. I took pains to stay as near them as possible so that I might not miss any of their talk. The Reverend McAllister was withered and singed and clad from head to toe in decent black. All that relieved his funereal attire was a gold watch chain across his convex middle from which hung a Phi Beta Kappa key. He was a dabbler in oddities. He knew, for instance, that the armadillo always bore identical quadruplets; he offered this news with a brief, factual account of the duck-billed platypus, but he went no further, although Mrs. McKenzie, who overheard him, was enchanted and pressed him for details. Or he would trace at length the development of spiritism, but far from discussing it in the light of his religious tenets, he merely presented the case as though it had no bearing on anything else. Gravely he would imitate the Fox sisters, "Ho, Mr. Slipfoot, are you there?" Or, if he were invited to express his opinion of Christian Science, he would repeat an anecdote he had heard about Mrs. Eddy which was perhaps illustrative of his feeling but which suggested, to his discredit, that that was all he knew about Christian Science. He was, as his son remarked of him once, the kind of man who came out ahead in pen and pencil games.

Miss Pride did not particularly like "the Reverend" though she respected him, for she had been taught that it was improper not to respect the cloth. She said in a low voice to a friend who had come to dine with her, "He is a very good Christian, I grant you, but he's a frightful bore."

The friend, a woman with a broad, innocent face, said, "I can't believe he's a bore, Lucy, though I've only met him once or twice. Why, I was dumfounded, when I dined at his house once, at the size of his theological library. And the books were so worn, so obviously *studied*. No, indeed, a man who has read that much can't be a bore."

"I don't think Reverend McAllister *has* read them all," said Miss Pride with a malicious glint in her eyes. "As for their being worn, my dear, haven't you heard of second-hand shops? But I'm not singling him out. I think the clergy has fallen into the sere and yellow leaf where learning is concerned. Last New Year's Eve, I went to Estelle Hornblower's at home and was literally forced by Lincoln Nephews to go into the little white parlor where six ministers were sitting about like a plenary council. Lincoln had said, 'Lucy, I want to show you something straight out of Trollope.' Three of the crea-

213

tures were Anglo-Catholics and were, I do believe, the poorest Latin-
ists I have ever seen. They were talking about *On the Sublime and
the Beautiful* by Theophrastus! Well, the Reverend was there. 'Hold
on,' says he, 'Theophrastus isn't your man. He wrote those little
vignettes you call *characters*.' 'Nonsense,' said one of the Anglicans,
'I'm not so rusty on my English as not to know those little things—
sometimes I believe they're called hornbooks—were a seventeenth-
century invention. But if Theophrastus didn't write *On the Sublime
and the Beautiful,* who did, pray?' Do you know not one of them
knew and Lincoln Nephews had to set them right?"

"Well, *I* wouldn't have known," said Miss Pride's friend. "I'm so
ignorant I would never be able to criticize the clergy in that way.
But in case I'm some time asked, who *did* write it?"

There was an imperceptible pause. "Why, Lucretius," said Miss
Pride. "I thought everyone took that in with his mother's milk." But
a little later on, she interrupted an anecdote her friend was telling to
say, "You'll tell me that people who live in glass houses shouldn't
throw stones. Didn't I just say Lucretius wrote *On the Sublime and
the Beautiful?* I must have been asleep, for as I perfectly well know
it was Longinus."

However much she deprecated in private his want of education,
she was so cordial to the minister when he took a meal with her that
I began to wonder if the old ladies' conjecture had not been in part
correct, that is, that she was anxious to make a match between her
niece and his son. For it was only in the presence of these two men
that she had nothing but good to say of the girl. Hopestill's defiance
of convention was transformed at these luncheons into her "high
spirits, her vigor." Her beauty, ordinarily spoken of as "something
about her that her extreme clothes brings out which I find very
strange," was alluded to with respect. She became "intelligent" instead of "foxy." But the Reverend was deaf to all these virtues of
Miss Mather because he wanted to inform the company that some
things had not changed with the times at all, that in reading Emerson's letters he had discovered that the train fare from Concord to
Boston was exactly the same in 1860 as it was today. The young
man, to whom Hope's graces were not news, as soon as possible effected a transition to another subject, less, I thought out of embarrass-

ment than annoyance because he knew Miss Pride spoke with shameless insincerity. Usually, he would inquire of her how she was progressing with her memoirs. "Hush!" she would say in real consternation. "You must not broadcast that. I'd be the laughing-stock of Boston if anyone knew. But since you ask, I'll tell you quite frankly that at times I despair. There is more to writing even of this sort than meets the eye. If I had a secretary, I feel that I could simply fly through them. The difficulty is that my sentences look so undistinguished when I see them in my own handwriting." She would glance at me as though to say that she had not forgotten our conversation in her library, and the young doctor, following her eyes, would briefly ponder me.

It was a midsummer night, cool after a sultry day. Gonzales had picked a bouquet of tea-roses and bridal wreath for my mother and I was taking them home, after work about nine o'clock. My mother, her face streaming with perspiration, was sitting beside the stove in which she had built up a raging fire that roared through the open damper. For further warmth she was wearing the old hooded wrapper and my sheep-lined slippers.

"Why, Mamma, why have you built a fire? It's like a furnace in here!"

I saw that despite her dripping face she was shivering and her teeth chattered between her words as she said, "Maybe you don't feel the cold if you're full of brandy. Not everybody has the good luck to have a little something to warm them up on the inside." The steady accusation in her eyes did not waver, and then I observed that the kitchen was in disorder. The shelves had been ransacked and half their useless objects had been thrown down so that broken glass and monkey wrenches and empty cans lay in a nondescript heap on the floor. Weeks before, at Dr. McAllister's injunction, I had taken the bottle of brandy to the shop. I said nothing.

"I suppose fairies drank it," said my mother. "I suppose the same little fairies that stole the golden egg so a person couldn't buy so much as a thimbleful of wine when they were dying of the cold. I guess they locked the door so a sick woman couldn't get a breath of fresh air if she needed it. It couldn't have been the invalid's daughter, oh, no."

I had often rehearsed my speech but as it issued, it sounded flat and false. My unsteady voice belied the words: "Yes, Mamma, I did lock the door. I didn't want to worry you and so I didn't tell you. A lot of houses have been robbed this last week and I didn't want the burglars to come here. You know how you lose yourself in your work and sometimes don't even hear me when I come in. I didn't want you to be taken by surprise."

She rolled her head crazily round and round, stopped, grinned at me, and rolled it again, repeating in what I suppose she thought was an imitation of my father, *"Ja, ja, ja, ja, ja, ja!"* Though the effort of moving in this inferno was exhausting, I started to clear the table, for usually at this hour we had a glass of lemonade and a sandwich of sardines or cheese. "Don't touch my belongings!" cried my mother. "Don't you dare!"

"Oh, Mamma!" I said, hoping to hide my alarm under impatience. "Don't be silly, Mamma. I'm not going to do anything to your lovely table-runners. I'm only going to fix us a little supper."

"Come here a minute, Sonie," she wheedled. "Come over by my chair. I want to tell you a secret." I advanced with dread and knelt down when she touched my shoulder. "Closer, sweetheart. There." She pushed back my hair and pressed her lips to my ear. "I hate you!"

I tried to rise, but she had put her arm around my shoulders, holding me against her with prodigious strength and I felt that she had barely tapped her resources, that if she desired, she could crush my bones. And as she had used to do when my father was her victim, she repeated her words half a dozen times in a monotone but with a crescendo which was meant less to convince me than herself. Sweat poured from our close faces and I felt its tickling rivulets down my back inside my dress. I begged my mother to release me, but she was not sure that we both understood yet and she continued to reiterate her declaration until, like my father, I cried, "Then leave me alone! Let me go!"

She did let me go. She jerked me to my feet with her superhuman strength and, like a skilled wrestler, hurled me to the floor. My head struck the leg of the sink and dazed me for a minute as she stood looking down. I implored her to believe that I had not locked the door to torment her, that the brandy was all gone, that the golden egg had been spent years before. At each of my attempts at speech, she again rolled her eyes round and round and hooted, "*Ja, ja, ja, ja!*" She drew her chair to the sink and sat down, daring me to try to stir. I lay still. In a few minutes, I could feel the sweat spreading in a pool all about me. My mother leaned across to the table and turned down the lamp, but by the starlight from the window I could still see her glistening face, beatified in the repose that had settled for a time on her lips and in her eyes. If I rose up on my elbow or stretched my legs or rubbed my head which still ached, her crazy skull commenced its revolutions and the "*ja, ja!*" came forth like the rasping of an imperfect machine.

The heat made me drowsy and though I fought off sleep I surrendered to it for brief, troubled fractions of the hours my mother guarded me. Then I awoke, my head throbbing, my flesh swollen and drenched to see her shining eyes which, so far as I could tell, had not left me for a second. Each time, I heard a loud popping or dripping somewhere outside the house, like water falling drop by drop on metal or like a sheet of tin cracking with expansion. Confused, I imagined it to be hot outdoors and I dreaded the morning and the progress of the day towards noon, that debilitating hour of fire when the heat shimmered in visible undulations over the grass and the sun, the tyrant of the bright blue skies, roasted one like a sucking pig, unstuck the pores of the body so that the sweat poured forth like water from a tap, slackened the senses, and benumbed the mind. It was as if the streaming of my flesh was in anticipation of that hour. Then my mind cleared; I remembered that there was a fire in the stove. I heard the ocean and longed to bathe my scorched body in it; my throat was parched; I conceived the sound as the slow leak of an ice-cold spring. Once I murmured, "Mamma, can I have a glass of water?" but my plea evinced only her derisive grimace and her absurd "*ja, ja!*"

A little while after the church bells struck midnight, my mother fell asleep in her chair, her head resting against the corner of the sink. I sat up slowly lest I rouse her, took off my shoes and then I crept, inch by inch, backwards to the door. As I passed the stove, its dying but still ferocious fire made me feel faint and ill. I gained the door and stood up; I could see her still in the light from the window. She had not stirred. I slid back the bolt and went out, brought the outer key from my pocket and locked my mother in, and then, revived by the salt breeze, I ran in my bare feet over the sandy path to the shop. The shop was cool and damp and I shivered with the sweet change. I put a piece of smooth leather to my cheek, then pressed my forehead against the windowpane, then coiled the cold rosary into my hand. Coolest was the bottle of brandy which I held in the crook of my arm. I did not go to sleep again for fear my mother, waking up, would find some way out of the house. I remembered how Ivan had told me that if he ran to the shop to escape her, she came to the window and peered in at him. I sat at my desk playing Patience by candlelight. Maudie had taught me half a dozen variations and I played them all, winning often and easily. The dawn was an eternity in coming and yet it was not four o'clock when the gray impinged upon the black shadows and I could see the dim outlines of the Boston water front where lights still burned. In another hour the lobster men set forth; I saw their green dories and their small, white motor boats and heard their terse greetings to one another. But the signs of normal human activity and the faithful daylight did not, as they used to do when I was a little girl, rout my fear. My legs were bruised where I had fallen, and my head ached, no longer from its blow against the sink but from the beginning of a cold. I sneezed and wished for a handkerchief. I knew that I must leave the shop before it was any lighter, for I did not want my mother, waking, to see me through the window, but afraid that she was already awake, I lingered a little longer in indecision.

At the first flush of the sun I slipped out, stooped down low as I passed the house, then ran till the wind whistled in my ears, in the direction of the hospital. My bare feet stung and my temples throbbed, but now that I was actually escaping her I was conscious of nothing but my terror, and if I had paused, it would not have been to stop my little pains, but to look back to make sure that she was not coming. I flew down the street where Nathan and I had dallied by the lilac bushes and noticed that the dead flowers were rusty among the green leaves, but just beyond them on lattices or against the walls of the houses, morning glories had opened up their bright blue horns. Taking the short-cut, I ran past Mr. Greeley's mortuary where a green neon sign burned still in the front window: "Chichester Funeral Parlor." In a moment, when I had turned a corner, I saw the hospital at the end of its concrete driveway and to my relief, saw that the operating room on the top floor was illuminated with a livid blue light. I remembered that Dr. McAllister was the anesthetist. Uppermost in my mind then was my need for a handkerchief before I presented myself to him.

# 3

Dr. McAllister called for me every Sunday morning to drive me to Wolfburg. West and south of Boston, the asylum was not far from a farm where his aunt, with a large staff of gardeners and farmers, grew apples, roses, wheat, cows, and guinea hens. She, her nephew told me, would have liked to believe that she pitched hay, milked cows, churned butter, and cooked for the harvest men. Although the young man freely joked about her to me, almost a complete stranger, he was very fond of her and told me that he would not miss his Sunday luncheon with her for the world. I had not believed him at first, thinking that the aunt was apocryphal and manufactured to allow me to accept his charity. But Miss Pride, who knew of our expeditions, said, "I dare say Philip McAllister likes having company when he goes to see his aunt. You must ask him sometime to drive you past her place. Her roses are so splendid that I have often said she should go into the florist business."

While the drive to Wolfburg was either tedious (if I wished the visit to be over quickly) or too swift (if I particularly dreaded this day with my mother), the drive back was delightful. It was the late afternoon when the air was unburdening itself of the weighty heat and the tight sky was split with pink clouds. I would have liked to walk a little way into the groves we passed, where twisting avenues, flowery and humid, opened sometimes in a delta at the highway. But the desire was a lazy one and equal to it was the wish that I might go along this way hours longer, my obligations behind me, and all about me the embracing summer, most tranquil at this cooling hour, gentlest on this kind of road where the sheen upon the leaves proclaimed the heat and the shade between the tree-trunks proclaimed its compensation. The opulent overflow of verdure, berries, flowers, was arrested like the subject of a picture.

When we reached Chichester, it had been dark half an hour and Boston was alight. I stood on the steps of our house, watching the doctor drive away, and stood a little longer looking up at the Barstow where Miss Pride's three front windows were rosy with the light that came through her striped curtains. It was then, when I entered the house that I realized more clearly than when I had been with her that my mother was no longer here, but in the vast, labyrinthine asylum where she was known by number and species. The mustard-yellow enameled walls of the main corridor were lined with hard benches where we, the visitors, sat bolt upright with cold, fixed faces as if we wished it clearly understood that we had no desire to sympathize or compare notes with one another. The blatant squawk of the girl at the address microphone came through ubiquitous concealed outlets: "Dr. Sho-ort." Or, in nasal ridicule, "Dr. *Fink*elstein." I could tell by the impatience with which they sometimes flung down their magazines that the other visitors detested the bodiless parrot as I did, and I wondered if they, too, desired to talk back to it, or, even better, to seek it out in its vociferous den and, if necessary, strangle it. One by one we were summoned to the gray cubicles where the jovial doctors in charge of our "case" glanced through a manila folder at typewritten sheets, the slowly accumulating history, the record of the arduous battle. As I passed down the corridor in the wake of a matron, silent with ill-nature or boredom or perhaps with the mere consciousness that she was sane, I peeped through the open doors of the offices and saw that all the other doctors looked like mine: their broad, red faces glowed with health; rimless spectacles sat on their neat tan noses; their grandiose condescension gave their voices a vast range of pitch, from a high amiability to a deep-toned expression of totally indifferent regret.

But it was neither the waiting nor the short visit with my mother that distressed me. It was the knowledge, after I had lighted the lamp in the house where she had always lived, that I had left her behind and that perhaps at this very moment she was imagining what I was doing. It was usually an hour before I was quieted, and then I began to read. Later, if the memory of her empty, staring eyes or her incoherent words came to me, I rationalized, said that she did not suffer as much as I since she was barely aware of her surroundings. I repeated to myself the doctor's exhortation that I must not feel guilty. His advice called him forth to replace my mother, and I searched the conversation we had just concluded for clues of how he felt towards me, if I were anything more to him than an element of a case that had been foisted upon him.

I had been nervous, on the first of these drives to Wolfburg, recalling that Miss Pride had said the young man was "brainy" and I feared that he would discover that I was ignorant, that he would report his finding to Miss Pride, and that I would fall from favor. Consequently, I spent the Saturday evening before the trip poring over the several copies of *The Atlantic Monthly* which had come and memorized certain facts about Russia, about overproduction, about co-operatives. But my preparation was unnecessary. Dr. McAllister shaped the conversation to suit himself and I was relieved of any responsibility. He was principally interested, I found, in religion, but I was never sure whether he was religious or merely inquisitive. When he spoke of the survival of the churches in the Soviet Union and said he longed to go to Russia to see how religion accomplished its ends under official atheism, he spoke as someone might who wished to visit Heidelberg to hear medieval drinking songs in a country where only German was spoken, or to see pagan rites in Christian Mexico. I had told him once that my father was a Catholic and he questioned me in detail on fasting, confession, and holy days of obligation. Only occasionally could I give him an answer, and he marveled at my want of knowledge but marveled even more at my father's neglect of my spiritual education. He had heard (again his information was a tourist's) that no nation had bred a more devout species of Roman Catholics than Germany. And he observed, "If you had been brought up a Catholic, you'd know how to feel toward your mother, I dare say. You'd know so much better than I, a doctor, that you'd have no need of the advice I've given you." On another occasion, he asked me if I had ever heard my father speak of the

Cistercians. "If I were a monk, that would be the order I would choose. I sometimes think there would be nothing pleasanter than a vow of silence."

I had noticed on my first visit to him in the hospital that his posture made one think his bones were of an unbending substance and when I observed over a period of time that he never relaxed, I inquired of Miss Pride if she did not admire his carriage. "Not at all," she returned, "but I do admire his fortitude." She told me then that, afflicted as a child with infantile paralysis, he had been able to assume only two positions, that one perfectly erect, the other bent nearly double at the waist. When he settled upon medicine as a career, he wished to be a surgeon and subjected himself to an operation of great delicacy which, if it were successful, would allow him to move freely. A surgeon could not be limited to a perpendicular position and a forty-five degree angle. The operation, involving the replacement of some of the atrophied spine, was followed by a period of twelve months in a cast from which he was released, totally unbenefited. He had had then to abandon his ambition. He did not reveal his disappointment to anyone, said Miss Pride, and refused to recognize his "handicap" or to refer in any way to what he might have been if his luck had been better. I think he endured a great deal of pain, at times, and I pictured him when he was alone, giving in to the agony that he had reined in all day just as I, on Sundays, delivered myself to the dejection that had been engrafted in me by the visit to the asylum earlier in the day. And as this gloom seemed to await me in my house, like a devilish creature that I had promised myself to on the condition that it would not come out into the light when I was still with my friend, so I thought that Dr. McAllister unleashed his tormentors in his room and permitted them to do as they liked with him for the season of his solitude.

Unlike Nathan whose disfigurement had given him a morbid appetite for abuse—turned either against himself or against those who he imagined laughed at him—Dr. McAllister had taken his much greater deformity almost as a gift of Providence, for, forced by the needs of his body into frequent hours of leisure, he had had the time to read extensively. But the leisure was work and if he relaxed his sickened muscles, he allowed his mind no rest. He slept no more than four hours, originally for the sake of discipline and later because his strict self-denial produced in him a habitual insomnia. He had told me, when I came to the hospital at five in the morning, that he had only just been preparing for bed when he was summoned to the operating room at four o'clock. The evening, he said, he had spent in studying a Russian grammar, suggested to him by the inconsequential babblings of my mother.

It was perhaps because he knew the whole of my story and had even lived through a chapter of it himself that he took an interest in me which was disproportionate to any offering I was capable of making him. Or it might have been, instead, that the Sunday drives were a prolonged but unconscious apology for his unjustified rebuke on the occasion of my first visit to his office when he thought I was seeking an abortionist. No mention was made of his mistake again, not, I am sure, because a review of the incident would have caused him any embarrassment, but because he had forgotten it when I ceased in his mind to be the kind of young woman liable to the charge. He thought that the principle of my being was a fanatical filial piety, carried to a degree that necessarily excluded the sort of selfish attachment which could terminate in so sordid a dilemma as an illegitimate pregnancy. His misconstruction, his over-simplification of my relationship with Mamma made me suspect, sometimes, that he had not the insight into people which is, we are told, the prerequisite of the successful physician. Now neither had Dr. Galbraith understood our household but for a different reason. He had been a blind man leading the blind. But Philip McAllister, through an intellectual, an almost literary faith in the perfectability of human nature, believed that had I not been completely devoted to my mother, I should long ago have run away from home. Thus, assigning to me the sanguine humor in distinction to the bilious or the choleric, he neglected to take into account the fourth, that is, the phlegmatic, which made up at least half of my composition. But whatever his motive was, he succeeded in my gradual reformation. By respecting my loyalty to my mother, he unwittingly shamed me into a real loyalty whose articulation was my faithful weekly visit to the asylum which came, in time, to be essential to my life. Although nothing was accomplished and frequently I was not allowed to see her (For she had seasons of bitter hatred for me as the cruellest of all her persecutors. These came when something sharpened her senses and she realized where she was.), I was determined to regain her love just as the sometimes uncertain communicant is determined to learn faith through his reception of the holy wafer and his prayers.

Yet I sometimes confessed to myself that I was exactly the opposite of the altruist. The renascence of her love would gain more for me than for her; mine was a craven peace-making. I was further hypocritical in that I acted for the young doctor's applause. Just as I had concealed from Miss Pride the marks of sleepless, undisciplined nights, in the doctor's presence I feigned joy at seeing my mother again after seven days' separation, and, on the return, grief at her unhappiness. We can be over-scrupulous, beg our confessors to double our punishment since they, we declare, have been too innocent to grasp the magnitude of our sin. We can, in love, doubt that we really love and suspect that we have bluffed our lover into the passion which will at any moment perish when he sees we have won him with half lies; or, brooding over a slip of the tongue, a misstatement, we can convince ourselves that our minds are really stupid and that all our words are fraudulent. Our conscience is speaking to us in parables. Thus, my desire to become once more the center of my mother's life was earnest. What was contemptible was my publication of it to the doctor as if it could not stand alone, or as if since it could engender no reward for me I must seek his praise for compensation.

His education of me had its more practical specialties. Where I had heretofore read at Miss Pride's prescription and had felt false to her standards if I had chosen something not primarily useful, I now, at the doctor's advice, followed my own inclinations, and was even persuaded that the writers she most admired, that is, James Russell Lowell and Emerson, were by no means inviolable and that the mortar of her ivory tower was chauvinism, not knowledge or taste. For observe, Dr. McAllister counseled me, she was uncritical of style and uninterested in a writer's conception of truth, but if he had been buried in the Sleepy Hollow Cemetery at Concord or lay in a less illustrious but still New England graveyard, he was a great man. She believed neither in Emerson's oversoul nor in Thoreau's religion of blueberries and Walden Pond; she was unimpressed by Henry Adams' genius, had even remarked once that he was a little too long-winded for her liking. I was not disillusioned by this exposé, but on the contrary delighted in her consistency, deplored by her demigod as the hobgoblin of little minds. But at the same time, I was liberated from the tyranny of *The Atlantic* and of Harriet Martineau's peregrinations.

It was towards the end of the summer that Dr. McAllister first asked me what I proposed to do after the Hotel had closed. I told him that Mrs. Brunson had invited me to be Maudie's successor. (Maudie had gone to Idaho as soon as the Brunsons left for Provincetown. She went by bus, taking with her a quart bottle of whiskey and parting from me with a hearty handclasp and the exclamation, "Idaho, here I come! It's round-up time for this here old bench.") The doctor said, "Is that what you want to do?" As if I were speaking to him in his professional capacity and telling him the symptoms of a disease which I knew to be incurable, I told him that since I could remember my goal had been Boston, that the only career I had imagined for myself was serving Miss Pride as her housemaid or her laundress or her lady-in-waiting.

"I dare say that could be arranged," he said. "She spoke to me the other day of getting a secretary and I'm under the impression that she had been thinking of you. She is very fond of you, you know."

I was not so pleased as I felt I should have been. It was as if she had sent the doctor as her ambassador for some obscure purpose of which even he did not know. And I was invaded by the same doubt of her that I had felt when she brought the cyclamen after Ivan's death and I had seen her in the winter sunlight for the briefest moment as an old, ugly woman inspired by a tenuous and urbane evil. But the doctor's blue eyes, in which were registered many thoughts in no way connected with me, were so ingenuous that I was convinced he spoke the truth and that she was, indeed, fond of me.

"That was good of her," I said. "But it doesn't help me, because I have no qualifications to be her secretary."

"But even that is of no importance. I've told you, I think, that she's thought to be one of the most generous women in Boston and there is no reason why she shouldn't send you to a business college."

On an impulse that I regretted and in which I heard myself speaking with Nathan's irascible and naïve resentment of wealth, I told the doctor how Miss Pride had conveniently arrived in Chichester the day after Ivan was buried in the potter's field, although I was certain she had got my letter sometime before. He answered with a laugh, "You don't understand the first article in the philanthropist's code which is that one never takes suggestions but always hunts on his own hook for the places where his money will do good. If it weren't for that, I would have suggested myself that she send you to a business school. As it is, we must simply wait and see if it occurs to her. And if it doesn't, that still won't mean you can't go to Boston. I'm a native of the place too and have ways of getting young ladies jobs. I might even hire you as my receptionist, though you wouldn't like that."

Our conversation took place on the last Sunday he drove me to Wolfburg. In the middle of the next week he was leaving Chichester for a vacation in Manchester where, as I knew, Hopestill Mather was spending the summer. Afterwards, he was going back to Boston to begin his practice in an office, outfitted by his doting mother with glass brick partitions, a costly imitation Kashmir, lucite magazine tables where would lie what she called "the leading periodicals" and the alumnus bulletins of Groton and Harvard. He had described the appointments of his office with what I felt was an unwarranted sarcasm and had told me that if I were ever ill, after I had come to Boston to live, I must allow him to examine me with his Shreve, Crump, and Low stethoscope kept in a Mark Cross case.

He shook my hand when he had stopped before my house and said, "Good luck. Perhaps we'll meet again in Boston." But I felt no promise in his words. I felt that he was already absorbed in the mainland while I was re-dedicated to my insularity and as, from the corner of my eye, I saw the lighted window at the Kadishes' and the shadow of Nathan's younger brother, I read the doctor's optimistic sentence as the epilogue to my long, feverish dream. A few hours later, reasoning that actually I had never been closer, that he was a more persuasive advocate than I could ever have been myself, I realized that I had not felt my isolation from the house on Pinckney Street confirmed forever, but that I had known I should never navigate the space between his planet and mine. The acceptance, without the least titillation, of the window which had once enshrined my first lover's birthmark, on reflection brought me, like a slow-working liquor, to a luxurious intoxication and I knew that for a second time I was in love.

My house was cool and it smelled of oranges that had faintly rotted in the window-sill. I wished that I had asked Philip McAllister to come in to drink some brandy so that in the course of an hour I might feed upon his mobile face and his rich voice. I went no further in my demands, but I knew that so long as I remembered him, the light from the window next door would have no power to make me regret or desire or stew in anger.

On the Sunday after Dr. McAllister left, Miss Pride came to my house, catching me, to my consternation, reading the comic strips instead of, as we would have both preferred, finding me ensconced behind the last issue of *The Atlantic Monthly* or Mr. Emerson's *Self Reliance*. I had been lying on the floor, moreover, on my belly and had been breakfasting, as I read, on a banana and a jellied doughnut. When I sprang to my feet at the sight of her standing primly at my kitchen door, I put the inflated doughnut, oozing out its raspberry heart, on the shelf amongst the pipes and tools and empty jars. My guest had never been in the house before (or anything like it, I suspected) and as we talked, she examined everything, not overlooking the remains of my disgraceful meal, with extreme care as if she were trying to find one object less dreadful than the rest. With a candor that was both brutal and complimentary, since it assumed that my taste was akin to her own, she asked me if I did not find the two pictures above the table appalling. I agreed and she said, "I knew you wouldn't mind my speaking plainly. It is one of the privileges of age." Now I had some years before acquired an animadversion to the little girls and the springer spaniels and to the barnyard and, because I idealized him, I could not imagine what had possessed my father to buy them. But I concealed the identity of their purchaser by saying, "They were in the house when my father came. He always hated them but my mother was fond of them." She ig-

227

nored this false and cowardly aspersion on my mother and stated the purpose of her visit.

"I thought, since Sunday is not one of my motoring days, that perhaps I could lend you Mac and my car for your trips. I told Dr. McAllister that he was rude not to warn me sooner that he was leaving. It only occurred to me this morning when I was served by the substitute waitress. I had forgotten it was Sunday."

I thanked her, not without noting privately that she herself was leaving Chichester a week from today. But she went on, "And something else came to my mind at the same time. Perhaps I mentioned the memoirs I hope to write this winter? And didn't I tell you I needed a secretary to do the 'dirty work'? I know you haven't the qualifications but after all you could go to a school of some sort to learn, couldn't you? The fact is that my niece who, as you know, has been living with me, is going to New York for the winter and I shall quite rattle about by myself in my house. I would like to offer you your lodgings as well as the trifling gift of your tuition. Would you be interested?"

She rose and drew on her gloves as if the matter had been settled and her question had only been rhetorical. I stammered, "Oh, Miss Pride, you are very kind to me!"

She glanced at the floor where my rainbow funny papers lay and I was not sure that she would not retract her invitation. But she said, looking up at me again, "Not at all. Now Mac is right outside and I'm going to walk back to the Hotel so you can start out to see your mother." She started to the door but turned. "My dear, you won't bring your pictures to my house, will you?"

# BOOK TWO
## PINCKNEY STREET

# CHAPTER ONE

The Back Bay Business College was a morose establishment in a once fine house on Dartmouth Street, now infested with tongue-tied girls who seemed always on the verge of tears under the persistent scoldings of the mistress, a vulpine woman in her forties who regarded herself as an educator. Had we been a little younger, I am sure Mrs. Hinkel would have rapped our bungling fingers with a ruler, for incompetence inspired in her the most ardent displeasure. At the very beginning, she had singled me out for especially lusty maledictions, insisting that I was wasting my money and her time, for I would never in a thousand years learn to operate a typewriter with any more skill than a dog. What aggrieved her the most in me was the "reach stroke" of my right fourth finger for which she held a marveling contempt: "Class, gather and observe! Observe the fantastic reach stroke Miss Marburg deludes herself into thinking is the *proper* reach stroke. Learn by this example if you ever hope to make an asterisk visible to the naked eye!" In other branches of my commercial education, I was somewhat abler, being at the top of the class in Business English (because I could immediately distinguish between the nominative and the objective cases and because the subjunctive mood did not baffle me) and being known as a "good worker" in the shorthand class.

The student body strikingly resembled the staff. They were all torpid and bird-like by turns and their humor consisted in such expressions as "I see, said the blind man," and "Well, laugh, I thought I'd die." I ate my lunch at a drug-store with five or six of my classmates who discussed silk stockings and serials in the *Ladies' Home Journal*. They could talk for three quarters of an hour, without any waning of interest, about the confections peculiar to the Boylston Street Schrafft's. The intimacy of the group (they referred to one

231

another's sisters by their given names and inquired after mothers and fathers and aunts) made me suppose that they were old friends and had gone to school together and I felt, therefore, that my exclusion from their talk was not my own fault. I learned in time, however, that they had never met before the first day of classes at what they jokingly called "dear old Back Bay." The discovery made me feel immature and when I could, I avoided these womanly lunch hours, not through snobbery, but through a sense of maladjustment.

I detested the business college, but at the same time it afforded me a contrast to the rest of my life without which I might have come to regard as habitual those things which gave me keen pleasure. I enjoyed the retreat I made each day from the gray plaster walls, the methodical accent of the typewriters, and Mrs. Hinkel's dour face in which her acerbity was coagulated in a large, asymmetrical nose. I went slowly through the Public Gardens at the hour of the exodus of the nursemaids who wheeled out the infant Cabots and the recalcitrant Chandlers. I crossed Charles Street and in traversing the asphalt boundary, entered dissimilar territory: the Common where orators and their satellites and their hecklers yelped and gestured with impotent passion. My own latchkey, fitted to the burnished lock of the white door, admitted me to the silent vestibule, in the dim light of which the mahogany tables, identical and facing one another, gleamed smoothly. Not a sound greeted me. As I pushed open the door to the empty drawing-room, I heard the crackling fire that had just been started. In another hour and a half, this room would be the scene of the comings and goings of Miss Pride's callers whose voices were carried up the stairwell and into my room.

Some afternoons, I stepped across the threshold and wandered about the drawing-room for a quarter of an hour, musing on how it would be when it was occupied by Miss Pride's friends. At first I had thought of the room as altogether Victorian, but after a few investigations, I saw that its objects were disparate and that the only really Victorian part of the room was the bay-window, furnished with an uncushioned love-seat of some stony black wood, the arms carved and embossed and curled; the feet of a stunted lion had been calcified and grafted on to the slender ankles of the seat's well-developed legs. On either side, stationed on the floor where presumably they got the morning light, were a variety of house-plants, no one of which laid claim to beauty. They were kept there and were replaced when they died (this happened rarely, their chief virtue being longevity) because they had been there forever just as a Pride or a tributary to the family had always lived in the house. Miss Pride detested them but would not have dreamed of having them removed; she was especially offended by one species which had large flat dusky leaves chased with pink striations. She did not know its name but called it after a kind of cookie it reminded her of, "Aunt Alice's Birthday Trifle" which had figured in her childhood. Evidently some former owner of the house had been a Francophile and another had fancied Oriental handiwork, for upon the ormolu top of a tulip-wood commode there sat a golden Buddha and above him on the white New England wall hung two Japanese prints of long ladies, long herons, and long sprays of wistaria. Yet at the Buddha's feet, as if to confirm the nationality of the commode, lay aimlessly an ivory-handled dagger of which the blade was inlaid with slate-blue *fleur-de-lis*. The sofas, high and stuffed with an inelastic substance, and the slipper chairs, low, velvety, resilient, had, like Aunt Alice's Birthday Trifle, grown up with the house and their removal was unthinkable although even Miss Pride admitted that they were hideous. Cluttered and inarticulate as it was, I preferred this room to the library, for it was lighter, being at the front of the house and carpeted with a buff rug sprinkled with rich, blue flowers, and its anachronisms imparted to it an atmosphere of geniality as if each heir had accepted the vagaries of the one who preceded him with good will and added his own in the same spirit. The library, on the other hand, was a formidable, masculine province, dominated by Mr. Pride and by several umbrageous ancestral portraits. The furniture was plain, solid, useful. Miss Pride had told me that on Christmas Eve when the revelers and carolers thronged Beacon Hill and one's door-bell rang a hundred times whether or not one had intended to hold open house, her father had read aloud to the servants from the Gospel according to Saint Matthew while in the drawing-room his daring wife, trembling with fear at her own importunity, served sillabub and *lebkuchen* to the visitors. In the library, too, President Eliot had been in the habit of spending two or three evenings a month playing chess with Mr.

233

Pride. His daughter described to me one such evening. "My mother sent me down to ask Papa if they would have some Brazil nuts with their sherry. She was never content to let well enough alone. She was a regular doter. The gentlemen were in the midst of their game and my father, very much annoyed at the disturbance, put his finger to his lips and motioned to me not to move a step nearer the table. President Eliot looked up and through me; my father finished a play and said, 'Sir, for your sake, I regret the brilliance of my rook's performance, for it has won the game for me.' 'You apologized too soon, sir,' said Mr. Eliot and bending forward with a smile like the Cheshire cat's, he captured the rook and checkmated Papa. Then, without any further talk, they set up the men again and to my question would they like some Brazil nuts with their sherry, Papa curtly replied, 'No.' But President Eliot, without looking at me though he glared at my father, said, 'Speak for yourself, Mr. Pride. I, for my part, would relish Brazil nuts as a reward for my triumph.' "

After I had heard this story, I never went into the library without being intimidated by the ghosts of the scholarly chess-players, for their sturdy square table and the board and men remained beside the fireplace, and a decanter of sherry with two glasses stood waiting on a cabinet. At first I thought the preparations were a memorial, as important in the history of the family as the silver christening cups and the yachting trophies on display behind the glass doors of the cabinet, and that in time, when the house became a museum, a copper plate, attached to the table, would inform tourists that President Eliot had played chess there. But I was quite wrong: the table was in readiness for Miss Pride who, with a manual of famous gambits, worked through game after game by herself every Sunday morning before church, and the sherry, too, was kept there for her when, having defeated the white men with Philidor's Defense, she took her own reward and, braced, went off to King's Chapel. Occasionally she would play a game with one of her friends, but these trifling conquests took place in the upstairs sitting-room, for the namby-pamby stratagems of the amateurs would have desecrated the ivory and ebony men of the library who had been in the service of brilliant generals.

The contrast between the drawing-room and the library was not, of course, accidental. Their distinct gender dated from the time the house was built and the drawing-room was still the "withdrawing room" to which the ladies repaired after dinner. The curious thing to me was that Miss Pride, being without a master for her parties, played both rôles. One morning she asked me to fetch her an aspirin tablet for she had a headache as the result of "combining spirits." The evening before she had been detained in the drawing-room by a boring nobody so long that when she finally arrived in the library to unlock the liquor cabinet for the gentlemen's brandy and whiskey (she would never in the world have allowed her servants to perform this duty), they were quite languishing and the delay made them drink twice as much as they would have ordinarily, to her appreciable financial loss. And she, although she had already had her Cointreau with the ladies, was so loath to go back to the tiresome guest (she was one of those creatures who late in life had become domestic and on Thursdays experimented in the kitchen with such materials as junket and peanut butter, and on all the other days tired out her friends with forcing her barbarous receipts upon them) that she "took a breather" with the men.

Each day, I saw the first tea guests arriving, for when the sun began to set, I took up my post at the window of my bedroom and did not leave it until the momentary yellow light just preceding darkness had made all the leaves of Pinckney Street declamatory. I longed to see from the outside these windows through which I looked, but I could not relinquish the prospect I had of Louisburg Square, its dead grass and dumpy statues enlivened by the rich light while the iron palings reasserted their dead, absorbent blackness. At this hour, the letter-slots and knockers blazed; the marble lintels seemed as cool and old as something from an ancient palace. Long and lean, the houses deepened into purple with the decline of the sun. Far up the street, forming the background to a pattern of golden elm leaves, was a bright blue door. From time to time, a man in a derby and a black Chesterfield would briskly cross the square to our house, and in a moment I would hear the door-bell. Or a chauffeur would hand out a lady from a gleaming automobile. Talk and laughter presently surged up the stairs.

When the arc lights came on, I left the window and turned on the lamp beside my bed. My room sprang forth, enlarged, entirely changed by the light. The ceiling seemed immensely higher, the wide, polished doors as tall as a castle's portals. Even my single bed with its lace counterpane and folded puff was more luxurious. To the left of my double windows was a massive, flat-topped writing desk with deep drawers on either side which had been filled with watermarked paper, yellow second sheets, onion skin and carbon paper. Its surface was furnished with silver tools: letter openers, pen-knives, scissors, boxes of paper clips and rubber bands, and postage stamps. In a small upper drawer, there was pale green stationery with our address embossed in small white letters. The typewriter on which I practiced my home-work had its own stand at the right corner of the desk so that I had only to turn my chair to be facing it.

The joy my room gave me was, each day when I switched on the lamp, so intense that my being required its articulation and some-times I could not see the deep mole-colored carpet and the silvery draperies at the windows for my tears. Again, the Breughel and the Vermeer and the Rembrandt prints, hanging on the ivory walls in double frames, could make me smile smugly. As large as a room, my clothes-closet was equipped with shelves for my expensive shoes, with padded hangers for my evening dresses, and with a ceiling light so that I could see to choose my costume. My bathroom was not adjoined but was down the hall a little way. Six thick, white towels, monogrammed "L P" hung about the gleaming tub. The medicine chest was filled with bottles of cologne, Miss Pride's soap, with a tooth-powder made up by a Dartmouth Street pharmacist, and with cans of faintly scented talcum powder.

On the left wall of my bedroom, near the fireplace, was a locked door leading to Hopestill Mather's sitting-room. And the windows above my bathtub gave on to a shaft across which I could see the windows that corresponded to mine above her bathtub. It was not until I had been in the house ten days or more that I saw her apart-ment. A maid was preparing it for her return from Manchester, and as I passed through the hall, I stopped to ask the girl some needless question about my laundry. I saw that it was true, just as I had imag-ined it, that the room and the one beyond it to which the door stood ajar was carpeted with green. In the generous bay-window was a wine-colored *chaise-longue*. The fireplace was in the same position as the one in the drawing-room, and in Miss Pride's room directly below this. Over it hung a portrait of Hopestill as a child. She wore a full-skirted white dress, ballet slippers, and a green hair ribbon in her red hair. It was so striking a likeness that I could hear her voice calling across the dining-room, "Waitress! Water, please." On either side of the hearth were wing chairs upholstered in green and wine-red stripes. Beside each was a table underneath whose glass top showed bright Italian tiles and upon which stood *cloisonné* cigarette boxes, match-holders and ash-trays. Against the wall opposite the windows stood a delicate Victorian writing desk, flanked on either side by low shelves filled with books still wearing their glossy, gaudy jackets. Through the distant door, I caught sight of a mahogany highboy and the corner of a four-poster bed.

An hour after the tea guests had gone, I would join Miss Pride in the upstairs sitting-room where we had a glass of sherry and a light conversation, after which we went down to dinner. Sometimes she repeated an anecdote she had heard during the day or summarized a colloquy that had struck her fancy. Usually, though, she questioned me about my attitudes, interspersing her interrogation with pointers on conduct. One Friday night she requested me to come downstairs at tea time the following afternoon to be, as she said, "broken in," an unfortunate phrase since it was also the one she used in speaking of servants whom she had trained. I was never, she admonished me, to regard myself as a servant. But at this phase of my career, when I had learned little more at the commercial school than which were the "home keys" on the typewriter, she could not truthfully call me her secretary. Moreover, being a woman completely sufficient unto herself, she could not introduce me as her "companion" without discrediting herself or making her friends suspect that her eyesight was failing. Nor could she pretend that I was a distant relative or the daughter of an old friend who until now had been in boarding school in Switzerland, for it would take no more than one conversation for anyone to know that I had no connections with Boston and therefore none with herself. What I was, in point of fact, was her "case" or her "project" or whatever the word was that was then in fashion to describe the beneficiary of that allotment in a rich woman's budget called "Miscellany." But wishing to spare my feelings (and also because practicing charity under one's roof was seldom "done" unless the recipient was the orphan of a friend or relative who had been left with no money), she did not fancy my presentation in these terms. At first, it had been her intention to keep me imprisoned while she tutored me in etiquette and until I was able to operate a typewriter, but this plan soon appeared impracticable owing to the fact that my residence in the house had leaked out, presumably through the servants.

She had hit upon a solution at last. Until I should be qualified as a secretary and until she saw fit to admit publicly that she was going to write her memoirs, she gave me to understand that I was to offer no unsolicited information, but if I were pressed I was to say, quite truthfully, that I was studying to become the amanuensis of a writer whose name I was not at liberty to give, that she and I had met through Dr. McAllister and she had invited me to share her house which, in Hopestill's absence, would be too lonely even for her. I was permitted to say I was from Chichester but almost all the rest of my background was to be obliterated from my memory. Quite understandably she did not want it known that my mother was in an asylum. No more did I. There was little danger of the fact coming to light, for the summer residents of Chichester did not move in Miss Pride's circles nor anywhere near them, and the only link presenting any danger was Dr. Barker, who not only had a bad memory for names but was also opposed to gossip and would certainly never dream of repeating anything so banal as his sister's report of Chichester's insane woman.

Having set the hour for my début in her drawing-room, Miss Pride went on frankly to clarify her plans for me. I say "frankly," but the word is inexact, for her confessions were so subtly put and she displayed so ambiguous a wit that it was only after I had left her and had gone to my own room after dinner that I realized how stark had been her projection of the future. She was mortally afraid of growing old; if she were to dodder into half-crazed and ludicrous senility, as both her father and her mother had done, she wanted a caretaker to silence her, to dissuade her from both the crabbed and the maudlin antics of old age. She feared blindness (she, whose eyes at seventy had never been fitted with glasses) and dreaded being deprived of reading and of walking. "I don't fancy taking up phonograph records to amuse me at my age," she said scornfully. She was not sure I was the right custodian for her; that, only time could tell, but she wished me to consider whether I should like to think of myself as permanently installed in her house, and she implied that I would not be forgotten in her will. I was grateful and happy at the prospect, even though it was impossible for me to imagine her so changed as to need the services of what amounted to a nursemaid. I told her that and she replied grimly, "My dear, we're all fools before we're fetched by the pale rider."

She dismissed me with that, but as I was passing through the door, she said, "Hope returns tomorrow. I fancy she'll come in about tea time."

"I am anxious to meet her."

Miss Pride looked directly into my eyes. "I am sure you are," she said. "I have the feeling that you have a preconceived notion of my niece."

"I saw her once, you know. She came to the Hotel some years ago. Perhaps you don't remember."

"My life has not been so helter-skelter that I do not remember its events, Sonie," she replied. "Nor have I forgotten Hopestill's dancing slippers."

A blush raced to the roots of my hair and my voice broke as I said, "My father didn't finish them."

She smiled wrily. "Hope refused to go to the party without them. I dare say if you had known that she spent that evening in her room, howling for her slippers, you would have sent them on." But while she twisted her dagger in me, her smile changed to one of great friendliness and she added, "The battle must begin early in our lives if we are to be victorious, isn't that right?"

## 2

I had dressed with care, but although I had been leisurely, I had a full hour before I could go down. Miss Pride had told me that she had no intention of "presenting" me, that I was merely to appear and "take things as they came." It would be better, she told me, not to be too prompt. I moved impatiently about my room, sat at my desk awhile and read one sentence over and over in *The Rise of Silas Lapham* without ever comprehending its meaning. Moving to the window, I sat for a while on the ledge, shivering at the icy air that came through the cracks, and stared at a boy, dressed like a Harvard student, loping up Mount Vernon Street across the square. Something in his carriage reminded me of Nathan. Without any transitional thought, I turned back into my room and standing, one arm on the foot rail of my bed, I opened *The Confessions of a Young Man*. When I had promised myself, on the night Nathan and I sat in the fog on the steps of the Hotel Barstow, that I would have the best, I had allowed destiny to choose the circumstances for me. I had at no time doubted that the choice of Boston by my guardian angel had been supreme wisdom, that this was the soil in which my gifts, whatever they were, would fructify. And thus, when I read George Moore, and I read him constantly, I did so out of the desire to prove to myself that the "best" Nathan had wanted for himself and for me was in reality only second best. My talents were not artistic, not creative. I felt that they were assimilative and analytical, that what I saw in Boston, what I had seen in Chichester I understood, but that I could not reassemble my impressions into something artful. I could not ennoble fact. It was experience of the most complex order that I desired, and while there were times when, exploring the narrow streets of the back side of the Hill, I wished my knowledge to include the cafés and *ateliers* and the quays of George Moore's Paris, the wish was diluted as I turned toward home and thought of my room, of Miss Pride, and of our conversation over the sherry glasses. She, I thought, was worth all the freedom and all the abandon, worth, indeed, all triumphs.

I closed the book. Opening the door, I heard many voices rising up, and I knew it was time.

A dozen people were already drinking tea when I went into the drawing-room and were deep in conversation so that my entrance passed unnoticed save by an elderly gentleman, seated upon an ottoman though his years should have got him an easy chair. He rose at once and came toward me, fumbling in his coat pocket. "Hello, there!" he cried. When he had got midway and had put his eye-glasses on, he halted and said, "Oh, I thought you were Hope."

"No, sir, I'm Sonie Marburg."

He murmured something like "Well, that's nice," or "Well, I declare," but kindly offered me his hand anyhow, though he did not come nearer and I was obliged to go after it. I should have liked to prolong our handclasp since his plump fingers were warm, and I was chilled to the bone after this first day of cold weather in the Spartan temperature of Miss Pride's house. As I had come down the stairs just now where drafts blew out of the very walls, I had had to stop several times to rub my stiffening fingers together and to check the clatter of my teeth. But the weatherproof Bostonians, seated in the drawing-room which was not perceptibly warmer than the upper floors, were not only comfortable so that their bright cheeks glowed with excellent circulation, indeed, they had even suffered someone to "crack" a window through which came an unflagging blast of late fall air.

The old man's fingers abandoned mine too soon. He introduced himself as Admiral Nephews and then returned to his ottoman, leaving me where I had been intercepted, still faced with the problem of what to do with myself. I felt that I was undergoing a radical physical transformation and was sure that if I could look at my feet (I was prevented by the unshakeable rigidity of my neck) I would find them twice their normal size and that my hands, pendulous at my sides, had likewise doubled their proportions, while my neck and face were suffused with a rashy red. I was further certain that if I were called upon to speak, my voice would issue either croaking or inaudible. I was rescued by a sign from Miss Pride who, lifting neither a finger nor an eyebrow nor speaking my name, commanded me to come directly to the tea-table where she was officiating. So peremptory was her aspect which alone had beckoned me, as it had done in the dining-room of the Barstow, that had I been in the middle of a sentence or had someone been in the middle of one addressed to me, I should instantly have obeyed her.

"Take charge for a while," she said when I came to her. "I must speak to someone." Then, bending over as if to inspect the plate of lemon slices, she said in a much lower voice, "I think you should be more sparing of lip rouge." This was by no means the first reproof I had received since I had been in Boston. She had taken it upon herself to civilize me, or, as she called it, to "caulk" me, for, she said, not even the sturdiest vessel could weather such storms as I had without some damage. The "storms" were not so much the facts of my father's desertion, my brother's death, my mother's calamity, as they were the omissions in my upbringing. She had sent me out when I first arrived to buy my winter wardrobe and when I had returned with what had struck my fancy, she had at once sent for her car, taken me and all my purchases back to the shops and chosen my clothes herself. For, although I had bought four pairs of gloves, I had not bought a hat, and although the coat I had picked out was a formal Chesterfield, my shoes were all flat-heeled oxfords.

Out of sorts with the cold, terrified by the roomful of people, I might have risen at her criticism—not from resentment but from despair—and left the house had not Miss Pride immediately retired, placing in my hands the custody of the tea-table, and allowing me, by her quick departure, no time to worry my smart into a real state of mind. I was quite bewildered by the array of shining vessels before me and especially nonplussed at the sight of three pots of about the same size, any one of which might contain tea. Before I had time to lift up their lids to determine what was inside, the old man who had mistaken me for Hope Mather tottered up and extended his cup, winking so broadly that one whole side of his face was stitched up, and saying in a humorous stage whisper, "It's my fourth! I thought I'd get my refill when Lucy wasn't here, what?" I chose the wrong pot and filled his cup with hot water.

"Here, here!" he cried, laughing and turning away from me. "I say, Lucy! Did you tell this young lady here to give me water if I asked for any more tea? That's a good one! It's like the orderly I had on the *California*. He liked his gin, that chap. Well, ma'am, he drank so much of it that towards the end of an evening, his mates used to slip a bottle of water in front of him and if he said it tasted queer, those rascals told him his taste buds were paralyzed!"

By the sparse but indulgent laughter that followed the mild little anecdote, recited loud enough for anyone to hear, I judged that it was not a new one, and that the interest which lighted up the eyes of all the guests was not in the story-teller, but in myself who had been discovered, as if by accident, within the Admiral's orbit. Miss Pride alone did not laugh. She stood by the door to the dining-room, and it was only after she had transfixed me with a gaze of exasperation for my mistake, that she attended to what she had gone for and rang the bell for a servant. The others resumed their talk, but now and then stole a tactful look at me, pretending to be glancing at the portrait on the wall behind the sofa where I sat or to be merely making sure that the Admiral was still there.

"I beg your pardon," I said to him. "I really didn't intend to do it." I filled a new cup with tea and handed it up but neglected to offer him any accessories. "Oh, come, dear girl," he said, "you're treating me shabbily. I take two of sugar and *copious* cream. You youngsters these days don't believe much in tea, what? It's all cocktails for you, what? I remember, ma'am, that when I was a boy I had carving lessons and my sisters had lessons in the technique of the tea-table. Don't they teach that any more?"

"I don't know, sir."

"Where did you go to school, mademoiselle?"

"In Chichester."

"I didn't know there *was* a school in Chichester. I didn't know there was anything in Chichester except those humdinger cherry-stones and that scuttled hotel Miss Lucy Pride risks her life in every summer. Was it day or boarding?"

"It was a public school," I said apologetically.

"Oh!" said Admiral Nephews, drawing up a chair. "I dare say you wouldn't get anything fancy there. Perhaps it's just as well. Perhaps we all learned folderol, who knows? I expect you had practical things like manual training and geology, what?"

"Why, no, I think we had the usual things."

"Latin, I suppose. I guess *Arma virumque cano* isn't Greek to you!" He chuckled, wrinkling up his pleasant, rosy face. "And French. Everyone does a good deal of French. *I* did. It's a good thing. One goes to Paris after all and doesn't want to look like a booby. And English? You're up on your English, I wager. Let's test you. Now I'll give you a fleet of quotations and you tell me what they're from. Ready? First:

> Shall I compare thee to a Summer's day?
> Thou art more lovely and more temperate.

Well?"

"Shakespeare," I said, but in a voice that shook with dread of his more difficult questions. "It's the beginning of one of the sonnets."

"Good! Second:

> When in disgrace with fortune and men's eyes,
> I all alone beweep my outcast state."

"That's Shakespeare, too," I said.

"Where do the lines occur?"

"In a sonnet, sir!"

"Good! Good! Excellent! Once more:

> That time of year thou may'st in me behold
> When yellow leaves, or none, or few do hang."

"Shakespeare!" I cried, hoping he did not intend to go through the whole sequence.

"I'll give you *E* for excellence, young lady. But now I think I may be able to stump you. Try this one:

> She shall be sportive as the fawn
> That wild with glee across the lawn
> Or up the mountain springs:
> And hers shall be the breathing balm
> And hers the silence and the calm
> Of mute, insensate things."

My luck continued, for in the year past I had learned my English from an effusive woman whose adoration of Wordsworth had made her give all the rest of literature nothing more than a lick and a promise while upon her exigesis of *Ode on Intimations of Immortality* and *The Prelude* she had spent nearly six months.

"Bravo!" cried the Admiral, putting his hand on my knee and continuing confidentially, "Do you know that I committed every line of those Lucy poems to memory in honor of Miss Pride? Perhaps she'll tell you some time how I recited them to her in this very room on the occasion of her twenty-fifth birthday. You may not see this in her, but I still think of her as just what the poem says, 'as sportive as the fawn.'"

The garrulous creature's eyes were dewy and I wondered if he had been a rejected suitor, for I was sure that if he *had* been a suitor, Miss Pride would have rejected him straightaway after his recitation of the Lucy poems. She must have been born hard-headed, I thought, and at the substantial age of twenty-five would have given anyone what-for who compared her to a "sportive fawn." The fawn herself was moving in and out amongst her guests and there was in her carriage such a vigorous uprightness, and in her face, from which her exasperation with me was not altogether obliterated, so formidable an aloofness that I was on the point of laughing out loud at the old man's metaphor. As she halted before each of the little groups, I observed that she treated her friends with very little more warmth than she did me or her chauffeur. She did not bend towards them, but stood erect, looking down upon the interrupted talkers and perhaps rewarding them with a cool smile. Her smile had about it the same economy that had her speech and her eating habits and her apparel. I do not mean that she lacked either cordiality or humor and no doubt she was genuinely fond of many of the people gathered here. But she was never, so to speak, surprised into a smile, and she allowed her smile to last only so long as it was justified by the nature of its provocation. I noticed, however, that she was not the only one who husbanded her responses, for often one of her guests cracked open and resealed his mouth as perfunctorily as she. I admired their abstention, regarding it as a kind of hallmark of the Puritans, like the haemophilia of the Bourbons. I had noticed, from the beginning, that Miss Pride was extremely frugal of her laughter. Now and again, she was amused enough to emit two muted barks of the same volume and duration, as if she were actually saying "Ha! ha!"

As Admiral Nephews followed her course with his nautical eyes, I warmed towards him for no other reason than that he admired her, and had not the very nature of my own admiration insisted upon discipline as its principal component, I would have exclaimed, "Isn't she wonderful!" in order to hear his corroboration. She was, in truth, more wonderful today than she had ever been. Although her guests were as pedigreed as she, and no doubt owned the famous names I had read on the calling cards, she outshone them all just as she had outshone Mrs. Prather and Mrs. McKenzie. Her pre-eminence came partly from the mere fact that she was the hostess and therefore the star performer, but even more from the *noblesse oblige* with which she had turned me loose in her drawing-room despite my over-painted lips. A lesser lady would have sent me back to my bedroom to remove the rouge lest my bad taste reflect upon herself.

The Admiral, having satisfied himself that I was tolerably edu-cated, did not inquire further into my background but after con-gratulating both me and himself on our learning (for he found it as remarkable that he, an officer of the navy, was versed in poetry as that I, educated at a public school, was) said, "Hope Mather would have known them all, too. She's a clever one! I heard she was coming home today. Where is she?"

I told him she was riding horseback in Concord where she had spent the night, having only just come back from Manchester. Thus far, I had not seen her.

"Now there's a girl that can ride a horse. I suppose she's the best horsewoman I know barring Mrs. Nephews, who was perhaps a shade more prudent. I well recollect when Spencer Mather's daughter was no higher than a table, she managed a two-year-old that Mr. Apthorp had in Bedford. She was a caution! She had a way with the groom, that little spitfire had, and she got him to saddle the horse that wasn't really broken yet, and before a fellow could say Jack Robinson, milady was on the horse and out of the stable, riding him into the ring. We were just coming back to tea—I expect we had ridden to Carlisle that day—and what did we see but that red-headed baggage putting the colt through his paces. When he frisked too much for her taste, she gave him his comeuppance with a whack over the nose with her little crop no longer than my forearm. She sat like a lady! Well, ma'am, while Spencer Mather was giving the groom a piece of his mind, the governess was leading Hope away and I believe" (the Admiral, overcome with laughter, could not go on for a moment), "I believe she must have been *living* in the stables for the vocabulary she used on that poor little Parisian spinster. It was too funny, you know! Hope swearing to beat the band while

246

the little mademoiselle was crossing herself. I dare say Hope doesn't remember those words now!"

After a few concluding chuckles, he sobered and went on to list Hope's further accomplishments. I gathered that she not only "sat a horse well" and "knew a good mount" when she saw one and had numerous other equestrian talents, but that she was an excellent swimmer (the statistics of the length of time she could stay under water, the distances she had swum, and the sensational dives she had executed, were quite lost to me who could not swim), could not be defeated on the tennis court, and was a girl who could jibe her boat into a sixty-mile-an-hour breeze with the skill of a veteran mariner. Indeed, what the girl could not do, he, for one, didn't know. "Why, she could milk a cow if she was asked to!"

Since he apparently knew her family well, I wanted to inquire of him whether Hopestill was descended from the famous Mathers, but I had no opportunity, for his praise of her athletic exploits led him to tell me about his grandson who was a lieutenant commander, stationed in Hawaii and who was also "no slouch" on a horse. It was the Admiral's dream that through this young man, Hope might be annexed to the Nephews family. "But neither party," he said with a sigh, "seems to want my will to be done."

I said, "Perhaps that's because they're so far separated?"

He replied, "No, no. It's a case of 'east is east and west is west and never the twain shall meet.'"

I was to learn that the Admiral could not get through a day without using at least one quotation and that because he had given up reading poetry some ten years before and now took his entire supply from Bartlett's, half the time his tags had nothing to do with the context of the conversation. But he was known in Miss Pride's circle as having a colorful and individual speech, the flavor of which derived partly from his literary allusions and partly from his use of polite address which, to ladies, included *"Fräulein,"* *"Señora,"* *"Madame,"* as well as "Ma'am," "Miss," and "Madam."

I thought Miss Pride must find his gabbling ludicrous and I was astonished when she came up to us and greeted him most affectionately: "Lincoln Nephews, you're too old to be flirting with this young lady. Now tell me what you've been up to. Evelyn Frothing-

247

ham just told me you had been to a dance at the Country Club. What an old beau you are!"

"I was and I had a thumping good time. So often the Country Club is stodgy, but this time, ma'am, it was superb. Why, Lucy, I tripped the light fantastic until two o'clock in the morning."

I could not think what criterion of stodginess old Lincoln had set up, any better than I could imagine him "tripping the light fantastic," since all three words were so peculiarly inapplicable to his embonpoint. It gave me great pleasure to hear of "the Country Club," "the Chilton Club," and "St. Botolph," as though I were peeping through the windows of those chaste establishments where, in the libraries and the ballrooms and the parlors, the thoroughbreds of Back Bay and Beacon Hill were engaged in fashionable diversions, the nature of which was still unknown to me, though I pictured the Admiral nursing a breather of brandy in the company of his pink-faced and bald coevals, while Miss Pride and members of her "reading circle" traced genealogies over their tea. On the Saturday before this, when Miss Pride was lunching at the Chilton Club, I had received a telephone message from her which obliged me to go round there to deliver her calling cards which she had left behind. When the door had closed upon me and I was actually on the premises of this sanctum sanctorum, I could not have been more stirred if it had been the residence of queens and princesses, though I saw only the vestibule with its cloak booth, presided over by a matronly woman in spectacles and a starched white cap and apron who, with her cultivated speech and her remote manner, could have been a member of the club herself. Through the half-open door directly in front of me and at the end of the hall, I saw the edge of a dining-table and a thick gray rug and half a portrait of a lady. From the room issued talk and laughter so that I knew the ladies were still at lunch and I would not, therefore, be allowed to hand Miss Pride her cards, but must entrust them to the custodian of the wraps. A waiter, as distinguished in his swallowtails as an ambassador and having a foreign accent, said he would have someone remind Miss Pride in "Meesis Saltonstall's party" that a parcel was waiting for her, and he went off to elect a responsible member of his staff to bear these tidings to my mistress. Afterwards, as I walked home along Commonwealth Avenue where the bright early afternoon sun displayed to their advantage the genuine and the false violet windowpanes, I chose the houses where she might go that afternoon to drop her card when Mrs. Saltonstall's party, like a courtly banquet, had been adjourned. Until then she would be inaccessible to everyone but those whose lineage entitled them to push open the door in the Chilton Club and pass between the portals into the dining-room.

Miss Pride and Admiral Nephews briefly and malevolently discussed the Evelyn Frothingham who had informed Miss Pride of her friend's revels and was, I gathered, still in the room and possibly within earshot. Miss Pride said she was resembling a toad more closely each day and the Admiral agreed, adding that her model was an especially unsightly specimen. Having demolished the poor woman, they proceeded then to what I soon discovered was the favorite topic of their generation in Boston: namely, the Irish politicians who had "taken over" the city, and were an even greater menace in Cambridge. Today Miss Pride had the openers: she had heard that afternoon that a young lawyer, distinguished for his illustrious family connections, for his irreproachable court record, for his manners and his charm, had suddenly taken it into his head to campaign for the mayor of Cambridge, and had been seen, only the night before, at a roadhouse near Weston in the company of six Irish politicians. And the same unnamed source had informed her that far from being ill at ease in their midst, the renegade from the Republican party whose name was Carew or Carey, I could not tell which, was in his element, was actually the ring-leader and was so disheveled from drinking and shouting and lolling about that he was barely recognizable.

The Admiral had a counter: another man, of Mr. Carew's (or Carey's) generation and kidney had recently, to curry favor with these same Irish politicians of Cambridge, been overheard panegyrizing the Roman Catholic Church in the presence of certain notorious gossips who were sure to spread the word. "What would our great grandfathers have thought if they had known Boston was to become a Popish stronghold?" said Miss Pride, appalled at this "case."

"Well," replied the Admiral, "I don't know the answer to that one as I never had the pleasure of knowing my great grandfather.

But I know that my grandfather would have said aplenty in strong words, ma'am, after the ladies had retired. My grandfather, you know, used to be acquainted with Matthew Arnold's mother, and when he learned that she turned all the pictures to the wall Sunday, when he came back from Oxford and had children of his own, he did the same thing. He was an exceedingly pious man and I dassen't imagine the way he would have scored the Catholics. In those days, of course, they hadn't become a problem. The old order changeth."

I stopped listening to the conversation, and while I was still digesting the fact that Admiral Nephews' grandfather had known Matthew Arnold's mother, I heard a sharp-faced, diminutive woman, who was sitting near-by, say to a young man, "Oh, a man and his books are quite separate things *I* think. I never knew anyone more charming and affectionate than Henry James and he was always one of my dearest friends, but I can't abide his books."

I could not evaluate accurately the aspects of this select world: whether the personal connection of these people with the immortals, or their poised arrogance in regard to such issues as the contemptible political machine of Boston, or their stylish language, or their blue-blooded ugliness was the more impressive. The roots of Miss Pride's guests were so deep and tough that I thought they were eternal, and the word "decadent" that Dr. McAllister, a traitor to his intended destiny, had used so often in speaking of Boston when he was trying to depress my expectations, was misleading. Decay must come from within and I could imagine nothing but an external calamity, a social revolution that could eradicate this solid society. Perhaps that was the aim of the ultra-montane newcomers. It was not, I concluded, that what they said and the judgments they passed were of any profundity or of any insight (on the contrary, they often sprang from a primitive and passionate ignorance of the opinions of the rest of the world but which, despite their egotism, contained a measure of self-distrust) but that the manner of these pilgrims' heirs was so fearless and direct that one was not struck with their fatuity. The woman who had been fond of Henry James spoke, a little later on, to the woman I identified as Mrs. Frothingham (she was, as her critics had described her, a reptilian, puckered, misshapen person), of her opinion of people who experimented with flowers. "Really, I do feel," she said, "that this craving for a *tulipe noire* is ridiculous. It debases nature." I believed her implicitly, though this was a subject I had never before pondered. Immediately thereafter I was won to the side of her adversary who, with as forthright a tone, rejoined, "I can't agree, of course. One might just as well say that formal gardens are a debasement of nature. Or that grapefruit is."

"I think grapefruit *is*. I don't care for it at all."

"But not formal gardens?" inquired Mrs. Frothingham drily.

"Ah, you have me there, you clever woman," laughed Henry James' friend, and I gathered that she had a formal garden. "I'll 'bone up' on that poser as my little Stephen says and tell you my answer Thursday at Sarah Cushman's."

"Shall you be there too?" said the other in surprise.

"Certainly. We have declared a most just armistice. I dare say it's in our blood, and no doubt we'll be far more battle-scarred than we are now before we die. But for the time being the white flag is up."

I was intrigued by this feud, so publicly alluded to, and was disappointed when later on I learned that the two warriors were sisters. Mrs. Frothingham and her friend, having shelved their differences on flowers and grapefruit, now exchanged views and reminiscences, having in their retinue a regiment of names as they traversed miles of drawing-rooms, summer residences, and the parks of foreign cities, dignifying the most trifling detail with a judicious and clear-voiced appraisal that made life and the world singularly leveled down and homogeneous. The small, sharp woman hated the new Pompeii for the same reasons (though these reasons were not stated, were, she said, "self-evident" so that I, who could not discover them, felt stupid) that she hated *tulipes noires* and grapefruit. Mrs. Frothingham maintained that these same mysterious reasons, which she readily apprehended and despised, were meaningless and that exactly the opposite was, in each case, true.

# 3

I rose, intending to make my way to the bay-window and try covertly to close it for I was suffering acutely from the cold. Miss Pride detained me. "I want you to talk with Amy Brooks, who is over there by the fire. She's about your age and a very suitable person."

"She's literary, ain't she?" asked the Admiral.

"No, she paints. But she's about Miss Marburg's age."

She indicated a person whom I had noticed before and had taken to be about forty-five. Now I subtracted a few years, but could not believe she was any less than thirty-eight. She had been in conversation with a stout old woman who now got up and was about to leave. I heard her, in parting, say, "I wish I had been half so clever as you when I was your age, Amy. You must come to me soon and bring some of the thingumabobs you were telling me about." With this, refusing assistance though she was very lame, she began a labored journey with her cane towards Miss Pride, and as I observed her, waiting a moment out of respect for her age before I took her place beside Amy Brooks, I recollected a scene that each fall repeated itself in Chichester. In the afternoon, it had rained, but the air had cleared by evening. As I walked home from the Hotel after dark, ahead of me I heard the steady, three-legged walk of old ladies with sticks over the wet gravel road, and voices, strangely sweetened by the waves or by my distance from them, deliberating the further necessity for umbrellas, even though they did not stray far from the veranda and could immediately have got to shelter if the rain began again. Children of the village, playing Run Sheep Run, passed me and overtook the strollers, scampered through the weak circle that the flashlight of one cast on the ground, and ran on, giggling.

I stood aside to let the old lady, who was dressed in mourning, pass. She gazed at me with dreamy, half-blind eyes and gave me a smile, the sincerity and sweetness of which momentarily disrobed her of the concealments of age and revealed her as she once had been. "How d'you do?" she said. "I know all about you, my dear." But before I could reply, she had taken the Admiral's arm and was being eased into a chair beside Miss Pride.

My appointed interlocutor was ruinously plain, wanting both an adequate nose and chin, but having, for compensation, large square glossy teeth and hyperthyroid eyes. She was small and nervous and given to giggling as well as to sudden fits of seriousness when her whole organism tensed to apparently agonizing statements like, "I have been reading Eugene O'Neill!" or "Last week I went to T Wharf and spent an afternoon sketching!" Then for a few seconds she would stare at me with her high, blue, mammiform eyes.

I said, "Were you sketching boats?"

"Yes! All kinds. Even a dear little Chinese junk! Not from China, of course. It belongs to some arty people, I think, but that doesn't keep it from being cunning, does it? Do you sketch?" I regretted that I did not. "Oh, but you should! There's really nothing like the satisfaction it gives one. Don't you think one ought to have an outlet? I do! I think it's so important these days, especially. I don't pretend to be an artist, you know!" She was visited again, distractingly, by giggles which delayed her. She continued, "I mean, I think it's so necessary to be in touch with art, don't you?"

I supposed that it was, but I could not expatiate for I was tonguetied before this ebullient spinster whose upbringing had taught her to say the most platitudinous things to a complete stranger but to say them so firmly and courteously that they sounded indisputable. Her zest—she said in a few minutes that the reason she sketched was that she wished people to know what she thought of life—was a consistent style, plagiarized and monotonous and eminently respectable.

Sorrowfully from Miss Pride and admiringly from Dr. McAllister, I had heard that Hopestill Mather filled her leisure time with none of the mild artistic enterprises commonly undertaken by young ladies who had been "out" for sometime, the water colors, the humorous poetry, the informal essays, the sculpturing in plasticine, the rendition of Chopin. Yet, although she had repudiated the conventional patois and honestly acknowledging that she had not even the mildest of gifts, her opinions were by no means poles apart from those of Miss Brooks as I realized, recalling the doctor's further comments. For I had been told that Hope did not want to "lose touch" with art and desired to be one of its patronesses. Dr. McAllister's irony came to me only now, for I had not perceived that this innocently overbearing notion was not unique in the girl I had set out to dislike. Art, to the Misses Brooks and Mather, was a custom: one "kept up" with the newspapers and fashions, was on the alert for word of engagements, marriages, births, débuts, and similarly, one did not like to "lose touch" with art.

Miss Brooks informed me that her stepmother, the Countess von Happel, had done a great deal towards bringing good exhibits to Boston. "Don't you think Europeans have more *feeling* for art than we do?" she said. "My stepmother is Viennese. She may be here later on today." Nor had the Countess neglected contemporary artists, struggling in Boston and New York; she visited their studios and hung their paintings in her dining-room and very often sold one, for a small sum, to a guest who admired it. "It might be only fifteen dollars, but you know even fifteen dollars will give an artist a lift. Oh, I think it's wonderful the way they keep on in their horrid little studios!" "They," a grubby and deserving species, sounded like prisoners serving a term for a felony they had not committed, to whom a gift of cigarettes or chocolate bars meant a new lease on life. I said I had heard Hopestill Mather was another good Samaritan, interested in the artist's welfare, though no doubt not on such a grand scale.

"Well, with Hope, it's different," said Miss Brooks. "She's more *Bohemian* about it. I mean, Hope is almost more interested in the artists themselves than in their work. You know! She's interested in *people*. We call her the 'psychologist.' She wants to find out what makes an artist and not what an artist makes. It all depends on one's point of view. Now the Countess is a great admirer of Van Gogh, but she doesn't care a bit for all those scandalous stories about his ear and so on. But how Hope loves them! Art is my stepmother's life, art," she added, "*and* dinner parties." This last was offered with a freshet of giggles which I took to mean that the Countess' predilection for dinner parties was of notorious proportions.

This girl, so inferior to my ideal conception of a Bostonian, and yet, with all her cordiality, so aloof, unwilling even to inquire what my business might be in that drawing-room (For how could she have failed to sense immediately that I was an outsider?) had, when she began to speak of Hopestill Mather, changed her tone from nervousness to calm, as if she were held in check by a powerful emotion which had put a stop to the vertigo of her introspection and had made her temporarily critical. I said, "Do you know Miss Mather well?"

"Oh, of course," she replied. "She's my cousin."

In the course of that day, I discovered a Bostonian general principle: namely, that everyone was related to everyone else, or if blood kinship did not obtain, something else almost as binding did; people had gone to dancing school together or their fathers had been law-partners or their mothers had been Red Cross nurses in the same village in France. But this kinship, even that of blood (perhaps actually it was true more of this than of the other kind) was so taken for granted that it was almost uninteresting. It was important to know who had married into what family and who were the forebears of the bride and groom and whether the bride's mother were the Martha Endicott who had gone to Winsor School with Priscilla Bradley but had married into Philadelphia. All of this was of vital concern, but half the time, the performers of that drama, coiled about itself innumerable times, were known most vaguely to their commentators. And the relation of twigs to the trees had become so complicated that no one could straighten it out immediately: the whole rigamarole must be gone through each time. Cousins were not appreciably more kindred than friends, and friends never knew when they would discover that they were really cousins, the fact being established only by an accidental remark dropped by a former Bostonian, who now lived in London, and relayed home in a casual letter by her visitor. Thus, Miss Pride had not told me that Amy Brooks was Hopestill Mather's cousin and Miss Brooks herself had supplied me with the information almost as an afterthought, really only to explain why she knew Hopestill as if their being cousins (since obviously they were not friends) was the only thing that would induce them to know one another.

Still, she had not spoken disloyally of Hopestill—perhaps, again, because her etiquette, the guardian angel of people in society, directed her, not her feeling—but she had spoken coolly and appraisingly as of a slight acquaintance and one whose "philosophy of life" was opposed to her own. But I suspected that there were other grounds, less intellectual, for the enmity, and that the divergence of their paths toward art was merely symbolic. It struck me that this poor ill-favored, twitching girl envied her cousin's good looks, or that she would really have liked to mingle with the Bohemians as

Hopestill did but, being spurned by them, had to cloak her disappointment in an indifference to the "psychology" of the artist.

I said, "Perhaps Miss Mather spreads the word about her artists just as your stepmother does."

"Oh, certainly!" she cried vigorously. "You mustn't misunderstand me. Hope doesn't trifle with them. She *believes* in them, you know. It's her catering to them that I don't see."

"Her catering?"

"Yes! Literally! She takes them strong cheese and rye bread and marinated herring and beer. And don't think for a moment she does her shopping in any usual place like Pierce's! No, she must have the shabbiest delicatessen on Revere Street! Oh, Hope is all of a piece."

This time I joined in Amy Brooks' laughter and when we had finished, I looked up to find that we were being approached by a pair of extraordinary young men, introduced to me as Mr. James and Mr. Pingrey. They appeared to have been turned out on the same wheel and in the same proportions and differed only in their decorations, like "basic" vases which may be painted appropriately for a particular décor. They were the tallest men I had ever seen and, though they must have been no less than twenty-five years old, were still unused to their height, as if they had shot up overnight and had not learned how to steer themselves. Their knees were in a perpetual state of semi-genuflection and they thrust their heads forward and afterwards tossed them back in an agony of clumsiness. One was dark and a little bald, sallow, thin, strained, but the other was blindingly fair, as shining as a Swede and having the color of new apples splashed recklessly about his broad, bony face. I had not witnessed their arrival and the shock of seeing them suddenly before us unnerved me: it was as if, like genii, they had vapored forth through the floor.

Miss Brooks, when she had presented her friends to me, travailed again in the mirth of her nervous system, and Mr. James and Mr. Pingrey were sympathetically infected, twisted and turned and bent their knees like two damaged snakes as between their giggles they all three reviewed some esoteric anecdote of their last meeting which, as nearly as I could make out, had been at a masquerade ball given by the Countess von Happel. I could not help thinking that the most elaborate costumes would fail to disguise any of these freaks in the slightest.

"And what have you been doing since?" said Mr. Pingrey, the fair young man.

"I was just telling Miss Marburg that I have been sketching. I was at T Wharf last week, Edward, and do you know there was actually a *Chinese junk* there?"

"I don't believe it! Truly I don't believe it! I must have proof! You must show me a picture of it!"

"*Do* come to see it. I value your criticism, you know. Come to tea soon, you will, won't you? And you tell me what *you've* been doing since that disgraceful party."

Edward Pingrey drew up a chair as Mr. James goggled uncertainly at me, not sure whether the *tête-à-tête* which was about to be launched between Miss Brooks and his companion would exclude us and necessitate a separate conversation. He also drew up a chair, to my side of the sofa, prepared for the worst. But Mr. Pingrey, though he bent toward Amy quite intimately and now and again emphasized a point by laying a huge, spatulate forefinger on the arm of the sofa within an inch of her hand, and addressed her solely, did not lower his voice and even glanced at us occasionally as he talked as though to make sure we were listening.

"Well, I've been doing something perfectly delicious, Amy. I have become intrigued with politics, of all things! You would never guess, would you, that a confirmed old ivory towerite like me would ever get involved in politics, but I have, my dear, up to the neck!"

"But what kind of politics, Edward?"

"By no means the usual kind! Not these tedious" (he pronounced "tedious" with a "j") "municipal squabbles. Don't misunderstand me: I realize the appalling state the city is in, of course, but there are so much bigger things! Such universal problems! I've joined an extraordinary group called '*Les Chevaliers de la legion de Lafayette*' which will eventually be *the* international party. We wear red shirts, and I just wish you could have seen us, sixteen of us, marching through the Mill Dam in Concord the day we were formally sworn in. Amy, they're bright red, really scarlet!"

Miss Brooks laughed. "I can't take you seriously, Edward. I don't believe for a minute you marched down the Mill Dam. They wouldn't *let* you in Concord!"

"Oh, wouldn't they though! You can never guess who is the leader of our group. Guess!"

"Someone proper? Someone I know?"

"No one but your esteemed Uncle Arthur Hornblower!"

I burst into laughter, an attack which came upon me quite unawares like a disease that strikes without preliminary symptoms. Until I heard Mr. Pingrey say "your esteemed Uncle Arthur Hornblower," as if "your esteemed Uncle Arthur" were his given name to match his absurd surname which came directly out of the *dramatis personae* of an Elizabethan comedy, I had not altogether been aware that Mr. Pingrey and his sallow shadow, Mr. James and Amy Brooks were three superb, natural clowns. Now I was shaken to the soul with the circus and felt that if I heard again a mention of its patron, Youresteeemedunclearthurhornblower, I would roar uncontrollably. The three performers stared at me in amazement. I was silenced. At last I said, "I beg your pardon. I was only thinking I used to know a terribly peculiar person named Hornblower." But as I uttered the name again, I was overcome.

Mr. James bent a reproachful gaze upon me. "It's not at all a common name," he said.

At that moment I was saved, for I saw Dr. McAllister coming into the room. He paused on the threshold and surveyed the guests and when he saw me, smiled. He gestured toward Miss Pride to indicate that he would join me when he had spoken to her. I rose from the sofa. "I'm very sorry I interrupted you, Mr. Pingrey. I was ever so interested."

The two lengthy young men stood up and bowed gravely. Miss Brooks giggled and said, "I think Uncle Arthur *is* comic, for that matter. It's been so nice to talk with you, Miss Marburg. We must have another nice long chat about sketching." And she extended to me a smooth, dead hand.

## 4

In the earlier part of the afternoon when, each time the door opened, I thought Dr. McAllister would surely enter now, I believed that he would be distant, no longer interested in me since he was in the center of a web woven about him by metropolitan society. For while in Chichester he could combine the offices of friend and counselor, here, I thought, his science would be separate from his social manner and that still unable to see me in any rôle but that of factor in "the Marburg case" he would shun me, not uncharitably, but to spare me the repercussions of a chance remark that might be dropped by one of us and apprehended by some stranger who happened to be within earshot. But his smile, which was transmitted to me like a message in code, intended for only my perusal, assured me that his generosity had not been modified. On the heels of this sense of security, and at the moment when, deliberately turning his back toward me, he sat down beside Miss Pride and the Admiral, came a searing jealousy of the dozen people in the room who one by one broke from their conversations to cry out their delight at seeing him again or to go directly up to him with the request that they be allowed to "have" him next. For I had failed, in my portrait of him, to particularize the background, having painted it before I had studied him in all kinds of light and from all angles. I had been literal and knowing him out of his *milieu* had been blind to the fact that he belonged to a type from which he could never extricate himself though he might denounce it. As he himself had told me, among the idiosyncrasies of this type was a simultaneous craving for and aversion to society, so that a complete break could never be effected. These were not merely the habits of a lifetime, he had said, but were the habits of two and a half centuries. In the renegade who has extirpated his New England accent and has espoused the life of the new frontiers, there is still the Puritan within his unalterable bones: a forward young lady at a house party in Winnetka, Illinois, importunately makes eyes at him, and if he recovers from his surprise sufficiently to make love to her, his performance will be cold, utilitarian, and intemperate.

At the same time, I should have disliked it if, after his brief salutation to Miss Pride and the old lady in mourning, he had come at once to greet me, for I passionately desired to have evidence that he "belonged." Yet, because I believed myself to be in love with him, I was nettled to discover that he was a great favorite. Thus, at the same time that I admired him as an aristocrat (the critical "I" did this, the I who was not in love), I wanted him to be a superior plebeian, a sort of polished edition of Nathan Kadish. Now, on the other hand, I had no desire to emend Miss Pride; her text did not bewilder me, and I was confident that I could imitate her style. In order, however, to meet the demands the doctor would make upon me if that extra-professional friendship I so coveted were ever to mature, I would have either to add something original to my translation of the old woman (I knew that he privately deplored my choice of model) or practice a certain dishonesty in deleting the elements in her that especially annoyed him. I wished to do neither, and it was for this reason that I hoped he might shoulder the responsibility himself and discover to me a strain in himself which matched my own.

It was ten minutes before he glanced towards me again and even then he did not come to my isolated place in the bay-window. Attentively and with a charming smile or as charming a look of commiseration, he listened to gossip, complaints and reminiscences, making no distinctions, as far as one could judge from his facial expressions, between youth and age or between old friends and slight acquaintances. As his tour (as impartial as his visits to ward patients) brought him closer to me, I could hear his replies to remarks addressed to him.

"Why, all I know of Germans is that in general their anatomy is similar to the American variety. That's all I'm required to know in my profession," he said to a woman who had just returned from a Bavarian watering place and confessed, with mock caution, that she had great faith in the Nazis (she pronounced the word with a scrupulous *tset*) as the liberators of the nation from her post-Versailles quandary. Now, in fact, I knew that the doctor had very strong opinions of the Nazis, but he refused to discuss the subject with this frivolous Germanophile who chose to esteem in the new system its most obvious, most spectacular, and most ambiguous virtues: the superbly trained Storm Troopers, the powerful health of the children in the youth movements, the touting of Wagner. He had deliberately made his reply as stupid as her observation, but if he hoped thereby to make her own words echo to her shame in her ears, he was disappointed, for she said, "Do you know I don't really believe you? I think there is some secret of strength in the German body that exists in no other. Why, half of them, I should say, eat oleomargarine and have for years, and yet they're the healthiest people in the world."

Not because he was in the least interested in the conversation, but because it was his moral duty, imposed upon him by his knowledge, to correct her, he replied, "Not only is margarine not unhealthful to anyone, but you would find if you cared to make a survey that an enormous percentage of the American people never use butter at all."

Vexed, the woman dropped the subject of the German physique and said, by way of dismissal, "At any rate, I think we all must recognize eventually that they are the leaders of the world." Further infuriated by a remote, ironic smile on the young man's face, she abruptly turned to her neighbor and shouted venomously, "What is the shocking tale I hear about your nephew and the Communists in Cambridge?" Dr. McAllister made his escape and came to the love-seat.

"I've expected to see you here long before this," he said genially. "I thought you looked forward to tea-parties."

I explained that I had not stayed away by choice but that Miss Pride had been educating me up to this afternoon. I intended no disloyalty because, far from being indignant, I was grateful for my preparation: had I not had it, the discomfort I had felt when I first entered the drawing-room would have continued and my talk with the Admiral would have fared much worse. But the doctor was contemptuous. "She drives a hard bargain," he said. He inquired about my business training and he asked me if I had found Boston up to my expectations. I told him I could have asked for nothing better.

"And Miss Pride? She's teaching you the useful arts, I trust?"

"Oh, indeed!" I said. I told him of the early morning conferences at which I was present. We took our breakfast together in the dining-room (Miss Pride was never tempted to be served in bed, a practice almost universal amongst her friends who, she told me, took as much care in selecting their bed-jackets as they did in selecting their dinner dresses) and at the end of it, Mary, the cook, was summoned from the cellar. Miss Pride was like a general previewing, with his aide, the campaign about to be started, the ammunition being money aimed where it would do the most damage to the enemy, for the Messrs. Pierce, Anderson, Rhodes, and the anonymous gentlemen entrenched in Hood's Dairy, Lewandos' Cleaners, and the Megansett Fish Market were, to use her own expression, "to be watched untiringly." The flattering telephone voice of Mr. Campbell of Rhodes' might win someone off his guard to buy oranges at eighty cents a dozen by describing the properties of the fruit with such a wealth of mouth-watering adjectives that one might believe it was cheap at double the price.

Miss Pride had requested my presence at the meetings of the economists because she thought I should learn to run a house. If I proved to have any common sense, she might in time confer upon me the high honor of running *her* house. She had long been desirous of some such assistance, for her other affairs kept her busy. These other "affairs" included not only her extensive social life (I had been agreeably surprised that she dined out so often and went to so many concerts and luncheon parties, for I had supposed that she was as ascetic in this department as in any other) but also with a great many negotiations with her lawyer over her real estate, with her affiliation with divers philanthropic organizations interested in women's prisons and in Christmas dinners for underprivileged children (whose fathers, no doubt, were those impassioned speech-makers in the Common who were after the blood of Miss Pride and her kind). She had recently, also, been in collaboration with the widow of a Harvard professor, preparing his correspondence and lectures for publication, and this took her to Cambridge for one full day each week.

When I mentioned the work in progress, Dr. McAllister interrupted me. "Have you heard that the correspondence has become a thorn in her side and she only does it now out of a sense of duty?"

"Why, no, you're quite wrong. It's exactly the sort of thing that suits her, she tells me."

"She tells you very little. But she tells me very much. She took umbrage last week when she found a reference to herself in one of the early letters. She copied it down and it was so priceless I learned it by heart. But I won't tell you."

"Why not?"

"Because you'd be furious."

My curiosity made me promise that I would keep my temper. But as he quoted the letter, my skin tingled with rage. It read, "Several of us dined two nights ago at Mr. Everett Pride's who, as you know has one of the most elegant houses on our fair Hill. His treasures include a superb Copley, an indifferent Badger, three Homers that they tell me are fine (you know I never get anything from him but *mal de mer!*) and an excruciating creation of his own, his daughter Lucy. Awful to look at, tormenting to hear, she reminds me of nothing so much as a curlew."

"What a fool he was," I said, "to write that down!"

"I will say for Miss Pride," said the doctor, "that her wit is always ready. She told me what she had said to the widow after she had run across the passage. She said, 'Bosworth was pretty damned gawky himself, Mildred.'" He laughed at the sally which I found less amusing than I would have liked, and then asked me, "What do you think of Admiral Nephews? He says you're a pippin."

"I liked him. Is he . . . Nothing."

"Come, is he what?"

I flushed but plunged in. "I was going to say, is he fashionable?"

"The most fashionable you could find in his generation," returned the doctor with a smile. "Not in the one just after him, though— he's a Unitarian."

Because most of my information about Boston came from schoolbooks, I did not know, until Philip McAllister told me, that Unitarianism had been out of style for more than half a century. Most of its present-day supporters remained in the fold because that was the environment to which they had been, as the psychologists say, "conditioned." The Admiral, who was by nature a sensualist, would far rather have gone on Sunday to the Episcopal Church, the higher, the better. But an atavistic conscience held him in check and he made only a minor concession to his idiosyncrasy: he attended services at King's Chapel where, despite its dedication to that doctrine indigenous to Boston, retained still a Royalist flavor, and old Lincoln Nephews could listen without shame to the organ, choice of Handel for King George, and fancy himself in the presence of ecclesiastical pomp.

I was about to ask another question about the Admiral, but the doctor diverted my attention to a miniature which he had picked up from the table near us. Handing it to me, he said, "Boston *was* something in those days." The faded miniature in its napless, maroon velvet frame presented a solemn, forthright girl. The central part in her straight hair was as precise as a clean wound. It was a face that made no compromises and in which no rounded lines appeared save those essential to the cheeks; her eyebrows were straight, her lips were straight, her nose was like a blade. The painter's colors seemed artificial, for one thought that the original had been a study in black and white. The high, round collar was pinned with an oval brooch, and the invisible ears terminated in smaller matching ornaments. She was an Endicott, he told me, related distantly to Miss Mather's father. He meant that Boston was something in the days when hell was immediate, altruism was ruthless, and justice was Mosaic. Now, cured of its chills and fevers, its blood watered down, it was no longer exciting. Still puritanical, it tried to imitate Sodoms and Gomorrahs in their decenter fashions, but the result was only dowdiness. Consider the Admiral, my friend commanded me, who had sunk in his rosy obesity upon a sofa and was telling the old woman dressed in widow's weeds a joke at which neither laughed aloud although the exertion both of the telling and of the listening made all four wattles wag and the two heads nod. He was no cavalier! His cavorting at the Country Club was so respectable, so circumspect! His affectation of French phrases and his Latin, employed to give him a cosmopolitan piquancy, so marked him as a citizen of Boston!

"I find him charming," I said.

"So do I," replied the doctor. "But preposterous. That's my grandmother, by the way, whom he's regaling. She and Miss Pride are currently enemies."

I asked him why this was and he said, "Chiefly because my grandmother is a possessive old woman and next to her house in Concord, I am her favorite possession—her only grandchild, you see."

"But surely Miss Pride has no designs on you!"

"Oh, but she has. When you meet Hope, you'll see her aunt is barking up the wrong tree though. She wouldn't have a dozen of my kind."

At that moment, there appeared before us an anxious little man like a caricature of Terror, for his feline green eyes were immensely magnified by a pair of very thick lenses and his small mouth trembled beneath the insufficient ambush of a sandy mustache. He was a new-comer and said hastily that he intended to run right along as soon as he had spoken to the doctor whom he drew aside and talked with in a whisper for a few minutes.

The room was less densely crowded now for it was a quarter past six according to the delicate china clock on the mantel which, after it had made a sound like the last quiet purr of a cat before it goes to sleep, gave forth a single, bell-like chime, sustained and ques-tioning. I had not noticed the clock before as it was dwarfed by the tremendous Copley incongruously placed above the narrow marble mantel. I discovered that I had not been conscious of the room at all until now, had not observed, as I had always intended to do, its transformation when it was occupied by guests. Now, at this late hour, dimly lighted, its walls pink from the fire in the hearth, it seemed surpassingly feminine and agreeable. I looked towards Miss Pride, handling her dainty Bavarian tea china and deftly replenishing the hot water in the silver tea-pot, conversing the while with her friends, so much the lady that both processes were carried on with-out any interference to each other. It came to me, so deliciously that I wanted to clap my hands together and crow, that I had never seen Miss Pride in the library without her green beaver hat: thus she had given me my tea there on the first day I had been in her house and thus she was, ready for church, every Sunday morning when I went in to pay my respects as she was playing chess against herself. I re-called the way my father had always worn his hat in the shop but left it there when he went into the house. While I knew that Miss Pride had been bare-headed the night she joined the gentlemen in their brandy, I was sure some other appurtenance, conversational perhaps, had disguised her feminine nature so that the bequests of her male ancestors were more apparent than those handed down from the mothers of her line.

Dr. McAllister's alarmed little man scurried away, looking straight ahead as though he were afraid of being trapped. He was like a rabbit running through a clearing. He did not make it, for Miss Pride caught sight of him and cried, "There he is now! Stop, Otis Whitney!" Obediently and out of breath he trotted to her side. My friend sat down beside me on the love-seat and watched the scene: Mr. Otis Whitney had been pushed by a thin but powerful forefinger into a chair beside the tea-table and was undergoing an inquisition about the health of his son who was under Dr. McAllister's care.

Abstractedly the doctor said, "By the way, I told my grandmother a little about you. Nothing you wouldn't want known, but she's a kindly old soul and you might like to visit her sometime when you want country air."

Just as I glanced toward her, there came a lull in the conversation of the group that sat between us and the tea-table and I heard old Mrs. McAllister say to the Admiral, "The report from Manchester this year is the same as ever. Hope Mather had all the beaux. Isn't she a heart-breaker! But you know she comes by it honestly."

The Admiral, not only to flatter Miss Pride who had half turned away from Otis Whitney, but also because he believed it, replied, "Indeed she does that. Why, the only young lady who could hold a candle to Lucy Pride was her sister."

But the old lady, with the sure touch of malice, said, "I quite agree, but actually I was thinking of Spencer Mather at that moment more than of his wife."

I knew already the basis of the slanderous remark, and Dr. McAllister filled in some of the details for me. Hopestill's father had been a notorious libertine, had married Charity Pride for her money, had flaunted in her face his philanderings with common women, and had died most disgracefully at a house party when, drunk, he had been thrown by a spirited horse that he could barely have managed sober. His wife died shortly afterwards of humiliation, it was believed. The doctor pointed to the grand piano at the left of the love-seat. "Miss Pride keeps this, mind you, not in memory of her sister who was quite accomplished but in memory of Spencer Mather's brutality. It has a dummy keyboard. He was extremely sensitive to noises and could not bear to hear scales. After he got her this travesty —and she was so mild she didn't protest—he used to say, 'Look at poor Charity. She plays all day long and never gets anywhere.'"

In reply to my suggestion that the ill-will between Miss Pride and her niece stemmed from the former's dislike of Spencer Mather, Dr. McAllister said with a smile, "We don't speak of 'ill-will' between them, my dear. To use my grandmother's phrase, we say they are both 'strong characters.' But, yes, that is perhaps why they don't get on. That and the fact that Hope is said to resemble her aunt as she was at twenty—don't ask me why the similarity annoys her. One would think she'd feel the opposite when people say of Hope, 'She's the image of you, Lucy.'"

Miss Pride had leaned over the diminutive and still fidgeting form of Otis Whitney and was saying to Mrs. McAllister, "I heard you mention Manchester. I understand the summer was, as they say, a 'dud.' Hope wrote that if it hadn't been for your Philip's little visit the whole season would have been a total loss."

"Don't flatter me, Lucy," laughed the old lady and, turning to the Admiral, said, "Isn't she the purest Christian to compliment me on that no-account grandson of mine! There's nothing I'd rather believe. Why, I would be overjoyed if I could think that wild young rascal occupied the least place in Miss Hopestill Mather's heart! No, Lucy, my dear, *I* know and *you* know that she's a sensible girl. Look at him"—she pointed to my companion and at the same time sent him a conniving and adoring smile to indicate that she was merely playing a game, merely looking out for his interests—"he's barely civil! And I see he has already victimized the youngest lady in the room. I give you my word of honor, he has been boring her with some awful descriptions of his interminable 'cases.' Really now, Lucy, admit he's not nice."

Philip flushed and shook his head at his grandmother like a reproving parent. His gesture was unfortunate for she cried, "Now he's signaling me to hush! You see, he has a bad conscience. Admiral Nephews, what would you do with such a rogue?"

Miss Pride, who knew perfectly well that Philip was the apple of his grandmother's eye and who took as an insult to her intelligence this deprecation of him—so false that the voice with which she ran him down was brimming over with love—said, "I can't say I see eye to eye with you. What you say of Philip applies much more to Hope.

Perhaps we're both right, though, and in that case . . . well, birds of a feather flock together."

The old lady was outwitted, for she could not admit that what Miss Pride said was precisely what she meant, that Hopestill was the unruly, fickle egotist that for the sake of her campaign against their marriage she had pretended her grandson was. She rose, fumbled for her stick, and said in a voice audible to everyone in the room, "Perly, Amy Brooks is coming to dinner with me next Tuesday. Can I expect you too? We can't get along without you if we play 'I am a famous man.'" And to Miss Pride, she added, "I dare say I couldn't engage Hope for that evening, could I?"

"On the contrary," rejoined Miss Pride, "she likes nothing better than to go to your house. Shall I give her a message?"

"I thought she was going to New York immediately," said the foiled grandmother.

"Not until next week." Then, with a slight sharpening of her expression, for evidently she had changed her tactics and had decided that it was better for the time being not to expose her niece to the determined old woman, she said, "But she will be occupied with packing. No, perhaps I'd better not mention it to her, for she would want to come and she really wouldn't have the time."

Mrs. McAllister sighed with relief, blew her grandson a kiss, and hobbled from the room on the Admiral's arm. Her place was filled at once by Mrs. Frothingham who asked for another cup of tea and said, "I'm lingering disgracefully long. I want to see Hope and hear all about what she's planning to do in New York. I do think she's too clever to go off all by herself. Can she really be serious about studying psychology?"

"You must ask her, Evelyn, for I'm too ignorant of the subject to know. Can anyone be serious about it? I must confess I can't. I have no more faith in dreams and the like than I have in Sally Hornblower's spirits. By the way, have you heard her latest? She swears that at a séance not long ago a Japanese girl was present and asked to be connected with some departed relative and, my dear, not only did the connection go through but the medium gave the message in colloquial Japanese!"

"Odd as that is," said Mrs. Frothingham in a lowered voice, "it's no worse than the way Arthur Hornblower has been cutting up. Have you heard . . ." But Miss Pride put her finger to her lips and motioned toward Mr. Pingrey who was still talking excitedly to Miss Brooks. "Is he . . . ?" queried Mrs. Frothingham. Miss Pride nodded and I caught the whispered words, "Berthe and I are campaigning in that sector."

Philip McAllister covered his smiling lips with his hand and then, on the pretext of examining a pot of philodendron, murmured to me, "My grandmother would like me to marry Amy Brooks. As you've probably deduced by now, our free will is purely relative. My mother had first say about where I was to go to school—there was a great to-do about it, I've been told, when I was two hours old —and my grandmother agreed on Groton instead of St. George only on the condition that I marry Amy who was then sixteen months old."

"And you don't like her?" I asked.

He did not answer. In less time than it had taken for the sound of my voice to carry to him, he had moved into a world poles apart from mine. I knew by the eager light that suffused his pale face, until this moment drawn and mask-like with fatigue, and by the tensing of his fingers from which arose a hygienic odor, that what had galvanized him and was still invisible to my eyes was some private shock. I had heard the front door open and a feminine voice say, "Good afternoon, Ethel." The interval between the salutation and the appearance of the guest in the doorway—during which I identified the voice as the same one I had heard in this room when Miss Pride had left me in the vestibule—was an ordeal for both of us and in order to hide, on the one hand his impatience as a lover, and on the other, my curiosity, we began to exchange views on the probable success of Miss Pride's memoirs as if it were the subject we had wanted to bring up all along but had been prevented by the intrusion of gossip which we could not help overhearing. And when Hopestill entered, even though nothing could have torn his eyes away from her, my friend, in an untroubled voice, was telling me that he liked nothing so much for bedtime reading as personal reminiscences and hoped Miss Pride would take Saint-Simon as her model.

Hopestill Mather, whose autumnal hair I remembered from the day at the Hotel, paused at the door like an actress overdoing her entrance in the fear that the audience would not applaud. And then she pressed forward, leisurely, through the assembly of guests and bandy-legged slipper-chairs. Her eyes were astray as she murmured courtesies which marked her as a person of poise and breeding, as though she were ambling through an art gallery, untouched by what she saw but knowing, with a firm, sure, aristocratic knowledge, that what she saw was right: that the Rubensesque woman, who had been seated all afternoon beside the fire-place in conversation with a distinguished middle-aged man, was not to her esthetic taste, but that she recognized genius in the composition; that her cousin Amy Brooks belonged to an eminent school though she lacked the characteristic color that marked even the lesser works of Rembrandt. Though she might despise her aunt and her aunt's friends, she seemed not to question their essential mettle: they were the authors and the stewards of reality. For the time being, I had gathered, she had chosen to visit other worlds, both real and unreal, by which she had been remembered in the last will of a larger order than New England. Between these greetings (the uniform warmth and urbanity of which, exactly like that I had observed in Dr. McAllister, made me see, with a pang of envy, that to start with they had a fundamental fraternity), as she held up her manners like the emblem of a secret cult, she showed by a smile in our direction that she was sorry to be detained in her progress to us who were, she promised, to receive the whole heart of her vivacity and not merely these pulsations which she allowed to the others.

Even from this distance and unable to distinguish her voice from those chattering others, or to see, because of the dim light, what sort of body encased the person I had envied for so many years, even so I had a feeling of that allurement that had been hinted to me in various ways, for though she was not beautiful (there was enough light for me to see that) she emanated a terrible femininity, like a soporific perfume, so that the men, while they rose promptly to their feet, allowed her to speak first as if they needed time in which to collect their wits.

She bent down to kiss her aunt as Admiral Nephews stood up

"I'm next," he cried. "Hope, you outshine yourself. When are you going to have dinner with me?"

The girl turned up her smiling face to him and received his kiss. "You name the night, Admiral Nephews. For you, I'm always free, sir." She sat down beside her aunt and they began to talk so amiably that I doubted if, after all, they really were enemies. But they spoke formally as if, while they were good friends, they were not altogether intimate. Hopestill complimented her aunt on the sandwiches and Miss Pride congratulated her on her costume, even though she had once told me in disgust that the girl spent nine-tenths of her time and all of her money on clothes, an indulgence shocking to a woman whose wardrobe consisted of four identical black broadcloth suits and two dark red evening dresses, one made of velvet and the other of crêpe. Her niece had converted a simple yellow dress into a "costume" by the addition of an Indian belt made of great silver conches. Her arms were laden with bracelets and her fingers with turquoise rings. Her long hair hung as straight as rain, an angelic, down-burning fire that parted for her small, perfect face which disdained the pastes and pigments of the cosmeticians, but was pale where God intended it to be and shone where He had burnished it. She was tanned from the seashore sun and from her ride this afternoon, retained the last glow of rosiness in her cheeks. She was tropical like the surcharged parrot; one felt that her flesh was hot to the touch and that her small feet, shod in white buckskin moccasins, were furnished with velvet pads like a cat's. When I first took her in, I did not recognize her belt as Indian or her yellow dress as being of a particular cut and fashion: it was rather as though she were clothed in some natural, unpurchased habiliments like a leopard or a Luna moth.

"Oh, please don't third-degree me," she said, laughing, to Mrs. Frothingham. "I don't know anything about psychology. I'm taking it up because I've soured on painters after this summer. It would shock Auntie if I told you why."

"Shock isn't the right word, my dear," said Miss Pride. "The nonsense of Wainright Lowe hasn't shocked me for years, but no one bores me more to hear about."

"Hope!" cried Mrs. Frothingham. "Don't tell me you picked *him* up!"

"How was I to know? Of course I *did* know the moment I stepped into his studio. But I simply couldn't shake him."

"He paints his pictures in half an hour," said Miss Pride. "As a matter of fact, I think I could do them in fifteen minutes."

The Admiral said, "I must confess, Hope, that I'm glad you've gone in for something besides all this painting hanky-panky. Psychology is a little too new-fangled for me, but still . . ." He rose and kissed Miss Pride's proffered hand. "As always, I've enjoyed it, ma'am, and unless I'm dead before then, I wager I'll show up again next week. I'm well pleased you've got yourself a companion for the winter since this intellectual young lady insists on going off to Babylon." The whole group at the tea-table glanced toward me and the Admiral said, "We talk the same language, Miss Marburg and I. I'm going to steal her some afternoon for a walk around Fresh Pond. Far from the madding crowd's ignoble strife, we'll revel in the English poets. Good-by, Lucy, good-by, Hope, good-by, Evelyn. Good-by, you three graces!"

Mr. Otis Whitney, who for the past few moments had been invisible, being blocked out by the Admiral's bulk, stood up and implored, "Lincoln, if you've got your car, would you be so good as to drop me?" But Miss Pride pulled him by the coattails and said rather sharply, "You only just came, Otis. You haven't told me a thing about Frank. Now do begin from the beginning. Where did he get that disgusting disease?"

Hopestill excused herself from her aunt and Mrs. Frothingham and came to us. The doctor rose and, erect as he was because of his deformed back, gave the appearance of leaning forward. The hand he offered shook and the voice with which he greeted her was unnaturally high and diffident. He was not used to her yet, I thought, and his eyes had not accustomed themselves to her ferocious radiance. Oblivious to all save this ignited tulip, he raised his hand and touched her hair. I sighed without meaning to, as if the inhalation were the vehicle for this strange scene. The doctor introduced us and, sensible of my presence for the first time since he had heard the front door open, reinstated me as his friend. "Sonie will be glad you've arrived at last. She's been here a month and this is her first public appearance."

"How do you do?" said the girl, smiling warmly at me. "I'm sure it's been awfully dull for you, and I haven't a doubt that Philip hasn't lifted a finger to amuse you."

The doctor made the lame excuse that he had been busy, although, had he thought back, he would have known that I—who until this moment had not resented his neglect—could hardly swallow it since he had intimated that he had come to tea here several times when he expressed surprise that he had not seen me before. But I was more embarrassed by Hopestill's scolding than he, feeling that he found me a bore or that he had avoided me because he pitied my misfortunes or dreaded my complaints.

Hopestill looked restlessly about the room. "Five minutes of this sort of thing and I'm at the end of my tether. Don't you think we should have cocktails?"

There was a good deal of Miss Pride in her, I saw. Her eyes were similar, small and nacreous like painted ornaments. She had been allotted less than her share of flesh and it was as dry as paper, and so pale her mechanism seemed to run by something other than blood or else in her the blood was really blue. And her voice, which her cold spirit permitted to be merely tinged with cordiality, had the same metallic opacity, lacking resonance and melody but having instead a vast range of pitch.

"I would be delighted," said Philip. "But doesn't your aunt belong to the school of thought of my sainted grandmother which holds you mustn't drink for pleasure but for the sake of your appetite?"

Hopestill smiled vaguely. "If they're similar in that respect, they wouldn't admit it, would they? Why, if Auntie knew that, she'd either turn teetotaller or dipsomaniac."

"Or else tell everyone that Grandma got the idea from her and was secretly an old soak."

"I need a drink." She had been toying with the foliage as she sat on an ottoman. She was dismembering a spray of fern. "I hate this hair-like vegetation, don't you, Miss Marburg? It fits though. My horse threw me twice today in the ring, in the mud. My trousers were ruined. I beat hell out of him. *That* I enjoyed."

A pained silence followed her confession of sadism. To consolidate our awkward triangle and to change the subject, I said, "I met your cousin and her two tall beaux this afternoon." And then, because she seemed to think I had something more to say, I told her of the predicament I had been entangled in by Your Esteemed Uncle Arthur Hornblower. Her face, instead of reflecting the amusement I had expected, hardened against me and anger brightened the flare of her eyes. I learned my lesson in the silence that followed my joke's collapse, but sick with humiliation, thought my experience would never benefit me, that this defender of her relatives whom she could not, nevertheless, abide, would refuse to have me any longer in the house. She looked away from me. "Have you heard the marvelous thing Uncle Arthur did? He changed his will last summer and left something like a hundred thousand to Vanzetti's sister. Isn't that really *good* of him?"

The doctor, perhaps not realizing that her chief purpose had been to reproach me, said, "Why, what a turncoat you are! I thought you were the most rabid supporter of the Committee's decision. Don't tell me you've got some inside information about their innocence!"

"On the contrary, I'm perfectly sure and always will be sure that they were guilty, but that doesn't mean Vanzetti's sister was. And Uncle Arthur, after all, could be prompted simply by generosity, couldn't he?"

"No," said the doctor with a smile. "But I say, about those drinks? Does she keep the makings in the library?"

"We'll have to have second best and that's in the pantry. Look, there comes the Happel. What a pity she has just missed seeing Amy flanked on each side by a tall beau!"

The scorn of her remark, far surpassing the acidity of mine, was deliberately aimed at me, and by it she gave me to understand that she was at liberty to say what she liked about her dowdy cousin, but that it would behoove any outsider to keep a civil tongue in his head. I was distressed when Dr. McAllister left us to confer with Miss Pride, for, since she had imposed upon my conversation a prohibition that applied to the only thing we had in common, that is, the guests, I had nothing to say to Hopestill. But she realized that it was her duty to select a subject for us and she gave me a sociable smile which only made me uncomfortable because it showed that she had now put me in my place and, confident that she would have no further trouble with me, could proceed.

"Aunt Lucy's house isn't the gayest in the world, is it? Has she sent up Mercy to keep you company?"

"Mercy?"

"She's my aunt's cat. Since her last accouchement, she's been rather peckish. Even so, I'm surprised Aunt Lucy hasn't introduced you. Do you like our house?"

I answered abstractedly, so overcome was I at the idea of Miss Pride's cat. There was something perplexing and a little unpleasant in her concealment of it. (When, on the following morning at breakfast, I confronted her with my knowledge, saying that I would like to see Mercy, she said, "She is nervous. Perhaps in time she'll be up to society again," quite matter-of-factly as if the person in question were a friend for whom a long sea voyage had been too much. I said it was strange that I had never heard the cat cry. "Oh, no," answered Miss Pride, "she's not much of a talker. She's well satisfied with her bedroom just off mine.")

"I'm sorry I must go on to New York so soon," said Hopestill. "Tell me, do you think you'll be able to stick it out?"

"Stick it out?"

"Yes, I mean it's rather a grim prospect, I should think, to be shut up in this gloomy old house where the ghost of my blue-nosed grandpa walks every night. Or perhaps you have friends in Boston?"

"A few," I replied warily.

"In that case, then, you won't be lonely. Where are you from, by the way? Auntie told me, but I have a rotten memory."

"Chichester," I said.

"Oh, of course. I know nothing about the place. I haven't been there since I was a very little girl." She paused and looked closely into my face, and then went on. "Chichester has produced a very objectionable person by the name of Betty Brunson."

"I know her."

"She turns up on Christmas Eve, at places she'd never be invited, with an entourage of horrible boys from New York. She's exactly like a guide and says, 'Now this is typical of Boston,' or 'You'd never

275

find this outside Massachusetts,' and all in the world she's pointing out is someone's Cape Cod lighter or a Currier and Ives."

I was so panic-stricken at the thought that I might some time encounter Betty Brunson in Boston that I could make no comment. Hopestill gave me a second of her searching looks.

"Have we met before?"

"No," I replied firmly.

"Your face is so familiar. Were you at the Porcellian dance last spring?"

"No. I'm sure we haven't met. I would remember you."

"I couldn't forget *you*. We *have* met, Miss Marburg. It was ages ago, wasn't it?"

Again I denied it. But she pursued. "Perhaps you were in Chichester one time, a hundred years ago, when I had a nasty meal with Aunt Lucy and Cousin Josie."

"Perhaps," I grudgingly allowed.

"Look here," she said, "I must get this straight. Auntie has been so damned mysterious about you. I know you're going to do the famous memoirs but what else? Are you somebody incognito? As they say, scratch a Russian waitress and you find an archduchess. I suppose it works the other way too, scratch an archduchess and you find an upstairs maid."

Taken off my guard by her unconsciously shrewd guess, I made a slip of the tongue which, had her attention not at that moment been diverted, would have let her know instantly all she needed to know about me, for I said, "No, ma'am, I'm not either of those."

"Look, Philip has seduced my aunt. What a perfect butler posture! There—I've shocked you." She laid her hand on my arm. "*So* sorry."

The girl was aboriginal and had eaten the whole apple. A pagan priestess in her yellow vestments, she moved her supple arms and torso as if in an abortive dance, turning now to the infatuated doctor who was bringing the drinks like sacrificial libations, and now to me, her face a plastic substance that alternately showed derision or aggrieved boredom, or, if she had a moment before glanced at her aunt, a profound and muddled rebellion. In order to lower the tone of our conversation I said, "Do you sketch, Miss Mather?"

"No. Neither do I write nor take part in amateur theatricals. But I *am* literate. I'm what my long-suffering aunt calls 'advanced.'"

My question had been a happy one and she talked for some time, even after we had been interrupted by the arrival of the drinks, with a real enthusiasm which made me think she had, after all, some sort of inner life and that her interest in dress and horses was no more than a trifling avocation. She had recently "discovered" psychology and now felt she had wasted her whole life on trivialities. "The pious doctor calls me heathen because I believe in dreams and the *anima mundi*. You know, don't you, that identical twins have been known to have the exact same thought at the same moment even though they have been miles apart?"

The moment she had excitedly uttered the statement, her interest vanished. She sighed and said through a vapor of ennui, "Of course that sort of thing is trimming. What I'm interested in is the good of psychology, that is, the advertised good: no one, they tell me, needs to be neurotic."

"I quite agree. I wish you would tell that to your friend Pope," said the Countess von Happel who, with another woman, crowded into our little recess. Hopestill introduced me to the large, fragrant Viennese and to the other, Mrs. Choate. The Countess, speaking to her friend and to me, explained, "Pope is a surrealist, ladies, but I call him a fool. Hope, he brought me a gouache called 'When Lilacs Last in the Dooryard Bloom'd' though it was just a great gray study of nothing at all. If you turned it upside down, you got a sort of feeling that a goose was squatting on a picket fence. I asked him why on earth he had picked the title and he said that the rhythm matched the 'color cadences' but, my dears, there was no color in it!" Fashionably dressed and set with colossal jewels, the Countess reached across to squeeze Hope's hand and with an equine laugh cried, "Admit it's a damned fraud."

"Oh, Berthe, *don't* let's have that all over again. You know I'm *quite* able to see the virtue of your Davids and Rembrandts and Bellinis. You just judge them and modern painting on different psychological levels."

"That's the fraud! Psychological levels indeed! But, darling, let me tell you the rest of the story about Mr. Pope. He came to my last Friday wearing bathing trunks, galoshes, a figured waistcoat and an enormous tam-o'-shanter. Naturally we ignored him. We're not amused by such clowns, at least not in a small music room."

"He was pulling your leg," said Hope.

"Well, my soul, don't you suppose I knew that? But he got no satisfaction out of his performance and he's ruined himself so far as I'm concerned. I shouldn't dream of letting him come again. Annaliese Speyer was quite faint when she saw him. Really, she was! I had to send for aromatics."

The Countess resembled photographs I had seen of Empress Augusta Victoria. Blond bangs, arranged beneath a little green velvet hat, imperfectly concealed a high, wide forehead which, as the conventional sign of intelligence, was enhanced by a pair of large blue eyes, half-closed with a superciliousness which also infected the well-shaped, slightly curving mouth. Dominating the whole was a noble nose, too large, but soundly and handsomely built, and that this eminent organ, in which all the pomp of her history was centralized, might be displayed to its fullest advantage, she carried her head at a backward tilt. Less fine than the elevated nose but more commanding was the Germanic bosom of which the velvet covering was like the hull of some fictitious fruit. The voice, initiated in some other region, traveled through the buried core and was flavored with a stout sweetness as though her words were sopped in rich, old wine. I should have guessed that she had been a singer from the massive bust, the voice, and the carriage. I did not, but she told me. She took the cocktail I handed to her and with her free arm encircled my waist so that I was gently drawn to her.

"You make me think of a pupil I once had in Vienna. Do you like Schubert?" I said I could not distinguish one composer from another and that I much regretted my bad ear. "Well, then, we'll train that ear. No one in Boston has a better gramophone or more gramophone records than I. You come to see me always."

The word "gramophone" misled me: I imagined a small box with a black enameled horn, shaped like a morning glory. Such an instrument had been kept in a far corner of the lobby at the Hotel Barstow, and occasionally in the afternoon when the guests had had their naps and had gone out for a brief "constitutional," I put on *Der Tannen-*

*baum"* or *"Ich Liebe Dich"* or "Drink to Me Only with Thine Eyes" sung in a sad, rippling tremulo which brought tears to my eyes. I told the Countess I was grateful, but this was a lie: her loving gesture, though it was only a part of her patronizing, impersonal manner, had made me think of my mother and had returned me directly, by no détours of specific memory, to the horror of womanly affection which I thought I had outgrown. As in a long moment when I rested against the firm pouch of her bust and inhaled the odor of lilac, as fresh and springlike as if it came from the living bloom, and my only thought was how best to disengage myself from her embrace, Dr. McAllister, from across the room where he had taken a cocktail to Miss Pride and Mr. Whitney, shot me a look of warning or disapproval and simultaneously I felt the Countess' strong arm tighten about my waist. Before my mind's eye, like the immobile tableau of a dream, she and I appeared in this fond attitude, alone, before the sorrowing tin morning-glory in a dim, overheated room. I said in haste, "But I'm not often free. I'm studying stenography and my classes last all day!"

She let me go and laughing on one rich, contralto note, chided me, "Go on then, dissembler! You don't regret a bit that you can't tell Bach from Offenbach."

Everyone laughed at her play on words. Miss Pride smiled and said to me, "You mustn't miss an opportunity like that, Sonia. Not everyone is admitted to that famous salon." Horribly embarrassed by my blunder as well as by my egotistical assumption that this resplendent personage had an ulterior motive in her cuddling, I protested, and the hearty woman, speeding me on with a resounding smack on my backside, forgave and engaged me to come two weeks hence to a *Kaffeeklatsch* where I would find other people "in the same boat" with myself.

Miss Pride at last released Mr. Whitney, who for the past half hour had been fussing on the very edge of the sofa, so anxious to return to the hospital bedside of his son to congratulate him on the good tidings he had received from Dr. McAllister. He had, being at the end of his patience and ready to scream with vexation, finally risen and squeaked like a schoolboy, "Lucy, I *have* to go!" Clutching his hat, which he had refused to give up when he came in, in the hope that he would be able to make a flying visit, he dashed from the room. Miss Pride left her post and came over to speak to the Countess.

"I hoped you would come in," she said. "I rang you up earlier to make sure, but you weren't home. I have a bit of news for you. You know what I mean. I had a telephone call from New York this morning."

"Indeed!" cried the Countess and a flush of excitement illuminated her already well-lighted face. "Well, darling, can't we step over there?"

They moved off arm in arm toward the tulip-wood commode and stood there talking gravely for some time. I thought it singular that these two should have a secret. Hopestill, perhaps sensing my curiosity, enlightened me. Both of them, being shrewd business women, were in the habit of exchanging tips on the stock market, but did so out of earshot of everyone else, partly because they knew their passion for finance (which they had managed to dissociate from "cash" and "money" and approached as a pure science) would be considered in bad taste, and partly because they were frankly unwilling to share with anyone else the precious information that their Wall Street brokers periodically hissed over the wires. They were subscribers to the daily forecast of the Dow-Jones averages and to Barrons, and when they met, if it were at a dinner party, in Stearn's department store, or in Mrs. Gardiner's palace, they instantly locked arms and conversed in whispers, comparing notes on the vagaries of the Greyhound Bus Company, like doctors consulting on a difficult case.

Mrs. Choate, stranded with the three young survivors of the tea-party, glanced from one to another of us and chose me to receive her first remark. "I know you must be a capable young woman. Just fancy learning stenography! Why, it's ever so much cleverer than my little avocation!"

She studied me brightly. Hopestill and Philip, refusing to come to my aid, began a private conversation and I was obliged to inquire what Mrs. Choate's avocation was.

"I have taken up cookery. You know I'm a southerner and though I've been here for many years, I've never got used to Irish servants. I simply can't manage them! My cooks won't cook as I tell them to.

And last year, I had gone without hoe-cake as long as I could bear it, so I simply went to the kitchen one Thursday and made myself hoe-cake. Ever since then, I've spent every Thursday experimenting. I'm always saying to Hopestill that she ought to take it up."

The woman gave Hope a humorous wink which missed fire and received no response. She went on, "Of course *no* one north of the Mason-Dixon Line knows how to cook."

Hopestill's voice was suddenly raised and I had the feeling that what she said had no part in her conversation with Philip but was merely thrown out as a bait. "It's a nuisance finding a restaurant when one's dining with a Negro."

The doctor, taking up her game, maliciously replied, "An awful nuisance. It's simpler just to dine at home."

Mrs. Choate paled. But though her face, a large and youthful one, wore a hurt, quizzical look, she said determinedly to me, "Perhaps you'll come to me some Thursday for a meal of greens and spare-ribs. My soups and desserts are not strictly southern, for I invent things, but the main course is always authentic."

"I had a splendid time at his apartment in Harlem . . ." Hope was saying.

Rebuffed, Mrs. Choate rose. "I'm going to interrupt that conference of the experts over there. I want to tell Miss Pride my latest discovery. I have invented a divine egg, poached in thinned tomato paste."

Hope grimaced, composed her features, and said to the outsider, "Oh, Mrs. Choate, I hear you've turned cook. I'm fascinated. Do you really make corn-pone and all those amazing things?"

But the woman was on her guard. "It is nice to see you looking so well, Hope," she said. "Philip, how is your dear mother?"

"Mother is very well," he replied. "She has almost lost her British accent."

Mrs. Choate smiled sickly and took her leave.

"She isn't southern at all," explained Hopestill to me in a whisper. "She's just a terrible fake. You'd think she'd been born with a mint julep in her hand and a fine old southern grudge against the damned Yankees that did in her granddaddy's plantation. My Aunt Lucy, who can't stomach her and couldn't from the very first, found out that she lived in New Orleans for ten years before coming here but before that lived in California! But did we sound too beastly?"

They had, indeed, sounded beastly to me and I had suffered as much discomfiture as Mrs. Choate. I could not answer but instead inquired, "Is she the Countess' friend, then?"

"She's nobody's friend. She either just shows up at tea time and manages to walk in with someone else, or she makes everyone come to perfectly horrible parties—she uses marshmallows in her salads and starts off with hot wine and I'm sure none of *that* rot is southern—so that she has to be asked back."

Miss Pride had observed the approach of the bore and quickly guided the Countess along to meet her, then seized Mrs. Choate and marched her back to us. "Of course I think," said Hopestill, "that the Negroes are the coming race."

The Countess leaned over and embraced Hopestill. "To use that word you're so fond of, Cousin Hope, you're too 'advanced' for me. So I'm going to leave before I hear why you think the Negroes are the coming race. You have frightened me enough already with your threat that Dali and Chirico will come into their own and reign for-ever. I couldn't bear to have the blackamoors reigning too! I love you! Good-by! Come along, Mrs. Choate, I'll drop you."

Miss Pride, to my astonishment, murmured to me, "From the top of a high building, I hope."

Our hostess went out with the ladies and from the vestibule, we heard her say, "Mrs. Choate, there is an article on New Orleans in a recent issue of *The Atlantic* that ought to interest you."

"Really? I never read *The Atlantic*. I just skim it the way I do the Bible." The Countess chuckled, but Miss Pride said coldly, "Some other day I must ask you to explain that provocative remark." There were brief adieux and afterwards Miss Pride went upstairs to dress.

The emptied room seemed smaller, for it was now quite dark at the windows and the pale lamps revealed only their immediate en-virons. We moved toward the fire. I knew that I should leave Hope-still and the doctor, but the cocktails had made me careless and drowsy. I did not want to lose my warmth by going up to my room where the fire had probably died.

282

"Sonia—that's all right, isn't it?—made a conquest of the Countess, Perly."

"That's only Berthe's way."

"You mean she loves *all* young girls?" said Hopestill with a laugh. "Tell me: How did you find us?"

"Oh, Hope!" protested the doctor.

"Don't be absurd, Philip! She didn't miss anything. Haven't I the right to know the total impression she's got?"

"I had a pleasant afternoon," I said. I could have added that this termination of it was as disagreeable as anything I had ever encountered.

Hopestill extended me her small hand which, in my clasp, was as lifeless as the hand of a sawdust doll. "It's been so nice to meet you, Sonia. The best of luck."

I had not expected to be dismissed so soon and, clumsy in my surprise, I knocked over an ash-tray on a small table by the hearth. I bent to pick up the cigarette stubs but Hopestill said, "Oh, for goodness' sake, don't bother about that."

Reddening furiously, I started to the door. The doctor walked across the room with me. "I wanted to ask you," he said, "if you still go every Sunday?"

"Of course," I replied.

"That's right. You're awfully good. By the way, don't think we're giving you the cold shoulder. The fact is I . . . we haven't seen one another for quite sometime. We're *very* old friends, you know."

"Yes," I said, but my voice was unconvincing and he must have known that I was offended.

"Believe me," he said anxiously, "you *are* a good girl."

The door closed behind me. My goodness remained in the library with its advocate while I put my eye to the keyhole. The doctor was kissing Hopestill's neck. She paid no attention to him but poked the fire and at last, lifting up her head to address the Copley, "Great God, it's just like dancing school except that then you didn't have that ramrod down your back! Perly, Sonia is just the girl for you and the battle is half won because she's obviously mad about you." She flung back her head so that her hair reached to the middle of her back and laughed heartily.

283

"Hush!" said Dr. McAllister. "She may be in the hall."

I stood up quickly and went to the stairs, but I heard Hopestill pause in her laughter to say, "I meant absolutely no harm. I'm just a little giddy, and she was so *incredibly* solemn!" And then, as solemn as I had been, she added, "Imagine Aunt Lucy not telling her she had a cat! I swear I think the woman's mad."

# CHAPTER TWO

In order to make my appearance at the Countess von Happel's *Kaffeeklatsch,* an attention to her I felt imperative since it was my first invitation in Boston, I had been obliged to negotiate with Mrs. Hinkel so that I could be excused from the last class, Business English. (The Countess kept European hours, serving her afternoon refreshments at four instead of five, a custom Miss Pride regarded as so novel that she almost never went there to tea.) Mrs. Hinkel was furious at the presumption of her "laziest would-be professional woman" and said, "I suppose you think you know all about correct usage! I have not been headmistress of this college for fifteen years without observing, Miss Marburg, that the graduates of public schools, with the exception of those from the Latin schools, know next to nothing in regard to grammar. You may think now that dangling participles and 'due to' and prepositional phrases are the least of your worries, but the time will come when you will ask me for a recommendation and I will have to say, 'The candidate under consideration left much to be desired in her work in Business English.' However, as the useless expenditure of my time and your money doesn't bother you, run, amuse yourself, go to the movies, go to the beauty parlor! Respecting your language, don't worry! Don't let business interfere with pleasure!" She dispatched me to my debauchery with a military salute and returned, secretly delighted with the rhetoric of her diatribe, to the book she had been reading called *Hints to Commercial School Teachers and Administrators.*

I would have liked to explain to her that the prospect of a musical afternoon afforded me no pleasure, that I could far better endure the boredom of the class in Business English (in which, as she perfectly well knew, I was the only literate pupil) than the snares I was bound to fall into at the Countess'. But I knew that I would only enrage her further, and I held my tongue. My hand was on the door knob when she burst forth again. "I may as well tell you, Miss, that I am so displeased with your work here, and feel so strongly that this expenditure of *my* time and *your* money is useless that unless I am informed of marked improvement in your attitude, I shall have to ask you to leave. My time is simply too valuable to be wasted." The threat was purest nonsense, for she would not have dreamed of parting with my money which came in regularly each week, but she was a great believer in intimidation as an academic principle, and having very soon discovered that I received her recriminations with just the degree of terror she needed to nourish her sense of power, she never let a day pass without summoning me to her office or cornering me in the corridor to remind me, exultantly, that my ignorance and lassitude were eating up her time.

I was on the point of tears, not so much from her scolding as from what was in store for me as I left the building and closed the outer door behind me, massive, black, embossed with a wreath. I was not only convinced that what Mrs. Hinkel had said was true, but also that the whole of my Boston enterprise was a fiasco. But just at the moment when I was wishing myself back in Chichester, I saw, mincing uncertainly down Dartmouth Street, a figure so familiar, so instantaneously reminiscent of the stuffed birds, the rocking chairs, and the chilled farina pudding at Friday luncheon, that its appearance was like an ominous symbol, and for a second or two I thought it had no substance or else belonged to a stranger and not, as I had at first thought, to Mrs. Prather. There was no turning back, for she walked quickly and was upon me before I could contrive an escape.

"Of all things," said Mrs. Prather, taking both my hands. "What on earth are you doing so far away from home? Do you and Mother live in Boston now? Around *here?*" I replied that I lived here, but by myself. Her weak eyes begot two tears and she squeezed my hands. "I'm the limit! Imagine not recalling that sad, sad story. Now, child, don't tell me a thing, I can read it in your face: you want work."

She opened her handbag which contained, I saw, an apple, a Hershey bar, and a great many loose lozenges, and withdrew a calling card on which she begged me to write my address so that when she heard of something she might get in touch with me.

"But I don't need work," I protested, making no move to take the proffered pencil.

She was surprised and, for the first time taking in my new, expensive clothes, she said forgivingly, "Dearie, it doesn't need to be all over for you. You write down the address and I won't hold it against you. We'll get you out of there just as quick as we can and no one will be the wiser. I would take you straight to Arlington this minute rather than have you spend another night in one of those places, but for the time being, I'm crowded for space."

Without mentioning Miss Pride, I made it clear to her that I was not living in a brothel. She was greatly relieved and said that in that case I might come to call on her some day and tell her "all about it." "Whenever you get tired of your present place, I know just the house for you. A dear friend of mine has never had a good second maid and I know she would take you in a minute if I recommended you to her. You would have a room to yourself, I happen to know, and two afternoons off not counting Sunday."

I was anxious to be off for I had just heard the bells at Trinity chiming a quarter past four, but Mrs. Prather held me another five minutes, describing the excellent treatment I would receive at the hands of her friend who, at last it appeared, was an invalid and in spite of suffering horribly from one of the digestive disturbances for which the Hotel guests had such an affection, had the "sweetest nature in the world." In parting, she tried to give me her Hershey bar which I refused, but not liking to seem rude, I asked if I might have one of the horehound lozenges. She then released me. "Good-by, good-by. I'm glad it's not what I thought. Now remember me and when you need me, come to Arlington. I'm in the phone book. I expect it's time for Cinderella to run home to her pots and pans. You know, the French people have an expression when they take leave of one another. Instead of saying 'good-by,' they say *au revoir* which means 'till we meet again.' So that's what I will say to my little Chichester friend, *au revoir*."

I did not stop running until I was two blocks from the Countess' house, and it was only then that I tasted the full flavor of the bitter, not unpleasant horehound. It was a taste that belonged exclusively to Chichester and the summertime, and it made me a little nostalgic. Although I realized that I had had a narrow escape and that I must henceforth be troubled by the knowledge that I might meet Mrs. Prather again round any corner and the next time might not be alone, this return of the past through the candy, despite my homesickness, restored my eagerness to continue the present time, and I was grateful for the old lady's errand that had carried her down Dartmouth Street in time to save me from a craven retreat.

The meeting had rendered me a service by taking my thoughts off the entrance I was about to make into a strange house, so that when I opened the street door, I rang the bell at once without having to wait for courage to lift my finger to the button. I was admitted by a manservant into a vast lobby lighted by three iron candelabra and a number of sconces placed at intervals like arc lights. I had heard of the Countess' prejudice against electricity, the effect of which, she claimed, was to destroy shadows, and shadows, like echoes and like the aftertaste of Moselle wine, were sources of inspiration to her. She had succeeded in creating with her candles a theatrical effect, and through some optical illusion made by the long shadows against the walls, which a highlight here and there revealed as lustrous and would have shone under electricity, the hall seemed much larger than it actually was and the ceilings loftier. I was guided over a Persian carpet and past "occasional" groups of high-backed chairs and console tables upon which stood vases of yellow rosebuds whose outer petals were ruffling into full maturity. Then, as though entering a bay from an estuary, we turned to the right into a wide, square room, dominated on the left by a staircase, illuminated like the entry with sconces, and on the opposite side by a portrait of the Countess in a double frame. She sat at a spinet in a pale blue Empire dress with her golden hair piled high, her head held well back to set off her nose. It was impossible to tell whether she were about to play or had just finished, for her musicianly hands rested in her lap, and the expression on her face gave no clue since all the other features were tyrannized over by the nose, sufficient unto itself. Just as the candlelight, perhaps intentionally, hinted that the owner conserved imported customs, older than the old Boston house, older than her own experience, dating from times before the fall of princes and the commercialization of palaces, and by its metamorphosis of the hall, otherwise so like all other halls on Beacon Hill, sharply designated the mistress as a member of a different species, so the portrait, pompous with the self-importance of the ruling class, gave those who viewed it to understand that an even further distinction was to be made between the Countess and her neighbors: that in that species she was a unique specimen, for she was not only aristocratic, but she was beautiful and talented as well, and, implied the station of the picture, according to standards that were not local, the *most* beautiful and *most* talented woman in Boston.

As we reached the foot of the stairs, the manservant spoke for the first time. "The name, please?" When I had told him, he repeated my name, putting an interrogation mark after the "Miss?" not in contradistinction to "Mrs." but to "Princess" or "Baroness," as if he were not in the habit of announcing the untitled bourgeoisie. I took a dislike to him partly because of his tone and partly because of his impassive, coarse, cunning face in which I seemed to read condescension as if he had divined that until recently (or perhaps even now) I had been "in the service" like himself. I said sharply, "I am expected."

"Certainly," he said, a flicker of a smile adding, "Don't be so naïve as to think I will take your word for it," and he indicated a divan, wide as a bed and upholstered in yellow satin, where I might wait, and left me, sending his dignified shadow ahead of him between the misshapen parodies of the balustrades on the uncarpeted marble stairs.

The yellow sofa was so placed that from it one could look nowhere but at the portrait of the Countess; and so, in my enforced contemplation of it, I was amused to see that upon the spinet there stood a vase of yellow rosebuds, the duplicates of which were set in such fresh profusion upon the tables in the entry. But a second discovery was even more amusing: I had been struck by the radiance of the canvas because the nearest sconce to it was several feet away, and now I perceived that craftily concealed under the inner frame at the top was a long, fluorescent tube sending a smooth shower of light over the whole surface! This in a Puritan house! In the hall of a great lady so sensitive she could not abide electricity! It occurred to me that other people had not seen what I had but had simply taken for granted, or had not noticed at all, the extraordinary visibility of this one object in the shadowy lobby, for Miss Pride or Hopestill, when they had told me of the candelabra, would surely have told me of this inconsistency if they had ever observed it. For, although they were both fond of her as were their friends, they found Berthe von Happel irritating and would most likely have been delighted to learn that at least in one particular she was a fraud. "I don't mean to criticize Berthe's taste," Miss Pride had said, "because on one level it is superb taste, but I must say that there is something *malentendu* in the way she has turned poor Ralph Brooks' house into a museum. And not to put too fine a point on it, frankly, when I go there and the last thing I have seen is the Common, if I'm coming from Pierce's, or General Hooker, if I'm coming from Goodspeed's, I feel very much as if I were going into Loew's Orpheum."

The butler was gone so long that I began to think I had come on the wrong day or that the Countess was offended by my tardiness, or, worst of all, that she had not really meant her invitation, could not remember any Miss Marburg, and would instruct the servant to turn me out, a commission that would delight him. The first time I reproduced the scene in Miss Pride's drawing-room, the date and the hour of the engagement were perfectly clear, "Friday week at four o'clock," but, as minutes passed and the porter of my banal name did not reappear and I again and again rehearsed the Countess' words in an effort to determine who was to blame for my mistake, I became so confused that had not the word *Kaffeeklatsch,* which I had never before heard spoken, been audible in each revision I made, I would have believed that the invitation was imaginary. Presently I heard the door-bell and stood up, thinking that the butler would come down to answer it and on his way would inform me of my verdict, and indeed, in a moment there came to me the sound of music as if a door had suddenly been opened on a floor above. Still, he did not appear. Yet I heard voices in the entry and immediately the treacherous butler, who had evidently come down another way in order to tease me, came into sight but vanished as soon as the visitor had turned toward the stairs. The visitor appeared tremendous, for he

290

was magnified by the shadows: his pale hair, which might have been blond or white, lost and then regained its glow as he passed the first sconce. I stepped forward, still in the shadow, intending to ask him if this were the day for the *Kaffeeklatsch*. He wheeled, startled, and peered through the dimness.

"*Doch, ist's so spät?*" he said.

"*Nein, es ist früh, glaub' ich.*"

"*Warum denn . . . ?*" He came closer. "Oh," he said, "oh, forgive me. I thought you were my daughter, Annaliese. It's so dim here. I expect I'll find her upstairs. Excuse me!"

"*Ich bin auch deutsche.*"

"*So?*" Impatient to be off, his eyes wandered up the stairs.

"I mean, sir," I said, "that for a moment I, too, was confused and I thought you were my father. But I see now that your dueling scar is not the same."

He gave a short, unamused laugh. "That's the way to tell, *nicht?*" And he ran up the stairs two at a time.

I had not, of course, mistaken him even though he did, in a general way, resemble my father, but I had been seized by a terrible longing to speak German and to be allowed to enter the upstairs room from which the music issued and which I conceived of as a world separate from Boston, the one to which I belonged and the only one in which I should ever be happy. But it was not only the man, apparitional and fugitive, that snatched me from the present time and Boston which I had hoped would be as familiar to me as a native habitat, it was, even more than him, the music. It was of a sort and played upon an instrument which I had never heard before: its academic precision was so intellectual, belonged so much to that altitude where mathematical progressions and retrogressions were animated by imaginative genius that, just as one cannot look directly at the sun, so I could not submit the part of the mind that hears without the protection of the part that sees. Thus, my pleasure came to me attended by memory of scenes or objects, my mother's face, the beach at Chichester, my father's rosary hanging in his shop, the summer drives to Wolfburg, so that the passage of the music to my heart was insulated, roundabout, enriched. And I saw, as though I stood upon it and not upon the costly Persian rug, the sweating sand at Chichester, pawed by the surf on a glaring August day, where my father and I had stopped to watch a plover. The amber-clear, archaic notes, plucked from the siccative strings of the instrument I did not know, and the stranger's voice, and the somnolent waves cast out and entrapped my father's exclamation: *"Ein Regenpfeifer! Still!"* My longing to speak German was then elaborately if minutely satisfied by the redemption of *"Regenpfeifer,"* a word I had heard only that one time, twelve years before.

The cessation of the music reminded me that I had been waiting an unconscionable time and was no closer to the Countess von Happle than this romantic representation of her, larger than life size. I wondered if, by hanging it here, she had meant to tantalize as well as impress visitors who, unknown in the house, were not allowed to go at once into her presence. It was a mistake, if this had been her purpose, and an insulting one to prolong their suspense, for, like the magazines in the busy dentist's office, it became an unendurable bore, and one's temptation was to leave and come back on another day. The postponement of a disagreeable affair and the self-righteousness in which it has had its genesis afford as much relief as if the pain or the embarrassment has been undergone, is finished, and can be forgotten. But just as we throw down the magazine, so trashy it seems like a calculated insult to our intelligence, and prepare to announce cuttingly to the secretary that our time is precious, we had assumed, when we made the appointment for four, that we would be attended to at that time, the door opens and the dentist emerges smiling, disarming us with a genial apology and a word of sympathy about the suffering our wisdom tooth is causing us. I had reached the turn in the hallway and had just annexed a new feature to my grievance, for I was hungry and my vitals informed me that it was past the hour when it was my secret and shameful custom to eat two crullers and drink a cup of coffee in a small, steamy café at the top of Pinckney Street, an indulgence into which I had been forced by the meager fare at Miss Pride's tea-table. The butler, coming through a door at my right, which I had not noticed, stopped me, and said that I might go up now, that Madam had been playing and he had been unable to announce me at once. Then, by way of apologizing for his suspicions, he said flatteringly, like the dentist, "Madam is waiting for you."

2

"How d'ye do?" said the Countess who stood in the doorway and drew my arm through hers, the vegetative softness and fragrance of her person and the intense heat of the small room making me think of summertime. "It's a pity you had to wait. Tell me, how did you like that little likeness of me in the hall? Did you notice it?" She turned her profile to me, waiting for my answer, and when I gave it, saying that I had been charmed, she continued to pose a moment longer in imitation of the "little likeness" as if she were not in the least concerned with my opinion, the anticipation of which, in fact, had set every nerve in her body tingling. Then, pressing my arm against her, she said, "It's an excellent painting, even if you don't like the subject, isn't it? I debated with myself a long time before I hung it at all: Will people want to look at poor me? I said to myself. But what nonsense! The painting is the thing, you goose, people won't even recognize you, you're simply incidental to the composition." I agreed that the painting was excellent (for all I knew it was, but it had struck me as being remarkably dull), but that she was wrong in thinking people would not recognize her, for she, not the composition, was its *raison d'être*. She could not deny my praise, but brought up from her interior an exultant purr: "Did you look at the hands? They are divine!"

This toll was levied upon every newcomer; some, less green than myself, added a gratuity to the set fee. Twice during that afternoon and many times thereafter, I observed the transaction carried out on the part of the Countess with a sort of childlike poise which made one feel that she was not so much vain as honestly amazed at her endowments. And when she had made her concluding remark, to one person about the hands, to another about the throat or the eyes, in a lowered voice as though she were praising someone within earshot, she became an amiable, solicitous hostess dedicated to the wants of her guests. Like the hypodermic injection of adrenalin that instantaneously relieves the asthmatic, the Countess' hospitality at once made me forget my annoyance and my hunger. She now allowed me to pass through into a small, bare room which in no way conformed to the speculations I had made about it when I was half submerged in the yellow satin sofa. It was an ascetic's cell on the top floor and at the back of the house, presenting a view from the uncurtained dormer windows of chimney pots and blind brick walls. Central in the room and, unlike the portrait, requiring no contingents to play up its merits, stood a rosewood harpsichord from which had been plucked the brilliant, incisive tones I had heard downstairs. The owner's seal, a silver pitcher full of yellow roses, had been placed on the wing directly in the player's line of vision. The other decorations of the room were testimonial: uncolored photographs of Mozart, Bach, Haydn, Handel, with perukes and lacy jabots, hung in a row upon one wall and opposite, between two bookcases, a deep square frame preserved a letter signed "Franz Liszt." Here and there stood high-backed, uninviting chairs without arms or cushions. The music, the wild log fire, and the table of refreshments were the only provisions for comfort. A few of the chairs were occupied, and several people stood around the table by the windows where they helped themselves to coffee and cakes.

The Countess, leading me to the table, said, "You must have been late, for I began sharp at four. There's no point in coming at all if you miss the music."

"I'm very sorry," I told her. "I met someone on the way. But there will be more, won't there?"

"More?" she repeated incredulously. "Well, you *are* a baby!" But she patted my hand kindly and chuckled. "No, after I've played one opus I'm through, for I won't mix composers and I won't overindulge in one. But you didn't know. All's forgiven. Next time you'll know better and not let yourself be waylaid."

"Then I may come again?"

"If you don't, I won't forgive you. Now let me get you started and I'll come back to you later on. Just now I must speak to *Herr* Speyer and his adorable daughter. I'm losing them. They're sailing for Germany, naughty deserters!"

The Countess plucked a boy by the sleeve. "I want you to meet this unfortunate young lady who got here late and 'sat out' the whole of the minuet."

The boy, a tall, frail Jew with a womanly grace in his long, supple fingers and a transparency of skin, turned eagerly at the sound of her voice, but not to meet me. "Oh, Berthe, you were wonderful today! When I closed my eyes, I could have sworn it was Landowska playing. I was overcome!" He was, in truth, dumfounded and gazed at her with famished, radiant eyes. The Countess puckered her brow in annoyance. "You're a trifler, Gerhardt, but you don't take me in. I'm improving, yes, but I'm still a greenhorn. Now be good and give Miss Marburg a cup of coffee." His eyes implored her retreating figure to come back, but simultaneously he said to me, "Will you have cream and sugar?"

I was surprised at the Countess' treatment of *Herr* Preis who was obviously head over heels in love with her. And being certain, from my own observation as well as from remarks dropped by Hopestill and Dr. McAllister, that vanity was the principle of her being, I could not understand why she had taken his compliment with so much displeasure. I thought perhaps he knew nothing of music and, being devoted to it almost as much as she was to herself, she could not accept homage to one and not to the other. But then I learned, in our ensuing conversation, that the unhappy boy had himself taught her how to play the harpsichord.

Because the room was small, it seemed crowded with people. There were, in fact, less than a dozen. They had not gathered into groups but wandered with their coffee cups to examine the letter from Liszt or the unrewarding view from the windows or to smell the roses on the harpsichord. A hush prevailed like that in an art gallery. The Countess, engrossed in a whispered conversation with *Herr* and *Fräulein* Speyer, made no attempt to remedy her guests' unease. I had no choice but to remain with Gerhardt Preis who would have liked to leave me, like a wounded animal, to nurse his hurts in solitude. Feeling that for the time being at least, he was incapable of talk, I made the opening remark myself, expressing my surprise that the guests were not, as I had expected them to be, in the midst of a spirited discussion of music. I had supposed, I said, that the company would be made up of experts and of ambitious amateurs.

Preis gave me a pained smile. "Berthe does not allow us to talk music here. Why should she? What more can be said than she says when she plays?"

"But surely," I said, "she must like to talk shop. I thought all artists did."

He shook his head. "Not the Countess von Happel. She's above it."

"Well, then, I'm more comfortable. I thought, when I came, that the talk would be too intellectual for me to follow."

"Intellectual!" he exclaimed to himself and for a moment drank in his own scorn. Then facing me with a civil smile, he changed the subject. "Your name is the name of my father's town. Do you know it?" I told him I had never been to Germany. "I shall never be in Germany again. No doubt you guessed that I am a Jew. I was born in Marburg, but I have no memory of it, for my mother took me to Paris when I was very small and we only visited Germany in the springtime. My father was a manufacturer of surgical instruments and as you Americans say, he 'made a fortune.' I'm therefore of that species Berthe finds so odd. She's completely above money, you know." I smiled, recalling her parleys with Miss Pride.

The young man continued. "Have you heard about the time she met the millionaire department store owner from Chicago? It's the most *Happelisch* story in the whole Berthe *Sammlung*. This Croesus was house-guest of someone she had invited to one of her Saturdays and he had to be brought along. As they were starting in to dinner, she said to him, 'You must go first, for I understand that you are a "merchant prince" and my only other noble guest this evening is nothing but a poor little Russian baron.'"

A pretty, dark-haired girl beside us took a step closer and frowned at Preis. "I was at the dinner-party. It was appalling, because, you see, Mr. Bruce was my mother's guest and it was very trying to us. For he was by no means a stupid man and he perfectly well knew he had been horribly insulted. You know, she ought to inquire into people's histories before she plays such a joke as that. We all think he is a fine man and not at all coarsened by his money. And anyhow, he came from Boston in the first place and went to Harvard. I think the Countess goes too far."

"I disagree," returned the young man sourly and his tone implied that the girl had taken far greater liberties than their hostess had done with Mr. Bruce. "It's of no use to criticize Berthe. She's unique."

"You forget that this is Boston," said his adversary. "To be quite blunt, Mr. Preis, what I mean is that we New Englanders were here a great many years before you refugees started arriving."

Immediately she regretted her tantrum since, though she had enjoyed it, it had been a breach of manners. But instead of apologizing, she simply left us and vanished from the room without telling the Countess good-by. I remarked to Mr. Preis that she seemed to have had enough of the salon.

"No, she hasn't had enough at all, and unless Berthe overhears her sometime, she'll be back every Friday all winter long. No one refuses invitations to this house. Berthe shouldn't live in Boston, of course, for it's very bad for her. She only does it because she's fond of the way she's done her house, though I've told her a thousand times she could have done a better one in New York. She's made for a Central Park penthouse. I hope you appreciate her, as I see you're not a native. If you have the good fortune to be asked often, I *beg* you to see how adorable she is. I'm afraid this is my last afternoon here! I've offended her somehow. She's as sensitive as the princess who could feel the pea."

His misery was so acute that he clasped his head in his hands and did not stir but sorrowed behind the handsome façade of his Hebraic face, his eyes closed, his full red lips parted as if in illness. I was deeply touched. "Perhaps things will come all right in the end," I said.

"Oh, you don't know her at all or you wouldn't talk about things coming all right in the end. No, when she's through, she's through once and for all. I could no more get her to forgive me than you could get her to play again this afternoon."

"But what have you *done,* Mr. Preis?"

"I fell in love with her, and that's against the rules. You can remember me as the first exile from Berthe von Happel's Fridays you ever knew. It's no consolation to me to know that you will see a good many more like myself in the course of time."

The Countess had gone to the door with the Speyers and allowed *Herr* Speyer to kiss her hand. Then, drawing Annaliese to her, she kissed the girl on the cheeks and on the lips and cried, "Don't change a particle while you are gone. I shall die of a broken heart if you cut off that golden tail about your head! Good-by! I love you!"

Above the heads of the embracing women, there appeared the face of a young man which, as the girl submitted to a final kiss upon her mouth, registered a virile horror, a response that the scene did not elicit in my companion who had not taken his eyes off the Countess for a second. The Speyers left and the head which had materialized out of the shadows in the hall acquired a body. The Countess smiled radiantly and had already forgotten her grief at the farewells. She told the young man she was sorry he had been kept waiting, that she supposed he had got sick and tired of her "little likeness" in the lobby. I turned my head in embarrassment at the repetition of her welcoming speech and told Mr. Preis that I would like to look at the view from the windows.

"Well, I shan't go with you. As for myself, I find that kind of view uninspiring. Do you really like to look at dirty chimney pots? Anyhow, I must speak to this low character."

The low character, having acquitted himself of his debt, hastened to greet his friend. "You're still here, then. I must talk to you. Can't we go now?" He started, seeing me. "Oh, I'm sorry. I didn't know I was interrupting."

"I was just leaving."

"Don't on my account, please." His bashful smile, as he blushed, so delighted me that although I should have left him at once to his confidences which he was perishing to impart to his friend, I did not move aside. He looked no older than a schoolboy and I could scarcely believe Preis when he introduced us, describing Mr. Garvin as a Harvard graduate student of philology, and went on, to the boy's discomfort, to tell me that his formal study of language was not enough, but that he was now about to tackle Japanese.

I said, "I am living now with the daughter of a Sinologist, or so I've been told he was. He had a large library of Japanese books too."

The two young men laughed and Gerhardt whispered to me, "He wants only a *speaking* knowledge of it, Miss Marburg."

"That's what I wanted to tell you about," said the other. "He's beat my time, just as we predicted."

"Who? Kadish?"

"Who else? He ran her down yesterday. And mind you, he had just left me five minutes before."

I could not help my outcry of surprise, but having no wish at that moment to acknowledge my acquaintance with Nathan, I turned abruptly and filled my cup from the large silver urn on the refreshment table. But I did not move out of earshot of the young men who, pausing for a moment after my ejaculation, continued their talk.

"And let me tell you what else he's done," said Garvin. "He is contracted to teach one Harry Morgan of Park Avenue, Long Island, Beverly Hills, and Sun Valley enough German to get him through the course he flunked last year. Where the hell did he get the German is what I want to know."

"Oh, he knows German," said Preis. "He speaks it like a native."

"Are you pulling my leg? I didn't know he knew a word of it."

"There's a lot you don't know about him. And a lot I don't know. But tell me how he got the *Japanerin.*"

"Not here. Later."

"But how with that . . . Oh, all right. We'll go in a minute. Let me stay just that long since it's the last time I'll be here."

Gerhardt's face had lighted as he saw the Countess bearing down on us, sending her resonant laugh ahead of her. "Come along, Preis, you can't accomplish any more here than you can at Jacob Wirth's," whispered Garvin.

The Countess, without glancing at Gerhardt, took me by the arm and as she led me away, called over her shoulder to Garvin, "Come next Friday, won't you?" Then, in a lowered voice to me, "I didn't ask him to come for the music as I'm sure he hasn't got an ear. I'm trying to drop the other one, and I thought I might get his friend to take him away with him. I'm sure he won't show up again next week."

I said, "I'm sure I shouldn't want to 'drop' anyone who admired me so much as Mr. Preis does you."

The Countess shuddered. "Ugh! I can't bear it. Really, give a refugee an inch and he'll take an ell. You understand, I hope, that I am not a refugee?" I took her question as meaning, "You don't think for a moment that I have Jewish blood, do you?" or else as implying that she had come here of her own free will from a society that was not in the least threatened by the upstart revolutionists who had played the devil with people of Gerhardt's class, definitely inferior to her own.

I flattered her a little on her excellent English and asked her then how long she had been in America. I listened to her voluble reply with only half my mind while the other turned over the remarkable mention of Nathan Kadish's name. I had been titillated at the sound of it, but without immediately being jealous of the Japanese girl whom he had "run down" I devoutly hoped I would not see him. With a coldness that startled and even alarmed me, I knew that at this juncture in my life, other things—indeed, *all* other things—were more important to me than being in love and, particularly, in love with Nathan.

The Countess was saying, "I have been here seven years and I've been a widow five, so you see I've had to make my own way like all the immigrants. How precious you are to praise my English! It's all right for ordinary chatter, but you'd never guess how it fails me when I'm confronted with a conversation about music: I can't understand a word. And consequently, much to my sorrow, I've had to avoid friendships with my fellow-artists. You can imagine how painful that has been."

The Countess puzzled me and from time to time the thought flashed across my mind that she was a fraud. Yet, I had it on what was probably good authority, that her talent was prodigious. Miss Pride had told me that before her divorce from Count von Happel and her marriage to Ralph Brooks, she had enjoyed a brilliant reputation in Vienna both as a singer and as a pianist. Hopestill Mather believed that her practice of filling her salon with people ignorant of music was sheerest snobbery, that she was the victim of the common European delusion that Americans had no taste and no artistic principles. And still, as Miss Pride pointed out, she had, with the sagacity of good breeding, made several concessions to Boston. True, she had remained aloof from its musical enterprises (tyros, asking her opinion of Koussevitsky, received the damning faint praise, "He's all right, though by continental standards, these conductors in America are a society of mountebanks.") but had gone in whole-heartedly for its art. Rather too effusively for her fellow-citizens who knew better, she declared that the Fine Arts Museum was superior to the Luxembourg. Miss Pride said that her concessions reminded her of the Greek who had set up the statue of Aristides in Louisburg Square and then to conciliate the rest of the community had faced it with one of Christopher Columbus. "Two negatives don't, in that case, make a positive," she said. "If we *must* have Aristides, whoever he may be, why can't we at least have Daniel Webster?"

I was curious to know why the Countess had left her Viennese husband, but nothing she said enlightened me. Except for brief interruptions when she told her guests good-by, that she loved them (this was her unvarying epilogue as the reference to her portrait was her opening gambit), she would not let me go but for three-quarters of an hour interrogated me minutely. She appeared disposed to regard my candidacy to her salon with favor. To my relief, she was incurious about my background and when, in connection with something she said about a room at the Chilton Club, I told her that I had never been there for I did not belong to society, she laughed and squeezed me closer to her.

"American society! The nobility is made up of 'cattle kings' and 'wool barons' and 'merchant princes' and between you and me, you're just as good as the rest of 'em, whoever you may be. I must confess a great weakness for New England, but try as I may I cannot take any stock in its society. Why, my people, when they are calculating time reckon in centuries, not in decades. It so amuses me to see Lucy Pride (I love her dearly and I hope you do too) show off her tea service which belonged to some governor or other in the eighteenth century. I don't call it 'old,' though I do call it pretty. I brought very little with me from Austria, only a few knickknacks, among them a set of tankards that have been in my family since the thirteenth century. I think them fairly antique. I'm going to tell you a story on myself before you hear it from someone else who might make me sound brutal. I had only been in this country a few years and I had heard so much about the 'wool barons' and so on that I thought perhaps the government *had* established a peerage. You're laughing at my innocence and I don't blame you! Well, a man named Mr. Puce (I have to chuckle at the name because it reminds me of the gloves I have always had my chauffeurs wear) came to dinner here and the person who brought him introduced him as 'the Chicago merchant prince.' How should I know any better? American names are so exotic, you know, to a foreigner, that it's not a bit strange to think of a 'king of Wyoming' or a 'grand duke of Iowa' or 'prince of Chicago,' so poor me! I had him go in first to dinner. He was flattered half to death, and the only reason the Baron Kalenkoff didn't leave at once in a fury was that he thought I was playing a joke!"

I could make no counter to this, and instead went back to the beginning of her anecdote. "I would like to see your tankards, Countess."

She laughed richly. "I'm no collector, darling! I'm not interested in *things*. Art is *my* life. Make me happy and tell me that it's yours too!"

"But I'm very green," I told her. "I would like to make you happy, but I'm afraid all I can do is read."

"Oh, but that's marvelous! I hope you aren't so modern that you will find what I like *démodé*, as Hope Mather does. I can still cry at *Père Goriot*. As for modern novels, they don't touch me. Either they're cold or gross. And *need* they be so difficult?"

I could not resist the temptation to advance myself with the Countess. "Balzac is sublime," I said. "He has touched all passions and given the commonplace the stature of tragedy. I cannot feel that Shakespeare is any greater." I was quoting from George Moore, a passage which had at first captivated Nathan with its audacity and then had filled him with derision. Since I had read very little of Balzac and worshipped Shakespeare with the fine rapture of adolescence, I visualized inverted commas about my words, but my voice did not convey them to the Countess who cried, "Lucy said you were clever, but she didn't prepare me for this! What an addition to Boston you are!"

My voice shook with shame as I replied, "Oh, I have only a few tags."

"By the way, I don't understand your name, Sonie. Is it short for

Euphrosyne?" Through a misreading of the word, she had metathe-sized the vowels and pronounced it "Euphrysone." I explained that Sonie was my own childish corruption of Sonia. "What a pity," she said. "Not that I don't love Sonia for you, but it would have been so delightful if you *had* been named for the goddess of Mirth. Your eyes are so merry." She held me off at arm's length. With a supreme effort I obliged her by grinning, hoping to infect my eyes with the merriness I put into my lips. "There! Isn't it the image of Euphrysone!"

A woman and her daughter came up to us at that moment to say good-by. "Amelia and I have so enjoyed the afternoon, Berthe. I love your nest and your cunning little harpsichord. You're like a sirocco to warm our cold New England."

The Countess glowed. "You're a fibber," she said, rising and taking both hands of her guest. "But you must come and tell me the same sweet-sounding fibs every Friday you possibly can. Next week I'm going to play the Haydn Opus 21 in D Major."

"I don't believe I know it," said the woman who did not, in that sense, *know* any music. "But if you will let us, we will come, won't we, Amelia? Amelia is wild about music, aren't you, Amelia?"

Amelia, fourteen years old, a gawky girl with long legs and knobby knees who was, obviously, at this stage of her life, an enemy to music and to mankind, nodded in agreement and said in a high, rushing voice as if she had got it by heart, "Yes, I am, Countess von Happel. I don't know anything about it, but I know what I like."

The Countess took them to the door, kissed them and proclaimed her love to the furiously blushing and twitching Amelia. She re-turned and settled down beside me again to resume her inquisition. But at that moment, she perceived that Garvin was edging toward the door, leaving Gerhardt Preis still standing by the refreshment table. "Well," she said resolutely, "I may as well do it now, make it quite clear he can't come again. Lou," she called to a girl who was reading the titles in the collection of record-albums and turned at the sound of her name, "will you come meet Miss Sonia Marburg?"

Lou, who did not supply her surname, sat down beside me and laughed softly. "She's had to take steps at last, poor Berthe. You're new here, aren't you?" When I told her that I was, she asked frankly, "May I ask how you met the Countess?"

"At Miss Pride's, at tea the other day. Do you know Miss Pride?"

"Oh, gracious yes, though I haven't seen her in a month of Sundays. Has Hope gone on to New York yet?"

"She left on Tuesday, but she'll be back tonight. She's going to spend week-ends here."

The girl laughed. "I dare say that was her Aunt Lucy's idea. Poor girl, she does hate Boston so. You didn't know she hated it? She has a perfect complex on the subject."

"I can't understand that. I've seen very little of it, but that has seemed charming."

"You mean you've never been to Boston before? But where . . ."

The Countess had dispatched Mr. Preis and returned to us. "I heard you tell Sonie that Hope has a complex. This child hasn't been here long enough to know all our complexes and reflexes and prefixes, Lou, and I don't want you to let our cat out of the bag. She'll detest us and run away."

"Berthe, you're priceless! Why, that's what makes us so interesting."

"Do you know what Amy and I think? We think Hope is going to change her tune and fall in love with Boston after all."

"Why that prediction?"

"Don't *you* think she'll marry Philip McAllister?"

"I'm sure I haven't the least idea," returned the girl coldly and rose. "Berthe, I've had a wonderful time. May I come again next week?"

"But, darling, don't go yet! I want your opinion. You know he went to Manchester for his holiday this year. Don't you think *that* indicates something?"

The girl merely smiled and drew on her gloves. "Will you ask Amy to ring me up? I want her to do Monadnock for me from the top of Prospect Hill. No, don't get up. Good-by."

When she had gone, the Countess put her arm about my waist. "Now I have you all to myself. Tell me, don't you think we're right about Cousin Hope and that nice young man?"

"I don't know Hope at all well. She seems a little . . ."

"A little highly seasoned for Philip? Of course we all think that, but that's precisely the reason we think he'll pursue her to the end. His mother and grandmother are so opposed, you know. Everyone talks about it *ad infinitum* so I'm not telling tales out of school. Haven't we got mean little minds?"

A hysterical laugh from the doorway announced Amy Brooks' breathless arrival. "Berthe, *darling!*" she cried and skipped across the room to kiss her stepmother. "I was so engrossed in doing the Oyster House that I completely forgot it was Friday. Mr. Pingrey was along and we've already had our tea. Do you forgive me?"

"I don't mind anything you do so long as Mr. Pingrey is your chaperon. We were just making a match between Hope and Dr. McAllister, and I was also on the very point of saying I'm betting on another marriage of a certain young lady not a thousand miles away to a young man whose name begins with P."

Amy Brooks collapsed in shaking laughter, her eyes brimming with tears, and I got up, unnerved by the spectacle and aware suddenly that we three were alone. The Countess permitted me to go only after she had got my solemn promise that I would come to her every Friday for the rest of my natural days. "And now, good-by, come back to me. I love you!"

# 3

Dinner was served punctually at seven, and nothing would have induced Miss Pride to delay it by a minute. She regarded tardiness at mealtime as the same sort of self-indulgence as illness. But as she insisted that I dress each night (she did not herself, but thought that I should "learn how to manage an evening frock against an evil day," the evil day presumably being the one on which I should be invited out somewhere) I could not help being late, and she had finished her soup when I entered the dining-room. "We dine at seven, Sonie," she said, laying down her spoon. "You shouldn't have changed."

"I thought you wouldn't like it if I didn't."

"When two rules conflict, the important one is the one that should be obeyed. It is commendable in you to remember to dress,

305

but punctuality is infinitely more important. I understand that you were late to Berthe's today." She leaned forward so that her face was framed by the white candles as she confronted me with this astonishing information. Was I so simple that my very actions could be read in my face? I dared not question her and for some minutes she pursued the subject without hinting at the identity of the scout who had lurked about the doorway on Beacon Street to time me. But she was not angry. She smiled. "It was a mistake. Berthe is rather lax about everything except her Fridays. I suppose it meant you didn't hear the music and that never sets well with her. But she wasn't offended. She telephoned me the minute you left the house to say how pleased she had been with you. She referred to you by some foreign nickname that I did not catch. I was rather surprised you were already on such intimate terms."

I explained how she had come to call me Euphrosyne (rather, Euphrysone) and while Miss Pride said nothing, I was sure she was taking in every word in order to repeat it the next time Berthe's name was brought up amongst her friends. I went on then to tell her that I had been delayed because I had encountered Mrs. Prather on Dartmouth Street.

"Who is Mrs. Prather?"

"Why, you must remember her. She has come to the Barstow every summer for years. At least as long as you have. She sits under the ptarmigan in the dining-room."

"Oh, yes, I remember. For a long time I thought her name was 'Mather' and wondered if she were a relative of Hopestill's. I did not inquire. I don't understand why you should have been late on account of her, though. She's simply the kind of fright one stares through if one's in a hurry, ain't she?" In a sense, she had forgotten who I was and that I could not possibly have cut Mrs. Prather. I went on to tell her of my conversation with the stupid but kindly old soul who believed I had become a prostitute. Miss Pride was vexed, not because of Mrs. Prather's delusion, but because I had spoken unguardedly in front of the maid. She rebuked me while the girl was still in the room. Upon her mischievous Irish face appeared a grin of malicious pleasure, so that I knew the scene would be reproduced in the cellar as soon as we had left the dining-room. "For a moment I couldn't place Mrs. Prather," she said. "But now I recall that she is a woman of great breeding, and if she thought you were pursuing the oldest profession as it were, she probably had good reason. I have often warned you, as you can't deny, that the excessive rouge you use on your lips is far from good taste. And I should remind you that in scorning Mrs. Prather's offer to recommend you as an upstairs maid may, in time, prove to be the greatest folly. If I were you, I would not be at all sure that I would not end up as an upstairs maid or even as a 'useful' servant."

She had never spoken so harshly before. In my agitation I took far more meat than I could use and it occupied so much space on my plate that when Emma came round with the vegetables I had to push it to one side and in doing so pushed it off onto the table altogether. Miss Pride, whose avian eyes had not rested for a moment in their barrage of killing looks on me, said, "Oh, my soul! Emma, bring a clean mat for Miss Marburg." The girl, nearly overcome, rushed to the pantry and banged the door shut, there, as I imagined, to giggle at my bungling. But when she returned with a clean napkin, the scolding was over and Miss Pride was genially telling me of her morning which she had spent with her Cambridge friend, the widow of the Harvard professor, in the Concord burying ground.

"And that reminds me that Philip McAllister called this afternoon and said that his grandmother would like to have you and Hopestill come to tea tomorrow. He'll drive you up. If you have time, do take a stroll through Sleepy Hollow. But don't put it off until after tea. Laura McAllister is such a chatterbox you won't get away before dinnertime." (Later that evening, she said, "When I spoke of Mrs. McAllister I didn't mean anything unfriendly by calling her a chatterbox. She's a charming woman, and it would displease me to hear that you had repeated what I said." With an antediluvian notion that marriages could still be made by families rather than by individuals, she was anxious to stay on the right side of Philip's grandmother.)

The account of her day amongst the graves alleviated only the suffering she had inflicted by humiliating me in the presence of a servant, but the other suffering that came from the fear that this was to be only the first of such occasions lingered as a dull but obtrusive ache. And because it was a symptom common to many diseases, there was no way immediately to identify it. It was inchoate fear, the first sign of all those irascible emotions that include hatred, contempt, despair, and so on. And after dinner, as we sat for an hour, according to our custom in the upstairs sitting-room and twice Miss Pride corrected my pronunciation of a word in the article I was reading to her from *Harper's Magazine,* the pain became acute for a moment and when it had gone I felt the vague nausea that accompanies shock.

We did not have our coffee until I had finished reading, at eight-thirty. It came up then on the dumb-waiter and Miss Pride established herself behind *The Boston Evening Transcript* while I filled the cups and brought a bottle of Benedictine from a closet in the "office." My mistress was proud of saying that she took no medicines but "vinous and spiritous liquors" which she called "the medicaments of Nature," and while she drank very little at a time, she had a glass of something at regular intervals throughout the day: at eleven in the mornings of week-days, she had a glass of port, but on Sundays, after her chess game, she had dry sherry. Before luncheon and dinner, she had two glasses of sherry and in the evening with her coffee a liqueur or a measure of rum which she took neat. The best of her liquor was kept in the den just off the upstairs sitting-room, and this was reserved for her own use. Less excellent whiskeys, brandies, liqueurs, and wines were kept in the library and given to guests when she entertained formally. The pantry and the cellar were stocked for the rank and file with domestic dry wines, low-priced Bourbon, and gallon jars of gin. I was not invited to pour myself a glass of Benedictine, but invariably she said, as she folded the newspaper but continued to read it and as I handed her the tiny green bowl on a thin gold stem, "Perhaps you'd like a glass of sherry. I won't offer you any of this, for I'm sure you wouldn't care for it, and it's so dear I can't allow it to be wasted."

Tonight, drowsy with the rich wine, out of touch with Miss Pride since she never spoke once she had begun to read the financial page, I felt simultaneously dissatisfied and proud. The dissatisfaction I erroneously (and perhaps intentionally) set down to the sherry, the effect of which had been to usher in a memory of the beer my father had used to pour into my soup. I conjured up his youthful face, so like that of *Herr* Speyer, and wondered at its incongruity in this rich woman's parlor, and felt that I had betrayed him since my own presence here was no longer incongruous. It was as if I had supplied his attributes, plagiarizing those my creator had conferred upon me; or, conversely, that *I* was the chimera, the reflection in the flawed looking glass, the misquoted doctrine, and he the paradigm. His presence became as palpable as that of Miss Pride. The *du* of *Herr* Speyer's remark, that intimate address, lay like a ghostly hand upon my cheek. Like a pilgrim, used to sleeping out of doors and claustrophobic in a house, I inhaled jerkily as if the air within this silent, genteel room were poisonous to my lungs, as though, if I could, I would escape the carnivorous flowers and come again among the harmless edelweiss my father's fancies had picked for me as I sat hearing his stories in the shop in Chichester.

I rose. "I believe I'll change and take a little walk, Miss Pride."

She did not look up. "I hurt your feelings at dinner, did I not?" But there was nothing in her voice to indicate whether she were sorry or if she intended me to apologize for my milk-sop sensitiveness.

"No, ma'am."

"I've told you not to call me 'ma'am.' 'Sir' is all very well, but 'ma'am' I cannot tolerate. You mustn't take me seriously when I'm crotchety. I wouldn't let you be an upstairs maid for a dowager duchess, let alone for one of Mrs. Prather's hypochondriac friends. No, indeed, I don't intend to turn you out. Stick by me, Sonie, won't you, and put up with my flip tongue? My father used to tell me I wouldn't have a friend in the world by the time I was thirty. Perhaps he was right and the only reason people come to see me is that they're after the rum cakes on my tea-table."

"Really, Miss Pride," I protested, "I wasn't in the least offended. I thought perhaps you had been annoyed by something earlier and were just out of sorts a little."

"You guessed it perfectly. Now don't put a false construction on this, for on second thoughts I realized that I was quite wrong. I was annoyed by the way Philip McAllister asked for you on the telephone this afternoon. I had the disagreeable feeling that if you had answered, he would have asked you to meet him for tea, and I said to myself, 'Surely that child can't be having rendezvous with Philip who is virtually Hopestill's fiancé.' "

Until now she had been talking to me behind the rustling screen of the *Transcript,* but now she lowered it and as I earnestly denied that I had seen Philip at all except in her own drawing-room, I winced at the firm set of her jaw and the suspicious, narrowed eyes. Though what I said was true, I did not feel that I had been absolved of my guilt, but that she was reading my mind in which my sporadic infatuation with the doctor was trying in vain to flutter out of reach of her superhuman intuition. Her gaze was like a magnet that drew towards it my will-less secret. Five minutes before, I had not been conscious of my love which, at best, when I was not with him, was like the exhilaration the novice feels from drinking, not like the somnolent pleasure of the addict. But now I felt feverish and giddy. Thus, the innocent man on trial, under the skillful bombardment of the prosecution grows hot and quivers and finds his voice distant and shrill as if a subtler faculty than his conscious mind has been besieged and he is no longer sure that he did not commit the crime.

"Poor girl," said Miss Pride, "it's not easy for you. You're homesick, I expect, not lovesick. I'm not up on my psychology, as Hope would say. Tell me, did you meet any interesting young people at Berthe's today?"

I told her of Gerhardt Preis whom she had met and had not cared for. "When I was your age, I deplored race prejudice. To my dear, single-minded Papa's chagrin, I used to seek out your Israels and Rachels, the bigger the nose the better. But at last I admitted to myself that I was just like everyone else. I didn't get on with them . . . their aggressiveness distressed me in public and their money mania at last got the better of my idealism. Now, while I say 'live and let live' I must confess I sympathize with that particular of Hitler's program. Did you meet anyone else?"

With relief I spoke of Mr. Garvin—relief because I did not share Miss Pride's prejudice and while neither did I feel strongly partisan towards Jews, the subject always embarrassed me because, not being able to detect Hebraic blood at once except in a most obvious face, I was afraid that someone's toes were being trod on. And even here in Miss Pride's sitting-room where there was no one to be offended (unless I myself were partly Jewish, a not unlikely possibility), I disliked the openness of the attack because, by my ambiguous silence I was no doubt giving her the impression that I subscribed to her view, and later on, when a Jew was present, she might call upon me to confirm some anti-Semitic statement.

She was inordinately interested in what I told her of Mr. Garvin because, through my desire to hasten from the Jewish question, I exaggerated the scraps of information I had gathered about him through his conversation with Preis, and told her that he was a student of Japanese even though I had been corrected by the boy himself. "What a small world we have," said Miss Pride, beaming with pleasure. "To think that one of your first acquaintances in Boston should have the same inspiration that my father had. Perhaps he would like to look over the books here. Is he a presentable young man or is he one of those brainy people, like Hope's artists, who don't wash very well?" On the contrary, I told her, Garvin was, if anything, overwashed. His tanned, freshly shaved face had been as clean as a baby's; his dark blue suit and his white shirt, his blue cashmere tie and matching socks were so fresh from the cleaner and the laundress that he could have posed, with no subsequent touching-up on the part of the photographer, for an advertisement of Miss Pride's White Cloud soap. "And what is his background?" she asked me next, but I could not satisfy her. "Berthe will know, I suppose. We might ask him to dine with us some evening. I don't want to deprive you of all society, you know, but at the same time I don't want you to drift away from me."

"Oh, I can assure you," I laughed, "that Mr. Garvin and I didn't strike up an acquaintance at all." Actually I did hope that I would see the young man again but only because I was inquisitive to know what sort of friends Nathan had.

"The Countess gave me a surprising piece of news. She says you're sharp as a tack on the subject of French literature. How in the world did you come by that?"

"She's quite mistaken. I know nothing about it . . . I . . ."

Miss Pride rolled her eyes in a way that was at once so omniscient and so repulsive that I had to look away from her. "You're quite right, my dear child, most of us are credulous geese. To be candid with you, I'd rather have you like this than have you be a real but bumptious intellectual."

"Like this?" I repeated, feeling that I ought to defend myself.

"I said *most* of us are credulous geese. But *I* know what you know. All I ask is that you don't take your game seriously."

I saw nothing for it but to confess that I had, indeed, been bluffing at the Countess' and to my relief she dropped the subject.

"Am I right in assuming that this restlessness of yours—this wanting to go for a walk in the middle of the night—is just that same homesickness we were talking about earlier? And that you're not growing tired of your life here?"

I assured her that I had no different ambitions than to keep her company, but there flashed across my mind, set off by her uncertainty of me, a sense of power over her that allowed me to make a private reservation. I would stay with her *so long* as she upheld her part of the bargain and did not deprive me of my freedom in those hours which were not dedicated to her. For it had occurred to me that as she grew older she might become more demanding of my time. Indeed, she had prepared me for that in our conversation the night before my first tea-party when she had said, "I don't want you to make up your mind yet, for you may find me too exacting. It will not be my fault, for I pride myself on respecting other people's privacy in their leisure hours, but it will be the fault of senility, that wretched Mr. Hyde I shall become in my last days." I had then disbelieved her completely, even though a few days later, I heard Hopestill say to someone, "Auntie is so improvident in her choice of fixed ideas. She surely *will* dodder into crabbed old age if she keeps thinking of it."

Tonight, like a subterranean river, a senile complaint slipped through her words and it did not, at last, seem unlikely that in a while the undertone would become the minor key in which were played the jeremiads of those whose only future is eternity.

Laughing, when she spoke of the humiliating possibility of a wheel chair, I said, "Miss Pride, you should bone up on those Thibetans who claim they know how to live two centuries or so." I was recalling a photograph I had seen in a newspaper of a Hindu,

312

said to have been born in 1786, making him a century and a half old. The broad, bald skull had looked like a death's-head and the drooping eyes had been tenantless, mere vacant openings in round pits of black shadows. The long dark lips were stretched in a hideous grimace, not of scorn for the photographer but of a corrupt delight in the pyrrhic victory of flesh over time. The caption had read, "Says He Will Live Till 2000 or After."

"I should hope not!" she exclaimed. "Do you think I want to see Boston turned into a hive of Customs Houses and aeroplanes replacing automobiles? No, thank you. I don't fancy myself rocketing about in the air with Mac at the controls. A century is too long for anyone to live. To go beyond *that* is my idea of anticipating Judgment Day. Tomorrow afternoon at Mrs. McAllister's, you will possibly meet a Mr. Childreth who is the oldest living graduate of Harvard College. He was of the class of '67. Although he still has his own teeth—they're no beauties, however—he has quite lost his reason and reads books written for children. It always strikes me as ironical that on Commencement Day he marches at the head of the Harvard procession when he barely knows his A.B.C.'s."

"But *you* won't be like that, Miss Pride."

"I'm not at all sure. If I am, though, I hope you'll have the goodness to lock me up. Even my father, a most sensible man, got notions toward the end. He confused me with my sister Charity and believed that neither of us was his daughter but that our surname was Fleet. 'Charity Fleet,' he would say to me, 'I want you to take my green bag which is full of peanuts and go feed the squirrels in the Common.' He had never fed a squirrel in his life, and until he was in his dotage always referred to them as 'the Common rodents.' And of course his bag hadn't so much as a peanut shell in it, but only his rice-paper books."

She fell silent, thinking perhaps of her father, and I started toward the door to leave her to her reverie, but she looked up. "I don't know how I started on that digression. We were talking about your friends, or rather, your friends-to-be. I dare say it isn't my place to say this as it's the duty of one's mother, but since yours is not accessible, I must look upon myself as your guardian. To put it bluntly, Sonia, you don't consider marrying, do you?"

"I don't know. I suppose I've never thought much about it. Perhaps I shall want to after . . . that is, when I'm older."

"But, my dear child, don't you see? Hasn't Dr. McAllister ever discussed the matter with you? I think it's a pity he's your doctor. He's a perfect scamp in many ways and has *always* been a heartbreaker, but that's beside the point. He ought at least to guide you, knowing what he does."

"Do you mean that I shouldn't marry because of my bad heredity? Because, why, yes, he has talked to me about it and has told me I shouldn't think of such things." This was not quite true. He had one time compared me to himself and had said our misfortunes could be turned to good account if we looked upon them as symbols, perhaps of original sin or of mortality, like Dr. Galbraith's *memento mori*. However, this had been in one of his religious moods when he was gathering all manner of disparate elements into his train of thought. He had never actually spoken to me of marriage and I, who seldom thought of it, had not solicited his advice.

"Times change. Nowadays children aren't spanked, don't learn Latin, don't respect their elders. And I haven't a doubt it's thought old-fashioned to be wary of insanity in the family. But, Sonie, there have been *two* instances of it in your lifetime, very close to you. I must say it would give *me* pause."

Had Miss Pride been able at that moment to read my mind, she would have been convinced that my mother's idiosyncrasies were already cropping up in me, for as I listened to her, I lost my identity. I was invaded by the strange feeling that I was not myself, or rather, that this was a phantom of myself, projected into Boston by my real being, still in Chichester. I had had this sort of experience before: in the winter just past when the days were at their shortest, I had waked once at four o'clock but had had no way of knowing whether it was four in the morning or four in the afternoon. Even though my mother was still asleep beside me and though no sounds of life came from outdoors, I concluded that it was afternoon, that we had slept through the whole day, and I rose in haste, ashamed of my sloth. As I shook down the stove, live coals fell into the ash box and I knew that it was morning or no fire would be left. Although I was wide awake, I had the sudden feeling that I was still in bed and that the person or the thing that held the cold stove shaker was not a dreamed-up aspect of myself but was a clever imitation. It was not so much Miss Pride's wounding, though perhaps sensible, counsel that made me take refuge in this fantasy—for I suppose the psychologists would say that my lapse was in effect an "escape from reality"—as it was that it did not seem to be the first time she had spoken thus. On one level, that of my conscious memory, I knew that this scene had not been played before, but on a secondary plane, her speech, down to the very syntax of her sentences, was so familiar that I knew, or thought I knew, exactly what was coming next. And for that short space, I believed that I was in my bed at home, enacting a daydream. The fact that restored me —in itself absurd, far from conclusive, but nevertheless as quick-acting as the cock's crow that hurtles ghosts and goblins back to hell —was the chiming of the clock on the mantelpiece marking ten. Or rather, I heard only the tenth stroke but knew that I had heard all the others as well and that Miss Pride's "Times change" had been uttered just as the first note sounded.

"I'm so glad to be here!" I cried.

"That's a *non sequitur*," smiled Miss Pride. "But I take it as a compliment, and also as a sly hint that you've had enough of my sermonizing. Very well, you win. I shan't mention it again. Let your conscience be your guide."

I ran up the stairs and locked the door to my bedroom. Standing in the pitch darkness, I imagined what I would see when I snapped on the light. For this was one of the moments, most delicious because they came so seldom, that I realized I was in Boston. My eyes grew accustomed to the darkness, and I could see across Louisburg Square to Mount Vernon Street where a house was lighted up for guests who came and went with singsong greetings and farewells. Amongst them, perhaps, were the Countess von Happel, the girl named Lou, Philip McAllister. Immediately above a chimney there shone a star so large that I thought at first it was a light. Automatically, I said, "Star light, star bright, first star I've seen tonight; wish I may, wish I might have the wish I wish tonight. I wish that:" But I had got my wish and could find no other. The room was here and my signature was on it: my own pajamas and dark blue wrapper would be lying on the turned-down bed.

I groped for the switch. The instanaeous flood of light broke my tension. But the order of things, deranged by two chance encounters, first with Mrs. Prather and then with *Herr* Speyer, and by Miss Pride's admonitions, was set right again. The mechanism would not be so tight for the repair, would henceforth be more liable to collapse, but for all practical purposes, it would serve. I was engulfed by a wave of love for Miss Pride, and gone with the dissatisfaction I had felt earlier was the spontaneous and perverse desire to marry that had not occurred to me until she had implored me not to.

Again, I so strongly disbelieved that she would grow old I wished to run downstairs to assure her. How could she? She who, the day before, had walked to Pinckney Street from Harvard Square and showing less fatigue than I who had strolled slowly home from Dartmouth Street, a tenth the distance, had taken me to King's Chapel where for an hour we had admired the shabby gravestones in the burying ground, smirched with the droppings of impartial pigeons. She had looked at her man's pocket-watch which she carried in her handbag and said, "Oh, we have half an hour before tea. I suggest we take a walk to Trinity and back." I had lagged behind sometimes, but she pressed on, her ruthless pace diminishing at no time, not even at street crossings. As she often said, she had been a pedestrian long before automobiles had been thought of, and she was not one to give them the right of way. The light on Arlington Street had just turned red and cars were commencing to move along against us, but Miss Pride did not stop. A truck-driver, halted by her formidable approach, leaned from the cab of his monstrous machine and said, with certain awe, "Look at that damned old bird." The old bird gave vent to one of her rare laughs and said to me, "He's only envious. The great thing has lost the use of his legs from running that juggernaut. Come along, we must work up an appetite for tea, you know."

Rejoicing in my success at the Countess' and in my secure position in this house, I could not fix my attention on my shorthand exercises. I must have been daydreaming for some time when I became aware of voices in the room below me, that is, an unoccupied guest room where, as Miss Pride told me, she was sketching her memoirs. I opened my door and stood in the hall listening. I could hear nothing but an unintelligible murmur and was just returning to my room when a door downstairs was opened and Hopestill's voice came up to me. "But how peculiar you are about it, Auntie! Why isn't it possible that I saw her in Chichester?"

"She wasn't there that summer. But it's not of the slightest consequence whether her face is familiar to you, Hope. The important thing about Sonie is that she's contracted to me."

I could fairly see the girl shrug her shoulders as she replied, "I understand, dear. I shall keep my hands off."

"You do not become less vulgar. Good-night."

I slipped back into my room. Lying face downward on my bed, I could hear the eccentric fury of my heart-beat.

# CHAPTER THREE

Hopestill Mather, when she came home from New York for the week-ends, was so disarmingly attentive to me that I came to think of her as an ally though I would have preferred to look on her as an enemy. On certain evenings, usually Friday, when she stayed at home, she invited me to come to her room where she served me hot buttered rum which she prepared with water kept steaming in a silver pot under a cozy. Frankly impressed by the way the Countess had been struck with me (To my blushing delight she said once, "Aunt Lucy is going to give Berthe what-for one of these days if she doesn't stop telling everyone that *she* found you."), she was endeavoring, I thought, to discover for herself what it was that had so rapidly elevated me to a place of honor in the salon. It was not, she warned me, a very high distinction, for the Countess was a little too hyperbolical to be taken quite seriously. She was bound in conscience, moreover, to point out to me that I had arrived on the scene just at the moment that Annaliese Speyer's departure had, so to speak, left a vacancy. At the same time, she expressed her congratulations and told me that if I "handled" the Viennese properly I would find her a faithful friend. She had never been urged to entrench herself in the little society of the music room, possibly because, knowing too much about the Countess, she had never paid her the homage strictly required if one were to become a habitué.

Having gone this far, Hopestill decided to continue to the end and refilling my mustache cup with rum presented me with the bare and slightly scandalous facts about her cousin by marriage.

The Countess was a "natural," she said, having been blessed with a perfect ear and with perfect taste. But through an inertia, deeply hidden under nervous energy and physical tirelessness, she had never supplemented her native and very considerable gifts with any study, was and always had been totally ignorant of the science, the history, the criticism of music. And, although she had no intellect, she had the intelligence to realize that if she were to be happy in the kind of musical circles to membership in which she was entitled, she must learn to think about her art and how to talk about it. The task was too enormous and it did not occur to her guileless mind to bluff her way through, though she was not above setting herself up as an expert amongst people whom she knew to be worse informed than she. Thus, in Vienna, her peers and her admirers were never permitted to make her acquaintance. At the same time, because she had been born self-conceited, she craved to be spoiled by something more personal than the press and more objective than her husband the Count, her doting family, her aristocratic but inartistic friends. She was ambitious for a following of innocent people. Consequently, she had divorced the Count and married the New Englander (whose name, for obvious reasons, she did not take) and immediately on coming to America, instituted these little musical afternoons to which, as a rule, only young people ("preferably tone deaf," said Hopestill spitefully) were invited. And now, if she were threatened by one of her guests who was disobeying the rules and learning something about music, she could take refuge in her difficulty with the English language. The audacious guest was shortly dropped.

I asked Hopestill if this, then, accounted for her treatment of Gerhardt Preis. "In a way, yes," she replied. "But there's more to it than that. That part of Berthe is more complicated." She told me that the Countess had deliberately made the young man fall in love with her while he was teaching her the harpsichord, for, it was generally assumed, she far preferred his enraptured looks and his mash notes sent with the yellow roses he showered upon her to any formal discussions of the music she was studying, and because Preis spoke German she could not pretend not to understand him. Then, having extracted his usefulness from him and far outstripping him in her management of the instrument, she got rid of him. Here the second of her peculiarities entered in. Apparently it would have been simple enough to keep him on tenterhooks indefinitely, to make his lips always the vehicle of nothing more dangerous than professions of love. And it would have seemed that keeping him by her would be greatly to her advantage since everyone knew that his virtuosity promised him an eminent career. Why not, then, since his sting was removed, save him as an ornament for her salon? The fact was that she disliked men.

I must have shown by my face how shocked I was at this revelation, for Hopestill hastened on to assure me that her cousin was not a Lesbian, was probably not even conscious that she preferred women to men. (It had not, of course, occurred to me that she might be perverted in this way. What alarmed me was the thought that she might prove similar to my mother.) She did not fear them, but she recoiled from them in a frigid, old-maidish way, and unlike Miss Pride who could join the gentlemen almost as a gentleman herself, she was ill at ease in their company, embarrassed, often rude, because her vanity warned her that they would make love to her. The third gift of her fairy godmother (the first two being talent and self-esteem) was a stern, intuitive moral nature which kept her so under control that none but the most astute observer suspected anything irregular about her, but which allowed her to surround herself with girls, to caress them chastely, to send them presents, and to write them affectionate letters, indulgences permissible since they could have no consequences. I asked how her second husband had figured in this intricate pattern.

"Oh, poor Cousin Ralph was baffled by her, but he was grateful because she was so sweet to Amy. Aside from that, the marriage was a dud. She treated him like a butler—always called him 'Brooks'—and wouldn't speak to him before four in the afternoon when she was certain of having callers."

"Do you think she's taken me up because she's certain I'll never know the first thing about music?"

"She's not *that* naïve," returned Hopestill with a laugh. "Why, the Countess is certain of nothing, but she has her high hopes."

"And did my predecessor keep her part of the bargain?"

"To the letter."

The Friday evening conversations became, after a few months, an established institution. Hopestill told me frankly that she far preferred to hear my bulletin on the afternoon in the music room to going to parties. I obliged her, partly because I would not have known how to refuse, and partly because it was flattering to have so eager a listener and so open an admirer of what she called my "faithful eye."

We who put in a regular appearance at the Fridays were all girls. Occasionally there turned up a pedigreed young man from Harvard or a European man engaged in some enterprise far afield from art. The girls were second- or third-year débutantes, girls in that interval between the coming out and the wedding. They waited charmingly and passively for the materialization of a husband. They made no effort to shorten the period of their retirement, concealing, as nuns conceal their bodies, the aspirations that fluttered in their hearts, but showed, by deferential questions and mild, general compliments to the correct young men that, as it was proper in society girls, they respected men as a superior breed in whose eyes they did, indeed, wish to find favor, but neither hastily nor through their own maneuverings. Perhaps it was their modesty that made them aloof, eclipsed their individual history, lined them up alongside one another like those rows of bathing beauties whose real names have been changed to place names such as "Miss Rhode Island" or "Miss Great Lakes." Perhaps the modesty was their strategic principle and the one whereby they were the most successful because its employment was so unself-conscious. I sometimes reflected that they were like their ancestresses whose names and probably whose noses and eyes they retained, of whom we know through historical, sociological, even psychological studies as "the New England woman," and whose personal style, whose distinctive behavior have been leavened by time so that we see as sisters and coevals and identical specimens Priscilla Alden and Mary Chilton and Margaret Winthrop, all dressed alike in blue-gray homespun dresses with white berthas, seated before a spinning wheel, all combining in equal proportions in their characters the virtues in whose names Pilgrim daughters were christened: charity, prudence, hope, faith, patience, from which admixture emanated dignity, loyalty, thrift. Now in these twentieth-century women, there remained all those traits but to no end (rather, to no end of which they themselves were aware) like the appendix in our bodies that no longer serves us. They were like ancient vessels the archaeologists disinter which have been revised by time and the earth's chemicals so that the luster has been obfuscated by a patina, a marine green-blue encrustation, here and there punctured, as by a star, by a minute gleam of the metal underneath.

I had no communication with them. They behaved towards me with a warmth, a sincere interest which for many months deceived and flattered me so that I was at a loss to explain why they not only did not invite me to their own houses, when they were so cordial—even to the point of seeking me out in the music room—but that also, when I met them on the street, as likely as not they cut me dead. It was the very lack of condescension, the tactful omission from their conversation of anything which might remind me, to my embarrassment, that I was not of the sisterhood that finally enraged me. It was no ordinary snobbishness which inspired them, on meeting me, to acquire a burning interest in an object across the street, and, indeed, it was perhaps not any kind of snobbishness but merely another aspect of prudence, resident in them all, that like a fog concealed the roads branching off from the one they traveled which, because they traveled it in homogeneous company and had been set upon it by their parents whom they had no reason to distrust was, they knew, the right one. Prudence lighted them and made the pitfalls solid; prudence, like a composition teacher, assigned them "topics" to beguile the tedium of the journey; and prudence, like a duenna, supervised their romances. A palmer like myself, straying by chance and for a brief season across their path, was not invited, as a rule, to travel onwards, for they had been warned, as children are warned against accepting candy from strangers, that appearances are deceptive and one can no more be sure of the probity of a slight acquaintance than one can be sure of the purity of the substance under the chocolate coating.

They dressed well and without taste as if the caution of their forebears lingered yet. They had let modern fashion shorten their skirts in the daytime and lower them again in the evening, but had stayed the hands that would cut too daringly, would drape them too caressingly. So, at the Countess' dinner parties (her "Saturdays," as they were known) they appeared in evening gowns which were not memorable; pleasing, they might be, or quaint, or festive (which boneless adjectives Hopestill, if she were present, employed in her compliments to them.) Their tremulous chiffons and pale crêpes, enlivened but unrewarded by a locket or a brace of gardenias, passed muster and no one noticed them.

Similarly, their conversation was lacking in excitement, though it was grammatical and scrupulously took into account the interests and prejudices, so far as could be determined, of their interlocutors. They had no affectations, aired no scandals, and had no discoverable attitudes save those they had inherited, like their noses or their jewelry. Their differences of opinion gave rise to no choler when they found themselves beside the heir of a different type of estate. "Oh, I forgot you subscribed to the New Deal," would say the daughter of a laissez-faire liberal. "Don't tread on me and I won't tread on you." Or the devoted sister of a young man, who wrote abstruse poems, would reply blandly to the boy who had attacked the "cult of unintelligibility" in *The Harvard Advocate*, "*De gustibus*. I refuse to quarrel with you on that score."

I had acquired, through no endeavor of my own, the reputation of being "literary," and almost every Friday, I was approached by a Miss Hornblower or Coolidge (who the day before had failed to recognize me as we passed one another on the stairs of the Public Library) who would say, "I've been hearing the most interesting things about you. My mother, who is a dear friend of Miss Pride's, was telling me that you want to be a writer. Do tell me what you're writing, for I'm dying to hear." The notion, actually, was Miss Pride's own and was derived from an innocent statement I had once made to Admiral Nephews. He, because when I first met him I had recognized the passages of poetry he quoted, thought that I had the same taste in literature as his own, and he used to bring me, the moment he had finished with them, the novels he had borrowed from a lending library, and which I was obliged to read out of respect for his thoughtfulness. I had at last grown tired of pretending to share his enthusiasm for books that were barely plausible and were certainly not distinguished, and said of one I had just read, "No, sir, I do not think it is excellent. I could write a better one myself." This was not true, to be sure, and I did not say it with any intention of proving it, but the Admiral misconstrued my boast and acquired the conviction that I was secretly engaged in writing a book. He reported his suspicion to Miss Pride who did not bother to ascertain its truth and who henceforward told everyone that I was anxious to be a writer and even supported the fiction by such statements as, "But I know Sonie well enough to know that it won't go to her head. She's much too sensible to become one of your peculiar Bohemians." I felt like the person—the person we all are at some moment in our lives—who is asked to play the piano and who protests he does not know how, cannot tell one note from another, and who has never depressed a single key, but who is accused of false modesty and begged to run off just some simple piece. In vain the defendant repeats that he is ignorant, is let off with the threat: "Very well, but you won't get off so easily next time." To the girl who was dying to hear about my writing, I replied that she was mistaken, that I had no such lofty opinion of myself, and she would say, exactly like the hostess who swears she has often heard us play, "You writers are all alike. I suppose you won't even tell me where you publish your stories?"

The Countess, making the most of my imaginary calling, directed our conversation, during coffee, into literary channels and I sometimes found myself being posed a staggering question about French poetry, for example, on which I was said by our hostess to be an expert.

I was genuinely fond of the Countess and suffered considerable remorse after I had joined in Hopestill's laughter at her expense, just as I did when I listened, without protest, to trenchant comments on her aunt and on Philip McAllister. Nor had I any reason to suppose that I was not myself the object of that merciless judge of her peers, but on the contrary could fairly hear her say of me to Amy Brooks (as she had said of Amy Brooks to me), "She's such a *deliberate* fright." It was perhaps because of this sharp tongue that Hopestill did not get on well with other girls, like those, for instance, who came to the Countess'. She was not well liked and never had been. At school, she had broken rules, had been slovenly and disrespectful, and so lazy a student that she had failed to be graduated. At her début, one of the most lavish ever held at the Country Club (her grandfather had left twenty thousand dollars for this specific purpose), she had drunk so much champagne that she could remember no one's name, could barely dance in time to the music, and had been insufferably rude to several older people. She was, moreover, thought something of a slacker, because she had never sacrificed any of her time to "good works" and long after all the other girls, who had come out in the same season that she had, had dedicated themselves to nursing or visiting the poor or reading to blind old women, Hopestill continued to fritter away her time with all the indolent pleasures of the débutante. It had particularly annoyed her friends that she had steadfastly refused to take any part in canvassing for the Community Chest Fund but instead had "done her bit" by contributing a large check to the drive and putting the whole thing out of her mind.

Declaring that she found me a "relief" (I would have preferred to be a little more stimulating), she included me in most of her plans over the week-ends and shortly after our first meeting she proposed that she teach me how to ride. I had hesitated, fearful of the ludicrous figure I would cut on a horse, but she had been persistent and Miss Pride had welcomed the project with enthusiasm, for, as she said, "Anyone with your constitutional aversion to exercise must be *made* to exercise." And consequently we went to Concord each Saturday afternoon where I was slightly more competent than I had hoped. Philip had been as ardent a promoter of the lessons as Miss Pride to my slight resentment for I thought he regarded them as a therapeutic measure to distract me from thinking of my mother, something which I rarely did save on Sunday when I paid her my weekly visit. As a result of his interest, he arranged to have us change into our riding clothes at his grandmother's house and to have tea there when we came back from the stables. He nearly always joined us and drove us back to town.

The young man's gallantry was impartial even in Hopestill's presence and while I knew by the heightening of his color as he first caught sight of her that he was in love, he was no more attentive to her than he was to me. And I, having just come back from an expedition in which my performance had been at best tolerable and in which hers had been brilliant, was more nettled than if he had ignored me entirely. It was as if, on these occasions, he looked on me as an appendage to her. Curiously enough, I was conscious of being in love with him only when Hopestill came back to Boston. So long as she was in New York, I could hear his name spoken or even see him on the street or at tea without the slightest discomfort, but the moment Hopestill stepped into the house late Friday afernoon I was ignited with jealousy, made the more obstreperous because I knew she was not in the least in love with him. Particularly excruciating to me were some evenings when, Hopestill being otherwise engaged, he was asked to take me to the Countess' "Saturday" and while I had spent the whole afternoon in a state of tremulous anticipation, my pleasure ended as soon as he called for me. He was either too absent-minded to hear my answers to his questions or he assumed an avuncular manner, offering me the most banal and unwanted advice on how to converse with my mother. In either rôle, I sensed his dissatisfaction at not being with Hopestill.

On one clear February day, Hopestill persuaded the riding master to let us go alone. "I'll pay you double," she said. The man looked dubiously at me, one of his least accomplished customers, but Hopestill snapped, "What difference would it make if that wreck you foist off on my friend *did* break a leg? Besides, she doesn't go in for jumping." He reluctantly agreed and we set off. Ducking our heads, we cantered through the brushy bridle paths and then came out into the open russet fields. Hopestill ran her sorrel mare over a rise and down and out of sight; presently, far off, I saw her hair, sharp as a scream and sudden as a flame, fling up along the ridge and for a space it flew, bodiless and horseless like a burning bird. I sat on a flat rock under a wine-glass elm tree watching her, while my horse stood near-by with a languidly drooping head, as disinclined for exercise as I. This was the first time we had ridden since early in December for it had been too cold. Today there was sun and air as gentle as spring. It was like the day the year before when Miss Pride had come to take me in to Boston. There was little essential difference, I thought, between that version of myself who, shabby and with grimy fingernails, had sat bewildered in the gloomy library and this one, pranked out in costly jodhpurs, waiting in a cramped and uncomfortable position for my skillful friend to ride back. There was a gross and disquieting discrepancy between my expensive clothes and my luxurious pastime and my little brother's unmarked grave.

As I thought of Ivan, there returned to me the mood that had followed immediately on his death. It was a recollection, rather than a memory, a poetic farsight, a distillation of a feeling which was not watered down by physical details but was the dense experience of comprehending death. I did not envisage myself standing beside his cot nor did I, as I usually did when I thought of the scene, redeem the odor of the benzoin. It can be said that memory is a sort of *entrepôt* serving the busy traffic of the unreflective mind, and that its stores, behind an unlocked door, may be rummaged through and plundered at any time; thus I had found the footsteps of the old ladies walking in the sand at Chichester to match the lameness of Philip's grandmother in Miss Pride's drawing-room, and thus, also, confused by the music and by the stranger in the Countess' lobby, had brushed off the dust from a forgotten incident and by a misapplication of the styles of sensation, compared the music to the sunlight of that past day, and remembered *Regenpfeifer* because I had been addressed in German. But recollection, on the other hand, is in more formal custody, can be seen only at certain hours and those being far apart, the time of day or month or season being rarely, or not at all, repeated. Thus we say of people who were once in love that they cannot "recapture" their joy and the words "I was in love with that person" are an historical statement which may be attended by illustrations: a café visited by the lovers when they were in love, a railway carriage where they sat with arms entwined, a shop where they met one day by chance. So also, when one says, "I was ill at that time," memory shows him the mercury of the thermometer at 104 degrees, but neither the rapture nor the fever is revived. The essential has been extirpated, whereas it is the essential and only the essential that recollection values. Severe in its gleanings, it seeks to preserve our continuity: the old man recollects though his memory, we say, has failed.

With useless greed I tried to detain this temporary wisdom, this growing pain even when I heard the rush of Hopestill's horse's feet returning. But the sense of death was instantly annihilated by the sound. At the same time, the power that had generated the intense and total knowledge had not been all used up, and being unable, because the thing was finished, to repeat the process that had transported me to the past, I directed the residue towards an envious hatred of the girl who had now ridden into sight. It had occurred to me that if I were not obliged each week to compare myself to her, to my disadvantage in every particular, I would be appreciably more urbane than the chambermaid from the Barstow who had not known what to say when she was asked if she were an Anglophile. I could tell myself that Hopestill and I belonged to different species and should not, therefore, be judged by the same standards. But this was cold comfort. As she dismounted, I indulged myself in a feast of torment, taking in her green suède waistcoat under a silvery gabardine jacket, her slender legs in black breeches, her eloquent hair disordered by her ride to its benefit. I hated her the more for her good manners when she said, "I don't blame you for not coming. That bag of bones would drop dead of the shock if you made him run," because she perfectly well knew that I was afraid. We sat in silence for a few minutes. Hopestill lighted a cigarette and meditated the smoke.

"Are you going to Berthe's tonight?"

"Yes. Are you?"

She shook her head. "I'm going dancing."

I did not look forward to the evening. At the bottom of the Countess' invitation, a square of mellow vellum headed by a coat of arms instead of an address, the calligraphy of which was so elegant that the only decipherable symbols were the date and the hour (one could not possibly tell whether the guest of honor was to be a Belgian brain surgeon, an Italian poet, a Danish architect, or a Canadian bishop), she had written—this in a legible hand—"Nicholas Doman, charming, from Budapest, will call for you." I was tired of the young foreigners she "dug up" for me. Their difficulty with the language discouraged and then annoyed me as did the *Weltschmerz* that was a property common to all their eyes. Or, if they could speak well, I was irritated by another quality in them, one which I could not properly define: it was a staleness or a frustrated sensuality or a womanly tenderness, or perhaps all three that sounded in their voices, as if they were visiting an invalid surrounded by flowers that had withered but had not yet lost their fragrance. In the cushiony cocktail lounge of the Lincolnshire, over the yellow, arid popcorn and the dubonnet, rich, beautiful Gerhardt Preis, whom I had met by chance in the

Public Gardens, confided one afternoon in me that his ambitions were to live forever as a celibate (because he could not have Berthe von Happel) in a hotel in Paris and to write a book (he would give up music, inseparable from her) which would be the modern counterpart of Amiel's *Journal*. From his homeless, continental Jewish face emanated the odor of pomade. In the vestibule of Miss Pride's house, he kissed my hand and then withdrew into the dusk, stealing on his suave feet past Louisburg Square under the spiritless rain that had begun to fall. I was certain that Nicholas Doman from Budapest would not be as charming as the Countess testified. He would very likely be addicted, as most of her hangers-on were, to telling anecdotes in French.

I told Hopestill my dilemma. "Oh, well," she said, "you won't have to be stuck with him the whole evening. That's the beautiful thing about Berthe's parties, you can take your pick after dinner. Anyhow Philip will be there."

"Will he? After dinner you mean?" I said.

"Yes. Why, Sonie, you're blushing!"

I was not blushing. I had been too taken up with a plan to escape the Hungarian to care whether Philip came, but her accusation immediately elevated the temperature of my skin and my eyes began to smart.

"If you say so, I suppose I am," I said.

She laughed. "Why don't you skip dinner and go afterwards with him and avoid the Hungarian altogether?"

"I couldn't do that. But I'm very glad he's coming. At least he speaks English."

"And he's very fond of you, too." It was a serious statement and I could detect no ridicule in her voice. She put out her cigarette on the trunk of the tree. "You know, somebody like you would be good for Philip McAllister. He's a monkish bloke."

"Well, I'm not," I replied testily.

"Of course you are. If you weren't, would you have chosen to be buried alive in my Aunt Lucy's house?" And after a moment, as if to herself, "Jesus Christ! How you could do it I shall never know!"

"I'm satisfied," I told her.

"Oh, I know. And so is my aunt. Poor creature, she deserves some-

329

one like you after me. Have you noticed, by the way, how much we would like to murder each other these days?"

I had, indeed, noticed that the girl and her aunt had found it difficult to be anything more than civil. Arguments arose at the dinner table over such trifling matters as the advisability of giving the Countess a set of artichoke plates for her birthday which Miss Pride thought would be welcome, or an onyx deer that had caught Hopestill's eye. Or they railed at each other over the season of some cousin's marriage or another's début. Or Hopestill would contend that her aunt's salad dressing was unpalatable because it was made with lemon instead of wine vinegar. Often I was called upon to settle a dispute. Invariably I agreed with Miss Pride out of cowardice, and while she readily used me as a court of appeal, she sometimes forgot, in her periodic scoldings, that I had settled an argument which otherwise might have gone on indefinitely, and she told me that she was by no means flattered at my constant agreement with her opinions. "I am an old woman," she said once, "and it has taken me many years to develop my prejudices and my affinities. It is nothing short of impertinence in you to adopt them without doing any of the work." Now on the other hand, Hopestill frequently expressed her gratitude: "If you hadn't settled on the artichoke plates, we would have gone on quibbling for weeks."

"We've disliked each other more since you came," continued Hopestill. "But I suppose that's reasonable. Do you know what is making my aunt's blood boil now? She's afraid Philip is interested in you and she's perfectly wild that I'm not doing anything about it."

"Oh, drop it," I cried and got to my feet.

"As you say," she agreed, shrugging her shoulders. But she was not content to remain silent long and when we had got back to the bridle path, she said, "Really, I was quite serious when I said some one like you would be good for McAllister." Her use of his surname unaccountably put me at my ease and I asked her why. "Well, I'm sure I don't know if you're religious in the least, but you have a nice sort of tranquillity about you that might turn into piety. Philip's bound to get religion sooner or later and I'd be the worst kind of wet blanket. I'm like Aunt Lucy: I think of God as a great big man."

I laughed aloud for what she said was so absurdly precise. It was quite true that Miss Pride thought of God as a big man Who had, in misty times, drawn up the Ten Commandments, and about Whom it was in bad taste as well as half sacrilegious to talk. She had towards Him the same attitude as she had towards the figures of literature, save those who had died in her lifetime. They wore the same antediluvian halo which, if seen in the cold light of Boston, would have struck one as pretentious. And so, although it was fitting for one to have an acquaintance with God and with Milton, it was not proper to display more than the merest courtesy towards them. It was acceptable to discuss a literary person (or a religious one) to whose name could be affixed the title "Mr." Thus, Miss Pride spoke of "Mr. James" whom she had met several times and of "Mr. Emerson" and "Mr. Lowell" (she had caught a glimpse of these latter two when she was seven years old); but as no one knew anything about "Mr. Dryden" or "Mr. Goldsmith" it was best not to speak too cordially of them. God was no more adaptable. With no intention of disparaging her, I presented this observation to Hopestill and she agreed with an amiable laugh.

"Yes, God and Shakespeare frighten her half to death. I think that's why she's so bent on making you out a literary person. She can't ignore literature but wants it homemade and by someone she can eat dinner with. She tried very hard once to know Amy Lowell, but she never succeeded."

My disappointment at this statement was less than my surprise, for I had conceived Boston society as so closely knit that it was as strange that two members of it were not acquainted as it would have been if La Grande Mademoiselle had not known Madame de Maintenon.

By the time we had reached the elder Mrs. McAllister's house, I had recovered from my choleric attack and could look on Hopestill with equanimity. Fortified also with the knowledge that I could not possibly fare too ill at the Countess' that evening since Philip would be there by himself, I was almost buoyant.

The old lady always kept us waiting for at least a quarter of an hour in the library after we had been announced. Then, the rustle of her black skirts and the tap of her cane apprised us of her arrival and we stood up as she, after a formal, "Good afternoon, young ladies.

I hope you enjoyed your ride," sat down in a chintz wing chair under a portrait of her husband for whom she still wore mourning, though he had been dead for twenty years. She had no sooner put her feet on the chair's matching stool than she said, as if it had just occurred to her, "What do you say to a cup of tea? Perhaps they'll have something in the dining-room for us. My grandson promised to call on me this afternoon and I must have tea for him, you know."

Philip's grandfather had one time been headmaster of a school so imitative of Eton and Harrow that the whole house spoke with a British accent. It had been Mrs. McAllister's custom, in his lifetime, to have a "day" for chosen boys and because often as many as forty had dropped in, she had entertained them at an immensely long table in the dining room. Although now there were never more than half a dozen people to be served, twenty chairs were in readiness and as many cups stood before the tea urn. We were fed the simple food the boys had been fed: gingerbread squares, small sweet buns, and English muffins. On the preposterous plea that she could not handle "them all" by herself, she always placed Hopestill at the opposite end of the table so that the poor exile's voice barely carried to us, while I was seated on her right ("I never have time to get really acquainted with this young lady") and Philip on her left ("So that he can fetch and carry for me.").

Hopestill spoke of the old lady's "closed door" policy while the one employed by her daughter, Philip's mother, was the "open trap." The younger Mrs. McAllister joined us today a few minutes after we had taken our places. Her pretty, submissive face was framed with white hair, the overnight acquisition at the time her son fell ill of infantile paralysis. After kissing her mother and nodding politely to me, she went at once to Hopestill whose two hands she clasped as she cried, "How glad I am to see you! Here, let me feast on that exquisite frock. Who but Hope Mather would think of bottle-green velveteen this year when the rest of us are all in navy blue?"

Hope, complimenting her in turn on her hat, exchanged an amused glance with Philip while his grandmother said, "Bottle-green is very nice. Marian, would you look at this child's nautical costume. I swear she robbed Admiral Nephews for her buttons. Why, they're the real thing."

Her daughter nodded and turned again to Hopestill. "When are you going to let me have the honor of supplying you with a dressing room? I do think you're unkind to give my mother *all* the pleasure. I have three rooms that are never in use, and if you'd only consent I could have more than these five-minute glimpses of you. I'll tell you frankly that if I once got you, I'd kidnap you for a whole week-end."

Philip, knowing that his mother would make use of such an opportunity to satisfy so completely any curiosity the girl might have about him that she would never want to hear his name mentioned again, hastily interposed, "But, Mother, they would have to be driven from the station then, for they couldn't possibly walk to our house and the walk to Grandma's, as I understand it, is part of the expedition." Both Hope and I confirmed him, but his mother was stubborn.

"Does anyone have a more selfish son?" she cried. "Really, Philip, one would think you were afraid I intended to blacken your character." This, of course, was precisely what she would have done, by going into his inconstancy, his hypersensitivity about his back, his egotism, his carelessness, by exhibiting his ugly baby pictures, by telling damning anecdotes, by resurrecting instances of his devotion to herself and attempting, in the light of the latter, to make Hopestill realize that she must play second fiddle to her if the marriage ever came off.

The conversation, passing beyond the skirmish of wits, became general. Philip, casting a studious glance upon me who did not participate, said, "You must have given Sonie a run for her money today, Hope. She's got the wind knocked out of her."

"Oh, on the contrary," she replied with a laugh, "she gave me a run for mine." And she began to praise my horsemanship and to deplore my horse, inventing a fantastically untrue account of my bold jumping and running which I was too dumfounded to deny. Old Mrs. McAllister patted my hand, said she could tell by my appearance that I could manage any horse, called upon her grandson to agree that I was the very picture of a healthy athlete, hoping to embarrass Hopestill who, though she was sound as a dollar, looked frail, and had chosen, instead of normal pleasures, the ugly affectation of the bluestocking. "I think you're very wise, Sonia," she said.

333

"Why on earth our Hopestill wants to waste her youth and ruin her complexion investigating people's nightmares I will never understand. And as for 'repressions' and 'sublimations' and so on, I think the least said about them the better. Goodness only knows we have serpents enough in our gardens without importing any more."

The iciness of Hopestill's smile was lost on her half blind hostess as she replied, "But, Mrs. McAllister, all of us are not so fortunate as you. My own garden was swarming with serpents when I first stepped into it."

Philip's mother, leaning toward her, cried, "You clever thing! You know how to get the better of my mother! Tell me, Hope, what sort of thing do you *do?*"

"Oh, I . . ." For the first time since I had known her, I saw Hopestill hesitate. Momentarily she averted her eyes as she jerkily returned her teacup to its saucer. Then, with a smile, she explained, "I'm not studying formally, you see, but with a psychiatrist. I see his patients and study their case histories and so on."

"What kind of patients are they, Hope?" pursued the woman. "I'm really ever so interested."

"Well, my man is rather fashionable and most of his patients are idle women who don't like their husbands for one reason or another or else don't have husbands and think they'll go off the deep end if they keep on living alone."

Old Mrs. McAllister snorted gustily. "And what's the cure, eh?"

"They're analyzed, of course, and Dr. Ragsdale gives them things to distract them. Ice-skating, knitting, growing herbs in the kitchen window."

Philip's grandmother was silent with disgust and then, in order to hear no more of Hopestill's nonsense which she was pouring out by request to her companion, she turned to Philip and said loudly, "I want you to give your father a talking-to, Perly. He's set on selling the Bedford Road house. I would as soon cut off my hand as see it taken over by a stranger."

"And so would I," said the young man in sincere alarm. "What gave him that idea?"

"I can't imagine," returned the old lady. "But between ourselves, I have never felt your father had much sense of history." Philip whispered, "You have never felt he had much sense of any kind, have you, Grandma?" But Mrs. McAllister was not going to agree to such a judgment of her son in my presence, and she went on. "I have always wanted *you* to have the house when you marry. Did you see the enchanting little water-color Amy Brooks did of it for me last autumn?" Then, turning to me, "You must make Philip take you to see it some day this spring. You will not find a more charming place in all New England."

The conversation at the far end of the table was lagging. Hopestill, getting up, said, "We must go to see the house some afternoon. It's my aunt Lucy's favorite next to her own on Pinckney." She directed to me an ambiguous smile which I took to mean that she had not quite made up her mind to relinquish Philip altogether, but that she would let me know in good time if I might go alone with him to inspect the house.

"You three," said the younger Mrs. McAllister, "you three are inseparable, aren't you?" I knew by her tone and by the look of injury on her turned-down lips that she liked me no better than she did Hopestill.

"We are separating now," said Hope. "But Philip and Sonie will meet again at the Countess'."

As I was taking leave of my hostesses, Philip and Hopestill went into the hallway to get our coats. When I started out to join them, lingering at the door a moment to receive a final compliment upon my robust health from the old lady, I heard Philip saying, "I don't need a procuress."

## 2

The Countess' "Saturday" was a formal dinner party for rarely more than ten, followed by a soirée at which one met chiefly Germans and Austrians who had had the foresight to leave (and in some instances, to leave with their money) in the early days of Hitler's regime. There were, in addition, titled personages from other parts of the world: a Korean prince, a Russian baron, a Polish count. The Bostonians who came were either charmed by the illustrious company or outraged, the latter group maintaining that "these refugees" were impertinent and arrogant because they had the crust to criticize the

United States and even, with supreme bad manners, to imply that it was only through luck, not through wisdom, that we were not ourselves ruled by a Hitler or a Stalin.

The dinner, consisting of many courses, was served by two fat, frowning Alsatian matrons, while the wines were poured by a little Hawaiian houseboy, employed, the Countess acknowledged, because he was decorative. Otherwise, he had almost no qualifications and cried a good deal for a female monkey named Lilioukalani whom he had had to leave behind. Three bitches, a schnauzer, a Doberman, and a boxer, paced the floor beneath the table or stood between two chairs, gazing first at one guest until her wish was granted and he threw her a morsel from his plate, and then at the other until he likewise succumbed to the plea in the piteous eyes. Miss Pride who, characteristically enough, liked dogs "in their place" almost never accepted an invitation to dine with the Countess, but if she did, she overlooked the dogs as one would overlook a foreign object in the dessert. Unfortunately they were particularly attracted to her because she carried with her the odor of her cat, Mercy, and during the soup, when they had no pressing business in other quarters, the three of them clustered about her legs sniffing. Her aplomb was admirable: as she drank her soup, crumbled her bread, and listened to the man from the Rhineland who was interested in guilds, it was not apparent that a debate was going on within her, whether to kick the brutes once and for all or to endure.

As soon as the gentlemen joined us, the door-bell commenced to ring and rang at intervals until well past eleven o'clock, bringing to us fortunate ten, a varied assortment of entertainers. Our hostess, immense and blazing in a diamond tiara and a cloth-of-gold gown which sheathed her ample flesh like hide and of which the central interest was a green orchid growing out of her mountainly bust, stirred her guests about, dispatching me to a Norwegian painter, Edward Pingrey to a cloth merchant from Berlin, Mrs. Hornblower to a young Puerto Rican of ambassadorial connections whom, unfortunately, it was easy to confuse with the houseboy. We were not allowed to remain long on any assignment. The Norwegian woman and I would just be establishing a communication of sorts after several false beginnings, when the Countess would descend: "You two charmers mustn't monopolize each other! Sonie, go speak to that woman over there, the dark one, Frau Gross. She's perishing to meet you. You're much alike—imaginative, *spirituelle*. She's a little deaf." Frau Gross, more like her name than the Countess' description of her, had not wanted to meet me, did not know my name, had not, in fact, ever seen me before and could hear nothing of what I said. In this enforced rotation one could hear conversations on German air-power, on French food, on Roman relics in England, on American politics, on European and tropical diseases, on coin collections, on train travel in the interior of China.

If one flatly refused to talk, being stricken tonight with one of those moods of taciturnity that visit us all, the Countess suggested cards in the library. It was not too happy a substitute, for she forbade such banal games as bridge or hearts, allowed only recondite or obsolescent ones like omber, loo, piquet. It was nearly always my bad luck, if I were sent to "make up a table," to find Baron Kalenkoff and one other person preparing a deck for omber, the most bewildering of all the games. The Baron, a handsome, well-tailored man in his thirties, a cosmopolitan and sycophant of wealthy women, was, as someone said, a "rattlesnake" at cards. He had, in addition to that acumen known as "card sense," such perennial luck that his adversaries regarded him with suspicion, not as a shark, for he was clearly a gentleman, but as the darling of some prodigal goddess whose invisible fingers distributed the cards in such a way as to make him invariably win. Now the only two people who had mastered the rules of omber were the Baron and the Countess and of course the latter did not play on her Saturdays. Consequently, the two of us who were obliging the Russian floundered in terminology without having the slightest idea of the procedure and lost all our money, sometimes a very considerable amount as the Baron liked high stakes. I might learn the "basto" and the "spadille" and the "matadors" of one trump by the end of a hand, but my knowledge was useless in the next when a different trump was named. It did not bore the Baron at all to play with fuddled opponents. On one occasion the nightmare lasted three hours and a half and was only concluded because supper was announced.

After that calamitous evening (poor Mr. Pingrey and I each lost fifteen dollars and I had to borrow money from the Countess), I did not go any more to the library, no matter how indisposed I was to chat with the Korean prince who had acquired the remarkable notion that I was an ardent student of pre-dynastic Chinese bone inscriptions, on which he was an expert.

I remained in the large drawing-room, the setting for our ballet. It was furnished with the gleaming surfaces and floral furbelows of Louis Quinze, whimsically repeating the colors and the materials of the costume of the *première danseuse:* if she had chosen pale blue, it was to set off the chairs upholstered in azure satin or the skies in the murals inspired by Boucher and executed by a young relative whom she had sent home at once as soon as he had finished. Another night, as if the looped draperies at the wide bay-window had not been admired enough, the Countess appeared in a dress of olive velvet and remarked, "I got the idea from my windows, as you see." There was a profusion of bare marble infants attached by their umbilica to the central support of gilt tables, or sprouting from the center of their curly heads bronze candelabra with a dozen sockets, or standing in pairs on the tops of cabinets bathing one another or posing as if for leap-frog or simply peeking at space with their stone eyes. It particularly irritated Miss Pride that two spurious Watteaus hung on either side of the fireplace where formerly, when the first Mrs. Brooks had been alive, there had been a genuine Trumbull on the right and on the left a stuffed twelve-pound trout from New Brunswick, caught by Ralph Brooks at the age of nine.

This evening, Baron Kalenkoff at once set about to recruit five gulls for loo, among them Nicholas Doman who offered me effusive apologies in several Continental tongues. Out of the corner of my eye, I observed the approach of the Korean prince and fearing that if I were cornered by him, I would miss Dr. McAllister I cast about for an escape. To my relief, I saw Miss Pride entering with a young man whom I had seen here several times before, and I hastened to her.

"Your admirer is downcast," she said, nodding in the direction of the prince. (She had no use for any race but the Caucasian and she believed that no one these days was a prince and that no one would be until a son was born to the English king.) "Where Berthe finds them all one will never know."

The young Jew at her side gazed about the room with a supercilious detachment. "From an employment agency, no doubt," he said.

Miss Pride, regarding his witticism as inappropriate, gave him a lacerating stare. "And what is it you do, sir?" she inquired.

Several times I had been seated next to the boy at dinner and each time had experienced a pleasurable shock at the resemblance he bore to Nathan Kadish. He was intelligent and insolent, and his voice had in it the same overstimulated quickness that had my friend's. But I had always found in him something lacking but which I could not name. He seemed, despite his carefully composed effrontery, entirely innocent, like a hornet that has been disarmed. Tonight, a trifle not only showed me why I had never struck up more than the most formal acquaintance with him, but restored a scene in Chichester just as earlier in the day I had recovered Ivan's death. A girl passed by and a breath of her lilac scent loitered in the air. The fragrance brought to my mind the last time I had seen Nathan and what I had said to him: "I love your birthmark," but the words reverberated now with a new undertone and with the addition of two other words which had been elided, that is, "I love *you for* your birthmark." And I knew then that all that had fascinated me in Nathan was his disfigurement, solely that, for I had never felt protective of him, had desired more than anything else to touch, examine, and discuss what was taboo. This self-revelation so appalled me that with a rudeness equivalent to that of Miss Pride's companion, I abruptly turned as he was in the middle of a sentence addressed to me, and offering no explanation, walked away to a deserted corner of the room, where I stood, faking a brown study so that I would not be disturbed, as horrified at my sinister nature as if I had found the marks of a vampire on my throat. (On the following day, Miss Pride, never dreaming of the reason why I had gone away, congratulated me on my resolute principles—for she assumed that I had been offended by his insolence which, in her fervor, she believed was incarnate in all Jews—saying, "I would have done the same. Courtesy to a discourteous Jew is beating one's head against a stone wall. And

339

yet I, despite my strong feelings, could never have done what you did.") And I wondered if I would have coveted Philip McAllister if he had not been deformed. Dizzied by this symptom of an abnormal and somewhat repulsive nature in myself, I felt the need to be reassured, but paradoxically, the only person who could reassure me was Philip himself. The moment I had formulated the speech I would make to him when I asked his advice, I realized that I was really not in the least troubled by my perverse taste in men, that I had only been seeking an excuse to occupy his attention with my problems. I suppose that I was determined to be in love at whatever cost.

The Countess was surrounded by her guests who were pleading with her to play for them. The Korean prince had attached himself to Miss Pride and was no doubt lecturing her on bone inscriptions. No one noticed me as I left the room, picking up as I went out, a "fine" edition of Heine's poems, the sort of book to be found all over the house, expensive, delightful to the touch, kept pliable and burnished by a man who came to oil them twice a year. Reconnoitering at the foot of the stairs, I heard nothing save the voices above me, muffled into one, monotonous and fluid, and the occasional chime of metal from the subterranean kitchen. Then I sat primly down on the yellow sofa, letting the book fall open where a red ribbon marked a former reader's place. It was then that I was ashamed of coming down so frankly to waylay Philip, for, although I could not understand the poem, certain phrases, ironic, overharsh out of their context, stood out and served to dismantle me and the room of our reality, so that the lurching shadows, brandished by the candles, the histrionic portrait, the off-beat of my heart like a mis-set metronome became the properties of something third-rate and sentimental: I was like the hoydenish girl growing into womanhood who finds the foretaste of maturity cloying, drives back her unwilling body, partially relaxed in the bud of the bloom, to tomboy pranks. I wanted to get up from the sofa and go back to the drawing-room, but I did not move and told myself that it was absurd to regret what had not happened, that in all likelihood I would do nothing regrettable, but that it would be a test of my strength to remain.

The door-bell rang. I heard the butler pad out of the dining-room and his "Good evening, Dr. McAllister. You'll find them in the drawing-room." I had risen and could see, along the wall, his un-accompanied shadow advancing toward the turn in the lobby. My self-denial, in the half-second before we were face to face, held me poised, but when he had stepped around the corner, my resolve col-lapsed because the thought that came to me was not, "He has come at last," but "He has come alone for the first time," and I was less conscious of his presence than I was of Hopestill's absence. Thus, when I stepped forward, my gesture was annihilatory, was the action of jealousy so unreasonable and eyeless that neither love for him nor hate for her entered as items in its muddled contents. I stood, an awkward girl of nineteen, with one hand holding the book opened to "Enfant Perdu" and the other grasping the young man's shoulder, and I imprinted on his mouth a lightning-paced and pastoral kiss. There was not, as I wished, a pit of impenetrable darkness to receive me. I tottered back a step and let my hand fall from Philip's shoul-der. As if to steady me, he took my hand and I was again propelled towards him while, by way of recognition, he spoke my name, or as by way of prelude, admonitory or consoling, of the kiss with whose ruthless luxury he sought to shake the flesh from my bones. Its abrupt urgency was unmodified, but, like a sudden shaft of blinding light cast by a random luminary, it revealed to us both a principle, a basic form as simple, as abstract as the line between two points. We stepped apart, prepared to partition and bury the sheer serpent. He continued to hold my dry and bloodless hand.

Neither of us spoke, and I, glad that the incident was over and taking his silence as a token that what had just passed between us was not to be incorporated into our relationship (that, being an accident, it deserved neither apology nor analysis), started toward the stairs. But Philip detained me. "We'll go in together," he said.

"Oh, I think we shouldn't," I replied. "Miss Pride is here to-night."

"She doesn't own you. She certainly doesn't own me."

I was uneasy when we entered the drawing-room together, certain that the hubbub in my mind would be visible in my face. Miss Pride, still listening courteously to the Korean, missed nothing, but turned upon us those yellow and accomplished eyes which accused me of committing an outrage. I looked away but Philip returned her stare and said to me, "The effect was just what I wanted."

Miss Pride, scrupulously faithful to her word, did not deprive me of companionship. From time to time, she summoned to dinner a group of people near my own age who, although they were well-born and well-educated, did not belong, and never would, to her sphere, but to a frustrated imitation of it. The young men, who showed by their faces and their manners that they came from good families, revealed by their clothes that they were not well off, while the girls, students for the most part from Radcliffe, had sublimated their natural longings for dress and parties into a defiant intellectuality, terrifying to someone like myself. The dinner parties were formal and while we were having our cocktails and elaborate canapes in the drawing-room, Miss Pride, grouping us together, attempted to break down the barriers between herself and them and between them and me. And if she succeeded at all and with the help of the Martinis we were talking with a minimum of restraint, our discomfort immediately returned when she, our only leaven, set down her glass and announced, "And now I'm going to leave you to yourselves. You won't want to be bored by an old woman. As my father used to say, no Utopia can destroy the aristocracy of years and the older one grows the more inferior one's caste. Good evening, I must hurry on to my fellow plebeians." She left us. A quarter of an hour elapsed before dinner was served and the cocktail shaker was empty. As she had not commissioned me to refill it, I dared not go back to the pantry in the fear that the vermouth and gin had already been put away and that I would return empty-handed, unable to explain my failure to my guests. A hush then fell upon us and continued through dinner. The young men joined us before half past nine and by ten everyone had gone home. Ashamed, disconcerted by the erudition of the college women who had been discussing Hegel's antinomies, the *Faerie Queen,* and *La Grande Jatte,* I went up to my room to drug myself with typewriter practice.

But because I did not wish to appear ungrateful or incapable of acting as a hostess, I said nothing when Miss Pride planned another of these exhausting fiascos. And since she was a friend of their families, her recruits rarely failed to accept her invitations, usually issued over the telephone to their mothers. Certain that she had pleased me and furthered my interests, she remarked once to the Admiral who had inquired how I put in my time, "Why, she keeps a regular salon to which only the cream of the intelligentsia is bidden. I don't stay among them, they're so formidable, so I always arrange to have other fish to fry. I wouldn't like them to find out what a dunce I am."

It was difficult to reconcile her selection of my friends with her antipathy to "braininess" for these young people had nothing if they had not that. And if she hoped to launch me on a social career which would not interfere with her other plans for me but would satisfy the natural demands of my youth, she was doomed to failure. They were all too busy, too ambitious, and too learned to seek me out, but it did not seem to occur to Miss Pride that it was strange I never received a return invitation.

I easily divined that the principal reason for her supervision of my social life was that she wished to distract me from thinking about Philip. She was not, of course, protecting me from disappointment but was looking out for Hopestill's interests, or rather, for the interests she devoutly desired the girl to have. I had heard from the Countess that the doctor had the reputation of being not only fickle but catholic in his love affairs, and just the year before had been all but engaged to a nurse from Nova Scotia in the Salem hospital whom he had boldly introduced in Boston even though she had, said the Countess, "the table manners of a Bavarian, the opinions of a barbarian, and the looks of a Paphian." It was true that she had been only a passing fancy and as soon as he had broken with her, Philip had fallen in love with Hope all over again as he had done each time he had strayed away. Just as he had often threatened to abandon medicine and become an astronomer or a carpenter or a Trappist monk but always returned to his profession with renewed enthusiasm, so he had invariably come back to Hope after an excursion in another quarter. While it was Miss Pride's belief (relayed to me by the Countess who did not dream, of course, that I had more than the merest interest in the doctor) that he would never marry unless he married her niece, she viewed with trepidation any symptoms in him of infatuation with another girl.

Although she did not mention his name to me and made no comment on the incident at the Countess', her campaign was perfectly apparent. She made a point of never inviting Philip to her house unless Hopestill was there, of always going to the Countess' when he was my partner and on such occasions of taking me home in her own car, of taking any telephone messages from him to me, even though I was at home, on the pretext that I was busy studying my bookkeeping or my shorthand. He, on his part, was delighted to have a chance to tease her and all during the spring telephoned me almost every day, requesting her to tell me that he would meet me "as usual" at the Lincolnshire or that he would pick me up the following day at Mrs. Hinkel's. The messages were never delivered and he, of course, had not meant them seriously, but Miss Pride arranged to have me run an errand at the hour he had named and, in order to make sure that I was obeying her, telephoned my destination to give me a further commission.

I could have told her that her precautions were needless. We did meet surreptitiously but it was only their secrecy that made our evenings together more entertaining than those I spent with Miss Pride's academicians. We met once every two weeks in the Union Oyster House where, in an atmosphere of sawdust and the acrid rot of crustaceans' shells, Philip was by turns courtly and brusque, but neither the one nor the other to any degree that would have told me how he thought of me. Nor did I, indeed, know how I thought of him. It was as if both of us were engaged in a pursuit of phantoms. We parted formally at the door of Miss Pride's house, but in our short lingering there was a mutual inquiry as if we had seen for an instant that which we desired but which distrust immediately obliterated. We were like blind men who, through some somatic perspicacity, can accurately judge spatial relationships and sense the presence of someone in the room but cannot, without the assistance of their hearing or their touch, know who it is. So we were at once the blind men and were the coy creatures who would not speak and would not offer up their faces or their hands for the expert, identifying touch. Or we were amateurs after nightfall in a terrain we did not know, hearing the hounds bay their triumph; to our untrained ears the sound of these fanatics might come from any direction, and we stumbled, parting company, running this way and that, encouraged by the nearness of the sound which in the next moment was miles away. At last we were to find the captive in its dog-rimmed tree, the coon peering suddenly with its owlish eyes, the clever possom faking sleep; we had known this was the quarry, this quaint and useless beast, but we were disappointed, resented our fatigue and chill, wondered why hunters and dogs night after night returned to the woods for the absurd quest. But going back the way we came, we did not voice our foolish grief, merely commented on the sky and its omens for the next day's weather.

I would afterwards lie sleepless for hours in the double envelope of darkness and quiet. Sometimes my thoughts wandered to other things, but they returned to what most tantalized them, bringing back from the impersonal world, prosaic crusts by which to compare their banquet. I would consider Miss Pride, asleep on the floor below me, as stark as an effigy while Mercy, whom I had never seen, toured the room on considerately noiseless feet. Or I stared at the grove of sharp iron spikes outside my window to keep the pigeons away, like a full quiver in the arc light. Hearing the impatient whistle of a train about to depart, I thought of how, if it were leaving from the North Station, it would pass by Walden Pond and Concord. If it were leaving from the South Station, it would go towards New York, that unimaginable foreign country from which Hopestill dutifully returned each week-end. And I would ponder her in whom there was at work a ferment which neither Philip nor I could analyze. It was more, he said, than a love affair. She would not come back to Boston so faithfully every Friday afternoon if it were only that. Her whole life there was a secret she guarded so jealously that she had refused even to list her address in the *Social Register*. She gave no apparent signs of restlessness. We continued to go to Concord to ride and she as adroitly tortured the McAllister ladies as she had always done. The altercations between her and her aunt were a little more frequent but not much fiercer. But I knew, from our vague and slightly drunken conversations on Friday nights and from our sparse talk on the train back from Concord that she was on bad terms with herself.

For there was no longer the camaraderie between us which had allowed us to gossip, to communicate on the same level. The Countess' musical afternoons did not amuse her, nor did she welcome any of my observations on her aunt's friends which heretofore she had relished, saying, "It takes an outlander to trap us alive." We talked now and again of a book, or in a desultory way Hope would tell me of an encounter in a Harlem night-club. There was thus apparently no more between us than between two people whiling away an hour in a train by means of a spotty conversation. At the same time, there was a bond of sorts between us which, although she did not know it, went back to the day when I, a little girl, had first learned that she lived in this house. Sometimes, against my will, my eyes were drawn to the portrait of her as a child. Once, seeing my contemplation of its delicate and sentimental color, she said, "I was really a nasty little proposition although I look so winsome there. But what child wouldn't be nasty who grew up in this place?"

I was infected both by Hopestill's furtive trouble and by Philip's capriciousness and had it not been for Miss Pride's reliably unchanging manner, would have probably given way to a dangerous dissatisfaction. She, I was sure, had no idea that my life did not satisfy me in every particular. She herself was so pleased with my progress that she invited me to live with her again the following year. Indeed, she declared, she hoped I would take up permanent residence on Pinckney Street. She regretted that she could not offer me her hospitality for the summer, but could instead provide me with a splendid opportunity to put into practice my stenographic training. I was to work in her soap factory in Cambridge, an arrangement which everyone except myself regarded with the greatest enthusiasm. The plan was generally thought to be my own idea and Miss Pride would say to her friends, "Sonie is the cleverest person here. No summer stupor for her: she has got herself a job, mind you, and while the rest of us are loafing, she will be earning money." Only the Admiral expressed doubts. "Why, child," he said, "won't you be lonesome?"

I was extremely lonesome. Philip had gone back to Chichester, and all the people I had met at Miss Pride's or at the Countess' had left for the Cape or the North Shore. It was too hot to read. My furnished bedroom on Kirkland Street was under the roof and the air was motionless all night. I lay naked on the bare floor, the sweat tickling my legs and back like flies' feet and, stupefied, I thought of nothing. It was, in this season, almost a pleasure to visit my mother. Although the trip was complicated, including three stages, by bus, by subway, and again by bus, I made it with a sort of martyred delight. As I sat in the crowded subway train, nudged by people carrying fading flowers and boxes of cake to their Sunday hostesses, or fanning their streaming faces with the Boston *Globe,* or swaying half asleep from the heat, I was more at ease than I had ever been in Miss Pride's house. At ease, even though at the end of the torpid journey there was neither rest nor entertainment, but the disinfected madhouse where I sat with Mamma, bored, sleepy but required to be on my guard each moment.

On the few unseasonable evenings when a languid breeze stirred the papers on my writing table and my pores stopped gushing, I wrote letters to Philip and to Hopestill and to Miss Pride, but only the last did I ever mail. On the way home from the letter box, I would stop and buy a bottle of sherry and once again in my character-less room would steep myself in the harsh, unpalatable wine and stare gloomily at the crabbed, complaining lines I had written to the people I could not fathom, yet could not ignore.

# 3

The second autumn in Boston differed from the first only in that we had begun the memoirs. We worked each morning except Sunday from the time our consultation with the servants ended until luncheon was announced, but for all our diligence we proceeded at such a snail's pace that I saw we had before us a labor of many years, and I wondered if the final product would be worth it. For Miss Pride, shrewd, witty, and fluent in conversation, was inarticulate when she began to write. The juvenility of her diction and the crudity of her syntax surprised me, for her few letters to me had been as elegant as her speech. After floundering for some months with no success, we at last hit upon a plan. She would write me a letter, very care-fully in the style of Horace Walpole, of whom she was an assiduous student, which begged me to set down in "sound English" the anecdote which she then wrote out in her tumid language. As her calligraphy was obscure (not intentionally, as the Countess von Happel's was, but because she wrote in the heat of passion), it often took me a full morning to decipher a single sentence and in a short time my desk bore a formidable sheath of manuscript which I had not transcribed or edited. Thus, all morning we worked facing one another at two long desks which had been pushed together.

Hopestill came home less often than she had done the year before and when she did come, I rarely saw her. We discontinued our evenings in her room and our rides in Concord. She was apparently so uninterested in anyone in Boston that she preferred her own society and during her visits kept to her room, emerging only for meals. Gradually she became for me no more than a ghost, one belonging in a way to Chichester, and I was free at last of any envy of her. Her clothes, if they were more spectacular, were no more expensive than mine; if I did not have Philip McAllister's whole heart, as she had had it at various times in her life, I had his constant companionship which even Miss Pride had been forced to recognize and tolerate. In my good fortune, I could afford to pity her for her misanthropy, and for the solitude in which she inexplicably had immersed herself. It was therefore the more startling that we again came together without warning and with most savage intimacy.

Philip had not waited even long enough for a cup of tea, but had only come to arrange to call for me at dinner-time. We were going later to the Countess'. The business had been transacted within earshot of Miss Pride intentionally, and while she made no alternative suggestion, she said with great displeasure, "I hoped you would have dinner with me. Now I shall be all alone." Philip gave her a smile. "She needs a change of air every now and again, you know."

The younger Mrs. McAllister had been Christmas shopping and declared when she came in that the only thing which had relieved the tedium of the task was the prospect of a "reviving chat with Lucy Pride." She had, however, after a perfunctory, albeit effusive, salutation to her hostess, immediately sought out Amy Brooks and the two of them had sat, heads together, on the sofa where Amy was in the habit of holding court for Mr. James and Mr. Pingrey. Philip paid his brief compliments to his mother and left the room. I went to the window and saw him for a moment hesitating before he went down the street. I was surprised to see that he was wearing a bowler today and that he carried a stick, for usually his dress was of the most casual. I experienced a moment of peculiar distaste for him as I watched his grotesquely military bearing in which, it seemed to me, I had sensed a new element.

Half an hour after he had gone, Hopestill made an entrance into the drawing-room, pausing as she had done the first time I saw her, at the tulip wood commode to reconnoiter and to determine which of the guests after her aunt deserved her first greeting. She was dressed in green moiré, the severity of which did not check her flaming beauty but struggled with it in a magnificent combat, so that her sudden appearance in the doorway, unexpected, was like a chivalric, plangent war brought to our quiet gathering.

"Why, Hope!" cried Miss Pride. "I didn't expect you for ten days."

"I know," laughed her niece. "It was to be a surprise, Auntie. You're glad, I trust?"

Because she had never before "surprised" her aunt with a visit, the old lady looked questioningly at her, but smiled and said, "Delighted."

When she had kissed Miss Pride and the Admiral, Hopestill crossed the room to Philip's mother who, on seeing her, cried out, "Oh, how glad I am I dropped in today! I never dreamed you'd be here. Philip will be wild when he knows he missed you. He just this minute left."

"It's nice of you to say that he'll be 'wild,' Mrs. McAllister. But since Amy was here I imagine he had quite a full enough afternoon without me."

Mrs. McAllister bit her lip in vexation. Philip had only nodded to Amy. Moreover, Amy had dropped a few remarks that had intimated at a romantic attachment to Edward Pingrey. I had heard Mrs. McAllister say, "But, Amy, he's not really your sort of person, do you think so? I'm extremely taken with Edward, as we all are, but he has never really belonged to your set . . . to yours and Philip's, that is." Amy ingenuously replied, "Why, Philip and I don't belong to the same set at all. I believe he thinks I'm unconventional." Her giggles commenced and drowned out the older woman's next speech.

Now, unwittingly nettling Mrs. McAllister, she said to Hopestill, "He snubbed me completely. He only came to make a rendezvous with Sonie."

"Ah," said Hope, glancing in my direction. But she turned again to her cousin. "I like your dress, Amy." She could not suppress a smile for Amy, who had no judgment about clothes, was wearing bright red wool, most unbecoming to her colorless face to which she had clumsily applied orange lip rouge and excessive mascara.

"It's terribly red, isn't it?" cried Amy, beside herself with her strange nervousness. "Edward likes it! Hope! I have read Freud since I saw you last!"

Hopestill smiled condescendingly and turned to Philip's mother. "I hope your mother will still let me dress at her house."

"Will you ride in this weather?" cried Mrs. McAllister.

"It's just the kind I like. The colder, the better."

"Well, you know you're always welcome, my dear. You haven't changed your mind about coming to my house instead? But perhaps you wouldn't like to feel indebted to Philip for I should give you his old playroom and he's most sentimental about it. I don't blame you: I shouldn't like to owe that young man a thing. Tell me truthfully, Hope, don't you think he has a heartless nature?"

"Indeed I do," replied the girl. "And that's the reason we've always got on so famously, for I'm heartless too."

"What a fib! No one has a warmer heart than you."

Hopestill, outraged because Mrs. McAllister had raised her voice so that everyone in the room could hear her, took her leave but not before she had said icily, "It's kind of you to compliment me so, but I'm bound to disappoint you if you really think I'm warm-hearted."

They embraced tenderly and the older woman said, "You could never disappoint me, Hopestill Mather."

I had been on the point of going upstairs for I had a few letters to type out for Miss Pride, but Hopestill intercepted me and taking me by the arm, led me back to the love-seat in the bay window. As we sat down, I saw that she was shockingly altered from the last time she had been here: the violet glades were deep beneath her glaring eyes and as deep were the new hollows in her pale cheeks which had lost their luster and had the gray opacity of fatigue. And as she talked, hysteria expanded her nostrils and shook her lips.

"Where did Philip go? To the hospital?"

I told her I thought he had gone home to dress for dinner.

"I'll telephone him then. I'm awfully anxious to see him. I don't suppose he told you what his plans were for the evening?"

"Why, yes. I'm having dinner with him and afterwards we're going to the Countess'."

She raised her eyebrows in a faked surprise. "Oh! I didn't know you actually dined with him."

"Yes. I often do."

She repeated, "I didn't know you actually dined with him. But it's of no importance. I dare say he didn't know I was coming on today. I wrote but perhaps the letter was delayed. I should have wired."

"You wrote?" My alarmed question was involuntary. Then, flustered by her lofty imperturbability, I said, "I've got some letters to go off. I'd better go up now."

"Will you look in on me when you've dressed, Sonie?"

I rose and started across the room as Hopestill went to sit beside Admiral Nephews. Miss Pride, who had left the room just after her niece arrived, was returning and I confronted her in the hall. "I trust you're going back to the letters. They're urgent and must go off tonight by air." I promised that I would not fail to get them in the post and moved past her. "One thing more, Sonie," she said, laying her hand on my arm. "I cannot condone—and I certainly cannot overlook—your behavior with Dr. McAllister. Two people remarked to me today that you seemed to be flirting with him. For your sake, I denied the accusation though I regret to say that in doing so I was also denying the evidence my eyes furnished me. I speak only for your own good, believe me, Sonie. I don't blame *you*. What was more natural than for you to go to Berthe von Happel's little parties with him? But it shouldn't have gone beyond *that*, my dear. It's been imprudent of Philip to encourage you in this infatuation. If I had been he and saw what was coming over you, I would have left you strictly alone. Why, Sonie, you're too sensible a girl to hitch your wagon to a star like that. Surely you must have heard what sort of person he is—one can't count the girls he's trifled with."

"Oh, you needn't worry about me, Miss Pride," I told her. "I have my feet on the ground."

"That's the way to talk! I knew you had good sense. Well, we all must take our foolish holidays, mustn't we? But now, since you know people have talked—unjustly I do believe—you'll take care not to let them talk again, won't you? Run along now and don't forget the letters. Isn't it nice that Hopestill came back just in time?"

"In time for what?" I inquired dully.

"Why, in time for Berthe's party. This is her most elaborate one of the year."

It was still early when I went to Hopestill's room, but she was already dressed and was seated before her fire engaged in wrapping a Christmas present. Her small sitting-room was confused with suitcases and unopened parcels and in the window stood a locked wardrobe trunk. "As you see," she said, following my eyes, "I've come back for good. When I've tied this knot, let's have a glass of sherry. Can you believe it, I had the fortitude to take a bottle of Aunt Lucy's private stock." I said I would have none. "Oh, do!" She dropped her package and took hold of my wrist, digging her enameled talons into my skin, as if my abstention from the stolen sherry threatened a catastrophe. She filled two glasses and gave me one. "Here, take it. You've never tasted anything like it."

She took a sip from her glass and picking up the fallen ribbon and the shears, turned to her work again. "Sonie," she said, "would you mind awfully if I went to dinner tonight with Philip?"

I drank before I answered her. "Did your aunt tell you to ask me?"

"Auntie? Of course she didn't. What business would it be of hers?"

"I only wondered."

"Well, she didn't. It was my own idea. I knew you wouldn't mind and you don't, do you? Did he by any chance," she said, looking up from her package, "send you those camellias you're wearing?"

I said he had. "They're lovely on your dress and what a lovely dress it is, too." I could not return her smile. She went on matter-of-factly, "Look here, Sonie, you're not in love with him, are you? Because if you are, I'm devilishly sorry. I'm afraid I rather put ideas in your head."

"Oh, I assure you you didn't."

"Sonie, I simply couldn't stick New York any longer!" she burst out. "I don't think I'll ever leave Boston again. It's more than flesh can bear to be separated from the only thing in the world one gives a tinker's damn about."

"What do you mean? This house?"

"You know perfectly well I mean Philip." She gave me a quick, bright smile intended to tell me that I was the first to be let in on her secret. "By the way, would you rather have your Christmas present now or wait? You know this year, for the first time in my life, I'm actually looking forward to Aunt Lucy's Christmas tree even though there is something really revolting about the way she hauls the servants up and gives them ridiculous presents. Do you know that once she gave Ethel two decks of cards in a monogrammed leather case for Whist parties?"

Wishing to have these pointless preliminaries finished, I said, "I'd like to have my present now."

"Oh, darling! How impossible of me! I just remembered it won't be here until tomorrow. It's a phonograph and several albums of records."

I was touched by her generosity and when I thanked her, she said, "After all, it was the least I could do, wasn't it?" The remark erased the kindness from her gift, told me with its frank interrogation that it was even less than solace but was the payment of a bribe the necessity of which she had anticipated, even though she had declared a little while before that she was not aware I dined with Philip. Hearing then her condescending negotiations, I was like the child who is told that he may not go to the picnic but for his supper may have a cream-puff. In his grief he believes he is offered a choice and cries, "But I don't *want* a cream-puff!" and cannot believe that his franchise is specious, nor can he persuade the governor of the nursery that while he likes cream-puffs and any other night would welcome them for supper, this is not the night; he *wants* only the hard-boiled eggs and the cold chicken that are to be on the menu of the picnic. I

353

did not want the phonograph although for several months I had been wishing for one, and while I could not say, like the disappointed child, that I did not, I could, like him, point out certain drawbacks in the gift. The child would say, "I don't want a cream-puff and it's silly because nurse told me we were having steamed pudding for supper and we can't have both and I think they're horrid anyway," and I said, "But I wish you hadn't bought me any records because our taste is probably not the same at all."

"Oh, Sonie, I'm sorry!" I had really distressed her and thought I even saw signs of tears in her exhausted eyes. She said, "I've tried so hard!" and thinking that she meant she had tried so hard to please me and my ingratitude was more than she could bear, I quickly said, "Oh, don't! I've really longed for a phonograph, and I've no doubt the records can be exchanged if I don't like them."

"I didn't mean that. I meant I had tried so hard in other ways. Well, it was all lost a long time ago and it's useless to try to regain it. I mean my balance was lost, my integrity, whatever it is in the name of God that keeps one together."

She poured herself another glass of sherry. "Do you want to hear an ugly yarn?" she said. "I haven't been 'studying' in New York at all, as Auntie knew and everyone must have suspected. I was going to a psycho-analyst and paying out fifteen dollars an hour for his nasty mumbo-jumbo. He had shaded lamps and old copies of the *New Yorker* and big divans in his waiting room where we all sat, so scornful of one another, pretending, every damned one of us, that we weren't there on business but had just come to pay a social call or had just dropped in to rest our feet. He had two Siamese cats that I grew to hate so violently that the doctor declared I had a cat complex, and he was beside himself with triumph when I volunteered, merely to pass the time, that Aunt Lucy had a cat that she kept locked up in her bedroom. He really said 'Eureka!' as though the whole problem were settled and it would only be a matter of minutes to find the cure. It's exactly like a dream and I can't really believe that he advised me that day to go out and buy a cat, *not,* mind you, a Siamese but a Persian tortoise shell like Mercy although I kept telling him that I had no objection to Mercy and it was his own wretched animals that I detested. He said I had come to substitute himself for my aunt! I kept going back because it quickly became a habit and at the same time I was doing just the same things I'd always done before because now I had confessed my sins they didn't seem very bad. He told me I wasn't co-operating and I got the notion that I was getting by with something because I was deceiving him the way I used to deceive the teachers at school and then Aunt Lucy and I enjoyed it all the more with him because he was powerless. I took the keenest pleasure in doing all the things I pretended I hated. His name was Dr. Ragsdale and I would tell him my dreams in which it was changed to 'Dr. Ratsbane.' He was pigeon-breasted and so evil I always knew he was homosexual and alcoholic as well as clinically insane."

"But why . . ." I began.

"Why, indeed? I kept thinking, I suppose, that I'd develop such a horror of my nature and the way he mauled it that I would at last be able to change. But I didn't. And so I have come back to Boston. *Here* maybe I can. There's probably a devil in me, one straight from hell like those in the Salem witches my ancestors used to burn."

She was sincere. A silence followed her words in which that evil she believed in and urged me to believe in was like a third person in the room; or it was like an innovation in the furnishings which was felt but not immediately perceived. I remembered, in that quiet, a series of small incidents which had puzzled me but which I had put out of my mind: once, the year before, when we were on our friendliest terms, she had brought me a present of a chartreuse evening gown which she had bought for herself and had afterwards discovered was too large. Chartreuse was a color I could not possibly wear as there were tints in my skin inimical to any variations of green or yellow, and since Hopestill and I had discussed this very misfortune sometime before when we had been shopping, I was naturally surprised at her gift. But in order to please her I put it on and went down to the sitting-room. Hopestill and her aunt were both there. "For heaven's sake!" cried Miss Pride. "Where did you get that frightful dress, child? You're the color of bile! Run back up this minute and change to that pretty blue of yours." "Yes, do, Sonie," agreed Hopestill, "it's awful." I was glad enough to change and went out, but stopping in the hall a minute to glance over a pile of letters

I had put on the table to make sure they were all stamped, I chanced to hear Hopestill say, "I can't think what got into me when I bought it for her. I was so proud of myself to remember her size, but imagine my forgetting that she couldn't wear that color," so that I knew she had not bought it for herself as she had told me. Another time, she had told me that she wanted me to meet a very distinguished cousin of hers who had married an Oxford don and was visiting for a few weeks in Milton. She said she had arranged a small dinner party and particularly wanted me to come because she thought I would find Lady So and So very amusing. And yet, when the day arrived and I warned her that I might be a few minutes late as I had to run an errand for Miss Pride in Cambridge, she said, "As a matter of fact, Sonie, Aunt Lucy asked me to tell you to stay at the Cock Horse for dinner and she'll send Mac around for you at nine. We're having a little dinner party for a cousin of mine who's a great bore and a stickler for family and that kind of thing."

Her malice was conscious, but its genesis was abrupt and unplanned, or seemed to be, though actually it must have been calculated painstakingly in the craters of her subconscious mind, so that probably she had intended to buy the dress for herself but a sudden impulse had made her select my size rather than her own and she had forgotten, in her guilt, the story she had told me and had told her aunt quite another. Now, having discovered the diathesis predisposing her to these brutalities I looked upon her with detachment, and thinking that what she wanted tonight was not to be with Philip but to spoil my evening (a desire which came from the same mischief that had prompted her to give me the dress), I resolved to keep my appointment with him.

Her mood had changed from one of restive worry to a sort of mild elation. She stretched out full length before the fire, her hair like the beams of a monstrance as it lay gleaming on the green carpet. The arc of her wide turquoise velvet skirt was broken by her small feet shod in gold dancing slippers. About her throat she wore a tightly plaited gold chain from which depended a scarabeus fluted with lapis lazuli. We were so still we heard Miss Pride moving about her room on the floor below us.

"It's late," I said. "I'm afraid I must go down."

"Go down? But I thought you had agreed."

I stood up. "You know I didn't. But if you insist on it, take his flowers." As I unpinned them, I pricked my finger and I thought how ruinous and beautiful this jewel of blood would be if it were to drop and glisten on her blue-green skirt.

She received the camellias, but as she pinned them to her shoulder, a shudder streamed from her face to her frivolous feet. "I wonder if he . . ."

"If he what?"

"If when he bought them he touched them with his hands. Oh, God!" She covered her face with her fingers, but her eyes were visible through the interstices. She stared up at me with a plea which, being unable to fathom, I could not grant. But as I turned to go, leaving the issue constructed between us like a barrier with no purpose, the girl's seemingly diverse moods which she had addressed to me since our first words in the drawing-room at tea time now appeared as an unbroken concatenation, and I was enlightened as I saw the uniformity of her whims. I divined, through an intuition which had never been exercised in me before, either because of a physical immaturity or because of the want of circumstances, that there was a sole exigency that could drive her to this corner where, for all her insolence, she was terrified. And as I realized that not the satanic particles but the organic chemistry of her composition had led her to this replacement of myself for the evening (a replacement she was determined, I now knew, to make permanent), I was ready to withdraw any claims I might have had since her need was so much greater than my own. My delay at the door, occasioned by this certain understanding, may have communicated its derivation to her, although she said, to my surprise (for in this instant after I realized that my hand had been half a minute on the door knob, I almost expected her to confirm my suspicions, to admit frankly that she was pregnant), "Take back the flowers and go to dinner with him. I will see you all at Berthe's." I had not fully turned around and I envisaged the flowers, their magenta petals protecting the golden filaments of the core, and as I went back to retrieve them (though I no longer wanted them, for by their exchange of hands they had been bruised and their significance had been polluted) my eyes traversed the window where, by arc light from Louisburg Square, the cold December snow was falling, and I remembered, as we remember comfort when the crisis of our pain descends and hints of our recovery are given us, that Philip had told me once that camellias bloomed in midwinter in New Orleans.

The single peal, three flights down, preceded a moment the six bells struck by the nautical clock on Hopestill's mantel. "It's Philip," I said, as I bent over to take the flowers. My utterance of his Christian name, upon the heels of my recollection of his report that camellias bloomed this time of year in the south (for, unable to visualize such a phenomenon, I had merely thought the words, Philip said . . .) imparted to my flesh an inchoate, sensual delight, similar as I perceived to that I had experienced when, identifying my own body with Hopestill's to make my diagnosis of her altered nature, my comprehension had not been established by logic but by the completion of my own ripening. Hopestill still lay before the fire in her strategic immobility. It was strategic because she appeared transfixed by an invisible pinion to the floor as if, like the possum or the dung-beetle playing dead, she would come to life at once upon my departure. Her eyes, apparently shut, took in each motion it was necessary for me to make to unpin the flowers from her shoulder and, glancing at the bits of shining eyeball, visible through her long, sparse auburn lashes and seeing once in that brief space of my perusal, the gold-flecked iris that enshrined the eye's soul, I knew myself to be in the presence of desperation so rarefied at this climax reared up by the signal at the outer door that it resembled lethargy. And simultaneously, I knew that no one else would see what I had seen and that she would go scot-free. Although at this point in her there was ambush and a cause for it, both would be obliterated; the sins would be exorcised not by the psycho-analyst but by concealing custom.

When I had left her and had stepped into the corridor, the sensation that summarized the scene in Hopestill's sitting-room was not one of anger or indignation, had nothing in it more unfavorable to her than my old and now enfeebled antipathy to the child in the Barstow dining-room. I directed the movement of my body to partake of the grace of my dinner dress, desiring, as though Miss Pride's dim hallway were lined with spectators, my organism to proclaim through its flattering draperies that the force inspiring me was one of fleshly love, akin to the passion that had undone Hopestill and with devoted obstinacy still clung to her in her dilemma. The love I felt, which like a rapid poison circulated throughout me, had no object, and until I was on the last flight of stairs from the top of which I saw Philip's hat and gloves on the vestibule table, my desire did not focus, for until then, the elusive lover I had tried to construct was that unnamed, unacknowledged man whose impregnation of Hopestill was also an exigesis of my own changing self. Then, attaching my attention to a well-known object, for the space of ten seconds, I was determined to finish with him what I had so indecisively begun. But the moment my desire materialized, it vanished; the shame that recalled me to my usual timidity was incommensurate with its cause: at the same time that I took in the doctor's bowler and the gray suède gloves, I heard Miss Pride's voice through the closed door of her bedroom: "You may go now, Ethel. I am ready to undress." The direction, which was probably superfluous to the well-trained maid who knew by heart her mistress's habits, fell upon my ear like an injunction repeated to herself by a nun, and I could no more imagine Miss Pride in the deshabille she painstakingly kept for the eyes only of her mirrors, than I could have imagined a Mother Superior in her nightdress. I took no pleasure now in the décolletage of my new frock, and thought it would be improved by the addition of a shawl thrown about my shoulders. But the atavistic reaction was not complete as it had been formerly, when I was a child and had loathed my mother for those qualities I had now discovered in myself. For I had gone too far, by becoming myself a protagonist, to believe blindly any longer that Miss Pride's was the ideal pattern: there was, in the tone of her voice, cold and neutral, a suggestion of ingrown, conceited lewdness which, having no sexuality to modify, advertised the secret nudity of the old, arid carcass.

The doctor had been shown into the library where he stood inaudibly conversing with a large young man, shaped like an athlete, but one whose muscles had relaxed already and beneath whose chin a soft second growth had begun. They turned to greet me and Dr. McAllister introduced me to his friend, Frank Whitney. The doctor was nervous and would not sit down. He said, "I've just lost my first patient and if there's anything here besides Grandfather Pride's port, I'd like to resort to the traditional sedative. Do you keep any whiskey here?" We did. I brought out a decanter of whiskey and a tumbler. Philip poured the glass three-quarters full. "I can blame only myself, although some kind-hearted person said the x-ray reading had been at fault. It was a skull-fracture and I advised against operating." He drank half the whiskey and then, pausing, with the glass still in his hand, he said, "How stupid! I poured out three times as much as I wanted," yet his hand remained suspended, clasping the tumbler and I knew that he wanted the rest of it, indeed, probably wanted another double portion, but that his will denied it to him.

"Hopestill is here," I said. The response on his face to my announcement was a compressed version of what I had seen on the first afternoon I met her when he raised his hand and touched her hair. But his look was not one of surprise and I wondered again what she had written him.

"That's convenient," he said. "Frank decided at the last minute to come along. We can all go together. By the way, some friends of Hope's rang me up a little while ago and said they were stopping by here . . . perhaps we can offer them a drink, what do you say?"

"Hope wasn't expecting to have dinner with us," I said.

"I'm sure we can persuade her," put in Frank Whitney.

"Oh, yes, I have no doubt we can," I replied. "She's very anxious to see you, Philip."

"That's good of her."

"She's come back to stay. Did you know?"

Hopestill entered the room. The animal that had matured in Philip's disciplined person, despite the herculean efforts of his Puritan will, strained towards its meeting with that other specimen of the same genus that I had seen rioting in the cold prison of the girl recumbent before her hearth. I turned away as he went to greet her and discovered Frank Whitney's dreamy brown eyes regarding me with wonder. I had picked up Philip's half-emptied glass and downed it. "Do you often do that?" inquired the young man. "I mean, drink that much whiskey neat?"

"No," I told him. "But it's a good idea."

360

Philip was telling Hopestill that her friends were coming here. "The person who telephoned me was named Morgan," he said.

"Oh, yes, of course. I know him," replied Hopestill. "He's from Long Island. From a branch of the family famous for its lack of fame. Quite a barbarian he is, but I'm rather fond of him."

"Morgan?" said Mr. Whitney as if it were a name he had heard in some unsavory connection. "I don't know any Morgans." He uttered it as an accusatory epithet, as if its etymology had vested the name with respectability but its root meaning glared forth in the pronunciation; it was as if he had said, "A rum runner? I don't know any rum runners."

The door-bell rang, bringing us, in a moment, Mr. Morgan and a couple who were introduced with a great deal of laughter as the Cabots, the reason for the hilarity being that their name was really Babbitt. Mr. Babbitt who, because of an unfortunate obtrusion of his mouth, resembled an animal that rhymed with both Cabot and Babbitt (I pointed this out to Frank Whitney later and he said gravely, "That's not our kind of joke."), came up to me as if we had known one another all our lives and said, "Where's the booze, honey?"

"The drinks are coming now," I said. Ethel had brought in glasses and ice at Hope's order.

"That's dandy. Are you going to Berthe von Happel's shindig?" I replied that I was and remarked that I was sure it would be a very lavish party since the Countess had dispensed with the dinner party and had expended all her efforts on the midnight supper.

"Oh, she'll give us our money's worth tonight, bless her royal heart. I nipped in this afternoon for five minutes to see if I could lend a hand, and had a look into that gorgeous drawing-room of hers. Would you believe it, she has a Christmas tree—a *tannenbaum,* as she insists—reaching to the ceiling, an absolute smack in Louis Quinze's face. And she has poinsettias in green tubs all over the house, for all the world like a department store."

"She's really appalling," said his wife, "but it's impossible not to adore her."

This was a brazen untruth, but Hopestill, Philip, and Frank Whitney all enthusiastically seconded it. The irony of the expressions.

"Isn't that absolutely the case!" "I love her parties, particularly her Christmas parties," and "She's a jewel, I'm head over heels in love with Berthe!" was so deeply embedded that had I not known that the authors of these praises actually despised the Countess, I should have thought them a cult convening to eulogize a high priestess. Thus, when they described her drawing-room to someone who had never seen it, they appeared to find it enchanting, and it was only the initiated who knew that some such statement as "She has two spurious Watteaus which are so charming one doesn't mind their being frauds," was actually inspired by the most savage spitefulness. The stranger, whose ear missed the note of contempt, at once admired the Bostonians for their defense of the Countess and felt little interest in the house itself, believing the word "charming" had been used out of simple generosity.

"Do you suppose Kalenkoff will be there?" asked Mr. Babbitt and the whole room laughed. Accustomed to their own habits of inbreeding and holding the common notion that royalty east of Austria was worthless because it was so abundant, these American aristocrats seemed to frequent the Louis Quinze salon chiefly for the purpose of snubbing its titled habitués. An obscure professor of physics from the University of Paris fared better at their hands than an arch-duke, and the dashing Baron Kalenkoff was invited nowhere while a wealthy British manufacturer of photographic equipment had a standing invitation to the best houses and clubs. They were so perversely American, so vehemently uninterested in any culture but that which their ancestors had found acceptable that they even went out of their way to offend the Countess' friends by their intentionally inaccurate pronunciations of German place names or their smug misconstruction of political philosophy or even, though this was regarded as démodé, by bragging of the excellence of the American sanitary system. On the one Saturday the year before when the Admiral had put in an appearance, he had said to Baron Kalenkoff, "Is it true, mate, that you Russian chaps sleep with dogs in your bunks?" The Baron flashed him a friendly smile. "It is customary," he said. "And when our guests are shown to their rooms they do not find detective novels and magazines on the night table to amuse them but they find the master's best dog in the bed. If the guest is any kind of gentleman, he will refuse this extravagant kindness and will insist that he be given the *second* best dog. You may be sure, sir, that if he does not hesitate to climb into bed with his host's prize wolfhound, he will never be asked again." The Admiral was flabbergasted by this leg-pull and moved away, remarking gruffly to Mrs. Frothingham who quite agreed with him, "Those Russians have no sense of humor."

Mr. Morgan alone did not join in the laughter and I surmised that he did not know the Countess. He had said nothing after the introductions and I quite erroneously thought that he was ill at ease. But when the laughter had subsided, he stepped forward shakily and said, "Don't you know I'm to be congratulated?" Mr. Babbitt then informed us that Mr. Morgan was celebrating his coming into a vast fortune through the death of his grandmother. To my astonishment, I heard Philip propose a toast.

"Thank you, thank you," said the heir, bowing at his stocky waist. "Somebody is missing from this conference, isn't somebody? It looks like a damned little conference, and what is this place we're holding it in? The Atheneum?"

"The missing person," said Mr. Babbitt, familiarly nudging me with his elbow, "beg pardon, the missing link is Miss Nanny Brewster whom you left in the ladies' retiring room at the Ritz bar."

"Nanny Brewster?" cried Hopestill shrilly. "What do you mean by bringing that street-walker to my house?"

Morgan patted her shoulder and said soothingly, "There, there, she isn't in the Atheneum. Didn't you hear John say she was in the W.C.?"

Frank Whitney abruptly presented his back to the company, whispering to me, "I remember him now," and began to read the titles of a section of books on Far Eastern studies. In a moment I joined him, preferring his pastime to the discussion of Miss Brewster's whereabouts, but not before Mr. Babbitt murmured to me with a moist laugh, "I don't know which one of them is getting the runaround." We were some distance from the others, Mr. Whitney and I, when he growled, "Bad blood is the rule with those Long Islanders. How can Hope stomach a buffoon like Harry Morgan?" And then, because Mr. Babbitt seemed to be approaching us again, he said, taking a book down, "Here's a funny thing, a Japanese novel translated into German. I call that too much of a good thing." Then when we saw that we were to be left alone since Mr. Babbitt was joining his friends, Frank Whitney told me about Morgan.

Mr. Harry Morgan was thirty years old. His equine face was being elongated year by year by the withdrawal of his black hair, and was being softened year by year by good living which the death of his grandmother, happily coinciding with Christmas, was evidently to make even better. We read in the newspapers that scions of famous families have gone to Hollywood to join, usually in a social capacity, the "film colony," and it is hard to tell, from the impartial journalists, whether the colonists or the immigrant are hereby benefited. Mr. Morgan was such a person, although, if his credentials had been gone into, it would have been found that he was so distantly related to any of the celebrated tycoons whose name he bore that he was no more entitled to a share in their glory than is a person named Shakespeare entitled to the homage of literary people. But it happened that this Mr. Morgan was extremely wealthy and few knew that his money came from the maternal side of his family, named Schumacher, and had been made in a variety of enterprises, including brewing, the manufacture of artificial limbs, razor blades, hooks and eyes, and the breeding of longhorn cattle. But the fact of the money, not its history, was the important thing. It was likely that had his father's name been Schumacher and he had not used Morgan at all or had used it as a middle name, he would have been as readily accepted in California. However, "the wealthy young Morgan" was a title of more tone than "Schumacher, the artificial limb heir." At the same time that he maintained an establishment in New York near a café called the Lancelot Club which he owned, he not only frequently visited Sun Valley, Idaho, and while he was about it looked in at his Beverly Hills cottage, but he was also, and had been for years, a student at Harvard College. There was a rumor, Mr. Whitney told me, never confirmed, that he had once made application for a Rhodes' scholarship.

"I won't go anywhere if that tart is going along," Hopestill was saying. "Really, Harry! And you're drunk."

"Let's not anybody quarrel," he replied amicably. "You had a last five or six drinks too many in the club car, sweetheart, you can't fool Harry. And how come you weren't on the train you told me to meet?"

"I got off at Back Bay," she said shortly.

It was as though we had come into a moving picture halfway through and because we did not know the beginning of the plot, could not adjust this scene to the foregoing action. Philip McAllister, standing witness to the intimate tiff, looked suddenly faint. "Excuse me," he murmured and backed away. For the second time, he told Frank Whitney and me about the skull-fracture case, of whose fatal termination he had learned over the telephone just after he had left our house at tea time. "Let me show you," he said, taking a pencil and envelope out of his pocket, "what it was in the x-ray reading that deceived me," and he began to draw a skull, but his hand trembled so, either from his surprise at Hopestill's almost domestic shrewishness with Morgan whom she had pretended to know only casually, or from a relapse into his earlier shock, that the outline was pinked like a valentine. Above his insistent explanation, I could hear the others talking and I was so intent on their conversation that from the doctor I learned only that the skull might be likened to an egg, which, broken on one side, might break simultaneously on the other, that his patient, struck on the temple had "sustained" an occipital fracture which he had misread as merely the widening of a suture line.

The Babbitts and Mr. Morgan had grouped themselves about the chess-table and seeing the men set up on the board, in readiness for Miss Pride's Sunday maneuvers, remarked that this was the final touch which proved that they had strayed into a club. To create the illusion that it was a commercial club, they put the board and pieces on the floor and set up in their place the bottle of whiskey to which they freely helped themselves. Hopestill, who had been standing by the fire gazing abstractedly into the spurting logs, joined them when they threatened to put ice down her back if she didn't, and they sat, the four of them, round the little table, at play, as if they were in a night-club and had grown bored with their surroundings so that they had turned to their own private jokes and gossip for entertainment.

I interrupted the medical monologue. "Listen, Philip," I said, "this makes me nervous. What if Miss Pride should come in?"

"What if she should? Hope is her own mistress, isn't she?" he replied touchily.

"But such strange people," I said. Both young men stared coldly at me and I flushed.

"Helen Babbitt is Hope's cousin," said Mr. Whitney solemnly. "I must admit, though, that they *are* an unattractive lot."

Philip agreed with a laugh and turning to me forgivingly, he explained that Mrs. Babbitt had been a Miss Brooks and therefore related both to Hopestill and, by marriage, to the Countess, and while no one had ever liked her, for she was a fool and had not worn stockings to her wedding, people forgot this and came to believe that the interloper from New Jersey had made her into what she was. Admiral Nephews had remarked to her, "Madam, thou art mated to a clown," and ever afterwards it was the universal opinion that Mr. Babbitt had had the weight to drag her down. They came to Boston at Thanksgiving and Christmas to the great suffering of Mrs. Babbitt's family who were, ironically enough, related in several different ways to the Cabots.

"I suppose it's natural enough Hope's taken up with them," said Whitney. "She's probably lonely in New York."

"I would say the contrary," returned Philip drily. "I've concluded that Sonie is right: Miss Lucy would have epilepsy if she came in here now. I'll see what I can do." And he called across the room to the group at the chess-table, "Don't you think it's time we went on to dinner?"

"Why, doctor, what a childish idea," said Mr. Morgan, "we are just beginning our *apéritif*. It's my party and I name the hour. By the way, doesn't the Somerset Club serve meals?" He went back to his conversation, dismissing the interruption.

In spite of the objections one might make to his appearance or to his manner, whether one saw at once that he was crude or unscrupulous—for, although dissipation had obscured the sharpness of his face, a certain cunning remained in the eyes which did not look directly into other eyes—or whether he offended one's intellectual principles, there was about the young millionaire something so magnetic that exposure to the same air he breathed was similar in its effect to a love-philter. I had thought, in the first minutes of my admittedly enraptured regard of him, when my mind, operating simultaneously on two levels saw him on one as irresistible and on the other as repellent, that the sensuality manifest in his face was the forerunner of the corruption into which Dr. Galbraith had helplessly sunk. But presently I revised the prophecy that in twenty years he would be as damned a soul as the old doctor. For while he was sentimental—this was apparent from his slang, that badge by which we recognize the members of an egotistical and tenderly self-indulgent order—he was also shrewd, noncommittal, and even tonight when he was drunk, constantly on guard against involving himself with Hopestill, with Philip, in a sense, with this very room.

There are some people who we know at first glance will never marry. How we know, I cannot say, but we know as surely as we know that other people have taken a dislike to us at the moment of our presentation to them. Harry Morgan was such a man. What appealed then so strongly to me that it was only with an effort of will that I was able to look away from him was the challenge flung down by his self-sufficiency, which could not but rouse in any woman the desire to conquer him, and I felt a revival of that light-headedness—anticipatory, perhaps, it had been—in which I had descended the top two flights of stairs.

Hopestill, handing him a pair of ice-tongs, said something we could not hear and he replied, whispering in her ear as he put an assured arm about her shoulders. She lingered beside him the briefest time and then moved away. There was a look of outrage on her face, but not that he had been familiar amongst strangers, rather that he had with such facility, such untroubled certainty of where he stood with her, communicated to all of us: "I can take you or leave you alone," for his gesture had been at once possessive and indifferent.

I doubt if Philip or Frank Whitney discerned the agitation into which Morgan sent the three women in the room, for even Mrs. Babbitt, although she was obviously accustomed to him, looked at him worshipfully. Neither of the men could have sensed the source of his charm since it required the intuitive simplicity with which a woman perceives in a man the very embodiment of temptation. This is one of the mysteries of their sex by which men are infuriated for, being unable to solve it, they believe it to be a hoax: "Why, So and So is a perfect bounder. What can you see in him?" they ask of the women who can only reply, "I can't explain it."

"Listen, Harry," said Mr. Babbitt, "I want you to sing that song Miss Nanny Brewster taught you. You'll love it, Hope. It's funny as hell the way Harry does it."

"I'm not interested and I don't want to hear it. I think it's time we went on to dinner."

But Mr. Morgan had already risen to perform. He moved unsteadily across the room and stood before the Governor Winthrop and in a moment began to sing. Above his strange head, like a moon at half eclipse, Miss Pride's father stared at the trophy case. His loosely clenched hand rested on a table at his side as if he were about to make it into a fist and pound. The wavering Long Islander sang with a tuneless, distended insolence, rolling his eyes and suddenly closing them as, stopping dead in his song, he stroked imaginary female hips of extraordinary dimensions. The Babbitts, half in tears with laughter, kept filling his glass with straight whiskey, for at the end of each line, by way of punctuation, he drained off what he had. The lewdness came chiefly from his pantomime and his catarrhal voice, for the words that issued from his boneless face were only:

> I love to go swimmin'
> With bow-legged women
> And dive between their legs.

"Isn't he a scream?" shrieked Mrs. Babbitt.

Frank Whitney was pale. "Let's get him out, McAllister. He's drunk as a catfish." He started towards the offender, but Hopestill, who without trying to stop the song, had been gazing up at her grandfather as if supplicating him either to forgive this indignity or to put a stop to it, raised her hand in an apostolic gesture which said, "He has asylum here."

"He's perfectly all right, Frank," she said. "He's only gay. He inherited two million dollars yesterday and he has every right to sing if he wants to."

"Repeat refrain!" cried Mr. Babbitt, covering his face with his hands while his thorax hopped convulsively like a jumping bean. Mr. Morgan obliged him and the words traveled slowly through his nose.

The door to the library flung open and crashed against the paneling. Miss Pride, dressed for dinner in garnets and black silk, stood on the threshold appraising the terrain. The first to speak was Harry Morgan who, going towards her with the sober countenance that appears in certain stages of drunkenness, said, "Mrs. Mather, I presume?" Miss Pride's enameled lenses suddenly could focus only on distant objects. She looked at me and said, "The letters, Sonie, which you promised to mail," and held them out. Mr. Morgan's rejected paw faltered uncertainly to his side.

"Good evening, Helen." She addressed Mrs. Babbitt frigidly.

"Good evening, Cousin Lucy," said Mr. Babbitt, bounding toward her, "I'm glad to see you." Miss Pride did not share his pleasure but glared straight through his head as if the gimlets of her eyes could puncture the optic nerve. She came to me with the letters. "Hello, Frank. Is Mary coming on for the holidays?" and as she took his hand, she gave me the bunch of envelopes and adroitly, so that no one could see, she pinched the fleshy part of my thumb between two fingernails so hard that I nearly cried out with pain.

For half a minute she stood there while Frank Whitney gave her news of his family. She did not release my thumb until he was finished and then she said, "I must go this minute. Hopestill, bring Frank when you and Philip come to the Countess'. I know Berthe will be delighted."

"We're all coming, Auntie," said Hopestill. "This is Mr. Morgan, Aunt Lucy."

"Good evening, sir," said Miss Pride and glanced up at the portrait of her father. "Papa looks *en prise*. Do set his men up again, Philip." And she left the room. The only proof I had that she had been angry were the two white crescent marks on my thumb made, in her rage at something with which I had no connection, in the way one hurls a teacup to the floor because the contents of a letter have infuriated him.

"Waiter, bring me my bill," said Mr. Morgan with a foolish grin

369

"And cancel my membership in the Somerset. The bouncer gives me the creeps. Are you coming, baby?"

"No," said Hopestill. "Before you go, Harry, will you apologize to all of us?"

"Now I suggest," said Mrs. Babbitt in the voice of a peacemaker, "that Harry and John and I all go eat dinner by ourselves and let the ladies and gentlemen alone. Nobody's mad now but if we don't go right along everybody will be dreadfully mad except me."

"I won't be mad," pouted Mr. Babbitt. "And Olga won't be mad, will you, Olga?"

"Well, I'm damned," said Mr. Morgan, using his hands as binoculars and directing them towards me. "Is *that* Olga? Troika-ho, Olga!"

They left, Mrs. Babbitt's giggles leaving a wake behind. If I had been able to speak, I would have been profane, would have used every blasphemous and scatalogical oath I knew to tell Hopestill how I was affected by the knowledge that I had been the object of amused discussion. Olga! Her malice was so rich, so inventive that even now, exposed by the babblings of her drunken friends, she tried to hoodwink me. "I don't think Sonie looks all that Slavic, do you, Frank?"

The evening lay in ruins. My disappointments, my humiliation, and my scorn bustled through the branches of my nerves, created a tic here and a tingling there, an ache in my skull and fever in my eyeballs.

Mr. Whitney touched my arm. "Will you have dinner with me?" he asked.

Hopestill smiled. "Give the poor child a stout drink," she said. "She isn't used to the lower classes."

"Oh, I'll have a lot to drink," I said, and she and Philip laughed. They had forgotten us already before we had even reached the threshold. Hopestill was saying, "Well, darling, I've come home to stay. Aren't you glad?"

As soon as I could I left the Countess' salon and got my cape, but as I was starting down the hall towards the stairs someone laid his hand on my shoulder and I turned to find myself the captive of Mr. Pingrey. He said, "Sonia, Amy is in a tiz over your cutting her. You come straight along with me, you baggage. Mr. Hornblower is here and you have to meet him. He's just been telling the most delicious thing about Mr. Roosevelt. Did you know that the name is really Rosenfeld?" I was in no frame of mind to meet Your Esteemed Uncle Arthur Hornblower and told Mr. Pingrey that Miss Pride had asked me to run home to fetch something for her.

"Oh, stuff!" said Mr. Pingrey, flapping his hands limply in my face. "You're a perfect imp sometimes. Very well, but I will absolutely disown you if you don't meet him when you come back. Do you realize that he knows everyone of importance? Gandhi, Mussolini, Hitler, Trotsky, the Lord knows who. He's the most literate person here by far."

I felt this to be a slight exaggeration, but said I had not been aware that the Countess' parties were intended to be the meeting ground of minds.

"Well!" he gasped. "Frankly I don't know what you're talking about. Why on earth would one come otherwise?"

"Why, to drink," I said.

Mr. Pingrey did not drink or smoke, making his abstention from alcohol, tobacco, and highly seasoned food a fetish as obstinate as a vice. He put his hand to his heart as if he had been wounded there and might, after his valedictory, topple over dead at my feet. "I cannot, I simply cannot understand this transformation in you." His eyes, similar to Amy Brooks' (both of them were victims of excessive thyroid secretions, a bond which strengthened their friendship, I am sure, and played a strong part in their marriage and their subsequent production of two children with the same glandular vagary), bulged forth as he bent his ruddy face down towards mine to gaze upon the frog which, before the gods had been provoked to wrath, had been a charming maiden.

"Then go on to your . . . punch bowl!" he cried, and stepped aside to let me pass. Had I lingered a few minutes longer, he would have used such words as "wassail" and "negus" and "sack" to show that his acquaintance with alcohol was purely literary. Once, at an informal luncheon, he had inquired of his hostess if her servants made the mead themselves. "Mead? What is that?" she asked. He indicated the glasses of Chablis. "Oh," said the lady, who did not like him and was also vain of her learning, "No, my athelings have lost the receipt. This is a simple grape concoction made by the Christians in Gaul."

I was halfway down the stairs when he leaned over the bannister and implored, "*Do* meet Mr. Hornblower. He wants us all to come to tea at his house tomorrow. He's terribly anxious to meet you and says he will be ever so interested to hear your political conflicts—I told him, you see, that you were half Russian and half German."

As the next day was Sunday, I could not go. "I will be away tomorrow," I told him.

"Oh, but you must come," he protested urgently, "because Mrs. Hornblower will be there too!" as though, if it were a rare thing to meet Mr. Hornblower it was an even rarer one to meet his wife. I repeated my refusal and Mr. Pingrey withdrew his head but not before he had stuck out his tongue at me like a peckish child and flung out, "Crosspatch!"

I had gained the outer hall when the door to the dining-room opened and the chauffeur shot past me like someone on a surf-board. He was carried along over the carpet by the leashed Doberman and the boxer to whom he applied, under his breath, the word "bitches" with venomous accuracy. Through the door I could see the supper table with its dishes arranged as tastefully as if they had been bouquets of flowers and were to serve no purpose other than ornament. The Countess had been planning this for months, ordering the strangest of the foods through importers, scouring Boston and New York for the finest Liebfraumilch and Niersteiner and champagne, herself supervising the decanting of the sweet wines and the liqueurs, and living through each step of the lengthy preparation of the *daube glacé* as if upon the proper contents of the bags of herbs depended her social success.

I had hoped to find the Countess here alone so that I could make my excuses to her, and I was annoyed to see that she was not in the room at all, but that wandering back and forth before the table were Baron Kalenkoff and a Jewish brain surgeon who were making hearty meals of the *daube,* the cucumbers in sour cream, the herring and salmon and caviar, the cheeses, olives, salads. Every now and again they abandoned the table only to repair to the side-board where the wines were cooling. The two accommodators, hired for the evening, and the Alsatian waitresses stared stonily at the carnage, stood near-by the gormandizers waiting to pounce upon the empty dishes and bear them away to the dumb-waiter to be, if possible, replaced.

I entered the dining-room intending to seek the Countess in the pantry. This room alone had been left untouched by the new mistress of the house; its walls were hung with Audubon's eagle attacking the inflated white belly of a fish, his Iceland gulls and curlews, and interspersed amongst the birds were Currier and Ives Maine landscapes and paddle-wheel boats. Miss Pride said of it, "I could digest my food there as well as I did in Josie Brooks' day if only Berthe didn't let her livestock run free."

As I paused in the doorway, the Countess appeared, coming out of the pantry with the intention, probably, of having a last minute look before she allowed supper to be announced. It must have been shocking for her to come upon two guests who had gobbled up visible portions of the food and had destroyed the appearance of half the dishes by their wanton hunger and who greeted her with their mouths full, one hand holding a slice of bread piled high with a layer of pickled herring, a layer of jellied partridge, one of salt salmon, and topped by a round of marinated onion, the other hand clasping by its neck a liter of cold wine. But the Countess' hesitation was the briefest possible. Undismayed, she advanced and she said, as though she were delighted by what she saw, smiling, her large fair face aglow with hospitality, her diadem of sapphires forming for this perfect hostess an angelic halo, "Oh, you didn't find the Niersteiner. You're drinking that flat Moselle. Here, let me get you some real wine."

Then, having finished her ministrations to the vandals and having caught sight of me, she cried, "Ah, angel! I was just going to look for you. What are you doing with your cape? Going? But you've only been here five minutes!"

I told her I was feeling a little ill, I believed I was catching cold. "Oh, no! How shocking! I won't have you taking cold." She thrust a plate of lobster *en mayonnaise* in front of the Baron and said, "Try this, Alexy, and give me your honest opinion. Will you excuse me for a moment?" And taking me by the arm, she led me into the hall and towards the yellow sofa.

373

"Now!" she said, adjusting the camellias at my shoulder to her liking. "Now tell me why you're playing such a trick on me."

"But it's no trick, Countess. Really, I am all chills and fever."

"Oh, adorable monster! But I'll keep your secret. Is he gifted? Is he a gentleman? Darling, don't think I'm prying, but I love you! I could not bear it if my Euphrysone weren't treated well!"

Anxious to escape and afraid that if she kept me any longer I would blurt out the whole story of my wounded dignity, I put my cape around my shoulders and laughed, "He, Countess, is only Dostoievsky whom I shall read when I've taken an aspirin for my cold."

"Seriously," she said looking, indeed, very serious, "I am only thinking how Lucy Pride would feel about it. You know her anti-Semitism. But you do as you like, my dear pet! I will let you go *only* if you promise to be amused!"

"Oh, I do promise!" I assured her and I extended my hand in farewell, wishing to end this baffling dialogue. The Countess got up, kissed me, and went to the stairs. "How stupid of me! I forgot to tell you that he's waiting in the library."

I had known, even before I opened the door, that I would find Nathan Kadish in the library. He was standing in the lamplight, his birthmark towards me.

"Well," he said, "aren't you surprised?"

"Hello, Nathan. I'm glad to see you."

"I should hope you might be, you poor girl! What you must have been through! Had I only known I would have come to solace you months ago."

"How did you get in?" I said, amused and pleased that he had not changed.

"It was a very neat coup. I saw you come in here with that St. Bernard—what a moron *he* looks like—and waited a minute and rang the bell myself. I must say I was ready to give up when I got a gander at that butler. He was tough sledding, but the lady was a pushover."

I saw that he was going over, with an admiring eye, the details of my attire, and I likewise allowed my look to travel upwards from his feet in muddied white shoes, over his immaculate gray suit and bright red bow tie to his face.

"Well, Sonie? Well, how would you like to get drunk? I very much regret that as I am currently in love with someone else, this is the only amusement I can offer you."

It was the only amusement I was capable of enjoying. Even the prospect was sedative. As we went into the hall, Nathan said, "I assume that you won't mind doing the boozing in my sort of saloon?" We met the soulless face of the butler who, opening the door for us, said to me, "Good evening, Miss Marburg. I hope you won't find it too wet underfoot."

"Want to come along?" said Nathan to him, but the man, ignoring him, said to me, "Of course you have a very short walk home."

"She's not going home, you buzzard," said Nathan, looking closely into the snobbish face. "Slave!"

Both the man and I were too shocked to speak. The white door slowly closed and I was certain that I looked for the last time upon the Countess von Happel's brass knocker.

# CHAPTER FOUR

Now on the glossy Sunday after I had stayed until four o'clock in the morning with Nathan Kadish at a café in Scollay Square, I had as my traveling companions not only shame, jealousy, and despair, but in addition a headache that pounded and reverberated through each convolution of my brain and stretched to bursting each tunnel and cove of my skull, a tidal nausea, a chill as dry and plunging as a winter wind. Last night's snow was deep and glazed, played on by bright sun, and the pavement over which we drove was like a polished blade casting upward shimmering filaments of frosty light. The spruce, hibernal landscape, simplified like a conventional design in which the vitality and the heterogeneous shades of autumn had been discarded for a white and mortal rigor, gave to the condition of my body and the state of my mind an incisive accent, and I could neither see nor imagine a source of warmth (chilliest of any detail in this fixed scene was the dun tendril of smoke ascending from a white chimney), nor could I be reminded by anything presented here of the good, the gratifying, the ennobling, or the pleasing elements of life. For I could observe only contrast, and in personifying nature as one will sometimes do in illness or in melancholy or conversely in well-being or in joy, I saw myself rebuked by the immaculate, inflexible earth for having been the night before exactly the opposite, just as I had been rebuked earlier this morning by Miss Pride whose wintry eyes in her bone-clean face had extinguished my heart's heat so that I had stood like a stalagmite beside the chess-table receiving her terse lecture.

Nathan and I had revived and resealed our friendships with mixtures of rum and soda water, the number of which a persistent, unsolicited clerk in the back of my tortured head kept trying, this morning, to count from memory. And at sometime these scorched, half-blinded eyes of mine had seen a chorus of footsore girls dancing on a platform to a rompish paraphrase of "O, Come All Ye Faithful." They had been dressed like Santa Claus, if Santa Claus had been a girl in red, fur-trimmed underdrawers and a brassière of gold stars and had worn, in place of the smile of a kind-hearted old innocent, a grin of the most workaday lewdness. Either before or after this travesty, which at the time I had taken for granted but which this morning possessed the impossible quality of a comic dream, a sailor in His Majesty's, the King of England's, employ had briefly joined us and in exchange for my wilted camellias which he requested, declaring that he would preserve them to the end of his days in his mother's prayer-book, he gave me a picture post card that we all regarded as irresistibly droll. It showed, in vivid colors, a small, libidinous, middle-aged man staring at a bathing beauty about to dive into the ocean while his portly wife, surveying a group of new cottages, remarked: "Look at the seaside development, George." For some purpose, lost forever to memory, the sailor had laboriously printed his name, Sam Casserly, on the back with an obtuse blue pencil.

The iconoclastic antics of the dancing girls and the transaction with Sam Casserly together accounted for perhaps fifteen or twenty minutes out of the five hours we had spent in the crowded room where the green and red lights, veiled by smoke, made the atmosphere crepuscular. But I remembered that we had not been idle and that our intake of noteworthy amounts of rum had been accompanied by unflagging talk which, although its substance was irrevocable, seemed, on retrospect, to have issued altogether from my lips. I could fairly see Nathan's face patiently registering courteous sympathy with my complaints, amusement at my mirthless anecdotes, respect for my moral and literary judgments. And yet, gradually, as if I were reading a book which I had forgotten I had read before, so much of my companion's current history came back that it seemed impossible, in view of the fact that I had learned all this in just five hours, that I could have uttered a word, but that the solo voice had been his, interlarding the calendar of his love-affairs and his scholastic enterprises with expositions of his character, guesses about mine, and childhood reminiscences common to both of us. He was now, he told

377

me, at Harvard and had been for two years, studying literature with the support of a fellowship. He was also tutor to Harry Morgan and was making so much money (he lived very simply) that he had saved almost enough to go to Paris after his graduation. Before the flight from America, he thought he might marry a Japanese girl whom he described as superbly beautiful, or else an elderly French fly-by-night who had no attractions for him but who spoke both German and French and could therefore act as his interpreter. And I believed, though I could not be certain, that when I reminded him that I was also bilingual (this exaggeration had evinced no comment from him), he had accepted my application, but had made it perfectly clear that he was in love with the Japanese girl.

I could not, though I exerted a supreme effort, retrace the paths I had traveled in our conversation, but I knew, if from nothing else than from the simple observation of human nature, that I had not been silent this whole time. What troubled me, therefore, to the point of tears which bubbled out of my red-hot eyes, was that I had possibly so involved myself with Nathan Kadish that I dared not cut myself off from him at once, must see him immediately again to ascertain how much and from what irascible or sentimental viewpoint I had revealed. And yet, because I could not dissociate him from my malaise, I desired nothing so little as this second interview.

When we had traversed another mile, I remembered that we had made an engagement for that evening when, at eight o'clock, I was to call upon him at his apartment in Cambridge for the purpose of meeting the Japanese girl. Simultaneously, I recalled my astonishment at hearing him ask me, "Does Shura live by herself in Chichester now?" I had been in control of my wits sufficiently to tell him nothing but I had found, by careful questions, that he had not heard of my mother's commitment to the asylum, for he had been back to Chichester only twice in the past two years and by that time, I suppose, some new scandal was of more immediate interest.

I had no difficulty at all in calling to mind what had happened after we left the café in Scollay Square. Emboldened by my renewed friendship with this charming young man, this paragon, as I often told him as we ascended the back side of Beacon Hill, of sense and sensibility, I did not hesitate to adopt his suggestion, when we

378

got to Pinckney Street and I found I did not have my door key, that I call out to Miss Pride while he bombarded her window with snowballs. For Nathan said that the procedure was more practical than rousing the whole house by ringing the door-bell.

"Hello, up there!" I cried. "Miss Pride! I'm locked out!"

"Hey!" shouted Nathan. "Hey, lady! Come down and let a person in! It's cold out here!" To our delight, one of the snowballs went in the window. I congratulated Nathan on his marksmanship and we shook hands, gazing at one another with deepest admiration. Presently Miss Pride's head appeared. "Hush! I'm coming." Nathan backed away and as he receded into the whirling snow, I had the impression that like the Cheshire cat, he was leaving his smile behind. He whispered, "So long, madam," and vanished as the outer door opened and Miss Pride stood shivering on the threshold in a brown wrapper. Her scanty hair was unpinned and it bristled about her collar. I was not in the least frightened. On the contrary I felt loquacious and was on the point of asking Miss Pride to join me in a drink of her whiskey as I was suddenly urged to tell her what I knew about Hopestill. But before I had opened my mouth to speak, she said sharply, "Come in at once and go upstairs, you wretched girl. If one whisper of this reaches anyone, I'll turn you out of the house." She said no more, or if she did, I did not understand her. But in the morning when I went to the library, she spoke at length.

The sight of the glass of sherry beside the chess-board made me gasp and lift my eyes to Mr. Pride, but the thought was at once in my mind that he and Dr. Eliot had one time eaten Brazil nuts with their wine. There was no corner of the room without its alcoholic associations: here Mr. Whitney and I had stood drinking whiskey, there Mr. Morgan had constantly refilled his glass, and Miss Pride, mercilessly smelling the bouquet of her wine between leisurely sips, reminded me that I had been drunk, had been drinking heavily, had had too much to drink, had reeked of alcohol, that I must learn to refuse the third glass of whatever it was, whiskey, rum, gin, brandy, wine. She had learned from the Countess that I had pled illness and had left the party (I could have wept with gratitude for the Countess' discretion), but she had also learned from Mr. Pingrey that I had said I must run an errand for her. The latter, comparing notes with his hostess, had been furious. Moreover, I had made no apologies to Mr. Whitney who had been kind enough to give up his evening for my sake, and I had refused point-blank to be introduced to Mr. Hornblower who was Miss Pride's cousin and who had had the generosity to show an interest in what he had heard about me.

In view of my egregious misdemeanor, I was to be punished by exclusion from a series of parties to some of which I might otherwise have been invited. These parties were to be in celebration of Hopestill's engagement to Philip which had been announced at the Countess' shortly after I left. The marriage was to take place in three weeks' time. On the day following this, a dressmaker was coming on from New York and Miss Pride had planned that she and I, for these pre-nuptial weeks, would dine together at an early hour, and the rest of the time, she implied, we were to make ourselves as scarce as possible except in those quarters dedicated to our work.

Just as one cannot be surprised at death when it has been prepared for by a long illness, as the liar cannot be surprised by the consequences of his lies, so I was not surprised by Miss Pride's news, for I had known from the moment Hopestill spoke Philip's name the afternoon before that it was her intention to marry him by fair means or foul. And yet, want of surprise does not cancel out grief over the death nor regret that the lies have been found out, and I did not hear Miss Pride without desolation. I mustered up what politeness I could, said I was sure she was happy over the turn of events, that it must have been something of a thunderclap since it was so sudden. Miss Pride assured me that on the contrary no one had been in the least taken unawares, but naturally everyone had been delighted.

What a revolting business appeared my sodden, sentimental interlude in the slums of Boston! While we had sat in dirty tumult, Hopestill in her turquoise dress with fresh camellias at her shoulder which Philip had bought her (probably at the same stall where earlier he had bought mine) was elegantly, forthrightly playing her game and playing it with an éclat which disguised her guile even to herself.

I was too absorbed with my diversified pains to determine, from Miss Pride's manner, whether the damage I had done myself in her eyes was irreparable. I recalled the pinch she had given me last night when she had discovered Mr. Morgan in the library. It had been a sort of gesture of fellowship, as though she had wanted me to know that she knew that I, her pupil, shared fully her revulsion. How appalling then must have been the sight of my disheveled person, the sound of my thick voice as I stumbled into the vestibule!

No apology was forthcoming from my dry, swollen lips. I swayed, dumb and contrite, before the chess-table, awaiting my dismissal. She gave it finally and with a stingy smile, but one which made my heart leap for joy, she said, "I have been told that Bromo-Seltzer brings relief to your kind of suffering," so that I knew my exile would not be permanent.

If only the short space of three weeks would cure my other ill, my stifling and manacled envy of Hopestill! It was like a fretting child that having a limited experience of the mercy of time believes that the mumps and his imprisonment will last forever and that the time at playing he has lost can never be made up but must blight his whole life. Love, commingled with envy, confounds the mind like drink or fever and the world narrows to the size of one's own soul. Archimedes, if he could have got off the earth, could have moved it. The wretched person, if he could get outside himself, could find the proper physic. But one does not learn, believes with laic obstinacy that the efficacious remedy is the homeopathic one: the common cures, impotent as a broth of newts' eyes and bats' wool, are the escape from love into love, or into writing verses about one's love or reading other's verses, or into a recital to friends of one's love and its debacle. Our obfuscated faculties cannot comprehend that the addition of fuel to the fire will make the blaze brighter and the heat more intense. Thus, I desired to replace Philip with someone who looked exactly like him, who had the same sort of voice and the same kind of mind and had even the same stiff back.

## 2

Eleven o'clock each Sunday, when Mac and I started out for Wolfburg, was the hour at which the descendants of believers and a few believers gathered sociably before Emmanuel and Trinity, the furred issue of the limousines offering to each other hands in gloves, white even in the winter, or a caress that served as a kiss in these days of so many colds and "catching" coughs, but was rather the light pressure of cheek against cheek. Along Commonwealth Avenue, others briskly walked in typical pairs: the middle-sized man with a black mustache, a bowler, a Chesterfield, and gray suède gloves, was formally but devotedly protective of his wife or sister in a short mink coat, adorned with last night's gardenia for whose longevity the ice-chest was responsible, a dress of which the gentle-colored skirt showed beneath the coat, a small hat topped with a crinoline posy. Now and again, as we drove past, I saw someone I had met at Miss Pride's or at the Countess', and if my nod were acknowledged, even though its target showed by her thoughtful scrutiny that she could not "place" me ("That's Lucy Pride's chauffeur," said the perplexed eyes, "but who can the girl be?"), I felt mildly triumphant. But mildly, because the luxury which embraced me—the camel's hair lap-robe, the shining glass between myself and my impeccable driver, the thermos bottle of consommé provided me in case I should get cold, my own expensive coat imported from the woolen mills of New Hampshire—made these outward signs merely the superfluous confirmation of my good fortune. If my greeting to one of the Sunday promenaders was not received, I felt no disappointment for, if I needed them, I could summon any number of explanations for the slight, none of which reflected unfavorably on me: Mrs. Frothingham was without her spectacles, Mrs. Coolidge was flustered because she thought she would be late to church. Admiral Nephews did not fail to know me. "Hello!" he cried as we stopped before the red light on Exeter Street. "Where are you going on this day most calm, most bright?" He pointed me out to his frail wife who leaned upon a cane, and she nodded amiably but tugged at his arm to remind him that this was no time to dally.

On Commonwealth Avenue on fine Sunday mornings, there was an absence of children and of poor people, as if the territory were "restricted" like apartment buildings which will not let space to Jews or the owners of dogs. Down the mall towards the Public Gardens, there strolled the débutantes, airing their doe-eyed cocker spaniels, or laughing with their beaux whose cropped, uncovered heads and Cantabrigian costumes—long tweed coats with leather patches at the elbow, trousers that did not match, bow ties, cinereous summer shoes over the tops of which lazily cascaded woolen socks—were the badges of privileged youth who, having other things to do, did not go to church. A fair-haired, solitary girl in riding clothes, who was exercising a prancing black shepherd, called out a greeting to one of the older generation who kept to the sidewalk. "Good mahning, Mr. Pukins! I heah Billy's going to Chiner. I think it's mahvelous!"

Mr. Perkins, lifting his bowler, faced her across the engine of Miss Pride's car, his white teeth revealed in a smile that agreeably elevated his little mustache. "Good mahning, Susan! We're having a little dinnah pahty for him next week. You've been told to come, haven't you?"

"Indeed I have!"

They bowed and smiled again and as he replaced his hat, Mr. Perkins added jestingly, "I see you don't go to church."

The roar of traffic, commencing to move along again with the green light, drowned out her reply, but I had faith in her and knew she would not make a fool of herself with a serious counter. Probably at Billy Perkins' farewell party, when his parents made their appearance during cocktails, after which they would leave the "youngsters" to themselves, the sally would be repeated, and Susan would say something like, "I really enjoy church, you know! But Sunday is such a lovely time to exercise my dog!" making her neglect of religion rather endearing as well as temporary for, her gentle, wistful tone implied, she was prepared for the inevitable and would graciously assume her duties towards God as soon as she had settled down either as a matron or as a spinster. And Mr. Perkins, into whose glass was being poured a second cocktail while the girl extended her fingers over her glass to show that she had had enough, would say that he absolutely agreed with her and that when he was her age he probably would not have gone to church either if it had not been compulsory. "Things were so line and rule," he would say, making the staid girl's heart flutter at this testimony of her generation's liberty. "You wouldn't have had a cocktail, for instance," he would continue as she gazed proudly into her Martini in which the olive was still an inch from the surface of the liquid.

As one tenacious of sleep in the early morning, I hoarded the moments of the drive along the avenue against the time when we would turn off towards Boylston and then into the Fenway. For to me, as to those whom the Countess derided when she said, "Boston is a very small place," the city ended precisely at Massachusetts Avenue, and all the rest of it, the cold, uncrowded medical college, the spacious Brookline parkways, the large houses of new materials and derivative architecture, the wide modern drives, did not belong to Boston with its narrow houses and painted doors, and I felt that the expatriates dwelling in Jamaica Plain and Hyde Park and Milton were but wealthier versions of the bourgeois Brunsons. I admired the horseback riders along the bridle paths which bordered Jamaica Pond and the ice-skaters, but did so only because I thought they merely used the resources of these fertile outskirts but returned, at the end of their diversion, to Pinckney or Marlborough or Beacon Street. I felt altogether differently towards such towns as Concord, Lexington, Bedford, Lincoln, and these, together with certain parts of Cambridge and what I called "Boston proper" constituted in my mind "greater Boston" whereas everything in between, even though nearer to the State House, was clearly excluded. I could not revise my map even when I learned that eminent families lived, and had for generations, on Blue Hill Avenue in Milton, in Needham, in Newton.

In an hour's time, we had reached the country and drove between fog-filled woods. Fresh snow, still scathless, lay between the trees where only a few weeks before the stained leaves had lain; the natural paths, rejuvenated by the graduation of the landscape into winter, crept in their immaculate renascence back into the far blue shadows; and not too long from now they would waver forth in the marine spring. We had not gone more than two or three miles when to our left there rose up the high red walls of my mother's asylum; covered with woodbine that had caught the snow, they blended with the landscape. Presently they broke for an iron gate guarded by a fat, unpleasant man who let us in and said sardonically, "This way to the booby-hatch, folks." I had told Miss Pride of the gate-keeper's manner which no longer offended me but which I thought must horrify the relatives of other inmates, for I believed that Miss Pride, with the flourish of a pen, could have the man removed and a courteous one installed in his place. She did investigate and found that this greeting was only for our car, as Mac and the man had been companions in grammar school, though there was never the slightest sign of recognition on Mac's misanthropic face.

My mother came into the reception room, like a nun coming from the cloister, in her gray uniform, her eyes observing something beyond me or above my head. I nearly always took her flowers and as she sat down, her head bent to study them, she appeared to be waiting for the roses and the carnations to be given the gift of tongues. Then she lifted them to her ear. "Pretty *things*," she would say to them. She would turn towards me her lovely eyes that could see me only as a little child and drawing me to her she whispered so that no one could hear, "Darling, we're going visiting today. The flowers won't wilt if we wrap them in a wet newspaper." Then we rose and walked, arm in arm, down the long, gray hall, followed at some distance by an attendant, and entered the common room where the daffy, harmless women rocked and sang, nodding and smiling, their tender eyes roving private worlds which they sometimes found so amusing they had to laugh out loud. My mother's fancy-work and mine were brought to us; together we worked for an hour and my mother praised the tailless birds she had taught me how to make. "But, dearie," she would say, "there's something wrong with it, I don't know what. See mine, see how it goes?" And she held up the identical bird, bereft of its tail feathers, embroidered in green and yellow silk.

Sometimes my mother's affection (she would suddenly drop her work to kiss me) spread like an epidemic through the room and the demented creatures who that day had no visitors shouted and cooed and goggled their eyes and beckoned me with rapidly wagging fingers. One mild and motherly woman with white hair and dimpled cheeks would hold up a pink candy box that rattled when she shook it. "I'll show you what's inside, Ellen, if you'll just come to Granny," and when I shook my head, smiling politely, she would take a man's white handkerchief out of her bosom and cry a little and blow her nose. Once an attendant let her come sit beside us to show us her treasure, fifteen gallstones of varied sizes and shapes. My mother was charmed. "That's a fine one!" she cried as she picked one up, but the old lady snatched it out of her hand. "No you don't, my good woman," she said sharply. "Do you think they grow on trees?"

Most of the others had neither fancy-work nor gallstones to keep them occupied, and so they merely sat about, batting their eyes, grinning and purring like happy cats. The malcontents, arms crossed on their breasts, sat apart, muttering motley diatribes: "I called the police. No, couldn't make it, too busy they said. Busy, yes, no doubt of that, I said, busy taking the bread out of poor people's mouths, that's what you're busy doing. Called the newspaper. No, didn't handle such matters. Why not, I said. Do you mean to stand by and watch the people of your community suffer because dentists' brothers are politicians? Yes, ma'am, no, ma'am. Don't yes, ma'am, no, ma'am, *me,* I told them and hung up. It is a crying shame that you can't carry x-rays of your teeth in your pocketbook without gangsters, hired by dentists' brothers, following to steal them or substitute the real ones with other people's teeth or dog's teeth, for that matter. I merely walked into the restaurant and two men with revolvers were waiting. Merely stepped inside to have a cup of tea after the dentist's visit, and there they were waiting." The less articulate of the persecuted stared in silence at the attendants, their faces fixed in a monotonous sneer.

My mother no longer felt that she was victimized, for much had been deleted from her memory: if she ever spoke of a place other than the asylum garden or of the room we sat in, it was of Luibka's house or the officers' tavern, but not of Chichester. She did not forget me, although, because her sense of time had gone, she thought I was eight or nine years old, and the six days when she did not see me were like the six hours when formerly I had been at school; nor did she forget the cold, but she would rub my hands between hers in the old way and complain with sorrowful resignation that "they" put snow in the stoves instead of wood. "They" were unreal shadows, harmless, stupid, servile ghosts who required a good deal of pampering; because she did not wish to offend them, she always spoke in whispers. "A new one came this morning just after you left, darling," she would say, "and left the door wide open so the snow came in. That's why it's so cold."

She talked very little. For the most part we worked at our birds in

386

silence. And so long as I was there, with the living proof before my eyes that she was not aware of her surroundings, I was not depressed but was even comforted by the soothing, aimless motion of my fingers as they plied the embroidery needle. I would wonder, watching her serene face, if I would ever achieve the degree of her beauty, for, if I still looked upon Miss Pride as my model for character, I was no longer deluded by that old hallucination in which I saw her as a beautiful person, and, at least on Sunday, I was as ambitious to look like my mother as on all the other days I was to be like Miss Pride. Unfortunately, I had a variable face so that my mirror showed me a different person half a dozen times a day, for I had inherited some features from both my parents and each set of genes struggled for pre-eminence: my hair was black like hers but my eyes were blue like his, and though my mouth was a facsimile of hers, its pure outlines were corrupted when I smiled and showed my father's crooked teeth.

Gliding, these hours, in brainless daydreams, fashioned from anonymous places and times, I would sometimes hear, like an echo, a voice of a familiar timbre. Like the person who, awakened by a scream, deduces from the cold sweat on his forehead and the trembling of his arms that the sound has come from his own throat, so I, recognizing the voice as my own, thought I had spoken. But in a moment, the words, which my nerves had retained though my mind had not yet comprehended them, were repeated: "Poor little blue cold hands," and I knew that it was my mother who had spoken, not I. Conversely, when I was not with her, when, for example, I was at the Countess' on Friday and everyone was chattering loudly, I was thinking of something far removed from the conversation of which I was a part and I heard my mother speaking; yet when the words returned they formed the banal, effortless answer to someone who had asked me if I had ever been to Ipswich.

The hours in the bright common room were like those a solitary traveler spends in a strange railway station, after a sleepless night, so that his weary eyes impose a glaze on colors; half-dozing, he wakes suddenly, thinking he has been asleep for an hour and sees that the old woman on the bench across from him who had taken out her handkerchief when he went to sleep has now begun to blow her nose, and that the man who sweeps up the burnt-out cigarettes on the floor has progressed at the most two feet. He sleeps again and wakes to see the old woman returning her handkerchief to her pocketbook, the cleaning man twelve inches farther along. Or they were like those moments when, succumbing to ether, the conscious mind suddenly revives, rises like the bobbing head of a drowning man, and hears the end of the sentence the anesthetist had begun as he attached the cone. The boredom of the traveler and the horror of the patient are unendurable when memory makes them so and pessimism complains that they may happen again. I never failed to dread Sundays nor to be distressed as we left the asylum; but at the time I was with my mother, I had no feelings save sensuous ones and nothing from the outer world accompanied me here. On the contrary, when shame or jealousy or despair had dogged me like a shadow all the way to Wolfburg, the moment the door to the common room was opened to us, I was beholden to no one and to nothing.

Each time, my mother was allowed to sit in the car for a little while before I left. An attendant sat in front with Mac, glancing often at us in the mirror over the wind shield. The meeting of my eyes with his trained ones, keen as a surgeon's (the medical effect was enhanced by the mirror in which he studied me, like the mirror of a nose specialist), produced in me a self-consciousness that warmed my cheeks and dried my tongue, and I blushed when I made some reply to my mother, although the glass was closed between us and my voice was inaudible to the men in front. What disturbed me— and marked the end of the hypnotic state that had enabled me to endure the visit—was that those watchful eyes included me as well as my mother in their vigilance. When my mother had been led away after a final sighing embrace from which it would have taken me hours to disentangle myself if I had been alone, and Mac had started down the drive, the embarrassment became a vague, irrational fear which was then followed, as the dénouement to Ivan's fits had been a coma, by a benumbing, anarchical depression which possessed me until finally, late that night, back in my room on Pinckney Street, I fell asleep.

# 3

It had never been so great a solace as it was today to sit in my accustomed place beside my mother in the unchanged common room, having no need to make explanations to anyone, not even to myself. Gradually the aspirin tablets which I had begged from a nurse (I had not liked to ask Mac to stop at a drug-store for Miss Pride's prescription for me) began to take effect and my nausea and headache were replaced by a sweet, feverish sleepiness. I had brought my mother some apples as well as the customary flowers, and their clean, wholesome smell was drawn from their satiny hide by the excessive warmth of the room. The last time, she had asked me to bring them. "Bring me some red apples, darling," she had said. "I know how smooth they are." But today when I opened the paper bag for her to see them, she had said, "What are these?" "Apples," I had replied, "You asked for them." She had put the bag on the floor and every now and again glanced at it. After a while she had said, "Sonie, tomorrow if you can find me some apples. Bring me some little yellow apples. I've forgotten how they taste."

My mother was not well. For some Sundays past she had had a cold in the head and now today I saw that it had settled in her chest. She coughed considerably and her breath sometimes came with difficulty. An attendant had whispered to me that I must leave sooner than I usually did, for she had been in bed in the infirmary for several days, though she had been allowed to get up for a few hours each afternoon. Never talkative these days, she was more disinclined than ever to conversation, and we worked for a long time in silence. The lulling, soporific warmth, the wordless muttering of the woman persecuted by dentists' brothers, the odor of the apples, and the steady stitching of the birds so satisfied me as an opiate that I proposed to myself, with the seriousness that makes a dream of a five-inch man or a German-speaking dog or an encounter with a camel seem useful or irritating but not in the least strange, that I spend the next three weeks in this well-heated and peaceable place.

When I had finished inventing plausible lies for Miss Pride about where I should be and had imagined myself installed with a few books and my phonograph in one of the cells, something in the room, a voice or a falling object or the rattling of the gallstones, awakened me and I suddenly laughed. My mother looked up from her work and said, "You have caught my cold!" And when I assured her that I had not, she said, "But you just coughed. I heard you." She beckoned to an attendant who was sitting near-by reading the Sunday comic strips avariciously and without the slightest amusement and when he came she said, "Do you know where they keep the cough syrup? Sonie coughed and she'll be ill." I attempted to make a sign to the attendant but I was hampered by the fixed gaze of my mother as if she were waiting for the devil inside me to make me cough again so that she might pounce on him. He went back to his chair and from the table beside it, took a bottle from a box which seemed to contain first-aid equipment and returned to us, gravely offering it to me along with a spoon. My mother resumed her needlework and I said to the man, "But I didn't cough, I only laughed."

"Laughed?" he said, as if that were a kind of action unfamiliar to him. "Why did you laugh?"

"I don't know. But anyhow I don't need the cough syrup."

"Take it," he said, nodding in my mother's direction and he poured out a spoonful which he handed to me. It was strong and not unpleasant, tasting a little like Cointreau. I thanked him and he went back to his funny papers, but for the next hour he glanced at me from time to time over the top of Elmer Tuggle and Gasoline Alley (he read thoroughly and very slowly) as if he were trying to fathom my laughter.

For a long time there was no other interruption, and in this cataleptic tranquillity, my mind was blank, or, rather, was occupied by certain abstractions such as "warmth" or "absence of pain" or "motion." In demonstrating to myself the last of these, I felt myself sinking through boundless space; I was at once pressed down and pulled down, in the first place by a weightless force from above and in the second by gravity, of which the principle I experienced in a manner more entire than the simple, conscious observation of a falling object could ever induce, just as, at other times when I had been fatigued for some days together, I fancied I could sense in my tired muscles the slow vertigo of the earth. When I emerged from this ethereal baptism, I was more than ever at ease, and I was so freed of any anxieties, in this isolated place and in this parenthetical time, that my mind could roam like an innocent child, at will, through grouped reflections and through favorite daydreams.

I had been following a string of associated memories which began with a clam-bake held about this time two years before by the senior class of the high-school. I had seen Ruby Beeler filing a boy's right-hand fingernails, and I proceeded from that to Mr. Henderson who all one winter had had a blue nail on his little finger. Abruptly the concatenation was unlinked by the obtrusion of a single, clear-cut image which could not be worried into any sort of relationship with what had gone before. Irrelevant, impulsively independent, there was before my eyes a room which I had never seen, but a room in which there was hardly an object that was unfamiliar. It was possible that I had briefly fallen asleep and had dreamed of such a place, and yet it did not fade upon my scrutiny of it, but, static, pictorial, it was present to me like a projection on a screen.

It was a dark and rather shabby room in which the solid, heavy draperies were threadbare, blotched and rotten in the folds. One of two casement windows was open, giving onto a court, and from it were visible frail balconies where mop-buckets and potted geraniums stood, and all the tattered, dirty overflow of kitchens, the rags and cans and empty cartons. On window-sills were bottles, bowls, and sleeping cats. All the windows were red, reflecting a sunset; the light had an autumnal quality, discernible only through feeling since no other circumstance hinted at the season of the year. There were no trees in sight, yet had there been, they certainly would have been releasing their fissile yellow leaves. Probably if the room had been animated or if from its visible contours I had proceeded to list its likely attributes in other sensory perceptions, it would have included a coolness, a musty smell, and through the windows, the voices of boys loitering on the way home from school.

The furniture of the rectangular room was ponderous and dark and was crowded together, forming angles and recesses and deep shadows like hiding places. In the middle of the room, quite by it-self, was a small round table covered with a white cloth which was clean but limp, as if in the ironing it had not dried properly. A bottle of red wine, bearing no label, stood in the center. The book-shelves which lined one wall and extended nearly to the ceiling were full and contained well-worn volumes largely, it seemed, in French and German. The titles were arranged in confusion. Among them was a bound medical manuscript dating from the fifteenth century. There was a book called *Der Traum den Rote Kammer:* its binding simulated rice-paper and there was a singular discrepancy between the design (a delicate torii and a path scattered with the petals of red flowers) and the curly German script of the title. Between the two windows stood a little Victorian writing desk, open, and reveal-ing a portfolio of cheap Italian leather, dyed green; on it rested a horribly ingenious tortoise-shell letter-opener of which the handle was fashioned into a lobster's claw, cleverly grasping a solid sphere of agate.

It was like the room of some student of wonders and curiosities who had returned the books to their shelves for the afternoon and had got himself this bottle of red wine to enjoy as he looked upon himself in leisure, asking whether his study of prodigies had affected him in any way.

I reviewed rooms in which I had been, as far back as I could remember, but I could not place it, and while, as I have said, it was by no means unfamiliar and all the objects were as real as if I had owned them for many years, I could not, nevertheless, actually iden-tify any of them. I cannot say how long the "vision" of this red room lasted, but while it did, I experienced a happiness, a removal from the world which was not an escape so much as it was a practi-ticed unworldliness. And it was a removal which was also a return. The happiness was not unmixed: as I gazed at the red evening sun-light winnowed through the brick chimneys of the court, I was filled with a tranquil, mortal melancholy as if I were out of touch with the sources of experience so that I could receive but could not participate: that is, I could *assume* that boys were shouting on the street, but I could not hear them. The mitigation of the light seemed to sadden me even more, for it had a potential quality of "bursting" in upon me and yet upon my windows, it was a layer of rich opacity which did not, however, prevent me from seeing quite clearly the balconies and the sleeping cats.

From another world, from the streets of the anonymous city where the room had been in readiness for my return to it, a voice ascended and as the windows were blackened and the room disappeared in a darkness as complete as that immediately after the lights have gone off in a theater, I heard my mother say, "I'm in the crazy house!" Her eyes blazed with the anger of a terrified animal as she was forsaken by the merciful anesthesia which for these months had made her live burial tolerable to both of us. Those powerful eyes now saw the barred windows behind the coy, concealing blinds, saw the inimical, impassive strength of the attendants, saw the moonstruck women grinning and gurgling like babies and they saw, completing the circuit, wider with each new revelation, that I was not a little girl just home from school but was a grown woman whose fine tailored suit and costly shoes cried aloud my treachery. Her lips twitched with panic and vivid splashes, induced as much by fever as by her fright, appeared on her cheeks.

When she had spoken, it had been softly in a breathless voice, as though she must state her discovery but must do so quietly lest she not hear another noise, and she had not immediately looked for a door through which to escape but had surveyed cautiously her dangerous surroundings. But though I thought I alone had heard her, the vigilant attendant, trained to hear and see things that did not attract other people's attention, had laid aside his comic strips and sat poised on the edge of his chair, ready to spring forward. Thinking to adjust things quickly, lead her back to her world of tailless birds and little yellow apples, I put my hand on hers and said, "Mamma, will you rub my hands?" But she flung me off and seizing the flowers from their pitcher on the table beside us, she stripped the blossoms from the stems and hurled them like rocks into my face, spattering me with drops of water as a shower of petals fell into my lap and obliterated the embroidered bird. As in the faithful dog that turns on his master, the stimulus for her assault was mysterious. She wanted to inflict pain on me, and in her rage she could not see that the soft rosebuds touched my face as tenderly as snow, and as if blood from wounds was pouring from me, she hissed, "Beast! Cheater!"

I could not remember what I had used to do with her in her exuberant furies, and with relief I saw the attendant approaching us, casually so as not to alarm the other patients, and knew that he would capably manage to quiet her. I had forgotten to be grateful that I was no longer responsible for her, but just as a woman whose children are grown recalls, on seeing a baby, the nuisance of infantile care, and as we are sometimes profoundly thankful as we witness the seething turmoil of adolescence that we are not and can never again be sixteen, so I counted my blessings as I watched the attendant draw my mother from her chair and, gently embracing her, move towards the door. Upon a signal from him, immediately after her first outcry—though it had been little louder than a whisper it had sounded like thunder in his alert ears—the other attendants had busied themselves with the patients, fussing with their clothing or asking after their wants, so that the crazy calm, the disruption of which had been threatened when my mother, pelting my face with the flowers, had become the cynosure of inquisitive simian eyes, continued as if there had been no hiatus.

I brushed the petals off my coat and finding no other place to put them, dropped them into the bag of apples which I picked up intending to take home with me. With the stubborn health of a strong animal despite what had just happened, I was hungry, for I had had neither breakfast nor lunch and the smell of the apples had so tempted me that it was all I could do to restrain myself from biting into one as I left the room. The rattle of the gallstones reached my ears as I crossed to the door and turning, I saw the white-haired old lady smiling beseechingly as she crooked her index finger at me. "Come here a minute, Ellen," she said. "Granny has a surprise for you." But one of the wise and lifeless matrons sat down beside her, saying, "Mrs. Andrews, may I see what you have in your little box?" Delighted, the old lady opened it up and said in her kindly voice, "Ellen gets them all when I die."

As I went into the white-walled corridor down which my mother and her guard were strolling, like lovers, her head upon his shoulder, his arm about her waist, a doctor, who had been writing something in a notebook as he leaned against a radiator, stepped towards me. "Are you the daughter?" he asked. I replied that I was and I remarked that my mother seemed to be approaching one of those crises with which I was so familiar. The doctor, bluff, corpulent, with a large, limber face in which broken capillaries running in all directions made it look like crazed pink porcelain, shook his head and answered, "On the contrary. We think she is recovering."

Instinctively, as if to prove that he was wrong, I looked down the passage towards her and as I did so, she turned her head. "Sonia, Sonia!" she cried, sobbing like a child, but the attendant tenderly bent her head again into his shoulder and they disappeared into a doorway marked "Infirmary."

"Oh, no!" I said to the doctor. "She can't be getting well. Why, she's much worse today than she has ever been before!"

"No, you're wrong, my dear girl. Dr. Tudor and I have lately been much more hopeful about her. To a large extent, she has shaken off that intermittent amnesia, and a good part of the time she is at least semi-aware of where she is. We're now of the opinion that she will recover, perhaps not completely and not permanently. But it is possible and, indeed, very likely, that in another three months you can take her home."

I said nothing. My silence drew a smile of understanding to the florid face. "I've been over the case. I understand you had her brought here because you hadn't money enough to get someone to take care of her."

"Yes, I have no money."

He did not fail to scrutinize my clothes. "But you're well enough off now?"

"I am secretary to a wealthy woman," I told him, "but I have very little actual money."

"Mmm," he mused. "You're qualified to be secretary to someone else, I suppose? To someone who would pay cash for your work?"

"I can't!" My fingers tightened round the paper bag of apples as I imagined this future life he proposed for me: the rumpless birds gradually crowding us out of our house, the endless cups of tea before a fire so violent it threatened to burst from the stove, the incorrigible maudlin affection manufactured at top speed by the indestructible engine in her person, unvarying in its pattern. I could think only of my return after work in the afternoons: day after day and year after year of her pertinacious life, I would hear my name reiterated in different tones and in combination with a few simple phrases, falling from her lips like tears or like a molten substance used to solder one thing to another in obdurate unity.

"Why can't you?" inquired the doctor with interest.

"Because I am afraid," I confessed. Until I said the word, I had not been afraid. My feeling had been anger that I must give up my life in Boston as it was now for the lonesome, tedious sort the girls at the business college had been prepared for. And I was as defiant of my mother as if she had conspired against me with someone, perhaps with this optimistic doctor. But I knew, as soon as I had spoken, that I spoke the truth, that I was afraid, not of any harm that might come to my mother through my inexpert treatment nor of any physical harm that I might suffer at her hands. When the doctor asked me, I told him, "Because I think sometimes *I* might go insane."

Still, when he questioned me further, I could give him no reasons save that I could not bear to be alone in the room with the Countess because she reminded me of Mamma and each time, after she had kissed me, I ran through the Common to Boylston Street and then ran back again to Pinckney as though the whistling wind, my pounding heart, my smarting face, could efface the memory of that plastic bosom and those full, intemperate lips. Sometimes my distress was so acute that I was obliged to send down word that I could not eat dinner because of a headache, and all evening I was numb and visited from time to time by an abortive retching, a spasm of inexplicable terror. And I could tell the doctor how sometimes Miss Pride's eyes and sometimes Philip's were watchful and that the guard who sat with Mac in the car perused my face for signs of madness and that all these eyes, on certain nights, watched me from the corners of my darkened room.

The disclosure shocked me: it was as if I spoke of an absent person, sketched impersonally the strange behavior of a fictitious character. But I was not creating. These things were true but until now I had not articulated them nor even recognized them. For months, though, I had felt presences in my room which came in that hazy interlude that foretokens sleep, and I had had the feeling that I was being watched, but like my mother I confused one sensation with another and said that the hallucination had come from the sound of the fire which, dying, soughed like a forest wind.

I did not convince the doctor. Even to myself my story did not sound like history but like an impromptu fabrication. I had neither the vocabulary nor the analytical gift to state my case in full, arguing from the past as well as from these present idiosyncrasies. But he was not unsympathetic, although he smiled with what may have been contempt.

"You must control yourself. If you want your mother to be well, you've got to help, you know."

"But *well*, sir?" I said. "I mean, how far will she be cured?"

"Why, I should think you'd be as good a judge of that as I. She'll be restored, we hope, to her original state of mind. From what we've seen here, we know that she is by nature an unstable woman and for that reason could never be thrown on her own. If she had no relatives and were completely alone in the world, I expect we would keep her here, give her some little occupation like helping in the kitchen. But you wouldn't want that, would you?"

"Oh, no," I hastened to assure him. Then, against my better judgment I went on. "There was a time when I would have given up my whole life to her, but that was before I saw that nothing, no change of atmosphere, no improvement in our standard of living, could make her anything but what she has always been since I was a young child."

"And what is that?"

"A millstone," I whispered. "But I know I'm duty-bound. You needn't tell me."

"I had no such intention. I'm not a moralist."

I closed my eyes for a moment to shut out his professional smile and as I did so, I seemed to descend once more through the wide, moving air and then, purged, absolved, emptied of all that did not pertain to solitude, I saw the red room with its wedges of shadow, its prospect of eternally slumbering cats. When, with the opening of my eyes, the room disappeared, I thought of adding to my list of suspicions about myself which I had just given him, this phenomenal apparition. For whatever had been the emotions with which I had received the impression for the first time a few minutes ago in the common room, surprise was not one of them: the part of my mind, the spiritual optic apparatus, so to speak, had registered the details of the room so singularly tangible—down to the title of a book in German—when the details were some of them extraordinary, that the exercise could not be mistaken for a daydream or a dream and I knew (but how could I expect anyone to believe this subjective testimony?) that it was not a memory. But I concluded that this morning was *not* the first time I had seen it, but that something in the external world upon which I could not lay my finger had by accident dislodged it from the populous, diffuse, chimerical mazes of my subconscious mind. I had this second time, as before, felt safe and comforted. And it was because of this that I did not tell the doctor, out of the fear that if I told him, I would lose the room forever. Then as I looked again, straight into his eyes which regarded me with curiosity, I was visited briefly by a feeling of guilt and uneasiness like the thief who, having cached his plunder, feels that he has been observed though a second survey shows him that no one is near. When I spoke—and it seemed to me that a long time had elapsed since his last words—it was with a stammer: "I can't explain . . . I . . . perhaps you don't believe me . . . that is, perhaps there's nothing to what you say. You say she has had fever. Well, often before, when she had fever, she seemed rational. It's nothing more than that, I can assure you." I cursed myself for this unsure speech, so insolent in its ambiguity, and as my eyes faltered and fell away from his astonished stare, the doctor said, "Why, you *are* at sea, aren't you? You must stop worrying. Go on back to town and see a movie and try to get a good night's sleep."

I thanked him and apologized for my hysteria. "Good-by," he told me and, as I retreated down the corridor, I could feel his eyes still on me.

As we drove back towards Boston, I ate one of the apples. My thorough enjoyment of its flavor and its frosty grain bitterly amused me: my perturbation was not of heroic enough proportions to kill my appetite; it was even likely, I thought, that I would sleep no worse than usual tonight. The satisfaction of my hunger urged me on to further practical action, and I proceeded to sound out for their utility the several impulses that came to me. My first and strongest was to go at once to Philip. It would be possible to tell him honestly why I could not live with my mother again, for he did not draw a sharp line between sanity and insanity but saw innumerable nuances between the two poles. But would a conversation with him now be as easy as in the old days, now that our incompleted gestures, their instigation unplumbed, were between us like a transgression that was not confessed because, having the appearance of accident, its premeditation on the part of either of us could not be proved? On the other hand, perhaps if I appealed to him now in my trouble and now that he had entered into a contract which precluded the maturation of that fumbling, dumb desire which had fled from the one of us as soon as it had made itself known to the other, perhaps now we could step backwards and, starting fresh, proceed as before. *As before.* But could I, in this darkness, find my way back through the détour where shaggy shapes misled the eye: the shapes of *might have been* and *still might be?* And where, at such an hour, would I find him? Even if he were at home in his three large rooms on Beacon Street, would it not be highly improper for me to call upon him there even for advice? But he would not be at home. He would be somewhere with his fiancée. They were undoubtedly already being fêted. Someone would have arranged an impromptu cocktail party for them and they would be there now, receiving congratulations. Even if I went to him, even if he had nothing else to do but listen to me, he would not be able to keep his mind on what I said.

Would it be better to warn Miss Pride at once? Should I go directly to her bedroom where she would be resting until tea time and beg her for help, telling her that she alone in all the world could give it to me? She was angry with me; she had made it clear this morning that she did not want to be troubled with me for the next three weeks. Another time she might be sympathetic, might even suggest some way to preserve the separation from my mother, but the marriage of her niece was of more importance to her now than anything else; my life, beside it, was a project like the memoirs which must be set aside for the time being. I could not risk it. I would wait until the wedding was over, and then some evening, just before she picked up the *Boston Evening Transcript,* I would say, "Miss Pride, may I ask your advice?"

Or should I now at this moment pick up the speaking tube and say, "Mac, turn around as soon as you can and drive me to New

York." When I was alone in the car, Mac gave in to his temptations and drove both fast and recklessly. While sometimes I recalled with terror the talk of the old ladies who declared that he had heart disease and might suddenly die at the wheel, today his speed and his narrow escapes thrilled me as if he were already obeying my command to take me far away and swiftly to a new life. But the squat shops and movie theaters of Mattapan were already huddled on either side of us and we slowed down with the thick traffic. Nudged on one side by an endless line of cars and on the other by the trolley that lurched slowly forward with loud ejaculations, at times we barely moved and I was gradually invaded by claustrophobia so insistent that the ligaments of my arms and legs began to ache as if I were actually cramped into a small space. How patiently our moral nature bides its time, how adroitly sets its stage, parting its curtains suddenly. As unprepared as Gertrude or her king, we willy-nilly witness our own villainy played out. It had not crossed my mind until I felt myself hampered, buried alive by the creeping machinery all about me that perhaps what the doctor had said was true and that my mother fully knew she was a prisoner whose release depended on me. Was it not the meanest beastliness even to think of flight? I caught a glimpse of myself in the mirror above the wind-shield, and saw my black hair. What if I unpinned it some time as she did always in her frenzies? What if my own passions became hopelessly entangled in a desperate disorder and what then if Miss Pride cold-bloodedly, like me, disburdened herself by sending me off to an asylum and stopped her ears to my entreaties? For ours were not the kind of aberrations that Hopestill's fashionable psychiatrist could cure.

I suffered from my punishment. But I made a bargain with my sense of duty: I said that the red room would be my refuge, that when the time came I would resume the battle on the condition that I might always return to it, as a warrior pauses to pray. The milder, though not sovereign, wardens of my being, granted me permission, and a little comforted, I sank back on the cushions as we pushed on.

The house would be silent and my room would be cold. I did not want to go home. I remembered Nathan's invitation, and although it was not yet five o'clock, I directed Mac to drop me at the Copley

Square subway station. My reason for going to him was no longer to find out how great a fool I had made of myself the night before. It was that I wanted company and I could think of no one more appropriate than my old friend whom I had used to watch reading on early winter nights.

4

The overwashed young man, his birthmark veiled in a shadow, was hard to establish in the surroundings of last evening and equally hard to establish in this cold, filthy, malodorous subterranean suite of two small rooms densely populated with furniture so shabby, fractured in so many places, that it seemed to be totally useless rubbish. I saw, as soon as I went in, that on his sick and sober awakening, Nathan had had no stomach for the visit he had suggested and that probably he had hoped I would not come. Not without irritation, he said, "Oh, it's you. It's only five. I thought I told you eight."

"I know," I replied. "I just had nothing else to do. I brought you some apples."

Perplexed, he took the paper bag from me; as he withdrew an apple, a shower of rose petals fell to the floor. "What the hell's going on?" he said.

I looked brightly about his place, ignoring the question, and said, "Well, you're cozy here." He was anything but cozy. The only light came from two small, high windows through which I saw a steady parade of legs marching briskly past as if they had been amputated but had retained their power of locomotion. There was no rug on the cement floor and this accounted, I supposed, for the galoshes that Nathan had neatly fastened over his trouser legs. There was a couch, covered with a foul green blanket, burned and stained; two overstuffed chairs with ruptured seats from which batting and horsehair indecently protruded; a desk, littered with papers, orange rinds, dirty cups, soiled handkerchiefs; a bookcase; a standing lamp with a paper shade decorated with a sailboat on a blue sea as flat as a table top. In the corners there were bundles, the wash or merely rags I could not tell, and stacks of magazines and pasteboard cartons full of trash. The air was damp and weighted with a strong odor comprised, I thought, of stale cigarette smoke and scorched coffee and fried meat.

401

And yet the occupant of this squalid cell was cleaner than I had ever seen him. I thought at once of the young man, Mr. Garvin, whom I had met at the Countess' and who had impressed me because he gleamed so brightly with soap and water. I said, looking from Nathan to the unsightly blanket on the couch, "Do you sleep here?" and he turned down the cover to show me a pair of clean sheets.

"At present personal cleanliness is my principal fetish."

"Do you know a person named Garvin?" I asked.

"Certainly. And you knew I knew him. He reported to me at once that he had seen you at that fat German's house. And, yes, you're quite right, I got the washing habit from him."

"She's not German, she's Viennese," I said. "He did tell you he had met me? Why didn't you look me up?"

He shrugged his shoulders and with his old, still breathtaking gesture, drew his long fingers over his cheek. "Our last meeting—I mean in Chichester, not last night—didn't leave me with the feeling that you would want to see me again."

"But you misunderstood me!" I cried.

"I had hopes that that was the case, but since you never tried to explain, I assumed you didn't want to explain. And there's no use in your doing it now, because I have other fish to fry."

I was irritated that he thought I had come to resume our adolescent flirtation. "And what makes you think I haven't? You're as vain as ever, I see."

He did not reply. I sat down on the couch and for a time we were silent while he ate his apple. When he had finished he wiped his lips with the back of his hand and reaching down behind the desk brought out a gallon jug. "I suppose you want some of this? I haven't any glasses but I have some teacups. It is sherry, the poor dipsomaniac's drink. Well?" I thanked him, forgetting Miss Pride's admonition. He went on. "Yes, I am glad to see you. The past, that is, the past prior to that aforesaid encounter, comes back rather pleasantly. The fog, for instance. I hadn't thought of it for months."

His eyes narrowed dreamily to show that he was thinking of it now with enjoyment. Likewise, to me, the past came back, for he had presented me with the brilliant cheek and my fingers tightened

402

round the handle of the teacup, restraining themselves from reaching out to touch the skin.

"Oh, rest assured I didn't forget you. I merely set you aside as something completed, the way I did when I finally had to admit that your father wasn't coming back."

"You said last night you hadn't been in Chichester. Why not?"

"Why should I? Oh, I probably neglected to tell you my family moved to Lynn. But my family would never be a reason for my going back there anyhow. I did go back though, twice, just out of curiosity to know what the dump looked like. The first time it was in the summer and all I did was get a bottle of Moxie at Bennett's and get out as quick as I could. There was one of those Barstow hags in the store buying a stick of camphor ice. But the next time I went it was in the winter and it made me sort of nostalgic to walk past your house late in the afternoon. At first I thought I saw a light in the window but it was only a reflection of the sun. Does your mother live there by herself?"

"No," I said. "No, she isn't there any more."

He did not press me and while I longed to tell him where Mamma was, I checked myself and instead poured out to him the story of my meeting with Miss Pride last night and this morning, putting into my account all the feeling I had about my talk with the asylum doctor. Nathan, at first surprised that I had taken my scolding so seriously and then disturbed because he felt he was to blame, comforted me with sincere little speeches which I applied privately to my future with my mother rather than to the one with Miss Pride. He said such things as, "But it will all be over and forgotten," "No one in the world is that important," or "Things will be the same as ever in a little while."

"But you don't *know*," I said. "You don't know *her*."

"Why do you care so much? She sounds like a bitch. May I have another apple?"

"Certainly. I brought them to you."

"They're good apples."

As he ate, the fresh odor reached me through the other smells, and I said suddenly, almost without plan, "Look here, can I come to see you every Sunday?"

403

He looked at me over the apple in surprise. "That's a very peculiar request. How do you know you will want to come here or that I will want you to? Why Sunday? It's a very inconvenient night for me as I have an early class on Monday."

"I'm sorry," I said, blushing. "I don't know why I said it. Do forgive me."

"But what is there to forgive? You're very much odder than you used to be."

"Perhaps I am, but it's also odd of you to tell me so."

He smiled and filled our green teacups again. "I'll confess to you now—now that I don't feel the same way any longer—that I hoped you were so drunk last night you wouldn't remember that I asked you to come. I woke up thinking, Now I've done it again, got myself involved with the past again when it's all I can do to stomach the present. But I'm glad you did remember. And I'm touched by the apples. The rose petals mystify me, though."

I wanted to tell him how I happened to have the apples; I wanted each Sunday night thereafter, through the winter and the long spring, but I was kept silent by indecision, for I did not know how my words would sound to him, whether they would elicit fear or sympathy, or how they would sound to me, whether I would be ashamed or comforted. Though the hours before I came to his apartment remained my secret, so that Nathan was still a stranger to one half of my life, nevertheless to me he became connected with it just as a landscape will seem to be inextricably involved with a remembered event although, at the time, it was hardly noticed. It was as if by giving him the apples that my mother had fingered and had not understood, I had joined them in an alliance which, for all its artificiality, consoled me. It was not that I had felt any disappointment in my mother's not welcoming the apples, nor that I appreciated, by contrast, Nathan's enjoyment of them. It was not in my power to please my mother. It was more, also, than the comparison I naturally made in coming from a madhouse into the presence of a normal person. It was, in effect as a symbol, that I saw the execution of this kind of duty to be worthless both to the agent and to the recipient, for my mother derived no benefit from my gift and had I not brought it, she would not have been aware that I had failed to fulfill my promise. And I, being commissioned to bring the following week essentially what I had brought this week (smaller apples and yellow instead of red) was walking a treadmill. This was what I had wanted to convey to the doctor, but I had known that I would never be able to make him understand and therefore the only hope I had lay in the verdict handed down to myself by myself: whether the obligation, imposed upon us all by the Fifth Commandment, was to be taken literally or was to be interpreted. But since I knew of only one kind of action which could follow if my decision finally was that I owed my mother no more years of my life, that action being the flight I had thought of as we drove home, I could not tell anyone of my debate. For flight, no matter how it may be justified, no matter how necessary it may be to the maintenance of life, is an act of cowardice. One's alternative is protest; but to protest without fear, one must be convinced that right will win, and if it does not, must accept, at least temporarily, the triumph of wrong. The conscientious objector to war is generally regarded as a moral man, if too philosophical, and immune, through some strange means, to the infectious patriotism that sweeps his country in time of war; he may be criticized but only a few will call him a coward. But the man who kills himself, the man who hides himself away in the mountains or in the swamps to escape conscription, is abhorred by everyone. Yet it is possible that his refusal to fight is neither out of the fear of danger nor the dislike of regimentation, but that it stems from the same moral principles as those upheld by the objector.

I was not certain of this argument; yet, as I sat that afternoon with Nathan in his dirty room, I laid the foundation for the edifice that would please me, not the one that was sure to be the soundest. I was persuaded that when the time came, my decision would be impartial, that in the end I would not favor myself, but that in the meantime I was entitled to play with the idea of going away, as unconditionally as my father had done, as far, perhaps, as Nathan was going.

"What are you going to do in Paris?" I asked him. "Write?"

He laughed savagely. "I've got that nonsense knocked out of me. What a pipe-dream!"

"What are you going to do then?"

"You really want to know? It's not nice. It's a damned colossal bore."

"I do want to know."

"I'm going to study Old French and I'm not going in the fine, careless, romantic, high-spirited way I let on last night. I am going on a fellowship and it is my thrilling ambition to make a critical study of Bernard de Ventadour. On my return to America, one year later, I will present this study as a thesis for the degree Master of Arts. Then, oh, then, dear friend, I will be ready for that next step to glory, the Ph.D. And after that, if I am very well-behaved and keep my nose clean, I may get a job teaching beginning French to the boys and girls of the Chichester high-school."

But what had happened to his earlier plans, those he had made on the steps of the Barstow in the fog. "I just grew up," he said sorrowfully. "But this has its compensations. I get a certain sense of power making footnotes on my papers on various medieval subjects: 'Ysonde,' I write learnedly, 'is a rare Scottish form of the name, usually rendered *Ysolt* or *Isolt,* or sometimes *Iseult.*' You know I wanted to go in for *Mittelhochdeutsch* and work on Walter von der Vogelweide just as an excuse to go to Germany, but that's out now, of course. I'll show you what the University of Heidelberg sent me last year." From an untidy drawer, he produced a prospectus containing photographs of the baroque *Alte Gebäude* half hidden by flowering lime trees, of the Castle in its massive decay, of the Old Bridge spanning the river, and of the Protestant cathedral with bookstalls stuffed between its buttresses.

"There are hills on either side of the river, you see," he said. "Garvin spent a summer there a couple of years ago. The first thing I would do would be buy a rucksack and take a long walk. Or maybe before I did that I'd buy a bicycle and go to Heilbronn. I know the map of South Germany by heart and just what the distances are and just where I'd stop overnight." He broke off and took the prospectus from my hand. "It makes me Goddamned sore that I've got a name like mine. Do you think I look Jewish?"

"Not very," I said, thinking as I did so that I had never seen a more Hebraic face than this one.

"Well," he said dully, "let's change the subject."

I was surprised to find that Nathan was essentially unchanged but that my whole perception of him had altered. Where before I had seen formidable brashness, now I saw only a nervous arrogance which, at times headlong, was at other times so timorous that I had only to disagree in the mildest way to make him retract, apologize, abjectly humble himself. He began pontifically to talk of books as if he had forgotten that I could read, had, indeed, been instructed by him, and when I took exception to his enthusiasm for a writer whose short stories were then much in vogue and which had, he asserted, revolutionized the art, Nathan's face expressed his amazement that I had even heard the writer's name, then distrust of himself, and finally he said, "Of course! He's a charlatan! Why didn't I see that before?"

When, in our conversation, he hit upon a poet whom I also admired, he was overjoyed; he fairly frolicked with our kinship, treating me with a connubial warmth, congratulating both of us on this marriage of minds. Our enthusiasms were, indeed, so commonplace that he would have lived in limitless polygamy if he had courted further. His transports would be over Shakespeare's sonnets or Heine or Blake or Yeats whom he would come upon suddenly with as much surprise as a traveler who has been over a road many times will feel if, on one journey, he finds that a handsome new house has been built at the side of it since he last rode by. He told me that it was precisely because of his confusion that he had gone in for medieval studies. "Your taste doesn't matter much there. You don't have to commit yourself on whether you think *The Agenbite of Inwyt* is good or bad."

I asked him if he had ever gone back to the Communists. "No," he said, "but I hate the upper classes more than ever. Harvard College for Boys teems with them. I am employed by one of them, as I told you, a party named Morgan. I have tutored him in German for two years and I bleed him of a great deal of money and learn twice as much German as he does. But this is the kind of thing he'll do: we'll be translating along—he's a moron, of course—and he'll stop suddenly and say, 'Beg pardon, baby, I've got to make a phone call.' He *always* calls me 'baby.' He will call the air line and say, 'This is Morgan. I want a ticket on the five o'clock plane and I want to be booked through to Las Vegas. Put it on my charge account, will you?' His *charge account,* mind you. We go on with the translation—and you couldn't believe his illiteracy—and the telephone will ring. It will be a dame and Morgan will say, 'Honey, I love you, I love you, but right this minute I've got to hop a plane for the Golden West. I'll be back day after tomorrow. I've got ten drunks from Metro Goldwyn Mayer at my place and I've got to go out and police the joint.' We start out again and maybe do one, maybe two paragraphs of *Immensee* and his door-bell rings. His butler (butler, I said) comes in and says there is a little lady outside. 'Well, baby, let's let the Hun go for today. I've got to lay this little lady before I hop a plane. Come around next Tuesday. Tell my man to fix you a drink.' Need I assure you that I do not tell that fat, patronizing penguin that I want a drink?"

With some effort, I brought out, "Do you ever see any of the little ladies?"

"No. And I never want to. But I see their mink coats lying in the hall when I go out. And don't think for a minute I feel the least bit sorry for them. I would rather go to a whore-house myself. But why should he be successful with women? He's stupid and he subscribes to *Esquire.* Now I am extremely intelligent and once you get used to my face, I'm not really ugly. But do I have any success with women? Can I ever be sure of them? If I am sure of them, it's because they're too uninviting to be unfaithful and then they bore me to death. That middle-aged French baggage I told you about won't stir from my door-step and she annoys me so much I could strangle her without the least remorse. But on the other hand I never have been so in love as I am with Kakosan Yoshida and I can't trust her. She lies and deceives me and when I most want her she doesn't show up. And that was the way it was with you. When I specifically wanted to do nothing else in the world but drink Budweiser draft with you at Red's, you wouldn't do it."

We had been sitting in the dark for sometime and now he turned on the lamp. He was as angry, I saw, as he had been on the way to the Brunsons' house, but I was equally angry and rose to go. As I reached for my coat, he grasped my hand. "Don't go," he pleaded.

"Oh, you make me sick," I said.

"I know it. I'm sorry. But please don't go."

408

"But your friend is coming. Your beautiful Japanese lotus flower."

"She won't come, and if she does, what good will it do me? I want to ask you a question, Sonie. Please sit down again and drink some more sherry or I'll make you coffee if you'd rather. The thing is this, do you think it will work, my going to France this way? I mean, if I don't marry Kakosan? I was joking when I said I might marry Andrée, she's impossible. Do you think it would work if I went by myself?"

I could not have answered his question even if I had had the time, for I did not know what it was he wanted except to live in Paris for a year and for that length of time to have a holiday from Mr. Morgan and his kind. At that moment there was a delicate triple knock on the door and Nathan rushed to unlock it and to admit his Japanese mistress, Kakosan Yoshida.

"I can't stay," she said, remaining on the threshold so that, because the hall beyond her was dark, I could not tell what she looked like. I could see only that she was diminutive; the clear, dissonant notes of her voice were like a string of brilliant, hollow balls. "I cannot come in. I am sorry. You must not be angry, please. I promised to go to the séance. It can't be done without me."

"But you promised three days ago to come tonight," said Nathan.

She hesitated a moment. "Yes, that's true, I did. And I would rather stay with you. But they said they couldn't make the séance work without me and so I have to go. Please understand."

"Let me go with you, then."

"Oh, but you said you hated things like that. You hate me to go to them. I told them this would be the last time I would come. You wouldn't like to go."

"Yes, I would like to go," said Nathan firmly. "Is it cold out? Should I wear a coat?"

The high voice was desperate. "But you would hate it. It would be all right if just the *real* people were there. But riffraff is coming tonight. It's not by invitation tonight. Please!"

"That's all the better. If there are a lot of people I can leave if I want without offending anyone. Is it cold out or not?"

"Very well," said the girl angrily, "I won't go then. I told a lie. It's not for everybody. It is very exclusive. They wouldn't let you in

409

No, I won't go. I will sit here with you. But first I must call and tell them I'm not coming."

"All right," said Nathan. "You can use the janitor's telephone."

"No, I must go to the drug-store anyway. I must buy something. I will be back in a little while."

Nathan sighed. "Go on to the séance if there is a séance. But come in and meet an old friend of mine, an old, and up to a point, faithful, friend."

"I am too faithful!" she cried. Then, "Oh," she said as she saw me, "Why does he want me if he has company?"

She tipped her little saffron face up to him and smiled. He could not resist her, although he knew that there was no séance, that she was going to meet another lover, and taking her small, lovely hand, he kissed the lacquered fingertips. As she stepped into the full light, she seemed unreal, less human than animal material fashioned in the image of figures of painting and sculpture and the ladies of poetry so that it was almost necessary to understand the ideal in Oriental art before one could truly appreciate how authentic her beauty was. I would say of my mother's lips that they had the color of a rose, but of Kakosan I would have to say that her mouth was like a "mallow flower" for her loveliness was something so unfamiliar that the old words and metaphors would not do, and to say her lips were like a rose would be to say that they were beautiful but not to specify them as Oriental. She wore, under her incongruous American polo-coat, a dress of purple silk brocaded with gold. In the glowing blackness of her hair was pinned a white carnation, and on either hand she wore a jade ring. She was, with this costume, with her symmetrical, unblemished face, her tiny body as limber as a grass, something so conscious, so tastefully assembled that she was like a bejeweled ornament of incalculable worth. It was hard to imagine her in the arms of an Occidental man, harder still to imagine her as promiscuous as Nathan had implied she was and as I had gathered from her unskillful lie about the séance.

She sat down on the couch beside me and handed Nathan a parcel elaborately wrapped in white tissue paper and tied with pink ribbons. "It was to take my place," she said. "I found it in the store and thought you would read it tonight while I went to the séance. Do you know the spirits?" she asked, turning to me. I replied that I did not, and she informed me that I had missed half my life by not becoming acquainted with the supernatural. She told me that she had not only heard spirit voices imparting news of the other world, but had also been witness to the unaided peregrinations of chairs and tables and vases of flowers and, on one occasion, to the levitation by will alone of one of the sitters. "A year ago, my uncle, the tea-merchant, spoke to me. He died in Kobe three years before. He told me I must not marry according to my father's choice. I am a Samurai daughter. How can I disobey my father?" She laughed. There was in her laugh something controlled and artful as if it were part of a song. "*He* should be happy at what my uncle said, shouldn't he?" and she pointed her finger at Nathan who was undoing the ridiculous pink bows on her present. "What would my father say," she whispered to me, "if he knew I had a beau like him? In a place like this? I call him *Gacho*. It means 'goose.'"

"And I call her *'hototogisu'* which means 'cuckoo,'" said Nathan bitterly. He had succeeded in removing the wrapper from the parcel and he withdrew a book. "Oh, thanks," he said, "I've wanted to read it." And he put it down on his desk.

"Now I must go," said Kakosan. "I am so obliged to meet you, Miss Marburg. Will you please go to the movies with me sometimes? Do you love the movies?" I said I had no burning passion for them, but I would be delighted to go to a matinée some day.

"Let's wait until the Garbo comes. I love the Garbo best of all. If I were not a Japanese girl, I would most like to be a Swedish girl."

As Nathan accompanied her to the outer door, I went to the desk, looking for the prospectus from Heidelberg. The book which Kakosan had brought was lying face down and I picked it up, curious to know what kind of writer she would choose to keep her lover company while she was deceiving him. The title was in German: *Der Traum der Roten Kammer.* The cream-colored binding was decorated with a black torii between whose posts lay several scarlet flowers; beyond the gate three cedar trees were visible. Although it had been in the shelves with all the others in my imaginary room, and I had only seen the back, I had known exactly how the front panel would look! When I heard Nathan's footsteps returning down the hall,

411

I dropped the book suddenly as if I had done something shameful. But between the time I heard him and his entrance, the room appeared to me. This time, three positive things happened: I wondered if there were more rooms down the hall from mine and if the buildings forming the court had a continuous passageway. Simultaneously a German word, *Gesäusel,* came into my mind and I seemed to stand in the doorway of the room, remarking the onomatopoeia of the word which meant "murmuring." Moreover, I recognized the writing desk as Louisa May Alcott's, on display in the Alcott house in Concord which old Mrs. McAllister had taken me one day to see. Upon this desk and under glass, I thought, had been Miss Alcott's diary, opened to pages of small, unreadable writing with the coppery look of aged ink. The town, from the windows of this room, eternally dead amongst its elegant trees, had seemed grandly harmless, and the glassed-in meditations of the gentlewoman were like a last testament begun at birth, like a happy, lifelong requiescat, and I remembered feeling as if I were in a different century. My lame and wattled companion, smelling of some faint, old-fashioned scent, had said to me, "Do you like the room? It is what I call a *gentle* place." But Louisa May Alcott's was not my room and we had not gone there at sunset, but in the early afternoon. Philip and Hopestill had driven to Walden Pond after luncheon to watch the skating, and Mrs. McAllister had said to me, "We mustn't stay in on this golden day. Let me take you to the Alcott House. It is closed for the winter, but the caretaker will let me in." And we had gone out in the pure yellow light of the winter afternoon.

Nathan touched my arm. "A trance?" he asked me. "Isn't it revolting the way I let her lie to me? I should have told her never to come back again or else I should have beaten her to death. And that book! Do you see what it is? A Japanese novel translated into German. Can you tie that for a pure waste of time?"

But for me, it was not a pure waste of time. His words were but a slightly altered version of what Mr. Whitney had said as we stood last night in Miss Pride's library and he had taken down a book from the shelves. I did not remember having looked at it at all. I was weak with relief that I had seen another copy like Nathan's, and I began to laugh. It was a deep, interior, physical laughter, as beyond my

412

control as hiccoughs, the kind that afflicts children in grammar school who bend their little shaking bodies forward and hide their heads in their folded arms and want to stop but cannot even when the teacher reprimands them.

"But it's not funny!" cried Nathan.

I could only splutter a reply, and after a time when I was quiet, I explained to him that I had not been amused by anything, that I was only nervous, probably from all our drinking the night before and the dressing-down I had got from Miss Pride. He looked down at me contemptuously. "Nervous, is it? You're more fashionable even than I thought. I suppose you are being psycho-analyzed."

"Certainly not," I rejoined with some annoyance. "You want to know too much."

"I assure you that I have not the slightest interest in knowing why you laughed. If you are a giggler, more's the pity. It is particularly offensive when it comes late in life."

I wrapped my muffler about my neck, resolving not to come back again. Although a little earlier I had wished to explain why I had not drunk beer with him at Red's, I now wished only to expunge him and the memory of him from my mind. But, as often in the past, he disarmed me. He sat at his desk, his birthmark hidden by his hand and regarded me with a piteous entreaty. "Did you really mean it when you said you would go to the movies with her?"

"Oh, I don't know. Probably not. It seems very unimportant."

"You could help me if you only would. If you could convince me that she's a bitch, possibly I could eventually break off."

"I'm not interested, and now I've got to go home."

"I'll be lonely if you go. Will you come back again next Sunday?"

"No," I told him. "You're too rude."

"You can't hate a cat for killing a bird because it's the cat's nature, and you can't get sore at me for being rude because that's *my* nature. Please, Sonia!"

"All right," I said. "I'll try once more. It will be a little later next Sunday, I expect." We shook hands and said good-by with an exaggerated warmth.

I walked quickly between the banks of snow which lighted the streets like moonlight. A few doors from Nathan's building, I heard

413

someone playing a recorder and I paused for a minute to listen. It was a tender, doleful tune like some Irish lamentation. The bold blood rushed to my face and fingertips. I passed on and peered into the uncurtained ground-floor rooms of students, for no other purpose than to see that they were all clean and comfortable, all unlike Nathan's and unlike my red room.

The room had been a little random daydream which I could have again, or it was like a lengthened *déjà vue,* that evasive quasi-memory which is a sort of unlearned knowledge of the soul. I could, I knew, in time, name in its real place each object in the room, and I felt confident that even after my vivisection, the room would accomplish again its impeccable synthesis, a fused and incomprehensible entity. It was a sanctuary and its tenant was my spirit, changing my hot blood to cool ichor and my pain to ease. Under my own merciful auspices, I had made for myself a tamed-down sitting-room in a dead, a voiceless, city where no one could trespass, for I was the founder, the governor, the only citizen.

# CHAPTER FIVE

The dressmaker who had been imported from New York to make Hopestill's trousseau was known by her trade name, Mamselle Thérèse, which she herself always substituted for the nominative case of the first person singular pronoun, as though she were her own interpreter. "Mamselle Thérèse does not touch the potatoes," she said on her first evening to Ethel who frankly tittered. She said to me, "Mamselle Thérèse goes to a night-club twice a week in New York," by which I understood she wanted me to supply her with the Boston equivalent of this diversion, but I did not respond as she had hoped and thereafter she made no more such overtures but amused herself (and presumably me) in designing costumes which she said would "bring out" my personality. She spoke of Chanel, Lilly Daché, Main-bocher as if they were Brahms, Bach, Mozart, or Plato, Descartes, and Hegel. "Daché composed a superb number for an archduchess last month, a really revolutionary turban. People were simply swept off their feet." Like the bald barber recommending a hair restorer, like the dentist whose teeth are false, Mamselle Thérèse dressed most frumpishly. She wore a strange assemblage of seedy garments, too large for her spare, nimble frame, out-of-date, soiled, frayed, reminding me of the hand-me-downs that two or three times a year the Brunsons' Boston relatives sent them to be given to me. And it was not only that the little modiste had clothed herself out of a rag bag, but that she had very bad taste, burdening herself like a fancy-woman with gimcracks from the five and ten cent stores: wooden brooches in the unreasonable shape of a Scotty dog or of an ice-skate or of a Dutch shoe or of a football; enameled beetles or dragonflies or cobras made of tin, with blinding rhinestone eyes; earrings in the shape of oak-leaves or candlesticks; and with any costume, upon her right arm, she wore nine thin silver bracelets which she clanked interminably. Her shabbiness could not be explained by poverty, for she had a flourishing business, and the expensive dresses of her two assistants who had been lodged in a house on Joy Street, suggested that she could afford to be generous in their salaries. She was charging Miss Pride a shocking price for this assignment, as I knew from the estimate she had handed in on the day she arrived. She spoke quite openly of this as "a good thing."

"Now for you, angel," she said, "Mamselle Thérèse would sew for next to nothing, but for them, the price is in the hundreds, sometimes in the thousands. It is an art, *n'est-ce pas?* Wouldn't they pay ten thousand for a picture by Rousseau? Then why shouldn't they pay ten thousand for a dress by Chanel? Mainbocher? Mamselle Thérèse don't kid herself. She knows she isn't in that class yet, but she works slow and sure like a mole. Five years from now Mamselle Thérèse will be in the movies like Adrian."

Her ruling passion was business, and she could see nothing except in terms of its commercial value. Thus, when she learned that I had gone to a secretarial school, she said, "You must keep your eyes open and when the time comes, rush in and nab yourself a plum. Mamselle Thérèse's advice to a young girl like you that has a good head on her shoulders is: be a secretary to a big-time lawyer. There's the money! There's the prestige! I'm telling you. What good are you doing yourself fooling around up here with that *vieille furie* when you could be on Fifth Avenue, New York? Mamselle Thérèse has a girl-friend working at Number One, Wall Street, on the thirty-fourth floor and she makes fifty dollars a week. I'm telling you."

She talked ceaselessly in a hoarse whisper as if we were two business men making a slightly shady deal. Often she worked arithmetic problems with the tip of her finger on the polished table, so obsessed with the imposing figures of her last year's state and federal income taxes that she did not leave off even when I warned her that her nails would scratch the finish. It was of no matter to her that I contributed nothing to the conversation but answered only with a monosyllable or a forced smile when she put such a rhetorical question to me as "Does Mamselle Thérèse know all the answers in the business world?" Her chief ambition was to receive a commission from visiting royalty; it deeply thrilled her to imagine some queen or princess finding, after she disembarked, that she had not brought enough evening gowns: " 'I must run right to Mamselle Thérèse. She will make me a *chose merveilleuse* for the White House ball.' Wouldn't Mamselle Thérèse be knocked off the Christmas tree?" Sometimes, impassioned by the memory of a gown that Mainbocher had executed for some foreign personage or by the contemplation of vast sums of money owed her by her "élite clientele" she would pursue me to my room, having given a peremptory order to Ethel as we left the dining-room, to bring our coffee to the third floor.

Occasionally, out of self-defense, I would deliver her a little lecture, on how much I liked the town of Concord and its environs or on the splendor of the Countess' Saturdays, but Mamselle could attend nothing of what I said and the moment I paused, she burst in with a raging river of facts and figures to obliterate completely my little trickle of talk.

But she was not, as she seemed, out of touch with human affairs. She was not especially interested in them, but nothing escaped her shrewd French eye. Believing me to be Miss Pride's secretary and nothing more, she spoke unguardedly of the household. *"Mon dieu,* that bridegroom! Angel, he is a fool, I'm telling you. Mamselle Thérèse don't need to make his acquaintance to know that like she knows the palm of her own hand. She only has to contact the fiancée, *n'est-ce pas?* That rich *renarde.*"

"Why do you say she is a *renarde?*" I asked.

"You can tell by the eyes. They are sub-zero. You know? It is on her part a *mariage de convenance.*"

"And how do you know that?"

"Because they haven't slept together. And how does Mamselle Thérèse know that?" She tapped her forehead. *"Par intuition."*

"But perhaps it is a *mariage de convenance* on his part too?" I suggested.

"Maybe. Yes, maybe. It is a cold place, this Boston. He marries her because she is rich, beautiful, what-not. Because a doctor should have a wife. She marries him because she is *enceinte, n'est-ce pas.*"

I should have laughed and denied the charge, but I was so astounded at the woman's wizardry that I could not gather my wits

417

together for a moment and when I did, knowing that her conviction was not only right but that I could in no way shake her from it, I said, "You may be right, but I beg you to say nothing to anyone. It would kill Miss Pride."

Mamselle Thérèse was offended. "Why should Mamselle Thérèse gossip? She is here for the money. She don't care a damn about the *mariage*. Angel, it is a dirty business and not for me. This little up-and-coming *couturière* stays single, I'm telling you. Plenty of boy-friends and not a husband. Don't mix business with pleasure, angel. So why should she interfere with someone else's *mariage*? Mamselle Thérèse won't talk to the interested parties. She is interested only in the money from the interested parties."

We were sitting in my room at the time of this conversation and it was rather late, perhaps eleven o'clock. Both Miss Pride and Hope-still had gone out for the evening. Presently we heard light footsteps coming up the last flight of stairs and Hopestill's door was opened. Evidently she had come back to get something for in ten minutes, she went out again and back down the stairs. Mamselle Thérèse, not so much through the fear of being overheard as through boredom with the subject, dropped it instantly on hearing the footsteps and began telling me about a new costume she had designed for nuns which would be at once more sanitary and more beautiful than their present ones. She had interviewed innumerable Mother Superiors and had written to various bishops and to the secretary of the Arch-bishop of New York. As she had what is aptly known as "total recall," she repeated verbatim each conversation, each letter, and each reply, all of which seemed, on the part of the ecclesiastical authori-ties, to be stubbornly hostile to her proposition.

But the soliloquy, which lasted for half an hour after Hope left the house, did not prevent me from hearing through the wall which separated our rooms, the soft collapse of the girl's body on the *chaise longue* and a sob, stifled at once as though she had pressed her face into a pillow. The sound would probably have escaped me if I had not heard it before and had not come to expect it as the expression, in a sense, of the reason for her visit to her room during the evening. Almost every night when there were dinner guests, she came up two or three times, and usually I heard that secret, frustrated outburst like a checked curse. On such evenings, she might stay as long as a quarter of an hour and hearing her footsteps back and forth across the carpet, muted so that I could not be sure if I really heard them or only felt the vibrations of the floor, I sat at my typewriter unable to strike a key, embarrassed because she must have heard the clatter of the machine which stopped as her door-knob turned.

I could not immunize myself to her misery and pitied her for whatever punishment her conscience was meting out to her. I was impelled to go in to her in the way one may start, hearing a human cry in the night and think it is someone lost or hurt and in need of help. Beside a warm fire in a light room, an impression of the night's cold and darkness superimposes itself upon the altruistic impulse, and one rationalizes, says the cry comes from the throat of a drunk or of a cat that can sound like a woman or even that it is the lure of a thief. I would wait until I heard her going down the stairs again and then I would shrug my shoulders with a resolute indifference and say aloud, "It's her affair, not mine."

Before my brother was born, I could not bear to have my mother speak of miscarriages and of "the pains" because I was sure that pain must be much more terrible to other people than to myself. And when Miss Pride reproved the Gonzales boy for stealing her soap to carve his little Virgin, I would have been glad to exchange places with him in order not to see the shame in his downcast face and the limp arms hanging at his sides, the palms of his hands turned out in broken-hearted supplication. And now while I did not minimize the discomfiture of my own position and spent a good part of every day in sorrowing over my unjust luck and even thought that in the end, my lot was much the worse, I felt that I was somehow better equipped to endure than Hopestill. She, the frail sheep lost from the herd, could not find her way back nor could she make her way alone. She knew already, as these flights to the privacy of her room showed, that she could not carry it off, for even if the discovery of her deception were long postponed or never made at all or made only by a few people who would not blame her or, if they did, would keep silent, she had nevertheless ruined herself in the only *milieu* for which she was trained. She had ruined herself even though there might never be suspicions or rumors, for she would never be *sure* that she was not suspected: she would hear the most innocent remark as a *double entendre,* the most amiable question as put with an ulterior design. It was possible, too, I thought, that after the secret gratitude to Philip for unknowingly saving her from disgrace had expired, she would commence to hate him, as the impoverished libertine, her father, had hated his martyred wife whose rich dowry had provided him with the means for his philanderings.

Long before this, Hopestill had damaged herself, though not irremediably, by her connections with "the Bohemians." She had occasionally brought young men, who let their beards grow and who dressed most unusually, to the houses of her friends and her aunt's friends, exhibiting them like trained poodles. Unconventional and explosive, they alarmed the hostesses whose disapproval could not find its exact target and fired nervously upon all sides. The poverty of these barbarians was thought to be an intentional and Communistic affront; they were believed to be practitioners of free love, companionate marriage, and atheism; their painting or their writing was eyed with distrust as revolutionary or satirical. The Boston hostess, finding herself at the mercy of a novelist (she had not heard of him and therefore could not tell if he was a satirist or not) guarded her words against the escape of a stupid or a typical remark, yet most typically, most stupidly, said, "I hope you won't put *me* in one of your novels."

It would have been tolerable, everyone thought (according to the Countess, my faithful informant), if Hope had been content merely to bring her friends to parties for, despite their appearance, they behaved usually quite well. It was that Hope had given herself such insufferable airs, sprinkling her talk with the cryptograms of literary critics, explaining, unbidden, the meanings of abstruse poems. She had painstakingly studied out an erudite essay on "psychical distance" the year before and for several months judged thereby every book, painting, play, or movie that came up. But as someone remarked—someone who probably had never heard of the esthetic principle she used so boldly—she shot only at sitting birds, and she was openly laughed at when she was heard to say to Amy Brooks, "The trouble with your Oyster House pastel is the figure in the foreground, which is under-distanced. He is simply too much the pitiable bum. He actually brings tears to one's eyes, and that won't do."

To be sure, she was over her "intellectual" phase and no longer carried marinated herring to the obscure studios. But she had not become any more manageable. Exactly what she was doing in New York no one knew. Indeed, no one knew her address beyond the vague fact that it was "in the fifties." When someone said to her, "I wish you'd look up my friend so and so. She has a charming place on the Park and I know you'd find her amusing," Hope replied with a warm smile, "It's terribly sweet of you. Of course one *never* does anything one wants in New York, but do give me her address anyhow." Only once had anyone seen her and that only by chance. A Miss Bradley, an elderly spinster, idling away an hour between appointments in Central Park, had come on Hopestill staring raptly at the sea lions who were being fed. "Oh, aren't they beautiful?" the girl had cried. "Oh, aren't they wondrous! Oh, if only I had seen them when I was a child. You know, Miss Bradley, that Aunt Lucy never let me go to the zoo." Miss Bradley, reporting this uninhibited speech to Amy Brooks, said, "I expected her to give me a lecture on child psychology, but she spared me and we had a very pleasant little chat."

Now that she had made the full circuit and had returned to the starting point, she was generally forgiven all her past peculiarities, and there was universal rejoicing in Miss Pride's circle that the marriage, prophesied for so long, was at last to come off. In my exile, I was obliged to rely entirely on the Countess for my information, and she assured me that both Philip and Hopestill were ecstatic, that it made her quite giddy herself just to be in the same room with them. Hope, she said, had never looked so well or so handsome.

I would have been glad to believe the Countess, but I could not because of that testimony of Hopestill's misery that I heard nearly every night. As soon as her footsteps had died away, I would give in to a vicarious fear that set me trembling and, suddenly cold, would go to the fire to warm myself. I would muse into the brilliant coals and shut my eyes. The inner wall of my lids retained the clarified red of the flames like the surface of one of those freakish hot pools in certain places where minerals behave in a fanciful way. Willfully I would force myself downward through a red wind until the door to my imagined room was opened and I stood upon its threshold. Recently I had identified the lobster-claw letter opener as belonging to a very aged woman who lived in Chichester and had rendered some service to my mother when I was about five years old, so that we went to call on her one afternoon at tea time. I had been given the letter opener to play with and I was horrified by it, but I was bashful and did not want to be rude to the kind old lady, and so I had twirled the agate sphere and stroked the reptilian claws until I was nearly sick and had to refuse the hot cocoa which had been made especially for me. Still, the aged woman's room was not my room. I remembered distinctly that she received us in her bedroom because there were no fires in the rest of the house and that the spool bed had been covered with a blue and white quilt with a design of five-pointed stars and crescent moons, and that I had sat on an ottoman covered with scarlet oilcloth and that the tea things had been on an old-fashioned washstand through the half open door of which had been visible a chamber-pot with pale roses painted on the side.

My memories of rooms where I had been were delineated with the perfection of detail of truthful photographs. I saw Miss Pride's room at the Hotel as it had been one day after a windy rainstorm. A cherub pillow had been by the open window and one of the castles was dark with dampness; an elm leaf was flattened against the screen, and a letter which had been on the sill had been blown to the floor. One day I recognized the unlabeled bottle of red wine. It had been in the Countess' music room one afternoon, late, when I had gone there to listen to some records and had been alone. I had tasted the wine, but it had gone sour and I concluded that it had been removed from the cabinet to be taken downstairs but had been forgotten.

My visits to the red room were infrequent. Though I was convinced that there was no harm in it, that it was, if anything, an achievement of will that should be envied and applauded by other people who had not so sure a refuge, I was, at the same time, loath to make my seclusion there a habit. I entered it only (rather, I stood upon the threshold, for I was never actually in the room and could not visualize myself taking a book out of the shelves or sitting at the desk) when I felt that I could not withstand the onslaught of

422

worry or of loneliness. Whenever I realized that Sunday was approaching and I must go again to see my mother and probably to have another conversation with the doctor, whenever Miss Pride reminded me that I was in disgrace, and whenever I came to think of Hopestill, then I would turn to my ghost of a sanctuary as I might turn to a drug.

When there were no guests but Hopestill and Miss Pride had gone out and Mamselle Thérèse was in her own room working at her sketches of a renovated nun, the stillness of the house unnerved me and if by chance there was a wind lamenting in the trees of Louisburg Square, my heart was plucked quickly like a taut gut. It was not that I feared sneak-thieves or murderers or Kakosan's spirits, nor did I feel, at this particular time, the watchful eyes of people who thought I might repeat my mother's pattern. It was a fear I could describe only approximately as a fear of *myself*. It was not a new experience. Sometimes in Chichester, I had taken care of children in the evenings at a lonely house almost at the Point. An old, one-eyed Airedale kept me company, snoozing on the sofa. Abruptly he would waken and lift his head, pointing his nose toward the door, and then, assured that there was nothing outside after all, he would look at me with his one intelligent eye. This look, so companionable and preternaturally wise, frightened me more than his attention to the door, beyond which he had sensed the lurking of some unknown thing: I was afraid the dog would speak. This droll idea, of brief duration, was but the envelope for another fear: the fear of my own mind which had conceived so awful a possibility. Like the motorist through dense fog at night who has proof of only himself, his automobile, and the road, and must accept *a priori* the fact that the rest of the world has not been dematerialized, I could not demonstrate the external authorship of myself and the dog nor our independence of one another. What proof had I that the dog was not the creation of my own mind and being such might, if I willed it, speak to me; conversely, what proof was there that I was not the dog's idea, evolved in those mysterious, perhaps Olympian, brains behind the obtuse snout? What broke my ghastly reverie was the registration of sound on my mind, the footsteps of some later walker, or the rustle of a bed above me as one of the children turned in his sleep. I argued that since my mind had been altogether on the dog, it could not have produced a noise in the distance. My hearing re-established my spatial relation to the outer world's complexities and immediately thereafter my judgments were restored.

Similarly at Miss Pride's on silent nights, what unbalanced the poise of quintessential self (a play on words would come to me: the eye was the proof of I, not only of my own eye or my mind's eye, but the Cyclopean eye of the Airedale) was the protesting, bewildered cry of Miss Pride's cat shut up in her bedroom. It would come toward the middle of the evening and was no more than one prolonged off-key yet musical howl which petered out on a descending scale.

I had seen Mercy only once or twice in all the time I had lived with Miss Pride. When I first came, I had been told that she was jumpy and unfriendly because her kittens, begot by an unauthorized tomcat during the summer when she had been entrusted to the care of the Hornblowers in Concord, had been chloroformed as soon as they were born, and the mother, her instincts baffled, hunted them with piteous persistence, crying and snooping through the closets, the bedroom, the bath, and her own apartment, a storeroom no longer in use. Until her mesalliance and its results, she had been allowed to roam at will throughout the house, but Miss Pride, attributing a high degree of intelligence to her, thought that by way of revenge, she might now defile upholstery and rugs, in her search might overturn vases and clocks, might in her despair and anger scratch visitors and claw their stockings. By this time, she had surely forgotten her kittens, but Miss Pride had decided to make this limited arena permanent, for what reason I do not know. Each morning, I saw Ethel putting Mercy's sand-box (called by Miss Pride "the kitty-cat's water-closet" but by the embarrassed servants "the cat's carton") shrouded with last night's *Transcript* on the dumb-waiter to be emptied and filled with fresh sand. This and the lonely cry at night were the only evidence I had that there was an animal in the house.

One night I thought that it would do no harm if I let the prisoner out for an hour or so, bringing her up to my room which was not a spacious place to romp in but would at least be a change of scene. I went down. Miss Pride's room was dark except for the fire that had burned down to a rich glow and at first I could not see the cat. When I was accustomed to the shadows, I perceived a pair of sulphurous eyes which, seeming to be suspended in the air four feet from the floor, regarded me with the unflinching stare of the hypnotist. I switched on the night-lamp beside the bed and in its weak light saw the animal perched on a chest of drawers beside the fire-place. For a moment she did not move but only looked at me. She had a short, square face and silver whiskers that curved downward from her tawny cheeks, marked on each side with two black stripes. She sat with her front legs straight and her luxurious tail curled about her feet. I moved toward her and she started, thrusting her head suddenly forward so that I could see the pure white fur under her chin. "Kitty, kitty," I said. She leapt from the chest with a chirrup of fear and ran to her room, a streak of fur that blended shades of red and yellow and blue, all overlaid and softened with a cloudy silver and striped with black. As she ran, her tail dragged on the floor like a train. I did not pursue her, for there had been in her face as she saw me coming toward her a look of primitive terror that could, I thought, easily become the rage of a wild beast. I ran back up the stairs two at a time to my cheerful room where all the lights were burning. Three or four nights later, again hearing the cry and again wishing to bring her upstairs, I went down to try a second time. I found the door to Miss Pride's bedroom locked.

It was easy enough to explain the locked door. I remembered that in my haste the first time to get away from the cat and to end our mutual fear, I had neglected to turn out the night-lamp, and Miss Pride, finding it and realizing that someone—probably a servant, she would think—had been in her room, henceforth took precautions against Mercy's escape. She preferred to do that, I reasoned, rather than to shut the door to the storeroom. But ever after that, when I passed through the hall on the second floor, the fact struck me as potentially sinister that I had never heard Mercy's call until these last weeks when I, too, was virtually a prisoner, heard it only at night when I was alone except for Mamselle Thérèse and the servants who were all on the floor above me. As I went on and ascended the flight of stairs to the third story, my common sense returned and told me that heretofore I had been reading aloud to Miss Pride at this hour, and that on the nights when she was at home, I used my typewriter, the racket of which shut out all but loud noises or very near ones. But there is a side in us that courts and would like to believe in the fanciful. "Of course it was no more than coincidence," we say, but we would like our audience to share our wonder and reply, "Coincidence, certainly, and yet . . ."

## 2

By day our house was the scene of what Miss Pride crossly called "a needless hullabaloo" for which, as a matter of fact, she was largely responsible, for while Hopestill and Philip had wanted a small wedding, she had insisted that a step of this kind be taken with public pomp. It was typical of her to speak of it as "a step of this kind," as if it were some sort of sensible negotiation which had been undertaken after several other "kinds" had been discarded. It was she who had wired Mamselle Thérèse (recommended by the Countess and deplored by Hopestill who had her own modiste) and she who had sent out invitations to three hundred guests for the wedding breakfast, and she who had persuaded a notable clergyman who had left Boston several years before to perform the ceremony. There had been some argument about this last detail. Both Miss Pride and Dr. McAllister's father were Unitarians and did their best to dissuade Hopestill from being married in the Episcopal church in which, adopting her father's rather than her mother's sect, she had been confirmed. She was adamant and requested, moreover, that the minister from whom she had received the Eucharist at her first communion be brought back for the occasion. In only one other particular had she insisted on having her own way. She refused to be given away by her uncle Arthur Hornblower or any other relative and before even consulting her aunt, conferred the honor upon Admiral Nephews.

I thought that she wanted to be married in the Episcopal church out of a nostalgic attachment to her childhood, as it had been a better and happier time. I could find no other reason, for she was altogether without religious conviction and never went to any services. I divined, too, that in denying any member of her family the right to participate actively in the ritual, she was relieving them, symbolically, of any accessory responsibility.

In the week before the wedding, my duties were many and complex. I acted as the intermediary between Miss Pride and the representatives of florists, liquor dealers, caterers, and took great pleasure in ordering such things as twelve cases of champagne and thirty pounds of filet of sole. Miss Pride would have preferred to attend to these matters herself because all tradespeople were scoundrels and I was both gullible and extravagant, but she was occupied with other things, among them with ridding the house of kinsfolk who came in droves beginning at nine o'clock in the morning, expecting to be asked to luncheon and then tea and even dinner. They infuriated her by telling her that she looked "worn-out" and that they were going to make her go to bed while they themselves took over, lock, stock, and barrel. To such a suggestion, Miss Pride would say, turning her eyes like pistols on the offender, "If I want crutches, I'll *buy* them, Sally Hornblower." They were full of plans for what she would wear to the wedding (I knew what she would wear: a new black broadcloth suit and a green beaver hat) and for the most decorative way of arranging the display of gifts. She would nod her head and say, "I dare say that would be nice. But I shall just muddle on in my old way. You can't teach an old dog new tricks." Once, after this cliché, she gave a mirthless "ha! ha!" and sounded, indeed, like the dog that could not be taught but had learned in his youth the trick of biting trespassers.

The continual stir of the house was intoxicating. On my way out of the house to run some important errand, I would glance into the upstairs sitting-room where the presents gradually were accumulating. Hopestill might, as I passed, be unwrapping something that had just come. She would hold up for me to see a blue plum-blossom jar or a silver pitcher. We could hear the bee-like flurry of the sewing machine and the animated conversation of Mamselle Thérèse and her two assistants. The door-bell and the telephone reiterated their clamorous demands until the servants were beside themselves. Leaving Hopestill surrounded by her treasure, I would go downstairs to receive a final instruction from Miss Pride. Nearly always, on one of the tables in the hall, there was a silver bowl half filled with water on whose surface floated the disintegrating but still fragrant flowers that Hopestill had worn the night before. I was curiously moved at the sight of them, and imagined her coming in late, the dangers of another day behind her, Philip's car already pulling away from the curb. I wondered if she would not ponder her face in the mirror above the table as she unpinned the orchid or the gardenias just as I pondered mine a moment before I left the house. Which face would she see? The one with which everyone was familiar or the one I had seen on the day she had come home when in her distress she had seemed old and plain?

The churchly odor of old wood and stone was sweetened with the perfume and boutonnières of the wedding guests assembled twenty minutes early. A beam of sunshine came through the open door and extended the length of the central aisle until, at the sanctuary, it joined in a pool of opaline light with another laden shaft sifted through the stained glass windows, of which the three segments were so detailed that I could read in them no narrative but saw only brilliant colors throwing off the glitter of jewels. Then, through the gilded haze the altar was visible, furnished with a massive cross, two golden urns of white azaleas, and pale candles still unlit. The sun and the flowers and the open door made me think of spring, though I had only to look at the fur coats to remember that it was not yet midwinter and that the cool of the church was withal warmer than the outside temperature. The freshness of the bath I had just taken and the clean, acrid odor of my new clothes combined with this pleasure to give me a general sense of well-being and excellent health, as if I had shaken off the aches and miseries of one season and had entered upon the next under favorable omens, like the day on which we realize that our blood has expunged the last particle of disease. Two incidents the day before, which was Sunday, had lightened my heart. When I went to the library in the morning, I found Miss Pride more cordial than she had been since the night of my defection ("The night," she called it, "when you came home in such an informal state of mind."), and by way of showing that I was being recalled from exile, she gave me a glass of her fine personal sherry and told me that I must not fail to be at the wedding and the wedding breakfast the following day. Then, at the asylum, I was told that I could see my mother for only a few minutes as she was very ill and was confined to her bed in the infirmary. The doctor, the same one I had talked with before, admitted that he was not so confident of her cure as he had been. He was positive, he told me, of her ultimate recovery but thought she could not be moved for at least six months instead of three as he had told me before. The extension of time seemed like an act of benevolence performed by the doctor himself out of the goodness of his heart and I so ill concealed my gratitude that I drew from him a smile and a companionable pat on the shoulder as he wished me a Merry Christmas. I was, moreover, in good spirits today because the end of my suspense was at last in sight and henceforth I would not hear Hopestill weeping into her pillow nor catch in her face an occasional look of alarm.

From where I sat at the back of the chapel, I could see Miss Pride in the front pew sitting between the Reverend McAllister and his wife. She was wearing a new suit, but as it was made in the same pattern as all her others and cut from the same wool, perhaps I alone knew that it was new, for I had seen the tailor's bill. She had made one concession to her relatives, and in place of her green beaver wore a small hat planted with red posies which caused her so much consternation, because she thought it would fall off, that during the ceremony, as she told everyone later, she could think of nothing but the moment when she might take it off.

She and the clergyman, in their sober black, whose forbears had not taken passage on the same boat with the Tory Almighty who had lodged in this chapel since pre-Revolutionary times, sat rigidly, staring straight ahead with disapproval at the Popish paraphernalia of the altar which, as Miss Pride said, was "tantamount to a repudiation of the Declaration of Independence." Distrust of the high-church folderol as well as of her headgear gave her face the dour immobility of a Protestant martyr and she did not smile once or look either to the right or to the left from the moment Frank Whitney ushered her to her seat of honor until she left it. The Reverend McAllister, on the contrary, sent his eyes meddling into the nooks and crannies of the "temple," as he spoke of it, and glowered upon the kneeling attitudes of some of these first cousins to the Roman

Catholics, into whose ranks he was heartily disinclined to release his son. The Reverend was a man of extraordinary obtuseness and had he ever taken the trouble—as his wife and mother did—to observe his future daughter-in-law even to form an impression of her external appearance, he would have been freed at once of his suspicions that she was leading Philip to the Pope, would have been far more worried that she would lead him to atheism. I had heard that at the time Al Smith was running for president, Reverend McAllister had been the victim of a recurrent nightmare in which a company of dwarfs (presumably Catholic dwarfs) attempted to stuff him into a confessional box, and he remarked to several people that if Smith were elected, he would die. Very likely he would have. He had presented himself at the house this morning to pay his respects to Miss Pride and as she was then engaged, I went down to entertain him until she would be free. He was a teetotaler and refused the port I had been commissioned to offer him. For five minutes he listed some facts to me which he had gleaned from his reading the night before, among which was the sagacious custom of polar bears who, when stalking seals, covered their black noses with their paws so that there was nothing about them to show that they were anything but mounds of snow.

Philip's mother who, although she would have preferred to wear black as a sign of mourning for her son, had finally decided that it would be too much of a good thing if all four of the chief relatives were attired as for a funeral, and was dressed in pale blue, becoming to her rosy cheeks and her white hair and her blue eyes, which had not been reddened but made only prettily clouded by the incessant stream of tears they had released ever since the engagement was announced. She had lost her appetite, had been unable to sleep a night through, and had not appeared at any of the pre-nuptial parties. It was said by her husband that her heart was temporarily "out of kilter." She had several times written Hopestill begging her to come to Concord: "We have so much to talk about," she wrote. "I feel there are many things you must know about Philip which only I can tell you. The hastiness of your wedding has prevented us from getting really well acquainted, but perhaps we can make up for lost time if only you will agree to spend two or three days with me." Hopestill, either because she was harassed by the business which the wedding involved or because she could think of no way to refuse the invitation graciously, did not answer, a breach of manners that had already had serious consequences. The elder Mrs. McAllister had told the story everywhere and, making use of her daughter's unwittingly accurate phrase, repeated often, "The wedding is too hasty for me. Marian and I both wish they'd wait until June. It is breaking Philip's mother's heart that she can't have a garden party for them. And since the poor thing's ill now, she can't even have an indoor party for them. I do think it's inconsiderate." The heart-sufferer, through a supreme sacrifice of her health, had managed to come to the wedding, though she would not be able to come to the breakfast. Her excuses, "doctor's orders," had been made through her husband this morning, as if she could not bear even to speak to Miss Pride.

The Countess, resplendent in a gray suit and a fox scarf, was sitting with Amy Brooks some pews ahead of me but she had spied me and was mouthing something which I could not catch and so mouthed back, "I can't understand what you're saying." It came out later that she had been telling me to be sure to look at Mrs. Hornblower, who had oddly enough come in evening clothes. I had, as a matter of fact, been on the lookout for Mrs. Hornblower who had heretofore seemed mythical, for I had learned on asking someone why it was that the tea-party to which I had been invited was such a remarkable event because the host's wife was to be there, that while she was on the friendliest terms with her husband, she did not share his house or his servants but lived in her own establishment fifty yards from his, a path leading from one door to the other. I asked my interlocutor—it was, as I remember, one of the girls at the Countess' Friday—to explain this. "They're just cranks," she said, shrugging her shoulders. "Mrs. Hornblower used to come to tea with my grandmother now and again when she was in town and she was at that time wrapped up in spiritism. It made poor Grandma have bad dreams about Mrs. Hornblower's astral body, and once when she said, 'Mary, I can simply walk through that wall if you only have faith in me,' Grandma shrieked, 'Nellie!' at the top of her lungs and it made Mrs. Hornblower furious although Grandma passed it off very nicely by saying that she just wanted Nellie to bring some more muffins. After that she took up the cause of Sacco and Vanzetti, but she didn't come to call any more for, as she told someone who of course repeated it to us, she didn't think my grandmother was interested in ideas." She had given up the occult for more pressing matters, but every now and again she would put in an appearance at a séance for old-time's sake, and at one of them, Kakosan had met her. Mrs. Hornblower had been a tremendous success and Kakosan, who assumed that because I lived opposite Louisburg Square I was intimately acquainted with everyone of consequence, had begged me to arrange an introduction. Mrs. Hornblower was a person of fine bearing, a large woman of whose face one immediately said, "She must have been lovely when she was young," and now, pitifully palsied, her white hair stained with yellow, she was still handsome. Much larger than her chubby husband who, although he was her senior, was better preserved and still wore black hair in which there was not a trace of gray, she bent toward him the loving and respectful looks of the obedient young wife.

Sitting at the aisle in the middle of the church, casually dressed in tweeds, Mr. Morgan slouched against the side of the pew, his chin in his hand, his eyes closed. He had not been invited, as I well enough knew because I had checked over the list of guests. But I was not in the least surprised to see him although I could not be certain of his motive, whether he had come to tease Hopestill or if he was in love with her and wished to torment himself, or if it was that desiring to escape suspicion he had thought it the better policy not to hide himself away. He had, if this last was his intention, made a serious mistake in his costume and continued, throughout the ceremony, to make an even graver error in his indolent attitude and his drowsy grin, for he was most conspicuous in that church full of people whose dress (with the exception of Mrs. Hornblower) was all so similar it was virtually a uniform, and thus he was set down by everyone who saw him—and he escaped the notice of very few— as vain and impudent for in gainsaying the decrees of custom, he was usurping custom's power. His presence relieved me on one point and troubled me on another. Evidently Hopestill had not been seeing him, as I had suspected from time to time, for if she had she would have told him not to come. I had suspected meetings between them because I had learned from Nathan that Morgan was in town all the the time now and there was no falling off of his visits and telephone calls from young women. What disturbed me—vaguely because this morning I felt detached from the whole business—was that since he apparently thought there was nothing odd in his coming this morning and coming with so blatant an air of indifference, there was no reason to suppose that Hopestill and Philip and their friends would be deprived of his company in the future.

Nathan, after two years of anatomizing his pupil, had come to the conclusion that he was not really selfish nor cold-blooded but that he was one of those unfortunate people in whom is missing the talent for falling in love. Such people do not give up but suppose that love will come at last in the person of some now unknown woman, just as other people do not relinquish their hope that belief in God will at last batter down the impregnable battlements of the soul. He carried on two or three affairs concurrently and was equally tenacious of each of his women because it was possible that *she* was the one who would, under an abrupt and accidental change of circumstances, become his solitary objective. This being the case and if Morgan's need for the centralization of his life about one woman was as urgent as Nathan would have me believe, would not Hopestill's marriage be an obstacle of slight consequence to him? I could only conjecture what had taken place in New York, but I was sure that if Morgan offered to marry her (and I imagined that he did, for he was the kind of person who could, with the left hand, dispense a sort of sentimental honorableness at the same time that the right hand was composing a love-letter to another woman) Hopestill had refused, not because she did not love him, not even because she was unwilling to support his infidelities, but because her pride had been mortally wounded and its resuscitation could be effected only if the accessory to the crime were out of sight and, eventually, out of mind. The refusal (I continued my hypothesis) impressed her lover who had not reckoned on so easy an acquittal and after his first sweet sensation of relief, he became tantalized with the possibility that he might have fallen in love with her on the revelation of her stern character which, in spite of her yearning, had firmly dismissed him. Perhaps he had come today, then, for the simple reason that he wanted to see her, to refresh his memory of her beauty and to determine, from the expression on her face and the way she walked, whether his siege of her would be rewarding.

In the hush that forewarned the wedding march, a hush that fell upon the flesh as well as on the ears so that the guests froze briefly in their postures of kneeling or leaning towards their neighbors, a faintness passed over me, obliterating the vigor of a few minutes before. And as from its rich reservoir, the organ's voice ascended, translating the march from *Lohengrin* into its ecclesiastical language, I was apprised of the crisis of my complex feeling about this wedding, so similar to the sickness of the flesh that it was as if the very guardians of my body's fluids had told me of my disequilibrium. My dizziness had no cause more serious than excitement, was but another and more acute version of that agitation which caused the women in the church to apply handkerchiefs to their eyes. And yet, the anguish, that one moment inched like a cold worm through the tunnels of my flesh and the next kindled a fire that spread from branch to branch until I was all aflame, was so much fiercer than any emotional distress I had had before that for a time I believed I was really "coming down" with some disease. Tears boiled over my eyelids and half screened the four bridesmaids in their green tulle dresses, preceding the maid of honor whose medieval velvet gown, a deeper shade than theirs, was like the outer leaf and theirs the paler inside ones. As I was on the verge, I thought, of toppling forward over the back of the pew ahead of me, my mind, like a rapid finger flicking through a book to find a special passage, went over possible diseases and diagnosed my weakness by presenting to me Hopestill's face, shrouded in shadows, as I imagined it might look in the mirror above the table in the vestibule. Certain then that my symptoms were not physical, I sought to efface them by an effort of will. My eyesight, still somewhat deformed by the tears, cleared enough so that the maid of honor was less nebulous than her vanguard. With a smile directed towards nothing but an abstract point of the compass, she addressed to her gait as much science and regard for the rhythms of the music as if she were executing a step in a difficult dance. But although I saw her thus and followed her slender body and the head whose black hair was caught in a cap of gold and perceived that in her hands she carried a bouquet of yellow roses, I saw her also through the hot vapor of my tears as a mobile stain upon the undulating curtain that obscured the church and the wedding-guests. Similarly, while the music advanced from chord to chord, it clung, at the same time, in my ears, to one deep, roaring note everlastingly renewed by its infinite vibrations. Closing my eyes, I saw repeated on the black waves of my blindness, the same green smear which my sightless pupils pursued until it swam out of their ken, yet entered again at once when the ball rolled back to its central position.

With the passing of the maid of honor, I felt a temporary return of strength. The vertigo ceased and my mind cleared. Across the heads of the audience, who were turning to behold the bride, I saw Philip entering from the chancel, and through some unstudied sophistication, I saw him separate from the person I had known but instead, as a total stranger who, in a few minutes, could no longer lend himself in my imagination to romantic equations of which I was the other magnitude. He underwent a second metamorphosis and became "the physician." It was under the auspices and according to the rules of this genus that I should henceforth govern my relationship with him. In the service of my own interests, I was then able to transmute the smile of a young man about to be married, who at this moment had caught sight of his bride as she entered the chapel, into the smile of the understanding healer who by his attentiveness seemed to exist for me alone. And taking this clean-boned Yankee together with his opulent and august setting, I was, despite my frustration, glad that our flirting had come to nothing, that he would be unchanged when throughout the years I sought his advice.

The dazzled guests watched the proud flower for whose protection and enhancement the leaves had been created: a chaste and perfect column draped in satin as pure as the wax of the tapers on the altar and outdoing their flame with the hair that blazed through a calotte of pearls. Her face, white as her finery and her lilies, wore an expression of solemnity befitting the occasion, although, as I heard someone whisper, there should have been something of a smile in her countenance, if not upon her lips, then at least within her eyes, for joy should be in proportion equal to the other feelings of the partaker of this particular sacrament. Her look, to me, was one instinct with death, yet death less chill than that which now like a layer beneath her skin gave off a waxen luminosity and imparted to her movement a brittleness as if the soft integuments of skin and cloth concealed a metal mechanism. Her thin fingers were tightly curled on the Admiral's arm. Harry Morgan had turned, with all the others, and while I could not see her face, I knew by his, when she had passed by, that a sign had passed between them, for his mouth curved into a serene smile as if he had half won his battle.

It seemed to me, as they joined before the minister, that Hopestill shuddered as she had done when she took the camellias from my hand. If this was seen by anyone else—indeed, if it occurred at all—it was attributed to her nervousness, the understandable and appropriate reluctance of a girl about to relinquish her virginity by so public a ritual. With a tidal rustling, the audience sat down, arranged their hands in their laps and adjusted their spectacles like people anticipating a well-known and beloved piece of music. It was, to be sure, an artistic performance, for the minister, wreathed in benign smiles, posed his literary questions and offered up his prayers with the intonations of a Shakespearean actor, which grace of pitch and diction was afterwards to evoke from Reverend McAllister the remark that the service had been "nothing but rhetoric." I was astonished at the brevity of the cross-examination, and before I had accustomed myself to the idea that something of great importance was going on, the whole thing was over and the man and wife were coming back down the aisle, arm in arm, smiling to their well-wishers, their faces illuminated by the sunlight into which they were walking. Hopestill did not fail to include her husband in her dispensation of impartial smiles, but her hand that clutched the bouquet of flowers was clenched like stone.

The drawing-room, the library, the dining-room overflowed with cawing guests and the stairs were packed with two lanes, one ascending to view the wedding presents, the other coming down. As soon as I had offered my congratulations (the bride and groom were stationed before the bay-window. Both of them had protested against this lavishness and were so harried that they seemed not to recognize me at all), I pushed my way through the throngs who, because they blocked the way between myself and my room for which I longed, offended me as if they were being intentionally hard-hearted. Outside the drawing-room door, I met Miss Pride who had got rid of her hat and looked refreshed. I told her that I thought I was ill and wanted to go to my room.

"Nonsense," she said. "I've never seen you look better. There are two or three things I want you to attend to in the pantry. Come along with me and I'll show you."

I said, "I thought that if I went to bed now the cold wouldn't have a chance to develop."

"Oh, I know your kind of cold, you vixen. I'm not as easily taken in as Berthe, though, and won't let you off. What I think is that you're just concerned too much with yourself. After this is over, we must have a long talk and straighten things out."

I followed her docilely down the hall to the door of the pantry where she instructed me to post myself in order to see that the dirty dishes were immediately sent down on the dumb-waiter to be washed and sent up again so that everyone might be served. The waiters, who were perfectly capable of managing by themselves, regarded me with such wounded displeasure that for the half hour I stood on guard I did not utter a word, but leaned against the window where the sunlight was warm, drinking the remains of the champagne in the glasses that came out from the other rooms. Once I closed my eyes to feel the sun on my lids and when I opened them again saw Harry Morgan lounging up against the door giving me what I could only call "a once-over." Fearing that if Miss Pride chanced to come into the pantry and saw us there together she might surmise that I was responsible for this intrusion, and being, moreover, greatly perturbed by his prowling eyes, I exclaimed, "My God!" and he, straightening up, extended his hand as he said, "May I share your quiet inglenook, dear, just we two?" One of the accommodators, a portly middle-aged man with a bald head and a frowning face, turned on him a look of avuncular disapproval as he pushed past with a tray of glasses and I said, "It's very crowded in here."

"Well, then, let's find a place that isn't crowded. I can't go back into that crush."

"Nobody asked you to," I said, so nervous that I was obliged to

437

put down the glass I was holding for fear of dropping it. "Nobody asked you to come in the first place."

"What kind of talk is that? I am guest Number One. I came at the urgent invitation of the doctor himself. No one asked me, indeed!" He laughed openly at my perplexity. "Well, in that case," I said, "you ought to join the party."

I myself, feeling that my services in the pantry were dispensable, went out, taking up a place between the long buffet table and the doors to the drawing-room which had been slid back all the way there to examine the implications of the conversation I had just had. I was prevented from a long study by the Admiral who, with old Mrs. McAllister, appeared slowly making his way toward the refreshment table. "Ah," he cried, spotting me, "here we have an ally. Sonie, what could you do in the way of a hot bird and a cold bottle for two old fellows? I'm hungry as a bear. I tell you, giving away a young lady is hard work. It's a strain on the heart! Particularly if you wanted her for your granddaughter-in-law." He winked at his companion. "Well, all's well that ends well, as they say. And while I'm about consoling myself, ma'am, let me congratulate you on getting a pippin for the boy."

"Much obliged," said Mrs. McAllister coldly. "I think Hope looks ill."

"Ill? Why, ma'am, though you're a woman, you don't know women. What female creature ever looked well on her wedding day? I always say the expression shouldn't be 'white as a ghost' but 'white as a bride.' And the whiter they are, the prettier, what?"

Mrs. McAllister received a plate of sole and salad and a glass of champagne from me. Refusing from that moment forward to discuss the wedding, the wedding breakfast, or the bride and groom, she commenced on an analysis of Amy Brooks' water colors in which she displayed more affection than intelligence. "The sweet thing, knowing that I don't get about, brought a whole portfolio full of them to me yesterday and I was perfectly charmed. She has real talent." She went on to describe in particular a little scene Amy had done of the hemlocks in the Arboretum. While I nodded with interest and even volunteered a few comments ("How much I should like to see the picture. No, I have never been to the Arboretum, but I hope to go on

Lilac Sunday," etc.), I was actually engrossed in staring at Harry Morgan who had belatedly followed me out of the pantry and was in conversation with the Countess who, from her smiles and laughter, appeared to find him delightful. A surge of people presently obliterated them and I turned my mind again to what Mrs. McAllister and the Admiral were saying. The Arboretum had led her to her own garden in Concord, and Concord had led her to the bitter announcement, corroborated by her son, Reverend McAllister, who edged his way up to us, that "I suppose you've heard Philip Senior has given the young couple a handsome wedding present? That house on the Bedford Road left to him by my husband."

"I declare!" cried the Admiral. "That *is* handsome of you, Phil. Why, that's a humdinger of a house. Up on a hill, ain't it?"

Mrs. McAllister sighed deeply. "The loveliest house in Middlesex County, Lincoln. One of the loveliest in New England. I have always said we ought to turn it over to a historical society."

"No, Mother, not in my lifetime. I hope the children will get some pleasure out of it. I've never cared much for the house myself. Would have sold it long ago, Lincoln, but Mother here didn't like it's being in the hands of a stranger."

The old lady pursed her lips, said nothing, but obviously was thinking that the house *was* in the hands of a stranger.

Her son asked me then, "How much champagne would you say Lucy Pride ordered for this collation?" I told him exactly: twelve cases. He raised his eyebrows, appalled. "If all the money spent on drink were handed over to the missionaries, we would have a Christian world."

Mrs. McAllister, who had wanted her son to go into the navy, had often been heard to speak like a pagan. She snapped at him, "I hope that time never comes, son, for I feel that there are times when one *needs* alcohol. Now, for example. At weddings and at funerals." Her voice had risen to an impassioned shriek and her son put his finger to his solemn lips. "Hush, Mother, they say it takes very little to go to one's head when one is advanced in years."

The Admiral snorted, "Your mother can take care of herself, old man. She hasn't had enough to drink, that's her trouble. Hand me your glass, ma'am, and let me refill it."

"Good afternoon," said Miss Pride crisply from behind us. "Ah, Sonie, I see you're taking over out here. I don't know what I would do without you. Well, and have you seen our poor lambs, Sarah? They're complaining that their arms ache from shaking hands and their faces hurt from smiling. They groaned when I told them they must stay another hour at least."

"At least," rejoined the old lady, staring hard at Miss Pride. "Why, I dare say that less than half of Boston has had a chance to congratulate them. My dear Lucy, you have outdone yourself!"

Miss Pride smiled pleasantly and turned to the Admiral. "I haven't even thanked you, Lincoln, for contributing to the occasion, but I'm angry with you for not wearing your decorations."

"Not with mufti, ma'am. Not me, thank you!" returned her friend, beaming all over his pink face in gratitude for her mention of his medals.

Old Mrs. McAllister, determined to find one barb at least to pierce Miss Pride's composure, at this said, "How did Arthur Hornblower feel about it?"

But she did not fell Miss Pride who retorted, "I expect he breathed a sigh of relief when he knew he wouldn't have to perform in that church. You know his objection is not to the Romish atmosphere but to the English. He's a great Anglophobe."

"Oh, I'm quite aware of *that*," said Mrs. McAllister with considerable asperity. "We've had several disputes. I tell him he's provincial, he tells me I'm a snob and we get nowhere."

"You would have quarreled with Papa, Sarah. I have always been glad that he died before war was declared because, since he liked neither France nor England, I have no doubt he would have made himself talked about in Boston. Oh, I don't mean to imply that he would not have supported the Allies whole-heartedly as far as the United States was concerned, but he would have turned a cold shoulder on England, I'm sure. His sister, my aunt Josephine, had what Papa called 'the hebetude' to marry a baronet and to be called henceforth 'Lady Fulke.' It was the name, even more than her large and totally inconvenient country establishment, that struck Papa so ridiculous. And I recollect that at the time I was presented at court and we were perforce staying with my aunt and my uncle Geoffrey,

Papa consistently introduced her as 'Mrs. Faneuil' or 'Mrs. Fuller,' being unable to bring himself to say 'Lady' or to utter a name so peculiar as 'Fulke.' But I remember, also, that my sainted father was worsted on one such occasion by Mr. Henry James who turned to an English woman and said, 'One may forget other names, but Faneuil Hall is always on the tip of the tongue.' Papa was no backwoodsman: he blushed to the roots of his hair and never returned to England again or permitted the names of Mr. James and Sir and Lady Fulke to be spoken in his presence."

"Ha! Ha!" laughed the Admiral who was well-known himself as an Anglophile. "Lucy, you're a real raconteur!" But old Mrs. McAllister, pretending that she had not heard the story, groped for my hand which she pressed as she said, "My dear, do find Amy Brooks for me!"

As I went in search of Hope's cousin, the Countess, fragrant as a whole garden, came towards me with outspread arms, bumping everyone who stood in her way, among them the easily terrified Mr. Otis Whitney who immediately fled through the drawing-room in the direction of the door and was not seen again. She had nothing to tell me of any more consequence than that she loved me and that I was not to wear anything ever again but the same shade of green that I had on today and that if I did not come to hear the "Scarlatti I've dismembered, dismembered, my angel," at her next Friday, her heart would be broken into a thousand pieces. As she embraced me at our leavetaking—she had of course given me a welcoming hug and had let me go for only about a minute—she dropped her effusive tone and spoke as if we were contemporaries: "I'm not pleased, Sonie! I'm much distraught. I've been talking with a young man who has given me a real fright. You . . ."

But she could not finish for, to my great vexation, we were interrupted by one of the girls who came to the Fridays. Martha Dole was a large, plain bluestocking whose embonpoint was apportioned helter-skelter so that the thin, rectilinear legs did not harmonize with the bossy torso and likewise the long, willowy neck was inadequate support for the full-blown Norman face. She, like the other young ladies, had always shown me great cordiality in the Countess' presence, and had two or three times sent me tickets to the theater or to concerts with which, to be sure, she had parted because she could not use them herself but which were accompanied by a flattering note which told me I was more deserving than she to hear the music or to see the play. Only three nights before, I had gone, thanks to her generosity, to see *Hamlet,* but this had not prevented her, on the following day, from becoming suddenly so engrossed in her companions that she did not see me, even though I passed directly in front of her, when I entered the cocktail lounge of the Parker House to keep an appointment with Nathan and Kakosan. Yet, her first remark to me this afternoon was, "Who was that lovely girl, Japanese, Chinese, whatever she was, that I saw you with the other day?"

"At the Parker House, do you mean?" I asked experimentally, watching her face to see what degree of confusion would be recorded there. If there was any, it was too infinitesimal to be measured, and she said, "Was it at the Parker House? Yes, of course, that's right. She was exquisite! We were all quite enchanted and I was greatly set up to be able to say that even though I didn't know her, I did at least know her companion. She looked as though she had stepped out of a fairy tale. You would have fallen in love with her, Berthe!"

The Countess gave me an indulgent spanking. "What do you mean, you wicked creature, keeping all of this from me? No, no evasions! I want to know all about her. Oh, such a betrayal!"

I explained that Kakosan was a stenographer in some firm, the exact nature of which I had never determined, for she always referred mysteriously to "the commodity" which might have been anything from ink to corsets. I told them also that she was the daughter of a nobleman in exile, a cultivated patriarchal gentleman who preserved all the customs of his country and his class, writing *hokku,* painting water-colors of the Yanagawa from his faithful memory of it, sitting beside his pool in the American duplicate of his garden in Kyushu, in contemplation of the Zen-Buddha to whom, each day, he paid his ceremonial respects in the tea-house. As I observed the mounting interest in the Countess' face, I regretted I had made Nathan's mistress sound so interesting for I had no wish to bring her to the salon. My reason was that I could not trust her to exercise any restraint in her conversation. The several times that I had seen her (in my exile, I had welcomed her invitations to the movies), she had

442

been naïve enough to tell me, when we had stopped at Schrafft's for raspberry frappés, about her lovers previous to Nathan whose attentions she described with a thoroughness that made me blush. I had no reason to suppose that she would be less candid with the Countess and the Boston girls.

"But she sounds charming!" cried the Countess. "Just imagine a real Samurai daughter simply at large in Boston! I've never heard anything so exotic! I command you to bring her to hear the Scarlatti on Friday, and if you do not, Euphrysone, I'll think up some really humiliating punishment for you. I'll make you spend a whole evening with Kalenkoff playing omber!"

I agreed, with misgivings, to bring Kakosan, and started to take leave of the Countess to go in search of Amy when Mrs. Hornblower approached us and halted me with an upraised and trembling hand. Gently with a dreamy, timid smile on her face—entirely out of keeping with her reputation of being a firebrand in political discussions, of being a sly one, and possibly engaged in subversive activities on the behalf of the Third Reich and Mussolini, having long since lost her interest in Sacco and Vanzetti—she said, "Lucy Pride told me where I'd find you. Someone told me you were acquainted with a young lady whose address I'm very anxious to get hold of. I mean the little Japanese girl, Miss Yoshida, or, rather, I should say, Yoshidasan without the 'Miss,' shouldn't I?"

"Ah, it's an epidemic!" cried Miss Martha Dole. "Imagine Sonie being in the key position!"

I told Mrs. Hornblower that I did not know Kakosan's address but that I should be glad to give her a message as I often saw her in Cambridge. "I'm getting up a benefit party for the Rebels in Spain, and I want her to come, partly for decoration, partly because I suspect that she's a sympathizer. Wouldn't you like to come too? Or don't you believe in Franco?" I had no strong feelings for either party in the Spanish Revolution and agreed with Miss Pride who said, "When the pot calls the kettle black, I shan't back either one."

"No, I can't say that I do think Franco's right," I said, and the Countess, a rabid Loyalist supporter, squeezed my arm and said to Miss Pride's cousin, "Sonie and I would be driving ambulances if we could, wouldn't we, darling?" This was not in the least true. The

Countess supported "causes" solely in her drawing-room and the drawing-rooms of her friends, and I, for my part, was too ignorant of world affairs to be anything but apathetic towards them.

"What a pity," said Mrs. Hornblower. "I have not found many recruits here. Countess, have you stolen everyone for yourself?" And turning to me, she said, "I had thought that you . . . your name, you know, such *echt deutsch* . . . might be of our persuasion. *De gustibus non est disputandum.*" She moved off murmuring half to herself, "So few people are willing to take the long veiw, the *Weltanschauung*. But the time will come." These words, proceeding from a face so venerable and harmless, gave me such an unaccountable fright that for a moment I stood looking after her, and what occurred to me as she was swallowed up by a crowd of people in the doorway was that perhaps my father, if he had gone back to Würzburg, had become a Nazi.

Martha Dole, espying an old friend, left us and the moment she was gone, I said to the Countess, "You were telling me about Harry Morgan."

"But he told me something extraordinary! Something too really strange! Don't misunderstand: I like him although he's rather racy in his language. I'm only wondering how everyone will take it."

"Take what, my dear Countess?" I cried with impatience.

"Oh, it's probably nothing at all. It's only that he told me that Philip has asked him to take charge of doing over the Concord house, and it only struck me odd because of the way Mrs. McAllister feels about the place. And of course, no one *knows* him. D'you understand me, Sonie?"

"Yes, yes," I said. "But what I *don't* understand is why Philip asked him. He hasn't known him for longer than a month."

"Precisely!" said the Countess with a wink and then, perceiving that her stepdaughter was at her side, added, "It is precisely as you say: a 'four-square' sonata, as tedious as a wooden block."

Having delivered to Amy the message from Mrs. McAllister, I made my way into the drawing-room where the crowd was beginning to thin. Hopestill beckoned to me. "Go up with me, will you, Sonie?" she whispered. I glanced towards her maid-of-honor and she said impatiently, "I've arranged that, don't worry." Philip's face was fixed in a smile that revealed his teeth which were so regular and white they looked almost false. The adjective "sanitary" flashed across my mind as I took in his clear, intellectual eyes, his fair hair, his meticulously cared-for person, and in that moment, I preferred his bride upon whose cheek there was a light streak of dirt and who was frankly exhausted and was making no attempts to conceal the fact. I told her that I would meet her in her room and she left when she had said something to Philip who, looking at me as if he had never seen me before, formally shook my hand, not altering his grin in the least. I laughed uneasily and said, "I've already congratulated you once, don't you remember?" and he replied, "How stingy you are! Can't you congratulate a man twice on the happiest day of his life?" But there was in his voice a note of such staggering unhappiness, so taut an irony that I could make only a feeble rejoinder, told him I must hurry up to Hopestill, that I wished him all the happiness, that I . . .

Hopestill had flung her bouquet down the stairwell, but one flower, limp and ragged at the edges, was caught in the pointed cuff of her wedding dress. She was waiting in her sitting-room for me and she could have been waiting ten years, she had changed so much. The structure of her face was loose, as if the sagging muscles had weakened the mortised bones. There was a starched pallor on her thin lips, a narrow canniness in her eyes, and the skin, in the brief time since I had seen her in the church, had lost that shimmer which had seemed to be touched by the moon rather than the sun, to have been inoculated by the spring rather than the summer, was ashen now, darkening to a bruised blue beneath her eyes. She had had a drink and when I came in, put down her glass. There was a newly opened bottle of whiskey on the table near where she stood.

"By God, he can wait for me!" she cried. "I'll go down when I'm God damned good and ready." And she sank into one of the wing-chairs and poured herself another drink.

"It was a very nice wedding," I said.

"Lock the door, Sonie. I won't have any of them coming in here! I won't! I wish I were dead!"

I locked the door as she ordered me and reluctantly returned. She directed me to sit down opposite her and she said, "I really mean it:

I wish I were dead. Now if I were you, I wouldn't wish that, but strictly *sotto voce,* strictly *entre nous* I wouldn't predict what you'll be feeling if you go on living with Aunt Lucy for another two years."

"Well," I said, "it's not quite the same thing. It's not the same at all, Hope."

"Listen to me, you child, you baby, you innocent little girl: the time will come when you see through that woman and know her for the bitch she is. It's that she's got to have power. All of us do here: we are obsessed by it. Philip is. I am. As soon as Aunt Lucy saw she couldn't control me—up to a point she could because she was my guardian and doled out my money nickel by nickel—she got a cat! That's the vile perverted thing she did! And kept the cat locked up in a storeroom deodorized by pine-scent! Oh, she fed Mercy well: the best tinned salmon, the finest kidneys, the richest milk, and every now and again the 'Persian fat lady,' as she was revoltingly referred to, was allowed to come down and purr for Aunt Sarah and Uncle Arthur and Admiral Nephews. Until, mind you, she had a chance to perpetuate her species and have four hybrid kittens and then she was permanently incarcerated."

"Oh, that's not the reason," I said, determined to defend Miss Pride.

"Hush! Let me finish. But a pussy-cat wasn't enough, and now she's got *you,* and she intends to have the time of her life with you because you're helpless. You're dependent on her. No matter what *gaffe* you make, if you get drunk and use obscene words in front of Mrs. Frothingham, Aunt Lucy will find some way to keep you."

"I am not property!" I cried, angry with Hopestill and at the same time perturbed.

"Well, dear, that's beside the point. All of this is beside the point. I'll have a drink if you'll pour it for me, please, and tell you what *isn't* beside the point." I filled our two glasses. I was muzzy and out-of-sorts with this oblique diatribe. "What isn't beside the point," she continued, "is that all I've accomplished today, all I've accomplished in my whole life, is that I've transferred myself from one martinet to another."

"You didn't have to marry him."

She got to her feet and glared at me. "I'm sure I don't know why

446

I've taken you into my confidence, and you can jolly well forget this. Now I'm going to dress."

The crowd had thinned considerably when I went down. In the vestibule, I heard a woman remark, "I wouldn't mind if my income were cut to fifteen thousand. I'd just go out to my farm for the whole year." And another voice replied, "Of course it wouldn't go hard with you, Augusta. Why, you have a fortune in your roses if you'd only do something about it." Augusta, whom I immediately knew to be the aunt Philip had visited when he drove me to Wolfburg from Chichester, laughed heartily. "That's what my nephew tells me, but he's a pipe-dreamer. I'm so glad that at least one of his pipe-dreams has come true. Hope is the sweetest girl in Boston, I've always felt."

"Wasn't it strange," said the Countess to Miss Pride, "that Mrs. Hornblower brought her present with her?"

"I didn't know she did," said Miss Pride. "It was peculiar enough of her to come in an evening dress."

"That's not all. She unwrapped it herself as well, and what do you suppose it was? A dozen perfectly horrid souvenir coffee spoons."

"My dear!"

Hopestill was coming down the stairs and in her carefully composed face there was no sign of the fright and anger that had made her burst out to me in her room. She joined Philip at the door and they went out, sped on by the uproar of the guests who had lingered.

"At any rate," Miss Pride was saying at my elbow, "I haven't lost this one," and she slipped her arm through mine. Through the sleeve of her black suit, I felt her bone on my flesh like a steel wand or, as she bent it into a hook, like a thin, inflexible staple. "And now," she went on to the Admiral, "now I'm going back to my memoirs."

The Admiral smiled radiantly. "When is this celebrated volume to be finished?"

Miss Pride returned his smile. "I dare say it will be years. At least that's what I intend, for I want something to occupy me so that I won't get foolish, and to occupy Sonie so she won't forsake me. Am I selfish?"

"No, ma'am. You're the most generous woman in Boston." He

bowed deeply and then said to me, "And you, Mademoiselle, are the luckiest."

It was with a sort of sudden desperation that I saw that the drawing-room was empty and that the accommodators were taking down the extra tables in the dining-room and that through the open door to the library only Reverend McAllister was visible, holding open in his hands a large dark green book which I knew was a volume of the *Encyclopaedia Britannica.* Voices still came from the upstairs sitting-room, but presently a little group of people appeared at the head of the stairs and as they came down in a gust of talk, I could tell that even that room was empty now for Ethel, who had evidently been waiting for her chance, crossed the hall and went in with a tray to pick up the glasses that had been carelessly left there by the sight-seers. I wished to detain these last few guests but they were saying good-by. Gratuitously they told their hostess where they were going: to the matinee of *Richard II,* to the Country Club for ice-skating, to Brookline to shop at Best's. Amy Brooks and Mr. Pingrey, shy with one another because Amy had caught Hopestill's bouquet which she clutched tightly against her quivering breast, shaken with silent giggles, passed by me without a word because they could not see me or hear me though I called out to them, "Oh, don't go yet!" Their only thought was to get through the door and away, by themselves. They hastily told Miss Pride good-by and Amy screamed, "It was lovely! I caught the bouquet, Cousin Lucy! Edward and I are going to Agassiz! I am going to do the glass flowers in pastels for Mrs. McAllister!"

They were gone then, the last. Miss Pride, still holding my arm, linked her other in the Admiral's, and three abreast we went down the hall towards the library. "We'll quickly get rid of Ichabod," whispered Miss Pride, nodding in the direction of Reverend McAllister who was still absorbed in his book, "and then we three can have a nice talk."

"Right-o," said the Admiral. "Ain't it a pity my wife had to miss this! Why, Lucy, I haven't had such a good time since I went dancing at the Country Club, unless it was a month ago when Rose Park gave the cocktail party for her Community Chest people. I'm gay as a lark. Aren't you, Sonie?"

"Oh, yes, sir!" I cried. Miss Pride released us both and after she had gently closed the door behind us, switched off the ceiling light. The sun had gone behind a cloud and the library was shadowy and cold. "There now," she said. "It's cozy. It's just right to have this sort of *dämmerung* follow a wedding. It is the anti-climax to these affairs that I like most."

# CHAPTER SIX

Philip McAllister, I was thinking, was one of those men in whom there lingers the perfectionism of childhood, who, when his stature was Lilliputian, saw the world as titanic, saw love centered in a goddess as a principle of salvation, as the meaning of that large, floating life, seeming so shapeless and so wonderful, like the shifting clouds of summer which veil and unveil the sun, that life he thought might vanish before he had sprung forth from his dwarfish body. We say of such people erroneously that they have never "grown up." We should say instead that they grew up too quickly, skipping certain years and finding themselves flowering, alone, and in the snow, months before the spring. The phantom he had been pursuing all his life, and which he believed was at last entrapped in this girl whom he had loved intermittently for many years, had escaped him and the love with which he thought to imprison her had dematerialized, leaving him without love and without an object to try to love.

I was coming from the Countess' and was on my way to the young McAllisters' house where they were having a cocktail party and I was going over, with distaste, the conversation I had just had with my earlier hostess. Having summoned me over the phone that morning to have luncheon with her, she began, the moment we had left the dining-room for the library, to state her object. It was nothing more than simply to satisfy her curiosity. For some months past, indeed, ever since Philip and Hopestill had come back from a wedding trip to Canada, everyone had been slightly or greatly (depending on the extent of his prejudices) shocked by the almost constant presence in their house of Harry Morgan. The Countess von Happel wanted to know what I thought of it. Had I any idea why such otherwise attractive people set loose upon their guests a person of such execrable manners, such unrelenting buffoonery? He was addicted to imitations and in the course of a single evening recently, the Countess declared, had "done" President Roosevelt at a cocktail party, Katharine Hepburn at a psychiatrist's, a Negro on trial for murder, a priest confronted by Mae West. There was little to distinguish one from another and no one could understand how he could delude himself into thinking he had the least gift for mimicry. "If he's as inexpert at architecture as he is at imitations," remarked the Countess, "the Concord house will be a scandal." The Concord house was already in a sense a scandal, for Hopestill and Morgan spent a great deal of time there, often without Philip and without any more chaperonage than that of the carpenter or the gardener.

Did I believe, as some people did, that Philip was perhaps endeavoring to show Hopestill how detestable his predecessor was by forcing the man upon her, much in the way some mothers allow their children to eat their way into an indifference for candy? And was this newly announced pregnancy part of Philip's plan to tame the wild creature who had lived amongst wolves so long that she had come to howl like them?

I was disinclined to confide in the Countess my own opinion for she was a notorious gossip and was not above naming the sources of her tidbits, and so, to all her queries, I only replied, "Oh, I suppose he amuses them," or "He's not such a bad sort when he isn't clowning."

But I was not to be let off so easily. The Countess, who enjoyed nothing so much as contemplating people's motives, continued her anatomizing.

"I cannot accept the attachment between Philip and Mr. Morgan as altogether genuine. And if he is trying to teach Hope a lesson, isn't he a bit innocent? I mean, my dear Euphrysone, one can't help hearing things. One hears of Mr. Morgan's reputation."

We are instantly put on our guard by the effeminate man who, as if to dispel our suspicions, says, "You know, homosexuals interest me very much psychologically and I must confess I have a number of good friends among them whom I would like to have you meet," or takes an even bolder stand and says, "I am so amused by the rumors I have heard about myself that I have been tempted to give people really something to talk about by having my hair curled and my fingernails painted" (so that we know, in the first instance, that if the homosexuals have admitted him to their minds which he is investigating in the interest of his hobby, they have as well admitted him to their arms, and in the second that curling his hair and painting his nails are probably what he will shortly do, but not for the reason that he has prepared us). Just so, the confidence that Philip placed in Harry Morgan made the astute Countess suspect that he did not trust him at all, that he was jealous of those New York days and New York evenings to which the young millionaire so casually referred, calling upon Hopestill to confirm the name of a restaurant or of a mutual friend.

"Pretend you're a European, darling! I love you! Don't be shocked! Tell me, dear angel, if you don't agree with this evil-minded old woman that Philip McAllister has some reason—don't interrupt, Sonia—for being disappointed in that lovely bride of his? And . . . Come sit beside me. I don't know where that Filipino child of mine is. And that he does not really adore her so much as he appears?"

"I don't follow you, Countess," I said nervously.

My friend pouted and then laughed. "Of course you don't *follow* me, precious scamp, you're a mile ahead of me."

I was by no means averse to gossip but I did not enjoy it with the Countess who, for some reason unknown to me, was reined in by no inhibitions when she spoke to me although I was certain that she was discreet with others. She seemed to be under the impression that my moral view had the same generous, continental latitude as hers. My disquietude, as I fumblingly put down my coffee cup, was transmitted to her and a small silence came between us, as precise as a picture hanging on a wall.

The Countess went on, more gently. "Oh, I have not been nice at all! But you and I, Sonia, observe things other people don't. Don't we now? Wouldn't you agree with me that probably you and I are the only people, besides the principals, of course, who know that Mr. Morgan was Hope's friend before her marriage?"

"Friend?" I repeated. "But of course they were friends."

"I use the word in its European sense, darling, as you perfectly well know." She crossed the room to the bell-pull, and stood poised a moment, the light from the window enlivening her fair hair with brilliant undulations, her nose aloft. There was something at once so childish and so wise about her pose as well as about what she had just been saying that I smiled. She caught my smile, returned it, and said, "Don't try to pretend any longer that you're not a spy. You were spying on me just then. We will have some more coffee and something very special, a beautiful brandy."

Bit by bit, in the course of the afternoon, my hostess' conjectures came out. Some she revised, others she left intact; I proffered nothing new, but I was forced, by the sheer weight of her intuition which had synthesized random elements into a composition as clear as a case history written in a book, to agree with her. I did not, however, know any ease even with the assistance of the crystal-clear brandy, for I felt somehow that simply by listening I was letting Hopestill's cat out of the bag.

Berthe von Happel, through the same sort of almost physical insight that Mamselle Thérèse had employed, had known from the beginning why Hopestill had suddenly decided to marry Philip. In another sort of society, her guess would probably have immediately occurred to anyone who did not believe that the girl was in love. But it would never have crossed the mind of, for example, Amy Brooks. Hopestill might be disliked, might be criticized for her inability to get on with her relatives-in-law, for her sharp and often cruel treatment of servants, for her bland disregard of charitable works, but no one would have dreamed of accusing her of so great a crime as the one she actually had committed and the one the Countess took matter-of-factly. For whatever else she was, Hopestill was a member of a society which did not countenance illegitimate children, which, in a sense, did not believe in them, just as the prim Victorian who is told for the first time of sodomy says with a firm scoff, "I never heard of it before. I don't believe it. It's merely a bit of obscene nonsense." To be sure, shop-girls and servants frequently ruined their lives through such misdemeanors, but the people one lunched with and invited to dinner chose other means: dipsomania or betting on the horses. Bastardry was not acknowledged as a possible function of the upper classes. (I recalled, in a momentary flare of anger, how the first time I had met Philip McAllister, he had accused me of coming to him for an abortion.) But there had been a time, the

Countess declared, when New England had not been so naïve, when sin was looked for in every stratum and duly punished.

Had I never seen in Philip McAllister's eyes the fanaticism of a Puritan? Had I never noticed how, at a dinner party, his flushed face did not turn when he spoke to someone but was kept tensely in an attitude that allowed him to keep a constant vigil on his wife, as if he were trying to read the thoughts in her deceitful head, or as if he wished to convey to her some message that would inform her he knew everything and forgave her nothing? Oh, to be sure, most people took this as a look of love. Indeed, the sole criticism of him was that he prolonged beyond the point of decency, his look of nuptial rapture and the vagueness which rendered him, in conversation, slightly stupid.

It was true, as the Countess said, that in public his eyes, across the cerulean azure of which there passed a flare of hotter blue like the quick, staggering stab of sun to the heart of a diamond, never left his wife but studied her as the rapt jeweler studies a rare stone through the little magnifying glass enfolded in his eye. And while he watched her, he praised her to everyone within earshot: no one had her genius for dress, or her hair, or her enchanting voice in a high minor key, or had that pearly shining flesh in which only the mouth, the palest pink or, in some lights, faint lilac, broke the lily-like monotony. In these first months of her pregnancy when it had not yet made itself cumbersome, she had reached the pinnacle of her loveliness, like the forced flower, blossoming under glass and out of reach of the distractions of other flowers and the alteration of its color by the sun or by the shade. No less embarrassed than her guests was Hopestill whose protests only made her husband the more extravagant, the more hysterically flattering: "And her greatest charm of all is that she doesn't know how charming she is!" he would cry.

I told the Countess that I did not quite see the logic of her argument: if Philip was aware that he had been tricked, and if, as she maintained, he was a throw-back to early Puritanism, why did he not divorce her or punish her by depriving her of all society, or, at the very least, refuse to have Morgan in his house?

"Oh, don't think he wants anyone to know. He wants them to

suspect, probably. But he can't punish her openly, can't divorce her —for I have no doubt he feels strongly about divorce—can't burn a scarlet letter in her forehead. Darling, unconsciously he's imitating Dante: Don't you remember that the lovers' punishment is to embrace forever?"

I could not bear to listen to any more and got up. "I'm due at Hope's house now," I said, "though I'm sure I don't know how I'll face her."

And she replied, "Why, be that same inscrutable Euphrysone we know so well. You cannot fool me! You have known all along! I love you! Give Hope a kiss for me!" And she deposited a kiss on either cheek, one for myself and one for Hopestill which I did not propose to deliver.

The Countess' house, like her person, was overheated and over-fragrant, and it was a relief to be on the street. I idled, taking the longest way to Hopestill's house, and finding an organ-grinder on Marlborough Street, I stopped to watch his monkey. I did not really attend the sad little dressed-up animal, but I put penny after penny into his leather hand and dreamily looked at him and at his soiled old master who could easily have been his father. The trees had been out for some time and although now, in the twilight, it was cold, there was a quality of spring in the air. I wished that I were in the country or that, at least, I might stay out of doors until it was quite dark, doing no more perhaps than paying the monkey for the windy tunes.

I moved on. Undoubtedly the Countess was right. Philip's disappointment had made him hate Hopestill. And his hatred, coupled with his atavistic, vindictive morality, prompted him to torture her, to batten himself upon the love of the two sated and now unwilling people. But simultaneously, as he caused them to remain at their revolting banquet, though they were gorged, caused them, like Paolo and Francesca, to embrace forever and be embraced by hell, he, as overseer must also be in hell, must see to it that they rendered him the true accounts, and did not embezzle from eternity one instant of relief.

Only for Harry Morgan did I have no pity at all. The Countess, while she had deplored him, had seemed to accord him a measure of sympathy as the victim of Philip's persecution, although she could

455

not deny my charge that he was in no way bound to accept invitations to Hopestill's house. There was one reason and I suspected two why he continued to come. The first was simply that he was a snob and had no intention of cutting himself off from the one house where he was welcome; he was a climber and would have given a good deal to be "in" as he was in other parts of the country. A fortune, he had discovered, was not the open sesame in Boston that it was elsewhere and he had once observed to me with a sort of bitter wonder that he could count on the fingers of one hand the débuts he had been invited to in this "city of the dead, this town where human life is at a premium." But there was, I thought, another reason why he did not refuse to come to the McAllisters' dinner parties and that was the new addition to Hopestill's gatherings (and the Countess', too, for that matter), that is, Kakosan Yoshida. Whether they saw one another anywhere save on Commonwealth Avenue, I could not tell, nor did I know if their friendship had progressed beyond the raillery they engaged in over cocktails, but I had perceived that they nearly always separated themselves from the rest of us before dinner and, by the time the highballs were served, had drifted to the sofa at the end of the drawing-room farthest from the fire-place. What they talked of, I could not dream, for I was sure that Kakosan had not told her new friend that she was acquainted with his tutor. Certainly, I had not told Nathan of any of this. He would have been maddened with jealousy if he had known that they were ever in the same room.

Kakosan had been an immediate success on the first Friday she had gone to the Countess'. Her conduct, of which I had been uncharitably dubious, was exemplary and her beauty, set off by a yellow satin dress embroidered with white flowers and a white carnation in her hair, distracted everyone so much from the music that the Countess was a little reserved in her conversation afterwards and we left rather earlier than usual. But Berthe von Happel bore no one a grudge and in a very short time she appeared at the Fridays and the Saturdays as often as I did. Likewise, she was taken up by Hopestill, and even Miss Pride, on one occasion, invited her to tea, though she confessed afterwards to me that she "found it a very pretty head but uncommonly empty."

If I had not let it be known that Kakosan was a typist, no one would have suspected that she had any other occupation than that of arranging flowers in a bowl or playing jackstones in a garden complete with torii and tea-house. For she was one of those people who have the enviable knack of keeping their addresses a dark secret without appearing to hide anything, of answering ambiguously or not at all questions about activities, backgrounds, preferences, antipathies. If someone said to her, "Where did you live before you came here?" she would reply, "My father, you see, has copied his villa on the Yanagawa. You should see it! He is a great gardener. And how sorry he is he cannot have the *tsubaki* in this country he loved so much in his beautiful homeland. Do you know what it is? It is red like fire and sometimes it blooms in the snow. But he has some of the Japanese flowers, you know, wistaria and cherry trees and iris. He has to have flowers, of course, for he is a Zen-Buddhist and must decorate his tea-house. And do you know that even though it never snows where his villa is, just as soon as winter comes, he covers the lanterns with straw mats as he used to do in Kyushu?" A persistent busybody, charmed with this information but nevertheless determined to know whether the villa was in California or Florida or Louisiana, might say, "Where did you say he has his villa?" As if she had not heard the inquiry, she would go on, "Oh, yes, and he has two red pines which he sprays twice a year, for it is the custom to remove every single dead needle." This was a side of Kakosan that I never saw when she was with Nathan or when she and I made our expeditions to the movies. With us, she talked only of her chief interests which were the "spirits," film stars, and some disreputable young men with whom she often conversed in the Common on her way home from work on a subject she called "nationals" and which we translated roughly as "politics." Or she would tell us the little adventures that took place in her office which sounded so remarkably like those I had heard from my classmates at the Back Bay Business College that I automatically envisaged Mrs. Hinkel as I listened to her.

But in the Boston houses, she was remote from anything worldly or anything Occidental, and I, along with everyone else, was captivated afresh each time my eyes came to rest on her dexterously wrought face as, when a conversation was in progress into which she could not enter, her golden mask became immovable and the eyes showed her to be humble before her intellectual superiors while the proud arch of her neck showed that the nobility of her blood forebade her too free participation in the meaningless talk of people who were "without tea." She was apparently the "real thing" and seeing her thus, I longed for Nathan to possess her forever as the reward for his generous overlooking of her faults. But the moment she dropped her "company manners" and exchanged a few words with me in private, I hoped that the affair would be swiftly over. The repugnance I sometimes felt for her (when she revealed herself as being so far from the "real thing") was the kind one feels toward anything that is not true to its origin if its origin is admirable or attractive: the book that begins well and peters out in mawkishness, the picture which at first seems profound until, on further study, we find that it has only the virtue of brilliant draftsmanship. She used only as ornaments the Samurai code, her father's gentlemanly pursuits of religion and art, and they were as removable as the flowers in her hair.

Nathan, feeling that he was required to justify his love of her to me (rather, to himself, for he was sometimes agonized by the discrepancy between his vast love and its mean, elusive object) often denied that she was unchaste and stupid, not stating his denial with a negative but offering me instead instances of her talents which opposed and triumphed over her defects. He did not say, "She is not stupid," but he said, "In some ways, she is very intelligent," and as an illustration of her insight, he told me that she had once observed something in him he believed he had perfectly concealed. "No, really," he said, "since I'm so generous with her, how could she know that I'm a miser?" I did not point out that the very energy of his generosity gave him away. Nor did he say that she was not promiscuous, but that she had been "misled." At one time, he would declare that she was not a harlot because she had been in love with each of her bedfellows. At another time, in a fit of jealousy of all those unknown possessors of her, he said, "She has never been affected by any of it. I am quite sure this is the first time she has been in love."

In the past month, she had been required to go to so many séances (some of which I knew to be imaginary, to be, actually, the Countess' Saturday. For some reason, probably a clever one, she had never told Nathan that she had been "taken up" by Boston.) and had broken so many appointments with him that he had become hollow-eyed with anxiety, unstrung with the suspicion that she had another lover. It was this, combined with their very evident enjoyment of one another, that made me think Kakosan and Morgan had at least entered upon the preliminaries of a love affair.

2

I had no more than let myself in at Hopestill's unlocked door than I was confronted with the proof of my suspicion, and it resulted from an incident which, by one of those almost supernatural timings of chance, occurred within the same hour that Nathan, two miles away and across the river in Cambridge, made the same discovery, his evidence being but slightly different from mine. The hall, through the carelessness of a servant, was not lighted yet, although it was quite dark, so that I could not distinguish the two people standing at one side of the door, possibly in an embrace, possibly helping one another with their wraps, but I heard Kakosan's high-pitched voice, suffused with childish laughter, cry, "Gacho, don't!", the name by which, it will be remembered, she called Nathan. And Harry Morgan said, "Okay, baby, but wait till I get you home." I was shocked, not only by the frank implications of these elided remarks, and the foretokening in them of Nathan's heartbreak, but also by the boldness of this love-play, a dozen feet from the drawing-room door. I concluded that they had already been to the party and had been relaxed by the cocktails. This, at any rate, was an advantage, for I should not now be obliged to talk with either of them. It would have been too much, I felt, if I had had to be omniscient witness to the antics of these two as well as of the McAllisters'. I hurried past them and as I went up the stairs, caught Kakosan's terrified murmur, "That was Sonie Marburg!"

Hopestill's drawing-room was so spacious that despite her many guests, it did not seem crowded. As Miss Pride said of the room,

"It's not the temperature but the color that makes one think of an ice-chest. The fire in that pallid hearth gives no more warmth than the ones in the theater made with flashlights and red tissue paper." It was called the "blue room" in contradistinction to an even chillier chamber, "the white parlor." The floor was carpeted in silvery blue; the graceful chairs and sofas were upholstered in gray satin and heavy blue curtains hid the violet panes in the bay-window at the far end of the room. Bare of pictures ("I can't afford originals and one doesn't have prints," she had said), the white walls were striated with gray shadows, for the room was dimly lit by a single bulb under the blue-green shade of a Chinese lamp. There was, as the Countess complained, nothing to look at in the room, for Hopestill detested bric-a-brac, having had her fill of it in her life at her aunt's and, influenced perhaps by her prejudice against the maidenhair ferns and Aunt Alice's Birthday Trifle, did not even put flowers on the tables.

"Oh, it's California, very likely," Miss Pride was saying to a youngish woman I had met before. "Most of them settle in the west, you know."

When Miss Pride spoke of "the west," it was as if she said "somewhere." It was not quite a void, but it was something stretching interminably behind one's back. Yes, she replied to her friend, she had been "out" once, and had not the least desire to go again.

"I dare say their rugged life and bad climate make the people hardy. But I must confess I find the Rocky Mountains quite hideous, quite lacking in style. They're too much of a good thing, so to speak. Even if the landscape didn't offend me, though, I couldn't endure the place more than ten days at a time. There is a crackly feel in western speech that sets my teeth on edge."

Her friend had spent three months in Saint Louis and countered, "But you should go to the middle west if you want to hear really peculiar speech. Of course Saint Louis is neither fish nor fowl nor good red herring. I could not get the key to the city. Is it southern? Is it mid-western? Is it an imitation of a German industrial town? I don't know. But I do know that their accent makes it almost impossible for an easterner to understand what they say. If someone told you, 'I lived tin yars in Versales, Mazura,' would you have the least idea that he meant, 'I lived ten years in Versailles, Missouri'?

By the way, isn't Versailles an amusing name?" The woman, whose home was in New Canaan, pronounced "idea" with a clear final consonant.

I was curiously soothed by this colloquy which was the first thing that came to my ears, for Miss Pride, no matter what scandals and disasters were perpetrated under her very nose, would never change. I assumed that she and her companion had been wondering where Kakosan's father lived. Miss Pride's announcement, "Most of them settle in the west, you know," made the Japanese immigrants as remote and unconnected with the world in which she lived as if they had never left their native shores, and Kakosan Yoshida herself went up in thin air. So long as Miss Pride was here, I thought, I could face anything. I was comforted to see that while she disdained the tray of canapés held before her by a maid, she exchanged her empty glass for a full one when the butler came round, so that I knew she would stay a little longer at least.

Feigning great interest in someone's proposed walking tour through Britanny, and someone else's plan to present Hopestill with a set of lawn bowls for her Concord house, and Edward Pingrey's recent attack of bronchitis, I actually only heard Philip's voice, superimposed upon all the others. He was not yet drunk, but he had reached a stage of animation which often just precedes almost hysterical excitement.

"What so amuses Hope and Harry about my father," I heard him say to Mr. Otis Whitney, a life-long friend of the Reverend McAllister, "is the titles of his books." And he went off into a spasm of pointless laughter in which Mr. Whitney joined with only a pained smile. His father was well-known as a mountain climber and had written three small volumes called *To the Jungfrau and Other Adventures, The Challenge of the Medicine Bow Range of the Rocky Mountains,* and *A Hymn to the Himalayas.* The titles, of course, amused everyone. But what variety of madness was making Philip's tongue wag on in so embarrassing a *gaffe?* One immediately pictured his wife and Morgan poking fun at his father while he indulgently looked on. It was no secret that Philip had no respect for him, but he had never expressed his contempt, had been friendly and even affectionate in his occasional little jokes about him. It sounded now as if his wife, through some obscure wile, had so corrupted him that neither taste nor common decency was left in this erstwhile dignified young man.

Evidently they had been discussing the renovations of the Concord house and the Reverend McAllister's name had come up in this connection, for Mr. Whitney, putting his glass on the mantel and murmuring that he must be going on, said, "I shall want to see the place when it's done."

"Oh, it will be a gem, I can tell you, Mr. Whitney!" cried Philip. "You should see the fire-place Morgan has designed. It doesn't look any more like a fire-place than you do."

I hoped that others were not, like myself, concentrating on the over-pattern of our host's voice. When Mr. Whitney had excused himself, Philip moved on to another group and repeated the reason why Hopestill and Harry Morgan were so amused by his father. Alcohol flings back, almost illimitably, the boundaries of humor so that we can find uproarious things which our poor sober friends miss altogether. It is necessary, if the joke is really good and really should be shared, to repeat it time and again until finally it penetrates those solemn skulls. Philip had for the third time cried out the names of his father's books. "I had never realized how terribly funny they were until Harry Morgan and Hopestill pointed it out!" Hopestill, detaching herself from Amy Brooks and two other earnest girls, came swiftly to her husband's side and slipping her arm through his, said, "Darling, Admiral Nephews wants to talk to you. Do rescue the poor old lamb. He's over there, you see, with Mr. James who's boring him to death." Perhaps, in one of those flashes of sobriety that intermittently punctuate the state of drunkenness, he realized that he had gone far enough and he obediently followed his wife, pausing to speak to me and to say, in an undertone, "Is there something up between Morgan and your Japanese friend? I shouldn't like that at all. I'll talk to you about it later."

I could keep my mind on nothing that was said to me and I moved with my cocktail to the fire-place where Hopestill's powerful dog, a Doberman, lay on the hearth, lifting his muzzle to me as I approached. Kurt had once belonged to *Herr* Speyer, the German who had mistaken me for his daughter as I waited in the lobby on my first musical Friday. When he left the country, he gave Kurt to the Countess who, having three dogs already, had handed him over to Hopestill. Despite his savage appearance, he was gentle and welcomed the advances of strangers who could not fail to be impressed by his gleaming black coat and his sharp, intelligent face. I never saw him without being reminded of his owner and the encounter with him that had given me so keen and so long-echoing a pleasure.

I sat down to contemplate the play of the flames on the short black hair and in the wise eyes that were now amber and now jet, and to restore the Nordic face that I had seen that day through the flittering shadows from the sconces and the voice, overlaid as by a filigree, by the music that descended to us from the room above. "Here, boy," I said, patting my knee. The dog wagged the stump from which his tail had been amputated, lifted his head to me, but did not get up. I wheedled a moment longer, then said, "Kurt! *Kommst du!*" and he bounded to me to put his forepaws on my lap, his shorn hind-end prancing. I was deeply attached to the affable animal who, though he bore only this resemblance to them, that is, that he could not talk, inspired me with the same joy—best known in memory—that certain things in nature did, and, in particular, through association with *Herr* Speyer, the August day when my father and I had seen the plover. Frequently Hopestill, who knew I was fond of Kurt, asked me to take him walking. We would hurtle down Clarendon Street to the esplanade and race along the river-bank. His strength and grace were communicated to me through the leash by which I restrained him and I was exhilarated with the swimming speed he demanded of me. Suddenly he would stop, listening. A growl would purr in his throat, but the bark it heralded did not come and instead, he would turn his head towards me, his companionable eyes informing me that he would not desert me after all for the excitement he had heard or smelled, far off, and we would resume our run.

Now Nathan and I, dreaming of Germany, had borrowed from libraries innumerable of those travel books which are written with a missionary's zeal, quick to report slighting comments on their darlings in order to refute them. Amongst these enraptured Valentines to Baden towns, we had found one that was full of photographs, from long study of which we had come to feel familiar with the walks, the bridges, the castle gardens, the cafés, the parks, the University of Heidelberg. As I walked with Kurt (born in Garmisch-Partenkirchen and intended, with his siblings, for a career on the Munich police force), I imagined that I was on the north bank of the Neckar River, proceeding towards the suburb of Handschusheim, the hills rising to my right, while to my left, across the river, I could see the mansard roofs of the old University and the spire of the Cathedral of the Holy Ghost. Just as in Chichester, I used to fancy Miss Pride's house in the shadow of the State House dome, so, taking the cathedral spire (the *locum tenens* being Eliot House across the Charles) as my landmark, I placed my red room somewhere to the left of it. Unless he was too impatient, I persuaded Kurt to stop awhile and I sat down on a stone bench. I ran my hand along the space between his pointed ears and like a child speaking to a doll, I told him about the room which had now acquired a locality, which was Heidelberg, a town plucked at random, and a temporal dimension which, owing to the peculiar light that stained the windows, was specified as autumn. At some change in the tone of my voice, the dog, hoping that we would move on again, would part his jaws in a grin, and I would say, *"Ja, Kurt, Ja, Kurt!"* and then take pity on the imploring tilt of his head and the little whine that sounded like a puppy's.

*"Doch, ist's so spät?"* I said to Kurt who was nuzzling my hand with his busy nose. I repeated the sentence in imitation of his former master and as I did so, tried to hear my accent which Nathan declared was more Russian than German. Experimenting a third time, I heard my mother's voice and experienced the now familiar sensation that it was actually she who was speaking. Instantaneously, upon my image of her which accompanied the sound of her voice through my lips, she vanished like the will-o'-the-wisp and what stood before me was the red room. The apparition had never been quite like this before: through the windows, instead of merely other windows and sleeping cats upon the sills, I saw, framed by soiled and motionless curtains, in a flat opposite me, a real face but one which I could not see clearly since it appeared to be obscured by a sort of mist. It was an old woman's face whose eyes seemed to be urged from their

464

sockets a little, staring at me with malevolent fixity. The mistiness evaporated: Miss Pride was there, in the flat across the courtyard and the sunset had changed the color of her olive hat.

When I vainly tried to see not the room but Hopestill's bare white walls and gray chairs, when I strained to hear the voices of her guests and could not, I knew that my game had got out of control and that Miss Pride had found me out in my retreat and was judging me a lunatic. It occurred to me with a terror that elevated me to an unimaginable height, that the only remedy for my obsession was a desperate one: that I must find the room in the real world before the real world intruded, as Miss Pride's face was doing now and confused me to the point of madness. For at this moment—and it was only a moment that I was conscious of her scrutiny—I was seized with a madness that was like an intense pain and was something outside myself, a violent force which urged my footsteps for the first time across the threshold onto the threadbare carpet with its faint green design. The knowledge that something external had precipitated my entrance was confused by a vertiginous and inarticulate emotion and for the present, I could not name the frenzy that had threatened but had not yet gained entrance. Despite the agitation into which the watchful eyes had flung me, I thought I sat serenely at the writing desk and sometimes smiled and other times rubbed my forehead with the tips of my fingers and then turned in my chair to examine the books on the nearest shelves. I noticed that the chair was exactly the right height, made so by a cushion. I was proud of my medical manuscript so beautifully preserved. The voice of my remembering self, roused from its sleep, said, "It was on Dr. Galbraith's desk the day you went to get him for Ivan." But my peace did not last. As Miss Pride's face moved closer, leaning out the window, her eyes pursued me and I whirled like a spinning top, whisking from corner to corner, fleeing them. I was strung out long like a bright wire that ended in brittle rays of copper, shining and pointed and raw. The eyes, like a surgeon's knives, were urged into my brain. The edges of the knives screamed like sirens; their sound curled in thin circles round my hot, pink brains. I crouched in a corner of the room, down behind the bookcases, safe, I thought. But I was plucked up by the burning yellow flares that went in a direct path like a sure blade. Miss Pride blinked her eyes. The room vanished. I had not moved but I felt an overwhelming tranquillity as if my brain were healed again, was sealed and rounded and impervious, was like a loaded, seamless ball, my hidden and wonderfully perfect pearl.

"Well!" said Miss Pride jocularly. "What a profound slumber you've just had."

Her niece stood beside her and both of them looked at me so curiously that I quickly said, "I was trying to remember a name." I was still trembling from my shock and I wondered if my voice had betrayed me. What shall I do? my eyes inquired of Kurt. His elongated face was up-pointed, immobile, and alert. I answered myself, "I must find the room or I will be like Mamma and then Miss Pride will find out and lock me up!"

Miss Pride said, "Hope tells me she wants you to stay here for dinner. I must be going on now."

"Oh, don't go just yet, Auntie," said Hopestill, her eyes wandering away from us as she sought her husband.

"I must," said her aunt. "I am behind in my political articles. Do you follow Mr. Roosevelt, Hopestill?"

Hopestill, who prided herself on not reading the newspapers and who, at the moment, was too distracted to comprehend what Miss Pride was saying, replied, "I haven't seen him in ages. I had dinner with him two years ago in a very muggy place in Cambridge. Surely he isn't *still* at Harvard!"

"Oh, no," answered Miss Pride, winking at me. "He's in Washington now."

"Really? As I recall, he was driving a banana-wagon that evening."

Disliking the prospect of having dinner alone with the McAllisters, I said to Miss Pride, "You said this morning, you know, that you wanted to do a little work this evening. Perhaps I should come along with you now."

"Oh, work is out of the question. Hopestill has made me quite tipsy. You stay here and enjoy yourself."

She turned away and Hopestill, leaning towards me, said in a whisper, "Why don't you want to stay, Sonie?" .

"I didn't say that," I told her. "But the fact is that I wanted to make a telephone call. I . . . ."

"Go into Philip's study if you like. You won't be disturbed there. I especially want you to stay. That is, I'm afraid if you don't, I'll have to eat alone because Philip will obviously pass out before dinner."

I relished no better the thought of being alone with Hopestill. The Countess' conversation, my knowledge of Kakosan and Morgan, and the visitation of the red room had combined to put me into an unsettled state which I knew only a normal evening with Miss Pride on Pinckney Street could cure. And, still, recollecting how her eyes had tracked me down, I was not sure of myself, felt I might suddenly cry out as she opened the *Boston Evening Transcript* or, more dreadful yet, the room might take me unawares again as it had done this afternoon and I would be obliged to explain my trance to her. Abruptly, I was stormed by a claustrophobia so violent that every element of the scene before me assumed the proportions of destroying force: there was no reason for this gathering, no reason for this elaborate amity amongst people whose civilization had pruned down their impulses to a set of manners which imperfectly concealed a dead indifference, no reason why I should be sitting here in this wealthy drawing-room when I, so far from being embourgeoised, could find pleasure only in the society of the dog, Kurt. I was alarmed by Philip who, damaged, loud, unrecognizable, was repeating anecdotes he had heard from Morgan and, to the even greater horror of his guests, was telling professional secrets about his own colleagues. Under what influence, wifely, personal, friendly, it was not known, he had, for some time past, seemed discontented with his profession. But he had not discussed it; people had only had a "feeling" that he was going through some crisis which would undoubtedly be happily resolved. Equally alarmed was I by Hopestill in whose eyes, strikingly like her aunt's today, there was an insistent plea that I remain. She had selected me, I reasoned, because she was perhaps actually afraid to be alone with Philip and because I, of all the guests at the cocktail party, could be trusted not to carry my observations to the fastnesses of the Vincent and the Chilton Clubs.

If anyone was in need, I thought, it was myself. It had been true, as I told Hopestill, that I wanted to make a telephone call. It was, though I did not specify this, to Nathan, or rather, to the janitor of his building who would occasionally understand (he was quite deaf) what I wanted and call my friend to the telephone. For I felt that I must see him at once, must make him understand fully where the apples came from, must impress upon him the necessity of my finding the red room. Moreover, I wanted to see, simply by looking at him, that he did not know who his rival was.

And I did not want to telephone from Philip's study. I had thought of a booth in a drug-store on a certain corner from which, and only from which, I had always put through my calls to Nathan, so that I had come to associate with his distant, often blurred voice, the wooden counter visible to me through the glass door of my little cell, where a pharmacist of Hellenic beauty stood as if guarding his rows of amber glass jars full of pills, his curly golden hair occupying the place of greatest light under the neon legend: "Prescriptions." It was nearly always necessary, since several minutes elapsed from the time I got the janitor until I heard Nathan's dazed "Hello"— these calls were even now a surprise to him—for me to deposit a second or third nickel in the slot. The young god, pushing aside a ciborium of nuxvomica, called, as I hurtled out of the box, "Here, I'll change it for you," having two nickels in exchange for my dime already waiting in his outspread hand. I had not time to thank him, for I was afraid my connection would be cut off, but when I had hung up and was leaving, expressed my gratitude and made a vague promise that it would not happen again. His large, heavily-lidded hazel eyes twinkled, either because he felt he was in on a secret (perhaps he thought that my parents would not allow me to see the person I was telephoning and that I was arranging a secret rendezvous) or else because he was amused by my absent-mindedness or by the loquacity which made all my calls cost double. He said: "I always have change back here any time you need it," as if he had no wish to be deprived of the spectacle of my flurry. Once I had got Nathan immediately, for he was passing by the janitor's door as the telephone rang, and the original coin I had deposited sufficed, my message being short. The pharmacist, who had been slowly doing up a package, glanced at me through the glass door from time to time and when I came out, rapidly produced two nickels from a box at the end of the counter. I thanked him but said I had finished and he exclaimed, "You didn't get your party, then!" in a tone something like disappointment.

It was in that place where, creature of habit that I was, I wanted to make my engagement with Nathan. Superstitiously, I felt that if I telephoned from this house, its owners would be drawn into my maelstrom whereas the pharmacist could not since he knew nothing of me and I knew of him only his youth, his beauty, and his deep voice containing the vestiges of a Nova Scotian accent. I was afraid, moreover, that if I did not make the call and see Nathan tonight, my determination would wane and by morning would have perished altogether so that the day to which I opened my eyes would be identical to all other days save that the danger was nearer, but not near enough, in the bright sunlight streaming through my familiar windows, to make me remember clearly enough how terrified I had been by Miss Pride's eyes.

When Hopestill motioned toward my untouched glass and asked me if I did not like the cocktails, I realized with a start that I had been here only a few minutes. I drank quickly and guiltily, gave Kurt a parting caress and, at Hopestill's injunction, set out to find the Admiral.

Throughout the half hour that I exchanged quotations with Admiral Nephews and soberly discussed, with Frank Whitney, the horrors of Communism, listened attentively to a drunken middle-aged man whom I had never seen before who was writing a book on a subject which he did not divulge, one part of my mind was busily casting about for an excuse to leave before dinner. Why did I not now slip upstairs, get my coat, and leave without saying good-by, then go to the drug-store or directly to Cambridge? In reflecting on one's own or in considering another's frustrations, one sees them as unnecessary, forgetting that the amenities of society, arbitrary and often absurd, beset us at every turn and it is only in larger things that one's will is really free. Thus we cannot, unless we have expert tact, or unless we are resigned to being called rude or erratic, turn from our door an unexpected visitor who arrives in the midst of a quarrel or an intimate conversation which we are loath to break off, or when we are at work. Yet, by suffering the intrusion, we accomplish nothing but ill, for our visitor senses that he is unwanted and does not understand why and we, on the other hand, are so displeased with him for not understanding that we fill our stilted, sporadic talk with little barbs, deeply offensive, so that when he leaves he may be resolving never to see us again. For there is, in the patois peculiar to the guest-host relationship, an ambiguity that penetrates to the very roots. Thus, the hostess who for the past hour has been grimacing with swallowed yawns, has, almost unconsciously, been emptying the ash-trays and collecting the glasses, begs us, when we get up to leave, not to go yet, that it is still early, that she wants another drink and cannot have it unless we stay. If we do remain, there eventually comes back to us, percolated through our mutual acquaintances, the remark she has made over the telephone the next morning, "So and So is very nice but someone should explain to him that there is a time beyond which one does not prolong a visit," or, "Like all great talkers, he's quite unaware of time. I was simply nodding in my chair and he didn't notice at all for he was only conscious of the sound of his own voice."

Philip was studiously avoiding me, and while the last thing I wanted was to talk with him, I was disturbed by the way in which, whenever our eyes met, he seemed not to see me at all and, if he found himself by accident standing near me, he immediately moved away, sometimes in the midst of a conversation. Hopestill, on the contrary, was almost constantly at my side. Her voice became progressively louder, as if she were trying to drown out Philip.

Guests were beginning to leave and there were only a dozen or so left in the drawing-room, loitering over a last cocktail. There came a general lull which was broken by Philip's clear voice saying to a young woman, the wife of a colleague of his, "I can't persuade Hope to go to Dr. Masters. She goes to a New York doctor just as she goes to a New York modiste. Fortunately our good friend Harry Morgan is decent enough to drive her down for her appointments."

As everyone knew, Hopestill was under the care of an obstetrician who served all the matrons of her circle, whose office was a few blocks from her house on Dartmouth Street. This very afternoon, she had been comparing notes with someone who had recently had a child and who declared that the process, under the supervision of Dr. Masters, was actually a pleasure. Hopestill had agreed warmly that she was devoted to him. Moreover, it was known that she had been only once to New York since her marriage and that time in the company of the Countess and Amy Brooks for the purpose of shopping and going to a Picasso exhibit. Yet, if she denied what her husband said, it would appear to the guests that she was in the habit of making trips either to New York or to some trysting place with Harry Morgan (Concord! thought the guests. Would she have the *nerve?*), using to her husband the excuse that she was visiting a doctor. Consequently, although the young woman with whom she had discussed Dr. Masters was still in the room, she said, laughing, "Oh, I only go to Dr. Ragsdale for good measure. I am quite loyal to Dr. Masters." Dr. Ragsdale, evidently the first name that came to her, had been her psychiatrist.

Philip smiled innocently across the room at her and said, "Why didn't you tell me you were seeing Dr. Masters, darling? I would have been greatly relieved to know that the product was not to be labeled 'made in New York.'"

The guests stared in hopeless embarrassment, full of pity for this naïve cuckold and regretful that he was so trusting of his wife that he had all but published her shocking subterfuges, and full of indignation that he had reached such a state of mind that his social sensitivity had been completely dulled. Specific pregnancies were not and never had been openly discussed in so loud a voice.

I waited for no more but left the room and went directly upstairs. As I picked up my coat from Hopestill's bed, I heard women talking in the dressing room adjoining. "Isn't there something in the Hippocratic oath he's disobeying?" said one. "He has the taste, thank fortune, to mention no names, but, for example, there's only one person he could have meant when he was ridiculing plastic surgery. It's frightening to see how high and mighty he is." "I've never particularly cared for him," said another, "but I find him quite impossible now. And of course Hope has such strange notions. I dare say she picked them up in New York." "New York won't hurt a flea if it's a good flea," returned the first. "Mother says it's a question of blood. 'By their fruits shall ye know them,' says Mother." "Everyone was devoted to Mrs. Mather, you know, although I've heard she was a neurasthenic. And of course her father! No wonder Hope is what she is."

I was surprised by this comment on Miss Pride's dead sister for it was like the statement of the anti-Semitic, "To be sure I have known Jews whom I've liked. I was very fond of So and So, for instance, though even in him, you must admit, the objectionable characteristics of his race were not completely obliterated." Summary pronouncements upon personalities are common to people in society who, looking upon families as units almost as disjunct as nations, acquire a prejudice against or an affection for one member, make a declaration of war against or an alliance with the whole but make certain reservations in either case, in order to appear fair. In a moment, I overheard the first voice remark, "Miss Pride has always been rather underhanded, Mother says. It's perfectly absurd, at her age, to continue to regard Admiral Nephews as her beau especially when poor Mrs. Nephews is confined to her bed most of the time."

My departure, observed by no one, gave me a feeling of security, and painful as it might be to try to explain my dilemma to Nathan, I looked forward with pleasure to this evening which I would spend in his grubby rooms. On the way out, I bought a bottle of Liebfraumilch which came, green and dripping, out of an ice-chest, and, to take home later to Miss Pride, a bunch of mountain laurel which came, I was told by the vendor, from West Virginia. The jade-green leaves and the pink flowers like little bonbon cups made me think of Kakosan and her father's garden and the garden that Nathan had promised, in the delirium of his rapture, to build for her in some distant time and space, a castle in Spain, a vine-covered cottage, that shrine which varies according to the experience of the lovers, but is an essential of love's culture.

He had been trying for the last hour to telephone me and as I came through the murky basement, ducking under the obese pipes of the furnace that stretched out like the arms of an octopus, I found him emerging from the janitor's flat where he had been making one last attempt to reach me. I knew that he was in severe distress for it had been agreed at the beginning that he was never to call me at Miss Pride's. He told me tonelessly as his baffled eyes roved my face as if he half hoped to find there what he had lost, that two hours before, he had gone, by appointment, to Morgan's apartment to give him a lesson and had found that he was not there. But there was a note for him which the butler went to fetch. As he waited in the hall, he saw lying on the table a copy of the book, *Der Traum der Roten Kammer,* identical to the one Kakosan had given him. He could not decide whether to go away at once, leaving it untouched, maddened with uncertainty, or to probe its pages for evidence of her guilt, for marks, inscriptions, a chance slip of paper. He concluded that he must know, once and for all. First he opened it and smelled the pages which gave off, just as his did, a fragrance of her favorite scent (he had given her a flagon of it only a short time before), for it was her romantic habit to spray her letters and gifts. And then, upon the flyleaf, written with the curlicues of penmanship she effected only in notes to intimate friends, was the same girlish, warm-hearted endorsement that appeared in his—and both in red ink—"For dearest Gacho from his Hototogisu." He had then torn a page from his notebook and written to Morgan that the pressure of examinations would prevent him from giving any more lessons.

Somewhere the block-flute which we often heard gave out a waggish excerpt from *The Well-Tempered Clavichord.* The surface of our cool, golden wine was marred by floating bits of cork. Nathan's face was three-quarters turned towards me and his birthmark looked like a shadow. I was conscious of these things in terms of a painting. They were a flat surface with only a representation of dimensions and I projected them into Paris, pretending that we were there and presently would go out for a *pernod* at the café Nathan had always said he would visit first, the Closerie des Lilas. Or I imagined us wandering through the crooked streets and over the bridges of Würzburg where, at any moment, we might pass my father or jostle the elbow of my cousin Peter. Or I was in Heidelberg and the block-flute became the song of a foreign bird entering through the windows of my ruby room.

If Nathan had been listening to me as I told him what I had come for, if he had heard me taking off, layer by layer, the wrappings of my jewel, I might have lost it forever. To my own ears, my revelation sounded banal, my terror was flaccid, unimportant, trumped-up. And I was surprised that I could not make him see what I so clearly saw myself: this churchly, peaceable hallucination. I had reached the end of my account and said, "I want to find the room, you see." But I was not really conscious of this need which, until now, had seemed so urgent, and when Nathan said, "I'm sorry. I haven't been listening. What did you say?" I was comforted that I had not, after all, admitted a trespasser. I returned to his immediate and frenzied world, feeling wise, mature, and safe.

## 3

In the spring, the young McAllisters opened their Concord house where they spent week-ends. Frequently they entertained and their country parties were more successful than those they had had in town, not only because there were more things to do—Hopestill, although she could not participate herself, organized horseback parties by moonlight, fitted up a badminton court with lights, arranged half a dozen other diversions that appealed to her guests, and gained for her the reputation of being a highly resourceful hostess—but also because Harry Morgan was no longer in evidence and Philip had for all practical purposes become once more the person everyone had liked and admired.

Guests, approaching the house at night, were deceived by its size. Under the influence of the darkness, out of which the ell loomed suddenly, incandescent between the blooming apple trees, it seemed of manorial proportions. The impression, actually false, was strengthened by the landscape. On two sides, there was a wide sweep of lawn bounded by low stone walls in the shadows of which grew violets and lilies-of-the-valley. At the back was a grove of pines, the entrance to which had been cleared into a precise avenue where I sometimes took a walk in the early morning, relishing the blackened trunks of the pruned trees and the rich brown of the resilient needles out of which, here and there, a shell-pink mushroom thrust its tender cap.

It was not the house itself that had been renovated in Harry Morgan's startling manner, but a smaller building which had formerly been Philip's grandfather's study. No one, not even the older

McAllisters, could complain that there was anything amiss in the main house. The room into which one entered was ancient, stiff, yet withal charming. The wide, thickly knotted boards of the original floors were darkened to a rich red-brown. The dresses of some of the ladies and the hides of some of the hounds in the narrative wallpaper had faded from red to the color of a wine stain and from yellow to a sandy pallor. At one end of the room was a long fireplace whose white mantel was laden with pewter plates and tankards and, at either end, ivy cascading from amber bottles. It was not a room for casual lounging. The hostility to comfort seemed to have been intentional and every article of furniture had been designed to punish the flesh: the high-backed, cane-bottomed chairs, the cruel, three-cornered "roundabouts," the cherry settle, as harsh as a pew. But the eye was pleased by the pure white doors and by two corner cupboards facing one another at the far end of the room which showed, through leaded panes, old red china, silver goblets and a flurry of bibelots.

It had been a shock, on the night of the housewarming, to go from this eighteenth century parlor to the "studio." It was like the transition from one extreme of temperature to its opposite. The studio was a box in two stories, the lower one being given over to one large room, at the end of which was a completely outfitted bar, curved and equipped with a chromium foot-rail and high maple stools upholstered in red leather. On either side, French doors opened out, on one side to a path leading to the open slype between the main part of the house and the ell, on the other, to the pine grove. The new, waxed floor was bare. Here and there, scattered about its long expanse, were massive leather chairs of an obtuse structure, but one which afforded great bodily comfort. For tables, slabs of flawed plate glass with a greenish tinge lay on iron frames. Sofas, chairs, tables, bookshelves were low as if the people meant to use them had shrunk from a normal stature but had, at the same time, become uncommonly wide. The tall, thin guests, engulfed in the cavernous chairs, had seemed fragile and undernourished, no match for the thick, pint-sized and blood-red glasses out of which they drank.

A pair of pyramidal green vases stood on the mantelpiece and, with their insistent geometry, influenced the tulips springing from

475

them to resemble also a "new idea" so that they did not belong to the world of nature but to that of mathematical design. There was a card table in whose four legs were inserted wedge-shaped shelves to holds the drinks of the players; a pair of crystal andirons for the remodeled fire-place which, as Philip had once said, looked no more like a fire-place than did Mr. Otis Whitney, and which he referred to as "the antrum." It was a low, square hole overhung by a vast rectangular marble shelf. A fire there could be tended, Miss Pride said, only by a dwarf and even he would be in danger of dashing his brains out. On the hearth stood a sandstone carving which represented three plump women in a happy embrace and was entitled "Breadline."

The Reverend McAllister, leading his mother about the room, had been less distressed by the bar than he had been by three pen and ink drawings which hung over a bookshelf and which produced an optical illusion: from one point of view they seemed to be illustrations of the myths of Venus and Adonis, Orpheus and Eurydice, and Narcissus, but by a slight change of focus, one saw that their subject was phallic, an assemblage of genitalia in coy half-ambush behind fronds, lotus flowers, and broad leaves of palmettos. The pictures had been a present from one of Hopestill's former friends on Joy Street, and although she was quite aware of their intention, if someone gasped and whispered in an appalled hiss that she evidently did not know what they were, she replied, "You're not the first person to tell me that, and I'm beginning to think there really *is* something ambiguous about them, though for the life of me I can't see it." It was quite true: she had seen the symbols in her first glance but had thereafter refused to let her eyes see anything but Orpheus holding his lute and Adonis lying in Venus' arms. As the latter, they were wholly without distinction, so that people thought either Hopestill's taste had gone terribly downhill or else that she was lying. As the clergyman stood before them, a dark blush stole upward from his stiff collar and he exclaimed to his mother, "I seem to be seeing things!" The old lady fetched her lorgnette from her handbag and moved up close to the pictures, although her son made an abortive attempt to stop her. She turned away, ferreting Hopestill out to kill her with a look, made particularly baleful by its filtration through her haughty instrument. Afterwards she was heard to say, "I shall never go into poor Edward's renovated library again. It gives me the same feeling of distress that I would have if the Old Manse were turned into a Howard Johnson." Miss Pride, refusing to acknowledge Harry Morgan's authorship of the changes, said of it, "Berthe von Happel, for all her eccentric notions about decorating an interior in Massachusetts, could not have produced that monstrosity. I do believe that children are born with a mental disease these days." And the Countess, looking with frank horror upon a kidney-shaped writing desk with a bakelite top and two chromium legs, one obese, the other as thin as a rail, murmured to me, "I dream! There has not yet been devised a machine to make anything so out of the question as this."

It struck me that the studio was a rarefied extension of that state of mind which had sent Hopestill to Dr. Ragsdale's consulting room. It was the demonstration, in meaningless shapes, in dislocated structure, of the rebellion to which she had become addicted without volition. Rather, the volition had existed in the beginning as a defense against her aunt, but it had now evaporated. What had taken place between her and Philip after their cocktail party, I never guessed, but none of us saw Harry Morgan again, and from that time forward, Hopestill was altered. It was difficult to say exactly what was changed in her except her appearance. She seemed to have gone beyond fear and beyond rebellion, beyond, indeed, all feeling and to exist automatically. Perhaps she had surrendered completely to Philip's hatred and had allowed her physical being to share in her moral disintegration. The demolition of her beauty was, everyone thought, merely temporary. After her child was born, her skin would regain its luster and her eyes their animation; she would be as brilliantly organized as she had been before. I wondered, though, if she would ever again be beautiful, and I thought that perhaps what we had seen as beauty had not been beauty at all but another quality, an emotional or intellectual force so powerful that it actually appeared in her person.

It will be remembered that when I was a little girl, I thought Miss Pride was beautiful. Later on, I did not call her that, but neither did I call her ugly. It was that my feeling had changed: from admiration of her carriage and her clothes, I had progressed to love of her. If by saying "she is beautiful," we mean something more (as I must have meant even as a child), we mean this as a commentary on our relationship with her, we have actually said, "my gaze is freighted with feeling and my love has urged this face to resemble my sweet memory of it." And that "feeling," like the catalyst which remains stable, must remedy, through its unchanging agency, the imperfections of what we see. Conversely, when we hate, our hearts can deceive our senses so that we find hideous what has beauty inseparably in it. In this way I, at the time I had said Miss Pride was beautiful, had simultaneously said that my mother was ugly or else that her beauty was something gone bad.

Now it was not only Hopestill's illness that made me think she had always been ugly. There was a force at play in my altered perceptions that was subtler and stronger than that which had come from my expanding knowledge of beauty, or that gradual repudiation of childhood criteria, or that vision, enriched by maturity, which allows one to speak of "types of beauty." Rather, it was that I had slowly come of age in knowledge of her and of her *milieu* into which I had willed myself. What marked the advent of my adulthood was a moment when I, standing in the doorway of the studio, saw her lying bare-footed on the couch. She was alone and Kurt lay on the floor beside her. Her small, bony feet were busily prehensile, spryly fiddling with the cushions, the toes opening and shutting like a cat's claws, the arch bowed tightly. I thought of her green slippers and how I had longed to be Hopestill or a girl just like her. Now, receiving her greeting, hearing her barren voice, I thought, "Why, it is her life that is ugly and has been from the beginning."

"What shall I do, Miss Pride?" I asked.

She deliberated the chess-board, not my question, and replied, "And how do you feel about it? Do you think she will be cured?"

I told her my opinion and then I waited, my heart palpitating at the sight of her as in her green beaver hat and black suit, whose nocturnal sobriety was relieved only by the white collar of her mannish shirt, she moved the men across the board. I knew that today after church, she was to have luncheon at the house of a Coolidge and that the guest of honor was to be a Mrs. Roosevelt, née Cabot. "Thunder!" she said suddenly. "I've made a mistake. You've rattled me and it's all spoiled. Well, Sonia, I would regret parting company with you, my dear girl, for I find your services useful and your manners steadily improve. I suppose there are other establishments besides the one your mother is in now? Of a different character where one would pay her keep. At any rate, I shall investigate."

She had set the men up to begin again and was referring to her manual, holding it at arm's length in the far-sightedness of age which she would admit to no one but me. I believed I was dismissed and turned to go, but she said, without taking her eyes from the diagram she was following, "Sonia, let us say for the sake of argument that I *do* agree to set your mother up in a private sanitarium: What returns will you make to me?"

Thinking that she wanted to know how I would repay the money, I replied, "I don't know what I *can* do for many years, Miss Pride. But perhaps I could set her up myself. I don't spend what you give me, you know."

She squinted in my direction. "My dear child, the pin money I give you wouldn't go very far in one of those places. Mind you, I know all about them. They're run by bloodsuckers and don't be told anything different. Mrs. Eppington's oldest daughter, who is named something remarkable like Margarine, though of course it isn't that, married a Russian who went quite mad and was sent off to one of those fashionable bedlams at a ruinous cost that led her eventually to opening a little tea-room in Newport, where all you could get for love or money, was some horrid red soup and salads made of Bartlett pears. Not that the marriage wouldn't have been absurd anyway. They had an apartment facing Washington Square, furnished as we don't furnish apartments in Boston, with couches that became beds and a bar in a closet, and I believe he had an icon, though he wasn't that sort of Russian. But I wander. No, Sonie, returns of that sort are not what I have in mind."

I started to speak, to assure her that I would not leave her. But she held up her hand for silence.

"If I undertake to support your mother as well as yourself, I shall be doing it with no thought of being paid back. I must repeat—although I am sure you return my devotion—that this is, I know, not much of a life for a girl your age. You have your moods, as we all do in our youth, our sentimental dreams of adventure, our fancied love affairs. Here, I've moved the rook too far." She changed the man's position. "You're unusually steady to be sure. I have only had inklings of a certain restiveness at times. I had it, for example, one evening not long ago, when you brought me that charming mountain laurel." She paused and glanced up at me. "Sonia, my father, a blunt man, but one who husbanded his words, brought me up in the belief that silence was the ideal policy, that honesty was next best, and that falsehood should be reserved for state occasions. For example, the only lie I ever heard him tell was to Mr. Charles Francis Adams' secretary who, under the impression that Papa was Mr. *Stanley* Pride, Consul General of Madrid, asked him to renew his acquaintance with the Secretary of the Navy at a dinner party at the Yacht Club. Papa said, 'I shall be delighted to renew my acquaintance with Mr. Adams.' He claimed that this was an equivocation rather than a direct lie, for he did not say Mr. *Charles Francis* Adams, and he could have meant Mr. Richard Chilton Adams or Mr. Archibald Revere Adams, two perfectly bona fide Adamses with whom he lunched every day at the Harvard Club. But silence, silence was what Papa chiefly counseled, and while I have so far as possible followed his precept, I must confess that there are times when you are a little *too* silent. Sometimes I cannot compass you. You become a cipher. I am afraid you will disappear altogether, vanish utterly. On that evening, for example, that you brought me the mountain laurel, I had the feeling while we talked that you were paying no attention to what you said. I did not ask you where you had been, though I had heard from Hopestill that you had not stayed for dinner, and I do not ask you now. But, my dear child, I cannot live with an image of you! If you are troubled by something, I implore you to let me know."

"That night," I said, "I had had too many cocktails at Hopestill's."

"I'm not entirely satisfied with that, but we shall let it go. You will keep me company, help me with my little book in the twilight of my life? You will not go away from Boston?"

"But I have no intention of going away from Boston!" I cried.

She drew her game to a close and glancing up at the clock which indicated twenty minutes before eleven, she waved her hand toward the cabinet where I went to pour out her sherry. I noticed that her hand shook; she seemed to shrink as I watched and her hand, curled into a trembling, beseeching cup, was like a beggar's, asking for alms. It was not the sherry that she reached out to seize, but it was myself. Putting the glass down beside the chess-board, she extended her old claw to me. "Agree!" she cried. "Agree never to leave me until I die!" She smiled, but the terror of death was in her yellow eyes and in her voice, and although I took the proffered hand and smiled back at her, my whole soul retreated from her in the appalled vision of her awful dependence, her hideous cowardice. "Agree!" she was crying.

"I agree," I said, but my voice was unnatural and I could feel perspiration collecting on my upper lip.

"I thought you wouldn't fail me. Poor Hope failed me but I dare say it was partly my fault. Lord, I must get to church! I wish you could hear our new Reverend Jackson, from New Jersey, oddly enough, but he preaches admirably. Good-by." And she went from the room, her martial tread echoing with a decreasing resonance down the corridor until the diminuendo ceased with the opening and closing of the outer door. Ethel peered into the library to announce that Mac was ready.

On the way to Wolfburg, I was fretful, then scolded myself for my directionless discontent. My problem had been solved, and I could ask for nothing more. It was perhaps only the spring air that made me suddenly *wanderlustig*. Perhaps it was Nathan's preparations to leave for Paris that inspired me with thoughts of leaving Boston. He had often told me that he had money enough to pay my passage. I envied him his mobility; my double servitude, that to my mother and to Miss Pride, lay heavy on me, and now, since our conversation in the library this morning, the die was cast. I could not, morally, disappear. Just before we reached the asylum, I regained control of myself, said I loved my mother and I loved Miss Pride and Boston and that nothing could ever shake me from my resolve to live the rest of my life exactly as I was living it now.

My mother had been over her illness for some time, and as I waited in the corridor, I determined to outdo myself in tenderness and to tell her, if she was in despair, that she was to be moved soon to a house that she would like. One by one the visitors were summoned to the doctors' cells and I saw them then going off to the reception room, their hands full of flowers or fruit or magazines. And presently I was quite alone save for the tireless, ethereal voice warbling for Dr. Finkelstein and Dr. Short. A doctor crossed the hall and seeing me, said, "You aren't Miss Marburg, are you? Well, then, will you just step this way a moment?" We went into "my" doctor's office and my escort put his arm about my shoulder in a paternal affability. Another doctor besides mine was sitting on the window-ledge.

"Miss Marburg," said Dr. Tudor, "Dr. Burns, who spoke to you last winter about your mother, has presented his findings to us and we have been going over the case." He cleared his throat and said something in an undertone to his colleague at the window who then went to a filing case and brought back a bulging manila folder. "As you know, psychiatry is not a definitive science any more than medicine is. And diseased minds are as liable to relapse as are diseased bodies. And, if anything, they are more difficult to diagnose accurately. Now let us say we have concluded that a man with pulmonary trouble has fibrosis. His symptoms, blood-tests, x-rays corroborate our opinion. He is kept in bed sufficiently long to remedy the trouble and we let him get up. But his fever rises, he begins to cough blood. We put him through another examination and find that he has tuberculosis of the lungs. We were probably not wrong in the first place. He *did* have fibrosis, but the tubercula bacilli, present in everyone, were working under our very noses, so slyly that none of our tests registered their progress. And now we must change our offensive, go back to a point near the starting line and begin again. Sometimes this happens in diseases of the mind. Originally we called your mother a 'manic depressive' and we had hopes of her complete recovery by simple treatment. But recently, particularly since her last attack of bronchitis, she has at times revealed symptoms of another disease, that is, catatonia."

The doctors all were watching me, and I had the feeling that they

482

were taking note of everything, that they saw, and afterwards would discuss, the slight tic that began at the corner of my right eye.

Dr. Tudor continued, "I must tell you frankly that what we have concluded is not hopeful. No treatment we know of can certainly arrest the course of katatonia. Two days ago, your mother, who is now in a room by herself, was seized with a violent attack of vomiting, after which a muscular rigidity set in which has continued with rare intervals of relaxation. Sleep is possible only if we give her opiates. Her hallucinations have increased and have become so diverse that they appear entirely unrelated to anything we know of in her history. It is bad news, Miss Marburg, but like all bad news, it is better to know it at once."

"Do you mean, sir," I said, "that my mother will never be well again?"

"We can't talk in positive terms like that, as I have said. Patients have recovered. Many have made partial recoveries. Your mother may be one of those fortunate people who do regain their health. But it will take a long time and we can promise you nothing."

"Does she know? I mean, is she . . ."

"You mean, is she unhappy. Subjectively, that is. Let me assure you that she is in a world of her own. She is frightened, yes, but nothing we can do, nothing anyone can do, can remove the cause of her fright."

"Perhaps I could! Perhaps if I took her away, back to Chichester, she would be better."

The doctor rose and came around his desk, standing over me with a benevolent smile that was yet somehow hasty as if he wished to draw our interview to a close. "Believe me, there is nothing you can do. For the time being, your visits will be of no use. She is very sick."

"Poor Mamma," I murmured.

"You go on home now. When we have anything to report, we'll drop you a line. Some day you can see her again."

"Some day? But when?"

"That, I can't say."

"Will you give her my flowers?" I asked him, holding out the waxy Easter lilies I had bought that morning at Mr. Quince's. Dr. Tudor laid them on his desk and, finished with my case, led me to the door. The corridor was silent, for all the other visitors had gone to their melancholy meetings. My footsteps on the hard, rubbery floor sounded wet and loud, and the sunshine which stopped half-way from the door seemed remote, a golden bay. The indefatigable voice pursued me to the door, calling after me, "Doctor *Fink*-ull-stein! Doctor Shor-ort! Doctor Baaxter!" I was conscious of the terrible permanence of the asylum: forever, in the same inflections, the voice would chant and bleat the names of the same doctors, would echo through the glistening halls where every surface and every shadow was rounded, where even the doctors, at their most precise, smoothed down the sharp edges of what they said. Only the shafts of sunlight were sharp, but they were laden with round motes.

Poor Mamma! The red room, now that I needed it, would not come. Instead, there came to me the kitchen in Chichester and the hot night I had lain on the floor at my mother's feet. Suddenly, with the same kind of uneasiness I had felt when I thought Father Mulcahy said "God's warning," rather than "Good morning," I believed that her change had come about through my own treachery. For several days my conscience did not allow my thoughts to stray from my crime, and it tormented me, saying, "You must not believe them when they tell you she isn't conscious of her misery." But at last I conquered the moral voice, and when I told Miss Pride that henceforth I should be free on Sundays to accompany her to church, and she did not ask me for any explanation, the recrudescence of the pain and remorse was momentary. For the time being, I had walled up my mother into the farthest recess of my mind, knowing that the time would come when I must let her out again.

4

I had only just learned to smoke. Like most tyros, mistaking the habit for an exciting vice, I had elaborate equipment: holders, lighters, cases, and expensive, unusual cigarettes with which I sometimes vapored through a whole evening without requiring any other entertainment than that of watching the smoke I expelled ascending in lively indirection, the thin columns expanding or splitting, and of feeling an occasional pain in my diaphragm when I inhaled deeply as if a weight had plummeted downward through my esophagus and simultaneously had delivered to my skull a faintly dizzying blow. My imagination, consigning insidious properties to the cigarettes as if tobacco were cousin to opium, through its perhaps intentional error, rendered to my thoughts a dreamy quality, the reality of their objects being interrupted just as my vision of the walls, the windows, the furniture was interrupted by the smoke. I experienced, as in illness, an imperviousness to time, feeling that I was an inviolable bystander before whose serene eyes the raging world catapulted through arbitrary, mechanized hours.

I was sitting one afternoon in the Concord cemetery, leaning against a mossy tree. Below me was a green, stagnant pool into which now and again fell a twig or pebble but it made no sound for the surface of the water was velvety with mold. From behind me came the sound of the gardener's lawn-mower and the occasional click of a trowel on stone. The faintest wind soughed in the branches and brought me the smell of pine-needles and lilies-of-the-valley which grew in profusion there amongst the graves. As I had come up the slope called "Authors' Ridge," I had seen tourists gazing respectfully at Emerson's clumsy pink quartz gravestone and at the slabs marked "Alcott." I had known by their pronunciation that they were outlanders, for they accented Thoreau on the last syllable and pronounced Alcott with a short "a." Miss Pride detested sight-seers who visited the cemeteries. One day she had seen a man set up a tripod and produce a great lot of photographer's contraptions to make a snapshot of Longfellow's sarcophagus in the Mount Vernon graveyard. Taking the law into her own hands, she accosted him and said, "Look here, sir, this is not permitted." A rude man, he asked for her authority, and she replied, "I just stepped out of my house, Elmwood. My name is Mamie Lowell." No longer interested in Longfellow, he turned his camera on her and before she could collect her wits, he had taken her picture, saying, "This is even better. I'd rather bring 'em back alive than dead."

I knew that I should go on to Hopestill's house where I was to meet Miss Pride, but I was too languorous to move and repeatedly said to myself as I fitted a new cigarette into my carved holder, a present from Kakosan, that this would be the last. Between puffs,

485

I held the holder horizontal and mused on its giver. It had been a token of her gratitude for my introduction of her to the Countess and had been sent, fantastically enough, by messenger who, in the employ of the telegraph company, had appeared vexed to be the porter of a parcel wrapped in pale blue tissue paper through whose silver ribbons three dark violets had been passed. "It ain't a telegram," he said, not by way of information since there could be no doubt on that point, but to show me that the absurd kickshaw he handed to me was in no way comparable to the important yellow envelopes which it was his proper function to deliver and several of which now conspicuously protruded from his breast pocket.

Kakosan, along with the present, had sent a note in her characteristically inconsistent style: upon a calling card giving her name in Japanese characters which ran like red bacteria down one side, she had written in a neat commercial school hand, "For a swell pal."

She, like Morgan, had disappeared from the blue drawing-room after the cocktail party, although, as I knew from Hopestill, she still received invitations. I concluded that she did not want to see me, remembering her frightened whisper, "That's Sonie Marburg," as I went up the stairs. She had made several futile attempts to see Nathan who steadfastly refused to consider a reconciliation. I had seen her only once, by accident. We met at dusk one day as I was going home along Commonwealth Avenue and we stopped beside a false magnolia shrub that had just come into flower. The white petals were smudged with pink and a lilac color; the thick, broad leaves were stiff and glossy as if they had been varnished. We talked only of the flowers and of Ginger Rogers. But on the following day, she sent me a set of brushes in an ivory box which she asked me to give to Nathan in memory of her. She had promised, long before, to teach him to write Japanese.

Nathan was torn between the desire to keep the brushes and the desire to wound Kakosan by returning them. I persuaded him to keep them since they would be a souvenir of that aspect of her he had loved. It was some time before he ever used them, but when he did, practicing the few brush strokes he had learned from her, there came to the good side of his face a look of tenderness and longing, not for the person he no longer loved nor could love, but for the girl he had known in the beginning, had pursued like a bloodhound down the streets of Boston, hiding behind the subway kiosks as she, this still unknown beauty, stopped to buy fresh posies for her hair. Finally, after months of this delightful chase, he had accosted her at a street corner as they waited for the traffic to pass and had asked her if she knew of anyone who could give him lessons in Japanese. He would put down the brushes, pass his fingers over his marked cheek, and then would pour each of us a teacup of his violent sherry and tell me, for the thousandth time, that he would never love anyone but an Oriental woman again with the same kind of wonder that he had loved Yoshidasan in the first of those days.

I looked at my watch: at this very moment, Nathan's train for New York was leaving from the South Station. At midnight tomorrow, he would sail for France. I felt no particular sense of loss. This morning when I had told him good-by in his basement room, stripped of his personal gear, his books and trash and the photographs of Dostoievsky and Heine which had hung over his desk, I had, on an impulse, taken between my hands his mutilated face and kissed him on the lips, and my kiss was not only a farewell to him but a resolute farewell to the temptations he had put in my path which had attempted to make my staid feet nomadic.

I flung my cigarette into the slimy pond and got up. If there were time, before we went back to Boston, I would take Kurt for a run through the woods behind Hopestill's house. I hoped that I would be offered one of the rum cocktails which had been invented by Harry Morgan, the household's former *arbiter bibendi*. Miss Pride had been making a tour of the Concord gardens in the company of several people whom she did not like, including the Mesdames McAllister, and I was confident that she would find herself in need of a restorative and would suggest to her niece that she "concoct a little something for us."

The old lady, all alone, was sitting on the lawn in a cane-bottomed chair. She was reading and did not hear my footsteps on the driveway. I was struck by the singular composition of the picture before my eyes: the spare black figure central in the expanse of shining grass and behind her the white house with its pedimented windows flanked by green shutters and its paneled door which was slightly ajar; burnishing the whole scene, giving to it that final fillip which distinguishes art from nature, was the clear light of early summer as skillfully executed as Vermeer's sunshine. She looked up with a smile as I approached.

"I hope you have enjoyed Hawthorne's grave better than I have done the gardens. I have no horticultural principles, yet had the great misfortune of being taken in tow by Mrs. Bigelow who feels very strongly about *tulipes noires*. I could not comfort her at Charity Brewster's, where she was confronted by several specimens."

I laughed and asked if Hopestill had accompanied her and she replied, "No. I don't know where she is. There isn't a sign of life about the place. Not even her animal is here."

Turning her eyes once again to her book, she indicated that she had spent enough time on me and I left her, making my way round the house to the studio. I helped myself generously to whiskey from the bar and put a Brahms piano concerto on the automatic phonograph. There was a sweet flamboyance to the music; it was like a plump and tender hug into which I burrowed luxuriously. Whiskey and music, I reflected, especially when taken together, made time fly incredibly fast. When the long concerto was finished, it was growing dark. A little wind had come up, threatening a storm. The air itself, more than the dark clouds, presaged the arrival of the thunder and the rain. I went back to the house to see if Hopestill had returned. Miss Pride had gone inside and the lawn was bare again save for the deepening shadows of the apple trees along the drive. There was a note for me thrust into the knocker which read: "Undone by the gardens I have gone upstairs to rest. When our tardy hostess arrives, tell her that since we have been given no tea, we shall expect dinner. Lucy Pride."

An hour later, just after the storm broke, Hopestill, wild-eyed, tousled, burst into the studio. She did not take off her wet raincoat but sprawled in a vermilion chair and the legs she stretched out before her were clad in jodhpurs, a fact that did not strike me as odd probably because her whiskey had rendered me impervious to surprise. Nor was I taken aback when she asked for the decanter of whiskey and took three large drinks neat and with a masculine rapidity.

"Do you believe in supernatural things?" she said quickly in a shrill voice and leaned forward with an eager look in her harried face.

"Some, I suppose." I regretted that I had drunk so much. I felt that there was something amiss and could not capture it.

"I mean, do you think hate can kill? There is a story about a woman who makes a doll in the image of another woman and burns it and the woman comes to some dire end, I think. It's been so long ago that I can't remember, but lately it's been haunting me."

"I don't believe in *that*," I said.

"Where's Aunt Lucy?" she asked, sitting up. "I want to ask her something. I want her to give me Mercy."

"What about Kurt? He'd kill her."

"Kurt? Oh . . ." Although she had poured herself a fourth glass of whiskey, she put it down before it had reached her lips and her face became instantly as pale as moonlight. "Kurt is dead," she said.

"Dead?"

"He was killed this afternoon . . . run over on the Bedford road."

"Was he off his leash? Weren't you with him?"

"No. He had been with me. I was riding. I had been running my horse and he was keeping up with me. Something frightened Chiquita—you know that little Palomino mare?—and she stopped suddenly and reared. Kurt went tearing back, here I thought, but just now, as I was coming up the road, I found him."

"I wish you hadn't let him go with you," I cried. "Why didn't you follow him? Why were you a whole afternoon going after him, Hopestill? Didn't you care?"

"I had had a little accident and couldn't get back. Chiquita threw me."

Now I saw the riding trousers for the first time, wondered even in my alarm when she had got them to fit her now misshapen body, and my voice issued as a scream. "You are ill, then!"

"Yes, I suppose that I shall be very ill."

"I must call Philip." I stumbled to the door.

"Don't! He'll think I did it intentionally." She slipped off her short boots and her damp socks. "And of course I did. I made Chiquita do it. Once, I remembered, she threw me because I was wearing some Indian bracelets which rattled and the sound made her wild.

489

I wore them today." And she pulled up the sleeve of her raincoat to show me three thin silver bands.

"You hadn't any right!" I said furiously and ran out and round to the house where, without disturbing Miss Pride, I telephoned Philip in Boston. As I waited for the sound of his voice, I could think of nothing but Hopestill's nimble feet as they had looked just now on the bare floor. They were somehow aged, for the skin was stretched and blanched and over the sharply knuckled bones, the tracery of veins stood out, blue and vermicular. When I had got Philip and he promised to come at once, I went outside and stood in the drenching rain under an apple tree and over and over again hummed the phrase from *The Well-Tempered Clavichord,* the favorite of the anonymous block-flute player. And I did not leave my dripping sanctuary until, three-quarters of an hour later, the lights of Philip's car came bobbing through the trees.

When I went back to the cemetery in October, half a year after her death, I could not remember at once where Hopestill was buried. At the time of her funeral, I had not heeded any landmarks, and all I could see, in my mind's eye, was her grave as it was yawning for her casket and, a few minutes afterward, as it became a fresh mound and pile of flowers. Built on a hill, this graveyard of a small New Hampshire town was cut by a spiraling road into four or five sloping tiers, all similar in appearance. Identical paths ran parallel to each other and every tree, spruce, or cedar, or elm, was mimicked by a twin. Hopestill was at the very top, beside her father. They were farther up even than the graveyard's only mausoleum which, in a splendor of marble and genuflecting angels, housed the bones of a distinguished bishop, native of the town, who had returned from the wide world to settle in the dust of his last vestments under his boyhood's earth. Miss Pride, the connossieur of graves, had remarked as we drove away, "I'd *walk* if I were buried there. From what you can tell of his Grace's taste from that outrageous excrescence, he must have been a trying party when he was alive. I dare say he went in for parlor statuary."

It had begun to snow long before the bus that brought me had bumbled into the little town, and by the time I had found her stone, it was covered over by a deep layer of white which was replaced by another as soon as I had brushed it off. Indeed, there was no need for me to see it, for I clearly remembered the bare factual legend engraved on the plain granite oblong: that she had been born some time and given the name Hopestill Pride Mather, and, being married, had taken McAllister, and that she had died a little more than twenty-one years after her birth. Nor was I, uncovering it and shielding it from the snowfall by my hunched-up body, urged by this physical symbol into recalling her better. I could not, as I crouched there, gazing, feel any harmony with her soul as it existed now or with her soul as it was arrested when her breathing stopped. I had not the faith as had her loving old friend the Admiral that her "spirit" still lived, though what he meant, approximately, was, "I have faith that Hopestill's soul continues its existence. What I *know* exists is my faith." But I granted the possibility that a soul might continue to operate in some imponderable place. There was, though, no affective coloring to the hypothesis: the grave could not become to me more than a little elevation of the soil and a flat stone and the skeleton which I visualized could not be hers but merely "skeleton," merely "heap of bones," and it was almost an accident that these bones had been the framework of someone I had known. I wondered when, in her grave, her hair had stopped growing and when its gloss was gone and if its dust were gray or red. I could see it yet, blandished by every change of light, the only remnant of her loveliness left when she lay in the fern-fingered casket. I shivered with the cold and with the memory of my mother's obsession over Ivan's hair which she thought had grown long in the water and was tangled with seaweed.

I had come this long way in the cold to finish her history, in a sense. I thought that if I saw her simple, conventional grave, like all the others, I would be able to efface from my memory the unhappiness of her last days. Although passion was withheld from me as I knelt and I was conscious of the cold which, chilling the dramatic core of my errand, made it folly, tears fell from my eyes, as tame as the windless snow. But they were tears almost of ennui because the death for which she had made so wild a preparation, no longer shocked me but seemed a languid petering out, like the expiring fire from which there comes a final flare and hiss of resin and then is ash. My weeping did not last and when I stood up, I saw that for a moment the snow had stopped and the air was clear enough for me to see the village's green roofs and white church spires.

The snow returned, colder than before, and obliterated the hill opposite the one on which the graveyard was built. A wind came down from the north, swift and soundless. As clearly as though it were borne by the rushing air, I heard the block-flute piping *The Well-Tempered Clavichord,* and trembled, recollecting how, all during her illness I had sat in my room on Pinckney Street humming it over and over again so that I would not hear the telephone which at any moment might bring us word that she had died. That revenant, whose single tune had joined my very blood so that its floating through the canals of my body depended for the tranquillity of its progress upon the cadences of that passage of music, purling in my ungifted throat, brought back, as the sight of her grave had been powerless to do, the person of Hopestill, not as the shrunken creature in the casket nor as the handsome girl of Boston, but of the little girl with the long red hair in the dining-room at the Hotel Barstow. All the time she had lain in the hospital dying, I had been able to think only of her bare feet and of the green slippers which I had defaced and slashed and of her recollection, that night in the studio, of the effigy-burning in *The Return of the Native.* Reason told me I was laughable and self-important in feeling myself an element in her death, but superstition rebuked me, made me deafen myself to the telephone with Bach.

She had been unrecognizable in her casket: her hair had been curled when half its beauty had been its straightness. A little rouge had been put on her lips which had never before been so treated. She was dressed in her wedding gown; she looked pinked and cooked like a frivolous cake. Mrs. Frothingham whispered in someone's ear, "Such a pretty girl to make such a plain corpse!"

I sat behind the straight, black backs of Philip and Miss Pride. Once Philip's shoulders lifted with a sigh. The Countess and Amy Brooks, the Hornblowers, the Admiral, all the cousins, and the friends wept. The McAllisters were rigid like Miss Pride and Philip. The organ music seared me as it had done the day Hopestill married, and the bright, hot sunlight on the wooden floor of the little church stole into my very brain, burning it like liquid gold.

The minister said: "One thing have I desired of the Lord, which I will require; even that I may dwell in the house of the Lord all the days of my life, to behold the fair beauty of the Lord and to visit his temple. For in the time of trouble he shall hide me in his tabernacle; yea, in the secret place of his dwelling shall he hide me, and set me up upon a rock of stone." The even voice and the words were cooling and when we knelt to pray, I mouthed the word "tabernacle" against the smooth wood of the pew ahead of me.

Outside, in the merciless sunlight, the guests, with their faces streaming, were grouped about on the lawn. The white spire of the church pointed up to a sky where shiny cumulus clouds were approached by gray rain clouds. It was impossible to tell which went behind; the rain was coming, we all knew, and we waited impatiently for the signal to move on to the cemetery. It had been quite a nuisance for some people to drive all the way up on such an uncomfortable day. Of course, it was understandable that Hopestill should want to be buried by her father. Even so . . . Little conversations, far removed from the dead girl, had started up everywhere, and I heard a woman say to her companion, "He is very interesting, I suppose, but he is so alien to anything I have ever known. He has the word 'success' written all over him like the measles and his children have come down with it, too. The boy is very fat and was unmercifully teased at St. Marks, but somehow or other he has got in with Alexander Hornblower's son and they're as thick as thieves. So he gets on, you see."

The Countess, more moved, I felt, than anyone except perhaps myself and Philip, pressed a point-lace handkerchief to her eyes and said to Miss Pride, "Ah! Let us pretend we are children again and are being escorted by our mammas for the first time through the Tuileries. Wasn't it wonderful! Wasn't it bliss to be ignorant then and not . . ."

But now the casket was borne out and she did not finish. As we got into the automobiles, the merging of the clouds was completed; no blue sky was visible. A heavy rain fell, but in five minutes, by the time we had reached the gate of the cemetery, the storm was over.

Soon after the funeral, Miss Pride and I left Boston to spend the summer in Mattapoisett. She had not liked, she said, to leave me alone in Cambridge again and although it might seem strange, at her age, to begin going to a new place, she had been rejuvenated, she said, by our work on the memoirs. We had not spoken of Hopestill at any time.

I started down the graveyard hill. When I reached the road, my depression lifted and I was reassured that what I had just left *was* a tabernacle. I felt strangely energetic and as if I had completed a difficult task. It had not snowed here, but there was the bluish fog of autumn between the trees; there was the smell, acrid and like the moist hull of a walnut, of maple leaves that had begun to fall. From a second rise, the last little hill between the graveyard and the town, I saw that the mist was vanishing as I watched, and the sun was coming out. Snug and rubicund, splattered with scarlet and golden leaves, the earth lay at its meridian.

It was late afternoon when I got off the bus on Tremont Street and I hurried. Miss Pride was giving a little dinner party, in honor of the engagement of Amy Brooks to Edward Pingrey. She had invited the Countess and the Admiral, Baron Kalenkoff, Mr. James, the Arthur Hornblowers, and the Norwegian water-color painter. We were to start with cocktails made with the second best gin, but during dinner were to have the best champagne. "Champagne, you know, shouldn't be kept too long," she had said. "I have had this two years and I really must have it drunk up."

As I crossed the Common, where the leaves were curly underfoot and the squirrels were lively in their heyday, I glanced up at the State House dome still shining brightly in the last rays of the descending sun. I used it now as a sort of register for the light. My glance told me that if I made haste, that same glow burnishing the golden sphere would still be on my windows. I hurried on across Beacon Street, down Mount Vernon, then turned into Louisburg Square. For a few minutes I stood at the farthest corner, looking at Miss Pride's house through the high black iron palings with their tops shaped alternately like sword points and sword hilts. Every seventeenth bloomed with a flower on a stalk like Grecian drapery. Frost had made the beds of myrtle droop, but the stunted evergreens were bright. Small Aristides and Christopher Columbus regarded one another across the expanse of dead grass.

The sun had left the lower windows of our house, but mine and Hopestill's on the third floor, and the servants' above were red. I knew that within, the Cape Cod lighter on my hearth would cast forth blinding spears of light. For a moment, the scene seemed remembered, not perceived; it was as if some intelligence in my eyes themselves believed that they would take in the house with its green shutters, its brass letter-slot on the pure white door for the last time now and therefore saw all details overlaid by a film, by an impalpable smoke like the twilight which presently would absorb the sun. Perhaps the time had passed and I could not, save in imagination, traverse the short cobblestoned space between my vantage point and the door to which I owned a key. But then, immediately upon the full development of my feeling that Boston was a part of the past for me just as it was so completely for Hopestill, I was brought back to the present time and knew again that these realities had not diminished in size and in distinctness. Years hence they would perhaps, after Miss Pride was dead, and they would be like the trees of an avenue which perspective reduces and shrouds.

Through the doorway of the building on which an inscription read: *Per Angusta ad Augusta,* a man and woman emerged. The man put on his bowler, then drew on his gray suède gloves. Their voices carried across the quiet square.

"Is it too late to look in at Lucy Pride's?" asked the woman.

Her companion took his watch out of his pocket. "It's six. Wouldn't that rush us? I dare say it wouldn't, but even so I'd rather not at this hour. Lincoln Nephews is usually the only one left by this time, the old loiterer."

The woman laughed. "You're only angry because he gave you your comeuppance in charades."

*"Ulalume!"* cried the man with bitter scorn. "Who but the most egotistical pedant would act out such a thing as that!"

They moved on down Pinckney Street and I ran across to Miss Pride's house. As I fitted my key to the lock, I noticed that the last of the rosy light had gone and that over the steep street lay a topaz patina. Far below, the fragment of the Charles was pure, cold, blue, and across it, a single sail, like a perfect iceberg, moved slowly. From within the house came the Admiral's voice, so close to me I knew he was about to open the door and I withdrew my key to wait for him. "Good-by, Lucy. I'll be back in an hour. Back to Lucy's cot where she dwells in untrodden ways. Ma'am, that was a bang-up tea you gave me. I'm so stimulated I could go waltzing and not peter out till morning."

"Nonsense," came Miss Pride's voice. "My rum cakes have gone to your head, Lincoln. Run along now, do." The Admiral laughed and with him laughed his friend. "Ha! Ha!" her rare bark burst upon me and when the old man opened the door, he found me on the step laughing too, for what reason I was not sure. She was there, behind him. Under the lamplight, she appeared vigorous and even youthful, as if her age which she had passed on to her niece were buried along with Hopestill in New Hampshire. She looked again as she had done when I was five years old in Chichester; her flat, omniscient eyes seized mine, grappled with my brain, extracted what was there, and her meager lips said, "Sonie, my dear, come out of the cold. You'll never get to be an old lady if you don't take care of yourself."